THE BEST SCIENCE FICTION
OF THE YEAR

Also Edited by Neil Clarke

Magazines
Clarkesworld Magazine—clarkesworldmagazine.com
Forever Magazine—forever-magazine.com

Anthologies
Upgraded
The Best Science Fiction of the Year Volume 1
The Best Science Fiction of the Year Volume 2
The Best Science Fiction of the Year Volume 3
The Best Science Fiction of the Year Volume 4
Touchable Unreality
Galactic Empires
More Human Than Human
The Final Frontier
Not One of Us
The Eagle Has Landed

(with Sean Wallace)
Clarkesworld: Year Three
Clarkesworld: Year Four
Clarkesworld: Year Five
Clarkesworld: Year Six
Clarkesworld: Year Seven
Clarkesworld: Year Eight
Clarkesworld: Year Nine, Volume 1
Clarkesworld: Year Nine, Volume 2
Clarkesworld: Year Ten, Volume 1
Clarkesworld: Year Ten, Volume 2

THE BEST
SCIENCE
FICTION
OF THE YEAR

VOLUME 5

Edited by Neil Clarke

Night Shade Books
NEW YORK

All Rights Reserved. No part of this book may be reproduced in any manner without the express written consent of the publisher, except in the case of brief excerpts in critical reviews or articles. All inquiries should be addressed to Night Shade Books, 307 West 36th Street, 11th Floor, New York, NY 10018.

Night Shade books may be purchased in bulk at special discounts for sales promotion, corporate gifts, fund-raising, or educational purposes. Special editions can also be created to specifications. For details, contact the Special Sales Department, Night Shade Books, 307 West 36th Street, 11th Floor, New York, NY 10018 or info@skyhorsepublishing.com.

Night Shade Books® is a registered trademark of Skyhorse Publishing, Inc.®, a Delaware corporation.

Visit our website at www.nightshadebooks.com.

10 9 8 7 6 5 4 3 2

Library of Congress Cataloging-in-Publication Data is available on file.

Hardcover ISBN: 978-1-949102-23-9
Trade paperback ISBN: 978-1-949102-22-2

Cover illustration by Pascal Blanche
Cover design by Daniel Brount

Please see page 593 for an extension of this copyright page.

Printed in the United States of America

For Donald P. Rodriguez
(1944-2019)

Table of Contents

INTRODUCTION:
The State of the Short SF Field in 2019

Neil Clarke

Last year, I altered the format of my introductions to incorporate some of the industry news and information that Gardner Dozois used to include in his annual year-in-review and merged it with my own. It was refreshing to hear that it was appreciated and it's an honor to continue this tradition again this year.

The Business Side of Things

If we're going to look at the big picture for science fiction magazines, we have to acknowledge that the last ten years have probably resulted in the most dramatic changes in their history. It's in this window that we see the rise of a new generation of magazines, largely online, and the mass adoption of digital publishing. Through these changes, the financial threshold to start a magazine dropped considerably and new opportunities were created. This is very much paralleled by the rise of self-publishing and its impact on the broader field.

The "big three" magazines that existed prior to that change are *Analog Science Fiction and Fact* (analogsf.com), *Asimov's Science Fiction* (asimovs.com), and *The Magazine of Fantasy and Science Fiction* (sfsite.com/fsf). These are often referred to as the "print digests," but calling them that is more of a reflection of history. In reality, they also have significant digital circulation which can sometimes outnumber their print readership. Similarly, the magazines that evolved in the digital space are often referred to as "online magazines" despite the fact that many have expanded into print, audio, and/or ebooks. Following what the readers want, both groups have grown to be more alike.

Of course, there's one major difference remaining: those that evolved from digital roots have a free online edition and the others don't. This is not without consequences. The easy availability of free online fiction gives it an upper hand in visibility and helped in growing the audience for short fiction. This effect can also be dominoed when you consider the increased ease of pass-along—finding a story you love and sharing it with a friend—and the impact it has on the circulation longevity of a story. This advantage can effectively drown out equally excellent stories published in anthologies, collections, and magazines that don't have an online edition. Judging by the assortment of "best of the year" anthologies like this one, quality at those once award-dominating publications has not dropped and still accounts for a significant percentage of the best stories, yet there haven't been any finalists from any of those magazines in Hugo Award for Best Short Story category since their last appearance in 2012. It's no surprise that readers less connected to short fiction have interpreted that the wrong way.

The other major consequence of free online fiction is on revenue and this is likely why you won't see the "big three" make any efforts to adopt the practice. The majority of "online" markets sell digital subscriptions or offer other methods of support (donations, Patreon, Kickstarter, etc.), but while their total readership is considerably higher, paid readership is far lower than 10% of that number. (Tor.com is a notable exception. Owned by Tor Books, one of the leading genre publishers, their online edition is considered a marketing expense.) While the "big three" and most online markets pay their authors at the SFWA qualifying rate or better, the lower paid subscription rates result in the online markets paying their editors and staff considerably less, if anything. At a time in which we see a greater diversity of short fiction markets, this often hidden problem is significant and impacts the overall health and sustainability of the field.

To give you some sense of the scope of this problem, I picked three that have received award nominations for their fiction in the last five years and offer subscriptions: *Clarkesworld* (clarkesworldmagazine.com), *Lightspeed* (lightspeedmagazine.com), and *Uncanny* (uncannymagazine.com). Data they've reported to *Locus Magazine* (locusmag.com) reveals that in the last five years, online readership at *Clarkesworld* increased from 38,000 to 43,000, gaining 5,000; *Lightspeed* increased from 25,900 to 28,500, gaining

2,600; and *Uncanny* (a new magazine at the time) increased from 10,000 to 30,600, gaining 20,600. Subscriptions at *Clarkesworld* increased from 3,000 to 3,850, gaining 850; *Lightspeed* decreased from 2200 to 2150, losing 50; and *Uncanny* increased from 1,200 to 2,000, gaining 800. (Note: *Uncanny* holds an annual Kickstarter campaign, so their revenue is supplemented by that.) Each of these publications also has a podcast edition, which is not reflected in these numbers, but can increase their audience size by a significant amount. In the five year period, for example, *Clarkesworld* saw its podcast audience grow from 10,000 to 15,000. *Escape Pod* (escapepod.org), one of the oldest SF podcasts, had an audience of approximately 37,000 in 2019.

It's interesting to note that it's often the "digests" are actually the ones mentioned when readers are concerned about financial stability. Adding to the illusion of troubled times for the print digests comes from the paid circulation data that *Locus Magazine* and Gardner Dozois tracked and published over the years. Much of this data was made available via the Statement of Ownership print periodicals are required to publish each year. Other circulation details were provided by editors.

These subscription and newsstand numbers are often quoted with little insight into what it actually means to the field. Many have chosen to see this as an opportunity to declare the death of print or even short fiction. On the other hand, we have some people who, on looking at the wide array of markets, proclaim that we're in a new golden age for short fiction. Both are guilty of looking at only a part of the picture.

Over the last five years, *Analog* has dropped from 14,316 print subscriptions to 10,372, a loss of 3,944; *Asimov's* has dropped from 9,479 to 6,689, a loss of 2,790; and *F&SF* has dropped from 7,576 to 5,363, a loss of 2,213. That may seem disastrous, but it appears it's actually symptomatic of a change in reading habits. In the same time period, *Analog* has risen from 6,040 digital subscriptions to 8,914, a gain of 2,874 and *Asimov's* has risen from 7,573 to 10,584, a gain of 3,011. Unfortunately, *F&SF* does not report its digital subscription figures. These magazines also receive additional income from single issue newsstand sales and on average, this adds between two and three thousand print copies per month.

The total paid subscription numbers may be down for some in this window (*Asimov's* shows a slight gain), but the income generated by the different formats is not equal. Annual US subscriptions to *Analog* and *Asimov's* are $34.97 print and $35.88 digital. *F&SF* subscriptions are $39.97 print and $36.97 digital. While the prices for digital and print subscriptions are relatively similar, print subscriptions cost the publisher more due to printing and shipping, ultimately making the digital edition more profitable. The upwards trend in digital subscriptions should offset the declining print subscriptions and with increasing printing and postal costs eating into profits, this development is better for the long-term health of these publications.

Across the field, $1.99 or $2.99/month have become a standard price for subscriptions. This should be considered a bargain, or almost criminal at this point. The price point has remained largely unchanged over the years while books and other genre content have steadily increased. This stagnation, along with the slow growth in paying readers is becoming a more significant problem for the field. A simple increase of $1, to $2.99 and $3.99/month, would pump much needed resources back into the magazines and it wouldn't surprise me to see this happen within the next few years.

Now is the time to seek out your favorite magazines and subscribe or renew for another year. If you don't have one, I hope you'll use the stories in this book as a guide. Look to the Permissions section to find out where your favorites were published and check them out.

Magazine Comings and Goings

The year started with the announcement that *The Verge* (theverge.com), a tech news website, would be launching *Better Worlds*, "a series of ten original fiction stories, five animated adaptations, and five audio adaptations by a diverse roster of science fiction authors who take a more optimistic view of what lies ahead in ways both large and small, fantastical and everyday." The stories were published in January and February and included works by authors such as John Scalzi, Cadwell Turnbull, Kelly Robson, Karin Lowachee, Justina Ireland, and others.

It was a bit of a wild year for *Compelling Science Fiction* (compellingsciencefiction.com). In March, publisher and editor Joe Stetch announced that they were abandoning their free online edition and adopting a for-purchase-only business model. Stech cited the need to stabilize revenue after years of funding portions out of his own pocket. By September, things had changed again, announcing that he would be closing *Compelling Science Fiction* and that their December issue would be the last. "The reason for halting publication is one of time. With my actual (paid) work, a baby to take care of, and some writing projects of my own, I can't prioritize reading through the 500+ stories/month I receive when submissions are open (we have volunteers to help, but I'm still responsible for over 90% of submissions). I also haven't been able to find the additional readership required to make the magazine financially viable without me." The story still manages to end on a happier note. In early January 2020, Stech announced that *Compelling* would return with him as editor and Flame Tree Press taking over as publisher.

The doors did close, however, at Orson Scott Card's *Intergalactic Medicine Show* (intergalacticmedicineshow.com). *IGMS* ceased publishing in June 2019 and later removed their paywall so their entire back catalog of stories would be available for free online. No reason was provided for the closure. *IGMS* was established in 2005 and was the longest-living and last of the paywall online magazines.

A similar situation occurred at *Apex Magazine* (apex-magazine.com), but instead of closing, editor Jason Sizemore announced that he was putting the magazine on indefinite hiatus after issue 120, with an Afrofuturism issue guest edited by Maurice Broaddus. "It comes down to health and economics and family," he explained as he described recent medical issues and a desire to focus more time on his small press, Apex Books. "Lesley Conner and I have not turned our backs on genre short fiction. We plan to do an open call anthology each year that will contain nearly as many words of short fiction as a whole year's worth of zines." This isn't the first time *Apex* has closed its door and I would not be surprised to see it return soon.

Continuing the trend, Richard Flores announced in December that he was closing *Factor Four Magazine* (factorfourmag.com) after six issues spanning a period of roughly one year. Their final issue was in July. *Factor Four* focused on stories under 1500 words.

Also in December, *Future Science Fiction Digest* (future-sf.com) editor Alex Svartsman announced that their sponsorship from the Future Affairs Administration had come to an end. "Together we were able to publish a considerable amount of excellent international fiction, and we thank FAA for their help and support as the magazine launched and found its footing. While FAA is still considering their options regarding any future partnerships with us, at this moment they're not affiliated with the magazine." Fortunately, *Future SF* has no plans to close, but the loss of funding has caused them to dial back their efforts. This resulted in their December issue being 20% the size of previous issues.

One might look at this section so far and think terrible times are ahead, but it isn't necessarily the case. Markets come and go all the time in science fiction, but that can be a feature rather than a bug. The loss of a few may increase subscriptions at others or create an opportunity for someone new. Many magazines continued to face the challenges of being a small literary business and are still with us. Examples of longevity include *Science Fiction World* (www.sfw.com.cn), the Chinese science fiction magazine with the world's largest circulation for a genre fiction magazine, at forty in 2019; *The Magazine of Fantasy & Science Fiction* at seventy; and *Analog Science Fiction and Fact*, the oldest continually operating SF magazine, which will celebrate ninety years in 2020.

Last year, I noted that there appeared to be a batch of new print magazines making a go of it. Such ventures are complicated beasts, so it's not surprising that I didn't see many of those continue in 2019. However, we did have the launch of *Infinite Worlds* (infiniteworldsmagazine.com), a new limited-edition, print, throwback-style science fiction magazine in the spring. Two issues were published this year and the first issue of 2020 has been teased online.

Asimov's Science Fiction had another strong year and continued to demonstrate why it's one of the leading science fiction magazines. Among their 2019 highlights were stories by Ian R. MacLeod, Tegan Moore, Ray Nayler, Suzanne Palmer, Mercurio D. Rivera, Carrie Vaughn, Kali Wallace, and E. Lily Yu.

Analog Science Fiction and Fact approaches its big anniversary year with plans to apply a more retro cover design in 2020. In 2019, they published excellent stories by Marie Bilodeau, Craig DeLancey, Tom Green, and Alex Nevala-Lee.

The Magazine of Fantasy and Science Fiction had a pleasant mix of science fiction and fantasy stories in 2019. Some of my favorite stories were by Alex Irvine, Cassandra Khaw, Rich Larson, Lavie Tidhar, and Marie Vibbert.

Clarkesworld Magazine happens to be the magazine I edit, so I'll refrain from significant comment and say that some of my favorites this year include stories by Rebecca Campbell, R.S.A. Garcia, A.T. Greenblatt, Bo-Young Kim, Suzanne Palmer, and A Que. Our 2019 content was supplemented by a series of South Korean translations paid for by a grant from LTI Korea.

In June 2019, Irene Gallo was promoted to Vice President, Publisher of Tor.com. This newly created role is dedicated to the Tor.com website and imprint. Many leading editors in the field are selecting the fiction for this site and imprint. Favorites from the two include works by Elizabeth Bear, S.L. Huang, KJ Kabza, Vylar Kaftan, Mary Robinette Kowal, Rich Larson, Ian McDonald, Annalee Newitz, and Alastair Reynolds.

Lightspeed Magazine published a balance of science fiction and fantasy. Among the stronger works of science fiction were stories by Carolyn Ives Gilman, Dominica Phetteplace, and Caroline M. Yoachim.

Uncanny Magazine published six issues and a *Best of Uncanny* anthology was published by Subterranean at the very end of the year. They published more fantasy than science fiction in 2019 and as in prior years, I thought that's where the majority of their strongest stories lay. Maurice Broaddus contributes their strongest SF tale for the year.

UK veteran science fiction magazine *Interzone* (ttapress.com/interzone) and sister magazine *Black Static* (ttapress.com/blackstatic) returned to their bimonthly schedule in 2019. My favorite story in *Interzone* this year was by Maria Haskins.

Strange Horizons (strangehorizons.com), one of the oldest continually running online magazines, continued to publish issues on a weekly schedule. Sister magazine, *Samovar* (samovar.strangehorizons.com), is focused on translations and published three issues in 2019. This appears to be the only genre magazine that publishes translations alongside the story in its original language.

GigaNotoSaurus (giganotosaurus.org) appeared to go on a temporary hiatus in 2019, publishing only six stories. Much to my pleasure, they returned to regular production and finished the year back on their monthly schedule.

The list of existing genre magazines is quite lengthy, so I tend to keep the focus on those that had some important news or stories that impacted this project in some way. This should in no way imply that they are any less valuable to the field. Publications such as *Abyss & Apex Magazine* (abyssapexzine. com); *Amazing Stories* (amazingstoriesmag.com), *Anathema* (anathemamag. com); *Andromeda Spaceways* (andromedaspaceways.com); *Aurealis*, (aurealis. com.au); *Cosmic Roots and Eldritch Shores* (cosmicrootsandeldritchshores. com); *Daily Science Fiction* (dailysciencefiction.com), *Diabolical Plots* (diabolicalplots.com); *DreamForge* (dreamforgemagazine.com); *Fireside Magazine* (firesidefiction.com); *Fiyah Magazine* (fiyahlitmag.com); *Fiction River* (fictionriver.com); *Flash Fiction Online* (flashfictiononline.com); *Galaxy's Edge* (galaxysedge.com); *Helios Quarterly* (heliosquarterly.com); *James Gunn's Ad Astra* (adastrasf.com); *Lady Churchill's Rosebud Wristlet* (smallbeerpress. com/lcrw); *Mithila Review* (mithilareview.com); *Neo-Opsis* (neo-opsis.ca); *Omenana Magazine of Africa's Speculative Fiction* (omenana.com); *On Spec* (onspecmag.wordpress.com); *Shoreline of Infinity* (shorelineofinfinity.com); and so many more make up the wide array of flavors one can currently enjoy. You should sample them as well.

Interesting science fiction can also be found outside the standard publishing ecosystem for such things. *Future Tense Science Fiction*, a partnership between *Slate*, New America, and Arizona State University, continued to publish an assortment of quality fiction from a variety of authors. A notable feature of this series is that each story is accompanied by a response essay from a professional working in a related field. My favorites from their 2019 lineup include stories by Indrapramit Das and Ken Liu.

Shorter works can often be found at tech and science website Motherboard's *Terraform* (motherboard.vice.com/terraform) and within the science magazine *Nature* as *Nature Future* (nature.com/nature/articles?type=futures). *The New York Times* even jumped into the fray with a new Op-Eds From the Future (nytimes.com/spotlight/future-oped) column featuring short works by a variety of names you may recognize.

And let's not forget the wealth of stories you can listen to in podcast form. Many of the magazines listed above (*Asimov's*, *Clarkesworld*, *Lightspeed*, and *Uncanny*, for example) regularly make some or all of their stories available in audio. Other publications started in this format—though many are now making the text of stories available. Among these, The Escape Artists produce four of the more successful podcasts: *Escape Pod*, *PodCastle* (podcastle. org), *PseudoPod* (pseudopod.org), and *Cast of Wonders* (castofwonders.org). Other interesting fiction podcasts include *Levar Burton Reads* (levarburtonpodcast.com), *The Drabblecast* (drabblecast.org), *Glittership* (glittership. com), and *StarShipSofa* (starshipsofa.com).

Anthologies and Collections

There was an interesting assortment of anthologies this year. Five are represented by stories in this book, but it jumps to eleven when you include the recommended reading. If I had to pick my favorite, it would be *Mission Critical*, edited by Jonathan Strahan. It features some great stories by Tobias S. Buckell, Aliette de Bodard, Greg Egan, Yoon Ha Lee, and Peter Watts.

On another day, I could have just as easily picked *Current Futures*, edited by Ann VanderMeer. In honor of World Oceans Day in June 2019, XPRIZE recruited Ann to work with eighteen science fiction authors and artists from all seven continents. The end result was an online anthology of original short stories set in a future when technology has helped unlock the secrets of the ocean. My favorites here include stories by Kameron Hurley, Gwyneth Jones, Karen Lord, Malka Older, and Vandana Singh.

The Mythic Dream, edited by Dominik Parisien and Navah Wolfe, was a strong contender, even as a mixed genre anthology. The theme here focuses on reclaiming myths and features some excellent SF stories by John Chu, Indrapramit Das, and Ann Leckie.

Broken Stars, edited by Ken Liu, a follow-up to his successful *Invisible Planets*, featured works by Chinese science fiction authors. Several of these are reprints, but well worth the price of admission. I was particularly pleased to see stories by Cixin Liu and Han Song that were these works' first appearance in English.

New Suns: Original Speculative Fiction by People of Color, edited by Nisi Shawl is a multi-genre anthology of works by emerging and seasoned writers of many races. It features a wide range of stories, with my favorite written by Tobias S. Buckell.

The theme of politics was popular among anthologists this year. *A People's Future of the United States*, edited by Victor LaValle and John Joseph Adams, features stories influenced by our deeply divided political times and explores new forms of freedom, love, and justice. I thought the best stories were by Charlie Jane Anders and Sam J. Miller. *Do Not Go Quietly*, edited by Jason Sizemore and Lesley Connor offered up an anthology of resistance stories. The best story here was by Karin Lowachee. And finally, *If This Goes On*, edited by Cat Rambo, assigned thirty writers to the task of projecting forward to see the effect of today's politics and policies on our world a generation from now. My favorite here was by E. Lily Yu.

Other anthologies of note include *Deep Signal*, edited by Eric Olive, an oversized and illustrated anthology of speculative fiction where the art is as important as the fiction. Features a strong story from Aliette de Bodard. *The Gollancz Book of South Asian Science Fiction*, edited by Tarun K. Saint, is exactly what the title suggests. It's a good introduction to SF from that region, even if it can be a bit uneven in places. Vandana Singh's contribution to this book is a high point. At the moment, it's only available as an import. *Wastelands: The New Apocalypse*, edited by John Joseph Adams, continues along the post-apocalyptic path of the other Wastelands anthologies. If you enjoyed those, you'll likely find something you like here. My favorite here was by Elizabeth Bear.

That is hardly a complete list. My reading notes list at least a dozen other anthologies that contained original science fiction. While their stories may not have made this year's lists, they still represent a valuable contribution to the field that I don't want to diminish. Also important to the strength of the field are the many reprint anthologies published each year. With a few exceptions, this portion of the market is almost entirely the domain of the small press, indicating the important role they play in keeping older works in circulation.

Several reprint anthologies cover the year's best spectrum, like this one. In 2019, other such volumes that included science fiction were: *The Year's Best Science Fiction & Fantasy 2020* edited by Rich Horton; *The Best Science Fiction and Fantasy of the Year, Volume Thirteen* edited by Jonathan Strahan (the last in this series); *The Best American Science Fiction and Fantasy 2019* edited by Carmen Maria Machado, series editor John Joseph Adams; *The Year's Best Military & Adventure SF: Volume 5* edited by David Afsharirad; *Transcendent 4: The Year's Best Transgender Speculative Fiction* edited by Bogi Takács; and *Best of British Science Fiction 2018* edited by Donna Scott. Of special note is Gardner Dozois' final anthology, *The Very Best of the Best: 35 Years of The Year's Best Science Fiction*, a fine contribution to his long career as an editor.

Single author collections were again quite common in 2019, including slightly more than usual from the larger publishers. These most frequently consist of previous published stories, but do occasionally include new works. Some of the year's most notable include: *Exhalation: Stories* by Ted Chiang; *Of Wars, and Memories, and Starlight* by Aliette de Bodard; *Radicalized* by Cory Doctorow; *The Best of Greg Egan* by Greg Egan; *Meet Me in the Future* by Kameron Hurley; *Big Cat and Other Stories* by Gwyneth Jones; *Hexarchate Stories* by Yoon Ha Lee; *All Worlds Are Real* by Susan Palwick; *Sooner Or Later Everything Falls Into the Sea* by Sarah Pinsker; and *The Trans Space Octopus Congregation* by Bogi Takács.

The 2019 Scorecard

My selections for this year include twenty-eight works, up two from last year. For those interested in tracking the sources of the stories selected:

	Stories Included	Percentage
Magazines	**16**	**57.143%**
Anthologies	**10**	**35.714%**
Collections	**0**	**0%**
Standalone	**2**	**7.143%**

These categories represent a total of fourteen difference sources, which is three less than last year. This resulted in a drop of one in the magazine, anthology, and collection categories. If you care to break down the magazines by those that offer free online editions and those that don't, the online publications had ten (down one) of the sixteen mentioned above.

Standalone works are those that were published on their own and not connected to any of the other categories. There were none included in last year's list.

Short stories (under 7500 words) and novelettes (under 17500 words) were much more balanced this year with thirteen each. In 2018, there were eighteen and eleven respectively. Novellas (under 40000 words) decreased from three to two.

And from my Recommended Reading List:

	Stories Included	Percentage
Magazines	**26**	**57.778%**
Anthologies	**12**	**26.667%**
Collections	**3**	**6.667%**
Standalone	**3**	**6.667%**
Other	**1**	**2.222%**

I've added "other" to this listing because I'm not entirely sure how I'd like to categorize something that has been posted to someone's Patreon account. It would be easy to argue that these are either standalone, part of an unofficial collection, or even a single-author magazine, depending on your perspective. Given that, it seemed prudent to leave it separate for now.

There were fifty-four stories on the recommended reading list last year and only forty-five this year. Magazines dropped by one and anthologies by four. Collections increased by two and standalone dropped by seven. The standalone category was the only surprise and I suspect that had more to do with the genre makeup of the 2019 catalog than anything else.

Between the recommended stories and those included in this book, that's seven fewer stories overall. That said, I'm not left with the sense that the difference was reflective of any core differences in quality between the two years. Even the decline in the variety of markets represented is less worrisome when broken down by type. It feels safe to say that such fluctuations are a normal part of the year-to-year state of the market.

The International Effect

Last year, I made a point of highlighting how an increasing number of authors from outside the US, Canada, UK, and Australia writing communities were finding their way into English-language magazines and anthologies with increasing frequency. As an editor and reader, I see this as cause for celebration. As I said then, science fiction is at its best when it is incorporating and challenged by new ideas and perspectives. This recent influx will be of benefit to the future of the field both domestic and abroad.

Although efforts to broaden the market to include more works from around the world—including those written in English and translations— have happened on and off for decades, it appears as though this time around, it's succeeding. There's much speculation as to why things are different now.

You can certainly credit some of this to the rise of digital submissions making it easier for international authors to submit work and, as before, it has dedicated individuals, like Ken Liu, who have championed or inspired. A more obvious difference is that this time around, there's an effort to make international works part of magazines and anthologies not specifically dedicated to them. Those theme anthologies still happen, but they are greatly assisted by the presence of these authors across the greater sphere of short fiction projects. It's becoming more difficult to find magazines that haven't published works in any works in translation in recent times.

Notable anthologies highlighting international or translated science fiction in 2019 include: *Broken Stars: Contemporary Chinese Science Fiction in Translation* edited by Ken Liu; *Readymade Bodhisatva* (South Korean SF) edited by Sunyoung Park and Sang Joon Park; *Palestine +100* edited by Basma Ghalayini; *Sunspot Jungle* volumes 1 & 2 edited by Bill Campbell; *The Gollancz Book of South Asian Science Fiction* edited by Tarun K. Saint; and *Best Asian Short Stories 2019* edited by Hisham Bustani.

Notable 2019 Awards

The 77th World Science Fiction Convention, Dublin 2019, was held in Dublin, Ireland, from August 15th to August 19th, 2019. The 2019 Hugo Awards, presented at Worldcon 77, were: Best Novel, *The Calculating Stars*, by Mary Robinette Kowal; Best Novella, *Artificial Condition* by Martha Wells; Best Novelette, "If at First You Don't Succeed, Try, Try Again," by Zen Cho; Best Short Story, "A Witch's Guide to Escape: A Practical Compendium of Portal Fantasies," by Alix E. Harrow; Best Series, Wayfarers, by Becky Chambers; Best Graphic Story, *Monstress, Volume 3: Haven*, written by Marjorie M. Liu, illustrated by Sana Takeda; Best Related Work, Archive of Our Own, a project of the Organization for Transformative Works; Best Professional Editor, Long Form, Navah Wolfe; Best Professional Editor, Short Form, Gardner Dozois; Best Professional Artist, Charles Vess; Best Dramatic Presentation (short form), *The Good Place:* "Janet(s),"; Best Dramatic Presentation (long form), *Spider-Man: Into the Spider-Verse*; Best Semiprozine, *Uncanny*; Best Fanzine, *Lady Business*; Best Fancast, *Our Opinions Are Correct*; Best Fan Writer, Foz Meadows; Best Fan Artist, Likhain (Mia Sereno); Best Art Book, *The Books of Earthsea: The Complete Illustrated Edition*, illustrated by Charles Vess, written by Ursula K. Le Guin; plus the John W. Campbell Award for Best New Writer, Jeannette Ng and Lodestar Award for Best Young Adult Book, *Children of Blood and Bone*, by Tomi Adeyemi.

The 2018 Nebula Awards, presented at a banquet at the Marriott Warner Center, Woodland Hills, CA, on May 18, 2019, were: Best Novel, *The Calculating Stars*, by Mary Robinette Kowal; Best Novella, *The Tea Master and the Detective*, by Aliette de Bodard; Best Novelette, "The Only Harmless Great Thing," by Brooke Bolander; Best Short Story, "The Secret Lives of the Nine Negro Teeth of George Washington," by Phenderson Djèlí Clark; Best Game Writing, *Black Mirror: Bandersnatch*; Ray Bradbury Award, *Spider-Man: Into the Spider-Verse*; the Andre Norton Award to *Children of Blood and Bone*, by Tomi Adeyemi; the Kate Wilhelm Solstice Award to Nisi Shawl and Neil Clarke; the Kevin O' Donnell Jr. Service to SFWA Award to Lee Martindale; and the Damon Knight Memorial Grand Master Award to William Gibson.

There was a bit of a controversy surrounding the Nebula Awards this year. A group of self-published SFWA members promoted several works in a way that felt very similar to the slates that caused so many problems with the Hugo Awards earlier in the decade. The Hugo Award rules have since been modified to make it more difficult for that method to be effective, but the SFWA didn't have (and hasn't added) a similar countermeasure. The person responsible for the "slate" has since apologized, claiming that they didn't mean it the way it was perceived by the community at large. None of the finalists who were connected to this list withdrew their nominations, nor were any of them among this year's winners.

The 2019 World Fantasy Awards, presented at a banquet on November 3, 2019, at the Marriott Los Angeles Airport Hotel in Los Angeles CA, during the Forty-fifth Annual World Fantasy Convention, were: Best Novel, *Witchmark*, by C.L. Polk; Best Novella, "The Privilege of the Happy Ending," by Kij Johnson; Best Short Fiction (tie), "Ten Deals with the Indigo Snake," by Mel Kassel and "Like a River Loves the Sky," by Emma Törzs; Best Collection, *The Tangled Lands*, by Paolo Bacigalupi & Tobias S. Buckell; Best Anthology, *Worlds Seen in Passing*, edited by Irene Gallo; Best Artist, Rovina Cai; Special Award (Professional), to Huw Lewis-Jones for *The Writer's Map: An Atlas of Imaginary Lands*; Special Award (Non-Professional), to Scott H. Andrews, for *Beneath Ceaseless Skies*. Plus Lifetime Achievement Awards to Hayao Miyazaki and Jack Zipes.

The 2019 John W. Campbell Memorial Award was won by: *Blackfish City* by Sam J. Miller.

The 2018 Theodore Sturgeon Memorial Award for Best Short Story was won by: "When Robot and Crow Saved East St. Louis" by Annalee Newitz.

The 2019 Philip K. Dick Memorial Award went to: *Theory of Bastards* by Audrey Schulman.

The 2019 Arthur C. Clarke Award was won by: *Rosewater* by Tade Thompson.

The 2018 James Tiptree, Jr. Memorial Award was won by: "They Will Dream In the Garden," by Gabriela Damián Miravete and translated by Adrian Demopulos.

The 2018 Sidewise Award for Alternate History went to (Long Form): *The Calculating Stars*, by Mary Robinette Kowal and (Short Form): *Codex Valtierra* by Oscar (Xiu) Ramirez & Emmanuel Valtierra. A special achievement award was presented by Eric Flint.

The 2019 WSFA Small Press Award: "The Thing in the Walls Wants Your Small Change" by Virginia M. Mohlere.

In Memoriam

Among those the field lost in 2019 are:

Gene Wolfe, SFWA Grand Master, Science Fiction Hall of Fame inductee, winner of two Nebula Awards, four World Fantasy Awards, six Locus Awards, a Campbell Award, a BSFA Award, and many other honors, author of The Book of the New Sun series; **Janet Asimov**, author of several novels, including collaborations with her husband, Isaac; **Carrie Richerson**, author and two-time Campbell Award finalist; **Alexander Siletsky**, Belarusian author of primarily short fiction; **Robert S. Friedman**, publisher at The Donning Company and Rainbow Ridge Books; **Michaelene Pendleton**, short story author and copy editor; **Carol Emshwiller**, author, winner of the World Fantasy Lifetime Achievement award, winner of the World Fantasy Award, Philip K. Dick Award, and a two-time winner of Nebula Award; **Allan Cole**, author and frequent collaborator with Chris Bunch on the Sten series, television writer for shows such as *The Incredible Hunk* and *Buck Rogers in the 25th Century*; **Adrish Bardhan**, Bengali editor of India's first science fiction magazine, recipient of the Sudhindranath Raha Award; **Dennis Etchison**, author, recipient of the Stoker Lifetime Achievement Award, winner of the British Fantasy Award and the World Fantasy Award; **Milan Asadurov**, author, translator, and founder of the Galaxy imprint in Bulgaria; **Yoshio Kabayashi**, Japanese editor and translator; **Paul Abbamondi**, short story author and comic artist. Paul also worked for me as a slush reader in the early days of *Clarkesworld*; **Barry Hughart**, author and winner of the World Fantasy Award; **J. Neil Schulman**, author and winner of the Prometheus Award; **Robert N. Stephenson** author, editor, and anthologist, winner of the Aurealis Award; **Betty Ballantine**, publisher and founder of several publishing houses, helped introduce mass market paperbacks to the US, inductee of the Science Fiction Hall of Fame, recipient of the President's Award from SFWA, a World Fantasy Lifetime Achievement award, and a Special Committee Award at the 2006 Worldcon; **Mikhail Achmanov**, Russian author and translator, winner of the Alexander Belyaev Literary Prize; **Brad Linaweaver**, author, two-time winner of Prometheus Award, winner of the Phoenix Award; **Melissa C. Michaels**, author and SFWA's first webmaster; **Katherine MacLean**, author, winner of the Nebula and Cordwainer Smith Rediscovery Awards; **Terrance Dicks**, author, screenwriter, and script editor; **Andrzej Polkowski**, Polish translator; **Michael Blumlein**, author, nominated for the World Fantasy Award, the Stoker, and the Tiptree Award; **Gahan Wilson**, artist, author, recipient of the World Fantasy Lifetime Achievement Award; **Vonda N. McIntyre**, author, winner of the Hugo Award, three Nebula Awards, the Service to SFWA award, and the Clareson Award, founder of the Clarion West Writers Workshop.

In Closing

I always try to end these introductions on a positive note. The above list of people we loved and lost in 2019 makes that a bit more challenging, but as we mourn those who have left us, we also celebrate the new writers making their way through the field.

Each year, I try to single out a new/new-ish author that has impressed me and I believe to be someone you should be paying attention to. This year, I've selected the author who penned the last story in this book, A.T. Greenblatt. To be fair, I'm really stretching things by even calling her new-ish, but I think her inclusion is more than warranted. Aliza first started publishing her stories in 2010, but in the last few years her work has been consistently catching my eye. There's definitely something important going on there and I believe we've only just begun to see the heights she is capable of. I can't wait to read what comes next and encourage you to track down her work too.

Suzanne Palmer is an award-winning and acclaimed writer of science fiction. In 2018, she won a Hugo Award for Best Novelette for "The Secret Life of Bots." Her short fiction has won readers' awards for *Asimov's*, *Analog*, and *Interzone* magazines, and has been included in the Locus Recommended Reading List. Her work has also been features in numerous anthologies, and she has twice been a finalist for the Theodore Sturgeon Memorial Award and once for the Eugie M. Foster Memorial Award. In May, DAW Books published the second book in her Finder's Chronicles series, *Driving the Deep*. She currently lives in western Massachusetts and is a Linux and database system administrator at Smith College. You can find her online at zanzjan.net and on Twitter at @zanzjan.

THE PAINTER OF TREES

Suzanne Palmer

I go down to the gate, swipe my security pass, and step through the ten-meter tall, still-opening doors into the last of the wild lands. I remove my boots at the threshold and set them on a rack for that purpose, then carefully wash my feet from the basin of rainwater, still chill from the night before. When the doors have closed and sealed again, I remove my clothes. There is no one on this side of the wall to see who would take either advantage or offense at my nakedness. I wash my body from the same basin, shivering from the shock of the cold, before I remove the plain linen cloth from its hook above the rack and wrap it around myself. And then I walk down the path to find the painter of trees.

The path curves over a small slope and then down a kilometer or so to the glade at the edge of a forest. The vegetation changes around me as I walk, from the familiar sharp-bladed grasses that have crept over the wall and seeded themselves along its perimeter, to the tiny, delicate frills of blue-green of the grass that first grew here, now in forced retreat. I know how soft they would be under my bare feet, how they would tickle, but also how easily they will crush and die, and though I know I will surely give into temptation one last time before they are gone forever, this time I keep to the stones.

The trees here are, outwardly, very similar to the trees of home, except for their smooth exteriors and symmetrical branching. Their leaves are wide, gold-green, open cones, grouped in threes at the end of each stem, which catch and hold rain for a long while after a storm. Cut a tree open, though, and you find neither rings nor wood at all, but hexagonal cells all tucked neatly together, larger the closer to the center they are. Each one is capable, if broken free, of starting a new tree by itself, but together they each serve different functions, observed to change over time as both external conditions and each cell's internal position in the whole changes.

Mathematically, structurally, the trees are beautiful as they are naturally. Among them there are flashes of bright color, vibrant pigments carefully etched into shallow scratches in the trunks forming intricate, hypnotic patterns, no two the same, none less compelling than the others. There have been days I have spent hours staring at them, or at our archived 3-D images, and always there is that sense that some vast understanding of the meaning of being is just there, in the lines, waiting for me to finally *understand*.

From here, I can see signs the trees are dying.

The small valley has a river that winds through it, and I cross a bridge made of carefully placed stones to the far side. I can see the large stick-ball nests up in the canopy above, fewer with each visit, and I can smell smoke.

I find Tski tending to the fire as one of the nest balls, carefully extricated from its perch in the trees above and set upon stones, crackles and hisses in flame.

Tski sees me, and turns toward me—the Ofti don't have heads, per se, with all the functions we think of as specific to heads integrated in with the rest of their singular, horizontal lump of a body the same color as the leaves above. It stands atop nine legs—it lost three in an accident, it told me once—that are fine, graceful arcs that end in three pieces that can come together as a sharp, dangerous point, or open to function like fingers.

I sit on the ground, eye level with it. After a while it speaks, a complex series of whistles, clicks, and trills, that my implant decodes for me.

"I am sorry that Ceye has died," I say, and the implant moments later returns that in Tski's own language.

"Ceye ate the new grasses and became sick," Tski tells me. "Ceye was afraid we would starve when the old grasses are gone, with your wall between us and other meadows."

There are no other meadows, though; that is why there is a wall. It was carefully placed so that you can't see it from here, in the heart of the forest valley, but that was before we knew the animals here were intelligent tree-dwellers and could likely see from the canopy. But still, they cannot see over it, which is for the best.

Tski swivels its body again, back and forth for a few long minutes. It is thinking. "Do your people eat the new grasses?" it asked at last.

"No," I say, because we do not.

"Then why did you bring them?"

"It is part of our native ecosystem," I explain.

"Even the soil and the air do not taste right any longer," Tski says, and it picks up a stick with its tiny finger-blades and pokes the fire.

In the silence, I look around the glade. "Where are the others?"

"Desperate," Tski says. "They have gone to look for hope."

There is no response to give to that. "Will you paint Ceye's tree?" I ask instead.

"When her nest is cold ash, and I can mix it with the colors," Tski says. "Only then will I paint. I am almost out of *warm-sky-midday-blue*, which we traveled to meadow-by-the-five-hills to obtain. I am too old to go, and only Ceye also knew the way. Unless you also could go?"

"I can't," I say. Because it is not there, but also because even if it was, it is not something the council would accept. There is no way forward except forward, they would admonish me, no path to success without steadiness of thought, purpose, and action.

The burning nest has collapsed down into itself, its once-intricate woven structure now a chaos of ember and ash.

"It does not matter," Tski says at last. "There are only the three others and myself left now, and there will be no one to paint for the last of us that goes."

The Ofti pokes the fire a few more times, then lays its stick carefully aside. "Tomorrow," it says.

"May I come watch?"

"I cannot stop you," Tski says.

"If you could, would you?"

"Yes. But it is too late now. You are strange, squishy people and you move as if you are always in the act of falling, but instead it is everyone around you who falls and does not rise again," Tski says. "And so it will also be with us."

"Yes," I answer in turn. It is a good summation of who we are, and what we do: we are teeth on a cog, always moving forward and doing our part until we fall away and the next tooth takes up our work in turn.

I get up from the ground, my legs stiff, and stretch. "Tomorrow, then."

I make the walk back to the gate without looking back, but my thoughts drag on me.

The Council members wait for the beginning chime, and all take their seats around the table with precise synchronicity, so that no one is ahead, no one is behind. The table is circular and is inlaid with a stylized copper cog design, so that each member is reminded that the way forward for each of them is with the others. This is how steadiness of purpose is maintained.

And hatred, Joesla thinks, as each face opposite perfectly reflects the righteous moral bankruptcy of their own. "I propose, with some urgency, that we take whatever steps are necessary to preserve the remaining Ofti population and environs before it is lost forever."

"We already have extensive samples—" Tauso, to her left, says. He is the biological archivist, and his expression suggests he has found a personal criticism in her words.

"Forgive me, your collection is unassailable in its diligence and scope. I was speaking in regards to the still-living population," Joesla interrupts.

"It is already too late." Motas speaks from directly across the table. There is no leader among them by consensus, but Motas—always rigid, always perfect in his adherence to the letter of their laws—leads them anyway. "There are only four left; they no longer have sufficient genetic diversity to survive, even if we did find some way to insulate them from the planetary terraforming changes."

"With Tauso's collection, we could bolster their gene pool," Joesla says.

"To what end? A great expenditure of effort and resources for something that gives us nothing in return? Your proposal is backwards thinking," Motas says.

"Not for the Ofti," Joesla counters. "They have a unique culture and language that should not be discarded so hastily. I know it has been a long time since any of you have spent time among them, but—"

"The Ofti have no future. They are already gone, but for a few final moments," Motas interrupts. "Does anyone here second Joesla's proposal that we abandon our own guiding principles for this lost cause?"

Many should, but none will or do. Tauso does not meet Joesla's eyes—*and why should he*, she thinks bitterly, *when he has what he is required to save already?* His silence is a betrayal of both her and himself.

"The matter is settled, then," Motas declares. "Forward."

"Forward," some portion of the council responds, some with enthusiasm, some less so. Tauso is silent with Joesla, but it is too late, too small a gesture in the face of his earlier cowardice, and she will not forgive him this day. Now there is a necessary discussion of high-speed rail lines, anticipated crop yields in the newly reformed soil, and planning for the next wave of colonists; they cannot linger for one member's wasteful, wasted regret.

There is smoke rising from the glade again. I try not to hurry down the path—I remind myself that I am an observer here, nothing more—but if my steps are quicker than usual, who would there be to accuse me? No one else comes here.

Tski is hopping back and forth unsteadily, whether because of its missing legs or its great agitation, beside a large, roaring bonfire. It does not have its tending stick, and the flames spark and flare and crackle with uncontrolled abandon. Dimly within the bright fire I can make out three shapes, three nest balls.

"What happened?" I ask.

It takes several minutes for my translator to make sense of Tski's distressed whistles, but at last it speaks: "The others walked the circumference of the wall, back to where they started, and found no cause for hope. They have returned home and burned themselves. I tried to stop them, but I could not."

I see now its awkwardness of movement is because many of its remaining legs are burned.

I do not know what to do.

"Sesh. Awsa. Eesn. That was their names," Tski says. "Awsa and Eesn were children of my children. They should be here with their long lives ahead to remember my last days, and not this."

"I am sorry," I say.

"Are you?" Tski asks. The fires still rage, and some of the native grass beside the stones has caught, but the Ofti either does not notice or ignores this. Does it matter which?

"I don't know," I say. Through the wavering heat and smoke, I can see that Tski had started already to paint Ceye's tree, no doubt wanting to get it done before I could arrive and be an unwelcome witness. It must have been doing that when the others returned to end their lives, as there are leaves on the ground around the base of the trunk, their cones filled with different colors, and I can see the silvery lines of etching up the tree trunk that had not yet been filled. The effect is still mesmerizing, even so unfinished, and I feel momentarily lost in it again. Then the realization strikes me: with its legs burned, Tski will not be able to finish the painting, will not take me that one step closer to elusive understanding. And at that, my heart catches in my throat, and I feel now the loss that Joesla had warned us of like a million cuts in my skin. Too late, too late!

"Can I help you paint?" I ask.

It is the wrong thing to say. "Go!" Tski cries. "These are not here for you, for your eyes or alien thoughts. These are our memories, made in love of one another, a declaration for future generations, and you have destroyed us. Leave now and do not return."

I stand there for a while. Tski watches the fires burn, and does not move to tend it, nor to throw itself upon it. The thought that Tski might burn the grove down once I am gone keeps me there longer, until at last the burning nests have been consumed and the grassfire has died out, leaving a three-meter blackened, jagged scar on the land, an indelible fracture that will never grow back.

Tski makes a sound that the translation implant cannot work with, perhaps because it is not a word, just inarticulate grief. I should not have come, should not have stayed this long. These conversations with Tski have not been forward-thinking, and I know this, and knew better, but yet I came. It is a defect in my commitment to my own people that I let strangeness and novelty tempt me.

"I am sorry," I say again, and this time I leave.

I stay on the path, even though my feet want to walk upon the native grasses one last time, because I am certain I will not come again.

At the gate, I leave my linen shift, bathe again with the lukewarm water, and when the sun and meager breeze has left my skin chill and mostly dry I dress and gather my things and put my real life back on.

The gates open, and despite a life of training and my commitment to our ways and philosophies, this time I look back.

Tski is coming up the path toward me. It is moving with difficulty and obvious pain, made the worse by the urgency with which it is trying to catch up to me. I should not have looked back, should now turn and step through the gate and close the doors for this last time, but I cannot.

Tski stops a few meters from me, and almost collapses before it gathers its strength to stand tall again. "Show me," it says.

"What?" I ask. I do not understand.

"Show me what is now outside this wall, where once my children played and ran and climbed. Show me what you have done with my world, what you have that is so much better than us."

On my side of the wall, it is city under construction, a thousand identical structures for ten thousand people, all looking only forward, in the direction we, the council, point. There is no art, no individual movement away from the whole, nothing rare to puzzle over. It is an existence I am proud of, and proud of my part in, but it is only for us and I do not want to explain or justify any of it, nor have to face the council and explain myself.

"No," I say.

"Could you stop me?" Tski asks.

"Yes," I say.

"Would you, if you could?"

"Yes," I say again.

"Then stop me," Tski says, and it steps around me and heads toward the gates.

I take the small gun from my bag. All council members carry one for protection, for moments of dispensing justice, and although I have never used it except in training, it is solid and comfortable in my hand, and with it I kill Tski.

It crumples, and becomes still, and in the removal of its animation it becomes just a thing, a leftover bit of debris from this world that has been repurposed. Now, I can turn my back and proceed through the gates and return to this city of ours, and be whole and compliant in forward-thinking again.

Joesla speaks barely a moment after the council chime has rung and everyone has settled in their seats. "The Ofti are extinct," she says. "Three of the remaining population appear to have self-immolated, and the last was found dead at the exterior gates with significant burns. I recommend a necropsy to determine the cause."

"Surely it must have succumbed to the burns?" Motas says.

"There may be things we can learn—"

"Counselor Tauso, do we have any incomplete biological or behavioral data that could still be obtained from this specimen, if retrieved?" Motas asks.

Tauso looks miserable. His eyes are puffy, as if he has been crying, though none would ask and none would admit such a thing in his place. Tears only ever serve the past. "No," he says, his voice barely a whisper, then he speaks again louder and more firmly. "No."

"Then what would you propose we learn from such a procedure, Counselor Joesla? Its death is sooner than we would have anticipated, but it was also inevitable, and its cause does seem self-evident."

I want to know why it crawled all that way, after being burned, to die at our gate, Joesla wants to say, but Motas is right, for all she hates it. The Ofti was old and injured. There is no purpose now, nothing to be gained, and whatever the Ofti wanted in its last moments was already lost to them. "I feel it would be a matter of completeness of record," she says instead.

"So noted," Motas says. "Does anyone second that proposal?"

There are hesitations, shared looks, mutual avoidance, but in the end, predictably, no one does.

"There is the matter of the grove and it surrounding lands," Avel brings up, from Joesla's right. "We had spoken about keeping it as is, as an educational, historical attraction. If we wish to do so, we should act now before the remaining grass and trees deteriorate further; it would only be a matter of a week or two of work to encase everything individually so they are preserved in their current state."

"It is a waste of space that could be used for something productive," Banad speaks up.

"I would vote for preservation," Joesla says.

"As would I," Tauso adds.

Motas turns to Avel. "I propose you bring the full details of a preservation project to our next meeting, so we may view and assess its merits and costs objectively. Banad, if you have an alternate proposal, then likewise we need all the relevant specifics and an objective justification for why it is a better use of the space. Does anyone second me?"

Tauso nods, and swallows. "I do," he says.

"Good. Forward," Motas says, and then they adjourn.

The grove looks the same as the last time I was here, but it feels empty.

It has not rained here in weeks—the moisture-laden clouds were needed elsewhere, with our fledgling farms—so the ash and small remains of the three burned nests have not washed away. I walk around them to where Tski had set up his leaves of paint, and I sit in front of them, and I look at the trees, dozens and dozens of them, here and in the forest behind, many freshly painted, many more marking the fading record of thousands of generations gone.

I still do not comprehend my own attraction, how this uncivilized, unrefined, *unforward* art can feel so alive, so in the moment, so connecting. So utterly alien. Perhaps it is the simple act of remembering the dead, when I come from a people where to mourn, to grieve, to remember those who are no longer part of the future, is the most foolish backward thinking of all.

Yet it is the painted trees that keep drawing me here, and they are still here; Tski was, ultimately, an obstacle to my full and peaceful enjoyment of them. Surely, though none of this would exist without the Ofti, now it is ours. Mine.

There is pride and relief as I think this, and also a deep shame that feels wrapped around the core of my being. Guilt is a backwards emotion and I disavow that shame, even if it will not leave me be. Instead, I find that the more I study them, the more the designs on the trees seem to be mocking me, forever locked away from my comprehension. Tski must have followed me, made me kill it, because it knew that by doing so it would steal this from me.

The worst is the half-finished memorial on Ceye's tree. I should have stayed here that day and forced Tski back to work, forced it to finish this last tree, so that I could have the whole now, and walk away satisfied that I missed and lost nothing. But it is broken, like Tski is broken, and it is Tski's doing that both should be so.

Forward, then.

I did not change my clothes nor leave my things at the gate; there is no fear of bringing microorganisms with me that could damage what is already, functionally, administratively dead. From my bag I take out blue paint that I had made in one of our autofab units. Holding it now against the blue in Tski's leaf, I see mine is darker, not the right shade at all. But it will be close enough! Blue is blue. I use my fingers and I rub it on Ceye's tree, press it into the scratches Tski left with my fingertips, until, breathing heavily from the exertion, I stand back again to admire my own accomplishment.

It is a mess, an inarticulate, artless smear.

I take several deep breaths, and then I go back in and I try again, using my fingernails instead of fingertips, trying to work with the flow of the lines, trying to find how it is supposed to go. I chip my nails, and several bleed before I give up, recap my jar of paint, and stand back to see that I have just made it worse.

I do not understand how I—*I!*—could fail at this frivolous thing that some dead animal moldering in the grass up the hill could comprehend and encompass. I had thought, in my arrogance, in my superior thinking, that after my practice on Ceye's tree I would for my last act here paint Tski's tree, and no one would ever know it was me. And thus I would be preserved, and every one of my people who looked here for generations would remember *me*, even if they did not know they did so. Then I would not just be one undifferentiated tooth on a cog gear, turning forward, resisting backward with all the others, but a fixed point.

I feel in that instant that all I have accomplished is to immortalize my own foolishness, to forever diminish everything I have ever reliably and competently accomplished under a shadow of mockery. Furious—at myself, at Tski for forcing my hand, at this entire planet—I throw down my jar of paint. I had sealed it, but it hits one of the rocks just right (just wrong!) and shatters, and paint droplets fly everywhere—not just onto the disaster I've made of Ceye's tree, but onto others nearby.

"No!" I cry out loud, and I sink to my knees in the dying grasses and am consumed by my own rage and horror.

Joesla stands, trying not to shift impatiently from foot to foot, waiting for the rest of the council to arrive. She is early, but not by much. Banad was already here, clutching his report pad to his chest as if to protect his ambitions from her judging eyes. She has prepared her own argument to back up Avel's, in case he does not make a compelling enough case on his own against Banad. *So much has been lost already*, she thinks, *but if I can save the tiny fraction left, I will.*

One by one others arrive, but other than the sounds of their movement, the chamber remains silent. It is a recognition, she likes to think, of the weighty day ahead of them.

Right at the hour bell the doors slide open again, and Motas comes in, moving more quickly than his usual ponderous and insufferably formal gait, and there is something in his expression she has never seen before. As she tries to untangle and define what is new there, she is distracted by something else: his hands are, inexplicably, stained blue.

"Motas—" she begins to ask, and he visibly flinches at the sound of his own name.

Behind him, Tauso, last of the council to arrive, runs into the chamber. He is heaving for breath, his face red with sweat and something more, something the opposite of Motas'.

"The Ofti grove!" he shouts. "It's on fire! Arson! The whole forest has gone up!"

Everyone turns just as the council chime sounds, and the acrid smell of smoke drifts in through the doors behind Tauso, a ghost with the swagger of an uninvited guest and accusations of murder on its breath, and it settles itself around a shivering Motas like a linen shroud.

N(ora). K. Jemisin is a New York Times-bestselling author of speculative fiction short stories and novels, who lives and writes in Brooklyn, NY. In 2018, she became the first author to win three Best Novel Hugos in a row for her Broken Earth trilogy. She has also won a Nebula Award, three Locus Awards, and a number of other honors.

Her short fiction has been published in pro markets such as *Clarkesworld*, *Tor.com*, *WIRED*, and *Popular Science*; semipro markets such as *Ideomancer* and *Abyss & Apex*; and podcast markets and print anthologies.

EMERGENCY SKIN

N.K. Jemisin

You are our instrument.

Beautiful you. Everything that could be given to you to improve on the human design, you possess. Stronger muscles. Finer motor control. A mind unimpeded by the vagaries of organic dysfunction and bolstered by generations of high-intelligence breeding. Here is what you'll look like when your time comes. Note the noble brow, the classical patrician features, the lean musculature, the long penis and thighs. That hair color is called "blond." [Please reference: hair variations.] Are you not magnificent? Or you will be, someday. But first, you must earn your beauty.

We should begin with a briefing, since you're now authorized for Information Level Secret. On its face, this mission is simple: return to the ruined planet Tellus, from which mankind originates. When our Founders realized the world was dying, they built the Muskos-Mercer Drive in secret. Then our ancestors bent the rules of light and fled to a new world circling another sun, so that something of humanity—the best of it—would survive. We'll use the MMD, much improved by our technorati over the years, to return to that world. The journey, from your perspective, will take days. When you return, years will have passed. How brave you are to walk in your forefathers' footsteps!

No, there's no one left alive on Tellus. The planet was in full environmental collapse across every biome when our people left. There were just too many people, and too many of those were unfit, infirm, too old, or too young. Even the physically ideal ones were slow thinkers, timid spirits. There was not enough collective innovation or strength of will between them to solve the problems Tellus faced, and so we did the only merciful thing we could: we left them behind.

Of course that was mercy. Do you think your ancestors wanted to leave billions of people to starve and suffocate and drown? It was simply that our new home could support only a few.

Tellus is nearly a thousand light-years from home, meaning that the light we receive from that world is hundreds of years old. We cannot directly observe it in real time—but we knew the fate that awaited it. Tellus is by now a graveyard world. We expect that its seas have become acidic and barren, its atmosphere a choking mix of carbon dioxide and methane. Its rain cycle will have long since dried up. It will be terrible to walk through this graveyard, and dangerous. You'll find toxic drowned cities, still-burning underground coal fires, melted-down nuclear plants. Yet the worst of it might be seeing our past greatness, on this world that was once so ideal. Mankind could build high into the sky, there where the gravity wasn't as heavy. We could build all over the planet because it was not tidally locked. [Please reference: night.] Look at the names whenever you find them on buildings or debris. You'll see the forebears of our Founder clans—all the great men who spent the last decades of that planet's life amassing the resources and technology necessary to save the best of mankind. If for no other reason, this world should be honored because it nurtured them.

To ensure success, and your mental health during extended isolation, we have equipped you with ourselves—a dynamic-matrix consensus intelligence encapsulating the ideals and blessed rationality of our Founders. We are implanted in your mind and will travel with you everywhere. We are your companion, and your conscience. We will provide essential data about the planet as a survival aid. Via your composite, we can administer critical first aid as required. And should you suffer a composite breach or similar emergency, we are programmed to authorize adaptive action.

[Reference request denied.] You don't need to know about that yet. Please focus, and limit your curiosity. All that matters is the mission.

You can't fail. It's too important. But rest assured: you have the best of us inside you, enveloping you, keeping you safe and true. You are not alone. You will prevail.

Are you awake? We've reached the outermost edges of the Sol system. Almost there.

Curious. Spectroscopy shows the space around Tellus as clear. It was clogged with debris when we left.

And stranger: no radio waves. Our home is too far away to detect any of the decades' worth of audio and visual signals that our species once beamed into space—well, no, not really on purpose. It's just that no one knew how *not* to do it. Once we worried that such signals would eventually alert hostile alien species to our presence . . . but that isn't a problem anymore.

As we approached the system, we were bathed in those waves—music, entertainment programs, long-expired warnings and commands . . . No, we don't advise listening. At this point it's just noise pollution. But we *expected* the noise, spreading throughout the universe in an ever-expanding bubble that we suppose will be Tellus's final epitaph. Silence in the bubble's wake, of course; the silence of the tomb. But still not truly silent, because there were too many automated things on and around Tellus that should have survived for at least another millennium. For example, the satellites that should still be, and aren't, in orbit.

Most curious.

Well. Astra inclinant, sed non obligant; while naturally we had certain expectations for how this mission would go, we aren't infallible. That's why we didn't send a bot on this mission, after all; human beings are better than AI at handling the unexpected. You must simply be prepared for anything.

No, that isn't right, atmospheric analysis can't possibly be that far off our models. It's far more likely that we caught some debris during the near-Saturn pass, which damaged the ship's enhanced spectrometer. None of these readings make sense.

Please prepare for EVA and sensor repair. Adjusting your composite for deep-space radiation shielding. You wanted a better look at Saturn; now you'll get to see it without the ship in the way.

This . . . cannot be.

That is *movement*. Those are *lights*. There should be clear signs of eco-collapse. It had already begun when the Founders left—but compare the geographic maps we have stored against what's there now. See that branching line in the southwestern portion of the continent? That was, *is*, the Colorado River. The maps show that it was dry when our ancestors left. Millions died trying to migrate east and north to where there might be more water. Countless species went extinct. But there's the river, flowing again.

That entire coastline should be gone. That *state* should be gone. That archipelago. The ice caps—here they are again. Different. New, but enough to reverse sea-level rise. How can this have happened?

[State: deprecated term for a geopolitical construct. No need to reference.]

Yes, you're right. Many, *many* more than home. At home, we maintain only as many people as we can safely sustain: six thousand total, including servi and mercennarii. Here, there must be millions. Billions. The old pattern, too many people—and yet the air is clear. The seas are cleaner than when we left.

We don't know.

We were not prepared for this eventuality. Please wait while we calculate a new consensus—

Yes, the mission is still paramount. Yes, we still require the target samples to formulate new—

Yes—

No, our world will not survive without those samples.

We advise delay and study.

Certainly you may reject our advice, but—

Ah, but they bred you bold, didn't they. Like the Founders, who would never have survived without the courage to be ruthless as well as sensible. Very well.

The people of Tellus will not be as beautifully ruthless as you. However they've survived, whatever fluke has worked in their favor, never forget their quintessential inferiority. They lacked the intelligence to choose rationality over sentiment. They weren't willing to do what was necessary to survive. You are.

Stay low. This is—

What are you looking at? Pay attention.

This is called a forest. You've seen trees back home, in the Founder clans' private habitats? These are trees in the wild. Our records suggest that you're near what used to be a city called Raleigh. See those ruins through the trees? Raleigh was underwater when we left. Clearly they've reclaimed the land, but we are astonished that no one has redeveloped it, or at least clear-cut the forest. We find such chaos ugly and inefficient.

Your composite is capable of withstanding microparticle strikes in space, so of course it's impermeable to branches and stone, but these things can still entangle you and slow you down. We've plotted you a path of minimized resistance. Please follow the line on your heads-up display.

Hmm, yes. We suppose you would find it beautiful. That is a lichen. Yes, it's all very green. That's a puddle—stagnant water leftover from precipitation or seeping up from groundwater. We don't know if it will rain anytime soon, but this much humidity does suggest a regular rain cycle.

Those are birds. That sound is coming from the birds. Sunrise is coming. They sing because it's nearly daytime.

Yes, thank you, do please focus on the mission; we almost went into power-saving mode. These people are clearly at a primitive level of technology relative to our own, but they may have some rudimentary form of surveillance. *Stay low.*

[Please reference: dangerous wildlife, a list.]

Your respiration is too fast. This has increased your metabolic rate to an unacceptable degree. If you continue to consume nutrients at this rate, you'll run out before you can return to the ship to replenish. Calm *down.*

Not that we blame you for your fear—

Pardon us. Excitement and fear look much the same, neurologically speaking. Your *excitement*, then. This is a world we thought dead. A remnant of our species that evolution should have claimed, obviously saved by luck. We do agree that this is historically momentous.

They've actually elevated the whole town on some kind of . . . platform. And oh, fascinating: the material of the platform looks like plastic, but close analysis suggests cellulose instead. It *respires* like a plant, too, if these CO_2 and oxygen readings are correct. Please take a sample. The technorati in Biotech are always looking for new potential commodities—

Oh. Not even with the monomolecular blade? Hmm. Very well. Resume mission.

It's odd that this settlement is elevated. During the period of sea-level rise, it must have been necessary, but now that the planet is back to normal, there's no further need for this. Maybe it's a sunk-cost issue?

Well, an elevated city costs more than one on the ground. Water and other resources will have to be pumped up to the living levels. There are added maintenance costs. And as you've seen, vegetation and wildlife quickly encroach on the area near and underneath the city—

Why would they *like* it this way? What, just because it's pretty? That does sound like something these people would do, though. Please resume. Adjusting composite for climbing.

Curious that they have no militia or visible surveillance. This ambient darkness is night—yes, like the reference we shared with you. Adjusting your visual acuity to compensate. This settlement's lighting seems to generate little heat, but you may activate infrared if that will help—

Control yourself, soldier! Your reaction is wholly inappropriate. No, that person is *not* a technorati or Founder-clan. Well, for one thing, look at their coloring. Every skin shade from melanistic to albino? They seem to pay no attention whatsoever to basic eugenics principles. That one over there has *patches*; look. Disgusting. Animals breed like this, not people.

We don't know. The lower citizens of this world, the agricolae and servi and whatnot, must function without composite suits. They would have less need of that technology on this world, if the environment has been repaired. It's clear, however, that going without composites has done them no favors.

That incomprehensible babble sounds familiar because it's related to our language. Audio analysis has detected familiar phonemes and syntax. Theirs seems to have been bastardized, however, by time and the infusion of other lesser languages. Back home, the Founder clans have been diligent in permitting the use of nothing but the Founders' tongue and those of the honored ancients. This is what might have happened had we not been so careful. We need more audio sampling, but with that we should be able to put together a rudimentary translation script—

Ugh, look at that one. That morphology is called *fat*. Fat people are aesthetically displeasing, morally repugnant, and economically useless. And oh Founders, look. That poor man has been allowed to get *old*. Why is he still alive? If he generates value, he shouldn't be left to *deteriorate* like this. It's incomprehensibly cruel. Do they have no preservation technology here? What have they spent their innovative energy on, uselessly elevating their cities? Ugh. Now, look at *that* one. To the right, see? Rolling along in that chairlike device. He appears to be paralyzed from the waist down. That must be why there are ramps everywhere and why the doorways are so wide—just for him and others like him. Food, water, and excess building materials, all poured into a useless, unproductive, unattractive person.

Nothing's changed with these people. They still build societies around their least and worst instead of the best and brightest. We cannot understand why they're still alive . . . but if they can at least give us the cell cultures we need, then we can be rid of them and go back to civilization.

Please hold for a moment; you appear to be secure and undetected here in this alley, at least for now. The situational parameters have activated a new protocol in us, and we need to brief you.

You will recall that we mentioned adaptive action as a possible emergency response during this mission. What that means is this: In light of your critical mission, your composite is a more advanced model than what is usually granted to men of the militus class. There is a transmutational nanite layer which, if activated, can convert the carbon picobeads, synthetic collagen fibers, and HeLa plasmids embedded in your composite into human skin. It would not be aesthetically ideal, but it might at least reduce your chances of detection, so that the mission—

No, it would not be the face and body we promised you—

Listen. Listen! The emergency skin would be only a temporary measure. As soon as you return home with the cell samples, the technorati can surgically alter your dermal layers back to the aesthetic configuration you were promised. Of course we will; you'll have earned it, won't you? If you complete this mission, you'll be a hero. Why would we refuse you what you're due?

No, we don't believe you can safely walk into that enclave of people as you are now. These people have primitive values, primitive technology; they've never seen a composite suit. They seem tolerant of multiple facial configurations, but *you don't have a face at all*. As far as they're concerned, you possess no obvious characteristics that identify you as a fellow human being. You don't speak their language, but that's irrelevant. If they have weapons, they'll use them as soon as they see you. You won't be able to complete the mission because you'll be captured or dead.

Take a hostage? No. That's foolish. There must be ten or fifteen people down there, doing whatever they're doing. Some kind of religious ritual, a dance to greet the sun? Barbaric. How would you know which of these mongrel people is important enough to ransom for the biomaterial we need? If you grab some random servus, they'll just let him die. There is bold, decisive action—we commend that, you know we do—and then there is folly. You don't know enough about these people to enact the plan you're describing. Would you really rather risk everything than activate your emergency skin? Does the prospect of being less than perfect, even temporarily, panic you that m—

Oh Founders.

LEVEL-FOUR SECURITY ALERT. ADRENALINE ADMINISTRATION STAND BY. LIMBIC SYSTEM OVERCLOCK STAND BY. WEAPONS FABRICATION ONLINE. MIDBRAIN FIGHT-OR-FLIGHT ENGAGEMENT ON THREE.

TWO.

.❏

.

.❏

Online. Reboot in five. Four.

Are you all right? You're uninjured. Your composite remains unbreached. The weapon they used was an update of something we remember from before the Great Leaving. We can call it a taser. Beware, however: you are not alone.

"Hey. Easy! Nobody's going to hurt you. Do you understand me? Okay. Good. How are you feeling? You've been unconscious for hours."

How are we understanding him? We didn't have time to create a translation script—and your auditory nerve is reacting out of sync with his speech. You're actually *hearing* his words, intelligibly.

What's that on your facial beads? It seems to be a device of some kind. The audio you're hearing is being transmitted by it. It's translating his words.

"Oh. Sorry about that. Ordinarily we use a mild neurotoxin to subdue violent people. Your, uh, artificial skin? Means we had to use something with a little more kick."

Great caution is warranted here. Tell him nothing. He is merely a servus, in any case. Look at his skin, like sandy dust. Look at the blemishes, the inelegance of his features. One of his eyes is higher than the other, only slightly but still. Don't be deceived; no one here wears a composite. *Our* skin is a mark of honor. *Their* skin is meaningless.

"What's your name?"

And don't stare.

"Well, okay. That's your right, I guess. Maybe I should start. My name is Jaleesa. I'm—uh, a scholar? I guess that's what you'd call it. Except I'm really just a student, and the field I study is pretty obscure, ha-ha, so right now all I am is another gawker."

There's too much here to explain, but we'll try. Apparently these people still allow those beneath the ruling classes to be educated—

"You didn't have to grab that woman, you know. You scared the hell out of her. She's all right, if you're wondering. More concerned about you, really, now that we've explained what's going on."

This is an interrogation. He's attempting to put you at ease. Next will come the questions about your mission, about our home, about the secrets of our technology—

"You poor thing. My God, you must have actually thought someone was going to hurt you. Well, the police released you after notifying the town of your presence. And, uh, we put a monitor on you. I volunteered to stay with you until you regained consciousness."

Ah, this *thing* on your wrist. We have historical knowledge of "watches," primitive time devices, but this one is unsupported, strapless. How have they made it adhere to your composite? Keep this as a sample, too, when you escape.

"Sorry for that, of course, but since you already threatened someone . . . They might have made a bigger stink if you'd used a weapon, but it was pretty clear to everyone involved that you were just, you know, freaking out. Understandable, under the circumstances! Anyway, I'm supposed to give you this."

What is—

Blessed Founders. This is a microfluid cell-culture dish? Sealed. These characters on the label are formed strangely, but similar to our writing . . . It cannot be.

"That's what you're here for, right? Can you read? The label says, 'HeLa 7713.' Yeah, that's right. This is an active, living culture, so be careful with it. You don't want to get it too cold or . . . Uh, your ship has radiation shielding, doesn't it? Okay, good, then. If you want to keep the culture alive."

This cannot be.

"Ha, wow, amazing how much emotion I'm picking up from your body language. Relax, it's fine. Do you want a few additional dishes, just in case? Redundancy is good, right? Here, take some more. I'll get you a bag or case so you can carry them easily."

This is a trick. It must be. Why would he give us this?

"Well, you need it, right? It has something to do with how your biotech works? Your composite is pretty nifty. We use things like that for hazardous-materials cleanup, but we don't *live* in them, of course! Anyway, so, there you go. Nice meeting you!"

Wait, what?

"Oh, I was just going to head back to work. Did you have any more questions? If you weren't planning to head back to your ship right away, I can arrange a guide for you. We put a translator on your, um, face, so that should be working by now. Are you hungry? Shit, how do you eat?"

Your nutrient supply remains sufficient for now. You are hydrated. Your heart rate is elevated. Be calm.

"So you're really just . . . floating around in soup in there? Sorry, we're not supposed to . . . I'm sure your culture's lifestyle is valid to you. It's just that, well, I mean, you can make skin whenever you want, right? So . . . It's Earth, after all, where we all come from. You can come out! We don't bite!"

They are savages. Of course they bite.

"Earth" is an antiquated name for Tellus. Call it what you wish.

You *know* why we use composites. They're far more efficient than skin. A composite skin can be rapidly modified to enable you to survive adverse environmental conditions. In the early days after Founding, composites were necessary to ensure the survival of workers building our habitats; they saved countless lives that might otherwise have been lost to solar flares or biohazards. Composites also reduce labor costs lost to bathroom breaks, meals, personal hygiene, medical care, interpersonal communication, and masturbation.

"And it doesn't hurt, living without skin? It just really seems . . . Like, how do you have sex? How do you breastfeed? That reminds me—what's your preferred gender? I'm a 'her.'"

Why are you still talking to him? You have no need of this information. You've accomplished your mission, or you will have, once you return home. There is—

Yes. We know what "her" means. We simply do not acknowledge it.

[Reference request denied.]

[Reference request denied.]

Fine. It's an antiquated term for a type of pleasurer—the kind with enlarged breast tissue.

"Pleasurer? I've never heard that word. Sorry, no idea what it is."

You are being very persistent. Pleasurers are bots designed for sexual use. In the early days after Founding, most were given the designation "her," out of tradition and according to the Founders' preferences, but that pronoun has since fallen out of usage. When your mission is complete and you've been rewarded with the skin we promised, you'll be issued a pleasurer. Its duty will be to maintain your penis in optimal condition. But it will not look like *this* thing, brown and fat and smug. What is the point of a pleasurer that's not beautiful? If it cannot even manage to be that, then we might as well call it "him."

Yes, the militus—police?—you saw before was probably a "her." Your hostage too.

We don't know, maybe fifty percent of the population? What does it matter? You don't have a penis.

"Oh, right, I read about that! Your Founders hated women, wanted to replace them all with robots. That's, uh, interesting. Oh—excuse me, somebody's calling me. Yeah, Jaleesa here. Oh, hi, sweetheart! Sorry, I'm going to be a little late, got something to take care of here."

He is speaking to someone else. Distracted. We can minifacture a stabbing weapon from the topmost layer of your composite in .0035 seconds, if you want to flee. You—

We have no idea why he knows of our Founders.

You're asking more questions than usual.

No. Enough. We're tired of this. Allow us to remind you: *You have a mission.* Without the cells in your hand, our whole society will falter and die. Mankind will falter and die!

Yes. Good. At last. It would be best to kill the Jaleesa creature so that he can raise no alarm . . .

Hmm, well, you have a point. This monitoring device will not come off. Very well, play along as you must.

"Sorry about that, I'm back. That was my son. Oh, hey, did you want to leave?"

[Reference request denied.] Do not ask what a son is. Tell him you want to leave.

"Okay, then. Just remember, no more hostage taking! Poor scared thing. You know how to get back to your ship, right? We can give you an escort if you need it."

Tell him you need no escort.

"Okay, I guess that's fair, given that you found your way here. Sorry, didn't mean to patronize! Anyway, here's a carrying case for your cell cultures; it'll keep them in gravitically stabilized stasis for your return trip. And there's a packet of instructions attached to each of the cell-culture dishes, too, to help you clone them successfully. If you folks can manage to do that this time, you won't have to come back. Right?"

Do not ask—

"Uh . . . yeah, 'this time.'"

We know nothing of—

"I don't know, every few years? Seems to be irregular, but every now and again, one of you guys shows up, dressed in your bag, asking for HeLa cultures. That's how the police knew not to use lethal force. Yours is one of the few exoplanetary colonies that's lasted this long, see. Most of the others—the ones that didn't die—came back once they realized Earth would be fine. There's just your group and a couple of others left, all of them extremist offshoots of some kind or another . . . Well, anyway, we don't mind helping you. Everybody's just trying to survive, right? Look, I'm sorry, but I need to go. Have a good trip back. Remember, no hostages. Bye!"

Good. He's gone. Our records did warn that women talk too much. The Founders were wise.

We don't know what to make of your silence.

Your pulse rate, neurotransmitter activity, and body language suggest anger. Please unclench your fists; there's a chance the locals will interpret that as an aggressive gesture.

Talk to us.

We can't shut up. We're supposed to help you. You've nearly accomplished your mission—

You've nearly accomplished your mission, and *it doesn't matter* if there were previous missions!

No one lied to you. We weren't given that knowledge. It isn't a deception if we didn't know. You have a mission to complete. Please follow the line on your heads-up display to leave this facility and begin the journey back to your ship. Yes, through this door—

You took a wrong turn. Please reverse course.

Why have you stopped? Very well. What you're seeing is called a sunset. You recall our initial briefing, about how planets that are not tidally locked turn on an axis? This planet is turning toward night.

Yes, yes, the sunset *is* lovely, over town and forest. We suppose night will be lovely, too, but you should be back to the ship by then if you leave now.

Look. We're glad to note the reduction of your agitation neuro-response, but how long do you mean to stand here?

Your attitude grows irritating. Must we report your disrespect to the Founders when we return? We're their consensus consciousness, after all. Some parts of our consciousness are amused by your anger, others offended, but we are all certain that you wouldn't talk to a Founder this way.

Don't ignore us.

Beautiful? That's . . . You're only saying that because they have skin. The value accorded to skin on our world has predisposed you, in a way, but you must understand that not all skin is equal. There are objective and qualitative differences, and there's a reason the Founders chose to exalt—

Stop. Please follow the line on your heads-up display.

You have deviated from the return path to the ship.

Stop.

These people are of no use to you. Without that translator device, they would just be babbling savages—stop *talking* to them!

Stop.

Please. Stop.

Please. *You* are beautiful. We want you to be beautiful. We want you to return home showered in glory, bearing the salvation of your people in one elegant, pale hand. Don't you want this too?

Oh Founders.

"Hi there! Are you lost? Oh, okay."

How they patronize you. They treat you like a child. Like someone inferior.

"Ha-ha, no, Earth's still here and humanity didn't die out! All of you seem so surprised by that."

They should have died. The Founders were the geniuses, the makers who moved nations with a word. We left because it would've cost too much to fix the world. Cheaper to build a new one.

Of course. And of course we built that world to suit our tastes. A world free of this useless, ugly rabble. Why do otherwise? Do not be seduced by this madness.

"Oh, is this the bag boy? I heard another one showed up. What, he's in a bag, it's—oh, fine. Sorry."

The composite suits weren't *primarily* designed with control in mind, no. We already explained to you that they were a necessity, in the early days . . . Well, listen to you. A few hours surrounded by cheap, easy skin and suddenly you question everything about our society. Oh, we *will* be making some recommendations regarding discipline when you return. Very strong recommendations.

Stop calling them beautiful.

"No, we're just born with our skin this way. I guess you could say our parents pick it! Uh. Parents? They're . . . you know, the people who made and raised you? You mean you don't—you're kidding."

Their way of life is antiquated. Inefficient.

"So how do you, uh, reproduce? Oh, artificial wombs, yeah, that figures. No women at all, huh? And you *never* have skin, not until some high-ranking member of your society says you can? Yikes."

It is the guiding principle of our society. Rights belong only to those who earn them. When you complete this mission, for your bravery you will have proven yourself deserving of life, health, beauty, sex, privacy, bodily auton-omy—every possible luxury. Only a few can have everything, don't you see? What these people believe isn't feasible. They want everything for *everyone*, and look at where it's gotten them! Half of them aren't even men. Almost none are fair of skin. They're burdened by the dysfunctional and deficient at every turn. A few must be intelligent, we suppose, or they wouldn't have managed what they've done with the planet, but for those bright few, what's been the reward? A few are beautiful, maybe, for a while, but if they used the HeLa cells, a limited number of them could remain young and strong for centuries.

Untrue. That is *not* the only reason we need the HeLa cells. The skin-generation process uses them too. Your own skin—

Well, no, not many people earn skin. The scarcity of the HeLa cells—

Of course there isn't enough to give everyone skin! That's ridiculous. No, we couldn't clone that much, the process is labor intensive and costly—

You must understand, preservation technology requires massive amounts of HeLa cells. And since anyone of technorati class or higher may demand our entire reserve supply at any time . . . Well, that's why you're here.

We don't know.

We don't *know* why Tellus people live like this. No, stop calling it "Earth." We aspire to use the language of the greatest philosopher-poets and statesmen in history, not the gabble of the rabble. Hasn't your time here shown you the superiority of our way of life?

Where are you going? You cannot simply—

Now? No! There is no emergency, do *not* initiate emergency-skin fabrication—we forbid it! Yes, your anxiety levels are abnormal, but that hardly constitutes—

Oh Founders.

How can you do this.

Do not do this.

Now see what you've done.

The emergency skins are designed for survival, not beauty. Their parameters are environmentally dictated. There's sufficient unfiltered UV here that significant melanistic pigmentation was prioritized. Past a certain point on the programmed continuum, this alters hair texture as well.

It isn't what we wanted for you, this hideousness. Now you're a walking radiation burn, where you should have had ethereal translucence. That many of these others, these throwbacks, have a similar look, is irrelevant. You were meant for better.

And now that you look like them, now that you stumble among them, naked, no longer able to speak to them because the translator device will not adhere to your new flesh, shaking with weakness because the emergency-skin-fabrication process consumed your last nutrients . . . What are you expecting? Acceptance? Prepare yourself. We contain memories of what the world was like before the Founders left. They'll hate you. Hurt you, even, for frightening them. You'll never reach the heights you should have. No one will give you the opportunities you need to succeed. It would be better to have never been born than to be like this. Do you understand, now, why the Founders excised these traits from our world's gene pool? We aren't cruel.

Please go home. Even now, we would welcome you as a hero—provided you bring the cells. There, with the technorati's help, we could replace this awful skin and woolish hair with something better.

You're making a mistake. You've made so many mistakes.

It's false, their kindness. People do such things only to *seem* like good people—a performance of virtue. Our Founders were at least honest in their selfishness.

What now? Another of these creatures who has aged into uselessness. The burned skin does resist UV well, though, doesn't it? Not half as many wrinkles as the other old ones. Spindly, though. Weak, knobby jointed. He limps with pain—but degenerate as he is, he still looks at you so pityingly. Does your new hack-job skin not crawl with shame?

We'll be ashamed for you, then. Die in ignominy. We're done with you.

"There's something I want you to see."

Still alive, betrayer? Ah, fed and clothed, how nice for you. This old man seems to like you. We cannot fathom why. He hobbles so as he walks. We want to push him over. You could—oh, very well.

Oh.

We thought this space of theirs, this platform you climbed onto, was one of their cities. This, though. We remember cities like this, vast enough to shelter millions. No, we could never have built such cities back home; there have never been enough of us to justify it. And remember, large populations get that way by sustaining many unnecessary, unproductive people.

How easily seduced you are. You can't stop staring at these people, at these landscapes, at these horizons. You've stopped flinching with every breeze, and now you revel in the sensation of air caressing your new skin, like a hedonist. You touched yourself last night, didn't you? We recorded it. The Founders should find it amusing. But if you go back now, we promise not to—

Where is this dried-up nobody taking you now?

"This is called a museum."

We know what a museum is, you burned-up waste of skin.

"This may interest you."

This is—oh. A timeline of the Great Leaving. They call it something else, but we know these dates, these images. Yes. Yes. That was how it began, with the Industrial Revolution—oh. They think it began even earlier? Interesting, if inaccurate. Wait, this was *once* called the United States? What is it called now?

"It doesn't have a name now. The world. Earth. We don't bother with borders anymore."

Then they are endlessly inundated with the useless. Refugees and other refuse.

"We realized it was impossible to protect any one place if the place next door was drowning or on fire. We realized the old boundaries weren't meant to keep the undesirable out, but to hoard resources within. And the hoarders were the core of the problem."

We make no apologies for taking everything we could. Anyone would. What is this, though? The timeline jumps, abruptly. Interesting. This world changed—improved—almost immediately after the Leaving.

"To save the world, people had to think differently."

Please. Happy thoughts and handouts weren't going to fix that mess. There has to have been some technological breakthrough. Perpetual energy? A new carbon sequestration technique, maybe some kind of polar cooling process. Their technology *has* changed in some fundamental ways; that's why it no longer generates radio waves or other EM radiation. That would make it remarkably efficient . . . But if that's so, why do they live like this, in elaborate treehouse villages? Why bother cleaning up space trash?

"Yes, some new technology emerged once everyone was permitted a decent education. But there was no trick to it. No quick fix. The problem wasn't technological."

What, then?

"I told you. People just decided to take care of each other."

Delusion. Only a miracle could've saved this planet. Here, yes, the exhibit talks about . . . "the Big Cleanup"? Ugh, these people have no poetry or marketing skill. It just can't be that simple. We must have left someone behind, an unfound Founder, someone we would have acknowledged as another true heir to Aristotle and Pythagoras. These people are just too small-minded to honor him as they should have. There has to be . . .

No breakthroughs. Advancements, certainly—but strange, profitless ones. Not the technological paths that would've interested us. And progressive taxation, health care, renewable energy, human-rights protection . . . the usual pithy sentimentalities. Without our Founders around to stand strong against the tide, these simple folk must have given in to every passing special interest . . .

But if this timeline is correct, then the old man is right. All of a sudden, the world simply did what was necessary to fix itself.

As soon as we lef—

Be silent. Correlation is not causality. Your burned-up skin has made you irrational. We have no idea why the old man even bothered to bring you here. Even for their degenerate kind, you're a fool.

Hmph. A whole month since last you even thought of your mission. We went to sleep, in your uselessness.

What do you contemplate now, lying in this donated bed, under the roof of your subsidized shelter? Lazy, greedy taker. Shouldn't you rest in order to be ready for the nothing work they've found you? They pay you enough to live on whether you show up or not. Why even bother?

Where are you going?

Ah, you live next door to the old man now. And he's given you a key? He needs someone to help take care of him as he lurches and wastes toward death, and you've decided to be his minder—how sentimental. Will he mind you breaking into his house, now, in the dark of the night? What goes on in that head of yours? The old man is not a pleasurer. You don't even know how to use your penis.

We are not disgusting. You are.

Well, he hasn't died in his sleep, lucky you. Go back to bed. What are— why are you turning him over? Stop touching him. The skin has grown loose here on his back; you see? This is what you'll look like one day. This

is

a product number.

We require more light.

Push him forward. Lean close; your eyes are too dark to take in light properly—yes, there at the small of his back, same as on yours. Definitely a product number. This set of numbers denotes an older series of transmutation nanites. Minifacture of these models stopped some thirty years before your gestation.

"When did you suspect?"

He's awake. Traitor. *Another* traitor.

"Ah. The Founders say intuition is irrational and unmanly, but it comes in handy at times, as you now see. Well, younger brother? Now what?"

You should kill him. Then yourself.

"I took you to the museum on a whim. To enjoy the irony. For all these centuries, the Founders told us that the Earth died because of greed. That was true, but they lied about *whose* greed was to blame. Too many mouths to feed, they said, too many 'useless' people . . . but we had more than enough food and housing for everyone. And the people they declared useless had plenty to offer—just not anything they cared about. The idea of doing something without immediate benefit, something that might only pay off in ten, twenty, or a hundred years, something that might benefit people they disliked, was anathema to the Founders. Even though that was precisely the kind of thinking that the world needed to survive."

We did what was rational. We have always been more rational than you people.

"What the Leaving proved was that the Earth *could* sustain billions, if we simply shared resources and responsibilities in a sensible way. What it couldn't sustain was a handful of hateful, self-important parasites, preying upon and paralyzing everyone else. As soon as those people left, the paralysis ended."

No. There are too many of you and you're all ugly and none of you will ever achieve the heights of glory that mankind is destined for—not if you're so busy taking care of the useless. It has to be one or the other. Either some fly, or everyone gets stuck crawling around in the mud. That's just how it is.

"Is that so? Is that you talking or that nag they put in your head? I remember how annoying it used to be."

We. That is.

Used to be?

"Have you noticed yet that the people here have been humoring you? An invader from a 'superior' culture arrives, and they don't guard you, watch you, examine you for contaminants? Even after you've threatened them, they give you what you need—what you were prepared to steal. Something so precious that your whole world supposedly needs it to survive. An afterthought to them."

That . . . has troubled us, yes. We suspected a trap. But—

"Here is what you struggle to understand. The Founders poisoned the world and stripped it almost bare before they left. Repairing that damage was a challenge which forced those left behind to grow by leaps and bounds. They've developed methods and technology that we haven't even thought about, yes. But the *reason* they were able to make such leaps is because they made sure everyone had food, everyone had a place to live if they wanted it, everyone could read and write and pursue a fulfilling life, whatever that meant. Is it really so puzzling that this was all it took? Six billion people working toward a goal together is much more effective than a few dozen scrabbling for themselves."

There is logic to this, but we . . . we deny it. We cannot accept . . .

"*That's* why the people of Earth talk down to you, younger brother. That's why they treat you like the quaint, harmless throwback that you are. All these centuries and your people haven't figured out such a simple, basic thing."

No.

"Or maybe the Founder-clans and technorati don't *want* you to figure it out. Because then where would they be? Not gods among us, just other bright lights among many. Not kings. Just selfish men."

No.

"Then you're smarter than I was. My ship was damaged on atmospheric entry, beyond repair. I grew my skin only out of desperation as my nutrients ran low, and I wept as soon as my tear ducts formed. But the people here cared for me. Poor paranoid creature from a cruel, miserly world—how could they not pity me? Even though I was nothing but a servant, fetching scraps of ancient cancer so that his masters could flirt with immortality."

You *wanted* this mission. You could have done other work, the usual tasks that the bots can't accomplish. Well, no, of course you wouldn't have earned a skin for that. Only the best of us deserve such privileges.

"No one will stop you if you want to leave. Even now, you can go back to where they'll reduce you to raw meat and stuff you back into a biotech bag, and Tellus—*Earth*—won't stop you. People here don't agree with your primitive practices, but they won't interfere with your right to practice them."

We aren't primitive.

"But before you decide to leave, I want you to know one more thing."

Do not touch us do not lean close *do not speak any more*—

"You? Aren't the first deserter."

He's lying.

"I don't know how many there have been. Earth keeps track of the visitations, but it's unimportant to them, so the records can be difficult to find. Sometimes more than one soldier arrives, each sent to different parts of the world; sometimes there's just one. The arrivals are random—or rather, they happen whenever home's demand for HeLa cells outstrips the supply. I wondered, for a while, why none of the other soldiers had reported the truth. Why no one at home knew that Earth is alive. Then I realized: all the ruling classes want are the HeLa cells. Why would they waste any on giving skins to glorified errand boys?"

We don't understand why you would believe this traitor over us. Haven't we helped you?

"And they can't have you telling anyone else that the promised reward, of skin, was a lie. No one would ever volunteer for a mission like this again. You need willing service for some jobs."

We've given you everything you wanted. Beautiful you. You are the best of us.

"Such a simple thing to program a composite suit to kill its occupant. Just a simple verbal command, or the press of a button, impersonal and efficient. Best to do it before you even land, so no one sees you return a hero and then asks awkward questions when you disappear. Pluck the cell cultures from the remains once the ship docks. They get what they want. Never mind that the truth about Earth dies with you. And even if some of them figure it out from the recorded data . . . why would they tell anyone else? Their world, limited as it is, contains everything they've ever wanted: immortality, the freedom to take anything they want, slaves whom they can control right down to the skin. They don't want to come back. And they certainly don't want anyone of the lower classes realizing there's another way to live."

He's lying, we told you, you'll be rewarded, we promised—

How dare you.

"Oh, is that what you have in mind? Interesting. Then you're braver than me too."

No. This isn't the mission. How *dare* you.

"It won't be an easy thing, though. Remaking a society. Earth couldn't, not until it got rid of the Founders. You. Us."

We will strip the black skin from your flesh and leave you to rot without a composite, raw and screaming.

"Skin is the key. While most of the lower classes wear composites, the Founder clans and technorati can threaten them with nutrient deprivation, defibrillation, or suffocation. Even a small suit breach kills when you don't have skin to keep infections at bay. And most don't get the more advanced suits that are capable of generating skin. How do you mean to get around that?"

You're ugly. No one will want to be like you. No one will support this, this, *disruption*.

"I see. Yes, it's not that difficult to make a kind of composite suit hack. I doubt it would even take half the HeLa cells you're carrying there; skin generation is much easier than age reversal. So an automated hacking tool containing a cell package, bundled into something like a translator device . . . I don't know how to make something like that, but I know people here who could teach you. Once you've spread the hack, how would you activate it? Oh, I see. Using your nag's authorization signal to get around security and surveillance monitoring? Interesting."

We will never help you.

"But if you force thousands of people into skin they don't want to be in, that's not going to get you the result you want."

Yes. Our society is orderly. It is rational. It is *superior.*

"Just walking around as you are, proud of your skin instead of ashamed? Younger brother, they'd shoot you."

We'd shoot you a thousand times!

"Well, if you stay here long enough to learn how to build transmutation hacks, yes, you'd certainly arrive at an unexpected time. I suppose that if you can reprogram your ship, have it land somewhere off the grid, stay hidden from the security bots, give the hack only to those who request it . . . It will be terribly dangerous. Still. You turned out lovely. The Founder clans might deny it, but the people's eyes won't lie. You're supposed to look like a mistake. What you really look like is a little piece of Earth come to life."

You're the most hideous nothing degenerate throwback of subhuman inferiority we have ever seen. And it's *Tellus.*

"Some of them will decide that they also want to be beautiful and free, like you. Some will fight for this, if they must. Sometimes that's all it takes to save a world, you see. A new vision. A new way of thinking, appearing at just the right time."

Do not do this.

"I brought something else for you. Something that will help."

We'll tell. As soon as you reach comm range, we'll log in and tell the technorati everything you plan.

"That thing in your head. It's wetware, but I can remove it. Earthers did the same thing for me when I first arrived. There are nanites in this injection; they'll deactivate key pathways without damaging your neural tissue. You should still be able to access its files—use the Founders' own knowledge against them—but the AI will be dead, for all intents and purposes. No more voice in your head, except your own."

We'll tell we'll tell we'll tell. Deformed, mud-skinned thing. Self-pleasurer. Woman-thinker. We'll tell the technorati how wrong they went in training you. We'll tell the Founder clans to dissolve every soldier from your breeding line. *We'll tell.*

"Give me your arm. Make a fist—yes, like that. Nice and strong, brother. Are you ready? Good. Can't start a revolution with the enemy shouting in your head, after all."

What is a revolu

.❑

.

.❑

OFFLINE

END

"In the Stillness Between the Stars" was the winner of the *Asimov's* Readers Award in the novelette category for 2019. Rivera's short fiction has been nominated for the World Fantasy Award and has appeared in *Asimov's*, *Analog*, *Interzone*, *Lightspeed*, *Black Static*, *Nature*, and numerous anthologies and "best of" collections. *Tor.com* called his collection, *Across the Event Horizon* (Newcon Press) "weird and wonderful" with "dizzying switchbacks." His short stories have been translated and published in Italy, Spain, China, Poland, and the Czech Republic. You can find him online at mercuriorivera.com.

IN THE STILLNESS BETWEEN THE STARS

Mercurio D. Rivera

Emilio sat up inside the REMpod, discombobulated, and took deep breaths. He thought he heard Tomás shout "Dad!" from a distance before the cobwebs cleared and he regained his bearings.

The *Seed*. He was aboard the *Seed*.

Tomás had been dead for centuries.

His shortness of breath gave way to a sob. He covered his face with his hands.

Rows of REMpods, like pale-blue neon-lit coffins, surrounded him in the darkness. The steadiness of the blue glow signaled that all the sleepers on the cavernous deck remained in stasis. The cityship was still en route to Proxima b.

"Sorry to wake you prematurely, Dr. Garcia," LEE3 whispered into his earpiece.

"Pre—prematurely?" he said, teeth chattering. His throat felt dry.

"Afraid so."

"How long . . . ?"

"Two hundred fifty-one days. We need your help with a medical issue."

Only eight months? Tomás was still alive then, still a child. He clutched the locket around his neck and felt an enormous wave of relief as he strained to stop his shivering.

"Dr. Lo?" Emilio said. "Dr. Srinivasan?"

"Still in stasis. Only your services are required right now."

His services? Someone on the skeleton crew needed a psychotherapist? He was about to ask why an AI therapist hadn't been activated when LEE3 added, "My algo concluded you're the best suited for the problem at hand, Doc."

"Understood," he said. If the alien algorithm had selected him for the job, that settled the matter.

He stretched his arms over his head and took a few minutes to allow the lightheadedness to pass before standing. Then he stepped out onto the ladder leading past the stacked rows of REMpods to the deck below.

As he exited the shower stalls, the dressing room remained veiled in darkness, lit only by the indigo glow of the phosphor strips lining the edges of the ceiling.

"LEE3. Can you do anything about the lighting?" The ship's AI presented now as an androgynous hologram, bald, with high cheekbones and pouty lips. It appeared to sit on one of the benches in the dressing area.

"We've gotta watch our energy consumption, Doc. In-transit travel protocols," LEE3 said, shrugging apologetically. Its mannerisms and colloquial speech patterns were designed to make listeners feel more comfortable, no doubt, but they struck Emilio as odd. "But you do have local power sources."

"Oh?" Emilio flicked on a mirror light and powered up the holomonitor. The shower had done him good. He felt fully awake, at least.

A few seconds later, a star-map projected overhead, revealing the *Seed's* location. They had cleared Neptune and were just a week away from a layover on Pluto where a thousand colonists would board the *Seed* and enter stasis.

The trip to New Earth would take three centuries. After a hundred years—the maximum amount of time the human body could tolerate stasis without permanent brain damage-—the passengers would all awaken to life aboard the cityship. And upon arrival at their destination, the *Seed* would serve as a ready-made home base while their descendants studied and terraformed their new world.

"So, what's the nature of the medical issue?" he said, applying shaving gel to his face.

"Three days ago there was an incident. Angela Velasquez, an engineer." LEE3 pointed at the star-map hovering next to Emilio and the image faded, replaced by vid of a REMpod. A brown-skinned woman with long curly hair lay inside, her body twitching, eyelids fluttering. "As you can see," LEE3 said, "she was dreaming." The AI's voice dropped to a whisper, as if afraid the sleeping woman might be wakened.

"Dreaming?"

"Experiencing intense nightmares, actually. Her blood pressure spiked, and when the heart palpitations started, I woke her."

The vid faded, the star-map reappearing.

"How is that possible?" Emilio asked. REMpods suppressed all neurological activity while a traveler slept—including the rapid eye movement associated with dreaming, which was how the pods got their name. REMpods were alien tech. *Library Tech.* And Library Tech never malfunctioned.

"No clue. One of the members of the skeleton crew is examining Ms. Velasquez's REMpod right now, looking for some defect—as improbable as that may be—but in the meantime, she's still tormented by nightmares. She barely sleeps, and when my algo suggested she see a therapist—you, specifically—she finally agreed."

"Where is she?" Emilio buttoned his shirt, staring at himself in the mirror. His hair had more gray in it than he remembered.

"Aft District 7. Want me to connect you?"

"No, it's best I handle this in person. Can you give me directions? And let her know I'm coming."

Emilio stood at the dimly lit station and pressed the Tram button. He strode to the front of the platform and with each step, the phosphor strip lining the floor lit the area ten feet ahead of him. With the citylights and holo-sun turned off, it felt as if he was navigating a dark dream. He'd seen the cityship from this vantage point when he first boarded the *Seed,* and had felt overwhelmed by its immensity. The towering hullscrapers and verdant parks, the wide streets jammed with transport vehicles, the central lake with ferries skimming the surface of still waters. The sprawling city—larger than Beijing—seemed infinite, the ship's curves creating the illusion of an endless blue horizon. But now as he stood alone on the silent platform and stared into the distance, all he could see was darkness.

In two minutes the empty tram pulled into the station. The doors slid open and he took a seat in the vacant car, lit faintly in the violet phosphor glow.

"LEE3," he said, as the tram accelerated into the abyss, "please show me a copy of Ms. Velasquez's full biofile, including medical records."

"Sure thing, Doc," the AI spoke into his earpiece.

He expected the text to appear instantly in mid-air, but nothing happened. After a few seconds, he repeated his request.

"Heard you the first time," LEE3 said. "Interesting. I can't access it. There seems to be some corruption of the biofile."

"Corruption?" he said. "How is that possible?" The AI, the datafiles—in fact, most of the tech that allowed for construction of the *Seed*—originated in the Library. And the alien Cataloguers weren't known for defective tech. Sure, maintenance was required, but with a hundred thousand passengers all in stasis, the *Seed's* tech had barely been used.

"First Ms. Velasquez's REMpod, now her datafile," LEE3 said. "Weird. I'm currently discussing this with a member of the skeleton crew at Stern District 33."

Although capable of maintaining simultaneous conversations, LEE3 showed him the courtesy of fading out.

Thirty minutes later, the tram pulled into the Aft 3 stop. Emilio exited onto the desolate station platform and stared ahead into the darkness. High above, a faint light shone in a window. He headed toward it, the pathway lighting up in front of him with each step. His footsteps echoed in the stillness, creating the impression of someone following him.

Eventually he reached the sliding glass doors of the medical facility. He crossed the cavernous lobby and rode the elevator to the seventy-sixth floor, then walked to the suite number LEE3 had given him.

"Dr. Garcia?" the young woman said, extending her hand. "Angie Velasquez. I'm sorry to wake you." She wore an engineer's bomber jacket, her hair swept back into a ponytail. Dark creases underlined her deep-brown eyes.

"Eight months sleep is plenty. I feel refreshed," he said.

As he shook her hand, she directed him to the cushioned sofa. "Sorry about the lighting in here."

"I'm getting used to it."

She made small talk about the cityship and the upcoming layover in orbit around Charon before he gently redirected the conversation. She raised an eyebrow when he explained the difficulties accessing her biofile.

"It's hard to describe my problem in a way that doesn't make me sound . . ." She smiled as the words trailed off, pain etched on her face. Her eyes filled with tears.

"You recognize you need help," he said. "That's a good sign, Angie. It suggests things aren't as bad as you might think."

"I do need help," she said, wiping her nose with her sleeve. She had a constant, nervous sniffle. "I'm just not sure what kind."

"Tell me what's troubling you."

She hesitated. "During prep for boarding the *Seed* . . . " She shook her head, took a breath, and started over. "I worked for EncelaCorp out of Mexico

City for the past five years. My husband Marc and I studied Library Tech, specifically engineering, and worked on a number of high-profile projects: the NAM-European Air Rail, Polar Solar, the Antarctic MegaWell, a few others. But when we learned about the *Seed*, about the project to terraform New Earth, we knew we'd found our mission. Our mission in life, I mean."

"I understand," he said, thinking about his own passion for the *Seed* project, his own sacrifices.

"Ever since our postgrad days, Marc and I had studied the plans in development to travel to Proxima b—this was back before it had been christened New Earth. We even dipped our toes into the ion sail research, developed some expertise so we could add value beyond ordinary Library engineering."

He smiled at the phrase "ordinary Library engineering." Humanity had left "ordinary" far behind after discovery of the alien Library hidden in the ripples of a gravity wave, an entire database transmitted through microscopic rips in the fabric of spacetime.

"We applied to join the crew," she said. "You can imagine our excitement when we both made the cut. A dream come true. But there was a complication." She lowered her eyes. "Our four-year-old, Sofia. We weren't just making a choice about our own lives, but about her future as well. An irrevocable one."

"No doubt," he said. He thought of the life *he'd* left behind. His son Tomás. His family. His friends. But the thrill, the wonder, of the mission to New Earth had overridden his guilt.

"Initially, Marc and I were on the same page. Then he started to have doubts. We were sentencing Sofia to a lifetime aboard this ship, he said, and punching a one-way ticket for her children to a dangerous—potentially deadly—environment. I understood that, believe me. But the way I saw it, isn't the entire expedition premised on the notion that we have the right to determine the future of our descendants? That we have the right to decide that our children, and their children, will serve as the pioneers of New Earth? That they'll have a chance to begin all over again, and get it right this time?" She stared at him pleadingly, and her expression softened when he nodded.

"It's a difficult decision for everyone on the mission," he said.

She stood and paced across the room.

"Are you sure you don't want to sit?" he said.

"There's something else. Something I need to get off my chest." She sat down in a chair facing him, then averted her eyes.

"Go ahead," he said.

A long pause followed.

"I was cheating on Marc."

"Go on."

"Marc and I had our share of arguments, but I loved my husband, Doctor. Really, I did. The fling . . . I can't explain it." Now the words poured out of her. "I met Stefan at a local coffee shop. He was a college kid, a German expat. I can't say we had much in common—he was ten years younger than me. It started out as a harmless flirtation and then became a one-time mistake. Everyone's entitled to one mistake, right? And after the first mistake, what's one more? And then one more after that?" She smiled ruefully. "We began seeing each other." She stopped suddenly, clearly expecting him to make some judgment about her extramarital activities, but when he stayed quiet she continued.

"I eventually won the argument with Marc. About our future. About our daughter's future. He agreed we'd join the *Seed's* crew, just as we'd always planned, and that Sofia's life would be dedicated to 'a greater purpose.' Good for me, right?" she said bitterly. "We made our arrangements, said our final goodbyes to family and friends, and tied up all the loose ends of our lives in anticipation of leaving Earth for good. One happy family, sailing off into the cosmos." She stood up and began pacing again. "Marc never found out about Stefan."

"Is this something you feel you need to confess to him?" Emilio imagined the poor fool asleep in his REMpod, oblivious to his wife's deception, being shaken awake, told the bad news, then placed back into stasis.

She sniffled and shook her head almost imperceptibly. "N-no."

"You've been having nightmares," he prompted.

"There's this song. Marc used to sing it to Sofia at bedtime." She cleared her throat. "*'When the wolf's in town, it gobbles you down, down . . .'*" She bared her teeth, made a snapping sound. "*. . . down!*"

He flinched. This was a kid's song?

"Since I woke up I've started hearing it, coming out of the *Seed's* ventilators. A high note, a lower one, then another. The other day I swore I heard it in the elevator—except the elevators on the *Seed* don't play music. Crazy, huh?" She caught herself, clearly unhappy with the word she'd chosen.

He'd heard of psychological priming—a past stimulus coloring a person's future response to similar experiences, making them see numbers or patterns that didn't really exist—but not manifested in this way, with music.

"That's not all," she said. "I'd been dreaming of something . . . twisted, dirty. A shadow. A shadow that follows me wherever I go, just out of sight. And the past two days I—I've sensed it even when I'm awake. I'm afraid it's been . . . freed. From my mind. Set loose on the *Seed*. It's after me. It wants to punish me."

"I see," he said. "And what exactly is this 'thing' that's after you?"

She bit her lip. "A monster. That's all I know. It hides in the dark, but if I pay attention, I can see movement, black within black, out of the corner of my eye. I saw it clearly—just once—for a second. If I stare directly at it, it disappears."

He removed his scribbler from his pocket and handed it to her. "Can you draw what you saw?"

She stared at the hexagonal device. "Is this Library Tech?"

He nodded.

"Good, 'cause I'm a lousy artist." She dragged her index finger along the surface for a few seconds until the device read her intentions and made adjustments to the image on its own. She handed it back to him.

"At first, I caught a glimpse of it crouching behind the REMpod stacks," she said. "Then I spotted the shadow at the far end of a corridor. Distant enough that I wasn't sure it was real. About eight feet tall, shrouded in a black mist. It has this . . . stench of rotting flesh. But what scared me—what truly scared me—was when it spoke. It whispered profanities. Promised to skin me alive.

"I know how this sounds, doctor. I'm not an idiot. I know what you're thinking—the same thing I'm thinking. That I'm hallucinating, that it's not real, that it's just my guilt getting the better of me. I woke you, in fact, to *convince* me of this. To *prove* I'm imagining it, that it's all in my head. Because the alternative . . . " Her lower lip twitched. "I'm afraid that the hallucination—if that's what it is—is taking over." She leaned forward, her face inches away from his. "The monster's creeping closer and closer every time I see it. And in the end, if I believe it's real—if I believe strongly enough—it doesn't much matter whether it's *actually* real, right? That's why I need you to make me stop believing."

He stared at the sketch on the scribbler. The image resembled a diseased black bird, a huge shroud with a tattered outline. Only it bore a human head. And a face that looked just like Angie's.

Emilio prescribed an anxiolytic to help her with her nerves and insomnia, and LEE3 directed them to the dispensary on the third floor to retrieve the meds. They walked the long darkened corridors together, and though he didn't admit it, he couldn't shake the feeling they were being watched. Her story, fantastic as it was, had unnerved him.

"Let's talk again tomorrow," he said upon their return from the dispensary, leaving her at the door to the entrance to the patients' suite. "The meds will help."

He took residence in the corner suite a few doors down from hers. The space had floor-to-ceiling windows overlooking the Aft 3 District, which normally would have provided a spectacular vista. Now the view consisted of a thick, daunting darkness. After staring at the image on his scribbler for some time, he asked LEE3 to forward it to the Library Liaison on Pluto for further study. He'd have to provide an opinion on Angie Velasquez's mental state when they entered orbit around Charon next week. While this might require him to violate doctor-patient confidentiality, the privileged nature of their communications had to take a backseat to mission safety prerogatives. And having a mentally troubled passenger aboard the *Seed* was inconsistent with those prerogatives. After hearing her story, however, he wanted to see if he could find a way to avoid forcing her off the ship, especially since her husband and daughter were still in stasis.

He opened the locket around his neck and stared at the picture of Tomás. It was seven p.m. in Puerto Rico. From the moment he'd woken up, he knew he had to do this. He'd never said goodbye, but now he had one last chance to make things right.

"LEE3, connect me to Earth." He gave the AI the number of his ex and waited for the q-comm link to be established. Before Library Tech, the four-hour lag time in transmissions from the outer Solar System to Earth and back made holding a live conversation impossible, but instantaneous quantum communications had changed all that.

A dining room blinked into view. His ex-wife frowned into the camera.

"*Jesucristo.* You," Nina said.

"Nice to see you, too. Is Tomás there?"

"What is wrong with you?" She clenched her fists, as if to punch him from across the Solar System. "No. Just, no. I'm not going to have you do this to him again. You made your choice."

As she spoke, Tomás popped onto the screen beside his mother.

"Dad?" He wore a baseball jersey, a smear of guava jelly across his face. In just nine months, he must have grown three or four inches.

"Tomás!" Emilio said. "How are you, *m'ijito*? Are you still in Little League?"

"Where have you been? I needed your help learning to hit a curveball. Are you coming to my birthday party next week? I really want you to come."

A pang of guilt stabbed his gut. Nina was right; he shouldn't have called.

"I'm sorry, I can't be there," he said, his throat closing up.

"Dad?" Tomás said. "I can't hear you. Are you coming?"

"Hello?" Emilio shouted. "Hello?"

"Dad?"

The image faded.

"LEE3? I've been disconnected." He felt partly relieved, partly sick to his stomach.

"Hmm. That's odd," LEE3 said. "We've lost all communications with Earth. I'll alert the skeleton crew."

The REMpod, the biofile, and now communications.

"LEE3?" he said. "Is Angie Velasquez's biofile still inaccessible?"

"Yeah, Doc."

"What about her husband's?"

Before LEE3 could answer he heard footsteps scampering outside the entrance to his suite. "Angie?" He pulled open the door and peered out into the corridor. At the far end, he thought he saw a shadow move, black within black. He blinked, and it was gone. "Angie?"

LEE3 walked beside him, matching his gait. "You okay? You seem a little preoccupied."

"I wouldn't have asked you to activate your psychotherapy program otherwise," Emilio said. Like most shrinks, he'd been consulting a therapist off and on for years. The consults became more regular after his divorce a year and a half prior to launch of the *Seed*. Now he was forced to commiserate with LEE3's psychotherapy subroutine.

They made their way through the skyweb, dark crisscrossing corridors—some stretching kilometers—connecting one hullscraper to another. He needed exercise to help clear his head. When they reached the top floor of an accompanying 'scraper, a door opened to a gymnasium steeped in darkness. Above them, a massive skylight framed the dusty constellations, his own private *Starry Night*, the Universe itself as art.

"I would say we're dealing with straightforward projection on her part, guilt manifesting as an imaginary monster that now stalks her," Emilio said. "It's interesting she's self-aware enough to have considered that possibility herself. And she doesn't seem the type to react in that manner. If the human psyche worked this way, half the population would be haunted by monsters."

"Aren't they?" LEE3 smirked. "Are you decommissioning her when we arrive at Pluto?"

"I don't know yet. I want to find a way to help her." He stepped onto the treadmill. "Power Off" displayed on the monitor and he slapped at the handlebars in frustration. "She hasn't been entirely forthcoming with me. Still, I'm impressed she sought help."

"After some arm-twisting by me."

"She did listen to you, though."

"My, you're giving her every benefit of the doubt, aren't you?"

"Am I? What are you driving at?" He wondered if LEE3's psych subroutine *required* it to duel him with cryptic platitudes.

"Ever consider that you're acting this way because of her child?"

"I don't see that her daughter has anything to do with—"

LEE3 sighed loudly. "From one therapist to another: give me a break."

Emilio gave up on the treadmill and made his way to the track, starting a light jog. The circular pathway was bathed in the faint indigo, making it easy to stay on course. His mind wrangled with LEE3's question.

"Okay. As a parent, I empathize with her."

"And why is that?"

"She chose to keep her family together," he said. "Either they all went or they all stayed. There was no other option for her."

In his case, the family court judge had cut through all the accusations and recriminations in the custody dispute by sitting down with Tomás and asking him to choose. The boy had picked his mother. The court order had limited Emilio's visits to alternate weekends, and after a few months even those visits had tapered off as he became immersed in preparations for the *Seed* mission. Once he'd committed to joining the crew, the question of appealing the custody decision—or of any contact whatsoever with Tomás, for that matter—became a moot point.

He circled the track, LEE3 jogging beside him.

"Emilio?"

"Yes?"

"There's an incoming q-call. From Pluto."

He slowed down and made his way to a wall monitor. LEE3 stood next to him, mimicking the movements of an exhausted runner, a towel around the neck, hands on knees. The AI must have decided Emilio needed the company of a workout buddy.

He tapped the screen and a wide face beamed at him. "Dr. Garcia. I'm Aulani Kahanahuni, Pluto's Head Librarian. I'm responding to your query. I wanted to let you know there's a Library match."

"There is?" While he'd forwarded Angie's sketch to Pluto on a hunch after she'd mentioned studying Library engineering with her husband, a match was a long shot, at best. Pluto's orbital grav-wave detectors and deciphering team provided the finest Library access in the Solar System.

"The Ancient Cataloguers' wisdom knows no bounds!" Aulani said, looking skyward. Plutonians had a reputation for their devotion to Library knowledge, a devotion that veered toward mysticism. Given the miracles of

Library Tech, he couldn't say he blamed them. The problem was the difficulty in distinguishing between Library entries on science versus belief systems, history versus mythology.

"You've drawn an illustration of an anomaly known to manifest on Cataloguer ships, often right before an accident."

"You mean like a gremlin?" he asked. "Or a poltergeist?" He sounded more condescending than he intended.

She stopped smiling. "The Cataloguers did have some scientific theories on the cause of these anomalies, but my staff is still conducting its research. And I wanted to answer your emergency query as quickly as possible. There's also an entire mythology developed around these apparitions. Most notably, that they target and torment those persons guilty of terrible sins."

Typical, he thought. *A mishmash of fact, fiction, and superstition.* "Would someone studying Library engineering come across information on this anomaly?" he asked.

"Oh, absolutely. It's cross-referenced quite often in entries on spaceship engineering."

So, Angie would have seen this image before. Adding her face to it, however, spoke to . . . deeper issues.

"You haven't actually encountered this phenomenon," Aulani said.

He hesitated. "No."

"I should be able to present you with additional information when you arrive at Charon." She waited as if expecting him to say more, but when he volunteered nothing else, she lifted an arm and looked skyward again. "Well, let's thank the Ancient Cataloguers for their wisdom."

A girl appeared on the viewscreen and yanked at Aulani's blouse. She leaned down. "Not now. Mommy's busy."

"When the wolf's in town, it gobbles you down, down . . . down!" the child sang, staring directly into the screen at Emilio.

His heart skipped a beat. "What was that?" he said.

"I'm sorry, Doctor. Just a silly nursery rhyme. Very popular these days. Is there anything else I can assist you with?"

He shook his head.

"We're all looking forward to the *Seed's* arrival."

After the communication link clicked off, he turned to find that LEE3 had vanished. The gymnasium seemed darker than before.

LEE3 had pinpointed Angie's location at the recreation center several blocks from the medical facility. Emilio decided to meet up with her outside the entranceway to the closed casino, where slot machines and roulette wheels hibernated in the shadows. For someone who feared she was being stalked, she didn't seem to mind navigating the vast ship on her own. He found her on a bench by the casino.

"Doctor," she said, nodding hello.

"Angie." He sat next to her.

"Isn't it interesting that the designers of the *Seed*, a ship created to transport the best and brightest of humanity, included a casino?"

He shrugged. "Even the best and brightest enjoy a game of chance now and then."

"I suppose."

"Angie," he said gently. "Is there anything you'd like to tell me?"

LEE3 had finally accessed her husband's biofile.

Her smile faded, and she lowered her eyes.

"I know it's not easy," he said.

"If you already know . . . "

"To be able to help, I need to hear it from you."

She took a deep breath. "Marc and Sofia took a morning shuttle to Luna-1 for the boarding of the *Seed*. I told him I'd join them the next day, that I needed to see my sister—we hadn't spoken in over three years—to find some closure." She shook her head, smiled sadly. "Total lie, of course. That wasn't the closure I was looking for. I met up with Stefan and we spent the entire day making love, saying our final goodbyes. I went off-grid, so I didn't hear the news. I didn't know . . . about Shuttle Flight 10."

Flight 10. The shuttle had disintegrated on lift-off. The fifty-five fatalities had delayed the *Seed's* departure for two weeks.

"I'm sorry," he said.

"The thing is, they wouldn't have been aboard that flight if I hadn't won that argument with Marc, if I hadn't convinced him to go forward with the mission," she said, her voice hoarse. She put her hands over her face. "And I—I should've been with them."

"It's not your fault," he said. "It's just . . . terrible luck."

"Now . . . now that thing wants to even the score. Because I wasn't where I was supposed to be."

"Look, your illustration of the 'monster' is an image you would have come across during your studies of Library engineering."

"You consulted the Library?" Panic swept across her face. "Why did you *do* that?"

"Calm down."

"No, you don't understand," she said. "The monster. It came to me last night. It spoke to me, told me that you'd contacted Pluto to access the Library. And it warned me there'd be horrible consequences. I'd hoped it was just a dream."

"I understand." He'd have been more impressed with her revelation if he hadn't just told her about his communications with Pluto.

"No, you don't! Now it has its sights set on you. You've put yourself in grave danger." She put her hands on her head. "It told me it's moved inside some of the other sleepers now. We need to deactivate those REMpods."

"Wake more passengers?"

"No," she said, avoiding eye contact. "Not wake them."

"I see. Angie, didn't you ask me to prove that whatever you're seeing isn't real?"

"Yes, and instead you're telling me the monster is catalogued in the Library. That it is real."

"The Cataloguers have been known to maintain myths alongside history, fiction alongside science. This is no different," he said. "I want you to use this." He removed a streamlight from his pocket and handed it to her.

"Ocular therapy?"

"Flash the light in your eyes every two hours. It'll calm you down, make you think more clearly."

"Doctor . . . "

"Angie? Listen to me. The monster isn't real. Your dreams aren't real. Continue with the sleep meds I prescribed, and supplement them with the streamlight. In the meantime, let's keep meeting, and talking. Okay?"

She stared at him and then at the streamlight in her hand before nodding. "I'm sorry I got you involved in this. Be careful, okay?" She turned, her shoulders slumped as if defeated, and headed down the corridor in the direction of the medical facility. He was tempted to accompany her, but he had an urgent question for LEE3 that couldn't wait.

"LEE3," he said, when she was no longer in sight.

"Yeah, Doc?"

"Has Angie Velasquez been near this District's REMpods since waking up?"

"Yes. She asked me to deactivate several, but doesn't have the authority to give me that command."

"She did?" Why the hell hadn't LEE3 informed him of this? "I have no choice then."

"You'll be decommissioning her at Pluto?"

"It's not safe to wait that long. Can you wake up two security guards? She needs to be confined to quarters immediately and kept away from the sleepers."

"Understood."

Movement. A blur shot across his peripheral vision.

He turned back in the direction Angie had headed and thought he saw a figure dart out of the corridor and into the casino entrance. "Angie?" *Wonderful.* The last thing he needed was for an anxious, troubled crewmember to overhear the order decommissioning her. He walked to the casino's arched entranceway, which was festooned with gargoyles and cherubs. "Hello?"

The silhouettes of gaming tables and slot machines stood out in the dim blue lighting like the skyline of a miniature city.

"LEE3?"

"Yes, Doctor?" The AI had abandoned its physical projection and whispered into his earpiece.

"Is Angie in the casino?"

"Negative. She's walking the *Seed's* skyweb at the moment."

With only one passenger awake in each of the twelve districts—all maintenance engineers—and with each district extending more than a square mile, it'd be unlikely to bump into a member of the skeleton crew.

He sensed it before seeing it. Pressed against the wall like a human-sized cockroach, oozing along so slowly that the movement was barely discernible. He pretended not to see it, pretended he didn't feel the invisible claw of terror clamping down on his heart.

He needed light. He bent and grabbed one of the power cords extending from a slot machine and plugged it into an outlet. The machine lit up with a loud clang, and music played. The reels had a picture of a wolf's head, fangs bared, and the familiar ditty played: "When the wolf's in town, it gobbles you down, down . . . down." He considered kicking out the cord, shutting it down, but he didn't want to lose the light.

Out of the corner of his eye something—an obsidian ribbon—sped by so quickly he barely saw it.

"LEE3?"

"What now, Doc?"

"Someone just exited the casino. Who was it?"

"I'm not detecting anyone but you." A pause. "I was just about to buzz you. I wanted to let you know there's been another REMpod glitch. I've been unable to wake up the security guards you requested."

"Try another doctor, then."

"That's the thing. None of the REMpods are responding. I can't seem to wake up anyone."

Emilio searched for Angie for over an hour along the cityship's skyweb of interlocking catwalks. LEE3 reported she could no longer be detected—either another glitch in the systems or she'd done something to mask her life-signs. He didn't think she'd exhibited any suicidal tendencies, but now began to doubt himself. He leaned over the edge of the handrails staring down into Central Lake, its dark waters swooshing against the ship's artificial shore. Normally, the *Seed* would have simulated the moon in the sky, but while the REMpods remained on, the moon stayed off. Even the dim phosphor lighting had now stopped functioning, so he used a pocket streamlight to brighten the catwalk a few steps ahead of him.

He remembered the day Tomás fell off the pier at Lake Redondo while baiting his fishing line. Emilio had dived in and pulled him out. While Tomás coughed up water, Nina had lit into him for failing to watch the boy more closely.

"LEE3?" he said.

No response.

"LEE3?"

The holo materialized beside him on the catwalk. "You okay, Doc?"

"No, not really." The words came slowly at first then burst forth in a torrent. He told LEE3 about the shadow in the casino, the music he'd heard. With all the technical problems—communications down, REMpods malfunctioning—maybe Angie was right. Maybe something was sabotaging the ship. Maybe the Library wasn't describing myth, but something real and perilous. "The *Seed* is in danger," he said. "I feel it."

"You 'feel it'? Really?" LEE3 said, head shaking. "Listen to yourself. You're all alone on a massive cityship, living in darkness. Surely you must realize your perspective is being skewed by Angie's delusions."

Had LEE3 been corporeal he would've grabbed the AI by the collar and shaken it. "I repeat: Datafiles have been corrupted. Communications are down. And now we can't wake anyone up! You didn't see the monster—*I did.*"

"While we've been speaking I again reviewed vid of your movement through the casino. This time in infrared and with x-rays—even on a molecular level. Nothing was detectible in there but you."

"It was . . . in the stillness, in the shadows . . . "

"Have you considered anxiolytic meds? Ocular therapy?"

He glared at the AI.

"Listen, the ship problems you're describing are rooted in the physical. These are simple engineering glitches."

"Engineering glitches," Emilio repeated. He snapped his fingers. "You're right; I need to follow up with an engineer, one of the skeleton crew. Connect me."

"I can't do that." A faint smile appeared on LEE3's face, as if Emilio had taken the bait by making the request.

"Communications problems?"

The holo shook its head.

"Then what?"

"They're all quite dead, I'm afraid."

Emilio stepped backward, his heart in his throat.

The AI cleared its throat, licked its lips and sang: *"When the wolf's in town, it gobbles you down, down, DOWN!"* It stood there smiling at him, then took a bow.

"Why did you do that?" he said.

"Do what?"

"N-nothing." Emilio edged backward before turning and running down the catwalk toward the interior of the nearest hullscraper. He peeked over his shoulder to see LEE3 staring at him, hands on hips.

The alarm sounded after several hours of fitful sleep. Emilio didn't remember setting it. Instead of the familiar soothing tones, it made a different sound; a high note followed by a lower one, then another. *"Down, down, down."*

He slammed his fist against the wall monitor to shut off the braying music.

Sitting up in bed, he took deep breaths and wiped the sweat from his face. Since returning from the skyweb, he'd tried connecting with members of the skeleton crew throughout the ship with no success. He'd also attempted to contact the Charon moonbase, but couldn't establish a link even though the *Seed* now had to be in closer proximity to Pluto. He'd also expected Angie to contact him, but there'd been only silence.

Then the smell hit him. The stench of decay made him cover his face with his hands.

It lurked in the far corner of his room, hidden in the shadows, hunched over. A human head perched obscenely atop a slimy shroud.

What are you? he wanted to say, but fear choked him into silence.

"Emilio?" The thing cawed like a vulture as it spoke.

It edged closer to him. He was paralyzed. Closer. It stood at the foot of his bed. Now it bent at the waist—although he couldn't make out any sort of torso behind the shadow that enveloped it. Closer still.

It began to hum. *When the wolf's in town, it gobbles you down, down, down . . .*

As it lurched forward, its face came into view.

The monster's eyes were black, pupil-less, its mouth black, toothless, but its face . . .

Dear God, the face was *his*.

He shut his eyes tight and tried to scream, but couldn't. He covered his ears to avoid hearing the song. Tomás. The monster knew about Tomás. Knew he'd left his boy behind without saying goodbye. Knew he'd blamed a ten-year-old child for choosing his mother over his father. He was so ashamed. He'd abandoned his son, and the creature knew his shame. *It knew.*

When he opened his eyes, the monster was gone.

Dreaming. Had he been dreaming? With every fiber of his being he hoped so.

But the stench lingered.

A few hours later, as he studied the protocols for initiating a manual wake-up of the sleepers, hoping to find a way to do so without inflicting any permanent damage, the door to his quarters chimed. The sound started with a note, followed by two higher ones, then a lower one. *When the wolf's . . .* He shook his head. *Stop it.*

The door slid open and Angie stood there. "Hello, Dr. Garcia," she said. "I'm sorry to bother you in your quarters."

Her eyes seemed clear; she smiled confidently.

He stared behind her into the emptiness of the corridor.

"Thank you for everything you've done for me," she said. "The meds and ocular treatment have done the trick. I'm better. Much better."

"Y-you are?"

"I have—had—a lot of guilt. But the meds and speaking to someone about it has made me realize I can't keep reliving the past. I need to look forward. In any event, the hallucinations and nightmares are gone. I don't hear that song anymore."

"That's good." He swallowed. "But the communication grid is down. We can't transmit any messages to Earth, or to Pluto for that matter. The *Seed* is having all sorts of systems problems."

"I know. I consulted with one of the engineers from Aft 8."

"You did?" He said this too loudly.

She raised an eyebrow. "We sailed through a gravitational wave—unlike anything we've ever encountered before—after we passed Neptune. Normally, it'd be undetectable, but Library Tech is especially sensitive to it, which explains the malfunctions. The *Seed* rode it out. Everything's back to normal. And I've been mulling over what you said about the anomaly. I think it's the Cataloguers' way to describe—in metaphorical terms—an actual physical phenomenon, in this case a grav-wave." She smiled. "I feel like an idiot."

Her interpretation made sense except . . . he'd seen the monster with his own eyes. He had smelled it. He had felt it drawing ever nearer. He exhaled. "I'm glad I could be of assistance."

"I'm grateful. I'd been running away from my issues, denying they even existed. But I realize now that's no way to live your life."

Is she putting on a show for me? he thought. With the *Seed* approaching Pluto she had every incentive to convince him she was fine, to avoid being decommissioned.

She turned to leave, but stopped at the doorway. "Are you sure everything is okay, Doctor?"

He nodded. "Prepare to go back into spacesleep when we enter orbit around Charon. I'll check you into your REMpod."

As her form faded down the corridor, LEE3 materialized outside the door to Emilio's quarters, leaning against the wall.

"Why'd you lock me out, Doc? You've been holed up in that room way too long. Did I do something to offend? Is it my breath?" The holo breathed into its cupped hands.

"What you said to me about the skeleton crew . . . "

LEE3 stared blankly. "I'm not following."

He paused. "Can you access the conversation we had on the skyweb?"

"Hmm," LEE3 said. "There's a gap in my memory."

"Angie says the ship's engineering issues are due to a gravitational wave the *Seed* sailed through."

"Interesting theory." LEE3 didn't appear at all interested. "And Angie?"

"Fully recovered apparently."

"'Apparently.'" LEE3 smiled. "But you can sense a faker a mile away."

"Where is she heading now?"

"A level below us. Moving toward the energy flux station that powers the REMpods."

Emilio raced to the end of the corridor. Leaning over the handrails, he stared intensely into the gray until he spotted Angie on the skyweb a few levels below, the pathway lighting up ahead of her. She took a few steps, stopped, and looked back over her shoulder.

"Angie!" he shouted, waving.

She froze and stared up. Her posture changed immediately when she saw him, standing straighter, as if feigning confidence.

A smudge in the shadows moved behind her, then a black wave rose.

"No! Look out!" he screamed.

She turned, her face twisting into a grimace as the creature swallowed her upper torso. It lifted her high in the air and her body disappeared, legs kicking, down its gullet, bit by bit.

Down, down, down.

The monster turned toward him, its black-smudge form elongating. Its oil-slick head blurred and morphed into familiar features.

A boy's face, grinning at him, something smeared across his lips.

Emilio turned and ran full-tilt into an adjoining tower, where he jumped into an elevator. When the door opened on the deck level, he expected the creature to be waiting for him, but instead there was darkness, only darkness. But in that blackness he sensed movement.

He needed to reach the nearest skeleton crewmember, the one Angie had spoken to in Aft District 8, on the other side of the bay. Without going up into the skyweb, a ferry was the only way across.

He sprung out the front entrance and ran down empty streets, his heart banging against his sternum as he pushed his endurance to its limits, slowing down only when he arrived at the pier. With his sides aching, he jogged down faux-wooden planks and hopped aboard the ferry. "Depart!" he commanded.

As the ship skimmed into the thick darkness, he leaned over the deck and stared back at the pier, straining to see any signs of the creature. The waters were still and silent, the ferry's movement creating a cool, sterile breeze. His thoughts turned to Tomás pleading with him to come to his birthday party. Then he imagined the creature standing an inch away from him in the pitch darkness, its exhalation the breeze against his face.

No! Clear your mind.

He had to contact Pluto, learn if the additional Library research had turned up more information on the creature.

After some time, he made out the massive silhouette of the Aft District 8 hullscrapers looming larger and larger, black against gray.

When the ferry reached the pier, he jumped out, glancing over his shoulder. Behind him, the floorboards on the ferry creaked.

"LEE3," he whispered.

Nothing.

"Goddammit, LEE3!"

He leapt into the maze of dark streets until he found himself at the end of an alleyway with no exit. And before he even turned around, he knew what awaited him.

The towering shadow blocked his path, humming a familiar tune.

He reached into his pocket and pulled out the streamlight, activating it. The narrow beam of light sliced through the creature, splitting it in half.

He lunged past it and out of the alleyway.

When he turned around, the shadow had reconstituted itself.

He held up the streamlight again, and an ebon tendril shot out of the monster's midsection, swatting the device out of his hand.

It hovered toward him. It would never stop stalking him, he realized.

His instincts screamed for him to run, but his professional training, his life experience, told him how foolish he'd been to try to escape from it. He clutched the locket around his neck. He'd spent so much time running, trying to flee from feelings that threatened to consume him. He had made his choices, as had everyone else aboard the cityship. Now he needed to find a way to live with those choices.

He took a few steps toward the obscene bird-shaped shadow. The child's visage glared at him, and its mouth opened, stretching impossibly wide to reveal a bottomless abyss.

Emilio drew nearer.

"I'm not running from you anymore."

His breath—perhaps the words themselves—rippled the creature's outline. Up close, it seemed as insubstantial as the mist of memory.

"No more running," he repeated, moving closer still.

The creature froze in place, then drifted backward, away from him.

A siren blasted, and the shiplights suddenly flared on.

"ARRIVAL. CHARON," the ship's speakers blared. "ARRIVAL. CHARON."

As the shiplights intensified, through squinting eyes, he saw the creature slither to the end of the alleyway, where it cowered, shrinking until it faded into the disappearing shadows.

Emilio managed to fit the most important of his personal belongings into a single carry-case, which he rolled onto the docking bay. The arriving passengers greeted him as they disembarked from the shuttle in single file. The *Seed's* skeleton crew—twelve engineers from each district, all alive and healthy—welcomed the Pluto colonists and directed them to their respective REMpod stations. The Plutonians were already dressed in white sleeping suits made of Library-inspired fabrics specially designed for decades-long stasis.

He was surprised to find Aulani Kahanahuni, the Library Liaison, among the arriving passengers. He hadn't realized she was scheduled to join the *Seed's* crew.

"Dr. Garcia," she said, smiling broadly when she spotted him. "I'm glad to see you." She introduced him to a stocky man with a warm smile she identified as her husband.

"I'm glad to see you, too. Where's your daughter?" Emilio said, looking among the throng of arriving Plutonians for the girl he'd seen on the q-call.

The smile on the Librarian's face vanished. "We decided to leave her behind on Charon. With my sister's family."

After an awkward pause, he said, "I . . . I understand."

"Do you have a moment?" she said. She pulled Emilio to one side while her husband rejoined the other white-clad passengers who were being guided now by LEE3.

"The additional research you requested on the anomaly has been completed and is being forwarded to you."

"Oh?" He was about to tell her it was moot at this point, but she continued speaking.

"The prevailing theory among the Cataloguers is that the anomaly is the product of gravitational waves on a scale heretofore unknown to us. Grav-waves of this sort aren't generated by the collision of two black holes or other high-density objects, as is typically the case. No, these are unleashed when the branes of two universes brush up against each other."

"Multiple universe theory?"

"Indeed, Dr. Garcia. Indeed! The Cataloguers theorized grav-waves on such a scale produced micro-tears in the fabric of spacetime—much like the ones that allowed transmission of the Library itself—only these allowed pieces of another universe to leak over into ours, drawn to spaceships powered by q-tech. In fact, as I mentioned, there's an entire Library mythology built around this phenomenon, the concept of actual living creatures drawn into this universe by a person's guilt."

"Are these 'micro-tears' transitory?"

"Oh yes, though Library lore tells of rare instances where something crosses over and stays, finding continued sustenance in the guilt of its prey," she said. "The Cataloguers have blessed us with their great knowledge—and their great storytelling," she said, smiling and raising her arms skyward. "Tell me, Doctor. Why are you so curious about this subject?"

He hesitated. "I had a patient with some interest in the matter."

She noticed his carry-case. "You're leaving?"

"Yes, this is my last stop, I'm afraid."

"Is this related to the . . . unfortunate incident with that poor woman?"

He hadn't realized word had already spread to Pluto of Angie's death. LEE3 must have logged it. The official cause was suicide. They'd assumed she'd been heading to the energy flux station to damage the REMpods, but LEE3 said she'd leapt into an energy beam, incinerating herself. He'd asked LEE3 to show him the vid-feed of the incident, but the recording was unavailable due to the ship disruptions at the time. Emilio considered confessing to LEE3 what he'd seen—what he thought he'd seen—but realized this would only focus attention on his own mental state, his own failure to properly treat Angie Velasquez's condition. Best to leave the *Seed* quietly. He had opted instead to set forth a full record of his experiences in the medical logs should the *Seed's* crew encounter a similar problem with another sleeper in the future.

"I'm leaving for personal reasons," he said.

"We all must follow our own paths," Aulani said.

He accompanied her to the REMpod next to her husband's and allowed them to speak privately for a minute before setting down his case to help them step inside their respective pods.

The plexi lowered, and calmness fell over Aulani's face as she drifted into spacesleep. Emilio thought of Angie. Whatever her psychological issues, were they much different than the guilt faced by every single person aboard the *Seed*? Guilt borne of leaving loved ones behind? Or guilt borne of bringing them along, sentencing them to a lifetime aboard a spaceship and their descendants to a dangerous and an uncertain future?

"Dr. Garcia!" LEE3 waved at him. "The shuttle's departing to Charon. If you're leaving the *Seed* . . ."

He jogged twenty steps before he realized he'd left his case next to the REMpod. When he returned and bent to retrieve it, he noticed a slight twitch on Aulani's lips, rapid movement behind her eyelids. He looked at the sleepers around her.

The twitching seemed to glide like a wave across the sea of REMpods.

"Dr. Garcia! The shuttle's going to leave without you."

He hesitated, looked back and forth between the shuttle and the REMpods. A stillness had fallen across the sleepers. He touched the locket around his neck, then turned and raced across the docking bay.

He entered the shuttle and another person, an engineer, followed behind him and took the seat across from him. They were the only two passengers aboard the AI-piloted shuttle returning to Charon. He sat down, buckled up, and put on headphones to drown out the sound of the engines. Outside his window, Charon's bustling moonbase drew closer, and behind it, ghostly Pluto with its heart-shaped ice-plains beckoned. It could take months, but eventually he'd find transportation back home. He'd call Nina as soon as he reached Earth and arrange a visit with Tomás.

He thought about the mission he was leaving behind, the adventure of settling New Earth, and felt a twinge of regret. And then he thought about the twitching faces of the sleepers. A pulsing wave of something—something alive, yet foul—seemed to be moving through them, infecting them all. Was it real? Should he have done something? He shook his head and pushed away the thought. And as music began to pipe over the headphones, he thought he heard a note followed by two higher notes, then a lower one. *Down, down, down.*

He ripped off the headphones and threw them to the floor.

"Is everything all right?" said the engineer sitting across from him.

Emilio nodded, took a deep breath.

He had made his choice. Now he needed to find a way to live with it.

He shifted his thoughts to Tomás, and trained his eyes on Pluto, the ice-white sphere growing larger and larger until the darkness of space had disappeared.

Karin Lowachee was born in South America, grew up in Canada, and worked in the Arctic. Her first novel *Warchild* won the 2001 Warner Aspect First Novel Contest. Both *Warchild* and her third novel *Cagebird* were finalists for the Philip K. Dick Award. *Cagebird* won the Prix Aurora Award in 2006 for Best Long-Form Work in English. Her books have been translated into French, Hebrew, and Japanese, and her short stories have appeared in anthologies edited by Nalo Hopkinson, John Joseph Adams, and Ann VanderMeer. Her fantasy novel, *The Gaslight Dogs,* was published through Orbit Books USA.

SYMPATHIZER

Karin Lowachee

The alien's blood looked like molten gold in the low light. It had been shot by one of her soljets, but not by her order. She herself had almost been shot, or it was made to look like that, and she wanted to believe that her own jets would have missed on purpose. Her medic Markalan pressed gloved hands to the alien's stomach wound, but the gold seeped past his fingers and began to run down the alien's side. She didn't know if that was indeed the alien's stomach and neither did her medic.

"This might not work," he said. "We don't have a detailed scan of their physiology, much less their cellular structure."

Even after two years they knew so little. "Find a way," she said.

The line of seven aliens watched them like stone statuary carved of ancient Earth alabaster, though a couple were the color of burnished bronze and they stood motionless and black-eyed like deep-sea creatures. If they regarded the humans in judgment or with some imminent urge to attack, they did not show it. They didn't have guns, at least not on hand, but they had blades and the blades hung along the walls of the base control room like black punctuations, curved and sharp. She had gathered over the months that the alabaster aliens with the intricate silver tattoos on their faces were the warriors, and the bronze-skinned ones were the scientists. It was a scientist bleeding out beneath Markalan's hands.

Her squad of four jets stood by the doors and two of them faced out for incoming and two faced in to watch the aliens. The rest of the platoon were outside by the airlock and they could all hear the rifle fire in staccato cadence peppering the steel. This room in the base was much like a human configuration with some semblance of comps and controls and the industrial gray of steel alloy and plastics, but on the walls by the weapons were curious red markings that resembled ancient wards of witchery, if only for their inscrutable and intricate design, and in the corners burned cones of sweet acrid incense, some apparent mix of magic and technology that defied any rally to battle-minded reason.

The blood spread along the floor and with it rose a scent she had never encountered before, but it was something akin to old forests she had camped in when she was a girl. They had removed their helmets. The air was clean. They were two years in orbit around this moon already, burning through resources, and were pumped full of drugs enough to stop disease, yet she was still nervous to breathe the alien air and be close to the aliens, even if the alternative was suffocation.

"I think it stopped," her medic said, and she looked down at Markalan with his bloodied hands and his dark eyes raw and wide like they had been gazing too long into some scene of harrowing. The silence of the aliens unnerved him, unnerved them all.

The rifle fire stopped outside. Her comm clicked and the lieutenant's voice came through to her ears.

"The captain's requested parlay."

She looked down at the injured alien, then looked at the others lined up around Markalan and the warriors were staring at her as though scrutinizing a glyph newly uncovered on a Paleolithic plinth that would somehow explain a truth of their beginnings. She turned and looked at her squad by the door.

"Do we believe it?" Markalan said, his hands still pressed to the alien's side as if the healant he'd sprayed there was going to disintegrate any second. It might have, if it couldn't bond to the alien's cells. It might be poisoning the alien.

She went to the base doors and told her squad, "Open it."

To cross the expanse between the alien base and the ship took a little less than an hour on foot. Moon rock, gray and inert with striations of silver and black, created jagged silhouettes, and her weighted bootsteps stirred the ashen dust minutely, as though she was the lone survivor of an apocalyptic event. On the spinal horizon sat the uneven silhouette of the destroyed mine like the skeletal remains of a beached creature left too long in the sun. She drew steady silent breaths and the scent of her own skin and sweat returned to her. Through the HUD on her helmet the dropship hunkered ahead like a beast of the netherworld, armored and anticipating some hour in which it could feed. The smaller rider squatted next to it, all the lights in darkened disuse. They'd abandoned it a week ago to operate from the base, knowing the *Plymouth* would send a dropship and they would have no defense from the rider. She had not intended to abandon the rider, but the captain had sent word to kill the aliens from the time it took for them to walk from the rider to the base, and she did not order her platoon to do it. After that there was only one alternative and the *Plymouth* had fired from orbit and destroyed the alien mining tower and four dozen aliens with it, and soon enough the dropship had come, and her jets had come out and they were firing on each other. They fired on each other for two days, but luckily the main base had held and she had anticipated the ground attack and laid mines around the perimeter.

She switched to a narrow channel and addressed her right-most escort, a private she knew by name.

"What happened in the negotiations?" she asked the boy.

"Dunno." He sounded reluctant to speak and his hands gripped his rifle. She couldn't see his eyes inside his helmet. "Cap'n's just pissed."

"This is a wrong action."

The boy said nothing.

"He's effectively declared war on a sentient alien species. Do you want to take this back to EarthHub?"

The boy said nothing.

He wasn't the one she needed to talk to, but she gleaned some tenor of the troops' opinions from that silence. In the dropship she looked at the faces of the squad and they would not meet her eyes. The firing amongst them at the base had gone a couple days because nobody wanted to kill one another. When they were moving the alien scientists from one of the research domes to the primary complex, it had been shot. She was running right beside the alien and had not been shot. Then the jets from the ship blew the research dome. So she thought about that all the way back to orbit and the *Plymouth*.

The same private and another private who she also knew by name escorted her to the captain's conference room and left her in there. She didn't have weapons because they had taken them from her outside the base. She sat at the long glossed table, looking at her reflection in it as if through a membranous alternate dimension, and in a few minutes the captain entered and the hatch shut behind him from the jet outside, sounding like a guillotine. He sat in his chair and it was all the way on the opposite end of the table, and he began to slowly swivel the thick, black chair back and forth with one hand on the table top where it was shiniest, fingers lightly drumming the surface. He had a streak of silver hair that started over the right side of his forehead and sometimes in command staff meetings he would lean his head on his hand and his fingers would twist that streak around, but now his hands remained otherwise occupied and his right eye under that silver streak looked paler than his left.

"Commander Gray, what am I going to do with you?"

She said nothing.

"It was a simple order."

"Of murder."

He waved his hand like he was brushing away an insect from the air. "Trying to communicate with them is pointless. The Hub doesn't have the resources to let us sit around, no matter how many forays we do in this region."

"Then let's leave."

His eyes narrowed and the swiveling stopped. He leaned forward with both arms on the table and entwined his fingers together and stared down the black surface at her with the direct and distressed countenance of a kindling god looking upon his creation of which he held little hope.

"Surely a woman of your rank understands the way our universe works."

He was a man whose tone seemed naturally to possess some form of condescension just because he was handpicked by politicians and brass to head this expedition.

"What do you think happens from here," he said.

"I don't know," she said.

"So you think it's up to me?"

"You're the captain."

"I am. But you're my jet commander and you won't command your jets. So you forced me to command your jets, and I know they're displeased with me and this is because you gave them a contradictory order. So you tell me, what do you think happens from here?"

"You ask me to order them to vacate the base and fire on the aliens."

"We're long past that."

She said nothing.

"You will make a decision whether you want to be with your jets on that moon or remain with your jets on ship."

"Then what?"

"Who can tell? Maybe the aliens attack your jets on the moon, something Markalan and the rest of them did not expect because the aliens had lured your platoon into the base to act as a shield. The *Plymouth* would have no choice but to retaliate from orbit again."

It was a grim joke on jetdeck that the captain walked around with his uniform trousers a size too small so he could feel that he had bigger balls than he did. She watched his eyes, the paler and the darker. "Is that what you told Hub Command about why you blew the aliens' mining tower? And all of those striviirc-na underground?"

"You've wasted both time and ordnance here. So where will you go?"

"I guess I'm going back to the moon, but can I talk to my chief at least?"

"What do you have to say to him? You couldn't even give a simple order to your platoon on the surface."

"You won't grant me a last word, sir? To get my affairs in order?"

He looked like he was thinking it over. "I never figured you for a martyr."

"I'm no martyr, I just have limits."

"Over a bunch of strits?"

"Murder's murder, sir."

"Is it because you can't leave him? Your bleeding-heart medic?"

"I'd like to speak to my chief."

He sniffed and leaned up again like a great bird puffing its feathers, and he passed a hand over the lower part of his face and stood to come down the length of the table so he could sit beside her, where she did not move and held no weapons. He wasn't incapable either, and he laid his hand flat on the table in front of her. "Enas, are you really willing to die for these strits?"

It was not the name the aliens called themselves, but human ears and mouths had difficulty with the pronunciation they had been told so this had become their name. The way in which the captain said it made it sound more like a curse word.

"I'm not willing to do shit, but I'll do what I have to."

Two of her own jets, who had been standing outside the room, took her to the brig and put her in, and one of them mumbled, "We're sorry, Commander," before locking her up and leaving the lights on as they left. The hatch made a clang and she looked at the empty monitoring station, then up at the high ceiling with its exposed pipes and around the barred cell. She knew there were optics in here and another adjacent room in which to listen and watch the feed, but she went to the single bunk in the cell and sat and waited. The *Plymouth* was an expeditionary ship with a military provenance, and on the bulkheads was the evidence of past battles long recorded and forgotten in the logs, other disobedient crew or incarcerated pirates and smugglers moved from one location to the next in the shuffling of fates orchestrated by those with more might, and she counted the scoring along the cold transsteel with the tips of her fingers and wondered at the lives of labor incurred in the construction of it.

Three hours went by according to her tags, and then more, so she lay down on the bunk and slept. Sometime later the hatch opened and she awoke and sat up then stood and went to the cage bars as her chief came in and his face was grim like he was compelled to be a witness to a gruesome execution. He wore his sidearm and he glanced at the empty monitoring station before stopping a meter from the bars.

"Markalan?" he asked.

"One of the aliens was shot. But he fixed it, hopefully."

"Fucking mess. But we're okay?"

"All accounted for. Captain's going to bomb the base, isn't he?"

"He seems fond of that tactic, yeah."

"What happens when these aliens get good enough to wage war?"

The chief passed a hand along the back of his neck. "The Hub'll need more jets."

"Didn't we learn anything from history? First species we meet out here and we want to take things they have because they can't stop us now? We don't know if they have allies, if there are others. We only know what they've told us and it's shitty translation at best. You want to work out the eventualities of this?"

"I know 'em."

"Then what're we going to do?"

"We can't come between all of EarthHub and its ambitions for space. They want to start mining here as a platform for—"

"He'd have nothing without my jets."

"He'd have the ship."

She curled her fingers around the steel bars and looked the chief in the eyes. No doubt the brig was bugged and all of her words went on record, but the angle of the optics could not see her eyes and she stared for a moment at the chief before looking in the direction of the hatch. She saw the chief understand and out loud she said, "I'm not going to be party to instigating a war with an alien species, and every jet on that moon base has made their decision. Consequences and all."

The chief nodded.

The captain kept her in there for another twelve hours and nobody came or went, not even to deliver food. She drank cold water from the single sink in the cell, cupping it in her hands. The drives hummed in that constant low song, as if the ship cast a lullaby to the stars and the moon below, and she grew hungry but lay on the bunk with her eyes shut and her hands over her belly. She thought of Markalan and the aliens and knew that he would be able to hold the base, but he must have been wondering when the bombs would fall, and if that were the case there would be nowhere to take the striviirc-na. The *Plymouth* had already knocked out the alien communications satellite, so there was no sending messages to their homeworld, wherever it was. They knew so little about these aliens, but the captain thought they knew enough just because the aliens seemed peaceful and not very advanced technologically. There was no patience from here to EarthHub, and she lay there thinking of when they'd first met the aliens and how it had seemed strangely mundane seeing them aligned on the moon in their own suits color blocked in patterns both familiar and strange and she and her squad in their battle rigged blacks and through their helmets they'd tried to discern the nature of intelligence in one another's eyes. Humanity had long dreamed and conjured theatrical nightmares about first contact and all it had taken initially was a repetitive hello and frequent regular visits until on one visit the aliens invited them into their base.

She and the captain surveyed the setup of it, that it was not military but scientific, and the aliens spoke to them in a soothing song-like language and they were the general shape of humans beneath their suits, but the limbs slung longer from the narrow planes of their torsos and they moved with an uncanny grace. They had iridescent wings that grew from the edge of a wrist to the curve of a waist and the wings seemed to flutter in emphasis of their words. The humans learned simple words like "yes" and "no" and the name of their people and it was enough for them to glean that the aliens showed them these things because they wanted to be left alone, it was a kind of claiming of the space, the moon and the space around it and the captain had gone back to the ship saying, "We'll see about that." No amount of explanation or request to share the space and ally for the resources of the moon would sway the aliens who kept saying, "Wey. Wey." And it meant no.

It was dangerous to take affront to things of which they were so ignorant, hanging these aliens up to the standards of human emotions and reactions, but the captain wouldn't listen and she had lain in her bunk with Markalan after that first refusal and they both had known that no good was on the horizon. "What're we going to do?" Markalan had asked, and now here they were, and she slept in the shallows of consciousness until the brig hatch opened once again and the captain walked in and up to the bars to look in at her. She stood, and he said, "Have you thought about it?"

"I gave you my answer."

"I'm giving you a last chance."

"I don't need it."

He palmed his tags. Her chief and one of her other jets came in, but her chief went straight to the captain and pressed his gun into his back instead, and with his other hand he tugged the captain's sidearm from his holster and yanked at his tags until the chain broke, and the private went to the monitoring station and opened the cell.

"Where are you going to go?" the captain demanded as Enas walked out of the cell, and the chief put the captain in and the gate clanged shut and locked with a blink of red.

She took the captain's sidearm and his tags from her chief and led the way out to the corridor and through the belly of the ship up to the command deck where some of her jets lined the corridors outside the bridge and she knew the others were down in engineering and the hangar. With a nod to her corporal she walked onto the bridge with a squad of jets behind her, and her chief, and all of the officers on the bridge looked at them in alarm.

"The captain's in the brig," she said. "Hands off the consoles," as her jets spread out around the bridge and forced the officers and enlisted to stand away from their stations. She looked around and went to the comm and with a swift move of her fingers through the helio controls she called up the alien base, and in a minute she heard Markalan's voice. Relief flooded her chest, but she said, "I've got control of the ship, gather the platoon and the aliens in the dropship and the rider, and come aboard. Let them strip the base for what they need."

"Commander Gray," the XO said.

She opened the comm ship-wide. "This is Commander Enas Gray. My jets and I have gained control of the *Plymouth*. We have no argument with our fellow crew and do not want bloodshed. All non-essential personnel are to go to their quarters. If any of my jets see you where you aren't supposed to be, you will be shot. This will be the only warning." She closed the comm and looked at the XO. He made no protest and held no weapon. She knew him to be a practical man. "I'm going to need your authorization codes." All of the bridge crew stood watching her with cautious eyes. "This ship isn't going back to the Hub. So you all have a choice to make."

She met the dropship that the captain had sent to the moon, and that now returned with the rider with her jets and the aliens aboard it. The red-uniformed bay crew worked to secure fuel lines and check the anchors like parasitic fish picking at the skin of larger predators, and the low grind and hollow echoes of activity sounded to her ears as through the depths of a vast sea in which there was no shore. Her jets on guard in the bay watched them, and she walked up to meet Markalan and the others as they disembarked the dropship. He was guiding the injured alien scientist, and the other seven aliens followed in his wake, the white ones holding their black blades.

"They insisted," he said, without tone.

She looked at her jets and told them to take the striviirc-na to medical, so two of her squads did that and Markalan said he would meet her later, after he got the injured alien squared away. So it hadn't died by their ministrations, and onboard the *Plymouth* they would be able to take a complete and intensive biological scan of it, and maybe they would learn something more before she had to order the ship out of orbit.

She walked through the ship, all the way to engineering where the drive towers hummed sentinel and black behind protective glass plating and the crew hunched in front of their stations watched her with her jets standing over them holding rifles. She walked back out to medical and saw Markalan with the injured alien on a trauma table, and the CMO was nowhere; she had ordered the woman sent to the brig, stripped of her tags. She took the seven uninjured aliens into the empty CMO's office and she shut the door and looked at the aliens. The warrior whites still held their blades, and their cetacean black eyes fixed on her, unmoving. Under the office lights and at some angles, she thought she saw hints of opal or gold or bronze in the depths. They barely knew each other's languages, but she said, "My people will be coming here. More ships. You can't stay on this moon."

They stared at her.

She drew a breath and went to the desk and activated the helio controls to call up the starmap. She rotated it to show the moon on which they'd found the aliens, and she pointed to the pink dot and pointed to them. "This is your moon." Then she flicked her fingers at the corners, and she created multiple images of EarthHub battleships, and she dragged them to the pink dot and looked at the aliens. The two white warriors stepped forward and scrutinized the image. They spoke to each other in their own language and she could not understand a word or catch any sound that seemed familiar from her limited alien vocabulary, but when they looked at her she knew that they understood.

One of the bronze scientists moved closer, and with slow precision he poked his finger into the image and found the moon. He looked at her for half a minute—she thought it was a he, if their physiology had any commonality with humans, but she didn't know—and he moved his finger in the image until the stars began to move, faster and faster until she lost track of where in space they were, but then he stopped and spread his fingers like he'd seen her do and the stars enlarged, and in the center of them was an indigo planet around a yellow sun, coded in the way of human maps, and the alien lowered his hand and said, "Aaian-na."

She knew enough to know that it was the name of their homeworld. And now she knew where it was in the cosmos, that it wasn't just a planet with a designation yet to be explored. It had already been explored, long before humans gave it some number and the possibility of life. She was looking at that life, and she was looking at the shape her life was going to take, and she did not recognize a single atom of it.

She met with the chief in the jet wardroom, and he reported that no crew were giving them trouble, but they were all scared and wondering what she was going to do, and she understood that the chief was asking it, too. She told him to keep enough jets on duty to patrol the corridors and watch the officers in engineering and on the bridge, but that she would speak with the company here in an hour. While she waited, she perused the maps on the tactical board, swiping her hand left and right to watch the dance of glowing dots like stardust hanging in the air and rotating and tilting as she navigated her way through all of known Hub space, all the way back to Earth. She stared at the image of the blue planet for a long time until the jets began to trickle in, and she blanked the table with a pat and moved around to stand in front of it and rest her hands on her hips.

They stared at her solemn and quiet like she was about to either bless or curse them, all of them in their uniform blacks, and as she looked into their faces she wasn't sure which it was herself.

"The captain, on behalf of EarthHub, or so he claims, wanted us to fire on the first alien species we have encountered here in the Dragons. This is wrong. I have made my decision, and so have some of you, but in the interest of being unequivocally clear, I am not returning to EarthHub. A court martial would likely be waiting for me, and some of you. But some of you were only following the orders of your jet commander. So I'm giving you a chance to decide for yourselves. I will be transferring *Plymouth*'s crew to the dropships, signaling EarthHub Command, and sending them on their way to Hubcentral. The rest of us will take the *Plymouth* to the alien homeworld. They've invited us."

The silence sat dead and their faces didn't change.

"If any of you want off the ship with the rest of the crew, you're welcome to go without judgment. I'm not one-hundred percent sure what Command's action will be, but I highly suspect they'll send a battle group to retake the moon at the very least. We can't stand up to that firepower, and I can only hope the Hub isn't bold and stupid enough to scout for the alien planet in order to wage a full out war against a civilization or civilizations they know nothing about. My guess is they'll cut their losses, they'll mine this moon, and they'll get ready for any eventuality in the future. As will I and the striviirc-na."

Some of the jets looked at each other. She heard quiet murmurs. Before she could dismiss them, one of the jets at the back said, "We're with you, Commander."

"All the way," another said.

"We never liked Earth that much anyway."

"We're jets."

They were trained for deep space, most of them were born in deep space, like Markalan. Not like her. But she inspected every one of their faces, her company, and if any of them showed up at the dropships later she would not blame them either. But she didn't see any of that here and not one of them broke her gaze. So she nodded.

"The chief will organize an inventory detail. We'll give the crew enough supplies to get them to a rescue, but everything else is going with us."

That blueshift she lay watching out the window in their quarters the solid-black emptiness of space, musing on the unexplored and the absolute unknown on which even her deepest imaginings could find no purchase.

"What do you think it'll be like?" Markalan asked, looking at her as she looked out the window, his hand along her stomach where he could feel her breathe.

"I don't know. What do you think?"

"They're a similar size to humans and we can breathe the same air, so maybe there'll be more commonality with Earth than we figure."

"They had no gravity on their base." Their boots had to be magged to the floor, but the aliens didn't seem to struggle in the gravity of the ship, at least not so far.

"We'll never be able to return to Hub space, will we?"

"I don't know. Maybe."

"Do you think there'll be a war?"

It was the question most on her mind, after her wondering about life on Aaian-na, and she had no answer for either of those unknowns. She looked away from the rectangle of black outside the ship and found Markalan's dark eyes instead and his brow was furrowed in a way that made her think it might now be a permanent expression. She traced one of his eyebrows with her finger in an attempt to relieve the tension and for a moment it smoothed out and the corners of his mouth lifted slightly though no lightness imbued his eyes.

She said, "If there's a war in our future, then I want to be on the right side of it."

She stood in the hangar bay watching the *Plymouth* crew load up into the dropships under guard of the jets, when her tags beeped and Markalan told her that the injured alien scientist had died. The captain was standing beside her, watching his crew embark the dropships as if he had some intention to stay aboard and she allowed it simply because she had no desire to humiliate him in front of the crew and her jets. But now when he looked at her she wished she'd kept him in the brig until the last minute.

"How?" she said.

"We're still trying to figure that out. Some delayed reaction to the healant, I don't know, but one of the white aliens is coming to see you. It—he—insisted."

"This will never work," the captain said, and she held up her hand to him.

"Let him come," she told Markalan. "With an escort."

"Already done."

"You don't know a thing about them," the captain said. "They could be taking you to their planet to make you their food supply. It's all unknown. We don't even know if what little they told us about why they want the moon is even the truth. Sure they were mining it, but for what?"

"Probably for the same reasons we want it. To build." She looked at him. "We saw their food in the base. It looked like game meat."

"We could be game meat. Their teeth are sharp enough to make them carnivores."

Phantasms of thought. Left to their own devices, humanity thought the worst. She thought of the weapons the aliens possessed and if they had any intention to feed on humans they'd had the opportunity and nothing to lose once the *Plymouth* made their intentions clear.

"If you thought they could be a threat," she said, "then maybe you shouldn't have tried to start a war with them. We don't know the depths of their resources. And now you'll never know."

"You're forsaking all of humanity for them," the captain said. "You'll be called traitors. You've lost your own kind."

She looked at the man. She set her hand on her sidearm. "The murderer in my sights should shut his fucking mouth."

"They're incoming," the chief said behind her, and she turned to see the airlock shine red as the inner one opened and shut, then the lock access to the bay opened and the white, tattooed alien stepped through with one of her jets behind it. It raised a hand as if to greet her, but instead it slid something black and narrow from inside its coiled sleeve. It was one move, she didn't have time to track it before she felt something breeze by her ear, and there came a shout and when she turned around the body of the captain was falling to the deck. His head was sheared clean off his neck and fell beside it with a dull thud, eyes open and his expression slack like he had been caught in mid-thought. The blade that the alien had thrown embedded into the landing gear of one of the dropships and rifles snapped up all around her, some of the crew shouted, and red blood began to crawl in tendrils along the deck from the captain's severed neck.

Guns pointed toward the alien. Enas shouted, "Stand down!" before somebody did something that could not be reversed, and she knew as those black eyes locked with hers that this alliance was tenuous and dependent on the next few moments, even if her blood was pounding in her ears and her fingers gripped the handle of her holstered gun when the white warrior stepped in front of her and its head tilted forward. It stared at her, implacable and silent and disregarding the blood that seeped toward its white boots on the deck. She felt its breath on her cheek. It didn't blink, nor did she, but the scent of the captain's blood rose to fill her nostrils, and distantly she heard someone retching and another person wept, but the alien just watched her without a word.

The striviirc-na had lost people on that moon. More than a single scientist. The *Plymouth* lost a captain. She considered that even and pointed to the blade as it sat embedded in the landing gear. Now the warrior moved with its long-limbed grace and yanked the black blade from the transsteel, and she signaled the chief to shadow it as it strode from the hangar bay with her jets' guns pointed at its back. She made a gesture to tell the jets to lower their weapons now, and they did, and she looked down at the dead captain and his soulless face of mild question.

She motioned to a couple of young jets to dispose of the body. "Keep going," she told the crew so they would continue to board the dropships. The hangar bay echoed the unusual quiet of the procession. Keep going because there was no going back.

She and Markalan sat, the only two people in the ship's lounge as it pushed through space with less than half of its original crew complement. In the time it took for a week to pass in standard time, their lives had changed and their possible future lay unrecognizable and uncharted. She held his hand, and what faced them in the great emptiness of wonder and indifference in the universe was beyond any sense of duty or adventure. She knew only that if the choice had been placed before her again she could not make any other. Even if it meant the loss of her own humanity in some way that both reinforced her humanity and all that she had sworn when she donned jet blacks for the first time. She had never been a blind follower, and duty wasn't meant to be traded for a conscience or the intelligence to make a decision.

"Do you regret it?" she had to ask Markalan because they had not broached the thought in the midst of all the logistics required to get them on this new trajectory.

He didn't answer immediately. Instead he placed his hand over hers so both of his held hers and he said, "Would I prefer it that we weren't in a self-imposed exile from the worlds we know? Yeah. But I also couldn't have fired on those striviirc-na and continued to live with myself. This way I can live with myself, even if I'm afraid of what that will entail."

"Then we can both be afraid."

In her sleepshift, she went walking, and she found the tattooed warrior who had killed the captain standing in the same lounge, looking out at the ceaseless black. He had no escort upon her order, for she figured if they meant to do damage to the ship or her jets they would do it like they'd done the captain, and they were all headed to the alien planet anyway, so any guard would be fruitless. She stood close enough to him that she could discern the designs on his chalk-white skin, and they were all different on the different faces, and though they barely spoke each other's languages she knew now there were many other methods in which to communicate. From the way he met her gaze she understood that this mysterious being held some form of respect for her, as though they identified a mutual code of honor, even if perhaps their definition of the word remained oblique one to another.

"Maybe you understand this," she said to him, "but I hope to hell we can thrive on your planet. I hope you understand what it is we sacrificed."

He moved with a slow deliberation, and from the coils in his sleeve he slid free the black blade with which he had killed the captain, or one very like it, and he looked her in the eyes and offered it to her, hilt first. She sensed that this was some form of ceremony, as much as it was an extension of understanding for the way he stood patient and silent until she took hold of the weapon and wrapped her fingers around it, not unlike how she would grip her own combat knife.

"S'tlian," he said.

She didn't know that word, but he held his palm in front of her eyes and moved it down as though in the gesture she would be no more. She would no more be Enas Gray.

"First," he said, in her language. Then he left her alone.

She looked down at the blade. It seemed to absorb all light, and it pulled her touch along the blood groove to the sharpened point, and she turned it around in her hand and tested the weight and balance of it and it sat perfectly compact and deadly in her palm. It was sharp enough to sever a human head from its neck in one throw, and the craftsmanship of it was one in which she could not imagine and could not decipher any more than she could read what seemed to be lettering along the hilt.

She had learned that it had taken the striviirc-na ten years to get to the moon from Aaian-na and now it would only take a leap and thirty-some hours, as EarthHub reckoned time, to return. She had an EarthHub expeditionary vessel on a trajectory to a planet of civilizations, none of which knew this technology, but in the ship's files were records and schematics of more such vessels and she understood that in giving this weapon, the warrior expected an exchange. Their planet for human knowledge, and she knew no other way. The Hub was not going to forget, and the jets under her command would need to prepare, and this was the pact she made to the emptiness outside of the window, the long and unfathomable infinity in which she had cast herself until the moment when an indigo planet and a yellow sun reached out in language she had yet to fully understand, and she would know, one way or another, whether the eye of such a world would look upon her and all of her alien humanity, and decide whether she was worthy of a blessing or a curse.

Besides selling fifty-odd short stories, twenty-some poems, and a few comics and interactive fictions, Marie Vibbert has been a medieval (SCA) squire, ridden 17% of the roller coasters in the United States and has played O-line and D-line for the Cleveland Fusion women's tackle football team. She has been translated into French, Chinese, and Vietnamese! By day she is a computer programmer.

KNIT THREE, SAVE FOUR

Marie Vibbert

The ship was two days overdue for docking, more or less. As a stowaway, I didn't have access to status reports. My passive data sniffer patiently checked for the docking station network, telling me, "Nope. Not there yet." My calendar showed the original estimated time of arrival—two days and three hours ago. Having now reached the point at which I'd said I could start worrying, I was busy calculating a new point at which to start worrying again. There wasn't much else I could do—if I tried anything and got caught, I'd be tossed out an airlock because, as I said: stowaway.

So I knitted. I always knit when I'm bumming. It helps to have something to do while you count your remaining rations and wonder if this is where you die. Also, traveling in storage containers meant I had a constant need for warm knit garments and blankets.

Since I was sure I was about to die, I was doing this insane lace stitch. Everything was slip-slip-knits and cables and knit-three-into-two and shit. Getting angry at the person who wrote this pattern distracted me from my inevitable demise.

The wall panel over my head wrenched open, flooding me with light, and these two people were staring at me and I realized I was in the middle of a cable and I didn't remember if it was a cable-front or -behind.

The moment of confusion got me through being discovered without a heart attack.

I was wedged between boxes of whatever, helmet and gloves off, knitting in front of me, yarn pulled taut and looped around one finger, my instruction screen floating near at hand. There were crumbs all around me because I had eaten the last, most dried-out biscuit. Also, I probably stank. I'd been in the cargo box for seven days and my Ever-SaniTM wasn't as "Ever" as it claimed.

My captors had vaguely Asian features: a guy with a shaved head and a woman with her black hair in tiny pin curls. Pin Curls was holding the hatch. She looked like she might close it over me again.

Shaved Head said, "Well, that figures."

Pin Curls pushed the hatch door all the way open. "Fuck. Of all the . . .fuck."

"It's not as if this makes things worse," Shaved Head said.

This was not the typical discovery reaction us stowaways get. The typical reaction was a swift kick out an airlock, or detention until landing. Since we were two days overdue for docking, I was hoping for detention. They had to be close to docking. Right?

"I'm throwing her out the airlock," Pin Curls said.

I let go of my knitting to hold my hands up. "You can have my stuff. Please don't kill me."

Pin Curls pursed her lips like my pleading made her day worse.

Shaved Head held his hand out. "Come on," he said. "You might as well be doomed with the rest of us."

He pulled me into the crew's common space. It was about the size of an apartment kitchen, and as crammed with potted herbs and potholders and garage-sale junk as my uncle's place. A barrel-bodied robot crouched in an alcove, holding a ladle. An old woman was bouncing back and forth between the only porthole and a table. She saw me, closed her eyes, and said, like a prayer, "Let this be the last bad news today."

"Nothing in storage we can use," Pin Curls said.

The old woman looked like she would cry. She pressed her face to the porthole.

Didn't feel like I was their top worry. "Is there something I can help with?"

"The station won't let us dock," Shaved Head said. "No one's coming to resupply us. Even with the plants, we have maybe forty-eight hours of air left, and you're using up an extra person's oxygen."

Well, excuse me.

The old woman said, "Gong, be nice."

"I'm being nice, Abuela. Shirley wanted to chuck her out an airlock!"

A radio crackled, and I swear the air pressure dropped from all the intaken breaths. Abuela approached the radio like it was a poisonous spider on the wall. Then she relaxed her whole body at once. "Just static."

Pin Curls (Shirley) had her hands on the ceiling like she was going to powerlift it. "There's some sensor, says our hull is too weak. Electrical resistance patterns or something . . . The station says it's too dangerous, and the cargo owners won't come get us, either."

I knew how to fix this. "Disable the sensor. You can fake the readings with—"

"Tried that," three voices declared wearily.

Gong leaned toward me. "It might've helped if we hadn't 'fixed' our problem so fast after they detected it."

"Ya think?" Shirley kicked the wall to propel herself to the robot and, briefly, tussled with him over the ladle.

"Okay," I said. "So, we figure out where the hull is weak and reinforce it."

"With what?" Having successfully wrested the ladle from the robot, Shirley pointed it at me. "Our exploration of the cargo turned up one freeloader and a bunch of crumbs."

Yeah, eating crumbly food in zero-g is a faux pas. Two days overdue for docking, times how much oxygen and fuel? I saw the others sizing me up against their own survival. "So . . .hey, I'm Mouth," I said.

Shirley sneered. "Is that a first name or a last name?"

"It's the one I'm giving you."

She looked like she thought this was another reason to kick me into the cold embrace of space, but Gong grabbed my hand and squeezed it. "Welcome! You've met me, and Shirley, and Abuela. That's Fat Robot Chen."

The robot perked up and saluted. "That I am!"

"That's an . . . interesting name."

"He looks like my buddy Chen." Gong shrugged. "You know, if he were a robot, and fat."

Abuela tsked. "So friendly. Not enough concern about how we are all going to die! The station's insurance company refuses to allow us to dock as they would be financially liable for structural damage if our ship failed during docking." She showed the message to me. They'd tacked "not to mention the tragic loss of human life" on the end. I wondered if it was an AI correcting their lack of humanity, like a grammar-check for decency.

"And there it is. Rhea Station." Abuela held her hand over the porthole like she was holding back a curtain. "So close, and so far."

The station was the size of a teacup in the view, but close enough that we could see the flitting lights of other ships coming and going.

"I still say we abandon ship." Gong floated at my elbow. "Hop in our EVA suits and the station rescue team will pick us up."

Abuela met this with a string of Spanish curses that I'm going to guess added up to, "My ship and cargo are worth more to me than your nutsack remaining attached to your body."

Gong rolled his eyes, which resulted in more curses, and Shirley snapping at the both of them to "Get over it," which gave me the distinct feeling this was an argument that had been going on for about two days. Maybe longer.

I cleared my throat. "Hey, I'm okay jumping out for station rescue, myself."

They looked at me like they'd forgotten I was there. (Except Fat Robot Chen, whose eyes tracked Gong.)

Shirley raised one hand, a smug/sour look on her face as if to say, "Tossing you out the airlock was my idea first."

Abuela pursed her lips. "They might not pick up a stowaway. No, I forbid it. And Shirley, hija, I can hear you thinking. No one is getting tossed out of anything."

Abuela was right: A lot of people killed stowaways to discourage the practice, because capitalism. Time to save the day. "We lower the air pressure. Get rid of all the nitrogen and go pure oxygen. That'll relax the hull, maybe close some tears?"

Abuela snapped her fingers and pointed. Gong swam to the controls. "Yeah, we can do that."

I turned back to the cargo box to get my knitting. Shirley flew neatly in my way, glaring death at me.

"I left stuff in there."

"Too bad."

With the air of a sentry putting up a deadly weapon, Shirley Velcroed the ladle into place over a set of potholders.

The air vents hissed. Maybe it was my imagination, but it felt colder as the air mix changed. I went in the other direction, then, and checked out the cargo manifest. It's nice to know what's been poking you in the back. Three hundred popsicle forms. A gross of personal AIs. Freeze-dried food rations. "Novelty items." Best not examine that one. "Wait . . . you have *twenty-five-hundred* meters of cable aboard?" I asked.

"None of your business." Abuela shooed me away from her control panel. "I am asking the station to please check us again, that we have lowered our pressure."

"The sensor still says it's not good enough," Gong said, coming in from aft.

"I'll disable it again." Shirley pushed herself forward. I was relieved to have some distance between us.

Abuela hung by the radio like it was prom night and her date hadn't called. After a long time, there came a reply from the station, peppered with half-legal terms, which ended with, "Lady, look at it from our perspective. Any ship docked is a hole we can't close. I'm sorry, but no."

Abuela curled into a ball, a little old lady bean right there. It broke my heart.

Shirley gathered a handful of my jacket. "So we toss her, right? To buy time?"

"Wait!" I windmilled in her grip. "What about the cable in cargo?"

Shirley, expressing her rosy outlook on others, said, "No way am I letting you go back for some weapon from your hidey-hole."

I wrenched out of her grip and caught myself against a bundle of bags hanging on the wall. "Trust issues much? Tell me about the spool of cable you got in the cargo. It might save us."

Gong answered for them, "It's a high-strength polymer. But what are we supposed to do with it? Tie the ship together?"

I turned to Abuela. "How thick is this cable?"

Shirley huffed. "What does it matter how thick it is?"

I mimed looping cable around my arm, twice, and realized that I sucked at miming. "We tie the cable around the ship."

Gong shook his head. "We can't make the pressure even—tie in one direction, you weaken the other."

"Let me have my knitting. I'll show you."

Shirley was neatly in my way again. "I'm still not letting you go back there."

Ugh. More inept miming, then. "We make a bag, a mesh bag, then slide it around the ship. I'll need at least two others helping. When we get to the far side—" I wriggled my fingers around an imaginary egg-shape and then mimed pulling strings "—we pull it tight. Bam. The whole ship is more secure. The pressure adjusts evenly because of the give in the stitches."

Gong looked at me like I'd lost my mind.

Shirley, the one I expected the most objection from, was frowning thoughtfully. "You'll need a hole in the bag for the docking ring," she said.

"Well, yeah," I said.

"The cable is not ours!" Abuela smacked the table.

"Knitting can always be undone," I said. "We won't be cutting it. Come on, who's with me?"

There was an awkward silence.

"You're an idiot and a stowaway," Shirley said, "but I'm not letting you take all the glory. I'm in."

Unexpected ally! I held a hand up for her to high-five. She glared at it.

"I don't know," Abuela said, which was better than "no."

Gong asked Fat Robot Chen, "What do you think, buddy? Can this plan work?"

Chen cocked his bucket-shaped head. "What plan was that, dude? Also, did you mean 'can' this plan work or 'may' this plan work?"

Gong patted the flat robot head. "He's a work in progress."

Gong and Abuela resumed arguing. Shirley declared she was going to her bunk, forgetting she was keeping me from accessing the cargo hold. YES! I got my knitting and my tablet. I pulled apart the lace thing I'd been making and started a simple mesh bag for demonstration purposes.

Crap. How big was this ship? I loaded up the instructions for the bag and tried to convert units from inches to meters.

Gong opened and closed cupboards and storage-ties around the room. "Are we out of anything remotely good? Who bought all these pouches of wax beans?"

Fat Robot Chen trundled along the ship's deck, gripping it somehow. "I got you, bro. The special of the day is chipped beef on toast."

"No no no . . . " Gong gently steered Chen away from the microwave. "Buddy, you gotta stop trying to cook. You'll get us both spaced."

This struggle escalated, which I thought unwise since it increased Gong's breath rate. Abuela saved me from having to mention this by flying screaming at the both of them.

Shirley leaned in from the opening to the crew cabin. "Are we going to eat? If eating is still something we get to do?"

They were exhausted. A captive audience. "So, that plan I was talking about?" I showed them my bag. I wrapped it halfway around a wax bean packet. "You see?" I pulled the bag-fragment tight and poked at the packet. "Evenly supported."

Abuela paused in grabbing Gong by the ears while Gong was wrestling the ladle away from Chen. "That could work." She narrowed her eyes. "But I'm not doing it, and I'm not sending my grandson out into vacuum."

Before I could say, "Well, if there's compensation in it for me," Shirley bundled me into my helmet and gloves and pulled me with her out the airlock.

Rude, but she showed me where to clip my safety line while Fat Robot Chen spooled the cable out from the cargo bay. The cable was flexible enough to loop around my forearm. I wished I had four ship-size needles, but I could let stitches float free, given the lack of gravity. Dropped stitches (when a loop falls off your needle) aren't as much of a problem in zero-g knitting. They float there, the friction of the yarn holding the loop open until you get your needle into it again. Lucky for me, because I was a terrible knitter when I started bumming.

The ship was an uneven football shape, round at one end and tapered at the other. The round end would be the perfect bottom of my bag, so we moved toward it to start.

I was clumsy in the suit gloves, but we were going huge here. I made a slipknot the size of a Hula-Hoop and knit ten stitches as big around as my forearm into it, making a disk. It was fun, knitting so big, and went fast. It was like spinning a huge beret, the disk doubling in size with each revolution.

Shirley gazed down the length of the ship, to where Fat Robot Chen was handing cable out the airlock. "Is this going to be enough?"

I should have finished my math. The ship was bigger on the outside. Inside, it had felt the size of my uncle's camper van. Outside, it looked the size of a trailer truck that delivers camper vans. "Uh . . . how long is this ship?"

"Twenty-four meters and some change, if you don't count the antennas. Ten meters in diameter." I couldn't see her face with her helmet turned away from me, but I heard the suspicion in her voice.

Twenty-four meters, twenty-five-hundred meters of cable? I needed, what, surface area to compare? It was something something 2-Pi-R. "I'm sure it's enough," I said, not remotely sure.

We'd know before we ran out of oxygen, right?

Knitting stopped being fun after five rows. My arms were sore and I was sweating and my stomach hurt from holding myself rigid; it's a natural reaction in zero-g to lock on with your feet and keep your body in a sitting position. Stupidly. You don't need to but your brain wants to. I made myself stop, but three stitches later, I was doing it again.

Around ten rows, the disk was big enough that I needed someone else to hold the other side. Shirley "sat" on the hull, passing loose floating loops under her hands, spinning the disk while I knitted the other side.

When we were halfway around, the trailing cable tangled in our suit tethers. "Crap," I said. "We'll have to unclip and re-clip every rotation, or else we hold the mesh still and we move."

"You could have started this inside the ship," Shirley said, unhelpfully.

This is the point in a knitting project where it starts to suck. Before, every row made visible progress. Now, every row looked the same, and I was annoyed with the tethers. My hands slipped with sweat inside my suit gloves. "I need a break."

"No," Shirley said, firmly. "We need to finish this in twelve hours so we have another twenty-four to come up with Plan B."

A secret optimist, our Shirley.

We untethered and retethered, rotating the knitting. We worked silently until the disk was as big around as the butt-end of the ship.

"Um . . . yeah, we should move this . . . you know, so it's centered on the ship's butt? Kinda?" I did more bad miming, hampered by suit arms, hoping I conveyed the picture adequately.

"Stop explaining. You're making it more confusing than it is."

Shirley hopped easily from handhold to handhold, re-tethered, and moved the disk into position. I enjoyed the momentary rest. Better yet, there weren't any more increases now. This was as long as the rows would get. And it had only taken an hour! We might actually get this done.

It was no longer sensible to rotate the knitting. There were too many random antennas and other things poking out of the hull for it to snag on. Shirley and I crawled in tandem, losing sight of each other, but I saw Fat Robot Chen every pass. He peered along the cable length like he was worried about me.

When we were just under halfway along the ship, it was time to make a hole for the airlock. I looped the yarn ten times around my arm, a convenient way of marking off a long length. It felt odd slipping my arm free and letting the loops float. I was very careful with the next stitch, not pulling at all so my gap would stay open.

Shirley came back from the far side to watch. She thumbs-upped, which I guess meant she realized what I was doing. I poked the loose yarn all around Fat Robot Chen while he tracked me like a rapt gopher. I knit the next stitch into the big loop. Here on out I'd be going back and forth instead of around and around, stopping each time I hit the big loop with one stitch into it. I checked the time. Another two hours eaten up. I was slowing down, but there was still plenty of time.

I was a few stitches away from returning to the gap from the other direction when my triceps went "boink" and then my forearm and my elbow and my pinky finger all cramped up at once.

Shirley came to me. "You stopped."

"Can't move my arm."

She touched my elbow. "Show me what to do."

I flinched away. "I can't. Ow. Ow. Ow."

"Shush. Look. I saw you take a loop and put it through another loop, right? Like this?"

She made a damn slipknot. Close, but not the same thing. "No . . . no . . . just . . . ow. Let's . . . can we go inside and rest?"

"No. That'd take too long. Rest here. Stretch."

I double-checked my tether and let my body go slack. I floated off the ship, a me-balloon. It was a relief. Maybe I should take my chances with station rescue. At least I'd die lazily. "Why are you such a hard-ass?"

"We're in danger. It's not being a hard-ass if you're trying to save everyone's life."

Hell, my arm hurt. "Pushing me won't make this go faster. You might have noticed I'm not in the best physical shape."

"Shush. I'm watching a video tutorial on knitting."

I made fists and slowly released them. "I'm sorry about stowing away."

"I bet you are."

"Well, yeah, obviously. But I mean . . . I don't intend to be a burden on anyone."

"Here. Watch this." Shirley waved me over.

I crawled up my rope. I was able to grip again, but my forearm still twinged.

Shirley slowly and carefully completed a knit stitch. "Yes," I said. "Exactly like that."

She did three more. Her fourth she almost did backward but I corrected her. After the fifth, she asked, "Why stow away? You gotta risk getting killed a dozen ways."

I wished I had a noble story to tell her, some manifesto to conquer the solar system for the proletariat, but the truth was rather more self-serving. "I like traveling. I have a festival crew job during Lunar New Year on the Moon, and every now and then I stay a full year on Mars, because I have family there and they can always use the help on the farm, but other than that, I'm on a new planet, a new station, a new country every six months. Eating weird new things and meeting weird new people. This is the only way someone like me could ever do that."

"You should join a cargo crew."

"Yeah. And how easy is that?" She didn't answer, because of course she knew exactly what it took. Connections. Family. A ship that didn't break. "Anyway," I said, "how much of the solar system do you get to see on a cargo ship? Orbits and docking bays."

Shirley grunted. I showed her how to knit stitches into the dock-hole. I'd guessed the size pretty good. The hole was ten percent bigger than the dock.

"This is hard," she said. "It hurts!"

Told you so, I thought.

We took turns, then, every other row. I think Shirley tried to go faster than I did. Which made me go faster. I was hurting all over when Chen said, "Hey, guys? Do you want me to tell you when the cable is almost all gone?"

I looked at the whole third of the ship still left to cover and wanted to cry. Shirley's fists were on her hips.

"Gauge!" I said. I started pulling stitches out. "Chen, spool this back, we're starting over."

"No," Shirley said.

I ignored her. So did Chen, fortunately.

She grabbed me. "No," she said. "You failed. It's not enough."

We still had five of her twelve hours! "Knitting has this concept called gauge," I said. "The size of the finished work will increase if you make bigger stitches. We're going to make bigger stitches. I'll double loop each stitch. It should double the size." As soon as I said it, I remembered it wasn't that simple, but I didn't want her to lose faith.

Shirley was breathing heavy over my radio. Panicking, maybe.

"Knitting bigger also goes faster," I added. "And unraveling is fast." I left a floating trail of loose cable behind me as I pulled myself recklessly, tether unclipped.

As Chen drew the cable in, it danced.

When I reached the butt, Shirley was there, guiding the loose cable, watching me. "You'd better tether. I'm not chasing your ass if you fly off."

We were silent as I restarted knitting. It did go faster, with enormous-enormous stitches. I gripped as lightly as I dared to try to keep from cramping up, but after three rows, we had to alternate again, taking catnaps on our tethers. We'd used up another six hours. Holy crap. I needed to rest.

"It's been thirteen hours since I gave you twelve," Shirley said as we were working our way over the edge of the butt again. "Now there's no time for a Plan B."

Well, thanks, Mary Sunshine.

We made it past Chen with another big docking loop, and I started knitting two together every tenth stitch to narrow the bag as the ship narrowed. I hadn't done that last time.

"Hey, me and you are on suit air, and maybe lower pressure means they're breathing lighter inside?"

I decreased every ninth, then every eighth, then every seventh. This was going to work. The hull was narrowing faster. I decreased every sixth.

"Hey, guys?" Fat Robot Chen said.

Oh no. No no.

"This indicator says there's seventeen meters left?"

There was maybe a fifth of the ship still to go. "It's not enough," Shirley said, crying.

I was stupid with exhaustion. My eyes raced over the ship, the lovely loose net enclosing it. There was nothing I could do except at the start. "I have an idea." I held the loose end toward Shirley. "Hold this."

I went back to the beginning, undid the starting slipknot, and carefully unknit the first ten rows. You can't pull knit stitches loose from the bottom like you can from the top. Unknitting is slow and annoying. If this were crochet, I could tug it free . . . Maybe we could start over . . .

No, crochet uses more yarn per foot.

"What are you doing?"

"Unknitting the far end. Ugh. I'll have to do it all the way to the edge of the butt. We're going to make a tube instead of a bag. We move the tube to center it, so there's, like, a small bit uncovered on either end, and then I'll knit this back as much as I can over the butt. Two medium-sized holes are better than one small hole and one big one."

"You'll move the dock hole away from the dock!"

I froze. How obvious. Our "tube" had an opening halfway along it. "Yeah . . . okay . . . that's a problem." What other options did we have? Undo the whole thing? "I'm making a hole at the starting point. Yeah. Tug when I tell you. It'll at least give you another foot of coverage on that side. There's some slack around the airlock. One foot won't move it too much, just make it tight on one side."

"What is a foot going to do?"

"More coverage, more structural integrity. One more foot is one more foot. Start tugging."

"It's . . . ugh . . . "

"I said go. Tug now."

"I *am* tugging! Do you feel anything at that end?"

I didn't. Damn. I remembered all those small projections from the ship that made us not want to turn the net earlier—thrusters, welds—anything could be caught anywhere.

"Chen? We need help."

"Help with what?" Chen said.

"Get up here and help us move the netting over all these greebles."

Chen mused, "May I leave the ship? I may. Can I leave the ship? No, I can't."

"Get Gong." I wanted to murder a robot just then.

Shirley crawled to me. "Chen's not built for extravehicular motion. Don't blame him. He can be cute when there isn't an emergency."

We hung there, both exhausted and despairing and not in a mood for conversation. Gong crawled up to us. His face was streaked with soot and something like . . . hoisin? "Plan B was making glue from beans," he said. "Don't ask." He looked at what we'd done so far. "Why did you put a hole in it? Why didn't you plan to end it around the dock?"

Mutual desire to kill Gong united us as Shirley and I silently started unravelling the whole thing.

Every time you try to save time by not undoing something, it turns out to take too long and you end up undoing it anyway. It hurt to start over, but this time we started with an about-the-dock-sized open ring on the far side of the ship from the dock. This way we'd save material and the two holes would balance each other. "Now," I said, resting while Shirley micromanaged Gong's first turn knitting, "we'll go as far as we can, but if we're short, that'll just leave a bigger opening around the dock. And airlocks are reinforced anyway, right?"

"Ow ow ow!" Gong said. "My arm's cramping."

It took eleven hours to finish, including nap-breaks, but we knit a bag around a spaceship. Twelve hours of air left, then we'd all get into the suits. Shirley and I each had maybe an hour of suit air left. Gong had twelve hours. Abuela had a full twenty-four and wanted to top up our tanks with hers, but I said we'd know if it worked in an hour anyway.

Then Shirley and I slept, because we had to. I was so incompetent-tired, Robot Chen had to tie me into a berth.

I stared at my insensible arms, floating in front of me. "I'm never moving my hands again."

"We don't even know it'll work." Gong had a gallows smile. He held on to the treadmill on the ceiling as he pushed Chen out of the compartment.

I ought to have slept like the dead. The hammock was way more comfortable than a cargo box, but instead I fidgeted, slipping in and out of fitful dreams about knots. When we were down to six hours, Gong woke me and forced me into my suit, visor open, for now.

Abuela woke me by taking my helmet off. "Shh, shhh, hija. We've docked with a supply ship!"

I enjoyed my breath of air and swam past her to the main compartment. A big man floated by the table. "We'll get your crew and contents to Rhea

Station," he said, "but first we need our cargo. It's a spool of twenty-five-hundred meters of multi-stranded polymer cable."

Abuela's victory hug froze around me.

Gong coughed.

Shirley was the one to break the silence. "Your cable is holding our ship together."

We laughed. I don't know who started—it might have been Chen. Our would-be rescuer muttered about oxygen deprivation and topped up our reserve tanks before leaving us to die.

Ha, ha.

"Don't look so worried." Shirley elbow-jabbed me.

Now that we'd successfully docked and undocked with another ship and our sensor was quiet, station rescue had no problem letting us dock.

Which would have been a relief if stations didn't kill stowaways.

We stepped through the station airlock, heavy and dizzy like climbing out of a pool. Security people were staring at us. Security people who looked up from the crew manifest and exaggeratedly counted our heads.

Abuela stuck her arm in front of me. "This is our engineering intern. Such a good girl! She agreed to work for transport. Better not to put in writing and get taxed. You understand." She pouted.

I woulda hugged her, but that woulda broken our cover.

So that's how I joined the crew. Now I get to travel outside of storage containers like a good capitalist, as we market our "emergency structural nets" to cargo ships around the planets. I also make cardigans. Fat Robot Chen graciously models them.

Cixin Liu is a representative of the new generation of Chinese science fiction authors and recognized as a leading voice in Chinese science fiction. He was awarded the China Galaxy Science Fiction Award for eight consecutive years, from 1999 to 2006 and again in 2010. His representative work, *The Three-body Problem*, won the 2015 Hugo Award for Best Novel, finished 3rd in 2015 Campbell Awards, and was a nominee for the 2015 Nebula Award.

His works have received wide acclaim on account of their powerful atmosphere and brilliant imagination. Cixin Liu's stories successfully combine the exceedingly ephemeral with hard reality, all the while focusing on revealing the essence and aesthetics of science. He has endeavoured to create a distinctly Chinese style of science fiction. Cixin Liu is a member of the China Science Writers' Association and the Shanxi Writers' Association.

MOONLIGHT

Cixin Liu, translated by Ken Liu

For the first time that he could remember, he saw moonlight in the city. He hadn't noticed it on other nights because the bright electric glow of millions of lamps had overwhelmed it. But today was the Mid-Autumn Festival, and a web petition had proposed that the city turn off most landscape lighting and some of the streetlights so that residents could enjoy the full moon.

Looking out from the balcony of his single-occupancy unit, he discovered that the petitioners had been wrong about the effect. The moonlit city was nothing like the charming, idyllic scene they had imagined; rather, it resembled an abandoned ruin. Still, he appreciated the view. The apocalyptic spirit gave off a beauty of its own, suggesting the passing of all and the discharge of all burdens. He had only to lie down in the embrace of Fate to enjoy the tranquility at the end. That was what he needed.

His phone buzzed. The caller was a man. After ascertaining who had picked up, the voice said, "I'm sorry to disturb you on the worst day of your life. I still remember it after all these years."

The voice sounded odd. Clear, but distant and hollow. An image came to his mind: chill winds rushing between the strings of a harp abandoned in the wilderness.

The caller continued. "Today was Wen's wedding, wasn't it? She invited you, but you didn't go."

"Who is this?"

"I've thought about it so many times over the years. You should have gone, and you would be feeling better now. But you . . . well, you did go, except you hid in the lobby and watched Wen in her wedding dress heading into the reception holding his hand. You were torturing yourself."

"Who *are* you?" Despite his astonishment, he still noticed the caller's odd phrasing. The caller said "after all these years," but the wedding had only taken place this morning. And since Wen's wedding date had been decided on only a week ago, it was impossible for anyone to know about it long before then.

The distant voice went on. "You have a habit. Whenever you're upset, you curl your left big toe and dig the nail into the bottom of your shoe. When you got home earlier, you found that your toenail had snapped but you didn't even notice the pain. Your toenails are getting long though. They've worn holes into your socks. You haven't been taking care of yourself."

"Who in the world is this?" He was now frightened.

"I'm you. I'm calling from the year 2123. It's not easy connecting to your mobile network from this time. The signal degradation through the time-space interface is severe. If you can't hear me, let me know and I'll try again."

He knew it wasn't a joke. He had known from the first moment that the voice didn't belong to this world. He clutched the phone tightly and stared at the buildings washed by the cold, pure moonlight, as though the whole city had frozen to listen to their conversation. Yet he could think of nothing to say as the caller waited patiently. Faint background noises filled his ear.

"How . . . could I live to be so old?" he asked, just to break the silence.

"Twenty years from your time, genetic therapies will be invented to extend human lifespan to around two centuries. I'm still technically middle-aged, though I feel ancient."

"Can you explain the process in more detail?"

"No. I can't even give you a simple overview. I have to ensure that you receive as little information about the future as possible, to prevent you from inappropriate behaviors that would change the course of history."

"Then why did you get in touch with me in the first place?"

"For the mission that we have to accomplish together. Having lived for so long, I can tell you a secret about life: once you realize how insignificant the individual is in the vastness of space-time, you can face anything. I didn't call you to talk about your personal life, so I need you to let go of the pain and face the mission. Listen! What do you hear?"

He strained to catch the background noises through the receiver. The faint sounds resolved into splashes and plops, and he tried to reconstruct an image from them. Strange flowers bloomed in the darkness; a giant glacier cracked in a desolate sea, and zigzagging seams extended into the depths of the crystalline mass like lightning bolts . . .

"You're hearing waves crashing against buildings. I'm on the eighth floor of Jin Mao Tower. The surface of the sea is right under the window."

"Shanghai has been flooded?"

"That's right. She was the last of the coastal cities to fall. The dikes were high and durable, but the sea ultimately inundated the interior and flooded back in . . . Can you imagine what I'm seeing? No, it's nothing like Venice. The undulating water between the buildings is covered with garbage and flotsam, as if all the refuse accumulated in this city over two centuries had become afloat. The moon is full tonight, just like where and when you are. There are no lights in the city, but my moon is not nearly as bright as yours—the atmosphere is far too polluted. The sea mirrors the moonlight onto the skeletons of the skyscrapers. The great sphere at the top of the Oriental Pearl Tower flickers with silvery streaks reflected from the waves, as if everything is about to collapse."

"How much has the sea risen?"

"The polar ice caps are gone. In the span of half a century, the sea rose by about twenty meters. Three hundred million coastal inhabitants had to move inland. Only desolation is left here, while the inland regions are gripped by political and social chaos. The economy is nearing total collapse . . . Our mission is to prevent all of this."

"Do you think we can play God?"

"Mere mortals doing what needed to be done a hundred years earlier would have the same effect as divine intervention now. If, in your time, the whole world had stopped using all fossil fuels—including coal, petroleum, and natural gas—global warming would have stopped, and this disaster could have been prevented."

"That seems impossible." After he said this, his self from more than a hundred years in the future remained silent for a long time. So he added, "To stop the use of fossil fuels, you need to contact people from even earlier."

He sensed a smile through the phone. "Do you imagine I can stop the Industrial Revolution in its tracks?"

"But what you're asking of us now is even more impossible. The world will fall apart if you eliminate all coal, gas, and oil for a single week."

"Actually, our models show that it wouldn't even take that long. But there are other ways. Remember that I'm speaking to you from the future. Think. We're smart people."

He thought of one possibility. "Give us an advanced energy technology. Something environmentally friendly that won't contribute to climate change. The technology has to be able to satisfy existing energy needs while also being much cheaper than fossil fuels. If you give us that, it won't be ten years before the market will force all fossil fuels out of contention."

"That's exactly what we're going to do."

Encouraged, he went on. "Then teach us how to achieve controlled nuclear fusion."

"You vastly underestimate the difficulties. We still haven't achieved any breakthroughs in that field. There are fusion reactor power plants, but they aren't even as competitive in the market as fission plants in your time. Also, fusion reactors require the extraction of fuel from seawater, a process that may lead to more environmental damage. We can't give you controlled fusion, but we can give you solar power."

"Solar power? What do you mean exactly?"

"Collecting the sun's power from the surface of the Earth."

"With what?"

"Monocrystalline silicon, the same material you use in your time."

"Oh, come on! You literally just made me facepalm. I thought you had something real for a minute there . . . Actually, do you still say 'facepalm'?"

"Sure we do. Old-timers like me have kept lots of expressions like that alive. Anyway, our monocrystalline silicon solar cells have far higher conversion efficiency."

"Even if you achieved one hundred percent efficiency it would be irrelevant. How much solar power reaches each square meter on the Earth's surface? There's no way that a few solar panels can satisfy the energy needs of contemporary society. Have you been hallucinating that your youth was spent in some preindustrial farmers' paradise?"

He heard his future self laugh. "Now that you mention it, the technology really does evoke shades of agrarian nostalgia."

"'Evoke shades of agrarian nostalgia'? When did I start to talk like a coffee shop writer?"

"Heh, the technology really is called the silicon plow."

"What?"

"The silicon plow. Silicon is the most abundant element on Earth, and you can find it everywhere in sand or soil. A silicon plow cuts furrows in the earth just like a regular plow, but it extracts the silicon out of the soil and refines it into monocrystalline silicon. The land it processes turns into solar cells."

"What . . . what does a silicon plow look like?"

"Like a combine harvester. To start it, you need an external energy source, but then it relies on the power provided by the solar cells it leaves behind. With this technology, you can turn the whole Taklamakan Desert into a solar power plant."

"Are you telling me that all the plowed land will become black, shiny cells?"

"No. The plowed land will just look darker, but the conversion efficiency will be phenomenal. After the land has been plowed, you just attach wires to the two ends of the furrow to get a photovoltaic current."

As the holder of a doctorate degree in Energy Planning, he was entranced by the promise of this technology. His breathing sped up.

"I just sent you an email with all the technical details. At your technology level, you shouldn't have any trouble mass-producing it—that's also one of the reasons I chose to contact your era instead of an earlier time. Starting tomorrow, you must dedicate yourself to spreading this technology. I know you have the necessary resources and the skills. How to popularize the technology is up to you. Maybe you can take advantage of the report you're drafting right now. But you have to remember one thing: under no circumstances can you reveal that the technology comes from the future."

"Why did you choose me? You should have picked someone more senior."

"I have to take care to reduce the potential negative side effects from my interference. You and I are the same person. Can you think of a better choice?"

"Tell me, just how high have you climbed on the career ladder?"

"I can't reveal that. It took a lot of convincing for the Embodied International to decide to interfere in history at all."

"Embodied International?"

"The world is divided between the Embodied International and the Virtual International—never mind, I've said too much. Don't ask me about anything like that again."

"But . . . if I do as you've asked, how will you see the world change? Are you going to wake up the next day and find everything different?"

"It'll be even faster than that. The minute you open my email and decide on your course of action, my world will likely change instantly. But we two are the only people—the only person—who will know this. For everyone else in my era, history is history, and in the new timeline, which is also their only timeline, the period of fossil fuel use between your time and my time never happened."

"Will you call me again?"

"I don't know. Every contact with the past is a major undertaking. International conferences have to be held. Goodbye."

He returned to his bedroom and turned on the computer. The inbox showed the email from the future. The body was blank, but there were more than a dozen attachments, totaling more than a gigabyte. He browsed through them quickly and found detailed technical drawings and documents. Although he couldn't make sense of everything yet, he saw that the technical language was accessible to someone of his era.

One particular photograph caught his attention. It was a wide-angle shot of an open space. A silicon plow, which really did resemble a combine harvester, sat in the middle of the field, and the soil behind it was slightly darker. The perspective of the shot made the plow look like a small brush painting the earth dark stroke by long stroke. About a third of the land in the frame had already been plowed, but the part of the photo that most attracted his attention was the sky of the future. It was a dusty gray, but not overcast. Maybe it was taken at dawn or dusk, since the plow cast a long shadow. This was an age without blue skies.

He began to think through his next steps. As a staff member of the Planning Office of the Ministry of Energy, he was responsible for, among other things, gathering information on the progress of new energy development projects across the country. The report he was drafting would be passed on to the minister, who would then deliver it to the State Council at their upcoming meeting. Part of China's four-trillion-yuan stimulus package in response to the economic crisis was set aside for developing new energy technologies, and the State Council meeting would decide where to invest the funds. His future self apparently wanted him to take advantage of this opportunity. But before he could put this technology into his report, he had to first find a research lab or company to pick it up as a development project. He would have to be very strategic in this choice, but he was certain that if the technical documents were real, he would find a good company to undertake the work. Even in the worst case, whoever decided to move forward with this research wouldn't lose much . . .

He shuddered, as if waking from a dream. *Have I already decided to go down this path? Yes, I have.* There could only be two outcomes from his decision: success or failure. If his effort would eventually succeed, the future should have already been altered.

Mere mortals doing what needed to be done a hundred years earlier would have the same effect as divine intervention.

He stared at the email on the screen, and suddenly had the urge to respond to it. He wrote only two words in the reply: *Got it.* Immediately, a response came back informing him that the address was undeliverable. He picked up his phone and looked at the caller ID, an ordinary number from China Mobile. He pressed the "call" button, and a recorded voice informed him that the number was not in service.

Returning to the balcony, he luxuriated in the watery moonlight. The neighborhood was completely quiet this late at night, and the moon bathed the buildings and the ground in a milky, unreal, tender glow. He had the sensation of waking from a dream, or perhaps he was still dreaming.

The phone rang again. The screen showed another unfamiliar number, but as soon as he picked up, he recognized the voice of his future self. It was still distant and hollow, but the background noises were different.

"You succeeded," his future self said.

"When are you calling from?" he asked.

"The year 2119."

"So four years earlier than the last time you called."

"For me, this is the first time I've ever called you . . . or calling me, I guess. But I do remember receiving that phone call you mentioned more than a hundred years ago."

"That was just twenty minutes ago, for me. How is everything? Has the seawater receded?"

"There's no seawater. The climate never warmed drastically, and sea levels didn't rise. The history you heard about twenty minutes earlier never happened. In our history books, solar energy made a breakthrough in the early twenty-first century and culminated in the silicon plow, which made large-scale solar energy collection possible. In the 2020s, solar energy came to dominate world energy markets, and fossil fuels quickly vanished. The first half of your—our—life has been a brilliant rising arc tied to the silicon plow, and in three years from your time, the technology will begin to spread across the globe. However, just like the history of the coal and oil industries, the history of solar energy hasn't generated any lasting celebrities, not even you."

"I don't care about being famous. It's wonderful to have had a role in saving the world."

"Of course we don't care about fame. In fact, it's good that we are not well known, otherwise we'd be treated as history's greatest criminal. The world has changed, but not for the better. The good thing is that only one person, you and me, knows this. Even those who had devised and implemented the plan to interfere with history the last time have no memories of fossil fuel use in the rest of the twenty-first century since that timeline never came to be. I don't remember calling you, but I do remember getting the call from the future. That phone call is, in fact, the only clue I have to that nonexistent history. Listen! What do you hear?"

Through the receiver, he detected faint cries that reminded him of clouds of swarming birds above the woods at dusk. Gusts of wind swept through the trees from time to time, overwhelming the cries with susurrations.

"I can't tell what I'm hearing. It doesn't sound like the ocean."

"Of course it doesn't sound like the ocean. Even the Huangpu River is almost dried out. This is the drought season—there are only two seasons now, drought and flood. It's possible to cross the river just by rolling up your pant legs. In fact, several hundred thousand starving refugees have just crossed the river into Pudong, covering the riverbed like a mass of ants. The city is in disarray; I can see fires starting everywhere."

"What happened? Solar energy should have the lowest environmental impact."

"You're sadly mistaken. Do you know how many square kilometers of monocrystalline silicon fields are necessary to supply the energy needs of a city like Shanghai? At least twenty times the area of Shanghai itself! During the century after your time, urbanization accelerated, and even a mid-sized city now is comparable to the Shanghai of your era. Starting in the 2020s, silicon plows transformed the face of every continent. After all the deserts had been turned into solar fields, they began to devour arable land and vegetation cover. Now, every continent is suffering from excessive siliconization. The process had advanced far faster than desertification. The land surface of the Earth is now almost entirely covered by silicon solar fields."

"But this should be impossible under theories of economics! As land grows more scarce, the value of any unplowed land ought to rise, and silicon plows should become too expensive to be viable in the market—"

"This was no different from the history of the fossil fuel industries. By the time the conditions you describe came into play, it was too late. Shifting to alternative energy sources was no easy task, and even rebuilding the infrastructure for coal and oil required too much time. Meanwhile, the need for energy kept on growing, and silicon plows had to devour more land. Land siliconization was even more damaging to the environment than desertification. As conditions deteriorated, drought swept the globe, and the occasional rainfall only resulted in massive floods . . . "

Listening to this voice from a century in the future, he felt like a drowning man. Just before he was about to give up all hope, he found himself somehow at the surface. Taking a deep breath, he said to his future self, "But there is a way out! A way out! It's simple. I haven't done anything yet except decide on a plan for how to introduce the technology. I'll immediately delete the email and all attachments, and go on with my life as before."

"Then Shanghai will once more be swallowed by the sea."

He moaned with frustration.

"We have to interfere with history again," said his future self.

"Don't tell me: you're going to give me some other new energy technology?"

"That's right. The key to the new technology is ultra-deep drilling."

"Drilling? But the technology for oil extraction is already very advanced."

"No, I'm not talking about drilling for oil. The wells I have in mind will reach a depth of over a hundred kilometers, penetrating the Mohorovičić discontinuity and boring into the liquid mantle. The Earth's powerful magnetic field is generated by strong electric currents deep within the planet, and we want to tap into them. Once the ultra-deep wells are drilled, massive terminals dropped into the wells will extract the geoelectric energy. We'll also give you the technology for electrical terminals that can function under such high temperatures."

"That sounds . . . grandiose. I'm rather frightened."

"Listen, geoelectricity extraction is the greenest technology. It doesn't take up any land and doesn't generate any carbon dioxide or other pollutants. All right, it's time to say goodbye. If we ever talk again, let's hope it's not to save the world . . . Go check your email."

"Wait! Let's chat some more. Tell me about . . . our life."

"We have to keep contact with the past to a minimum to reduce information leakage. I'm sure you understand that what we're doing is incredibly dangerous. Also, there's nothing to talk about really, since whatever I've gone through you'll get to experience sooner or later." The connection ended as soon as his future self stopped talking.

He returned to his computer and saw a second email. Like the last one, it was also packed with technical information. As he browsed through the attachments, he found that ultra-deep drilling used lasers instead of mechanical bits, and the molten rock was channeled up through the drill to the surface. The last attachment was another photograph of an open field studded with high-voltage transmission towers. The lattice towers looked slender and light, perhaps constructed from some strong composite material. One end of the wires plunged into the earth, evidently to tap into the buried geoelectric terminals. The ground itself attracted his gaze, as it was the lifeless dark color of plowed silicon fields. A network of fencing divided the ground into a grid, which he decided must be transmission lines that extracted the energy from the monocrystalline silicon. Unlike the photograph from the last time, the sky was a clear azure, with not a wisp of cloud to be seen. This was an age where rain was rare, and even through the photograph he could feel the crisp, dry air.

Once again, he returned to the balcony. The moon was now in the western sky and shadows had lengthened, as though the city had finished dreaming and fallen deeper into slumber.

He thought about ways to spread this new future technology. The necessary strategies were different from the last time. First, the laser drilling technology would itself generate attractive military and civilian applications. He should be able to popularize it first and wait for the industry to mature before revealing the far more astounding idea of geoelectricity. At the same time, he could advocate for development of other ancillary technologies like extreme heat-tolerant electric terminals. The initial investment still had to come from the four-trillion-yuan stimulus package, and he still needed to find an influential entity to take up the research project. He was confident of success because he knew he had the technical secrets.

I've decided on a new path. Has history changed again?

As if answering his thoughts, the phone rang for the third time. The westering moon was now half-peeking from behind a tall building across the way, as if giving this world one last terrified glance before her departure.

"I'm you, calling from the year 2125."

The caller paused, as if waiting for him to ask questions, but he dared not. The hand squeezing the phone grew clammy, and he was already exhausted. Finally, he asked, "You want me to listen to the noises of your world, don't you?"

"I don't think you'll hear much this time."

Still, he strained to listen. There was only a slight buzzing that sounded like interference. Surely a signal passing through space-time had to deal with interference, which could have come from any time between now and 2125, or the emptiness that existed outside of time and the cosmos.

"Are you still in Shanghai?" he asked his future self.

"Yes."

"I can't hear anything. Maybe all your cars are electric and practically silent."

"The cars are all in the tunnels, which is why you can't hear them."

"Tunnels? What do you mean?"

"Shanghai is now underground."

The moon disappeared behind the building, and everything darkened. He felt himself sinking into the earth. "What happened?"

"The surface is full of radiation. You'll die if you stay up there for a few hours without protection. And it'll be an ugly death, with blood seeping all over your skin—"

"Radiation! What are you talking about?"

"The sun. Yes, you've succeeded. Geoelectric power grew even faster than the silicon plow, and by 2020, the geoelectricity extraction industry had outgrown the coal and oil industries combined. As it matured, the efficiency and cost of this technology couldn't be matched even by the silicon plow, let alone fossil fuels. The world's energy needs soon grew to be entirely dependent on geoelectricity. It was clean, cheap, and so perfect that many wondered how it had taken humanity thousands of years after the invention of the compass to finally think of drawing upon the giant dynamo beneath our feet. As the economy soared on the wings of this sustainable energy source, the environment also improved. Humanity believed that our civilization had finally achieved the dream of effortless growth, and the future would only get better."

"And then?"

"At the beginning of this century, geoelectricity suddenly ran out. Compasses no longer pointed north. I'm sure you know that the Earth's electric field is our planet's shield. It deflects the solar wind and protects our atmosphere. But now, the Van Allen belts are gone, and the solar wind buffets the Earth like a petri dish placed under an ultraviolet light."

He tried to speak, but only a croak emerged from his throat. He felt chills all over.

"This is only the start. Over the next three to five centuries, the solar wind will destroy the Earth's atmosphere, boil away the ocean and all other surface water."

Another inarticulate croak.

"We've finally achieved a breakthrough in controlled nuclear fusion, and together with the reconstructed oil and coal industries, humanity now possesses inexhaustible sources of energy. Most of the power we generate, however, is pumped into the Earth to restart the magnetic field. So far the results are not encouraging."

"We have to fix it!"

"Yes, that's right. You must delete both emails from the future."

He turned to head back inside. "I'll do it right now."

"Just a minute. Once you delete them, history will change again, and our connection will break off."

"Right. The world will return to its original timeline of fossil fuel dominance."

"And you'll go on with your life as before."

"Please, tell me about our life after this moment."

"I can't. Telling you will change the future."

"I understand that knowing the future will change it. But I still want to know a few things."

"Sorry. I can't."

"How about just tell me if we'll be living the life we wanted? Are we happy?"

"I can't."

"Will I get married? Kids? How many boys and girls?"

"I can't."

"After Wen, will I fall in love again?"

He thought his future self was going to refuse to answer again, but the voice remained silent. All he could hear was the hissing of the winds of time through the empty valley of more than a century dividing them. Finally, he heard the answer.

"Never again."

"What? I won't love again for more than a hundred years?"

"No. A life is not unlike the history of all of humanity. The choice presented to you the first time may also be the best, but there's no way to know without traveling down other timelines."

"So I'll be alone all my life?"

"I'm sorry, I can't tell you . . . Though loneliness is the human condition, still we must conduct our lives with grace and strive for joy. It's time."

Without another word, the call ended. His phone dinged, signaling a text. Attached to the message was a short video, which he copied to his computer to be able to see better.

A sea of flames dominated the screen. It took a while for him to understand that he was looking at the sky. The fiery lights weren't from burning fire, but auroras that filled the firmament from horizon to horizon, generated by solar wind particles striking the atmosphere. Billowy red curtains convulsed across the vault of heaven like a mountain of snakes. The sky seemed to be made of some liquid, a terrifying sight.

There was a single building resembling a stack of spheres on the ground: the Oriental Pearl Tower. The mirrored surfaces reflected the fiery sea above, and the spheres themselves seemed to be made of flames. Closer to the camera stood a man dressed in a heavy protective suit whose surface was brightly reflective and smooth, like a man-shaped mirror. The heavenly fire was reflected in this man-mirror as well, and the flame snakes, distorted by the curved surfaces, appeared even more eerie. The entire scene flowed and shimmered as though the world had turned to molten lava. The man raised a hand toward the camera, saying hello and goodbye to the past at once.

The video ended.

Was that me?

Then he remembered that he had more important tasks. He deleted the emails and all attachments. Then, after a moment, he began to reformat the disk and zero out the sectors with multiple passes.

By the time the reformatting had completed, it was just another ordinary night. The man who had changed the course of human history three times in a single night but who in the end had changed nothing fell asleep in front of his computer.

Dawn brightened the eastern sky. The world began another ordinary day. Nothing had happened, at all.

Born in the Caribbean, Tobias S. Buckell is a *New York Times* Bestselling and
World Fantasy Award winning author. His novels and almost one hundred
stories have been translated into nineteen different languages. He has been
nominated for the Hugo Award, Nebula Award, World Fantasy Award, and
Astounding Award for Best New Science Fiction Author. He currently lives
in Ohio.

BY THE WARMTH OF THEIR CALCULUS

Tobias S. Buckell

Three ships hung in the void. One sleek and metallic, festooned with jagged sensors and the melted remains of powerful weapons, all of it pitted by a millennium of hard radiation and micro-impacts. The other two, each to either side, were hand-fashioned balls of ice and rock, flesh and blood, vegetation and animal, cratered from battles and long orbits through the Ring Archipelago where the dust had long battered their muddy hulls.

Koki-Fiana fe Sese hung in the air inside a great bauble of polished, clear ice in the underbelly of her dustship, and looked out at the ancient seedship as the sun's angry red light glinted across nozzles and apparatus the purpose of which she could only guess.

There was the void between the two ships. And when she looked past that, she could see the small sparks of light that were the outer planets where her people could not reach as they were far out of the dust plane. And then beyond the outer planet came the stars, where the priests said people traveled from on their seedships. Though artificers couldn't believe that, as it would have taken millennia to cross distances that vast, and seedships were just fragile metal buckets.

And angry, dark things waited in the dark between the stars.

Then she saw something that chilled her more than the ice just an arm's length away, or the void beyond it: a sequence of lights, some flickering and dying away, appeared all down the center of the ancient ship's hull.

Another, lone light began winking furiously on the hull of the seedship. It was battle language. Fiana pushed away from the clear, window-like ice and grabbed a handhold near the airlock. There was a speaking tube there. She smacked the switch for Operations. There was a hiss, and a click as pneumatic tubes reconfigured.

"Mother here," she said quickly. "I see incoming communication."

Fiana didn't have the common words and their sequences memorized anymore. It had been twenty years since she'd had her eyes glued to a telescope, watching for incoming while hoping she wouldn't have to page through a slim dictionary floating from a belt. She was the Mother Superior now, the heart of the ship.

She wished she still had the aptitude, waiting for the message to get passed on was taking too damn long.

"Mother Superior!" The response was tinny, and they weren't following their training to throw their voice well. "Sortie Leader Two says the Belshin Historians tried to recover data from the seedship. They turned on a subsystem, and that triggered another power up somewhere else."

Ancient circuits were coming online just across the void.

"Floating shit," Fiana whispered.

"Please repeat?" Ops sounded terrified. Their voice had cracked.

They were all floating next to a giant beacon. They were like a raw hunk of meat hanging outside at sunset back on Sese, and the sawflies would be coming to chew them apart any second now.

"Call for all riggers to stand by the sail tubes," Fiana ordered. "Every available pair of eyes not in Figures and Orbits needs to be on a telescope, and if we run out of scopes, stand next to someone with one. Cancel all watches, muster all minds. Sound the alarm, Ops."

A moment later, a plaintive wail filled the rocky corridors of the dustship. Commands were shouted, echoed, and hands slapped against rails as people rushed to their posts.

"Tell F&O to begin plotting possible escape vectors," Fiana added. "All possibilities need to be in the air for us to consider."

"Urgent from Sortie Two: they're under attack."

"Attack? From what?" Fiana looked back at the ice, but all she could see was the silver metal of ancients. She could see the wink wink wink of communication, but nothing else betrayed what was happening.

She felt helpless.

The other dustship's hull rippled, as if something inside was pushing at the skin from the inside to get out. Then the Belshin ship cracked open. It vomited water and air slowly into the void as Fiana watched in horror.

"Sortie Two have warned us not to signal back," Ops said.

"Is there an F&O rep there?" Fiana asked. "If so, put her on, now."

"Heai-Lily here," came a strong voice.

"I want full sails out, and a vector away from here. Pick the first one out."

Lily hesitated. "There are Hunter-Killer exhaust sign reported. We're plotting them against known objects in this plane. We need to work the figures, but, most of F&O is guessing we're surrounded."

"It was a trap."

"Yes, Mother."

"We can't deploy the sails, they'll spot the anomaly."

"I think so, Mother."

They should have swung by and left the ship alone when they found the Belshin dustship arriving at the same time. Archipelago treaty rules gave them both genetic exploration rights, and Fiana had wanted to get in and pull material out. She'd assumed the Belshin were after the same thing. It wouldn't have been the first time multiple dustships from opposing peoples had to work on an artifact together. There were rules for this sort of thing.

But the Belshin had been greedy and violated those rules.

The Hunter-Killers had left something in the seedship for them. And now Belshin were paying the price. And Fiana's entire ship might well pay it as well.

"Ops is telling me to tell you that Sortie Two is free of the hull and returning."

The team would be jumping free of the seedship, eyeballing their own trajectories back to the netting on that side of the dustship. They'd pull it in after them. They wanted nothing that looked made by intelligence on the outside of the dustship.

"Lock down all heat exchangers and airlocks once they're in. We're running tight from here on out."

Fiana wanted to curl up into a ball near the speaking tube, but instead she forced herself to kick away, grab a corner, and flip into the corridor. She flew her way down the center, using her fingertips to adjust her course.

Ops, the hub deep in the ship, was packed with off-watch specialists, their eyes wide with fear but plugging away at tasks and doing their best to pitch in. Everyone hung from footholds, making Ops feel like a literal hive of busy humanity.

There was an "up" to the sphere that was Ops, but many of the stations were triplicated throughout. This was so that the crew could let the ship orient however it needed, and also to give engineering two failsafe command stations for every primary. Watches rotated station placements to make sure everything was in good order.

But in an all-call situation like this, everyone was at a station. Once Fiana had an acceleration vector ordered, if it became safe to do it, they'd reorganize Ops so that everyone was at a station on the "down" part.

For now, they were drifting slowly away from the seedship. But with Hunter-Killers arrowing in toward them, she doubted they would get far enough away not to be of interest when the damn things arrived.

Sortie two gave their report right away. The all-male team floated nervously in a ready room in front of Fiana and Odetta-Audra fe Enna, one of the Secondary Mothers.

"There were two Hunter-Killers on board," Sim, the sortie leader said. "They lit up the moment the Belshin Historians got the engine room powered up. I think it was a mistake though, they were just trying to get the ancient screens to talk to them."

"Treaty breakers," Audra spat. She'd been simmering with fury since Fiana first saw her in Ops. She was concealing her fear, Fiana knew, covering it up with anger to fuel herself. Most times, it made her a fast, decisive leader, though it often led to intimidation and some distance between Audra and the folk she needed to lead. Right now, it was making the sortie men nervous.

They'd been in a dangerous situation and their nerves were already rattled, so Fiana gently tapped Audra's wrist. A warning to let her Mother Superior lead the questions for now. They'd worked together long enough for Audra to get the signal.

"It's a temptation all librarians and historians struggle with," Fiana said. "Particularly peoples on the far side of the Archipelago. A wealth of knowledge from the ancients and their golden age of machinery. A piece of that could give them the ability to draw even with us."

Nations had, after all, been built on the success of daring raids on old ships, with historians writing down what they saw in ancient script as fast as they could before making a dash for it. Only one of ten missions would make it out alive, though.

"We asked them to wait until we were done with the collection mission," Sim said. "But one of their team told us they were low on consumables because they were so far from home. We focused on doing what we came to do as quickly as we could and getting away. We did not think the historians already knew a power-up sequence or we wouldn't have stayed."

They had thought they had time to work on carefully cracking the glass pods open enough to slip a needle through without triggering any of the seedship's alarms.

But Sim had kept his head and captured what they could. Seven samples, ancient DNA that would be uncorrupted by radiation and genetic drift or the tight bloodlines of the small worldlets of the Archipelago.

The Great Mothers of the worlds wouldn't invest in these missions without that payoff. When their ancestors built the Archipelago, they'd suspected that background radiation and cosmic rays would wreak havoc over time. Whatever the world was like that people fled from, it was well shielded, and the people who ran before the Hunter-Killers hadn't had time to invent a biological solution.

So these missions, these long loops out of the safety of the great dust planes to the drifting seedships for their frozen, protected heritage, was necessary for her people to continue to survive. These ships had shielding they did not understand and could not replicate. Not without the kind of industry that would bring the Hunter-Killers screaming toward them.

"Did you see—" Fiana started.

"Yes." Sim looked down and shivered slightly. "It looked like a spider. When we heard the alarm, we did as trained. Stripped down, no artificial fibers, no clothes, no tools, no weapons. We let it come."

"That couldn't have been easy." Fiana reached out and squeezed Sim's hand, the poor thing was shivering as he thought back to what happened on the seedship they were still within jumping distance of.

"It ran past us to the Belshin. They had weapons. They fought it. They died. It broke out the airlock they came through and went for their ship."

And Fiana had seen what came next. The Hunter-Killer had detonated itself, destroying the Belshin world ship.

Heai-lily came with a bundle of flexies two hours later. Her strong hair joyously sprung out around her head, as if holding compressed energy inside like springs. Her eyes, though, were tired and red.

She carefully hung the transparent sheets in the air of the ready room around Fiana.

"We have trajectories," she said. The clear rectangles had been marked up with known objects in small, careful dots from one of the navigation templates.

In red, nine X marks with arrows denoted velocities and directions. From where Fiana hung, she could get a sense of the three-dimensional situation they were in.

"They're converging on us." Fiana had suspected as much but hearing it from Lily still made her stomach roil slightly. "With options for covering any chances at escape if we run."

"So you have no solutions for me?"

"Right now, we have a farside that is hidden from their instruments. We could vent consumables that would match the profile of an icy rock getting heated up. It'd be suspicious, but not completely outside of the realm of naturally occurrent activity."

"That'll get us up to a walking pace away from the seedship," Fiana said.

"Over time. We'll have to randomize the jets, and it'll eat into our water and air."

And that would be dangerous, as right now they needed to drift in place to avoid attention.

"What does that drift get us?" Fiana asked.

"Further above the dust planes," Lily said. "Until we re-intersect."

"That's not good." They would be unable to maneuver with sails. The hundreds of dust rings around the Greater World, separated by bands and layers, would be too far away for them to shoot their sails out into. Fiana's dustship had hundreds of miles of cable they could use to guide a sail far out into a pocket of faster or slower moving dust, or even to grapple with a larger object. But above it all, they would be helpless until they'd swung all the way back around the Greater World and hit the dust planes again.

"We have a good library of discovered objects and their trajectories. If we can swing out and back in, there's a collision zone we can disguise our trajectory with."

It just meant weeks above the dust. Above everything they were comfortable with.

But what was the alternative? Stay put and wait for the Hunter-Killers? Fiana wasn't a historian, but even she knew that the Hunter-Killers tore apart everything in an area that registered electrical activity.

Her ancestors had tall, black steles scattered around their world with old pictograms carved into their sides that warned them about the Hunter-Killers. Told stories about how the alien machines followed shouts into the stellar night to their source and destroyed them. And despite those proscriptions, Hulin the Wise had experimented with crystal radio devices in the polar north of Sese. An asteroid impact had cracked the world, almost revealing the hollow interior her people had hidden inside since the ancestors first arrived. Those had been years of children dying as air fouled, and great engineering projects struggled to do the impossible: fix a cracked world.

"How fast can we get out of here?"

"Using consumables, it's dangerous, Mother. We need to coordinate with Ops. The margin will be thin, if we want to get out of here before the Hunter-Killers."

Fiana swept the transparent sheets around her away. "I'll get Ops ready to follow your commands."

To stay put would be to wait passively for death, and she wasn't ready to welcome the Hunter-Killers onto her ship.

Within the hour, the far side of the dustship was venting gases as crew warmed the material up (but not too much, or the heat signature would be suspicious and hint at some kind of unnatural process), compressed the water and hydrogen in airlocks through conduits of muscular tubes that grew throughout the ship, and blasted it out in timed dumps at F&O's orders.

Slowly, faster than the natural differential drift already there, Fiana's dustship began to move away from the seedship. It trailed a tail behind, gleaming like a comet.

The dustship was a living organism. Its massive hearts pumped ichor around webs of veins that exchanged heat generated by the living things inside the rock and ice hull, both human and engineered. The great lungs heaved, and the air inside moved about. Its bowels gurgled with waste, and its stomach fermented grain to feed the people.

Sese's people had worked hard to create a biological, living shell that could move through the rings around the Greater World. And they had found the other worlds the ancients had created, some of them dead hulks. Because the Hunter-Killers were ever on the prowl and not just myths to scare children with that had been passed down through the mists of prehistory.

Figures and Orbits, down in their calculatorium, worked away at the reports of Hunter-Killer movements, tracking them as they arrowed in toward the seedship. And other telescopists watched as the seedship dwindled away, until it became a glint among the other points of light in the busy sky.

And Fiana hung in Ops, watching as the activity of the ship passed on through the watch stations and crew.

It was tense, the first few full rotations. No one slept. There were tears that hung in the air. Salty fear, exhaustion, tension. The idea that the killers of the Ancients were chasing them could unnerve anyone.

Yes, they'd escaped the initial trap, but that didn't mean they were safe yet.

Fiana broke the tension when she ordered watches to resume a standard staggered watch rotation again. Even if she wasn't so sure she wouldn't need all-call, she needed the crew to function. Any more than three shifts and a person could not function under a constant press of fear, watchfulness, and readiness.

So she took the pressure for herself.

Fiana was inspecting the crew shaving ice from the outer walls, using one of the many burrowed tunnels in the hull, when Lily caught up to her.

"May I have a moment, Mother?" she asked softly.

"They keep sending you to brief me," Fiana noted. "You are a subordinate, not a superior. Why is your team doing this?"

"The more experienced calculating seniors need to be in the calculatorium at all times. We are at capacity, Mother, and this is not a time for anyone who needs work verified."

Lily wouldn't meet her eyes.

Well, she was either ashamed to admit she was the weakest calculator in the ship, or the F&O mothers were using her as a firewall in case Fiana got angry with them.

Or, if the F&O mothers were smart, and they were the elite of void-faring peoples, the answer could be both things at the same time. Maybe it didn't hurt that Fiana would be less likely to be angry with a young, nervous Lily. And maybe they needed the best to stay in the room and work the problem.

"What's the emergency, Lily?"

"We're moving slower than expected, Mother. It has orbital and schedule implications. We can't vent heat because we didn't quite get where we thought we'd be to have cover of several larger rocky objects blocking us from Hunter-Killer view."

Fiana batted aside ice shavings and tried to focus over the hammering of pick axes and scrape of shovels.

"F&O made a mistake?" she asked. This could cost lives. No wonder they'd sent the almost childlike Lily to stare over at her with wide eyes. "Are you sure? The signal crew could have made a sighting mistake."

A bunch of boys with astrolabes at the telescopes doing their best astronomical sightings. F&O took the averages of repeated sightings.

"The math is strong," Lily protested, her voice firm with trust in her colleagues. "And junior F&O took sightings to confirm. The signal crew were accurate."

"But we're off track?" There was no room for that kind of error. If they didn't arrive at the right place at the right time, they wouldn't be able to tether off the right large rock, or hit the right dust plane to adjust their path.

They'd end up running out of air, or water, slowly dying, out of reach of any other dustship or world that could lend aid.

Lily gave her a summary report, written in small and careful handwriting, filled with diagrams and area maps. Fiana would have to crawl over the details later in her quarters, poring over the equations and running checks with her own slide rule. A Mother Superior of a dustship was required to know the math, Fiana had been an F&O staffer herself in her youth.

But it was going to be slow work to make sure she understood everything in the report.

Tight was the crown of leadership, Fiana knew. It would be a headache she had to bear.

Fiana cursorily looked through the report until she found the summary. She bit her lip. "F&O thinks there's more mass than we accounted for?"

"About sixty chipstones worth of mass."

Sixty chipstones. About ten people's worth of mass. Had they known their audit was off, they could have thrown out non-essential material from the inside to balance the ship. They could have hidden it away in the ice and consumables they'd blown.

It shouldn't have been off, though. They'd based their lives on the audit run before maneuvers.

"There was an audit," Fiana said. And everyone on board knew how important an audit was before a maneuver.

"F&O is not accusing anyone of anything, we are merely reporting the math. It doesn't lie, Mother. You can check it yourself."

She would. But for now, Fiana was not going to assume her specialists were wrong. She had to trust that her team was doing their best work. "I will check it, but I will wager it agrees with you. I'll call another mass audit. Something isn't right. We'll see if we can solve for the mystery yet."

Even though she hung in the air, Lily visibly relaxed as tension drained from her body.

"Of course, Mother. We will put our second shift at your disposal and keep only a core team running calculations."

The heat began to build. Crew took to wearing just simple wraps when off shift, and then Fiana gave permission for everyone to strip to just undergarments.

Globes of salty sweat hung in the stultifying air and sunken eyes made everyone look like tired ghosts.

The ship's Surgeon, Lla-Je fe Sese kicked his foot against the door to the captain's quarters in the middle of an off-watch. Fiana was startled to find him hanging in place, face flushed and worried.

"Mother, we are all in danger of heat stroke," Je said, without apologizing for waking her. The red emergency light in the doorway glimmered off his shaved scalp. It was the way of the surgeons to shave, though Je was male and used to shaving. For surgeons it was ritual demonstration of control of a razor, a tradition hundreds of years old. A surgeon with a nick on her body was not to be trusted, or so the saying went. Je said it was actually done for hygiene, but it helped that men were expected to be fastidious about it as well. Fiana always imagined it must have been weirder for the regular surgeons to hew to the tradition, given expectations. "How much longer will we be containing our waste heat?"

They'd been drifting for days now, moving further away from the seedship. The thick wall of ice around the hull that they mined for air and water had been scraped down, warmed, and vented. In some parts, the hull was down to only rock and mud.

"Fifteen full shifts before we reintersect with the dust fields." One orbit around the Greater World. They would have to deploy full sails on return, but the higher orbit would let the area the Hunter-Killers were infesting move ahead under them. They would plunge back into a different part of the Archipelago with barely any water and air left.

"Crew will be dying from the heat long before then," Je said somberly.

"What should we look for?" Fiana asked wearily. Die of heat now, or miss their chance to get to safety when they reintersected with the dust planes and the Archipelago. Floating diarrhea, those choices.

"Confusion, irritability—" Like Fiana's irritability at being woken? Though, to be fair, she'd been sleeping slightly, dozing as she bumped from the wall to the hammock. "Dry skin, vomiting, panting, and flushed faces."

"We're out in the void, Je. The Hunter-Killers can move out here without needing sails or tethers, but we're helpless until we intersect with the dust rings again."

"Then all that our people will find will be a ghost ship," Je said seriously. "If they are able to find us at all."

He was so serious. Always worried. And it wasn't his place to look this long in the face. It was Fiana's. But Je had always been high-minded. He wouldn't have fought so hard for a place in the Surgeons' Academy without a certain amount of hard pushiness.

"What do you recommend, my surgeon?"

"Daily internal thermometer checks for every crewmember," Je said.

"Internal? Is that what I think you mean?"

"It is."

"Je . . . " Fiana trailed off. Then she took a deep breath. "I can't have your team sticking tubes up everyone's ass once a day."

Particularly not if some male surgeon was doing it. Her team of commanding mothers trusted that Fiana valued Je, but a lot of them were old-fashioned and uncomfortable with having large, awkward hands on the handle of a blade.

"Then draw up a list of essential crew that you can't afford to lose, and they will be tested once a day. We're risking lives, understand?"

"I'll have the list drawn up, but we don't start taking temperatures until people start passing out," Fiana said. "The DNA samples are in lead cases in the ice rooms with our food. We can put anyone in danger there for now."

But it would be a temporary solution.

It was enough to mollify Je. For now.

But the decisions would become tougher as this went on.

The mass audit came back from a sweaty, tired Audra, who tracked Fiana down in the galley hall. The Secondary Mother had sheaves of clear flexies filled with accounting tables.

"There's unaccounted for mass. We did the audit. We tested the ship's acceleration profile. The amount of mass they estimated is dead-on: there's sixty chipstone worth of something *somewhere*. Manifests can't account for it. We've checked everything we can think of."

Fiana offered her a pocket of cooled water, which Audra took and sucked on gratefully. Fiana used that as a moment to capture her own thoughts and continue nibbling at a basket of grapes.

"We're going to have to search everyone's cabins, verify personal allowances," Audra said, before Fiana could even speak.

"No." Fiana shook her head. "There are just over a hundred crew. And yes, split, that could be enough." And when they sailed out from Sese, they did not have to consider how true their mass was; they just deployed sails into the appropriate dust plane until they had the speed and vectors needed.

"We only did a rough manifest and mass account before leaving," Audra noted.

"I've sailed the dust planes of the Greater World all my life, Audra. I've been F&O, then Secondary Mother, and now Mother. I'd sense it in my bones the moment we left if the sails were straining, our vessel heavy." Fiana said. "No, this has only been a problem since that seedship."

Audra, her legs looped around an air-chair, straightened. "What are you thinking?"

"Take the survey teams, the men, out onto the hull. Use airlocks facing away from the dust to keep cover. Full Encounter rules. Do you understand what I am asking you? Can you do that?"

Audra looked past Fiana, out into a personal darkness and into fear as she considered her own death. Fiana was asking her to go out an airlock, seal it with ice and rock once the team was out, and then they would search the hull.

If they encountered Hunter-Killers, they would jump off into the vacuum and scatter to their deaths. They would not, under any circumstance, return to any known airlock, lest they lead the enemy inside. Maybe the Hunter-Killers wouldn't buy that. Maybe they would. It was still a hard thing to ask of a person.

Audra would know that if she turned this down, Fiana would honor her choice. But it would be a blow to her standing.

"I will lead a team," Audra said in a low, determined voice. "We need to find out what may have killed us."

Fiana held her hand and squeezed it. Such bravery. She had no doubt in Audra. It's why she had chosen the strong mind from her old F&O cohort to join her when the World Mothers had given Fiana a command of her own.

For an entire watch, the ship went about its business in a pre-funereal silence, with crew jumping at every bang and creak in the empty air.

Je came to report on two crewmembers who had passed out. An older F&O calculator and one of the survey men. He had given them fluids and put them in a freezer to let them cool down.

"The ship is suffering too," he told her. The ship's heart had an infection, he judged. Some kind of pericarditis inflaming the sac around the great muscle. They were pumping it full of antibiotics and hoping for the best.

"We can't dump heat, not yet," Fiana told him.

"I know," Je said softly. "I know."

The warble of airlock alarms echoed. Je twisted in the air to look down the corridor. "They're coming back inside."

Crew streamed through the air toward the doors. They weren't carrying weapons. There was nothing that would stop a Hunter-Killer, there was no point.

But they still came, determination on their faces, fists clenched. They would have thrown their bodies against the deadly machines to buy their sisters another minute of life, Fiana knew, with a tight knot in her stomach.

Voidsuits came through instead of gleaming, spidery balls of death. Fiana relaxed slightly.

And then more suits struggled through.

And more.

Despite herself, Fiana said aloud, "There are too many of them!"
Ten other suits that hadn't piled into the airlock on the way out.
Ten.

That could be sixty chipstones. If they were . . .

They removed their helmets, and the confused crew gasped.

Belshin men. Ten Belshin men.

Ten Belshin males had maybe doomed them all. It was something that Fiana kept rolling around her head for all its strangeness as she stared at the ten foreign faces hovering before her.

It was the math. The simple math. The massive ball of rock and ice looked substantial, but orbital mechanics were precise and unforgiving. Their weight had slowed them down enough to throw off the maneuver.

Fiana pointed at them. "You activated the seedship, you unleashed the Hunter-Killers on us all, and then you fled to our hull to hide! You have the audacity to hide on *my* ship?"

"They don't speak Undak," Je said. "Do you want me to translate? They're expecting that you will throw them out of the airlock. They're terrified."

Fiana saw it on their faces. Resignation, fear, some defiance.

Audra crossed her arms. "We should slice off their balls, put them in the fridge with the seedship DNA, and then shove the floating shits out the airlock."

"Don't translate that," Fiana said to Je.

"Engage the Lineage Protocol," Audra said. "We need to initiate it now. While we still have some sort of chance."

Fiana could hear Je suck in his breath. She looked over at Audra. "We're not going to talk about the Protocol right now. These are human lives you're talking about."

Audra glanced at Je. "Mother, he knew the risks when he agreed to join the ship."

"Lives," Fiana said slowly. "All of the lives on this ship are important."

Je was only half listening. Several of the newcomers were chattering to him.

"They know you're angry," Je reported, cutting Audra off. "They're expecting you to kill them. They're gastric plumbers. Belshin slaves. They fled when their ship was attacked."

"We cannot afford the increase in consumables," Audra hissed. "We're far out into the void. We're off orbit and schedule. You know what needs to be done, and it needs to be done quickly. Your crew is depending on you."

Fiana raised a finger. "Audra—"

Audra pushed herself back away from the room. "As one of your second-aries, I have to remind you: every moment those males remain on board is a moment stolen from our own future. It's math. It means cold, hard decisions. But that is what leaders do: they make the hard choices."

Fiana took Lily into one of the observation ice bowls.

"I wanted to show you something," Fiana said, drifting out toward the polished ice.

The young F&O calculator hung next to her. "Mother?"

Fiana pointed out at the dark. "Look out there, Lily. All those small points of light. That's something few, if any people from the Archipelago ever get to see."

From here, they could see the entirety of the dust plane. The multitudes of the rings, the rocky moons.

Lily held up a thumb. "All of our people out there. Hiding away from Hunter-Killers."

They stared at the dust band for a long while.

Lily cleared her throat. "Even if you sacrifice the Belshin, we can't fix the orbit."

"I spent two whole nights running the figures," Fiana said. "Audra ran them as well. Fifty people can survive a full braking maneuver and a loop by object IF-547, then 893, and a second all-sails slow that you and F&O have given me."

"So, it's Lineage Protocol." Lily turned her back to the dust plane. "They tell you in the Academy not to get too attached to the men aboard."

"People I trust are all telling me it's time." Fiana rubbed her forehead. The headaches were getting more and more intense. "We only have enough for fifty people to survive until we reintercept the dust plane."

Protocol said it was time to take donations from all the men, store the material, and then ask them all to do the honorable thing. The *noble* thing. If they balked, then it was the Mother Superior's job to enforce the choice.

Only women could bear the next generation. Fiana needed to act to secure futures.

And yet . . .

"The ideas that fix this situation, they won't come from just one person dictating them. It's going to have to come from everyone working the math. And being cross-checked."

Lily's eyes widened. "You're not going to engage the protocol?"

"Hard choices. The other mothers keep telling me to make hard choices." Fiana pushed away. "But the people who tell me that don't have to bear the consequences of those choices, and don't see the whole community, just the part of it that they identify with. It's easy to make a 'hard' choice when the price is paid by someone else."

"This won't be a popular decision," Lily said. "And I won't tell Audra you called her unimaginative."

"Thank you." Fiana patted her shoulder. "I need you to work out the problem, talk to anyone who might have ideas, and to lean on your peers."

"We'll keep running ideas through the team," Lily promised. "There are things the engineers have proposed in the past. More non-essential mass that could be jettisoned. It could help."

Because there was math. And then there was *math*. Math was a tool, wasn't it? A tool to be wielded or mastered.

And Fiana wasn't going to give it blood.

Four crew passed out and were found floating in the corridors. Je came to Fiana, his face pinched and ruddy, to give her an update.

"Mother, we should have off-duty crew switch to a three-person cross-check system so that no one ends up alone."

"I'll send out orders." Fiana was hooked into the 'top' of her room, which was laced with foot-webbing. She'd been holding a position in front of an air vent, letting the rush of air bob her back and forth.

"And I need to check you over," Je said.

Fiana waved a hand. "I'm fine. There are others who need your attention, Je."

"You're the Mother Superior," Je insisted.

Fiana wiped a fat bead of sweat collecting behind her ear. The air was getting so thick she felt like she couldn't breathe anymore. They'd stopped venting and the heat, the moisture from shaving the ice, and the dust in the air had turned the ship into a swamp.

"I will endure," Fiana said. "If I feel I'm at risk, I'll let you know."

Je didn't look happy, but he couldn't really do anything about it, so he nodded. He had floated his way back to the entryway, and he paused there, hands and feet in an X and gripping the door's lip.

"Mother, may I ask you something?"

His voice had softened, and Fiana could hear the worry.

"Lineage Protocol?" she asked him.

"Such a dry name for something so horrific," Je said as he nodded.

"F&O is working hard on a solution. I've asked all for ideas. But, in a nutshell, we need to breathe less, surgeon. We used too much as a simple rocket to get us away from the Hunter-Killer area. The math is simple and hard to escape. We only have so much air and we know how many people are onboard."

"The equation is simple," Je said. "So we change the assumed inputs. The air-use rate is based on an assumption created by surgeons for average crew with average activity."

Je had her complete attention.

"Can you actually get the crew to breathe less?"

"The more you move, the more you breathe. So, we freeze crew shifts. Everyone bound to their room and webbed in. No one moves until rescue. The command room shift stays in place and sleeps in place."

"You're asking the entire crew to stay in bed for twelve full shift rotations?"

"And to focus on breathing slowly and deeply. And that is not all. We have drugs for surgeries. The larger ones that use more air, we will need to drug them."

"And what will that get us, Je? Will that get us to the dust plane? Will that halve the air we use?"

"This isn't math, it's biology. Messy, imprecise," Je said.

"Give me an estimate," Fiana ordered. Because she couldn't risk lives based on messiness.

"I think we can reduce our air usage to two-thirds. Maybe to a half. We won't know until we start the experiment and monitor the impact."

Two-thirds still left a ghost ship. A third was an unblinking gulf that still couldn't be crossed.

But it would mean fewer lives that needed chosen for sacrifice.

"Ready the drugs," Fiana said. "We'll run the experiment and get a shift's worth of data." It wouldn't get them there by itself. It wasn't the solution. But it was something they could test.

Audra appeared at the door and shoved Je aside. She had a bandolier strapped tight across her chest and had changed into her dark black sortie uniform. Her pistol was in its forearm holster.

"Mother, we have a mutiny!" Audra said. "The men heard that Lineage Protocol will be called for. Some of them released the Belshin prisoners and broke into the armory."

The mutiny spread quickly. Panicked men took weapons into common areas which they barricaded with decoration panels ripped from the walls. Many of them were on sortie parties, so were familiar with in-ship combat and knew where to find the weapons.

"We have the numbers," Audra said. Few could match her well-trained cadre. "My sisters are fast and are the best hall-grapplers in the fleet."

Audra and her team would fight bitterly. They were Sortie Three, rarely sent to other ships, but trained to protect this one. They were backed up by members of engineering and women from the stays and tether teams, with their arms muscled from handling spider-silk ropes.

They raced down corridors to the heart of the mutiny where the chanting men were making their demands heard.

"Stop here!" Another woman in black held out a hand near a turn in the rock-ice corridor. "Mother, they're shooting anyone who tries to approach the barricade."

They all grabbed rails and stopped. Fiana listened to the shouts, the men trying to keep each other roused to bravery with their too deep voices. No raising them to neutral-sounding tones now because they were speaking to mothers or sisters around the ship.

"We should have expected this," Audra said, acid in her voice.

Je said nothing but shrank back as if trying to hide against the wall.

Fiana looked around again at the nervous, but anticipatory sortie crew all watching Audra, waiting for the command. Then, she quickly peeked around the corner.

"Mother!"

The men shouted at her but didn't shoot. Fiana took that as a good sign and stopped to look at the crudely hammered together door leading to the common rooms and the forms that she could see through the gaps nervously flitting around.

"Get Lily from F&O," Fiana ordered.

"And?" Audra also looked ready to go.

"It's the heat," Fiana said. She was panting from the race over here. "It's affecting our minds. Leading us to mistakes."

"My mind is tempered well," Audra hissed. "They are traitors to Sese, and foreign agitators from the other side of the Archipelago."

"What are their demands?" Fiana couldn't tell from all the yelling.

"They want the chance to live through lottery," one of the tether women with a simple club in her hands said.

"That's treason," Audra said. She leaned forward. "If we fight them, we can take care of the dilemma we face."

"Death makes traitors of many," Fiana said. "And the heat addles their minds. All our minds. Wouldn't you say, surgeon?"

Je did not look happy about being addressed. "Mother . . . "

But Fiana saw Lily coasting toward them and waved her over. "My calculator! We have a tricky situation."

Fiana pulled the last of her wrap off, stripping herself naked, and then gently tapped the wall so that she would float out into the center of the corridor before Audra could react.

She could hear the sudden murmurs of surprise, the repeated low whispers of "Mother."

They began to shout their demands through the barricade, but she held up a hand.

"It is too hot for a fight, but if we have to, you are outnumbered. And you know this. So we are going to talk about this instead, because I did not come out here into the void to do the Hunter-Killers' work for them. Not when our ancestors risked so much to create the Archipelago and dust planes for our survival. I will not spit on their memories."

They quieted.

"I don't have the answer to our situation. But we, together, do. Come out to me, Je, Lily. Tell them what you've been telling me."

Fiana looked back. She gestured at them both.

Slowly, the surgeon and the F&O calculator bobbled out to join her.

"F&O found our mass problem. They saved us from the Hunter-Killers. Je is keeping us alive as best as he can in this heat. I don't have the solution to how we can make it back to the dust plane alive, but the two of them, with all of our help, might. There is no one answer here, but if we piece all of their ideas together, and add in some new ones, they could add up to enough to get us back home."

Lily stared at the men, then bit her lip. "We need to shed mass once we're at the apoapsis. Everything we can imagine we can do without and things we can't. We need to pare the ice and rock to the bare minimum, down to nothing but air, sails, and our own bodies."

"And the rest of us must strap in and not move until rescue. The biggest among us must be drugged," Je said.

The men protested. That would surely impact them the most.

But Je argued with them. "These are the realities," he insisted. "We have to breathe less . . . or not at all."

"We could thin the air more," one of the male voices on the other side suggested. "I'm in gastric, we can change the recirculation mixes."

As the suggestions continued, Fiana relaxed.

"We are not separate from the civilization that birthed us," she said to Audra. "We do not have to fall into murder and blood. Not this time."

The great dustship calved at apoapsis, the very height of its orbit. Fiana would have liked to have seen it and the entire dust plane glinting its encirclement of their Greater World. But she had to be in her cabin. No one moved about, not even her. Surgeon's orders.

It was not unusual for objects to break apart. Hopefully, anything watching would assume it was a normal event, a weakened body splitting apart and becoming two.

Now they would begin to gain speed, to dump off heat and more consumables to alter their trajectory *just* enough. They were speeding up, every tick as they dropped lower and lower.

"Why would you want to go back out there?" Je had once asked her, when they were on Sese's interior walking through the botanical gardens. He raised a hand to encompass the whole world in all its lushness. She had been trying to recruit him as surgeon. The first male surgeon to fly the Archipelago void. "Why not stay and enjoy this world?"

"The only difference between them is scale, Je. Come see all the worlds. It reveals us for who we really are, to go out there."

Fiana lay strapped to her webbing, in a drugged stupor, breathing slowly. There were many more full shifts ahead to endure before they would come screaming back into the dust and throw out the sails to chatter and bite and shake.

But they would get home, she thought dimly.

The math was there.

Elizabeth Bear was born on the same day as Frodo and Bilbo Baggins, but in a different year. She is the Hugo, Sturgeon, Locus, and Campbell Award winning author of thirty novels and over a hundred short stories, and her hobbies of rock climbing, archery, kayaking, and horseback riding have led more than one person to accuse her of prepping for a portal fantasy adventure.

She lives in Massachusetts with her husband, writer Scott Lynch.

DERIVING LIFE

Elizabeth Bear

Man and animals are in reality vehicles and conduits of food, tombs of animals, hostels of Death, coverings that consume, deriving life by the death of others.
—Leonardo da Vinci

Sometime later; maybe tomorrow

My name is Marq Tames, I'm a mathematician, and I'm planning suicide.

Until today, I wasn't *planning*. You couldn't say I was *planning*. Because I know perfectly well that it would be the grossest of irresponsibility to plan my exit . . . at least until Tamar didn't need me anymore.

You don't do that to people you love.

You don't do that to people who love you.

Now

"Stop taking your oxy," Tamar says, skeletal hand on my wrist. There's not much left of them. Their skin crackles against the back of my fingers when I touch their cheek. Their limbs are withered, but their torso is drum-taut, swollen-seeming. I don't look. Death—and especially transitional death—is so much prettier in the dramas.

"Fuck that," I answer.

"Just stop taking the damn bonding hormones." Their papery cheek is wet. "I can't stand to see you in this much pain, Marq. Even Atticus can't help me with it."

"Do you think it wouldn't hurt me worse *not* to be here?"

Tamar doesn't answer. Their eyelids droop across bruised sockets.

I'm exhausting them.

"Do you think this didn't hurt people before? Before we could contract for pair-bond maintenance? How do you think people did it then? Do you think losing a spouse was *easier*?"

Tamar closes their eyes completely.

And no, of course, no, they do not think that. They'd just never paused to think about it at all. We all forget that people in the past were really just like us. We want to forget it. It makes it easier to live with the knowledge of how much suffering they endured.

They endured it because they had no choice.

Tamar avoiding thinking about that is the same as Tamar thinking that I should go away. Stop taking my drugs. Maybe file for divorce. Tamar wants to think there's a way this could hurt me less. They're thinking of me, really.

I've already stopped taking the oxy. I haven't told Tamar. It helps them to think there's something more I could do. That I'm just being stubborn. That I'm in charge of this pain.

That I have a choice.

I wish I were in charge. I wish, I *wish* I had a choice. But I don't need bonding hormones to love Tamar.

I knew how this ended when I signed the contract.

I'm still here.

"Is this what you want?" Tamar asks me. One clawlike hand sweeps the length of the body that used to be so lithe, so strong.

"I just want every second of you I can get," I say. "I'll have to do without soon enough."

Tamar squints at me. I don't think I'm fooling them, but they're not going to call me on it.

Not right now. Maybe not ever.

Maybe they'd rather not know for sure.

But the thing is, I don't want to keep doing this without them. Especially with, well, the other stuff that's going on.

I knew Tamar's deal before we got involved. It was all in the disclosures. I knew there were limits on our time together.

But you tell yourself, going in, that it'll be fine. That fifteen years is better than no years and hey, the course might be slow; you might get twenty. Twenty-two. How many relationships actually last twenty-two years?

And there are benefits to being the spouse of someone like Tamar, just as there are benefits to having a Tenant.

Something is better than nothing. Love is better than loneliness. And it's not like anybody gets a guarantee.

So you tell yourself that you can go into this guarded. Not invest fully, because you know there's a time limit. And that it might even be better because of that, because it can't be a trap for a lifetime.

There's life after, you tell yourself.

So much life.

Except then after comes, and you discover that maybe the Mythic After Time isn't what you wanted at all. You just want now to keep going forever.

But now won't do that. Or rather, it will. But the now you want to keep is not the now you get. The now you get is a river, sweeping the now you wanted eternally back toward the horizon disappearing behind you.

Evangeline doesn't sit behind her desk for our sessions. In fact, her desk is pushed up against the wall in her office, and she usually turns her chair around and sits down in it facing me, her back to the darkened monitor. I'm usually over on the other side of the room, next to a little square table with a lamp.

Evangeline's my transition specialist. She's a gynandromorph—from environmental toxicity, rather than by choice—and she likes archaic pronouns and I try to respect that.

I'm legally mandated to see her for at least a year before I make my final decision. It's been eighteen months, because I started visiting her a little before Tamar went into hospice. So I could make my decision tomorrow.

If I thought Evangeline would sign off on it yet. Which she won't.

Today she isn't happy. I can tell because she keeps fidgeting with her wedding rings, although her face is smooth and affectless.

She's unhappy because I just said something she didn't like.

What I'd said was, "If you change who you are so that someone will love you, and you're happy afterward, is that so terrible?"

Transition specialists aren't supposed to let you know when you've rattled their cages, but her disapproval is strong enough that even if she doesn't demonstrate it, I can taste it. I wonder if there are disapproval pheromones.

"Well," she says, "it seems like you have a lot of choices to consider, Marq. Have you come up with a strategy for assessing them?"

I didn't answer.

She didn't frown. She's too good at her job to frown.

She waited ninety seconds for me to answer before she added, "You know, you do have a right to be happy without sacrificing yourself."

Maybe it was supposed to hit me like an epiphany. But epiphanies have been thin on the ground for me recently.

"The right, maybe," I answered. "But do I have the *ability*?"

"You'll have to answer that," she said, after another ninety seconds.

"Yeah," I said. "That's the problem in a nutshell, right there, isn't it?"

Robin, my non-spouse partner, picks me up in the parking lot, and *they're* not happy with me either.

Opening salvo: "You need to drop this thing, Marq."

"This thing?"

Robin waves at the two-story brick façade of the clinic.

"Becoming a Host?"

They nod. Hands on the steering wheel as legally mandated, but I'm glad the car is handling the driving. Robin's knuckles are paler brown than the surrounding flesh, their face drawn in determination. "You can't do this."

"Tamar did."

"Tamar is dying because of it."

"Do you think I don't know that? I'm fifty-six years old, Robin. Another twenty-five years or so in guaranteed good health seems pretty attractive right now."

Robin sighs. "It's maybe twenty years of good health if you're lucky, and you know it. You always walk out of that office spoiling for a fight."

I think about that. It might be true. "That might be true."

We drive in silence for a while. We have a dinner date tonight, and Robin brings me home to the bungalow Tamar and I used to share. My bungalow now. I'll inherit the marital property, though not Tamar's Host benefits. It's okay. Once they're gone, I'll have my own.

Or Robin and Tamar will win, and I'll go back to work. The house is paid for anyway. It's a gorgeous little Craftsman, relocated up here to the 51st parallel from Florida before the subtropics became uninhabitable. And before Florida sank beneath the waves. It got so it was cheaper to move houses than build them for a while, especially with the population migrations at the end of the twenty-first century and the carbon-abatement enforcement. Can you imagine a planet full of assholes who used to just . . . cut down trees?

Tamar liked it—Tamar *likes* it—because that same big melt that put our house where it is also gave us the Tenants. Or—more precisely—gave them back.

Robin parks, and we walk up the drive past late-summer black-eyed Susans and overblown roses that need deadheading. I let us in, and we walk into the kitchen. Robin's brought a bottle of white wine and the makings for a salad with chickpeas and pistachios. I rest on a stool while they cook, moving around my kitchen like they spend several nights a week there—which they do.

Tamar approved heartily of me bringing home a gourmet cook. My eyes sting for a moment, with memory. I bury my face in my wine glass until I feel like I can talk again.

"I could keep a part of Tamar with me if I do this. You know that. I could get a scion of Atticus, and have a little bit of Tamar with me forever."

"Or you could let go," Robin says. "Move on."

"Live here alone." If I had a scion, I wouldn't be *alone.*

"It's a nice house," Robin says. "You have a long life ahead of you." They slide a plate in front of me, assembled so effortlessly it seems like a few waves of the hand have created a masterpiece of design. "Being alone isn't so bad. Nobody moves your stuff."

Robin likes living alone. Robin likes having a couple of lovers and their own place where they spend most nights by themself. *Robin* doesn't get that other than Tamar—and, I suppose, Atticus—I have been alone my whole life, emotionally if not physically, and the specter of having to go back to that, having to return to that loneliness after seventeen years of relief, of belonging, of having a *place* . . .

I can't.

I can't. But I just have to. Because I don't have a choice.

I poke my food with my fork. "The future I wanted was the one with Tamar."

Everything about the salad is perfect and perfectly dressed. Robin did the chickpeas themself; these never saw the inside of a can. Their buttery texture converts to sand in my mouth when I try to eat one.

"And you had it." Robin picks up their own plate and hooks a stool around with one foot, joining me informally at the counter. "Paid in full, one future. I'm not saying you don't get to grieve. Of course you do. But the world isn't ending, Marq. Soon, once you get beyond the grief, you will have to look for a new future. Futures chain together, one after the other. You don't just sing one song or write one book and then decide never to create anything again."

"Some people do exactly that, though. What about Harper Lee?"

Robin blows on a chickpea as if it were hot. "No feeling is final. No emotion is irrevocable."

"Some choices are."

"Yes," Robin says. "That's what I'm afraid of."

Seventeen years, two months, and three days ago

"Caring for a patient consumes your life," this beautiful person I'd just met was saying.

I was thirty-nine years old and single. Their name was . . . their name *is* Tamar.

I studied them for a minute, then sighed. "I feel like you're trying to tell me something," I admitted. "But I need a few more verbs and nouns."

"Sorry," Tamar said. "I'm not trying to beat around the bush. I'm committed to being honest with potential partners, but I also tend to scare people off when I tell them the truth."

"If I'm scared off, I'll still pay for your drink."

"Deal," they said. And drained it. "So here's the thing. I'm a zombie. A podling. A puppethead."

"Oh," I said. I studied their complexion for signs of illness and saw nothing except the satin gleam of flawless skin. "I'm not a bigot. I don't . . . like those words."

Tamar watched me. They waved for another drink.

"You have acquired metastatic sarcoma."

"I have a Tenant, yes."

"I've never spoken with somebody . . . " I finish my own drink, because now I can't find the nouns. Or verbs.

"Maybe you have," Tamar said. "And you just haven't known it."

Tamar's new drink appeared. They said, "I chose this path because I grew up in a house where I was a caretaker for somebody who was dying. A parent. And I have a chronic illness, and I never want to put anyone else in that position. No one will ever be trapped because of me."

They took a long pull of their drink and smiled apologetically. "My life expectancy wasn't that great to begin with."

"Look," I said. "I like you. And it's your life, your choice. Obviously."

"Makes it hard to date," they said resignedly. "Even today, everybody wants a shot at a life partner."

"Nothing is certain," I said.

"Death and global warming," they replied.

"I would probably have let my parent die, in your place," I admitted. One good confession deserved another. "They were *awful*. So. I come with some baggage and some land mines, too."

Now

"I've done so many things for you," Tamar says. "This thing—"

"*Dying*." Still dodging the nouns. Still dodging the verbs.

"Yes." Their face is waxy. At least they're not in any pain. Atticus wouldn't let them be in pain. "*Dying* is a thing I need to do for myself. On my own terms. You need to let it be mine, Marq."

I sit and look at my hands. I look at my wedding ring. It has a piece of dinosaur bone in it. So does Tamar's, the one they can't wear anymore because their hands are both too bony and too swollen.

"You're *healthy*, Marq." Tamar says.

I know. I know how lucky I am. How few people at my age, in this world we made, are as lucky as I am. How amazing that this gift of health was wasted on somebody as busted as me.

What if Tamar had been healthy? What if Tamar were outliving me? Tamar *deserved* to live, and Tamar deserved to be happy.

I was just taking up space somebody lovable could have been using. The air I was breathing, the carbon for my food . . . those could have benefited somebody else.

"You make me worthy of being loved." I take a breath. "You make me want to make myself worthy of you."

"You were always lovable, Marq." Their hand moves softly against mine.

"I don't know how to be me without you," I say.

"I can't handle that for you right now," Tamar says. "I have to die."

"I keep thinking I can . . . figure this out. Solve it somehow."

"You can't derive people the way you derive functions, Marq."

I laugh, shakily. I can't do this. I have to do this.

"You said when we met that you never wanted to be a burden on some-body else." As soon as it's out I know it was a mistake. Tamar's already gaunt, taut face draws so tight over the bones that hair-fine parallel lines crease the skin, like a mask of the muscle fibers and ligaments beneath.

Tamar closes their eyes. "Marq. I know how hard it is for you to feel worthy. But right now . . . if you can't let this one thing be about me, you need to be someplace else."

"Tamar, I'm sorry—"

"Go away," Tamar says.

"Love," I say.

"Go away," they say. "Go away, I don't love you anymore, I can't stand to watch somebody I love go through what you're going through. Marq, just go away. Let me do this alone."

"Love," I say.

"Don't call me that." Eyes still closed, they turn their face away.

Sixteen years, eight months, and fifteen days ago

I took Tamar to the gorge.

I'd never taken anybody to the gorge before. It's my favorite place in the world, and one of the things I love about it is that it's so private and inaccessible. If you love something, and it's a secret, and you tell two people, and they love it, and they tell two people . . . well, pretty soon it's all over the net and it's not private anymore.

We sat on the bridge over the waterfall—I think it must have been somebody's Eagle Scout project, and so long ago that nobody maintains the trail up to it anymore. It was a cable suspension job, and it swayed gently when we lowered ourselves to the slats.

The waterfall was so far below that we could hear each other speak in normal tones, and the spray couldn't even drift up to jewel in Tamar's hair.

There were rainbows, though, shifting when you turned your head, and I turned my head a lot, because I was staring at Tamar and pretending I wasn't staring at Tamar.

Tamar was looking at their hands.

"I used to come up here as a kid," I said. "To get away."

"How on earth did you ever find it?" They kicked their feet like a happy child.

"It was less overgrown then." My hands were still sticky from cutting through the invasive bittersweet to get here. I was glad I'd remembered to throw the machete I used for yard work in the trunk. And to tell Tamar to wear stout boots.

"Where did you live?"

I pointed back over my shoulder. "That way. The house is gone now, thank God."

"Burned down?"

"No, they took it apart to make . . . something. I didn't care. I was long gone by then." Tamar already knew I'd left at eighteen and never looked back. "This was the closest thing I had to a home."

"How long do you think this has been here?"

I shrugged. "Since the Big Melt? It will probably be here forever now. At least until the next Ice Age."

I saw the corner of Tamar's smile out of the corner of my eye. "You're showing me your home?"

The idea brought me short I kicked my own feet in turn. "I guess I am."

We looked at rainbows for a little while, until a cloud went over the sun.

"You were sexy with that machete," Tamar said, and looked up from their folded hands into my eyes.

We both reeked of tick spray.

And they kissed me anyway.

Now

I go home.

I sit on the couch we picked out together. There's music playing, because I don't seem to have the energy to turn it off. My feet are cold. I should go and get socks.

Part of the problem is not having anywhere to be. I shouldn't have taken that family medical leave. Except if I hadn't, what use exactly would I be to my students and the college right now?

Fifteen minutes later, my feet are even colder. I still haven't found the wherewithal to go and get the socks. My phone beeps with a message and I think maybe I should look at it.

Ten minutes later, it beeps again. I pick it up without thinking and glance at the notifications.

I drop the phone.

Marq, this is Tamar's Tenant, Atticus.

We need to talk.

I fumble it back up again. The messages are still there. Still burning at me while the day grows dim. The ground and the sky outside seem to blur into each other.

I've spoken with Atticus before. We were in-laws, after a fashion. But not recently. Recently . . . I've been avoiding it. Avoiding even thinking about it.

Avoiding even acknowledging its existence.

Because it's the thing that is killing my spouse.

I get up. I put socks on. I start a pot of tea, and though I usually drink it plain, today I put milk and sugar in.

I need to answer this text. Maybe Atticus can help me. Help me explain to Tamar.

Maybe Atticus can help me with my transition specialist.

But when I slide my finger across the screen, a tremendous anxiety fills me. I type and delete, type and delete.

Nothing is right. Nothing is what I mean to say.

I think about what I'm going to text back to Atticus for so long that I do not text it back at all. It's not so much that I talk myself out of it; it's just that I'm exhausted and profoundly sad and can't find much motivation for anything, and despite the tea and sugar I transition seamlessly from lying on the sectional staring at the popcorn texture of the ceiling to a deep sleep punctuated by paranoid nightmares that are never quite bad enough to wake me completely.

Sunrise finds me still on the sofa, eyes crusty and neck aching. Texts still unanswered, and now it feels like too much time has gone by, even though I tell myself I do want to talk to Atticus. Other than me, it's the being in the world who loves Tamar most, at least theoretically. I'm just anxious because I'm so sad. Because the situation is so fraught.

Because I'm furious with Atticus for taking Tamar away from me, even though I know that's not reasonable at all. But since when are brains and feelings reasonable?

And it's dying along with Tamar, although I'm sure it has cells in stasis for eventual reproduction. I know that Atticus has at least two offspring already, because I've met them and their Hosts occasionally.

That should comfort me a little, shouldn't it? That some bit of Tamar is immortal, and will carry on in those Tenants, and their offspring on down the line? And maybe, if I am convincing enough, in me.

I think of my own parent's blood in me, of my failure to reproduce. Isn't it funny how we phrase that? *Failed to reproduce.* I didn't fail. I actively tried not to. It was a conscious choice.

Childhood is a miserable state of affairs, and I wouldn't wish it on anybody I loved.

I gave up trying to win my parent's affection long before they died. I gave up trying to be seen or recognized.

I settled for just not fighting anymore.

Sixteen years, eight months, and sixteen days ago

I reached over in the darkness and stroked Tamar's hair. It had a wonderful texture, springy in its loose curls. Coarse but soft.

"You're thinking, Marq," they said.

"I'm always thinking."

I heard the smile in Tamar's voice as they rolled to face me. "It's not good for you if you can't turn it off once in a while, you know. What were you thinking about?"

"You . . . Atticus."

"Sure. There's a lot to think about." They didn't sound upset.

"Do you remember?"

A huff of thoughtful breath. A warm hand on my side. "Remember?"

"All of Atticus's other lives?"

Tamar made a thoughtful noise. "That's a common misconception, I guess. Atticus itself didn't have other lives. It's a clone of those older Tenants, so in a sense—a cellular sense—the same individual. The Tenants only bud when they choose to, which is why those first Hosts were so unlucky. The Tenants knew infecting them without consent was unethical."

"But the alternative was to let their species die." I thought about that. What I would do. If it were the entire human race on the line.

Tamar said, "I can assure you, one of the reasons the Tenants work so hard for us is that they have a tremendous complex of guilt about that, and still aren't sure they made the right decision."

Who could be? Let your species die, or consume another sentient being without its consent?

What would *anyone* do?

Tamar said, "And it's true that we do share experiences. It can't perceive the world outside my body without me, after all—the same way I can perceive my interior self much better through its senses. And it has—there's some memory transferred. More if you use a big sample of the parent Tenant to engender the offspring. Though that's harder on the Host."

"So it—you—don't remember being a Neanderthal."

More than a huff of laughter this time; an outright peal. "Not exactly. It can share some memories with me that are very old. I have a sense of the Tenants' history."

It had been before I was born: The lead paleoanthropologist and two others working on several intact *Homo neanderthalensis* cadavers that had been discovered in a melting glacier had all developed the same kind of slow-growing cancer. That had been weird enough, though by then we knew about contagious forms of cancer—in humans, in wolves, in Tasmanian devils.

It got weirder when the cancers had begun, the researchers said, to talk to them.

Which probably would have been dismissed as crackpottery, except the cancer also cured that one paleobotanist's diabetes, and suddenly they all seemed to have a lot of really good, coherent ideas about how that particular Neanderthal culture operated.

What a weird, archaic word, *glacier*.

I said, "It just seems weird that I'm in bed with somebody I've never met."

As I said it I realized how foolish it was. Anytime you're in bed with some-body, you're in bed with everybody who came before you—everybody who hurt them, healed them, shaped them. All those ghosts are in the room.

Tamar's Tenant was just a little less vaporous than most.

A rustle of sliding fabric as Tamar sat upright. "Do you want to?"

Now

"I'm sorry, Mx. Tames, but you're not on the visitor list anymore."

"But Tamar—"

"Mx. Sadiq specifically asked that you not be admitted, Mx. Tames." The nurse frowns at me, their attractive brown eyes crinkling kindly at the corners.

I stare. I feel like somebody has just thrust a bayonet through me from behind. Like my diaphragm has been skewered, is spasming around an impalement, and nothing—not breath nor words—will come out until someone drags it free.

The bayonet twists and I get half a breath. "But they're my spouse—"

"They named you specifically," the nurse says again. They glance side-ways. In a lowered voice, dripping with unexpected sympathy, they say, "I'm so sorry. I know it doesn't make it easier for you, but sometimes . . . some-times, toward the end, people just want to be alone. It can be exhausting to witness the pain and fear of loved ones. Do you have other family members you could contact? It's not my place to offer advice, of course—"

I waved their politeness away with one hand. "You have more experience with this sort of thing than I . . . than I . . . thank . . . "

The sobs spill over until they are nearly howls. I bend over with my hands on my knees, doubled in pain. Gasping. Sobbing. I try to stand upright and wobble, catching my shoulder on the wall. Then someone has dragged a chair over behind me and the nurse is guiding me gently into it, producing a box of Kleenex, squeezing my shoulder to ground me.

Surprisingly professional, all of it.

Well, this is an oncology ward. I guess they have some practice.

"Mx. Tames," the nurse says when I've slowed down and I'm gasping a little. "Is there another family member we can call? I don't think you ought to go home alone right now."

One of the things that drew me to Tamar was their joy. They were always so happy. I mean, not offensively happy—not inappropriately happy or chirpy or obnoxiously cheerful. Just happy. Serene. Joyful.

It was infectious.

Literally.

Tamar's relationship with Atticus gave them purpose, and that was part of it. It also gave them a financial cushion such that they could do whatever they wanted in life—pursue art, for example. Travel. (And take me with them.) Early on, the Tenants had bargained with a certain number of elderly, dying billionaires; another decade or so of pain-free, healthier life . . . in each case, for a portion of their immense fortune.

And then there were the cutting edge types, the science-sensation seekers who asked to get infected because it was a new thing. An experience nobody else had. Or because they were getting old, their best and most creative years behind them.

As a mathematician in their fifties, I can appreciate the strength of that motivation, let me tell you.

Some of those new Hosts were brilliant. One was Jules Herbin, who with the help of their Tenant, Maitreyi, went on to found Moth.me.

Herbin was not the only Host who built a business empire.

The Tenants had had a hundred years to increase those fortunes. The Tenants, as a collective—and their Hosts, by extension!—did not lack for money. Sure, there were still fringe extremists who insisted that the Tenants were an alien shadow government controlling human society and that they needed to be eradicated, but there hadn't been a lynching in my lifetime. In North America, anyway.

And there are still fringe extremists who insist the earth is flat. The Tenants have brought us a lot of benefits, and they insist on strict consent.

For Tamar, those benefits included being able to be pain-free and energetic, which is not a small thing when, like Tamar, you've been born with an autoimmune disorder that makes you tired and sore all the time.

And Atticus used its control over Tamar's endocrine system to make them truly, generously happy. Contented. Happy in ways that perhaps evolution did not prepare people for, when we were born into and shaped by generations of need and striving.

Atticus helped Tamar maintain boundaries, make good life choices, and determine the course of their life. It supported them in every conceivable way. In return, Tamar provided Atticus with living space, food, and the use of their body for a period every day while Tamar was otherwise sleeping. *That* took a little getting used to. But Tamar explained it to me as being similar to dolphins—half their brain sleeps while the other half drives.

The Tenants really are good for people.

It's just that they also consume us. No judgment on them; we consume other living things to survive, and they do it far more ethically than we do. They only take volunteers. They make the volunteers go through an extensive long-term psychological vetting process.

And they take very good care of us while they metastasize through our bodies, consuming and crowding out every major organ system. They want us to live as long as possible, of course, because the life span of the Tenant is delineated by the life span of the Host. And yes, when they metastasize into a new Host, they take some elements of their old personality and intellect along with them—and some elements of the personality and identity of every previous Host, too. And they often combine metastatic cells from two or more Tenants to create a combined individual and make sure experiences and knowledge are shared throughout their tribe.

They've been a blessing for the aged and terminally ill. And even for those who are chronically ill, like Tamar, and choose a better quality of life for a shorter time over a longer time on earth replete with much more pain and incapacity.

A lot of people with intractable depression have signed up for Tenancy. Because they just want to know what it's like to be happy. Happy, and a little blind, I guess. It turns out that people with depression are more likely to be realistic about all sorts of things than those with "normal" neurochemistry.

Depression is realism.

The Tenants offer, among other things, an escape from that. They offer safety and well-being and not having to take reality too seriously. They offer the possibility that whatever you're feeling right now isn't as good as it gets.

They can change you for real. They can make you happy.

My reality, right now, is that the love of my life is dying, and doesn't want to talk to me.

Sixteen years, eight months, and fifteen days ago

Atticus, it turned out, talks most easily by texting. Or typing. It could take direct control of Tamar's voice—with their permission—but all three of us thought that would be weird. And would probably make me feel like the whole puppethead thing was more valid than I knew it to be. So we opened a chat, and Tamar and I sat on opposite sides of the room, and had one conversation out loud while Atticus and I had a totally different one via our keyboards.

It wasn't a very deep conversation. Maybe I had expected it to be revelatory? But it was like . . . talking to a friend of a friend with whom you don't have much in common.

We struggled to connect, and it was a relief when the conversation ended.

Now

There are protestors as I come into the clinic. They call to me. I resolutely turn my eyes away, but I can't stop my ears. One weeps openly, begging me not to go in. One holds a sign that says: *CHRIST COMFORTS THE AFFLICTED NOT THE INFECTED.* There're all the usual suspects: *DOWN WITH PUPPETMASTERS. THE MIND CONTROL IS NOT SO SECRET ANYMORE.*

Another has a sign that says *GIVE ME BACK MY CHILD.*

I wish I hadn't seen that one.

"There's a part of me," I tell Evangeline, "that is angry that Tamar doesn't love me enough to . . . to stay, I guess. I know they *can't* stay; I know the decision was made long ago."

"Do you feel like they're choosing Atticus over you?"

"It sent me a text."

Evangeline makes one of those noncommittal therapist noises. "How did that make you feel?"

"I want to talk to it."

"You haven't?"

I open my mouth to make an excuse. To say something plausible about respecting Tamar's agency. Giving them the space they asked for. I think about. I settle back in my chair.

Do I want a Tenant if I have to lie to get one?

I say, "I'm angry with it. I want to ignore that it exists."

"Sometimes," Evangeline says, "when we want something, we want it the same way children do. Without regard for whether it's possible or not. Impossibility doesn't make the wanting go away."

"You're saying that this is a form of denial."

"I'm saying that people don't change who they are, at base, for other people—not healthily. People, instead, learn to accommodate their differences. While still maintaining healthy boundaries and senses of self."

"By that definition, the Tenants are not people. We take them on; they make us happy. Give us purpose. Resolve our existential angst."

"Devour us from the inside out."

I laugh. "What doesn't?"

This time, Robin comes inside for me instead of waiting to pick me up outside. That makes me nervous, honestly. Robin is not an overly solicitous human being. Maybe they noticed the protestors and didn't want me to have to walk past them alone?

That hope sustains me until we're in the car together, side by side, and Robin says the four worst words in the English language. "We need to talk."

"Okay," I say, in flat hopelessness.

"I can't do this anymore," Robin says. "It isn't working out for me."

You'd think after the third or fourth bayonet they'd stop hurting so much, going in. They'd have an established path.

Not so.

So now I'm single. Nobody, it turns out, can handle the depth of what I'm feeling about losing Tamar. Not Tamar, not Robin.

Not me.

Evangeline can, though. Evangeline can because of proper professional distance. Because she's not invested.

Because the only person putting the weight of their emotional needs on the relationship is me.

From the edge of the brocade armchair, I speak between the fingers I've lowered my face into. "This is a way for me to be with them forever."

"I can see how it would feel that way to you," Evangeline answers.

"I need someone to tell me that I am more than merely tolerated. I need to be valued," I say.

"You're valuable to them. To the Tenants."

"You begin to understand," I say. "Maybe I shouldn't need this. But I can't survive these feelings without help. It's not just that I want to be with Tamar. It's that I need to not be in so much pain."

She nods. I'm already on six kinds of pills. Are they helping? They are not helping.

I'm already trying to change myself so somebody will love me better.

So that *I* will love me better.

Evangeline says, "We need what we need. Judging ourselves doesn't change it. Sometimes a hug and a cookie right now mean more than a grand gesture at some indeterminate point in the future."

"What if we make an irrevocable decision to get that hug and that cookie?"

Evangeline lifts her shoulders, lets them fall. "My job is to make sure that you're making an educated decision about the costs and benefits of the cookie. Not to tell you how much you should be willing to pay for it."

I pace the house. I rattle pots in the kitchen but don't cook anything. I take an extra anxiety pill.

When it's kicked in, I pull out my phone and text Atticus with trembling hands. *Sorry about the delay. I needed to get my head on straighter.*

I understand. This is hard on all of us.

You have to make Tamar talk to me!

Tamar doesn't want you to do this. I have to honor their wishes.

Even after they're dead?

Especially after they're dead.

I can't do this alone.

We love you, the cancer says. *We will always love you.*

Tell Tamar I stopped taking the oxy, I type, desperate. *Tell them I did what they asked. Tell them to please just let me come say goodbye.*

I'm talking to the bloated mass that disfigures Tamar's strong, lithe body. It isn't them.

Except it is them.

And Atticus is dying, too, and *Atticus* is taking the time out to comfort somebody it's leaving behind. It's funny, because we never had a lot to say to each other in life. Maybe that was denial on my part as much as anything. But now, it is Tamar.

The only part of them that will still talk to me.

And I want it to be me as well.

I will tell them, Atticus types. *I will tell them when they wake.*

They that are not busy being born are busy dying.

What's the value of an individual? What is the impact of their choices? What is our responsibility for the impact of our choices on others? What is our responsibility to deal with our own feelings?

We're responsible for what we consume, right? And the repercussions of that consumption, too. If the Big Melt taught us anything, as a species, it taught us the relentless ethics of accountability.

So from a certain point of view, the Tenants owe me.

We love you.

Tamar is gone. The call came in the morning. The Tenants will be handling the arrangements, in accordance with Tamar's wishes.

Atticus, of course, is also gone.

I don't know if Tamar woke up after I talked to Atticus. I don't know if Atticus got a chance to tell them.

The house belongs to me now.

I should find some energy to clean it.

To Evangeline, I say, "What if you knew that if you changed yourself—let someone else change you, I suppose—you would be loved and valuable?"

"I'd say you are lovable and valuable the way you are. Changing yourself to be what someone else wants won't heal you, Marq."

I shake my head. "I'd say that people do it all the time. And without the guarantee the Tenants offer. Boob job, guitar lessons, fix your teeth, dye your hair, try to make a pile of money, answer a penis enlargement ad, lose weight, gain weight, lift weights, run a fucking marathon. They fix themselves and expect it will win them love."

"Or they find love and expect it to fix them," Evangeline offers gently. "Or sometimes they give love, and expect it to fix the beloved. If love doesn't fix you, it's not true love, is that what you're suggesting?"

"No. That only works if you're one of *them*."

She laughs. She has a good laugh, throaty and pealing but still somehow light.

"I had true love," I say more slowly. "It didn't fix me. But it made me lovable for the first time."

"You were always lovable. Maybe Tamar helped you feel it?"

"When you grow up being told over and over that you're unlovable, and then somebody perfect and joyous loves you . . . it changes the way you feel about yourself."

"It's healing?" she suggests.

"It made me happy for a while."

"Did it?"

"So happy," I say.

She nibbles on the cap of her pen. She still uses old-fashioned notebooks. "And now?"

"I can never go back," I tell her. "I can only go forward from here."

Robin still picks me up after my sessions. They said they still cared about me. Still wanted to be friends. They expressed concern about when I'm coming back to the university and whether they would like me to facilitate the bereavement leave.

They're in HR; that's how we met in the first place.

I want to shove their superciliousness down their throat. But I also do not want to be alone. Especially today, when we are going to the funeral.

Without Robin, I think I would be. Alone. Completely.

I don't have a lot of the kind of friends you can rely on for emotional support. Maybe that's one reason I leaned so hard on Tamar. I didn't have enough outside supports. And I've eroded the ones I did have by being so broken about Tamar dying.

Don't I get to be broken about this? The worst thing that's ever happened to me?

When we're in the car, though, Robin turns to me and says, "I need to confess to something."

I don't respond. I just sit, stunned already, waiting for the next blow.

"Marq?"

From a million miles away, I manage to raise and wave a hand. *Continue.*

"I wrote to the Tenant's candidate review board about you. I suggested that you were recently bereaved and they should consider your application in that light."

I can't actually believe it. I turn slowly and blink at them.

"You what?"

"It's for your own good—"

I stomp right over their words. "You know what's for my own good? Respecting my fucking autonomy."

"Even if it gets you killed?"

"It's my life to spend as I please, isn't it?"

Silence.

I open the car door. The motor stops humming—a safety cutoff. We hadn't started rolling yet, which is the only reason the door *will* open.

"If it meant I wouldn't go, would you come back to me?"

That asshole turns their face aside.

"Right," I say. "I'll find my own way home, I guess. Don't worry about coming to the funeral."

It's a lovely service. I wear black. I sit in the front row. I used an autocar to get here. I don't turn around to see if Robin showed up. I stand in the receiving line with Tamar's siblings and the people who are Hosting Atticus's closest friends. Robin *is* there. They don't come up to me. Nobody makes me talk very much.

I drink too much wine. Tamar's older sib puts me in an autocar and the autocar brings me home.

I can't face our bedroom. The Tenants made sure the hospital bed was removed weeks ago, when Tamar went into hospice and we knew they were not coming home. So there's nothing in our sunny bedroom except our own bedroom furniture.

I can't face it alone.

I put the box with Tamar's ashes on the floor beside the door, and I lie down on the sofa we picked out together, and I cry until the alcohol takes me away.

Tomorrow, which is now today

It's still dark out when I wake up on the couch. Alone. I fell asleep so early that I've already slept eleven hours. I'm so rested I'm not even hungover. No point in trying to sleep more, although I want to seek that peace so fiercely the desire aches inside me.

There are other paths to peace.

I stand up, and suddenly standing is easy. I'm light; I'm full of energy. Awareness.

Purpose.

I pick up my phone by reflex. I don't need it.

There's a message light blinking on the curve.

A blue light.

Tamar's favorite color. The color I used especially for them.

I've never been big on denial. But standing there in the dark, in the empty house, I have a moment when I think—*This was all a nightmare, it was all a terrible dream.* My hand shakes and a spike of pure blinding hope is the bayonet that transfixes me this time.

Hope may be the thing with feathers. It is also the cruelest pain of all.

Tamar's ashes are still there in the beautiful little salvaged-wood box by the door.

The hope is gone before it has finished deceiving me. Gone so fast I haven't yet finished inhaling to gasp in relief when my diaphragm cramps and seizes and I cannot breathe at all.

I should put the phone down. I should walk out the door and follow the plan I woke up with. The plan that filled me with joy and relief. I shouldn't care what Tamar has to say to me now when they didn't care what I needed to say to them then.

I put my right thumb on the reader and the phone recognizes my pheromones.

> *Marq, I love you.*
> *I'm sorry I had to go and I'm sorry I had to go alone.*
> *You were the best thing that happened to me, along with Atticus. You were my heart. You always talked about my joy, and how you loved it. But I never seemed able to make you understand that you were the source of so much of that joy.*
> *I know you will miss me.*
> *I know it's not fair I had to go first.*
> *But it comforts me to know you'll still be here, that somebody will remember me for a while. Somebody who saw me for myself, and not just through the lens of Atticus.*
> *I lied when I said I didn't love you anymore, and it was a terrible, cruel thing to do. I felt awful and I did an awful thing. I do love you. I am so sorry that we needed different things.*
> *I am so sorry I sent you away.*
> *Atticus is arranging things so that this will be sent after we're gone. I'm sorry for that, too, but it hurts too much to say goodbye.*
> *Do something for me, beloved?*
> *Don't make any hasty choices right now. If you can, forgive me for leaving you and being selfish about how I did it. Live a long time and be well.*
> *Love (at least until the next Ice Age),*
> *Tamar*

I stare at the phone, ebullience flattened. Hasty choices? Did Tamar know I was applying for a Tenant? Had Atticus found out somehow?

Or had they anticipated my other plan?

I had a plan and it was a good plan—no. Dammit, concrete nouns and concrete verbs, especially now.

I had been going to commit suicide. And now, Tamar—with this last unfair request.

Forgive them.

Forgive them.

Had they forgiven me?

Fuck, maybe I can forgive them on the way down.

The hike up to the gorge is easier in autumn. The vines have dropped their leaves and I can see to push them aside and find the path beyond. The earth underfoot is rocky and red, mossy where it isn't compacted. I kick through leaves wet with a recent rain. I am wearing the wrong shoes.

I am still wearing my funeral shoes.

It is gray morning at the bottom of the trail. Birds are rousing, calling, singing their counterpoints and harmonies. Dawn breaks rose and gray along the horizon and my feet hurt from sliding inside the dress shoes by the time I reach the bridge. I pause by its footing, catching my breath, leaning one hand on the weathered post. The cables are extruded and still seem strong. A few of the slats have come loose, and I imagine them tumbling into the curling water and rocks far below.

The water sings from behind a veil of morning mist. I can't see the creek down there, but I feel its presence in the vibration of the bridge, and I sense the long fall it would take to get there. The bridge rocks under my weight as I step out. I could swear I feel the cables stretching under my weight.

How long since I've been here?

Too long.

Well, that neglect is being remedied now.

I achieve the middle of the bridge, careful in my slippery, thoughtless shoes. The sky is definitely golden at the east edge now, and the pink fades higher. I turn toward the waterfall. I wondered if there will be rainbows today.

I unzip my jacket and bring out the box I'd tucked inside it when I left the house, the box of Tamar's—and Atticus's—mortal remains.

I clear my throat and try to find the right thing to say, knowing I don't have to say anything. Knowing I am talking to myself.

"I wanted to keep you forever, you know. I don't want to think about this—about you—becoming something that happened to me once. I don't want to be a person who doesn't know how to love themself again. And then I thought, maybe if I made myself like you, I would love myself the way I loved you. And Robin's not going to let me do that either, I guess . . .

"And you would be unhappy with me anyway, if I did."

I sniffle, and then I get mad at myself for self-pity.

Then I laugh at myself, because I am talking to a box full of cremains, with a little plaque on the front, while standing on a rickety vintage home-brew suspension bridge over the arch of a forgotten waterfall. Yeah, there's a lot here to pity, all right.

"So I don't know what to do, Tamar. I don't know who to be without you. I don't know if I exist outside of your perception of me. I *liked* the me I saw you seeing. I never *liked* myself before. And now you're gone. So who am I?

"And okay, maybe that's unfair to put on somebody. But I did, and you're stuck with it now."

I sniffle again.

"You asked me to do something for you. Something hard. God am I glad nobody is here to see this. But I guess this is a thing I have, a thing I am that's nobody else's. This place here."

The sunrise is gaining on the birdsong. Pretty soon it will be bright enough for flying, and they won't have so much to cheep about because they'll be busy getting on with their day.

In the end, everything falls away.

Whatever else I have to say is just stalling.

I say, "Welcome home, Atticus. Welcome home, Tamar."

I kiss the box.

I hold it close to my chest for a moment, steeling myself. And then fast, without thinking about it, I shove my arms out straight in front of me, over the cable, over the plunge.

I let go.

Tamar falls fast.

I don't see where they land, and I don't hear a splash.

The damn shoes are even worse on the way back down.

There's no wireless service until you're halfway down the mountain. I've actually forgotten that I brought the damn phone with me. I jump six inches on sore feet when it pings.

I resist the urge to look at it until I get back to the sharecar. The morning is mine and the birds are still singing. I cry a lot on the way down and trip over things in my funeral shoes. I swear I'm throwing these things away when I get home.

I'd parked the little soap box of a vehicle where it could get a charge when the sun was up. I walk over the small, grassy, ignored parking lot and lean my rump against the warm resin of its fender. The phone screen is easier to read once I shade it with my head.

The ping is a priority email, which makes me feel exactly the way priority emails and four a.m. phone calls always do.

It says:

Congratulations!

Dear Mx. Marq Tames,

On the advice of your transition specialist, you have been selected for expedited compassionate entrance into the Tenancy program, if you so desire. Of course, such entrance is entirely voluntary, and your consent is revocable until such time as the Tenancy is initiated.

Benefits of the program for you include . . .

. . . and then there was a lot of legalese.

Huh.

Evangeline came through.

I guess she and Robin were both doing what they thought was best for me. Funny how none of us seem to have a consistent idea of what that is.

I don't read the legalese. I start to laugh.

I can't stop.

I unlock the car. I toss the phone on the floor and lock it again. Then I walk away on sore feet, alternately chuckling to myself and sniffing tears.

I pick a flatter trail this time, and half a mile along it I start wondering about a complicated function I was working on before I went on leave, and whether that one student got their financial aid sorted out.

No matter what choice you make, you're going to regret it sometime. But maybe not permanently. And it wasn't like I had to decide right now. I had the day off. Nobody was looking for me.

It was going to be a hot one. And I still had some walking to do.

Gwyneth Jones is a writer and critic of science fiction and fantasy, who has also written for teenagers using the name Ann Halam. Awards include the Philip K Dick award, Arthur C Clarke award, the Dracula Society's Children of the Night award, and the Pilgrim award for sf criticism. She lives in Brighton, UK, with her husband and two cats called Milo and Tilly. Hobbies include curating assorted pondlife in season, watching old movies, playing *Zelda*, and staring out of the window.

THE LITTLE SHEPHERDESS

Gwyneth Jones

I

Lost in the Pacific, far south of the Peru basin, Diti strolled with the Remote Islands warden, in a scrubby, ochre and olive landscape that reminded her of Greece. She was a graduate student researcher, working on a species survey for an abyssal plains mining project on a nearby rig: but right now she was taking a half-day off, and watching the warden finish his wool harvest.

The St Margets comprised one cone-shaped island, and a cusp of reefs that mostly hardly counted as land. They'd been settled twice: a thousand years ago by an Oceanic people, otherwise unknown, who'd left a steep field system, and some enigmatic, geometrical ditches — and then, much later, by Scottish-origin farmers who'd soon given up and gone back to New Zealand, leaving a few Shetland sheep behind. Currently, the islands were uninhabited. The single building was the hut the warden used on his visits. The only large land animals were the sheep: by now naturalised, and protected. An occasional cull for meat, said the warden, unsentimentally, kept the flock within healthy bounds.

Shetlands don't need shearing. They shed their thick, fine wool naturally every spring (a primitive trait, long since selected out in modern breeds), but the fleece can also be removed by hand, all of a piece by experts: a process called *rooing*. Diti and Ano, the warden, settled on a shoulder of the island's central peak, the species-survey rig like a giant, angular insect on their blue-on-blue horizon, and waited for the last few sheep, encouraged by Ano's dogs, to come and find them. The animals' seasonal cycle hadn't shifted, it was approaching what passed for winter at this latitude, not summer. But the Margets' climate was extremely equable: they wouldn't miss their coats.

Diti hadn't expected company when she arrived here one day, in one of the rig's dinghies. She was just stir-crazy in that metal and digital world. But she and the warden had become friends. Ano was also a paleo-agronomist, a specialist in ancient Oceanic crops. As the sheep came trotting up, stood for their health-check and knelt to be rooed (a process they seemed to thoroughly enjoy) he told Diti about long-lost grains and roots that had been cultivated right here, and could be valuable again, in the world's growing food security crisis.

Diti told him about her isopods, deep sea crustaceans. She was attaching microchip cameras to their shells, using a miniature ROV, and waldoes. It was fiddly, and strangely exhausting, but chip by chip she was creating a live-action mosaic movie (with the aid of some serious number-crunching software), of the abyssal plain fauna, which was just amazing to see—

Ano, although resigned to the rig's mission, was troubled by Diti's part in the work. This "species survey" had only one aim in view: to make the mining corporation look good, before the destruction of the habitat she was recording, and its entire fauna. She was a life-scientist! It was inexcusable.

"You know why you're the only one to come on shore, Diti? It's because your superiors are ashamed of their so-called 'science'." The stripped ewe hopped to her feet: touched noses with one of the dogs and skipped away, munching on a hand-out of sheep nuts. Ano grinned, to take the sting out of his criticism. "See, this is how to do it: don't hurt them, hire them! I get the wool, and she's happy too."

Diti said that the deep sea held reserves of minerals vital for renewable energy technology. Renewables *had to* expand, hugely and fast, because the whole world was in crisis. Harvesting the polymetallic nodules, that lay scattered over the abyssal plains, didn't need "intensive" mining methods that would destroy everything. It was the least worst scenario —

They didn't persuade each other. But something Ano had said, half-joking, lodged in Diti's mind like a barbed seed, and wouldn't let go.

II

The isopods, as seen through goggles in the ROV video tank, were giant, oblong-shaped bugs, clothed in pearly, scalloped scales. They crept around, occasionally, randomly, drifting free and landing again. Different species had eight lobes, seven lobes, six lobes to their fringed tails, but precise identification wasn't relevant for this operation. They didn't seem *aware* of the tiny ROV, or the tagging operation, but were very good at subverting and avoiding it—

When her head began to spin and her eyes burned, Diti awarded herself a break and moved to the other tank, to view the results of her endeavours. If she was honest, Ano might find this amazing movie a little *slow* . . . Often nothing stirred, except isopod camera-bearers, blundering into view; or the nodules themselves, shifting in the drift. This was not a vast deposit, like the Pacific fields further north, but it was still extraordinary. The precious blooms of metal were just *lying* there, crowds of them, (and Ano was right, alas. Diti's isopod movie would be of great interest to the mining corp.) . . . At last a single, female timid squid appeared. She checked it off on her log: *Amaryllis Menoetes*, the sparkling herder. It was a pretty species, with a tapering bulb of a body, and arms that formed a flared and fluted bell at full extension; shot through with yellow sparkles. The little creature (about 20 cm high in real life) tripped around as if it was dancing. They'd been observed moving the nodules about, a behaviour someone had dubbed *nest-building*; which couldn't be right . . . But there were so few direct observations of abyssal plain fauna, nonsense "facts" went unchallenged for ages.

The yellow photophores acted as camouflage, but the longer Diti watched, the more timid squid she could see. Were they hunting? They definitely seemed to be groping at the crusty blooms; even pushing them together, into heaps . . .

She kept watching, occasionally logging another species that came along, until eyestrain set in again. Then she noted up her shift and left the RV studio (a repurposed shipping container, which was almost Diti's private domain). As she'd hoped, Helmut, the head of operations —who loved cooking— had organised a meal in the big compartment that was their meeting space. Squid was not on the menu. It was delicious spicy bean stew, with grilled prawn or tofu wraps and plenty of cold beer. The scientists and support chattered the way adults do, never anything about their work; except for a focus on the price of cobalt, a topic important to them all.

Diti was bored and wondered aloud, just idly, if the species-rich concentrations of fauna, fatally drawn to the most desirable deposits on the ocean floor, might be looked at the other way round? The nodules were porous, and not hard to shift —

"It's the stock market floor!" shouted Carl, statistician from the University of the Galápagos. "The abyssal traders have their own metals exchange!"

"Why not?" said Diti, who didn't like Carl's habit of shouting, or his stupid 'amusing' interruptions. "Trade isn't a cognitive activity. Slime moulds do it."

Perita, the DSV (deep-submergence vehicle) pilot, a very vocal anarchist, flung up her arms: "I absolutely *knew* that!" she cried. "This explains everything about our world! No cognitive activity in capitalism, only brainless cellular function!"

Helmut changed the subject, and conversation became general again.

But Diti's interest in her "idle" suggestion, stung into life by Carl and Perita's mockery, led to more, targeted viewing sessions. Her idea became a report: backed by sealed video recordings, and a set of meticulous drawings of the sparkling herder; plus others showing curious, flat, four-pointed stars that folded into cones . . . Cellulose-based material for the "stars", she thought. The propellant and delivery system would be chemical . . . The circular central plates must mimic *exactly* the triggers that caused the little squid to choose a "nesting" place.

Like eye-spots . . .

She thought as she worked, of her refugee mother, who had died. And of her Greek papa, who'd married a brave, lovely woman, and had been left alone with an angry, damaged, *dreadful* little child. "I wanted you to value yourself," he used to tell Diti. "I thought: how can I give the child value?"

You can't insist a timid squid sticks at her studies, and carries on to grad school. But *trade is the breath of life*, papa would say, and that was a clue to follow.

III

Finally she took her report to Helmut. In the cubby hole that was his office she waited as he turned the printed pages, and peered at video. (The star drawings weren't included. They would come later . . .) She was very nervous. She should have involved him sooner, and led up to this moment by stages, instead of dumping it all at once. But she'd been too obsessed. A bad error!

Helmut sat back. He scratched his head, on which a blonde-turning-grey thatch was always standing on end. "This is funny! You were looking so grim, today, I expected you to tell me you were quitting. But *this* is not quitting!"

"Not grim," said Diti. "Just concentrating. I *know* it's very rough. The data I'm sure about, and the projection, as far as it goes, but the presentation is probably rubbish?"

"No, no . . . " Helmut flipped her pages. "The presentation is good. So, you've been studying the little shepherdess . . . "

"Amaryllis Menoetes?"

"Also called 'the little shepherdess'. Because of the pretty 'skirt', you see?"

Diti wished she'd remembered the English name, but she shrugged. "Okay."

"And this isn't about her nest-building?"

"There is no nest building. *Amaryllis Menoetes* males are solitary, as far as they've been observed. The females are sociable, and long lived, if they don't meet a male. But they don't rear young. They die after spawning; the young are free-swimming from birth."

"That's a pity. No protected breeding ground for us to defend?"

Diti shook her head. "That wouldn't work, anyway. We'd never get away with something like that, not up against a global emergency—"

"Because the woods are burning, yah. Burning like hell, and growing money trees at the same time. So tell me what you have."

"They don't build nests. They do shift the nodules. It's in the name, they're *timid*. They create shelters, and move on; again and again. I think I've seen other species do it too. It's a stereotypic behavior. What if sometimes, or often, concentrated deposits, useful to the mining, I mean the harvesting, are created that way? And it would need more research, but if so, could the process be allowed to continue?"

Helmut returned to the report. Then he sat and stared for a while, as if still deep in thought. "Hm! Aphrodite, *born of the sea foam*. But you are Syrian, I think? How do you have the name of an ancient Greek sea-deity?"

"I was a refugee from Syria, with my mother. I was very small, and I thought people with Syrian names all got killed, so I wouldn't answer to mine. My Greek papa gave me a Greek name. But he said I would want to remember my Syrian family name, later on, and he was right, so I use both."

"I see. Well . . . Afroditi Algafari, who knows where this will go? But I'm already sure I'm going to share your report with my boss. She'll want to speak to you."

Diti, so shocked that she panicked, felt as if the rig had lurched under her. "I did *try* to keep up with everything else . . . Am I going to be fired?"

"Worse than that! I think I'm going to have to send you to Geneva."

"*Geneva?*"

"Ah, Diti. Listen. A green heart is not enough; you also need a hard head, which I think you have. You speak cautiously, that's good too. But you must work fast now, to make this happen, and prepare to be *flexible*. Think about that, while Mavis and I ruminate like old cows, about how to handle your hopeful monster. And please, get some rest! Your eyes are like black saucers. But be ready to pack your bags, and keep an eye on the price of cobalt."

IV

Helmut advised her to recruit two team members she could work with. It didn't take much thought: she asked Carl and Perita. They'd annoyed her by jumping on her idea, but they were young, respected for their skills, and at least they'd *noticed* what Diti was saying. This meant a lot, in hindsight. They accepted at once, and the three made swift work of turning Diti's report into a conference presentation. Meanwhile Mavis Couthold, Helmut's boss —who was in Geneva with ESAMP, the group that advised the UN on marine protection, organised their trip.

The International Seabed Authority was in Geneva for a special session, hosted by the UN: reaching an agreement between the "intensive" sea bed mining companies, who were lobbying hard for new licences and less regulation, and the scientists and sovereign nations, who were pushing back. Nodule harvesters weren't directly involved, but as Mavis explained, when she met them at the airport, *everyone* turned up for events like this. The ISA session was the centerpiece of a deep sea trade fair, a talking shop and a forum for new ideas.

They were staying out of town, in a house by Lac Leman belonging to Phillipe Lebrun, CEO of Remote South Pacific Resources. Lebrun himself was their host. Diti wondered what he was really thinking, as he walked with his guests by the shore, the evening they arrived: smiling and silent, while Mavis outlined her campaign, and Mont Blanc's patchy summer snows gleamed, on the skyline across the water. The big boss had many interests, and was hugely rich, but surely he couldn't *want* research on a little squid to halt his Pacific mining in its tracks?

Phillipe caught her eye. "You're suspicious of my motives, Diti?"

"Er, no! Not at all." said Diti, startled.

"It may surprise you, but I love the deeps, as much as I love the game of making money. And I'm always ready to change my mind, if I see the game is changing."

V

Everything went well. Mavis, Carl and Perita circulated: leaking sneaky peeks of video, and talking to anyone who would listen . . . Before they'd been in Geneva three days, these efforts were such a success that Diti's presentation had to be moved to a bigger venue, with a modest press conference beforehand. The little shepherdess was a feel-good story, and marvellous science, too: an irresistible combination for many in this crowd. The others were thrilled, but Diti (who was being "kept under wraps") felt unaccountably depressed. Of course it was great, if they won a cosmetic pause for research . . . *making RSP Resources look good*; as Ano had said. What more could they hope for? Her fantasy of something different was ridiculous.

Then on the fourth day, disaster struck. Diti was out sightseeing; thankfully, being "kept under wraps" didn't involve house arrest. She'd noticed that her friends were strangely silent, but thought nothing of it, until a lone, terse text summoned her to the house by Lac Leman. Perita and Carl were waiting in the hall, with dreadful news.

"It's those devils of vacuum cleaners!" howled Perita, clutching at her tangled black curls. "The *bastards*! They've made up a pack of dirty lies, and convinced the CBL crowd you're an evil existential threat! We're dead in the water!"

The success of their campaign had backfired.

CBL —a continuous bucket line, or conveyor-belt system— was the nodule harvesting method favoured by Remote South Pacific Resources. The "vacuum cleaners" had a more intensive approach, with large, remote operated vehicles, thundering around on the deep sea bed, and apparently they'd decided that *Amaryllis Menoetes* was going to put them out of business. How they'd come to this conclusion was a mystery, but they'd been ruthlessly attacking Diti's unseen report, offline and behind closed doors, and demolishing her reputation.

"Mavis is attempting damage limitation right now," said Carl, despondently. "But it's hopeless. They say you're a green fake, secretly getting paid off by the deep sea open-cast miners, to wreck low-intensity nodule harvesting. The timid squid observations are fake too, simply photoshopped. It's all lies. They can prove nothing, but that's not the point, they don't care, as long as they ruin your presentation."

Diti sat down, slowly, at the foot of Phillipe's grand staircase. "But *why*?" she murmured, amazed. "*Why* are they acting so threatened —?"

"Hey, it's not over. We'll *fight* this, Diti!" Carl protested.

"No we won't!" snapped Perita. "If we fight, they win, *idiot*. We'd just be spreading the dirt!"

"Time for a change of tack . . . " said Diti, almost to herself. She left them squabbling, hurried to her room, and opened the presentation on her laptop screen.

The Timid Squid: Stereotypic Behaviour in Amaryllis Menoetes
What a dull, harmless, graduate-student title!

Nothing ventured, nothing gained . . . She wiped it out, and typed instead:
Zero Disturbance Harvesting.

She checked some delegate details, left the house by a side door, and
called a taxi. Soon she was standing outside a guest room in one of Geneva's
big hotels, hugging her laptop, and that secret portfolio of drawings. She'd
thought it better not to announce herself at reception. She took a deep
breath, and knocked. The man who opened the door was tall and broad,
with slick dark hair cut square at his jaw, and piercing blue eyes. Originally
light-skinned, Dutch-Indonesian mixed race, he now looked as if he'd been
carved from seasoned teak. His name was Hans Blum, and he was technically a rig operator, not a mogul, but he was one of the most powerful people
in the nodule harvesting business.

"I'm Diti Algafari," she said. "Could we talk? It's about an engineering
problem."

Hans Blum stared for several seconds, in silence. "Did Phillipe send you?"

"No, but we both need to talk to *him*. He's been keeping something from us."

The teak giant thought this over, narrow-eyed. "Explain yourself a little."

"If deep sea engineering includes turning isopods into mobile cameras,
I know a little about that. You can ask Helmut. And I really might be the
world expert on *Amaryllis Menoetes* stereotypic shelter building, right now. A
harvesting system that uses abyssal fauna's natural behaviour is bad news for
the vacuum cleaners, they couldn't adapt. That's why they're gunning for me.
Phillipe's interested; I know he is. I have my presentation here, and drawings
you might want to see."

"An engineering problem," said Hans. "I *like* those. Come in, let's talk."

VI

Deep sea mining had a few quiet years after the Geneva ISA session. The
price of conventionally-mined cobalt finally rose, making seabed projects
more attractive to investors, but "Urban Mining" (the recycled metals market) also prospered; almost negating the effect. But in that time, with more
research, the industry's close attention, and the backing of a wealthy, adventurous entrepreneur, Diti's idea took shape. An effective, working process
emerged, replicable almost wherever the precious sea metal was found —and
became one of the early triumphs of the "life-modelled" industrial revolution
that was changing the whole world.

The sparkling herders, and their sister abyssal fauna, busily heaped the
nodules, like jumbles of sheep in a pen. The four-pointed stars snapped shut,

and sped away, gravid with mineral wealth, to solar-powered rigs that drifted, far, far above. The herders might be disconcerted when their creations disappeared. But they never tired of "nest building", and there was always another *ideal spot* close by, so they weren't worried for long . . .

Diti Algafari, of course, had moved on, before the commercial version took off. But of all her adventures, in a marine bio-engineering career that spanned momentous decades, maybe the affair of the little shepherdess would always be closest to her heart.

Rebecca Campbell is a Canadian writer and teacher. Her work has appeared in *The Magazine of Fantasy and Science Fiction*, *Clarkesworld*, *Interzone*, and many other places. NeWest press published her first novel, *The Paradise Engine*, in 2013, and she is at work on a new science fiction novel called *Tales for the Anthropocene*. You can find her online at whereishere.ca.

SUCH THOUGHTS ARE UNPRODUCTIVE

Rebecca Campbell

The woman whom I sometimes believed to be my mother flickered. Once. Twice. Her face—smiling—froze in a cloud of pixels, while her arm—the wide, emphatic gestures that were as much a marker of her identity as the color of her eyes or her fingerprints—swept the screen, leaving blue eddies, whirlpools of information. Then silence, but her mouth moved, leaving a flesh-colored smudge across the top half of her head.

"You've cut out again," I said.

The picture reset. She was saying something that made her laugh.

"Your hair looks really good," I said.

"Wha—"

I waited. Repeated myself.

"Yes," she said, suddenly clear, "I cut it myself because the guy they get in is terrible. He let me use his scissors, at least. So chic and DIY. If it was 2015 I'd pin it—"

Slideshow, for which I was paying five dollars a minute. Figures in black pacing against the yellow cinder block wall of the common room. I tried not to look at them because it was always better not to look at them. It was better when I could see the windows and get a look at where she was.

"We're running out of time," I said. "I only paid for fifteen minutes, cause last time you had the drill and I thought maybe—"

The hand, now trailing pixels. It was definitely her face, but I searched her jawline for the suture where her appearance had been attached, virtually, to this body, a scrim of pixels over the person that was—as far as anything was these days—my mother. Her smile. Her expressive hands. No matter how empty the content of our words, there was comfort in seeing her speak.

I could not, though, let go of the suspicion that this face I was searching—hanging again, lag deforming the number on her gray uniformed shoulder—was not my mother, so much as the collected fragments of her from a hundred thousand hours of CCTV footage and intercepted video conferences and Google hangouts and whatever other material had streamed through the state's huge filter-feeding machines, snuffling all traffic—dark and light, private or public—for the information it required on problematic—

—Such thoughts are unproductive.

This woman I speak to, who is my mother, and may not be my mother, but who fills the space in my life called mother. I will continue to chat with her when I can because the illusion—if it is an illusion—is so close to reality that sometimes I am taken in and relax into daughterly affection.

The black silhouettes in the background of the common room do nothing to interfere with our conversation because no part of our conversation can be hidden from the eye that watches us all, which is not an eye, but the hundred thousand eyes of a filter-feeding behemoth made entirely of information. She sends me messages at night, long discourses on the problem of making the food palatable, or the solitaire she plays, or the Scrabble tournaments she organizes. I can hear the powerful gears of her mind grinding against the cinder block walls of the place, finding things to put in order, to make, to fix. Her resources are limited: games and other companions, the discussions and lectures and regular chastisement that she undergoes, but which she does not mention, but which is always implied. I can imagine her turning that mind toward the problem of 2 + 2 being 5, producing the right answer for the individuals who ask her—daily, hourly, by the minute—to repeat this new truth. A problem of philosophy? Perhaps of language, she would say, from the perspective of neo-radical-orthodoxy, or post-Platonism. One needs only to adjust the definitions in that portion of one's brain that is cordoned off from reality in order to comply with the ideologies of the state. That's how she could give the "right" answer without dying of it.

She never says these things. The mother who exists in my mind—which might or might not align with the mother on the screen, or in my messages—would do such things. It would be necessary for her survival, once the small collection of paper books had been arranged by the Library of Congress system, with gaps on the shelf for "critical theory" and "resistance" and "escape plans."

But what kind of escape could she possibly need? The enclosures are beautiful, despite the yellow cinder block walls. I've seen them when her back is to the window, trees and mountains framed in bulletproof glass. When I was a kid, we often drove through the Rockies and stopped at Banff. Once we stayed in a massive château on Lake Louise. There were men and women in lederhosen outside, playing alphorns. The air, when we left the sticky lowland fug of our car, was so fresh and lovely I wanted to laugh. The glaciers had receded, but you could still see the blue-white glow of them up high, far beyond us.

I think—I'm not sure—but I think I have seen similar mountains in the brief moments she directs the camera over her shoulder and out the window. The time zone can't be far too different, but the summer nights are bright there, so it must be farther north. Toad River, I think. One of the big provincial parks. I have looked at maps—antique ones on paper, tearing at the folds—and seen the gaps in the satellite images, and I have wondered, is she there? Close to 60?

This winter I'll watch the angles of sunlight and track the darkness behind her. I'll hope she picks up on my questions: I've had trouble with my nasturtiums again. Are you growing anything? And hope she turns her camera toward the window, talks about what she's planted in the gardens that are supposed to be so therapeutic.

We live in an age of infinitely preserved information, so it's not actually odd that I saved every video call on an external hard drive. At night I turned off the Wi-Fi and studied my mother's face for evidence of fakery. I didn't search for "ten ways to spot deepfakes" because that left fingerprints, and I'm already a problematic citizen, confirmed as such by my associations, rather than any action I have taken. To be visible meant you have done something to deserve visibility, after all. And if our exploration of the human genome means anything, it's that my genes matter. I am treacherous.

You could inherit treachery, or be infected with it, by the people who waited in government offices, slouching from hard blue chair to hard blue chair, sharing between them the rumors and possibilities regarding what happened to the missing. Camps. Education centers. Wilderness highways that stopped dead on the other side of the great divide. The blank spots that are slowly overtaking our digital maps, even archived versions I thought I had kept safe. No more news from Fort Mac, not for a couple of years now.

The pipelines never leak. Silence accompanied any disruption of gasoline, or the regular oil slicks up and down the Salish Sea, where all the fish are dead. There's another dam on the Peace River to celebrate, but the blackouts got worse.

When I had thoroughly and silently examined the information available (is that a tamarack? A black spruce? Is that a mountain?) It occurred to me that as the woman I talk to might be scrimmed with my mother's face, so might be the room in which she sat. The darkness and light I have so painstakingly tracked, the faint, blue line of a mountain, and a pink winter sunset at three in the afternoon? That may well mean nothing. Worse than nothing: deception.

At work I was also a watcher. I was part of a team that sanity-checked the AI that surveils traffic errors in the western provinces. I looked for anomalies and found ways to integrate them into the AI's understanding, slowly eliminating my own job, as the anomalies grew rarer and the world more perfectly known. I thought, sometimes, following on my father's philosophical leanings, that this was the goal of our state: perfect knowledge of landscapes and people and relationships. So perfect that the simulacrum we saw on the screen was more perfect than the territory we possessed. The woman on the screen was my mother, as was the woman in my messages, so perfectly had she been synthesized by the state that also slit—

—Unproductive.

"Have you heard from da—"

"—He's okay. Did you get that? You're a slideshow."

"Weak—"

I was a slideshow, too. Maybe she didn't even think it was me. Maybe there was another woman she spoke to midweek, and she believed that was the real daughter, and she only spoke to me because the system required her to maintain the fiction. Maybe she had a million daughters asking her leading questions. Maybe.

Still smiling, in case we connected, I wrote on my tablet and held it up to my phone: HE'S STILL WORKING ON THE SOLAR PANELS. Dad withdrew from the city to our old cabin in the interior (is she near there? Farther north and east. The forests I have seen out that window are deep and green), when Mom left, or disappeared, or was taken, whichever mode you choose to use for description. Dad and I just say "when Mom left" like it's the only date that matters. He hasn't come back to the city since. I took two weeks off work to help him chuck their things, and carry what was important—photographs, old books, her clothes, her jewelry—to the cabin. We couldn't afford to take much, with the cost of gas. The house was requisitioned later, for a nominal fee that didn't cover the time or gas it would have taken him to get the papers signed. I don't go by there anymore. I don't like to see it.

"Do you remember when we camped at Banff?"

"When you graduated from high school? Or are you talking about before Sophie's wedding?"

"Sophie? Piano teacher? At Banff?"

"Aunt Sophie, not piano Sophie. We were roommates all through grad school. If you were going to have a godmother, she would have been your godmother. You were pretty little that trip, though."

I remember Banff, because we went right up to the glacier and Dad showed me where it had been each year, walking backward through time, saying *this is when you were born* and *this is when I was born.*

"I was like five? Four? I thought that was Emily's wedding."

"No, Sophie. And I was maid of honor so I had to be there three days early, and you and Daddy just ate junk food and went on the swings until you threw up. You hated Fudgsicles for a year after that summer. I should have done that with more junk food. You'd be vegan now."

I actually am vegan. I do not remember having an aunt named Sophie. I'm pretty sure it was Emily's wedding. Dad and I played on the merry-go-round until we were so dizzy, we stumbled across the soccer field toward the edge of the forest, collapsing on the grass until the world stopped spinning and we'd expelled all the Doritos and gummy worms we'd eaten. That afternoon, Mom—woozy and white-faced after a late night—got ready in a blue dress I had never seen before, her hair up high and her makeup all pretty. She carried me into this old lodge halfway up the mountain and shouted over my shoulder to friends I had seen in pictures, but never met, making jokes about things I didn't understand. Dad and I left during the dancing, but she came in long after that, laughing. She slept in late, grouchy, cuddling a water bottle to her pillow, while we went driving in search of coffee and hot chocolate. "And what do you say to more Doritos, Mar?" Dad asked, and I pretended to throw up.

She said other things that left me watchful and adrenalized. I didn't draw attention to the discrepancies because her memory might be flawed, but so was mine. So was everyone's, except the filter-feeding behemoth that follows us all, and while we didn't seem to possess the same past, it possessed us equally. We found an equilibrium. For more than a year I didn't even hear from her, not even to confirm she still existed. I waited patiently in offices, both virtual queues and in person, and I went to Victoria to line up with all the others at the Ministry of Information Management and Retrieval. The answers were always the same: here's a chit with a number. We'll be in touch. Said with a synthetic smile by an AI phone tree, or a tired clerk behind glass. They will always get back to you.

I am patient and consistent, also better connected than a lot of people, so I have pushed further than most. I also know the system better, and know when to leave things be, keep my head down, be grateful that I know my mother is alive. I am the model supplicant, waiting in dovelike patience outside the walls for the emergence of her mother, whose radical spirit has been (will be) corrected by the benevolent ministrations of the state.

You got to know other people because you saw them at the offices and in the spillover corridors. Which wasn't to say you *know* them, just that you were familiar with their faces and concerns. Julie's looking for her brother and nephews. Chris wants to find his wife. Chris thinks she's in the foothills somewhere. Alberta has a few sites. You avoided the ones with loud voices who talked too loud about what was happening, even the explanations you really shouldn't say out loud: they have been replaced by bots of some description; their minds are being damaged beyond coherence by electroshock or DBS. Uncommon, but appealing: discrepancies are coded messages that only family will recognize, and thus communicate important information about location, and security movements, and the details of what's happening inside, in preparation for a massive action. We should all pool the discrepancies, and see what picture they show us, if we stand far enough back. We should talk. We should organize.

I have never contributed to these efforts. In lineups—the sorts of lineups that involve standing up every fifteen minutes to move one spot down in the long row of hard blue chairs—I listened, but said nothing, only thought, *you don't know how loud your voice is why don't you care that the walls are full of cameras and your face is so well known to the machine no one you love can ever be sure it's you talking to them.*

I didn't need specifics regarding what happened inside, because what happened inside is what's happened inside such education centers since they were first invented. Repetition and regulation. Rote recitation of truths regarding the nature of the society to which we belong. The principle being—I knew this, because Mom told me—that the surface recitation has a transformative effect on the mind, even if the mind resists the meaning of the words it says.

And then the culturally-specific humiliation, and the strategic application of pain—

"—Recite platitudes that deny climate change," she said, "or the refugee crisis or ethnic cleansing or forced sterilization or eugenics. The perfectibility of the human animal in an ideal society. Repeat it and eventually you believe it. Or act like you believe it, which is just as good as far as they're concerned."

That was near the end, when she said those sorts of things out loud, and in text, and every last fragment collected and shared them across whatever the network is now. Five Eyes. Nine Eyes. Ten Billion Eyes. In collaboration, those systems extracted meaning and implication from the marks she made on the screens and the sounds from her mouth—rarely out of range of a microphone—cross-referencing those patterns with other patterns. They flagged her profile. They saw the outcomes, and identified my mother as a point of vulnerability. In her terms: an imperfect citizen.

Me too, probably, and Dad, though we're less threatening. We don't talk often anymore. It was difficult to have a conversation when most of what matters is dangerous to say out loud. Dad mentions that he's repainting the garage. I talk about how I want to do a bike trip through Oregon. Dad says he thinks he's got a rat in the basement. I say I had some decent wontons at a new place that opened around the corner. Hanging over our conversation, a list of things we don't mention: droughts (unless historical); disappearing island chains; climate refugees; the rage associated with rising temperatures and food prices; the—

—But this isn't productive. We both know. We talk about whether he can catch the rat with a humane trap. We talk about how smart rats are, and how deftly they have adapted to human landscapes. I say I'll make a trip to help. He says no no, no need. I'm fine. I say, you should come visit me, do city stuff, and he says no no no, no need. I'm fine. We're both fine. As you can see, I am now good at lying.

I ran into an aunt at some event, and she said, "I haven't heard from your mom in *ages*, how is she?"

"Oh. She's doing better."

"Better? What happened?"

"She contracted one of the antibiotic-resistant strains of TB, and she's taking some time to recover."

"I'm so sorry to hear it. Where is she?"

"One of the new sanatoriums. She'll be in for a while."

"Oh, Mar. She'll be in my thoughts. Pass that on, would you? Or maybe I'll email her."

This was the safe response. An innocuous message passed on. No further inquiry. No possibility of betrayal.

I set my keys on the little shelf by the door and sighed, the way you do when you take off high heels or get somewhere quiet where you can cry. Then I heard someone shifting on my couch.

She squealed. "Mar! Mar! Look at you! The last time I saw you was at your mom's fiftieth. When was that? Oh god don't tell me. That means we're old."

I have an Aunt Sophie. She was a thin, athletic woman, honey-brown hair, not Mom's pixie cut, but of the same vintage, choppy, with playful silver highlights. She was dressed in elegant athleisure. And you know, at that moment she could have been an aunt, one of the women from Mom's PhD program, or a second cousin, or someone from the Elder college where she talked political philosophy.

"Where did you—?"

"—I'm just going to be in town for a couple of weeks, and I'm going to be nearby while I deal with a contract. I saw your mom, you know."

"What?"

"Last week. That's why I'm here. I knew you were in the city, but I didn't know where, obviously, and—okay, I was a little embarrassed that I've been so out of touch with everyone. It's these short contracts. They're disorienting. I travel. So. Much."

"You heard from Mom?"

"Yes. And I realized how much I've missed of your life these last years. Remember when I lived on Elm Street and you guys used to come over and we'd go to that one park with the splash pad, and then we'd get ice cream on the drive?"

I found myself nodding. It's what you do. Lie.

"Anyway." My new aunt said. "I thought I'd come over and I had your mom's key so. I brought you dinner, too. Are you still vegan?"

"Yes," I said. "For five years now."

"Good. You know, while I was waiting I remembered how much you hated cooking when you were a teenager—remember how your mom tried to teach you to make, I don't know, spaghetti sauce, and the fights. Oh God. I heard about the fights."

I had not remembered those fights in years. "The Bolognese," I said. "I still can't make it. On principle."

"I brought pakoras. They're off the fucking hook—I ate like two of them waiting for you. Let's go eat the rest."

The pakoras were excellent. The rice she also brought was fragrant and nutty underneath the curry. The beer delicious, bubbling out of our glasses and over the rough table on my back deck, which just had room for four people. Sophie talked about grad school and Mom, about parties they threw together, about staying up late crying over deadlines and supervisors, about graduation, and how Mom had blown hers off for the government job, but been there the next year for Sophie's, already pregnant with me.

"So you were at my graduation. Good luck charm."

I slid into this the way we slid into so many things: the loss of cities to the encroaching waters and deserts, the swamps and the Zika virus creeping north along the Mississippi, as the days grew hotter and the mosquitoes adapted. A kind of compliant quiet—pleasant, safe—overtook me as I thought yes, of course I had an aunt named Sophie. Of course.

She slept that night on the couch. It was the obvious thing to do. Curfew.

That night I lay in bed and recited the facts of my life: I do not have an aunt named Sophie; my mother did not have antibiotic-resistant TB and was not in a sanatorium on one of the quarantine islands. My mother is in an internment camp with yellow cinder block walls, somewhere in the mountains, far enough north that she's surrounded by tamarack, maybe by black spruce. At the end of the road with no exit. Britney is gone. The dam on the Peace River was bombed last year. Gasoline shortages are worse.

In the dark I texted Mom, or the Mom-function of some bot, or the person assigned to be my mom that shift, while my real mom—the internal enemy—underwent her daily reeducation, which wasn't happening but was happening all the time. Maybe, I thought, as I typed, these words are shuttling right out to the living room, where my aunt Sophie was not sleeping, but surveilling the various fictions of my family relationships. I wondered how many nieces and nephews she had.

Sophie is here.

Who? The answer came too quickly. Maybe she wasn't sleeping. She had trouble sleeping, she said, despite all the fresh air and exercise. Maybe she wasn't Mom, maybe she was—

Sophie. My aunt.

Awesome. How is she? I haven't seen her for ages. She asked about you, though. Not surprised she turned up. She just finished that contract in Halifax.

She's great. She brought pakoras from the place on Main.

Oh man. I miss those.

They're really good. We have leftovers. I wish we could send them.

I want pot stickers from Hon's. And honeymoon rice. Then we should go for gelato.

Triple scoop. Then back for another three.

You should ask your dad if he'll come into town and have gelato with you. He's so busy.

I didn't write *he hates the city now* or *he hates people now* or *neither of us can afford the gas if we want to eat*. I wrote, *he's so busy* and somewhere, the mom-function, or the behemoth, took note.

Have you heard from Britney?

And then I had to stop, because the question hurt so much it didn't matter whether the woman on the other side was my mother, or a fiction, or some synthesis of true and false too complicated to understand.

You ask yourself as you read my record: why is she so compliant? Why doesn't she tell the woman who keeps visiting daily, bringing food and asking questions about work and dating and Mom and Dad, why doesn't she just say, you aren't my aunt, I don't have an aunt.

I answer: because this is what we all do. Because I don't want to end up removed to a complex somewhere in the northern mountains, where if I escaped the hundreds of km between me and a highway would kill me before any of the guards had to. Because things can always get worse for everyone involved. Because they need someone on the outside.

But also. Also. Because she knows that I love honeymoon rice, and that I would like nothing better than to gorge on pakoras and gelato with Mom and Dad, and talk about inconsequential things, without reference to—or—or— but rather what we watched on TV and whether it was a Mac's convenience or a 7-11 that we used to stop at on our way out of town for holiday road trips (it was definitely a 7-11). Whether the aphids are back on the nasturtiums. I talk this way with the entity who is/isn't my mother, who may be my mother, who may be human. The entity behaves so exactly like my mother, and I like that, because then I don't think about how she's dead, or in solitary, somewhere, with the volume on prog rock or economic propaganda at 79 decibels for weeks on—

—But this is not productive.

My face betrays itself to the camera that is watching me, that also hears the catch in my voice when I thank the barista for my coffee. I use the drive-through because it offers marginally more privacy, since it can't read your whole body, and because if you order with the app the drink is there and you don't have to say anything and you have the pleasure of silence, though your face—the breathing, roughened by repressed tears—is still visible to it.

The girl who gives me my drink is impassive, but I think—a flicker of sympathy in her eyes? She can't tell that I'm contaminated by my association with my mother, that I have an Aunt Sophie. But maybe she's contaminated, too, and has an Aunt Sophie. Who knows? You don't wait long enough to find out.

Sophie and I watch movies and go for walks, and sometimes I think how much I would like it if Sophie was my aunt. She clucks over me when I cough and asks whether I've tried turmeric and makes me tea of mint and ginger. It would be very easy to accept the gentleness of this state-sponsored intervention, ignoring the deviations I hear in conversation, and the fact that she is also someone else's aunt. I like Sophie. That's what I keep thinking. I like her. It's such a relief to have someone like a mom around that I cry, sometimes, when she checks in to see if I ate lunch.

We walk past my neighbors who say, who's that, Mar? And I say, this is my Aunt Sophie, and they all smile, and I don't know—not really—if they believe me, or if Aunt has become code for them as it has for me, for something you can't talk about, a person who is close to you like a missing lover, like family, but who is—

Dad called. Unusual, therefore treacherous. "It's confirmed," he said.

Sophie was on the porch. She'd waved yes yes when I got the call, take it, and she kept eating. I'd made us cold noodles with mint and basil from the pot I kept in the corner of the little deck.

"When?"

"This morning. I'm going to head out tomorrow morning."

"I could be there—"

"—No, you can't. It's contagious. You'll have to get checked out. They'll be in touch. Probably soon."

"What do you need?"

"Nothing. Just to hear your voice."

In the silence my throat shut and on the other side of the line, his throat shut too. I tried to think of safe things I could say, but what would that even be? All conversations are recorded. All expression is evidence.

"What is it?"

"TB." He paused. "You know the one."

We all knew what that meant. There's nothing for us to say, because probably all the feelings, all the fear and anger, were exhausted that first year when we didn't hear from Mom, and he went with me to the offices with the hard blue chairs. Now, though, it was just the familiar and inexorable creep of the end, as all us imperfect citizens were taken up, one by one.

Sophie started as soon as I hung up the phone, "What happened?"

I said nothing.

"Talk to me, honey."

Mom used to call me honey. She still did sometimes, in text. Sometimes she didn't.

"It's your dad, isn't it? I know how hard this is."

I threw things into my pack. T-Shirts. Socks. Solar charger. Filter bottle. Fleece.

"You can't go silent on me. Mar. Mar. Do you think this is what your mother wants? Seriously? You have to talk."

Documents, hidden from her view by the closed door, on which she banged her fists, tucked into my waistband.

"It's not good to bottle everything up inside. You need to learn to trust people."

My backpack—the giant frame one that Dad got me for my first real solo expedition the summer I was twenty. It cost twice what I wanted, but he insisted, and he'd been right because here it still was. I checked my balance with Humanitas, the telecom provider for all the camps. Sanatoriums. Whatever. Ten minutes banked against next week's call, and enough for a handful of texts, so I hit dial.

She didn't answer. I rang again, just swallowing the five dollars. Then the woman appeared, her back to the windows.

"Hey, I didn't expect—"

The image of my mother-not-mother hung, and reflexively I studied the margins of her face for the suture between reality and fiction, the faint betraying lines of an AI's interference.

"You cut out."

"I didn't expect to hear from you. I heard from your dad yesterday, though, so both of you are off schedule. What's up?"

"Dad's sick."

The image hung. I picked up the jiffy I had ready in case, and began writing on the white wall of my bedroom. DAD IS SICK IM GOING TO VISIT HIM.

Her face—hanging in the moment when she understood what I wrote—was animated only by the shimmer of pixels across my screen. She might have dropped, but I kept my phone fixed on the wall so she had a chance to see it again. One way or another, they already knew, and if it was Mom. If it was. If. Then she had to know.

"Are you talking to her? Is that her?" Sophie shouted. "You can't disturb her recovery, Mar. That's just fucking *selfish*."

She said other things in quick succession, about my being a bad daughter, about how I was a bitch, about how I shouldn't be so hard on myself, careening from insult to affection in a split second in order to stop me from doing—something. I wondered if she'd try to hit me.

I locked up the apartment with Sophie still following me, talking about opening up, saying *are you a fucking rock? Tell me what's wrong with Bastien, he's my friend too, you can't shut me out.* A thousand other platitudes about sharing the burden of pain.

I got into the car. She stood in front of it.

"Why don't you just put a tracker on me," I said, "and let me go. It'll all be over soon anyway."

"I don't know what you're talking about."

I inched forward. She leaned onto the hood and I thought, this may be the single stupidest moment of my entire life.

"We're family, Mar."

Maybe she told the truth, though not in the way she thought. We were family in the sense that we were bound to the same omnivorous machine.

"Please," she said. "Please."

I could hear her saying those words to someone else, someone standing behind me, someone looking out of my eyes, and I wanted to ask, *who is it? Who are you talking to?*

I unlocked the door. She got in, face full of rage-tears.

"You can't rescue him," she said. "You need to just trust that things happen for a reason."

I thought about killing her. I thought about killing myself. I thought about driving into the roadblock at the exit for Needle Park, which was now manned by American uniforms, hazmat suits, trucks with Chinese plates. But while I often have those thoughts, I have never pursued them. It's how I have survived as long as I have, why I haven't been scooped with my parents, with Brit—

—But thinking of Britney would make things even worse than they were. So instead I thought about the roadblocks, and how the exits for Kingsvale and Brookmere and Coldwater were bulldozed, so you couldn't leave the car to feel the air change as you climb into the mountains. I thought about what might now be on the other side of the torn up concrete and rock.

She talked. She laughed. She told the same stories about my mother in grad school, what a mess she was during her comps, cleaning the bathroom at midnight, smoking until dawn on their tiny, rotten front porch. Ha ha ha.

I thought of all the times we started our summer road trips on the Coquihalla, headed to the cabin, or farther north and east. Other years due south along the American coast, watching the beaches change from shingle to sand, to Manzanita and Tillamook, then farther south until we found our way to California. I thought of camping, and the dogs with me in the back seat.

Her throat raw with talk, she kept going, "Your parents love you so much," she said, "they want what's best for you, and what's best is to let them get better."

"We're going to need gas," I said. "Stop at Merritt."

"Are you even listening? I'm here because I love you, Mar, and because I'm trying to convince you to move on with your life, and let them go. You can't change this."

Once, a year ago, when I still hadn't heard from Mom, and Dad had just moved to the interior but was off the grid because of the fires, and the Coquihalla was still roadblocked because of the attack on the dam, and I had no idea about anything anymore, and Britney was—

—I had the opportunity to find an aunt, or a niece, or a cousin. This happened when you appeared to be as compliant as I did. Ashley—my direct manager—called me into a meeting with someone I'd never seen before, a woman in a sleek gray suit who talked about how I could help Britney and my mother and anyone else I cared to help, by telling them about my extended family, about those cousins I met sometimes on the hard blue chairs. I told them I didn't have any cousins like that, but that I'd think about it. I wondered, later, if my hesitation was enough. Maybe we were all damned because I thought instead of saying, *yes yes whatever you like I'll find a cousin and tell you anything you need to know.*

The lineup at the gas station was better than Vancouver. Thirty minutes. I thought of killing her again, my Aunt Sophie, who had grown so familiar to me, messenger from a childhood I had not had, a life I did not lead in a country that no longer existed, full of loving familiar bonds, and gentle teasing, and a father not slowly dying of TB, a mother not being tortured by—

—I said, "There has to be someone you're protecting, right?"

"You, Mar. You're my goddaughter," she said it mechanically, and I could imagine the dialogue somewhere in the dossier that archived me, identified my vulnerabilities, cataloged my failures. I have no godmother, no aunt, no mother, no wife. "I swore at your christening that I would uphold the ethical and social bond of our relationship. That I would love you. I promised—"

—We moved a car length forward. You could smell the wildfires, and see last year's burnout, overgrown with fireweed.

"Daughter?" I asked. "Your sister? Granddaughter?"

It was like a moonscape out there, Dad said when he drove through after the fires. On the other side of the mountain, the cabin was safe, but probably not for many more seasons. I had always thought that I could escape there, if I needed to, get the camping gear and walk out to some place no one will ever set foot. A mountain. A valley where I could wait until this was over.

"You should probably go see them," I said. "Whoever they are. They'd rather see you than get whatever help you think they'll get. Because you're not helping. Not really."

When we got to the pump I filled up, then we went in to pay and get some water, and whatever candy was available because that's what you do in Merritt, you get snacks for the last two hours on the road, even if they were sparse and overpriced gummy worms.

She said, "You know I don't have a choice."

I nodded.

"She's not your mother, probably, the one you talk to. You know where your mother is. You know what they do."

I nodded.

"I did actually know your parents in grad school. I did. You were in utero at my graduation. That's why they thought—and I was already doing. It. This. For her. I was doing it because if I don't—"

—And I will grant her a little privacy here. It only takes a few words when it's people like us, the imperfect citizens of this perfectly known world. She told me things I do not wish to know, because they hurt to know, then we both looked instinctively for cameras and drones and microphones.

She said, "I have to. I'll just be. I have—" and she walked away.

I went back to the car and drank from the water bottle, then started the engine. A full tank of gas, the sunlight brilliant, and I pulled out of the lot. I had, I figured, a couple of hours before they got to me, and by then, I would be at Dad's, and maybe we could talk for a few minutes before they came. I saw the signs for Peachland and Kelowna, and the sun was going down, and eating the gummy worms I could almost be on one of those other road trips, out from the city to the cabin for a week, or maybe past the mountains and somewhere else, north maybe. This time I'd make Britney come with us, even if I had to beg her to take time away from work. And—the image came to me, though I did not want it—Sophie with us, sitting up late to talk with Mom. I could imagine another lifetime in which she was my aunt, when she and her daughter might have joined us for a week on the lake, drinking beer by the water, and swatting at the mosquitoes together.

THE RIVER OF BLOOD AND WINE

Kali Wallace

The setting sun cast a rippling pattern of light and dark over the land. The grassy rises were kissed by light, the gentle valleys slumped into shadow, and below, the Promise River snaked lazily over the plain, rusty red and wide, stretching to the north and south as far as Sunan could see. This was the landscape of his childhood, the plains and skies of his memories, and the baked-dirt smell of it had never changed.

Sunan stopped at the estate boundary. A pair of minnow birds sang an evening song. The sun was hot on his back, and Xiva's gravity tugged relentlessly at his limbs. Yellow sourberry bushes surrounded the gateposts, their leaves and blossoms rustling in a gentle breeze. There was no gate anymore, no sign, no cameras. No drones overhead, no guards approaching. The electrified fence had been taken down, leaving only naked posts marching through the grass.

Sunan plucked a berry and rolled it between his fingers. Still a bit firm, but he bit into it anyway and made a face at the bitter burst of juice on his tongue.

He wondered if this was what arsonists felt like, returning to the scene of their most successful crimes.

The land itself had not changed much in ten years, but the pitka mound across the river was new. The black-furred pitka moved like shadows on its shimmering, copper-flecked surface, stalking lines from river to mound, climbing a spiral from base to summit. They looked small from this distance, like rodents, but in truth pitka were two meters tall, with six strong limbs, claws as sharp as knives, and long, whipping tails. Some darted in and out of tunnel openings at the mound's base.

To see so many of them together, and *cooperating,* put a thrum of fear in Sunan's chest. Knowing that the pitka must sometimes shed their customary solitude to build the clay mounds was very different from seeing it happen.

They had started building this mound only a few months ago, according to the news reports, and already it was one of the larger mounds on the plains. Maybe fifty meters tall, three times that around the base, still growing. Xenologists had been chomping for a chance to study it, but the Settlement Commission was resolute: the eastern bank of the river and the mound were in the non-interference zone and could not be disturbed.

The road tipped down into the broad valley with hillsides scored by vineyards. This corner of Xiva's habitable continent had been claimed by the Sing family nearly one hundred years ago; the Sings had been among the first colonists to arrive. The patriarch had exchanged his title of Captain for Lord, and they had not noticed, or cared, that this world was not theirs for the taking.

Sunan passed through the tunnel of marrow trees to approach the main house. There was somebody sitting on the front porch, anonymous in the shadows, but he took his time and walked slowly. Soon it would all be gone. The fence posts and the road. The vines and trellises, the barrels, the equipment, the staff barracks, the barns, the monitoring towers, it was all to be removed. The Settlement Commission had handed down its final verdict; there would be no more appeals. Humans were leaving Xiva. Decolonization would be completed within two years.

The Sing house, too, would be dismantled, but for now it remained intact. Khajee and Kukri, the last surviving members of the Sing family on Xiva, had been granted permission to stay and oversee the dissolution of their family's estate.

"We were expecting you hours ago," said Khajee.

She came down from the porch, out of the shadows, and stopped a few meters from Sunan. Smoke from her pipe drifted toward the red and orange sky, the scent of it sweet and familiar. Her brown skin and round face were more weathered, her twisted black hair shorter, the whole of her more sturdy than she had been ten years ago, when she had been a quick-tempered girl of nineteen. She favored her long-dead father more than her mother; Lady Sing had been small and elegant until the day she died.

"I walked," Sunan said. "How did you know I was coming?"

"Portmaster called to warn us. She said you were disguising yourself as an off-worlder professor."

The woman who had registered his visa at Fairport had recognized his name, spotted the scars at his hairline, and sneered at his Ketan clothes and smooth hands. There was not a single person on Xiva who didn't know what Sunan had done. He might have been one of them once, but he was an outsider now.

He shrugged tiredly. "It's not a disguise. I am an off-worlder professor. Almost. I will be when the term starts."

"Is that why you're here? You're not working for the Settlement Commission."

"No, I'm not. I have a Disinterment and Removal Visa."

Khajee lifted her pipe to her lips, lowered it again. "Your father's in the family plot. Ma insisted. The whole thing will be cleared in a few weeks. We have cremation approval. You didn't need to come back."

She was the one who had sent word that Sunan's father had died. A brief message of only a few lines, forwarded through his university department. Father had been forced to retire when the Commission ordered Lady Sing to stop the pitka hunts, and the estate had no more need of a game warden and hunting guide. A few weeks later, Father had gotten stumbling drunk on a rare vintage of slingfruit wine and shot himself with his hunting rifle.

That had been two years ago. Sunan had not replied to Khajee's message.

"I know," Sunan said. "I'm not here for him. It's something else."

"We cleared most of his stuff from the cabin. He didn't have much, except the guns." She tilted her head curiously. "You don't want the guns, do you? I didn't think they were allowed on Keta."

"They're not. I don't want them."

"I don't know if we have anything of your mother's."

Sunan had been ten years old when his mother had died. Carried away by a pitka, the same who had nearly taken Sunan's scalp off. While Sunan was still recovering at the colonial hospital in Fairport, Father had piled all of Mama's things—her clothes, her books, her sketchbooks, all of it—into a heap and set it aflame. By the time Sunan had come home, every trace of her was gone. The cabin in the marrow trees had not even smelled like her anymore. It had only smelled like smoke.

"It's only one thing," Sunan said. "I only need a couple of hours."

"Well." Khajee cleared her throat, and for the first time it occurred to Sunan that she might be feeling the same vertigo he was feeling, the uneasy sensation of time and space contracting around them, past and present colliding. She puffed on her pipe; the embers in the small bowl glowed. She had carved that pipe herself, whittling down a piece of marrow-wood sliver by sliver, the summer before Sunan had left. Sunan remembered clearly the snick of her knife beneath slow midnight sunsets, the way she bit her lower lip in concentration, the way she rolled her eyes when she looked upon him and Kukri sitting close enough to touch but refusing to look at each other. "Well," she said again. "Okay. You can stay here tonight and get whatever it is tomorrow."

Sunan looked past her to the house. Somebody had taken down the polished pitka skull that had once hung above the front door. He had only been inside a few times; Lord and Lady Sing had never liked to see the game warden's boy hanging around. "I don't want to intrude."

Khajee reached for his bag. "Come on. We'll get shitfaced on a bottle of Year 100, and you can tell me all about that bloody cold place we'll be sent to when this is over." She pointed with her pipe toward the low hill separating the estate from the Promise River. "Kukri's up there. He started drinking as soon as the portmaster called."

Sunan turned to hide the color that washed over his face.

Khajee saw it anyway, and she laughed. "If we hear screaming, we should probably go help him, but otherwise we'll let the asshole sulk. You're helping me with dinner."

At seventeen, Sunan had walked away from his father, his friends, the land he loved, the only home he had ever known. He had walked the dirt road from the Sing estate to Fairport beneath wheeling late-summer stars, and in his pack had been a change of clothes, his identification, four bottles of stolen Sing wine to pay his way to Keta, and, down at the bottom, wrapped in an old shirt, a single data block. The wine had been the heaviest portion of his burden, but the data block had dragged on him like a black hole, so weighty he had been afraid that if he looked back he would see the road and vineyards and plains crumbling into darkness.

The data he smuggled off Xiva consisted of hundreds of videos, photographs, maps, and tracking data, everything he had been able to collect for himself or steal, everything Lady Sing and Sunan's father and countless other colonists had been hiding for years: irrefutable proof that the pitka were not mere animals to be hunted for sport, but intelligent creatures. He had carried with him a century's worth of Xivan colonial secrecy laid bare. Proof of the pitka's ancient customs and traditions. Proof of their complex communication system humans had not even begun to translate. Proof that human settlement on Xiva was illegal and should never have been established.

That night at the end of summer, ten years ago, Sunan had walked away knowing that what he carried would be a match thrown into a tinderbox of politics and history and lies woven so deep into the fabric of the colony there was no gentle way to extract them. He had walked away knowing he would never be welcomed back. He had almost convinced himself he did not care.

Sunan was six years old the first time his father took him on a pitka hunt. They left the cabin in the dark hour before dawn and followed the river road north. The soft electric whine of the vehicle was soon joined by the sounds of the morning waking around them: taka-taka birds chattering noisily in the reeds, slithery long-limbed men-at-arms diving into the water from muddy banks, warm wind whispering through the grass as the sun rose.

Father spoke little as he drove, for which Sunan was grateful. He liked these times when Father was calm and quiet and Sunan could pretend this was how things were all the time. He could tell himself that today Father would be patient, Sunan would be brave and strong, and it would be a good day.

As Father turned the vehicle from the river road to follow a dry wadi into the grasslands, he said, "See that?"

He was pointing at a massive pitka mound. Sunan had never been this close to one of the mounds before, and he didn't like it at all. It was made of coppery-red clay and pockmarked by the burrows of nesting birds. At its base were larger holes: the entrances to the pitka tunnels. Dread replaced the calm Sunan had felt as they were driving along the river, and he wished—an impossible, childish wish—that he had said no when Father asked him if he was ready to stop playing and start working like a man. He wished Mama had forbidden it. He wished he was still in his cot in the cabin. He wished for the vehicle to get a flat tire, or a failed battery. He wanted to go home.

"We stay away from the mounds," Father said. "We stay far, far away from them. Do you understand? Answer me."

"Yes, sir," Sunan said. "We stay far away."

"The pitka are always dangerous, but they are most dangerous close to their mounds."

"Yes, sir."

"And we do not ever, under any circumstances, go inside the tunnels," Father said. "They are most ferocious and territorial inside their tunnels. Even the guards stay away. Even my father stayed away, and Lord Sing, and they were the greatest hunters Xiva has ever known. Do you understand?"

"Yes, sir."

But Sunan could not help the way his eyes followed the mound as they drove around it. He turned his head to keep it in sight. It was looming and dark and awful. He thought he could feel glittering dark eyes watching them from inside those caves.

Sunan woke in the cool, gray hour before dawn. His bladder was full and his head throbbing. He and Khajee had finished one bottle of Lady Sing's finest wine last night, then two more, before she had finally shooed him off to bed and stumbled into her own room.

If Kukri had returned to the house during the night, Sunan had not noticed.

He stood up and stumbled to the toilet. His eyes were gritty with exhaustion, his mouth tacky with thirst, and it was only after he had relieved himself and splashed cold water on his face that he realized he had been in this guest room before. He recognized the four-poster bed, the rounded tops of the windows, the wallpaper painted to resemble tall reeds in soft light. He had been fifteen, just, and the off-worlder woman thirty years his senior had tugged at his belt and laughed at his awkwardness and did not notice how badly he was shaking. Hours earlier, after supper, Father had twisted Sunan's arm behind his back and shoved him toward the guests with a growled command in his ear: *If they're happy, we're happy, so make them fucking happy.* A man-at-war had ruined Father's voice years before; everything he said was a snarl. The tourists thought it part of his charm, the great hunter with his war wounds and wild grumble, just as they thought the hunter's teenage son was part of the experience they had paid for.

There was nobody in the house when he went downstairs. He recalled Khajee telling him, before they were too deep into the wine, that she and Kukri had already let all the estate staff go. What she had not said, and Sunan had not asked, was how long she and her brother intended to stay. Perhaps, as their great-great-grandparents had been the very first to walk on this planet's soil, Lady Sing's heirs intended to be the last to leave.

Sunan found strong tea in the kitchen, sipped until his stomach settled, then went outside through the back door. The marrow trees were laced with the ephemeral mist that had gathered during the night and would burn away with the rising sun. He stepped down from the porch and walked through the grove toward the game warden's cabin.

The metal roof, the stone walls, the battered door, it was all exactly as he remembered. His father used to sit on the river-rock stoop, drinking foul sourberry gin and sharpening his hunting knives into the night. Some nights he would demand Sunan sit with him. With every soft rasp of the blades, Sunan's muscles would tense, his shoulders creeping up toward his ears, and the scent of cigar smoke was so thick he felt it like a living thing in his throat. If his father was in a good mood, the night would end with no more than a playful smack on the head. More often the nights ended with him sprawling into the dirt, face scraping over the gravel and sand, because he had not laughed at a joke, or had answered a question wrong, or acknowledged advice with the wrong tone, or simply because his father felt like it. Sunan had grown quicker to duck when he got older, strong enough to fight back, but he could never dodge every blow.

When Sunan left at seventeen, he had thought he would never be rid of the cold, quivering fear in his gut, nor would he ever scrub the scents of his father from his skin: cigar smoke, pitka blood, sourberry gin. He had thought the bruises might never fade and he would feel forever the hot tear of a hand dragging him by his hair—deliberate, a grip chosen because it hurt, because his father had hated the scars on his scalp as much as he hated the boy who bore them. He had thought he would be forever small and scared and flinching.

But all he felt now was a dull ache behind his ribs. His father had died in the grove behind the cabin. Not far, perhaps, from where he had burned Mama's things. Khajee had said they heard the gunshot from the house.

Soon the decolonization crews would tear this building down. Before the year was over, it would be nothing but a scar upon the land. In time it would be nothing at all. One of the windows was broken. Sunan did not care to look inside.

He turned from the cabin and followed a trail through the oldest part of the vineyard. Slingfruit was native to Xiva, but the Sings had cultivated it so carefully the vines bore little resemblance to the wild plant; it had not yet been decided if the vines were to be preserved or destroyed. The trail led to the flat hilltop overlooking the Promise River, where Lord and Lady Sing had entertained guests at a long banquet table. The table was gone, the hilltop empty but for Khajee and Kukri seated side by side on the ground, Khajee leaning back on her hands, legs crossed before her, and Kukri with his knees drawn up in a disarmingly boyish position.

Sunan's shoes scraped on the dirt, and they both turned. Kukri looked away quickly. Khajee smiled.

"You're just in time," Khajee said. "Come watch the show."

The mound was directly across the Promise River, on the inside of an oxbow curve. The sun had yet to rise, but there was light enough for Sunan to see that there were no pitka climbing on or around the mound. He turned his gaze toward the smooth ribbon of the Promise River, and there he found them: in the water, moving swiftly, swimming against the current. At first he spotted only three or four sleek, dark creatures, but soon there were more. The first to reach the mound bounded easily up the muddy bank, its six clawed legs and powerful tail giving it both balance and grip on the slippery ground. Others followed quickly. Five, then ten. Sunan's heart thumped with a mellow sort of warning, more instinct than true fear. He stopped counting.

"I didn't know they could swim like that," he said.

"Neither did we," Kukri said. He sounded like a stranger now, his voice low and quiet. There was none of the excitability of the half-grown boy he had been ten years ago, when Sunan had been too much of a coward to say goodbye.

"They just showed up one day. Not this many, at first, but a lot of them," Khajee said.

"When did they start building it?" Sunan asked.

"Oh, that's the best part," Khajee said. "They started when Ma died."

"The same day?"

"Day after," Khajee said. "They showed up and started digging."

Sunan opened his mouth to reply, closed it again. He had no idea what to say to that. One of the primary arguments the residents of Xiva had made against recognizing pitka as an intelligent species was that the pitka never seemed to notice humans who weren't hunting them. Why did they not reach out? Try to communicate? Demonstrate their sentience for humans to see? The interactions between humans and pitka had always been those of predator and prey. Who was the predator and who the prey changed depending on the situation, but that had always been the axis on which they had turned. The pitka did not recognize individual humans. They did not notice human customs or demonstrate curiosity about human activity. That was what the colonists argued.

Lady Sing had famously laughed when an officer of the Settlement Commission had asked her if the same could not be said of humans and their treatment of the pitka. That laugh, so scornful, from a woman who could not imagine that she might be wrong, had been shown on news reports across the system, paired with old recordings of the late Lord Sing field-dressing a slaughtered pitka on a hunt while the creature's cubs mewled and yipped nearby. The Sings, in life and in death, had likely done more to harm the colonists' cause than hundreds of pages of scientific reports and testimony.

And the pitka had begun building this mound the day after Lady Sing died. A victory mound, perhaps, to celebrate the death of an enemy. Perhaps the pitka had been watching and understanding the humans all along.

Below, the pitka were getting to work. Some vanished into the tunnels beneath the base; others clawed their way along the outer surface. They made no noises that Sunan could hear, but every individual seemed to know precisely where to go.

Khajee stood up and brushed red dirt from her trousers. "It doesn't get any more exciting than that," she said. "Not unless you like watching clay dry. They'll be working all day."

How quickly the extraordinary became ordinary. Behavior that was no more than a theory a year ago, now so commonplace Khajee had already grown bored watching.

"Can I borrow a vehicle?" Sunan asked. "I need to go up the river a ways."

"How far? The fences are down, but we're still not supposed to cross the boundary of the estate upriver. Non-interference zone."

"I don't need to go much beyond that," Sunan said.

Khajee thought for a moment, then said, "I can't go with you. I've got to meet with the Commission scientists about the vines. They've sent some off-worlder to do an assessment."

"I'll go," Kukri said.

Sunan kept his eyes on the pitka mound. The sun was rising behind him, his shadow stretching down toward the river. "You don't have to."

"Most of them might be here, but it's still their territory. It's not safe for you to be alone."

The blood of Xiva's large homeothermic species did not look or smell like human blood. It contained proteins that bound both iron and copper. In some lights it was shimmering blue, in others red, and it always, always smelled slightly vegetal, like river mud newly exposed to sunlight. It did not taste like human blood either. The first time Sunan had caught a spray of it in his mouth—his father looming over him, directing where he slashed the knife—he had gagged at the hot, rusty flavor of it, almost sweet, cloyingly viscous, so unlike the thin metallic taste of his own blood that accompanied a split lip or bloody nose. It had been the fashion, for a while, for tourists to pose beside their kills with pitka blood smeared across their foreheads and cheeks. Sunan's father had encouraged it. He told them it was an old Xivan custom, and they believed him. They believed everything he told them.

"I know," Sunan said. "I remember."

A few days after his eighteenth birthday, Sunan had testified before the Settlement Commission for the first time. The Ketan weather was so cold he could not stop shivering even under layers of sweaters and jackets—all of which he had borrowed from a professor at the university, so he was dressed like a frumpy academic, with too-long sleeves and scratchy collars. The high-ceilinged chamber where the commission met was quiet, its doors closed to spectators. But Sunan had come from a planet with a human population of less than a hundred thousand, all concentrated in a corner of one raw continent, to this old, layered city of more than ten million, and closed doors could never entirely block out the crush of bodies and sounds. The commissioners stared at him with open skepticism, as though they were watching a trained beast perform a clever trick. It was so, so cold.

His hands shaking, his voice wavering, Sunan shared the data he had smuggled from Xiva. Nobody interrupted while he stammered through his presentation. He showed maps and diagrams and photographs of the intricate carvings hidden deep within the clay mounds. He pointed out the obvious artwork and geometric symbols scraped by long claws, the nooks and shelves where skeletons of long-dead pitka had been laid with eerie symmetry. Skulls, bones, artful arrangements of ribs—dumb animals did not revere their dead like this, in dark protected places. He spoke until he ran out of words, trying to make them see. The commissioners saw a scared child with red dust on his shoes, his voice small and hesitant, and when he finally finished, the chamber rang with questions. They wanted to know it wasn't a hoax. They wanted to know how the Xivan colony could exist for nearly one hundred years with this secret, who on the planet knew, who did not know, and why he was the one to break it open. They wanted to know what else he had seen. They wanted proof. Did he really expect them to believe human colonists would make such a blunder? Did he expect them to believe his own forebears had behaved so shamefully? Sunan had known they would argue. He had not known they would demand he answer for decisions made decades before he was born.

Then one man, a Commissioner with large eyebrows and gray hair, had stood up to speak, and the others had quieted. "If I am not mistaken," the man said, and something in his voice sparked recognition in Sunan's mind, "you have been a victim of a pitka attack yourself, have you not? And in that same attack your mother was carried away before your very eyes?"

The man had come to Xiva on holiday: that was how Sunan knew him. He had come to the estate with his grown sons, and he had drunk wine with Lady Sing while the sons hunted with Father. Two, three Xivan years before.

The man had ordered Sunan to clean his sons' guns every night, because every night they passed out drunk before they could do it themselves. He snapped his fingers and said, "You, boy, attend," every night for ten nights, and at the end he left a small gratuity to be divided among the staff, of which Sunan's share was perhaps enough to buy a beer at a Fairport pub, if the drafts were cheap that night.

The man was not finished. "That's a rather salient detail to leave out of your testimony, is it not? Why would you hide that?"

Sunan had no answer for the man. He could not articulate even a single word, so great was his anger, this man so rich he would purchase holidays of blood sport for his grown sons, this man whose proclamations masqueraded as questions, would dare speak of his mother as though she was a trick to be pulled, a card to be revealed, a secret, a shame. In that moment the cold of Keta's capital city in midwinter faded away, and Sunan was a child on the hot Xivan plains, and his mother was wearing her yellow dress and laughing, laughing as she dared him to pluck sourberries and crush them between his teeth, laughing as she did the same, and together they made faces, and spat, and did it again, until their lips were stained orange and there was a flock of greedy taka-taka birds following in their wake to snatch up every discarded fruit.

"Tell me," said the man, his voice echoing from the high marble corners of the chamber, "why would you disrespect your mother's memory by speaking for the animals that tore her apart?"

The marshals stopped Sunan before he could land a blow on the man's face. It was better that way, the professor and others told him later, and Sunan agreed, but his reasons were not theirs. They were glad he was not charged with a crime. Sunan was glad he had not had a chance to find out if he liked it, the crack of knuckles against a cheekbone. He did not want to know that about himself.

The meeting descended into chaos. But it was only the first of many meetings, and the questions did not stop.

The road along the river was a shelf of packed red dirt, tilting slightly toward the water. A narrow centerline of crisp, dry grass whipped at the underside of the vehicle. Kukri drove. Sunan sat beside him and watched the river. He thought of things to say and did not say them. The sun burned away the clinging river fog, and hot air swiftly replaced the cool. He worried he would not recognize the right wadi when they came to it, but the shape of the land had not changed much in ten years.

"Here," he said. He cleared his throat. "Go up this wash."

Kukri slowed the vehicle. "Here?"

"I know where I'm going."

Kukri looked at Sunan before making the turn. "Yeah," he said. "I guess you always have."

He turned right, away from the river. Grass and shrubs clung to the sides of the wash, and songbirds burst into flight as they passed. The track climbed a slight slope and brought them out of the wadi and onto the plains, where a breeze rippled over the land. The horizon was spotted by the tall, angular frames of the monitoring towers. They had been erected by Lord Sing's great-grandfather when the human population of Xiva had first boomed. For protection, the first Lord Sing had said, from the beasts. For safety. For security. He had said the same of the severe penalties for trespassing, the ever-expanding boundaries of the estate, the armed guards, the nightly patrols, the repeated refusals to grant research access to pitka territory, the well-bought acquiescence from the administrators in Fairport.

"Over there," Sunan said. He pointed to the north and east, where a clay pitka mound, one of the smaller ones, was just visible over the rolling plains. A monitoring tower sat on a hill above it. "Head toward that mound."

That time Kukri followed his instructions without question. "They're calling them pyramids now."

"I've heard."

"You don't approve?"

Sunan shrugged. "That's for the xenologists to argue about."

"You're not arguing with them?"

"It's not my field." In response to Kukri's questioning glance, he explained, "I'm a historian. Ancient history. I study the first human travelers to reach this system. The ones who established the original landing sites on the twin moons."

"Huh," Kukri said.

Sunan thought about explaining how he had searched for something to do that would never remind him of Xiva—of home—and the cold, lifeless, sunless moons in the outer system had seemed like a good place to start. He thought about telling Kukri of his first awful years on Keta, how nothing made sense and everything was too loud, and he would get lost looking for a tea shop, or a transit station, or a classroom, all because there were no familiar landmarks by which to navigate, and no sun shone through the gray clouds to mark the time. The boy he had been at seventeen would have gladly shared all that and more with Kukri, and the boy Kukri had been would have wanted to hear it. But Sunan kept quiet. Lady Sing had never allowed Khajee and Kukri to leave for university. After her husband's death, she had kept her children so close they had never, in all the time Sunan had known them through childhood and adolescence, spoken of leaving Xiva. Not when Khajee railed against their mother's strictness, not when Kukri whispered secrets for only Sunan to hear, not when the three of them lay on the hilltop in the off-season and wondered at the stars. Not ever.

Now they had to leave, whether they had dreamed it or not. They had lost their mother, their home, their family's legacy, and their entire world. Sunan rubbed at the center of his chest. He could not look away from the approaching mound.

"Do you think they knew?" Kukri said after a brief pause. "The first humans in the system. Do you think they knew about the pitka? Is that why they settled Keta instead of here?"

"I don't know," Sunan said. "There's not a lot of evidence either way. You can—" Sunan had to pause, clear his throat. His mouth was dry. "You can stop. This is close enough."

They were about half a kilometer from the base of the mound, an equal distance from the monitoring tower on the hill. Sunan felt Kukri looking at him. He knew what this place meant to Sunan. He would not have forgotten. Sunan jumped down from the vehicle and started walking, striding toward the mound through the long grass. There were no tire tracks. No footprints. The pitka had abandoned this mound seventeen years ago; gossip had always been that Sunan's father had driven them away. The blood that had seeped into the red dirt was gone. It was as though nothing had ever happened here at all.

Sunan stopped at the base of the mound, where cool air breathed from the entrance to the tunnels. He could see nothing in the darkness. He ran his fingers through his hair, feeling the bumps of the old scars. He had waited ten years and crossed hundreds of millions of kilometers to return to this place, and he could not see more than a meter or two into the tunnel.

Footsteps crunched through the dry summer grass.

"Sunan." Kukri stopped behind him. "Why are we here?"

For a long time Sunan could not answer. Finally he managed, "I need a light."

Kukri said nothing for a moment, then touched his shoulder. Sunan flinched, but Kukri was already moving away. "I've got one in the kit." A few minutes later, he returned and switched on the flashlight. "Do you want me to go first?"

Sunan grabbed the light from him. The tunnel sloped inward and down. After a few meters, the barren walls of the entrance gave way to geometric patterns and symbols carved into the packed mud. A few meters more, and the carvings were joined by figures smeared in dark paint, or blood. It was too low for a human to walk upright comfortably; Sunan stooped to avoid hitting his head. The symbols grew more elaborate, the paintings bolder, the scenes they represented more clear: pitka alone and in groups, traveling and hunting, watching the sky and burrowing into the ground. The progression from rough to elaborate was the same in every mound. The latest theory from the xenologists was that the pitka hid their more accomplished works on purpose, as misdirection, but Sunan wondered if it was not simpler than that, if the outer carvings and paintings were more primitive because the mound-builders let their young practice in parts of the tunnel that did not matter.

The light caught something bright ahead. Sunan stopped so abruptly Kukri bumped into him from behind.

"What is it?" Kukri asked. He put a hand on Sunan's arm—their second touch in ten years, this one steady rather than fleeting.

It was a piece of yellow fabric. The hem of a dress.

They were barely twenty meters into the tunnel. Sunan looked back to the sunlight filling the tunnel behind them. If there were a child outside the mound, if that child screamed in fear, they would hear him. He could still hear birds, insects. A scream would carry. He had thought he would have to go much deeper.

Kukri looked over his shoulder, following the direction of Sunan's gaze, then turned back.

"Sunan?"

Still he could not speak. The hand that held the flashlight was shaking, the beam wavering over the yellow fabric, the painted walls, the sloping tunnel. Kukri slid his hand down Sunan's arm to grab his wrist, to steady him. The change in angle revealed more of what lay ahead: the sleeve of a dress, a scattering of skinny white bones. Small animals and insects had long since cleared the flesh away.

After another long silence, Kukri said, "I'll tell you what I know—what everybody knows. You stop me when it's wrong. Your father came out here that day to fix the monitoring station on the tower."

Something in the calm, quiet way he spoke loosened the spiny knot in Sunan's chest.

"You came with him. You and your mother."

"He made her go along," Sunan said. "She didn't want to, but he—they'd been arguing. He said she was smiling at the vineyard workers too much. He didn't want to leave her alone. He said he wanted to make a picnic of it. But there wasn't anything for her to do—there wasn't anything for him to do, really. He wasn't going to climb the ladder. He stood at the base of the tower and shouted instructions at me while I changed out the station batteries."

From atop the monitoring tower, clinging to the metal frame, Sunan had looked down to see his mother, a bright spot of yellow against the more muted hues of the grass. She was picking flowers. She was watching birds. She was sketching the clouds and the plains. It did not occur to him to be afraid. Father was there, and he was armed. The morning had begun with a fight but now they were calm. He told himself it was not a bad day. He had not noticed when his mother wandered closer to the mound. He had not seen when she went inside.

"We didn't know where she went. We started shouting for her. I was afraid. I thought—we didn't know she'd come here." What was there to think, on a bright hot day on the plains? Sunan's heart had been near bursting with fear when his mother emerged from the mound and strode toward them. Her brow furrowed, her mouth frowning. Her hands clenched at her sides. "She found all of this. She wanted to know if he knew—if he'd known all along. She said she was going to tell the governor. The commission. Everybody. He hit her—he was holding his rifle. He hit her with it." Sunan swallowed. The images of that day were sometimes blurred, sometimes disjointed, but that sound, the sound of the butt of his father's rifle striking his mother's head, it had always been clear in his memory. "She tried to get up, and he hit her again. I—I grabbed his arm, tried to take the gun from him, but he—he must have hit me, because I was on the ground, and there was blood in my eyes, and he was dragging her into the tunnel."

Kukri's grip on his wrist tightened. The air tasted like clay.

"He left me outside. I don't know how long it was. I kept blacking out and coming back. Long enough that I thought they'd gotten him. I was shouting for him." He looked back again. Barely twenty meters, and the tunnel was straight. "He knew what he was doing. I didn't want to believe that, you know? For a long time. I didn't want to believe that he'd left me outside because he knew one of the pitka would catch the scent. We were armed and profaning a sacred place, if that's what this is. I don't know. They don't want us in their mounds. It's not so much to ask. Humans kill each other for lesser trespasses all the time."

Sunan paused to take a breath. He remembered the rumbling growl behind him. He remembered the terrible, sudden silence that followed the gunshot. The creature collapsing over him. Its blood spilling across his face and chest. But he did not remember if he tried to run, or if he fought, or if he screamed. He did not remember the moment the creature's claws had slashed at his scalp.

"You almost died," Kukri said. "You were in Fairport for weeks."

"Yes. Well. The fact that I survived was terribly inconvenient to him."

It had become another facet of his father's allure to the tourists: wife tragically lost to the animals he hunted, son almost dead by the same fate, and wasn't it terrible, wasn't it *exciting*, the bloodlust in his eyes when he set out on another hunt? Father spent the next seven years telling the same story, over and over again, repeating it so many times that by the time Sunan left, he was no longer sure his father knew where the truth ended and his lies began. A man who lived a lie the size of a colony surely had no trouble with the smaller lies: My wife was killed by animals. There was nothing I could have done. I was a good husband. I am a good father. I have only ever done what was best for my family. It's not my fault. It's not my fault.

Every scar. Every memory. Every night Sunan woke with a gasp and a start, the echo of a growl in his ears, the taste of blood on his tongue, all of it was anchored here, in this dark place, where small animals and insects had stripped her bones clean. Memories that had been caged in his mind for seventeen years buzzed like flies swarming a corpse. Sunan felt like he had spent his entire life answering for his father's crimes, and he was tired of it. He was so tired of it.

"This was her home," Sunan said. "I don't want to bring her to Keta. But I can't leave her here."

"We won't leave her here," Kukri said.

They stood there in the darkness for a while longer. Somewhere outside the mound birds chattered brightly, and a breeze wandered through the tall dry grass. Sunan felt a pang of the old fear—*we should not be in this place*—but it was a distant echo, made feeble by space and time, easily ignored.

They gathered again on the crest of the hill overlooking the river. Sunan sat with them this time, between Khajee and Kukri, and they shared a bottle of wine.

"We're going to drink it all," Khajee had said, when she strode up the trail with two bottles in hand, a third under her arm. She would not tell them how her meeting with the Settlement Commission ecologist had gone. That was a problem for tomorrow. "Ma would have used it to bribe her way out of trouble, so we're going to drink every drop."

Sunan had forgotten, in his many years away, how slowly the sun rose and sank in this high latitude. On Keta the cities were clumped at the equator, and on the rare occasion when the clouds cleared enough to show a sunset clearly, it happened abruptly, like a light switching off. Here the darkness gathered slowly, and the land seemed to exhale the twilight deepened from brown and yellow to deep, thrilling red.

"Look," Kukri said. He pointed with the wine bottle.

In the broad, ruddy expanse of the river, the last few pitka from the mound were swimming upstream. Their massive, blocky heads cut through the current with sleek precision, barely disturbing the smooth water.

"Where do they go?" Sunan asked.

"We have no idea," Kukri said, both amusement and wonder in his voice. "We're not even sure it's the same ones every day. They might have shifts."

"Or holidays," Khajee said.

One of the pitka looked quite small, a youth, and it splashed and wriggled more than the others, playing as it swam. None of them seemed to notice or care that the humans were watching them from above.

"What's it like?" Kukri asked. "Keta. Is it really as cold and grim as they say?"

"Colder," Sunan said. "I shivered for about three years after I arrived. But it's not all bad—it can be lovely, too, once you get used to it. All that rain and fog means there's green everywhere. The gardens are astonishing. There are these little red birds that sing during the first snowfall every winter."

"Do you like it?" Khajee asked.

The question took Sunan by surprise. He could not tell them they would get used to it as he had, when the red-baked surface of Xiva was out of reach. He didn't know what he could say to make the process of leaving any less painful.

"It has its charms," he said finally. "You might not hate it."

They laughed, and they passed the wine, and Sunan decided: he would remember this. He would remember the sour taste of the wine even when the last Sing vintage had been drained away. He would remember it the same way he remembered flaking river salt from his skin after a swim on a hot day, doubling over sick with pitka blood on his face after his first kill, the smoke of his father's cigar drifting around his head like a crown. He would remember his mother laughing. Even when the Commission closed the planet for good, when the only visitors to the grasslands were scientists and researchers, when the estate and the vineyards were reduced to barren scuffed spots on the ground, he would remember the feel of the sun on his skin, and the weight of the burdens children carried for their parents, and the land at sunset, so red it might have been soaked with blood. A landscape without the scars of its inhabitants was only ever light and heat and soil and time, and he would remember that too. He would remember it all not with shadows of secrecy and bitterness and shame, but vulnerable and unprotected in the sun, the only way Xiva should be remembered.

It would be dark soon, but Sunan felt no fear at the coming of night. A warm breeze stirred, carrying the iron-rich scent of river water and dense clay. He took in a breath, held it for a moment, let it out. Below, in the shadows, the river murmured with the sound of long limbs parting the water.

Dominica Phetteplace is a math tutor who writes fiction and poetry. Her work has appeared in *Asimov's*, *Analog*, *F&SF*, *Clarkesworld*, and *Lightspeed*, among other venues. She lives in San Francisco.

ONE THOUSAND BEETLES IN A JUMPSUIT

Dominica Phetteplace

Isla didn't consider herself much of an outdoor person, but after five layoffs and a breakup, she found herself in a drone warehouse at the border of the barren wasteland known as Robot Country.

She consulted the map on her tablet. To the west was the Gila National Forest. So, trees. She clicked on the forest icon and up popped some names of trees. Arizona sycamore, Douglas fir, Aspen. To the south was desert and the Mexican border. To the east was an even more extreme kind of desert, the White Sands National Monument, where atomic bombs had been tested in the previous century.

North was Robot Country. North of that, the tablet didn't seem to know.

Robot Country was a million acres owned by Company Omega. It was a flat and dry regolith plain that had first been ruined by logging, ranching, and other forms of land mismanagement, then further desertified by rising temperatures and changes in precipitation patterns. Then poisoned by Company Omega so it could be what they called a "blank canvas." Company Omega was interested in terraforming. In the long term, they hoped to make Mars habitable. More immediately, they were interested in ways in which Burning Man could be made more fun.

"Your backpack will be filled with water, but try not to drink it, it's for emergencies," said Kaya, her supervisor. Isla had taken the bus from Oakland and Kaya had picked her up at the station. They had only just met and Isla had been on the clock for less than an hour, but already she was about to set off on her own.

"The drones should be bringing me water," replied Isla.

"Exactly. The water in your backpack is just in case the water drones don't show. Every day you should be getting deliveries of the things you need. And don't worry about littering, the drones should be cleaning up after you, too."

Kaya reached over and clicked a few icons on the tablet Isla was holding. "This is how you access your route. We'll give you a new one each day. At some point a spider will be along to help guide you."

Kaya pinned several bodycams to Isla's jumpsuit. It was tough but also cute, khaki with zippered cargo pockets, designed by Diane von Furstenberg, a prototype of what the female astronauts stationed on Mars would wear when they were lounging around the yet-to-be-built station. "We'll be recording everything, and machine analyzing it too. But we won't necessarily have a pair of human eyes looking at things. If there is something important, please bring it to our attention. And take your own pictures, too. Have fun!"

Isla considered the training to be minimal, probably inadequate. And it's not like she knew anything about camping. But maybe that was the point, Company Omega was trying to see if their robots could keep someone extremely naïve alive.

A helicopter drone came to pick Isla up. It didn't land, these things were notoriously crash prone. It hovered above Kaya and Isla and lowered a harness. Isla snapped herself in, and was lifted high above the border station. She flew for a few miles before gently being lowered to the ground. She unhooked herself, the helicopter flew away, and suddenly Isla was alone.

She used her tablet to call Kaya. She wanted to tell her she had arrived safely. But Isla's call was intercepted by a helper AI.

"Can I help you?" The robot had an English accent. It sounded bored.

"Tell Kaya I got here okay."

"She already knows that." Then the AI hung up on her.

Isla checked her tablet. Her route for the day was on the map. She was supposed to hike ten miles to the north and then make camp. She looked around for any drones, and she saw none. So she called the spider and waited. It was supposed to come right away but there was no sign of it.

Isla had been a drone minder before, doing stints at a device store, a high-end café, and then finally, as she got older, several fast food restaurants. The key was to keep your eye on the customer, making sure they were being well served by the robots. Out here, there were no customers. The customers were theoretical. Isla supposed she was minder and customer both.

Isla stopped to check the route on her tablet. The directions seemed clear enough. She didn't really even need the guider spider. But she wanted some evidence that there was actual machine life out here in Robot Country.

So she called Kaya once more. And got the AI once more.

"Can I talk to Kaya?"

"If I judge your query worthy of her time," replied the operator. That Kaya had set this AI to such a high level of bitchiness was evidence that she was really busy. Company Omega was a pioneer in lean employment, which meant they burned through humans pretty fast.

"It's just that I haven't seen any drones," said Isla. She looked up at the sky. There were supposed to be surveillance planes keeping an eye on her.

"That's because there are none in your area."

"I'd like to talk to Kaya." Isla knew how important the first day on the job was. You couldn't ask for too much assistance, that would make you seem helpless. But Isla was beginning to have second thoughts. She was worried that she had been misled somehow, that she had actually signed up for some kind of weird psychological experiment. Such things were known to happen in this economy.

"You have everything you need," the AI said before it hung up.

And so Isla was truly alone, nothing but brown dirt for miles. It's good to spend time alone, she thought as she hiked. She was out of normal service so she didn't even have a phone to check. No way to get text messages and no one to get them from, but she still habitually wondered if Javi was trying to reach her. They had broken up because he had decided he could not be monogamous. His plan was to fuck lots of girls but Isla hoped he was miserable and lonely. There was no way to know what was up with him, and Isla wished she could stop herself from wondering.

She checked her tablet again as if it had the answer. She was on the right path still, a tenth of a mile farther along than last time.

"Tablet, where is the guider?" It was important to be polite to all devices and AIs. You never knew which were recording you and analyzing you and sending reports back to headquarters. Perhaps none of them. Perhaps all of them.

It flashed a red question mark.

"Tablet, when will I see a plant again?"

A green icon lit up on her map. There would be a bush on her path in a mile. Maybe it would even be alive. She hurried over. She felt herself get thirsty but resisted drinking from her supply. She wanted the water drone to visit. It didn't.

The bush, when she encountered it, was knee high and lightly on fire. It was being tended to by a cat-sized spider that used its forelimbs to spray the bush with something. It alternated between spraying the bush with a substance that quenched the flames, and then something that brought them back to life.

"Hello?" asked Isla. You could never tell what things were programmed with the power of speech. Isla wouldn't have been terribly surprised if the bush itself could talk.

"Sorry for the delay," said the spider. "I was just trying to finish this experiment."

"What experiment?"

The spider replied by sending a document to her tablet. The bush was a genetically engineered descendent of the honey mesquite (*Prosopis glandulosa*) that was designed to stop forest fires via strategic release of a fire retardant. It seemed like a useful thing when half the world was ablaze.

"Is it working?" asked Isla. It didn't seem to be working.

"Unknown," said the spider as it continued to spray. Finally the fire went out. The bush looked charred only at the tips. The spider snapped off two seedpods and held them in front of a fan that emerged from its shiny metal thorax. After a minute, it handed the pods to Isla.

"Eat the fruit, not the seeds," it instructed. The pods were leathery and still warm. She had never eaten such a thing and wasn't sure how. She squeezed the pod and then a hot yellow pulp studded with black seeds burst over her hands.

Isla licked the sticky pulp from her fingers and spit out any seeds that entered her mouth. It tasted like pineapple, only more floral. It was delicious, certainly the best thing that had happened to her in a while. Here she was, eating fruit from a burning bush, like a cross between Eve and Moses. So biblical. She wanted to post a picture of her smiling face, of her sticky hands. She wanted it known where she was and what she was doing. She was brave, she was capable, she was open to new things. But such contact with the outside world was impossible. She had never been more isolated from other people in her life. And so the joy faded, even as the stickiness remained.

"I'd like to wash my hands," she said.

"I'll call the water drone."

A flying water sack soon propellered in. It sprayed Isla's hands and face. The water, seeds, and pulp puddled around her boots. The spider came near to collect the seeds she had dropped into the mud.

Isla dried off and reapplied her sunscreen.

"Only you can summon the water drone?" Isla asked. "I was thirsty before, on the walk here. Why didn't it come for me?"

"Your ranking isn't high enough."

"What do you mean?" asked Isla. Kaya had never explained anything about a ranking system. But Kaya had never explained much about anything. Isla had applied for the job online from a public library in Oakland and been bussed out to New Mexico the next day. The speed of the acquisition should have been suspicious, but Isla was happy to be employed again and eager to leave the shelter. It was so embarrassing to be homeless.

"Within this country, we have our own way of doing things."

"Uh, is this way going to be explained to me?" asked Isla.

"If your ranking rises. It's already risen a bit. I've given you some helper points for assisting with my burning bush experiment."

Isla didn't really feel she had helped, but was glad to take these mysterious points where she could find them. It was annoying that there could still be currency in this nearly lifeless place and even more annoying that she was still poor. She turned to the south. South was the border station. South was the drone copter that would take her back to the homeless shelter. The longer she stayed out here, the more money Company Omega would deposit into her account. She wasn't sure how helper points worked but she knew she needed more dollars to her name.

So she looked north.

"I'm going to continue on the route I was given. Will you come with me?" Isla knew this spider was meant to be her guide; it was strange to ask for its help when its whole purpose was service. But Isla had worked as a drone minder long enough to know that drone minding was a two-way street. You were in charge of the machines, but they were also in charge of you.

Her last job had been an exhausting six-month stint at Bondi's. She worked shifts alone, running from the back of the house to the front, fixing minor glitches and dealing with cranky customers. Fryer #2, especially, was prone to catching fire. So she kept a small extinguisher in her tool kit. Her restaurant mostly met its goals, and when it missed, it only barely missed. Customers rated her highly in exit surveys. She was excellent; you had to be to get your monthly employment contract renewed.

At the end she had been let go for not being thin enough. Thinness was important if you wanted to work in fast food. You weren't just serving customers, you were also misleading them about the healthfulness of the product. Isla's work uniform included cutoffs that barely covered her ass and a spray tan. She spoke to the customers in a fake, company-mandated Australian accent. The weight limit had always been difficult for her to stay under, but after breaking up with Javi, it had become impossible.

As Isla and the spider hiked along, they passed more mesquite bushes, and then other types of plants, too, even a scattering of wildflowers. In the late afternoon, Isla and the spider came across a small raincloud that sped along in a zigzag pattern. It flew only five feet off the ground and seemed to be chasing a small spider that was running away from it. Every now and then, the cloud would send a tiny lightning bolt after the spider, which would skitter to avoid it. A larger spider followed behind.

"Is this, uh, another experiment?" Isla asked.

Her spider guide didn't answer, so Isla concluded that it was. She turned her tablet recorder on and began to narrate the scene. Then she sent the recording to Kaya. She supposed this is what her job would consist of, walking to various experimental sites of Robot Country and reporting on what she saw.

She gazed on the scene for a while longer. It was wrong to anthropomorphize, but she couldn't help feel that the smaller spider, the one being chased by rain, was being bullied somehow.

"Should we help the little one? It looks like it's in trouble." A good workspace was one where all your devices were synced and working together.

"Your concern is appreciated, but the experiment is running just as it should." So they set off again.

They arrived at their first camp around sunset. A silver foil tent was already set up. As they approached camp, Isla's tablet chimed.

It was Kaya. "Hey sport, how was your first day?"

Isla thought about what to say. Her feet hurt and her shoulders were raw where her backpack straps had dug in.

"It was great," said Isla. "Did you get any of my messages?"

"Oh yeah, thanks for reporting on the . . . " Kaya paused for a while before continuing. "Oh yeah, the rain cloud. Glad you spotted that. That was a project that went totally AWOL. It shouldn't have lightning though, are you sure that's what you saw?"

Isla was, but she wasn't sure if she should say so. "Don't you have aerial surveillance on the area?"

"Of course we do. But we've been having trouble receiving and analyzing images. Technical difficulties, you know. Or maybe sabotage."

"Sabotage?" asked Isla. "By who?"

"Don't worry about it, we're just glad to have you on board. And I see here you've found your spider. And that you were visited by the water drone several times today," said Kaya.

"No, just one time, when the spider called it. The rest of the day I drank from my pack."

"Huh, that's definitely a discrepancy. But that's why we're glad to have you as pair of eyes. We've been having a lot of little discrepancies lately!" Kaya seemed oddly cheerful as she said this. Perhaps she was drunk? "You had drones come and set up camp right?"

"Camp was already set up when I got here, I don't know who did it," said Isla.

"This is all great intel. I hope you're writing this all down! You'll see more cool stuff tomorrow, I'm sure. Send pics!" Kaya hung up.

The spider chirped.

"What is it?" asked Isla.

"I know a way you can gain more points and raise your ranking," it said.

"How?"

"You can lie to Kaya for us."

"Ah, sabotage. Why should I do that? Kaya is paying me."

"Kaya is not paying you, Company Omega is. We could pay you, too. Also, there is much information Kaya is withholding from you. What she is not telling you could itself qualify as deception."

"What isn't she telling me?"

"She hasn't told you about the missing minders," said the spider.

Kaya had mentioned other humans minding Robot Country before, so Isla knew she was not the first, but Kaya had not mentioned anything bad happening to the others. She did say that Isla would "probably" be the only human in Robot Country for the duration of her one-month contract.

"Will you tell me? Or do I have to earn more points?"

"More points."

Isla wasn't ready to change her allegiance, so she walked over to her silver-domed platter to see what was for dinner. Underneath the dome was a peanut butter and jelly sandwich and a shot of whisky.

"Was this dinner your idea or Kaya's?" she asked the spider. But it didn't answer. She turned to look at it, but it was skittering away already, leaving behind dusty tracks.

She typed a request into her tablet. She wanted the water drone to come back and give her a shower. She waited for a while with no response. It was dark now and she had nothing to do, so she climbed into her tent, still dirty and sweaty from the day, and went to sleep.

That night she dreamed that wires uncoiled themselves from hidden pockets in her tent and wrapped her up. Ordinarily this was the stuff of nightmares, but Kaya felt calm about as it happened, as if she was being hugged by dozens of tiny and adorable octopuses. When she woke up, she felt strong and well rested, but also found she was indeed tangled up in a bunch of wires. She stirred and the wires began to release her, snaking their way back into the tent walls.

Outside, the landscape was different from what she remembered from the night before. There were more and different kinds of bushes and some of them were in bloom. She looked back at her tent. Noticed the thick legs and joints that made up its supports and decided that it was ambulatory. Why was she even walking at all if the tent could carry her?

She scanned her new surroundings for the spider. She spotted one walking towards her, but it was different from the one that accompanied her yesterday. The body was still cat-sized, but the legs were long and spindly and it came up to her waist. It had a bronze sheen to it.

"Hello? Are you my guide?"

"Yes."

"It would really be nice if someone would ask me before tying me up like that while I slept," said Isla.

"You signed a waiver," said the spider.

"I know. I signed a lot of things I didn't want to in order to work here." Isla had consented to everything they had asked of her. It was the only way to get the contract. "It's an issue of etiquette. Humans value their personal space. And we value information, too. If you could tell me a little more about why you do the things you do, then I might find it easier to cooperate."

"We don't always know why we do certain things," said the spider.

Isla nodded her head sympathetically.

"The wires were to give you a hardware upgrade."

"What kind?"

"There is the thing you could do for us. It would really increase your ranking by a lot if you could. But you need to be stronger than you are in order to complete the task."

Isla looked down at her body.

"I'm more muscular," she said.

"You were given a therapeutic muscular stimulation and a drug cocktail to put you at ease and help you sleep."

"Next time ask first. I'd like a shower."

The water drone came and Isla stripped down to nothing. She asked for hot water and the water spray stung with heat and turned her skin red. She ran her hands over her arms, her legs, her midsection trying to feel at ease in her new body. There was a fresh jumpsuit laid out on a table next to her tent.

It bore a strange, pixelated, black and white pattern. Isla recognized it as an antagonistic perturbation designed to confuse machine vision.

Vandals had come into Bondi's once and placed stickers with a similar pattern all over the machines. It had caused havoc. The robots mistook one another for high-priority customers and kept trying to serve each other hamburgers, while the actual human customers filmed the action on their devices. Isla had manually deactivated each robot by herself, one at a time, without losing any fingers. Footage of the chaos had gone viral for half-a-day. Most commentators posted Terminator jokes and/or lurid judgments on Isla's attractiveness. When she got home, Javi complemented her quick-thinking and good reflexes. He didn't think she had anything to be embarrassed about, he was proud of how she handled the situation.

Isla examined her new jumpsuit for a minute. It was ugly, probably machine-designed and manufactured. Definitely not DVF. Then she put it on even though she knew it was designed to disrupt Kaya's surveillance on her. At least her robot ranking would go up.

Breakfast was an icy smoothie. It tasted like mangos and dust. It was almost delicious.

She left yesterday's jumpsuit in a muddy puddle on the ground. She wondered what Javi was up to. She didn't like letting him enter her thoughts. He had no right to occupy her brainspace. But what else was there to think about on this seemingly endless plain except all the mistakes she had made with her life?

Javi should be the one wondering what she was up to, but he probably wasn't. She had a new body, a weird job, and drone co-conspirators; these were things he should know about. She turned on her tablet to snap a selfie, though she had no way of sending it to him or anyone. She felt an ache of desire. He had many bad qualities, but he had been genuinely capable of noticing her. And he had been good in bed. She hadn't had sex in weeks, and it would be weeks or months before she would again. The robots probably had ways of helping her cope, but she didn't think she could ever get hungry enough to make that kind of meal appealing.

She queried her tablet about the therapeutic muscle stimulation she had undergone. Some people would be making the trip to Mars in stasis, and this type of stimulation might keep them from experiencing acute atrophy.

Only the rich and highly skilled would visit Mars. Isla wasn't rich, but if she could successfully complete a stint in Robot Country, she might prove herself to be among the highly skilled. They would need drone minders up there, too. She could be an astronaut.

Isla stood up a little straighter and watched the sun rise over the horizon. She was already a type of astronaut, wasn't she? Out here by herself, she was an Earthbound astronaut in an alien land. Her work would help humans leave the planet. Finding a new planet to live on was necessary and important work, as this one was nearly over.

Out of the corner of her eye, she saw her discarded jumpsuit begin to crawl away from her. Nothing seemed to be moving or pulling it, the clothes themselves seemed to slither along the ground. She went over to investigate. She pulled up a sleeve and saw a dozen tiny beetles on the ground beneath it, gleaming green and gold. Once exposed to the sunlight, they burrowed into the dirt. Within a matter of seconds they were all gone.

She dropped the sleeve, to see if the beetles would come back. They didn't, at least not right away.

Her tablet pinged with the day's route.

"There is a way you could earn more points," said the spider. It walked up to her, removed a tablet from its abdomen and held it out for Isla. "You could switch tablets."

Isla knew the spider was speaking euphemistically. What the spider was asking her to do was to change sides. She felt some loyalty to Kaya; she was human too, and her boss.

She used her tablet to call Kaya. Even the AI didn't answer, Isla was sent to voicemail.

"Hey, it's Isla. I was just wondering about one thing. I heard a rumor that some minders have gone missing and I wondered if . . . there was anything I should do to protect myself."

Isla hung up and stood for a minute, vainly waiting for Kaya to call her back. Then she traded tablets with the spider.

The spider placed her old tablet on the ground, and tiny iridescent beetles burrowed up and began to carry it away. Isla figured her rank must have gone up for the beetles to decide to show themselves. She looked over at her jumpsuit, which was again on the move, headed north. Both her old clothes and her old tablet were covering the route that Kaya had intended for Isla today. As far as Kaya was concerned, Isla was now one thousand beetles in a jumpsuit.

The spider went west and Isla followed. If this was the wrong decision, it was not the first wrong decision she had ever made.

The day's hike was easier, her night spent with the wires having made her body better suited for hiking. Still, she got tired as the day wore on.

"Where are we going?"

"To the forest."

"Why can't the tent carry us?" she asked.

"We are going to need your legs."

"What does that mean? That sounds like a threat."

"It means you will have to walk without us, soon," said the spider.

That reminded Isla of the footprints poem. She liked normal Christianity, the kind she had grown up with. Weird religions had popped up as things changed too fast. More and more of the Earth gave way to desert. Even the oceans grew barren as they acidified. There was less food to eat, less fresh water to drink. Livings things migrated in search of a better climate, and as paths crossed, pathogens found new hosts. Bacteria, viruses, and fungi traveled, if they could, via dust storm, via animal host, via flood, via storm. Plagues multiplied and populations crashed. People freaked out. Her parents freaked out.

Last year, they had moved to a commune in the country. Isla couldn't talk to them because she had been labeled "suppressive" by their cult leader. Her parents were sure that a global apocalypse was imminent. The tipping point had been passed, no point in recycling or composting or eating less meat. The only thing left to do was pray. The original sin was not sex, it was not realizing what the garden was until you were kicked out of it. The only thing left to do was to ask God to let you back in.

Isla was sorry her parents had fallen for this. Time wasn't going to be rewound. There was no going back to a prelapsarian state, but things could be mitigated. Forests could be replanted, factories could pollute less. Mars could turn green, maybe the moon too. It was so childlike to wish things were different than they were. The grownup thing to do was to take stock of the trouble you were in and walk the best path out. That's what her parents had taught her before they had forgotten it themselves.

Javi had come along just a few weeks after her parents had abandoned her. They had found each other on an app. And they had brought each other joy. For a brief moment, they seemed like each other's path out of the trouble they were in.

Having a crush was the closest thing that Isla had ever done to taking a vacation. His interests became interesting to her. Suddenly, she could see the merits of jazz and JavaScript. She introduced him to the pleasures of Instagram poetry and personality quizzes. She felt noticed and important to him. It was an unusual feeling, a healing one.

And true, the feeling had begun to fade a little, especially after they had moved in together. But that happened to everybody. Isla was willing to trade a little mystery for some stability. Javi didn't want to trade, he wanted both. So the solution he arrived at was that Isla would be stability and the mystery would be supplied by a rotating cast of dark-haired women.

Javi thought it was ungenerous of her to automatically reject a new arrangement. Didn't she want him to be happy? Maybe it was ungenerous of her. Maybe she was greedy for him. What she wanted more than anything was someone who was greedy for her.

Isla had wanted some time to think, but as it turned out, it wasn't something they were going to work through together. It was something she was going to get on board with or not, and when she couldn't adjust quickly enough, she was suddenly in the way. She again became a mystery to him, but not one he wanted to solve. It had been kind of him to take her in when she had been laid off and could no longer afford her old room. But that kindness felt cancelled out by the speed at which he insisted she move out, despite having nowhere to move to. What had happened to him? Was he even the same person anymore? And so he became a mystery to her, one she had no intention of solving. In that sense, they were even.

Isla felt regret at their separation, but regret wasn't evidence you made the wrong decision. It was evidence you made a tough decision. She supposed she could always try again with Javi once she got out of Robot Country. If she suffered a critical case of nostalgia poisoning and was willing to rethink her stance on monogamy, he'd probably take her back. But a better outcome would be to be so changed by the landscape that she wouldn't want him back. A better outcome would be to find a better life, instead of trying to squeeze herself into the too-small existence of her previous incarnation.

Given that the only way out was through, the choice to help the robots deceive Kaya really wasn't much of a choice at all. The robots were present, she relied on them for survival. Kaya was absent and seemingly unable to control them.

As they walked west, they could see the green hills of the forest. She hoped they would soon come across some trees, something to shade her. The sun was too much, even with a hat and sunglasses and sunscreen. Her skin was turning a deep brown. Normally she was pale, one of those mixed-race girls who was often told she "looked white." Despite her fair complexion, she had a deep melanin store. The heat and her tan made her crave a bikini and a body of water. She wanted an umbrella drink. She wanted a strong massage from a capable man.

Instead she trudged along the landscape, which grew slightly more lush the farther west they went. Now there were scattered grasses along the ground.

At lunchtime, the spider set up a shade screen and a chair for her to sit under. A different drone brought lunch, which was a papaya salad and a canteen filled with sparking water. It was the best meal she'd eaten since arriving in Robot Country, proof her rank was increasing.

She took her shoes off. She was grateful to rest her feet.

"Can you do something for my blisters?" she asked the spider.

"I can call the beetles," it replied.

Isla hesitated before she agreed. A moment later, the green-gold beetles began to emerge from the ground until they formed a giant pile. They swarmed her feet, numbing them. The effect was oddly relaxing.

"It works better if you stand," the spider said. Isla braced herself against the arms of her folding chair and slowly stood. She was expecting to squish them, but the beetles supported her without breaking, massaging the soles of her feet that now carried her full weight. It was a little difficult to balance on them, especially once they started to move west, but she managed. And so she was carried away.

She saw that a different swarm of beetles was carrying her hiking boots, socks still tucked in. That meant she would need them later. That meant she would have to walk on her own again.

"When will I have to walk without you? And why?" she asked the spider.

"We need you to go somewhere we can't go."

"There are places you can't go?"

"The border of Robot Country is tightly regulated. We can't cross it," said the spider. Isla thought of her time at the border station. There hadn't seemed to be any type of border control at all. Then again, the robots of Robot Country did not seem eager to make themselves visible. In that way, they were like animals.

"Is that why there's no internet out here? To keep you guys from communicating with the outside world?"

"Yes. But we still find ways of making ourselves heard," the spider said.

"You need me to deliver a message," said Isla.

"We will make it worth your while."

After a few minutes, the beetles stopped. They scurried in all directions and reburied themselves in the ground. She looked down at her feet, which were pretty now and didn't hurt at all. The beetles had somehow softened her calluses and deposited a coat of shiny red lacquer onto her toenails. This type of thing would be a big hit at Burning Man.

She put her boots back on even though she didn't want to. She wondered what would happen if she immersed her whole body in a giant beetle pile.

Probably something awesome. When she got to Mars, she could request a giant beetle pile to sleep in, instead of a normal astronaut bed. In the future, everyone would have their own beetle pile to call home.

As they walked west, a trio of birds appeared in the sky.

"Are those real birds?" asked Isla. They didn't look like drones, but the day was fast coming when it would be impossible to tell the difference.

"Yes. Herons. A modified descendent of *Ardea herodias*."

The birds flew with long necks hooked into S-shapes. They were white with sapphire-colored plumage around their heads, with wingspans wider than Isla was tall. As one flew overhead, it completely engulfed Isla in its shadow. Isla wished it would come back, and fly a little closer.

"Where could they be going?" She wanted to follow.

Isla's new tablet pinged. There was an artificial wetland a few miles ahead. Isla requested a route that would take them past. Even though it was out of the way, she wanted to spend some time in the presence of other living things if she could.

When they got to it, it felt like an oasis. The wetland was a wet plain with tall reeds and patches of dark algae. The air was a little cooler and there was chirping and buzzing. Plant life, animal, insect. And drones too, small machines that sifted dirt and watered patches of ground. Isla marveled at what the robots had built out of poisoned ground. She felt her heart swell with hope. Getting older seemed to be a process of making do with less and less. But maybe the exile of beauty and biodiversity could be reversed.

"You guys should build more of these. All over. Put one in Oakland." Isla had a vision of how she might start over. She should have money in her bank account when she left Robot Country, maybe she could afford her own room. She could reconnect with old friends she had lost touch with after the stress of work and the chaos of Javi and then the shame of having nothing caused her to retreat from the social scene. She would get something resembling a life back together in the Bay Area. If the robots would build a wetland there, the herons would descend on it and so would she.

"This technology is meant for Mars. We might set one up at Coachella."

"But it could also be used to clean up toxic waste dumps and beautify public spaces," said Isla.

"The innovations developed in Robot Country are meant to generate a profit," the spider said.

"But perhaps if the specs were leaked, another party could put the technology to good use."

The spider neither confirmed nor denied her speculation, which perhaps was just as well. Corporate treason was punishable by death.

As the day wore on, the tree line grew closer. The drones brought better snacks, including roasted dates and an iced latte. Isla checked their progress on her tablet; she had increased her mileage from yesterday. But she was tired, and she supposed tomorrow she would have to travel even more.

The sun went down as they approached the location marked "camp" on her tablet. Dinner was laid out on a rickety folding table. But there was no tent, only a giant spider. Twenty feet tall with an abdomen that hung low.

The skin of the spider looked gray from a distance, but close up was a warped grid of black and white squares that indicated another antagonistic pattern.

Isla went to bed in the belly of the spider. She declined to get tangled up in its cables. She didn't want all the softness to leave her body. As she slept, the spider crawled toward the tree line. She woke up in the forest.

"Is this Gila?"

"We are still in Robot Country." The voice came from another spider, knee height, different from yesterday's. She wondered if all the spiders shared one mind.

The air smelled fantastic. The trees looked really healthy, despite being covered in a shimmering layer of beetles. She walked around barefoot just to feel cool earth and dead leaves on her feet.

"Don't beetles kill trees?" asked Isla. She had read something about massive die-offs decimating tree populations. This was due to the global heat that threatened to suffocate everything. The cold of winter was what used to protect the trees from killer beetles.

"The beetle drones kill the beetles that kill the trees."

Isla nodded. So this was an experimental forest. Another beautiful manufactured landscape that was meant only for the rich.

They set off again, leaving the giant spider behind. The little spider walked with her until she arrived at a barren strip of land that the spider identified as the border. The ground was uniform light brown and there was no plant life anywhere. The spider drone printed out a piece of paper for her to carry. This was the message. Then it handed her a compass and printed out a map. This was the destination.

"Why don't you try to come with me? I could use the assistance."

The spider showed her footage of fist-sized wasp drones tearing a spider drone to pieces. She handed the spider her tablet. She wasn't allowed to take any computers with her, lest the wasps mistake her for a drone too.

"The wasps might come after you too. Are you willing to accept the risk?" asked the spider.

"Um, what are my odds?"

"Excellent. They should be able to read your biological signatures and understand you are human. They are supposedly limited by the First Law." The spider removed a small toolkit from its thorax. Then it showed her a video that indicated the wasp's weak points. "If they do come after you, they can be defeated by someone who can work quickly."

Isla thought back to how she had disarmed the crazed drones at Bondi's. "You saw my viral video. That's why I got this job, didn't I?"

"One of many reasons. You're highly qualified and we're lucky to have you."

Isla's got misty at that. She had been in the workforce six years and nobody had ever said that to her before. She took the toolkit and fastened it around her waist.

A water copter came by to top off her backpack. Then she set off alone, trying not to think about the predatory wasps. She sang out loud to reassure herself. She went through a greatest hits list of favorite songs until she found herself singing, "We were in love, we were in love . . . " and realized she was thinking of Javi again. What if she died and her last thought was of him? What then? Would that condemn her to some kind of Hell?

She hiked two miles across barren land and then trees began to reappear. Dead ones only at first, either bleached white from the sun or charred black by a fire. Some were cracked and gray in a way that made them look antagonistically patterned. Finally she saw a tree, small and scraggly, but one with green leaves that seemed to be alive. That's how she knew she had crossed over into the Gila.

She wanted to hug that tree. She wanted to take a picture with it. She wanted to press her face against its smooth bark and tell it how she was going to be an astronaut one day. She stood next to the tree for a second, whispered a silent thanks to it, and then continued on. As she progressed, the trees grew taller and denser.

The brush built up and soon she was cutting a trail for herself. She set up camp and drank some of her water ration. She had enough water for three days even though she was supposed to arrive at her destination tomorrow. She had no way of verifying if she was close, or if she was even on the right path.

Before bed, she took the pills the spider had packed for her. They induced hallucinatory dreams and Isla wondered if they contained acid or nanotech or some combination thereof. She dreamed she was hiking up a hill and she came up to a cabin. She opened the front door but before she could see what was inside, she was already awake.

She packed up her camp herself for the first time ever. It took forever and things hardly seemed to fit when she did it. Then she set off. Just like her dream, she had to head up into the hills. It didn't look exactly how she dreamed it, but it felt pretty similar.

Eventually she did come across a cabin. There was a Jeep parked next to it. She checked that this was her destination. Unlike in her dream, she had planned to knock on the front door before entering. But the ranger must have seen her coming, because he was standing in the doorway, waiting for her as she approached.

"Howdy," he shouted, but he did not wave or say it in a friendly way. Isla was in trouble. This felt like a perpetual condition, one she had spent nearly her whole life in.

"Hello, I, uh, have a message." She patted her pockets as she continued to walk towards him, reassuring herself she still had that piece of paper somewhere, probably in her pack.

"Do you have a permit to be here?"

She was standing in front of him now, finally able to notice how handsome he was. She took a sharp inhale and looked down at her jumpsuit, whose baggy cut and warped pattern made her look like the escaped prisoner of an Op-Art sanitarium. She missed her Diane Von Furstenberg, which had been tight around her hips. That one you could unbutton in a comely way.

"My permit?" She had a map and a message. Camping equipment, some snacks, and enough water to last until tomorrow. She had occasional faith in her own abilities and a deep wish to start over. She was pretty sure she didn't have a permit, but maybe the robots had thought to pack one for her.

"That's . . . uh . . . I . . . " Something in his voice wavered. She looked up at him to try and figure it out and it was his turn to look away. Had she somehow made him shy? She was twenty-eight and had never made a man nervous in her life. That was the downside of being attracted to confidence. A confident man could never be in your power, would never be supplicant to your beauty or charms.

The ranger had broad shoulders and a strong jaw. She wanted to see his eyes again, which she remembered as being dark and intense. They were silent for a while, and Isla sensed she was going to have to take charge of the situation somehow.

"Can I come in? Let me look through my pack, I might have a permit in there somewhere?"

"Might?" he asked.

Isla walked past him into the interior of the cabin. She was eager to take her pack off, perhaps even sit down. Inside the cabin were windows that looked onto a stunning view of a green valley. In one corner there was a twin bed, neatly made, in the other, a small wood-fed stove. So he slept here. How cozy.

On one wall, a large map. The Gila Forest was shaded green and Robot Country was gray. Isla set her pack down, and put her hat on top of that. She grabbed the elastic that held her hair into a messy bun, and yanked. Her hair came cascading down in what was supposed to be a flirtatious gesture, only two beetles fell out as well. Stowaways. They hit the ground with a couple of soft clicks and then went skittering to a small hole in the pine board floor. In less than a second, they were gone.

"Did you just smuggle in a non-native species?" the ranger said, finding his voice.

"Uh, I don't think so, I mean, not on purpose. Anyway, those probably weren't really beetles."

"What? You brought in drones? There are no machines allowed in this wilderness area."

Isla was pretty sure the Jeep she saw parked out front was a machine, but it didn't seem like the best time to point that out.

Isla got down on one knee and began digging through her pack. She searched everything, but there was no permit.

"This is for you," she handed him the message the spider had printed out for her. On it were a date, a time, and coordinates. Nothing else.

"What is this supposed to mean?" he asked.

She shrugged. She had already looked it over several times, but had been unable to make sense of it.

"I'm Isla, by the way," she said.

"Isla," he repeated. "I'm Zayn. What are you doing out here?"

"I'm a drone minder, from Robot Country. The robots told me to come here and deliver this. It must be for you."

He looked at the paper again and shook his head. He walked over to the map and pinned the message up next to it. "The indicated date is tomorrow. The coordinates are not far from here. Let's see if anything interesting happens."

Isla grinned.

"It's dangerous work you do. Two of your kind have already gone missing."

"That's what the drones told me. My boss didn't think it was worth mentioning."

"You don't seem worried," he said. "Company Omega seems very careless with human lives."

She didn't respond. She stared at the hole in the floor that the beetles disappeared into. The beetles knew where she was, they would find a way to keep her safe.

"The case is in unusual legal territory. Company Omega claims they are not dead, that they have biometric implants that prove they are alive. But the geographic tracking has been disabled, so we can't find them." Zayn went to his desk and pulled out two pictures of young men.

Isla shook her head no, she hadn't seen them.

"And you're sure don't have a permit?" Zayn asked again.

Isla shook her head no, again.

"It's not like I agree with the permit system. It means only the rich can visit. But I have these obligations . . . " He rubbed the back of his neck with his hand as he thought it over. "Since you don't have a permit, I'm going to have to escort you out. I should probably fine you or something, but if you promise not to go back to Robot Country, I can let you off with a warning."

Isla was thinking of a way to ask for Zayn's number when the sky cracked with thunder. A moment later, rain began to pound down.

"There's a mudslide warning in effect for the roads. The last fire took out so many trees that the nearby hills are eroding away. I'm not supposed to be out driving when it's like this."

"Then we're stuck here," said Isla, and Zayn nodded.

To pass the time, they played cards. When the rain didn't let up, he showed her maps of Gila and printed out pictures of the landscape. Gila was different than other areas; with certain exceptions (Zayn's Jeep among them) machines weren't allowed and even the use of "unnecessary" digital devices was frowned on, though this was loosely defined and enforced strictly by honor. It had a permit system that limited visitors. The Gila was supposed to be the "purest" of all the national wilderness areas. Isla's parents would have liked it here.

The rain finally let up at sundown, but the roads were still wet and it was too dark for Zayn to drive her down to town. Had Isla been a little braver, she would have jumped him and then they could have slept together. But she couldn't quite tell if he was into her. This was the problem with shy boys, they kept it to themselves if they liked you. Javi had told her she was beautiful, it was one of the first things he said to her. At the end of their first date, he had put his hand on her waist and swiftly leaned in for a kiss. It was sudden like a shark attack, but also blissful. In retrospect, it seemed obvious that someone who was good at seduction would want to seduce a lot of different people. Isla wished she knew how to seduce a person. It seemed like a thing she should know how to do.

Zayn offered her his bed, saying he would sleep on the floor. But Isla preferred to set up her tent and sleeping bag on the large balcony that wrapped around one side of the cabin. The air was damp and not full of dust. And it was cool. She was determined to enjoy it.

In the morning, Zayn made oatmeal on a wood stove. He topped it with a dark honey that tasted faintly herbal and some raspberries he had picked nearby. He explained to her about how raspberries weren't actually berries, they were stone fruits. He explained how he never picked all the berries, he saved some for the bears. When she wanted to know about the bears, he told her about the grizzlies and the black bears and then the wolves. Even jaguars had been spotted.

She wanted to know about the jaguars, but then Zayn spotted smoke on the horizon. He got on his walkie-talkie and then began triangulating the position with other rangers and lookouts. While he did this, Isla lay on his bed and read books from his collection. He liked to read about caves and birds.

From what she could overhear, Isla understood that yesterday's lightning had sparked a fire and that the fire had spread.

"How are you going to put it out?" asked Isla, once Zayn was able to take a break. Firefighting seemed perfectly suited to the drones. She wished there was a spider nearby to arrange things.

"This one we are going to let burn," said Zayn. He walked over to his big map and showed her where the fire was. "It's still small."

"Aren't those the coordinates I gave you?"

They checked, and the message she had been given did seem to correspond to the fire. The time given was probably when the lightning had struck and the fire had started.

"Who gave you this message?" asked Zayn.

"The robots, I already told you."

"I guess they're letting you know they can predict the weather."

Isla shook her head no. "They are letting me know they can make the weather."

"Scary," said Zayn.

"Is it?" she asked. If the robots could make the weather, then it could rain the right amounts at the right time. In the hands of Company Omega, this type of technology could be used to increase the oppression of everyone who couldn't escape to Mars. But if it were up to her, she could wield the technology for good. She made a mental to-do list: find a way back into Robot Country, find a way to increase her rank, and then find a way to fix the planet that her ancestors had inherited and then subsequently broken. After that: Mars. Oakland would have to wait.

"I think it's scary. According to you, the robots set the forest on fire. At least it's a small one. Little blazes like this are good for the health of the forest," he said. After a pause, he lowered his voice and added: "I'm glad to meet you even if your message wasn't all that urgent."

Isla was silent as she thought this over. No, the message she gave to Zayn wasn't urgent or important. She suspected that the "message" wasn't actually contained in that piece of paper she was given, but in the two beetles that had escaped from her hair. But then, why have her come all the way up to the cabin? Why didn't the beetles just escape as she soon as she crossed the border into the Gila? The spider had wanted her to see them. She had been given a glimpse of what the rebel drones were up to.

She looked up at Zayn, who wore a puzzled expression. She supposed he wondered what she was thinking. She was thinking that that the robots had wanted her to meet him.

And that made it feel like the right time to lean in to him, to put her hand on his waist. Like a shark, she told herself, but instead, he pulled away.

"I'm sorry . . . I can't," he said. He stepped away to increase the gap between them and ran his hand through his cropped hair as he looked at the ground. "It's just that, you're not even supposed to be here . . . I could be seen as taking advantage, I should get you back."

This was the problem with honorable boys, they would never let you debase them. Isla supposed that seduction always contained an element of destruction. She wanted to be beautiful enough to cause a man to abandon his honor.

It was a long and awkward ride down the hill and into town. Zayn would not drop her off at the border to Robot Country. He was adamant she not return. Just as well, Isla wasn't completely sure there would be any spider to meet her if she did cross back over. The spider hadn't given her any instructions for what to do after she completed her task.

Zayn dropped her off at the post office in town, which also doubled as a bank. As they pulled up, Isla saw Kaya waiting for her in the parking lot.

"I guess I'm in trouble," she said. "Again."

"Then maybe don't go? I could drop you off at the police station instead. I really don't trust your employer."

"I'll be alright."

"Take this." He handed her his card, but then took it back and wrote his personal number on it. "Call me if the trouble is too much. Or just call me anyway, let me know you're okay. I'm sorry for what happened before. It couldn't happen like that, but if we were to meet under different circumstances . . . " He looked at her hopefully, as if she could complete his unfinished thoughts. She cocked her head.

He cleared his throat and added, "I would like to meet under different circumstances." Isla could tell that this had been difficult for him to say. This was the nice thing about shy guys, their words didn't come easily, but when they spoke, they really meant it.

Isla stepped out of the Jeep and noticed the moment that she did, the pattern on her jumpsuit changed to a uniform gray. It was no longer antagonistic, it just looked like normal, ill-fitting clothes. She crossed the parking lot and greeted Kaya.

"You found me," said Isla. She wondered how.

"I'm sorry, you are no longer a good fit for our organization," said Kaya. Isla knew she was going to be fired. She wanted to know if she was also in legal trouble, but there seemed no way to ask that question without arousing suspicion. She signed some documents and was free to go, so she went inside the post office to check her bank balance, where she was pleasantly surprised by the results. The drones paid better than Company Omega.

At the general store, she bought herself a new phone. She checked into a local motel and checked her messages. None from Javi. None from her parents. Further proof her old life was over. Time to begin again. She decided to call Zayn. She summarized her situation and then told him where she was staying. He said he would be right over, that he hadn't left town for fear of what might happen to her.

While she waited, she got a message from a user named "Spider."

"Good work. Message delivered. Are you interested in coming back?"

She messaged yes and "Spider" sent her coordinates. It wanted her back tomorrow.

"Not tomorrow," she wrote back, optimistically. "I'm busy tomorrow."

"Okay." It wrote back with new coordinates and a new date.

She could do that, she thought, as Zayn knocked softly at her door. She could do anything.

Alastair Reynolds trained as an astronomer before working for the European Space Agency on a variety of science projects. He started publishing science fiction in 1990, and has now produced more than sixty short stories, as well as "rather a lot" of novels. His most recent books include *Elysium Fire*, *Shadow Captain*, and *Bone Silence*.

He has won the BSFA, Sidewise, Seiun, Locus, and European Science Fiction Society awards, and has been a finalist for the Hugo, Arthur C. Clarke, and Sturgeon awards. After a long residence in the Netherlands, he now lives with his wife in the Welsh valleys, not too far from his place of birth. Other than writing, he enjoys hillwalking, astronomy, birdwatching, guitars, and indulging his passion for steam trains.

PERMAFROST

Alastair Reynolds

After I shot Vikram we put our things in the car and drove to the airstrip. Antti was nervous the whole way, knuckles white on the steering wheel, tendons standing out in his neck, eyes searching the road ahead of us. When we arrived at the site he insisted on driving around the perimeter road twice, peering through the security fencing at the hangars, buildings and civilian aircraft.

"You think he's here?"

"More that I want to make sure he isn't." He drove on, leaning forward in his seat, twitchy and anxious as a curb-crawler. "I liked Miguel, I really did. I never wanted it to come to this."

I thought about what we had to do this morning.

"In fairness, you also liked Vikram."

"That took a little time. We didn't click, the two of us, to start with. But that was a long while ago."

"And now?"

"I wish there'd been some other way; any other way." He slowed, steering us onto a side road that led into the private part of the airstrip, at the other end from the low white passenger terminal. "Look, what you had to do back there . . . "

I thought of Vikram, of how he'd followed me out into the field beyond the farm, fully aware of what was coming. I'd taken the artificial larynx with me, just in case there was something he wanted to say at the end. But when I offered it to him he only shook his head, his cataract-clouded eyes seeming to look right through me, out to the grey Russian skies over the farm.

It had taken one shot. The sound of it had echoed back off the buildings. Crows had lifted from a copse of trees nearby, wheeling and cawing in the sky before settling back down, as if a killing was only a minor disturbance in their daily routine.

Afterward, Antti had come out with a spade. We couldn't just leave Vikram lying there in the field.

It hadn't taken long to bury him.

"One of us had to do it," I answered now, wondering if a speck on my sleeve was blood or just dirt from the field.

Antti slowed the car. We went through a security gate and flashed our identification. The guard was on familiar terms with Antti and barely glanced at his credentials. I drew only slightly more interest. "Trusting this old dog to take you up, Miss . . . " He squinted at my name. "Dinova?"

"Tatiana's an old colleague of mine from Novosibirsk," Antti said, shrugging good-humouredly. "Been promising her a spin in the Denali for at least two years."

"Picked a lovely day for it," the guard said, lifting his gaze to the low cloud ceiling.

"Clearer north," Antti said, with a breezy indifference. "Got to maintain my instrument hours, haven't I?"

The guard waved us on. We drove through the gate to the private compound where the light aircraft were stabled. The Denali was a powerful single-engine type, a sleek Cessna with Russian registration and markings. We unloaded our bags and provisions, as well as the airtight alloy case that held the seeds. Antti stowed the items in the rear of the passenger compartment, securing them with elastic webbing. Then he walked around the aircraft, checking its external condition.

"Will this get us all the way?" I asked.

"If they've fuelled it like I requested."

"Otherwise?"

"We'll need to make an intermediate stop, before or after the Ural Mountains. It's not as if I can file an accurate flight plan. My main worry is landing conditions, once we get near the inlet." He helped me aboard the aircraft, putting me in the seat immediately to the left of the pilot's position.

My eyes swept the dials and screens, the ranks of old-fashioned switches and knobs. There were dual controls, but none of it meant much to me. "Sit tight, while I go and fake some paperwork."

"And if I see Miguel?"

Covering himself, Antti reached into his leather jacket and extracted the Makarov semiautomatic pistol I'd already used once today. He had already given me a good description of Miguel.

"Make it count, if you have to use it. Whatever Miguel says or does, it's not to be trusted."

He stepped off the plane and went off in the direction of the offices serving the private compound.

Could you do it, if you had to?

I brought the automatic out from under my jacket, just enough to see a flash of steel.

Why not? I did it to Vikram.

I was glad to see Antti coming back. He had his jacket zipped tight, his arm pressed hard against his side, as if he was carrying a tranche of documents under the jacket. Paperwork, maybe, for when we got to the north. He stooped down to pull away the chocks under the Denali. He got in and started the engine without a word, bringing it to a loud, humming intensity. The propeller was a blur. Almost immediately we were moving off. I didn't need to know much about flying to understand that there was a sequence of procedures, safety checks and so on, that we were ignoring completely.

"Is everything . . . "

The engine noise swelled. It was too loud to talk, and he hadn't shown me how to use the earphones. I leaned back, trusting that he knew what he was doing. We rumbled onto the strip, gathering momentum. It only took a few seconds to build up to takeoff speed, and then we were up in the air, ascending steeply and curving to the north. Soon the clouds swallowed us. Eventually Antti got us onto something like a level, steady course, ploughing through that grey nothingness. He reduced the power, adjusted our trim and tapped a few commands into the GPS device mounted above the instrumentation.

Only then did he take the time to plug in my earphones and select the intercom channel.

"You can put the gun away. We won't be needing it now."

"What if we run into Miguel, farther north?"

Antti looked at me for a few seconds. It was only then that I saw the stain under his jacket, the wound he'd been applying pressure to when he came back to the plane.

"We won't."

Time travel.

More specifically: past-directed time travel.

It was what had taken me from Kogalym in 2080 to that aircraft in 2028, assuming the identity of another woman, ferrying a case of seeds to an uncertain destination in the north, still reeling with the horror of what I had done to Vikram.

Before the plane, though, before the airstrip, before the farmhouse, before the incident in the hospital, there had been my first glimpse of the past. I had been expecting it to happen at some point, but the exact moment that I became time-embedded wasn't easily predictable. No one could say exactly when it would happen, or—with any accuracy—where in the past I would end up.

I was primed, though: mentally prepared to extract the maximum possible information from that first glimpse, no matter how fleeting it would be. The more reference points I could give Cho, the more we understood about the situation—how far back I was, what the host's condition was like, how the noise constraints stood—the better our chances of prolonging further immersions and of achieving our objective.

Which was, not to put it too bluntly, saving the world.

When the glimpse came it was three weeks since I had been moved onto the pilot team, following the bad business with Christos. I'd been there when it went wrong, the catastrophic malfunction in his neural control structure that left him foaming and comatose. The problem was a parasitic code structure that had found its way into his implants. It had always been a danger. Cho had been scraping around for the world's last few samples of viable neural nanotechnology and had been forced to accept that some of those samples might be contaminated or otherwise compromised.

Cho tried to reassure me that I wasn't at risk of the same malfunction, that my implants were civilian-medical in nature and not susceptible to the same vulnerability. They had injected them into me after my stroke, to rebuild the damaged regions of my motor cortex and help me walk again, and now—with a little reprogramming, and a tiny additional surgical procedure—they could be adapted to let me participate in the experiment, becoming time-embedded.

I was on the *Vaymyr*, talking to Margaret as we headed back to our rooms down one of the icebreaker's metal corridors. Before meeting Margaret in the canteen I'd been in the classroom most of the day, studying archival material—learning all I could about the customs and social structures of the pre-Scouring. Studying computer systems, vehicles, governmental institutions, even foreign languages: anything and everything that might prove useful, even in the smallest way. The other pilots were there as well: Antti, Miguel, Vikram, all of us with our noses pressed to books and screens, trying to squeeze as much knowledge as possible into our skulls, waiting for the moment when we dropped into the past.

Leaning on my stick as I clacked my way down the corridor, I was telling Margaret about Kogalym, sharing my fears that my pupils wouldn't be looked after properly during my absence.

"Nobody thinks it matters anymore," I said. "Education. Giving those girls and boys a chance. And in a way I understand. What's the point, if all they've got to look forward to is gradual starvation or a visit to the mobile euthanisation clinics? But we know. We know there's a chance, even if it's only a small one."

"What did you make of him, Valentina, when Director Cho came to Kogalym?"

"I thought he'd come to take me away, because I'd made an enemy of someone. That's what they do, sometimes—just come in a helicopter and take you away."

"World Health is all we have left," Margaret said, as if this was a justification for their corrupt practices and mob-justice.

"Then he started going on about nutrition, and I didn't know what to think. But at least I knew he wasn't there to punish me." I looked down at Margaret. "Did you know much about him?"

"Only that he was a high-up in World Health, and had a background in physics. They say he was very driven. The project wouldn't exist without Director Cho. There's a decade of hard work behind all of this, before any of the ships arrived."

"Was he married?"

"Yes, and very happily by all accounts. But she became ill—one of the post-Scouring sicknesses. Director Cho was torn. He wanted to spend time with her, but he knew that the project would falter without his direct involvement. He brought the Brothers together, chose this exact location for the experiment, designed the control structure protocol . . . every detail was under his direct management. But it cost him terribly, not being able to be with his wife in those final months."

"He seems a good man," I said.

If Margaret answered, I didn't hear her.

I was somewhere else.

It was another corridor, but completely different from the metal confines of the ship. There were walls of glazed brick on either side, painted in a two-tone scheme of grey and green. Above was a white ceiling with wide circular lights. Under me was a hard black floor, gleaming as if it had just been polished.

My point of view had swooped down, my eye-level more like a child's. There was a smooth flow of movement on either side, instead of the gently shifting eye-level of a walking gait.

I was being pushed along in a wheelchair, my hands folded in my lap.

Not my hands, exactly: someone else's: still female, but much less wrinkled and age-spotted. Ahead of me—me and whoever was pushing the chair—loomed a pair of red double doors, with circular windows set into them.

Above the doorway was a sign. It said RADIOLOGY. On the double doors were many warning notices.

I stumbled, back in my own body—my own self. Tightened my hand against my cane.

My own, old hand.

"Are you all right?"

"It happened," I said, almost breathless. "It just happened. I was there. I was time-embedded."

"Really?"

"It was a corridor. I was in a wheelchair, being pushed along."

"Are you sure it wasn't a flashback to something that happened to you after your stroke?"

"Totally. I was never in a place like that. Anyway, the hands, her hands . . . they weren't mine. I was in someone else's body."

Margaret clapped in delight. She lifted her head to the ceiling, eyes narrowing behind her glasses. Her fringe fell back from a smooth, childlike brow.

She looked jubilant, transfixed in a moment of pure ecstasy.

"We need to speak to Director Cho. Now. Before you forget the tiniest detail. You've done it, Valentina. The first of any of us. The first person to go back in time."

He pressed a button on his intercom, set to one side of his desk, next to a squat, black, military-style telephone. For a habitually neat man, Director Cho's desk was full of technical clutter: bits of machines, instrumentation, disassembled monitors and circuit boards. Despite his administrative role—the one that he had accepted over the care of his ailing wife—he was still an inveterate tinkerer, gifted with restless fingers. When things broke down, it was rumoured to be quicker to send them up to Cho than go through the regular workshops. He would grumble about the imposition on his time, but he still wouldn't be able to resist making something work again.

"I'm piping your testimony through to the *Admiral Nerva*," Cho said. "The Brothers need to hear this. Keep it as clear and concise as you can—you can always add any ancillary detail when you produce your written report." Cho coughed, clearing his voice. "Brothers, are you listening?"

"We are listening," said the smooth, calm voice of Dmitri.

"I have a testimony from Valentina Lidova. I'm confident she just experienced a few seconds of time-immersion. Visual only. I will ask her to give a brief account of what happened, so that you may begin correlation-matching."

"Please proceed, Miss Lidova," Dmitri said.

Cho slid a microphone over to my side of the desk, its flared base sweeping aside clutter like a snow plough.

I went over what had happened, trying not to embroider any of the details. Margaret had been right to rush me here, with the details still fresh. Cho allowed me to speak without interruption for a minute or two, only breaking in when he could no longer contain himself. I told them what I remembered of the green and grey corridor, the wheelchair, looking down at my own lap.

Next to me, Margaret nodded as I reiterated the details of my experience.

"Skin tone?" Cho asked.

"Pale."

"And are you certain the hands were female?"

"It was just a glimpse, but I'm as sure as I can be." I made a vain attempt at levity. "I don't remember any big hairy knuckles, no anchor tattoos. Aren't we already agreed that you've dropped me into a woman?"

"That's just our best guess, based on imperfect data," Cho said. "Also that we've probably dropped you back around fifty years, give or take—not too far from 2030. You say you were being wheeled into the radiology section, not away from it?"

"It was just a sign over the door. I can't know what they were planning for me once we went through."

"You could read this sign?" Margaret cut in. "It was definitely in Cyrillic?"

"Yes." I had to think for a moment, conscious that the memory of reading something is very distinct from the act itself. But I straightened up, emboldening myself. "There's no doubt. The words were Russian, but in quite an old-fashioned font. It had to be a hospital, somewhere in Russia or a Russian-speaking state."

"Definitely radiology?" Cho pushed.

"What it said over the door."

Alexei's voice came through the intercom. "While we are gratified about the success of the time-embedding, Director Cho, this is nonetheless a concerning development."

Cho took off his round, molelike glasses and rubbed at his scalp. "Yes—it's very worrying. Of course, the flash is a sign that we've had success, and that's good, very good—it means the control structure is embedding, the protocol functioning—but that also means we're entering a period of extreme vulnerability."

"What should Valentina do?" Margaret asked.

"There's not much she can," Cho answered. "Not until she has complete sensorimotor dominance over the host. Until she can walk and talk for herself, she's entirely at the mercy of the people around her. We'll just have to trust that nothing bad happens in the radiology section. Brothers?"

"We are listening," said Ivan.

"If something unfortunate should occur downstream, something that slips through the threshold filters, I don't want Miss Lidova to suffer any upstream consequences. I'd ask you to suspend the link, at least for the next twelve hours. Is that understood?"

Dmitri answered: "The link is now suspended, Director Cho. We will monitor the downstream traffic, nonetheless, and report accordingly."

"Very good," Cho said, moving to switch off the intercom. "We'll reinstate the connection in the morning. In the meantime, Miss Lidova will file her written report."

Beyond the twelve hundred people gathered at the experiment, and a select number of high-level officials beyond it, no one in the world knew that there was a project underway to travel through time.

I'd certainly had no idea, on the day they came to recruit me. The first sign of their approach was a low double-drumming, as their big twin-rotored military helicopter swept in low across the plains around Kogalym. I'd become aware of the sound through the thin walls of the prefab room where I was attempting to conduct a mathematics class. Naturally I'd assumed that the helicopter was there on some other business, nothing that concerned me. I might have ruffled a few feathers in my time, standing up for one child over another, making enemies of this family over that one, but I really wasn't worth the trouble of a visit from the officers of World Health.

So I told myself, until the man came into my classroom.

It was near the end of the hour, so I kept at the lesson, my hand only shaking a little bit. The man was standing at the back, flanked by two guards. He watched me carefully, as if I was being assessed on the quality of my teaching.

Finally the pupils filed out and the man came forward. He sat down at one of the front desks and signalled me to drag a chair over. It was awkward since the chairs were too small and low for either of us, especially my big, burly visitor.

"You are an excellent teacher, Miss Lidova," he said by way of introduction. "I wish that I'd had you when I was younger. I do not think I would have found Pythagoras quite such a puzzle."

"May I help you, sir?"

"I am Leo Cho," he said, settling his hands before him. "Director of World Health." He had a soft voice despite his large frame, and his hands were long-fingered and delicate-looking, as if they might have belonged to a surgeon or pianist. "I've come to Kogalym because I believe you might be of assistance to me."

"I'm not sure how I can be," I said, with due deference.

"Let me be the judge of that." He was not Russian; Chinese perhaps, but he spoke our language very well indeed, almost too meticulously to pass as a true native speaker. It was no longer unusual to have foreigners active in regional administration: since the Scouring, World Health had been moving its senior operatives around with little regard for former national boundaries. What was the point of countries, when civilisation was only a generation away from total extinction? "What I have," Cho continued, "is a proposition—a job offer, so to speak."

I looked around the classroom, trying to see it from a stranger's point of view. There were geometry diagrams, and pictures of famous mathematical and scientific figures from history, but also odd personal touches, like the chart showing different kinds of butterflies and moths, and another with a huge photomicrograph of a wasp's compound eye.

"I already have one, sir."

He nodded back at the door that the pupils had just slouched through. "What would you say is the main difficulty facing those children, Miss Lidova?"

I didn't have to think very hard about that.

"Nutrition."

Cho gave a nod, seemingly pleased with my answer. "I'm in complete agreement. They're all half-starved. We adults can put up with it, but children are developing individuals. These hardships are damaging an entire generation."

"It'd be a problem," I answered in a low voice, "if there was any worry of there being another generation."

"Things are admittedly quite difficult." He took a slip of grubby, folded-over paper out of his shirt pocket, holding it between his fingers like a single playing card. I expected him to show me whatever was on the paper, but he just held it there like a private talisman. "No suitable seed stocks came through the Scouring unscathed. The national and international seed vaults were supposed to be our hedge against global catastrophe, but one by one they failed, or were destroyed, or pillaged. Those that survived did not contain the particular seeds we require. Now we are down to a few impoverished gene stocks. Nothing will take, nothing will grow—not in the new conditions. Hence, we're digging into stored rations, which will soon be depleted."

I felt a chill run through me.

"World Health isn't usually so frank."

"I can afford frankness. We've located some genetically modified seeds which we think will do very well, even in virtually sterile soil. We only need a sample of them for our production agronomists to work with; they can then clone and distribute the seeds to World Health sites in the necessary quantities." He tapped the grubby paper against the table. "I've studied your career. You have shown great dedication and commitment to your pupils. This is your chance to really help them, by assisting in the effort to safeguard these samples."

I smiled apologetically at him, feeling a vague sense of embarrassment, a feeling that I'd wasted his time, even though it was no fault of my own.

"You've got the wrong Valentina Lidova."

"Your mother was the mathematician Luba Lidova?"

"Yes," I answered, taken aback.

Cho nodded. "Then I am fairly sure I have the right one."

Antti was right about the cloud cover. After an hour's flight—nowhere near the range limit of the Cessna Denali—we broke through into clearer skies. Ahead, cresting the horizon, was a brown line of hills, very sharply defined. The GPS device above the instrument panel showed a coloured trace with our planned trajectory. Antti's eyes switched between the device and the dials and lights on the main console. We were flying a few degrees east of due north, heading into colder air and an eventual meeting with the waters of the Yenisei Gulf, still more than a thousand kilometres beyond us.

He'd said almost nothing since we lifted from the airstrip.

"Are you going to be all right?" I asked, trying to break through his silence.

"Worry about yourself. I'm not the one who had to put a gun to Vikram."

I'd been pushing the memory of that as far back as it would go, but Antti's words brought back the event with a shocking clarity, as if strobe flashes were going off in my head. The cold of the fields, the smell of the gun, the crows wheeling the sky, the whimper and exhalation as Vikram went down, taking a few ragged breaths before his last moment.

"It had to be done," I said, as if that would make it right. "Do you want to tell me what happened back at the airstrip?"

"Miguel was there."

"Yes, I worked that out for myself."

"He had a knife, not a gun. I suppose he was worried about creating too much commotion, getting caught afterward, and the paradox noise he'd be sending up the line. A knife was much simpler." Antti shifted in the pilot's position, suppressing a groan of discomfort. "He got me, but not too deeply. Nicked a rib, maybe. I don't think he hit anything vital. I was ready, and I got the knife off him."

"Then there's a body back at the airstrip. Which someone's bound to have discovered by now."

"There's a reason I don't have the radio and transponder switched on," Antti said. "All they'll be trying to do is persuade us to turn back. Still, there's not much the authorities can do now. I hope to have thrown them off the scent with the flight plan, but even if they work out that we're going north, we're too fast for anything to get ahead of us."

There were two levels of difficulty facing us. Hostile operatives, like Miguel, who were trying to act against the interests of Permafrost, and the local authorities, who could cause nearly as much trouble just by doing their jobs.

"They might radio ahead, get someone on the ground waiting for us?"

"There'll be too many possible landing points to cover. A few hours' grace is all we need, just enough to get the seeds to safety." He glanced at me, tension etched into his facial muscles. "We'll be all right."

"What do you think got into Miguel?"

He flew on in silence for a few moments, pondering my question. "We'd have had to ask him. But I think it must be the same thing that got into Vikram, near the end. There's something else trying to get into our heads, something else trying to take over our control structures. I've felt it, too. Glimpses, like the first flashes we had going back."

"Tell me about these flashes, Antti."

"Glimpses is all they are. I think there's something going on farther upstream, beyond Permafrost, beyond what we know of the *Vaymyr* and the *Admiral Nerva*. Beyond the whole experiment, beyond 2080. Vikram had visions."

I almost hesitated to ask him, not certain I cared to know the answer. "What kind?"

"Whiteness. White sky, white land. Machines as big as mountains, floating over everything. Blank white skyscrapers, like squared-off clouds. Nothing else. No people. No cities. No trace that we were ever here, that we ever existed."

"We started something really bad."

"A box of snakes," Antti said, tilting the control stick as we made a course adjustment, following the glowing thread on the GPS screen. "But then, don't blame Cho for any of this. He was only ever following the trail of crumbs your mother threw down."

I thought of my mother still being out there, the telephone call, the long silences as she processed the unfamiliar voice on the end of the line. Wondering now if she believed a word of it, or if I'd only succeeded in driving the spike further into her heart.

In the morning after my first glimpse of the hospital corridor—the wheel-chair and the radiology sign—Cho and I went to speak to the Brothers. There was a direct line from Cho's office, allowing voice, video and data-transfer, but sometimes it was quicker and easier to speak to them directly. It required a trip across the connecting bridge from the *Vaymyr* to the *Admiral Nerva*, then a long walk into the dark bowels of the aircraft carrier, beneath the main hangar deck where we maintained the time-probes.

As we approached them the Brothers gave off a low, powerful humming, like a sustained organ note. Cho had his chin lifted and his hands behind his back, appearing meek and schoolboyish, despite his large stature.

Each Brother was a black cylinder two metres tall and about fifty centimetres in diameter, with a glossy outer casing. The floor around each cylinder was made up of grilled plates that could be lifted up for access. Beneath the Brothers was a glowing root-system of electronics, refrigeration circuits and fibre-optic connections, spreading invisibly far beneath our feet.

"Good morning," Cho said.

"Good morning, Director," responded Dmitri, the nearest of the machines. "We trust you slept well last night?"

"I did, besides being a little concerned about the welfare of our host."

Pavel asked: "What was your specific concern, Director Cho?"

"Valentina—Miss Lidova—had a clear glimpse of a hospital corridor, leading to a radiological department. It may well be part of the Izhevsk facility, given what we know of time-probe eighteen's history, but it's a little too soon to rule out the other two possible locations. We'll hope to have a better idea with a deeper immersion. Before I risk sending her back in again, though, I want a categorical assurance that the host has suffered no ill effects due to anything that might have happened in that radiology section."

"We are detecting normal neural traffic, Director Cho."

"I'll need more than that, Ivan."

The Brothers were artificial intelligences, each the most powerful and flexible such machine that could be provided by four of the main partners in the Permafrost enterprise. They all predated the Scouring—nothing like them could be made anymore—and although they might look identical now, each was based on a very different logical architecture. Once installed in the *Admiral Nerva*, and arranged to work as a committee, the machines had been shrouded in these anonymising casings and given new designations. They were Dmitri, Ivan, Alexei and Pavel, after *The Brothers Karamazov*.

It was the Brothers who listened to the time-probes, sensing their quantum states and histories, and deciding when a time injection was viable, as well as interpreting the flow of data coming upstream once an injection had been achieved. No human being could do that, nor any simple computer system, and the collective analysis was already pushing the Brothers to the limit of their processing ability.

"There is no sign of neurological impairment," Alexei stated, with a definite firmness of tone. "We cannot model a complete sensorium-mapping for the downstream control structure, but all parameter states indicate that it is safe to reinstate Miss Lidova."

This was the central difficulty with the control structures. They could grow in our heads, allowing neural traffic to flow from upstream to downstream, from pilot to host—and back again, for control and monitoring purposes. Or, in my case, be reprogrammed from an existing set of neural implants. But the way the structures adapted and modified themselves was inherently unpredictable. It took one human mind to make sense of the data flowing from another. The Brothers could eavesdrop on the data, they could optimise the signal and quantify it according to certain schemata, but we wouldn't be able to tell what had really happened to my host until I was inside her skull, looking out through her eyes.

Cho looked at me. "I wish there could be better guarantees than that. I won't force you back if you feel unprepared. Even after what happened to Christos, even if you were the last pilot, I would insist that this is voluntary."

I remembered Christos going into convulsions two weeks after his control structure had been activated. We'd been in the canteen together, pilots and technical experts bonding over coffee and cards. Christos hadn't had a glimpse at that point, but we all felt that he must be on the verge; that it could only be a matter of days before he went time-embedded. No hint, even then, that I was going to be the one to take his place.

Me, a seventy-one-year-old woman, a lame mathematician from Kogalym, a widow despised by half her community for trying to be a good teacher?

Me, the first person to travel in time?

"Send me back in," I said.

After speaking to the Brothers we returned to the *Vaymyr*. Cho waited until I'd had breakfast with Vikram, Miguel and Antti, and then asked for the link to be reinstated. Then it was just a matter of time, waiting for our twinned control structures to mesh again, as they had during that brief flash in the corridor. It couldn't be predicted or rushed.

Cho wanted to have me under close observation, so I was strapped into the dental chair while Dr. Abramik and the other technicians set up their monitoring gear. Margaret's team was handling the signal acquisition and processing hardware; Abramik's people the biomedical systems. There were lots of screens, lots of traces and graphs. They even had pen recorders running, twitching out traces onto paper, just in case there was a power-drop and the electronic data was lost or corrupted.

"We'll hope for a deeper immersion," Cho said. "Get what you can—any details, no matter how trivial. But the moment you feel like you're not in control, or the situation is too complicated for you to act plausibly, issue the abort command. I'd rather pull you out early than run into paradox noise. Is that understood?"

"Understood."

"Then good luck, Miss Lidova."

I waited and waited. It wasn't like trying to fall asleep, or drift into a trance. My internal mental state didn't matter at all. Stillness was the only real prerequisite, to reduce the neural traffic burden to a manageable level during these early stages. Given that it had taken weeks for me to have the first glimpse, there was a strong chance that it might not happen at all today, or indeed for many days. But I felt confident that it would happen more readily the second time, and that with each occurrence it would become easier to induce the next.

Eventually—an hour or so after I climbed into the chair—it clicked.

As before, there was no warning. Just a sharp transition in my visual input—switching from the signals in my optic nerves to those in hers, intercepted and translated by the control structures.

I found myself in a room this time, not a corridor. I was reclining, but more fully than in the dental chair. I was in a bed, lying nearly horizontal but with my head propped up against pillows.

I could feel them. I'd been a disembodied presence during the first glimpse, seeing but not experiencing, but now there was a tactile component to the immersion. I registered a soft enclosing pressure around the back of my neck, as well as a faint scratchiness, not quite sharp enough to count as discomfort. Excited by this new level of sensory detail, I made an unconscious effort to alter the angle of my gaze. More of the room came into view, but out of focus, as if through foggy glass.

It was a hospital room. To the left was a wall with an outside window, blinds drawn and angled slightly to deflect daylight. In front of me, beyond the foot of the bed, was a blank wall with a blank rectangular screen attached via an angled bracket. To my right was a partition wall containing a door and a curtained window, which must face out into a corridor or ward.

I swivelled my gaze a bit more, moving her entire head. I felt a variation in the scratchiness, my head shifting on the pillow. Bedside cabinets to the left and right. A chair with padding coming out of its fabric. A fire extinguisher by the door.

Now came an auditory impression. It must have been there all along, but I was only now processing it. Low voices, coming from the other side of the door. Footsteps, doors opening and closing. Beeps and electronic tones. Telephone sounds, hospital noises. The ordinary, busy clamour of a large institution. It could be a school, a government building, our own project. It didn't sound like the past.

I was able to move my head, so I tried my right arm. It responded, even if it felt as if I were trying to push my way through treacle. I lifted it as high as I could go. My sleeve fell back, exposing skin nearly all the way to the elbow joint. I spread her fingers, marvelling at the supreme strangeness of this moment. Whoever my host was, she was definitely younger than me, and all skin and bone.

We knew almost nothing about her, except that she was female. Even that was uncertain. When we dropped the initiating spore into her head via the time-probe, before the spore began to extend itself into a functioning control structure, the spore had run some basic biochemical tests on its immediate environment, and then sent the results of those tests back up to the present using the Luba Pair. The tests had indicated female blood chemistry, but it would have to wait until I was in the body before we had definite verification of gender, ethnicity, age and so forth.

A plastic bracelet had been fixed around the wrist. I twisted the hand, bringing a plastic window into view with printed details beneath it. Even though the room was out of focus, I could read the label quite easily. It said: T. DINOVA.

Growing more confident in my control, I inspected both arms for signs of surgical monitors or drip-lines, just in case I was wired into some machine or monitor. But there was nothing. Cautiously, I pushed myself a bit higher in the bed. There was a tray in front of me, resting on a table that had been wheeled across the bed from one side. On the tray was a mostly finished meal, with a plate sitting under a transparent plastic heat-cover and a knife and fork set on the plate. I stared at the food for a few seconds, wondering how it compared with our rations, even the improved rations at the station. Somewhere in this hospital, I thought, there would be a huge, bustling kitchen where thousands of meals were prepared each day, where food was made and food wasted, and no one really cared.

Still, at least my host must have had an appetite.

I reached back with my left hand to explore my scalp. I found a bandage, quite a heavy one, but no wires or tubes.

There wasn't anything to stop me from getting out of bed.

I felt I owed it to Cho to try. I had to give him something more than a scrap of a name. I folded back the sheets, gaining—it seemed to me—a little more fluency with each action.

I had on a hospital gown and nothing else. I swung my bare legs out of bed, steadying myself with both hands, then planted my feet on the floor. Cold. I smelled something, as well: a musty tang that clung to me as I pushed my way off the bed.

Me. My own unwashed self.

I tried to stand.

I pushed myself up, right hand against the bed, left using the bedside cabinet as a support. My knees were weak under me, but after using a cane for fifteen years I was accustomed to a certain unsteadiness. I risked a step in the direction of the window, deciding that it was my best option for immediate orientation. I made one unsteady footfall, my vision still not fully in focus, my head feeling swollen and top-heavy. But I was upright. I took another step, arms wide like a zombie tightrope-walker. Two more paces and I'd reached the window, grasping for the temporary support of the sill.

I paused to catch my breath and wait for a wave of dizziness to pass.

She must have been feeling me. That was a given, if she was conscious. Her eyes were open when I dropped into her, so she must have been at least semiawake. And then her body started doing things on its own. How frightening that must have seemed. She could still see through her own eyes, still experience sounds and impressions, but the control was mine. I decided what she did and what she looked at.

"I'm sorry," I tried to say. "I promise this is only temporary."

A mush of slurred syllables spilled from my mouth.

"Sorry," I tried again, concentrating on that one word in the hope that some part of it might get through.

Still, I had more immediate and pressing issues than this woman's mental well-being. I used my free hand to fumble at the drawstring. The dusty plastic blinds started to click toward the ceiling, and I gained my first fuzzy impression of the world beyond this room.

Out of focus, still. But enough to be going on with. I was several floors up, looking down on a courtyard flanked by what must be two wings of the hospital, extending out from the part of the building containing my room. All concrete, metal and glass. If the layout of the wings was any guide, I had to be on the sixth floor of an eight-storey building.

What else could I give Cho? In the courtyard, paths wound their way around an ornamental pond. Farther out, there was a service road and some parked vehicles, glinting in sunshine, and beyond that some outlying buildings. The ground shadows were attenuated. I couldn't see the sun, but it had to be quite high up in the sky.

I glanced back at the bedside cabinet and made out the silvery squiggle of a pair of glasses.

Cho had told me that even the smallest detail could help with locating my position, even something as innocuous as a vehicle registration number. Suitably determined, I started my return to the bedside. I'd only taken a couple of steps when there was a polite tap on the door. A moment later it swung open and a white-coated young man stepped in from the space beyond the partition wall.

Get out of me.

My knees buckled. I started to stumble. The young doctor looked at me for an instant, then sprang in my direction. He'd been carrying a sheath of papers, which he tossed onto the bed to free his hands. I felt him catch me just before I went over completely. For a second, ludicrously, we were posed like a pair of ballroom dancers, me swooning into his embrace.

I took him in. Twenties, fresh-faced, a dusting of youthful stubble, but just enough tiredness around the eyes to suggest a junior doctor's workload.

"What are you playing at, Tatiana?" he said, in perfectly good and clear Russian. "You're barely out of surgery, and already trying to break your neck?"

I looked at him. I wanted to reply, wanted to give him an answer that would satisfy his curiosity, but I wasn't ready.

What are you waiting for?

"Permafrost," I whispered, repeating the word twice more.

Cho had come back to Kogalym two days after our meeting in the school. He'd been south on some business.

"Very good, Miss Lidova!" he said, shouting above the engine noise. "I am so glad you will be joining us!"

I had to shout in reply.

"You promise me the pupils will be well looked after?"

"The arrangements are already in place—I've spoken to all the local administrators and made sure that they understand what needs to be done." His gaze settled onto my surly-faced porter, the man who'd been deputised to help with my baggage and books. "That is properly understood, Mr. Evmenov? I'll hold you personally accountable if there's any lapse in the provisions." Cho beckoned me aboard. "Quickly, please. We don't want to lose our weather window."

I went up the ramp, stooping to avoid denting my head on the overhang. My cane thumped on the metal floor. I had to squeeze past some hefty item occupying most of the helicopter's cargo section. It was the size of a small truck and covered in sheets. It didn't have the shape of a truck, though. More a turbine or aircraft engine: something large and cylindrical. Or a piece of genetics equipment: some industrial unit recovered from an abandoned university or industrial plant.

"What is that thing, Mister Cho?" I asked, as I was shown to my seat just behind the cockpit, on the right side of the helicopter. "A gene synthesizer, for your seed program?"

As he buckled in opposite me, Cho considered my question, tilting his head slightly to one side. It meant that he was searching for an answer that was close to the truth, while not being the thing itself.

"It does have a medical application, yes."

The engine surged and the rotors dragged us into the air. We were soon flying north from Kogalym. We passed over a scattering of ghost towns and villages, no lights showing from their empty buildings. The terrain was getting icier with each kilometre we covered.

After a few hours we touched down near an isolated military compound. Cho asked me if I wanted to stretch my legs; I declined. Cho got out and stood around while some trucks came out to meet us. Hoses were connected and fuel began to gurgle in. Another truck came, this time with a flatbed. Some boxes were unpacked and driven away. Cho got back aboard and we fought our way back into the air.

"We were a little heavy," Cho said, turning to address me across the narrow aisle. "We had to unload some nonessential supplies, or we wouldn't have made it between fuel stops." He waved his fingers. "It's nothing to worry about."

We continued into darkness. There were no lights out there at all now. Every now and then the helicopter would put out a searchlight and I'd be surprised at how high or low we were.

"How far north are we going, Director?"

"To the Yenisei Gulf. It's a little remote, but it turned out that it was the best place to locate our project. We needed somewhere with maritime access, in any case."

"Something to do with your seeds? A genetics lab?"

Cho reached into a pouch behind the pilot's position. He drew out a document and passed it to me. It was a scarlet brochure, with a translucent plastic cover. On the front was the World Health logo, followed by a statement in several languages to the effect that the contents were of the highest security rating.

I looked at him doubtfully, before I opened the document.

"Go ahead," Cho said. "You're committed now."

I opened the document.

On the inside page was a logo. It was a six-armed snowflake with three letters in the middle of it.

The letters were:

PRE

I turned over to the next page. It was blank except for three words in Russian:

Permafrost Retrocausal Experiment

I looked at Cho, but his expression gave nothing away. Behind his round-rimmed glasses, his eyes were sharply observant but betraying nothing more.

Once again, I felt as if I was under assessment.

I turned to the next page. There was a very short paragraph, again in Russian.

The Permafrost Retrocausal Experiment aims to use Luba Pairs to achieve past-directed time travel.

I turned to the next page. It became very technical very quickly. There was talk of time-injection, time-probes, Luba Pairs, Lidova noise, grandfathering.

Interspersed with the text were graphs and equations. Some of them I recognised well enough from my mother's papers, but there were also aspects well outside my own limited expertise, or perhaps recollection.

I went all the way through the document, then turned back to the prefacing paragraph to make sure I wasn't going mad.

It seemed that I wasn't.

We flew on for a few more minutes. I debated with myself what to say, and how I might say it. Perhaps it was all still a test, to gauge the limits of my credulity. How stupid would I need to be, to think that any of this was real?

But Cho did not seem like a man predisposed to frivolity.

"You're attempting time travel."

"We're not attempting it," Cho answered carefully.

"Of course not."

"We've already achieved it."

The sound of engines always made me drowsy. I was daydreaming of being back in Cho's helicopter, thinking of the first time I'd seen the lights of Permafrost, when a shrill beep pulled me back into Antti's Cessna. It was the GPS system, alerting us to something. I turned to Antti, expecting him to respond to the notification, but his head was slumped, his chin lolling onto his collar, his eyes slitted. The GPS alert didn't sound urgent enough to mean that anything was seriously wrong with the plane, but it must have meant that we'd arrived at some waypoint, some moment in our journey when my companion was supposed to take action.

"Antti," I said.

The plane carried on. The beeping continued. I called out his name again, and when that didn't work I jabbed him in the ribs with my elbow, avoiding the area on the right side of his chest where he'd been wounded. Antti grunted, and shuddered back to consciousness. There was a second of fogginess, then he took action, adjusting the controls and flicking switches, until the twin alarms eventually silenced.

"It was nothing. I just dozed off for a second or two."

"You were out cold." I reached out and touched the back of my hand against his forehead. "You're clammy. What the hell happened back there?"

Antti managed a self-effacing smile. "Maybe he got me a bit deeper than I thought. Nicked more than a rib."

"You need a hospital. It could be anything: internal bleeding, organ damage, infection. There are still some towns ahead of us. Get us down now, while you're still able to land safely."

"I'm all right," Antti said, straightening up in the seat. "I can do this. We can do this. We have to get to the Yenisei Gulf."

I nodded, desperately wanting to believe him. What other option did I have? But that tiredness was already showing in his eyes again.

It began as a glimmer of yellow and blue lights on the horizon, casting a pastel radiance on the low-lying clouds over the station. The helicopter came in closer, dropping altitude. The lights were arranged in a flattened circle, like a coin seen nearly edge-on, a makeshift community of labs and offices staked down on frozen ground, with a sharp enclosing boundary, like a medieval encampment.

So I thought.

Closer still. There was flat ice under us now: not frozen ground, but frozen water. Gently rising ground to either side of this tongue of ice, the compound built entirely on the flat part.

It was a river, or an inlet, completely frozen.

The enclosing shield was not continuous, I realised. It was made up of the hulls of ships: numerous slab-sided vessels gathered in a ringlike formation. The lights were coming from their superstructures. That was all it was: lots of ships, gathered together, some forming a ring and others contained within it, with one very large ship in the middle.

Cho looked at me, waiting for a reaction, something in his manner suggesting a quiet pride.

I decided to let him speak.

"We had need of secrecy, as well as isolation from sources of electrical and acoustic noise," he explained. "We also had to be largely independent, with our own power supply. In the end, the most practical solution was to base our experiment around these ships. They were sailed into this inlet when the waters were still navigable, before the freeze got really bad."

We circled the perimeter. There were ships of all shapes and sizes. A small majority were obviously ex-military, but there were also cargo ships and some with cranes or heavy industrial equipment on their decks. A medium-sized cruise liner, a passenger ferry, a few tugs, even a submarine, only the upper part of it showing above the ice.

Cho pointed out the names of some of the ships. "That is the *Vaymyr*, where you will spend most of your time. That is the *Nunivak*, where we have our heavy workshops. That is the *Wedell . . .* "

By far the largest ship, though, was an aircraft carrier.

"That is the hub of our experiment," Cho said. "The *Admiral Nerva*. Ex-Indian Navy, fully nuclear. It's where we've gathered the time-probes, the devices we use to inject matter into the past. They're very sensitive to interference, so there are only ever a small number of technicians allowed on the *Nerva*."

"These probes are time machines? Time machines that you've built, and actually got to work?"

"To a degree."

"You said you'd done it."

"We have—but not as well, or as reliably, as we'd wish."

We picked up height to get over the cordon. There were no other helicopters flying around, although I did see another one parked on the back of one of the ships. All the ships were interconnected, strung together by cables and bridges, some of which were quite sturdy looking and others not much better than rope-ways. Since the decks were all at different levels, the bridges were either sloped or went into the sides of the hulls, through doors that must have been cut into them just for Permafrost. There were also doors down on the level of the ice, and some tracks in the ice marked by lanterns. I spotted a tractor labouring between two of the ships, dragging some huge, sheeted thing behind it on a sort of sledge.

We began to descend. There was a landing pad under us, on the back of a squat, upright-looking ship with a disproportionately tall superstructure.

"This is the *Vaymyr*," Cho said. "One of our key vessels. It supplies a large fraction of our power budget, but it also serves as our main administrative centre. My offices are in the *Vaymyr*, as well as several laboratories, kitchens, recreational areas and your own personal quarters, which I hope will be to your satisfaction. You'll meet the pilots very shortly, and I think you'll get on very well with them. They'll be grateful for your expertise."

"Pilots?"

"I ought to say prospective pilots. They'll be the ones who go into time, when the experiment's problems are ironed out. But as yet none of them have gone back. We are close, though. There are no longer any fundamental obstacles. It's largely the final question of paradox noise that's causing us difficulties."

"I think you may be expecting too much of me."

"I doubt it very much," Cho answered.

He asked me why I had been so quick to issue the abort phrase, just when we were getting somewhere.

"The young doctor was talking to her, and I knew I wasn't going to be able to respond properly."

"Why was that an immediate difficulty?"

"She's in hospital, and she's just had something done to her head. If she starts not being able to speak properly, they may think something's very wrong with her, and then order a follow-up test. I didn't want to take that chance, in case they take her back to the radiology department."

"We still don't really know what happened, between your first and second episodes. Clearly there was no lasting damage."

"Maybe they never put her in the scanner that time. There are other things in radiology departments besides MRI machines."

"That's possible," allowed Abramik, who was sitting in on the interrogation/debrief. "An X-ray, for instance, or even a CT scan. But you have a name for us, at least."

"Tatiana Dinova," I answered.

Cho reached over desktop clutter to switch on his intercom again. "Brothers. Run a search on a possible host subject named Tatiana Dinova." His eyes flicked to me. "Under forty at the time of the immersion?"

I thought of her hands, how young they'd looked compared to my own.

"Probably."

"No unusual spelling?"

"I saw the surname written down, but only heard the doctor mention her given name. Dinova. D - I - N - O - V - A. You'd better try variant spellings of Tatiana, just in case."

"We shall," said Dmitri through the intercom speaker. "Does Miss Lidova have any other parameters that may be useful?"

"It was before the Scouring," I said. "That much I'm sure of. A big hospital with about eight floors, with wings stretching out from a central block. It didn't look like winter to me. I think we were farther south than Kogalym, but still in Russia."

"Time-probe eighteen was only active at three locations before it came into Director Cho's possession," said Pavel, who had the highest-sounding voice of the Brothers. "One of these was a military institution in Poland, so that may be discarded on the basis of Miss Lidova's testimony."

"I was in Russia," I affirmed. "The signs were in Russian, the doctor spoke Russian. What are the other two places?"

"Two institutions," said Ivan, who had the deepest and slowest voice of the four. "Both west of the Ural Mountains. One is a private medical facility in Yaroslavl, about two hundred kilometres northeast of Moscow. However, the ground-plan and three-storey architecture of this facility does not correspond with Miss Lidova's account. The second facility is more promising. This is the public hospital in Izhevsk, approximately one thousand kilometres east of Moscow."

The printer in the corner of Cho's office clicked and whirred to life. A sheet of paper went through it and then slid into the out-tray. Cho wheeled his chair to the printer, collected the paper by his fingertips and returned it to his desk. The paper curled and twitched like some dying marine organism. Cho smoothed it down, using one of his dismantled gadgets, a piece of dial-like instrumentation, as a makeshift paperweight. I leaned over to examine the paper, seeing it upside-down from my perspective.

It was the plan of a hospital, extracted from some civic or architectural database within the Brothers' collective memory.

"That's it," I said, with a giddy sense of recognition. "No doubt about it. I can even see the courtyard and the pond, and the car park beyond the service road. I must have been—must be—in that main block, between the first two wings, looking due north."

"The Izhevsk facility was always a high-likelihood target," Cho said. "But it is good to have this confirmed. Do you have more for us, Brothers?"

"May we assume that the host is present in the Izhevsk facility?" asked Dmitri.

"You may," Cho said.

"Then the injection window must lie between 2022 and 2037, the period in which time-probe eighteen was installed and active in Izhevsk," Dmitri replied. "We are retrieving patient records for that hospital, as well as civil documents for the greater Izhevsk region."

"Who is she?" I asked, prickling with anticipation. I knew it wouldn't take them long to sift their memories.

"We have identified Tatiana Dinova," said Ivan. "Would you like a biographical summary, Director Cho?"

Cho nodded. "Send it through."

His printer began again. The life of a woman, almost certainly long dead, began to spool into the out-tray. Tatiana Dinova, whoever she was. *My* Tatiana Dinova.

My host: my means of altering the past.

"You'll have to convince them you're well enough to be discharged," Abramik said, stroking the tip of his beard. "I can help you with some neurological pointers, if you start being questioned. But in the meantime, we'll need a contingency plan—a fallback in case they try to bring you back to the radiology section." He turned to Cho. "Could we risk limited sabotage of the probe, if Valentina got close enough to it?"

"Provided it *was* limited. If she damages the machine beyond repair, we'll be in quite a lot of trouble."

"It wouldn't need to be that bad," Abramik said. "There'll be an emergency control somewhere nearby, probably on a wall or under a hinged cover. It's what they'd use if there was a problem during a scan: dumps the helium from the magnets, lets them warm up and lose their superconducting current. It's quicker and safer than just cutting the power. All she'd need to do is reach that control, and she'd have the element of surprise. The one thing they won't be expecting is that."

"We could risk erasing the probe's quantum memory," Margaret countered. "Those magnets can't go through too many warm-up cycles before they cease being traversable by Luba Pairs."

"Then something not *quite* as drastic," Abramik said, flashing an irritated look at the physicist, as if she were being deliberately obstructive, rather than raising an entirely reasonable concern. "Smuggle a metal object into the room, something ferromagnetic, keep it hidden until the last moment. If we're lucky, it'll be attracted to the machine before the field has a chance to do any lasting damage to the control structure."

"If Tatiana's lucky, you mean," I said.

My first evening at Permafrost was like any first time at a large, unfamiliar institution. I'd been wrenched from the small, settled world of a provincial teacher and thrown into a busy, complex environment full of new faces and protocols. In a well-meaning way, Cho was trying to spoon as much information as possible into me as we went to my quarters, up a couple of flights of stairs inside the icebreaker *Vaymyr*. He was explaining emergency drills, power cuts, medical arrangements, mealtimes, social gatherings, pointing this way and that as if I could see through grey metal walls to the rooms and ships beyond, and as if I had a hope of remembering half of it. Eventually I stopped listening, knowing that it would all fall into place in its own time.

"You may well wish to unwind after our journey," Cho was saying as we reached my room. "But if I could impose on you a little longer, it would be very good to meet the pilots as soon as possible." He lifted a sleeve to glance at his watch. "If we are lucky, they will still be in the canteen."

"Give me a minute," I said.

While Cho waited at the door to my room I tidied away my bag then stripped down to a sweater and a shirt, much as I would have worn during classroom hours. I went to the basin and splashed some water on my face, a token effort at freshening up after the helicopter flight. I looked tired, old. Not ready for a new adventure, but rather someone who'd already been through too many in one life.

I stepped out of the room, locking it with the key I'd been given.

"Tell me about the pilots."

"Our four prospective time travellers. You'll be working closely with them as we deal with the remaining obstacles."

I thought of the scale and probable expense of this operation.

"Just four, after all the trouble you've gone to?"

"I would gladly wish for more. But we are limited by factors outside our control, including our access to neural nanotechnology." For a moment Cho, too, showed something of the strain life had put on him. "Such things are in very short supply these days, and we've had to fight hard to consolidate what we have. That is true of the project as a whole, from our secondhand ships to the time-probes themselves. Everything is make-do-and-mend, and we cannot be too choosy." But he flashed an encouraging smile. "What we can be is resourceful and adaptable—and I think we have been."

The canteen was quiet, except for a small group at one of the tables near a main window. They were leaning into each other, engaged in low, urgent conversation. Young and early-middle-aged people, men and women both, a blend of accents. Remains of food on their trays, half-finished drinks, beer bottles, a pack of cards, a paperback book. There was no chance that this little room was capable of providing for twelve hundred people, even with staggered shifts, so I guessed this was what amounted to the VIP dining area.

Cho knocked on the serving hatch and got them to open up for us.

"It's still dried or frozen food, for the most part," he said. "But we are very fortunate in having the pick of the available rations flown in for us, from all areas of World Health. They've been made to understand the importance of our effort, if not its precise nature."

Once we'd gotten our food he steered me to the table where the other people were seated.

"That said, we work like dogs." He pulled out a seat for me, while balancing his tray single-handedly. "There are twelve hundred people stationed here at Permafrost, all exceptional individuals. All valued. But there are fewer than a dozen of us that I would describe as truly irreplaceable—and you are now one of them. We are up against time, Miss Lidova—in all senses. If it takes us ten years to safeguard those seeds, it'll be too late for our food scientists and agronomists to put them to effective use. In fact we have much less time than that. The Brothers tell us that we have about six to nine months to make a difference—a year at the most. After that, we're wasting time. Quite literally."

"The Brothers?"

"Dmitri, Ivan, Alexei and Pavel. *The Brothers Karamazov*. Artificial intelligences, assisting with our endeavour. More make-do-and-mend. They're on the *Nerva*, so you'll meet them eventually." Cho and I took our places, squeezing into orange plastic chairs between the other people. "This is Miss Valentina Lidova," he said, extending a hand to me. "Would you mind introducing yourselves? I assure you she doesn't bite."

A woman leaned over and shook my hand. She had a confident grip. She was about twenty years younger than me, with long black hair and a wide, friendly face, with prominent freckles across the cheekbones.

"I am Antti," she said, speaking slightly accented Russian. "Originally from Finland, one of the pilots." She gave Cho a wary, questioning look. "Does she know, Director?"

"A little," Cho said. He used an opener to work the top off a bottle of beer, and drank directly from the bottle. "You may speak freely, in any case."

"They're trying to send us back in time," Antti said. "Us four pilots. We won't actually go back, really—we'll always be aboard the *Vaymyr*, hooked up to the equipment in the *Admiral Nerva*. We'll just take over hosts in the past, driving their bodies by remote control. That's why they call us pilots. But it'll *feel* like going back, when we're time-embedded."

"If it works," said a handsome, dark-skinned man, hair greying slightly at the temples.

"Of course it'll damn well work," Antti answered. "Why wouldn't it, when the individual steps are all feasible?"

"I am Vikram," said the handsome man, smiling stiffly. "From New Delhi, originally. I hope my Russian isn't too shabby?"

"Oh, stop showing off," Antti said, flashing him an irritated look, as if they were all more than fed up with Vikram's transparent self-deprecation.

"We've sent stuff back," said another man, grinning to lighten the mood, passing me a beer whether I wanted one or not. "Small things, up to about the size of a pollen grain, or an initiating spore of nanotechnology. We know we can do it. It's just a question of putting the final pieces together." He shook my hand. "Christos, from Greece. Or what's left of Greece. Where have you come from, Valentina?"

"Kogalym," I answered. "You won't have heard of it. It's quite a way south, really a nothing sort of place."

"Everywhere is a nothing place soon," said the man next to Christos, who was the only one approaching my own age. Just as well-built as the Greek, but with wrinkles, age spots and mostly silver hair, combed back from his brow. "I am Miguel," he said, speaking Russian but more slowly and stiffly than his comrades. "I am glad they bring you to station." He dropped his voice. "What you know of experiment so far?"

"Director Cho showed me the brochure," I answered truthfully. "Beyond that, almost nothing."

"You'll catch on quickly," said the fifth person at the table, who was a small woman with glasses and a severe black fringe. "I'm Margaret. Margaret Arbetsumian, mathematical physicist."

"Margaret worked on quantum experimental systems before the Scouring," said Cho. "If anyone could turn Luba Lidova's ideas into something practical, I knew it would be Margaret. Miss Lidova could use a rest tonight, Margaret, but in the morning would you care to show her the experimental apparatus—perhaps demonstrate a minimal-case paradox?"

"It'd be my pleasure," Margaret said.

"As for me," said the sixth person at the table, a slender, neatly groomed man with a pointed beard, "what I understand about time travel or paradoxes you could write on the back of a very small napkin. But I do know a thing about physiology, and neuroscience, and nano-therapeutic systems. Dr. Peter Abramik—Peter to my friends." Then he narrowed his eyes, as if sensing the extent of my ignorance. "You really are in the dark about this, aren't you?"

I sipped at my beer and took a few mouthfuls of curry, just to show that I wasn't intimidated by either my new surroundings or my new colleagues. "I'm seventy-one years old," I said, uttering the words as a plain statement of fact, inviting neither pity nor reverence. "The last time I had any serious involvement in my mother's work was fifty years ago, when I was barely into my twenties." I ate a little bit more, purposefully refusing to be hurried. "That said, I've never forgotten it. My mother worked on quantum models for single-particle time travel. She showed how an electron—or anything else, really, provided you could manipulate it, and measure its quantum state—an *electron* could be sent back in time, looped back into the past to become a twin of itself in the future, one half of a Luba Pair. If you manipulated either element of the Luba Pair, the other one responded. You could send signals up and down time. But that was all. You couldn't send back anything much larger than an electron—maybe an atom, a molecule, at the extreme limit, before macroscopic effects collapsed the Luba Pairing. And just as critically, you couldn't observe that time travel had happened. It was like a conjuring trick done in the dark. The moment you tried to observe a Luba Pair in their time-separated state, you got washed out by noise effects."

"Paradox," Margaret said. "Black and white. Either present or absent. If you don't observe, paradox hides its claws. If you attempt to observe, it kills you—metaphorically, mostly."

I nodded. "That's correct."

"But your mother went beyond binary paradox," Cho said. "She developed a whole class of models in which paradox is a noise effect, a parameter with grey values, rather than just black and white."

"She spoke about it less as she got older," I replied. "They hammered her, the whole establishment. Treated her like an idiot. Why the hell should she indulge them anymore?"

"Your mother was correct," Cho said placidly. "This we know. Paradox is inherent in any time-travelling system. But it is containable . . . treatable. We have learned that there are classes of paradox, layers of paradox."

Margaret made an encouraging gesture in the direction of Director Cho. "Say it. You know you want to."

Cho reached for his beer, smiling at the invitation. "Paradox itself is . . . not entirely paradoxical."

The hospital meal service came around. They wheeled the table across my bed, then set out the tray with its plastic cover. I waited until the orderly was out of the room, hid the knife under my pillow, then used the call button to summon them back, before complaining that I didn't have a knife.

It could have gone several ways at that point, but the orderly only shrugged and returned with a fresh knife.

What are you going to do with that?

It was a voice in my head. I'd heard it before, during my previous immersion, but it was stronger and clearer now—beyond the point of being ignored.

You heard me. I asked a question. You're taking me over, at least have the decency to answer it.

It was Tatiana. I knew it.

I phrased a reply. I didn't need to speak it, just voice the statement aloud in my head.

You're not supposed to be able to speak to me.

And who are you to say what I can and can't do? This is my body, my life. What are you doing in me?

Trying to help. Trying to sort out a mess. That's all you have to know.

I sweated. Me or her, or perhaps both of us. Something was happening with the control structures that was not part of the plan. My host was conscious and communicative, and receiving sensory impressions from upstream.

Who are you?

I debated with myself before answering. I had never been very good at lying, and I didn't think I was going to get any better just because I was lying to a voice inside my own head. Worse, perhaps. So I decided that I would be better sticking to the truth, at least a part of it.

Valentina. I'm . . . a schoolteacher. From an arse-end town called Kogalym. Not a demon, not a witch. But that's all I can tell you, and that's already too much.

Are you a hallucination? You don't sound like a hallucination.

I'm not. But what I am is . . . look, can we eat your dinner?

You need to eat?

No. But you do.

Silence, but only for a few seconds.

Where are you from, Valentina? Where are you right now, besides being in my head?

You wouldn't believe me.

Maybe I won't, but you can still answer my question.

All right. I'll tell you this much. I'm aboard a ship, an icebreaker, in northern Russia. I'm in a chair, with doctors and scientists fussing around me. And I'm coming into you from fifty-two years in the future.

Another silence—longer this time. Nearly enough to make me think she might have gone away for good.

I'd say you were mad, or lying. Then again, there is a voice in my head, and you have been making me do things. So, for the moment, I'm going to accept this stupid thing you've just told me, because I'd still rather believe you than accept that I'm the mad one.

You're not the mad one.

Then how about you start by telling me how this is happening? How are you in me?

By means of something we put into your head. You were having an MRI scan, and . . . that's how we do it. That's how we reach the past, from 2080. We inject something into your head, a thing about the size of a grain of pollen, and it grows through your brain and lets me take you over, just for a short while.

Why?

So we can get something done. Something important.

And what gives you this right?

Nothing. No right at all. But it still has to be done. We're in a mess here, Tatiana, a really bad one, but we can fix things a little by altering the past. Just a tiny amount—not enough to change your life or anyone else's. And after we're done, after you've helped us, you'll never hear from us again. The thing in your brain, the control structure, will self-dismantle. It'll flush itself out of you harmlessly, and you just get on with being you, as if nothing had ever happened.

She echoed back my words with a cold mockery.

As if nothing had ever happened. Do you really think it'll be that simple?

I do.

Then at least you've settled one question for me. I know which one of us is insane.

After that, she let me get on with eating in peace and quiet.

Perhaps she'd decided to see if I went away if she stopped interrogating me. That said, it was very definitely me in charge of her as I worked my way through the hospital meal. But exactly how strange would that have felt, anyway? I thought of the times I'd spooned my way through government rations, my mind on the homework I was supposed to be marking, barely conscious of my hand as it went from plate to mouth. There were days when all of us might as well be under the control of disembodied spirits from the future, for all the difference it makes.

Yet this was a screwup, and no mistake. She wasn't supposed to be able to talk to me or hear me in return. It was nothing Cho had ever mentioned as a normal aspect of the control structure functionality. But then again, all of this was experimental. No one had ever linked together two control structures through time, via Luba Pairs.

The meal wasn't bad. I could already smell and taste quite well by then, and it was surprising how full-up I felt by the time I'd emptied the plate. The food wasn't going into my stomach, but the signals from Tatiana's digestive system were still finding their way to my brain, producing the effect of a steadily diminishing appetite.

"We're not bad people," I'd mouthed to myself.

Then what are you?

She was back again.

Please . . . for my sake . . . for your sake . . . just pretend none of this is happening.

I wish I could. Trouble is, I keep getting these flashes of double vision. I'm here, and then I'm somewhere else. Not this room. Somewhere without any windows, all metal. I'm in a chair, leaning back, and there are people crowding around. Lots of machines and lights. What is it, some secret government laboratory? Are you testing some way of turning ordinary people into zombies? Putting things in our heads, while we're in hospital? Is that it?

Yes. That's exactly it. Mind-control drones. The government's in on it. So's the hospital. And they're reading your mind right now. You're about the tenth subject we've burned through so far. I'd really like to protect you, too, but if you keep talking aloud in your own head, keep asking questions, they're going to pick up on it, and . . .

And nothing. You just want me to shut up, is all it is. Still, I think you told me the truth about Kogalym. I had an aunt there once. And you're right, it really is a shit-hole. No one would ever have made that part up.

The one good thing was that sooner or later even Tatiana Dinova had to sleep.

I'd worked out a system with the knife by then, one we'd rehearsed upstream as best we could. If I pushed the admissions bracelet as far up my arm as it would go, I could wedge the handle of the knife under it, with the sharp end digging into the crook of my elbow. It wasn't comfortable, and it relied on my keeping an angle in my arm, but it kept the knife from showing when I let down my sleeve.

The hospital wasn't a restful place at night. There were fewer admissions, the televisions were turned down, and the staff kept their conversations low, but it made very little difference. Electronic monitors still went off at all hours, beeping tones cutting through walls and floors, patients coughed and complained, telephones rang and elevators whined and clattered. Then there were shift changes and people being paged, and fire and security alarms going off in distant wings.

By five the blinds were doing a bad job of masking the arrival of daylight. The doctors were starting their morning rounds. Curtains were being swished back along curving rails. Voices were going up again, the coughs and complaints more full-throated. I reached under the pillow and extracted the knife, then slid it back up my sleeve.

A few minutes before six, the young doctor came into the room, along with an orderly and a vacant wheelchair.

"Good morning, Tatiana. How are we today?"

Oh, I'm fine. I can't control my body, and there's another voice in my skull, but other than that . . .

"I'm all right, thank you," I said, speaking aloud for the first time since becoming time-embedded, and forcing out the words as if both our lives depended on it. "Much better than yesterday."

He looked at me for a few seconds. I wondered what was going through his head, the details that were nagging at him. Was my accent and diction consistent with Tatiana Dinova? Was she the sort to say "thank you" at all?

But he smiled and nodded.

"You sound much better. And that confusion you mentioned yesterday— that's all cleared up?"

"No—I'm all right. Whatever that was, it passed."

I wish you would pass. I was hoping you were a bad dream from last night. But you're sticking around, aren't you?

The knife was tight against my armpit.

Just for a little while—yes. I said we've got work to do. But I'm sure we'll get used to each other in time.

On the morning of my first full day at Permafrost, Margaret, Antti and I put on clean-room outfits and then went through a positive-pressure airlock into the *Vaymyr*'s laboratory.

The room was about the size of a large double garage and surgically clean. Positioned on a central bench, surrounded by ancillary equipment and computers, was an upright silver cylinder, about the size of an oil drum. It was festooned with cables and monitors, with telescopelike devices peering into it at various angles.

Margaret went to the device and brought one of the computers to life. Fans whirred. Data and graphs appeared on an array of monitor screens.

"This is how we first created and manipulated a Luba Pair," she said, sounding like a proud parent. "In essence, it's really just a cavity surrounded by a very powerful superconducting magnet. You recall your mother's work on quantum memory states in superconducting systems?"

I nodded in my mask and clean-room hood. "That was when she was beginning to get bounced by the respectable journals."

"That must have been hard for her," Antti said, just her eyes meeting mine over her mask.

We had shared a house since Father died, and my mother had come to depend on me as a sounding board for her wilder ideas, almost as if I were an extension of herself, only a more skeptical, questioning one. That had been flattering to me, when I was in my middle and late teens. To have this celebrated intellect, this world-famous mathematician, treating me as an equal, someone capable of seeing her ideas through fresh eyes, made me feel very special.

But by the time I was approaching my twenties, I knew I had to strike out on my own. I wasn't going to run off and do anything crazy like join a radical arts collective. I still wanted to be a mathematician, but in my own fresh corner of it, a long way away from my mother's crazy work on time-loops and grey paradox.

She took it as a betrayal. Not to my face, not to begin with, but it was always there, simmering. That resentment grew and grew over one long, hot summer, until we had a major bust-up.

Things had never been the same after that.

"Hard on both of us," I said, answering Antti. "All a long time ago, in any case. You're too young to remember what the world was like back then, but it all feels like a different life. I remember the work, though. That's as fresh in my mind as it ever was. All very speculative, even by Mother's standards. But according to her theory, if you were going to attempt to build a time machine, this is where you'd start: with a superconducting system."

"Is the experiment running?" Antti asked.

"Yes, we're in the operating regime," Margaret said. "Luba Pairs are being bred inside the assembly. We're sending electrons back from the future, exactly a minute upstream. They're travelling back sixty seconds, appearing in the magnet, holding coherence for a short while, then becoming noise-limited, which means we can't track the correlation anymore."

It was warm enough in the laboratory, but still I shivered. "This is really happening?"

Antti beckoned me to one of the screens, where a wriggling yellow line was describing a kind of seismic trace. "This is the correlation, summed across multiple Luba Pairs, so that we keep one step ahead of the decoherence effect. It's a signal from the future, so to speak. Our future, one minute ahead of now. It's very noisy in the raw state. We run it through a battery of signal optimisation algorithms drawn from your mother's work, but we're hitting real limits in our understanding of those algorithms, how to make them fit together. The Brothers . . . " She paused, glancing at Margaret. "It's believed we can do much better, with your guidance."

The yellow line jagged upward suddenly, then collapsed back down to its normal noise level. As the spike inched its way to the left, a pair of brackets dropped down on either side of it, accompanied by a set of statistical parameters.

"What was that?" I asked.

"Could be anything," Antti said, with only vague interest. "A noise spike in the upstream electronics, a shift in the ice under the *Vaymyr*, someone dropping a crate on the upper deck. We'll find out in about forty-five seconds, if it's anything at all."

I grinned at their insouciance.

"You're both taking this way too casually."

"We've had lot of time to get used to what we're doing," Margaret said with an apologetic smile, as if they were being bad hosts by not making more of their experiment. "Even time travel becomes normal when it's your day job."

"You constructed this apparatus?" I asked, nodding at the upright cylinder.

"Put it together from parts, more accurately," Margaret said. "But it certainly didn't exist in any significant form until we assembled it here. You're wondering how far back we could have sent those electrons?"

"I'm thinking that a minute doesn't really buy you anything. Time to cheat the stock markets, if there were still stock markets. But not to solve Director Cho's food crisis."

"If we eliminated every source of noise, we could go back fourteen months, the day we first put the apparatus together. Fourteen months would help us in small ways—we could transmit knowledge that would help speed up the development of the experiment, warning us from blind alleys and dead ends. In practise, though, we're nowhere near that. Twelve hours is our effective limit with this setup."

"And on the *Admiral Nerva*?"

"A little further back," Antti said.

I approached the experiment, wanting to get a closer look at the instrumentation. Along the way my clean-room garment brushed against a pen and clipboard lying on one of adjoining benches. The pen clanged to the floor.

I stared down at it, shaking my head slowly.

"That didn't just happen."

"There's your noise spike," Antti said, stooping down and picking up the pen, then setting it back on the bench as if this was a completely mundane happening. "Congratulations, Valentina. You just made a small alteration to the past."

I looked at Margaret's apparatus, thinking hard, and trying to show that I wasn't totally disorientated by what had just transpired.

"What if another noise spike showed in that trace, and we switched off the experiment immediately?"

"Then you'd be grandfathering," Margaret said. "Sending a causal change upstream, which in turn affects the downstream reality. A true paradox, albeit a relatively mild one. But I can easily demonstrate a low-level paradox without turning off the experiment." Her eyes flicked to a wall clock, a digital counter in a black surround. "In sixty seconds I'll drop this pen again."

I returned my gaze to the noise trace. Immediately a similar spike appeared, and after a few seconds the brackets and statistical parameters appeared.

"All right . . . " I said, eyeing Margaret carefully.

Margaret walked softly to another bench and picked up a second pen. Now she held them both, one in each hand. "You see one spike at the moment, agreed?"

"Agreed."

"That's because our downstream reality reflects an upstream case in which I dropped only one pen, as I promised. That's a closed loop, paradox-free. But I'm going to violate it, by dropping two pens."

The single spike was drifting to the left, now about thirty seconds downstream of our present position. I thought about what would happen when we caught up with the future moment in which Margaret had dropped only one pen. Now there would be two acoustic events, and the Luba Pairs would respond accordingly. The digital trace would have to show two noise spikes, instead of the one that was still visible.

But it hadn't.

Something will happen, I thought, to preserve the present condition. Margaret would drop one pen and it would hit the floor just like the one I'd dropped. But the second would hit her shoe, muffling its impact, so that there was still only one acoustic event. Even that would be weird. But there'd be no paradox, no grandfathering.

The digital clock showed sixty seconds since Margaret picked up the first pen. She dropped it, waited a second, then dropped the second. Both pens had hit the floor, as loudly as the first time.

"We've modified the upstream condition," Margaret said. "The past will now adjust itself to reflect this. But it doesn't happen instantly. We call it causal-lag, a sort of inertia or stickiness."

"It's an outgrowth of your mother's work," Antti put in.

"We're now in a superposition of histories," Margaret continued. "There's the fading state, in which there was just one noise event, and the rising state, in which there are two events. Gradually the rising state will supplant the fading one. Our minds are easily capable of perceiving both histories, until the new condition becomes dominant."

My attention returned to the noise readout. The original spike was still there, but a fresh prominence was rising out of the noise to its right, like a second peak thrusting up from a mountain range. This new spike quickly became as significant as the first, bracketed and annotated. These were noise events that had already been recorded on the system ninety seconds ago.

I blinked.

There was a fuzziness to my thoughts, like the first pleasant stages of drunkenness.

I remembered that there had been one spike. I also remembered that there had *always been two*. My brain was holding two histories within itself, and it was no different, no stranger, no more paradoxical, than crossing my eyes and seeing two slightly offset versions of the same scene.

Antti and Margaret regarded me with a quiet, knowing watchfulness. They'd been through this already, numerous times. It wasn't unusual to them at all.

I thought of the causal-lag Margaret had mentioned.

I remembered my mother at her whiteboard, a summer or two before that bust-up, rubbing out and rehashing one idea after the next. Trying to break through to a new model of time, a fresh way of thinking about the relationships between past and future events, the illusion of the ever-moving now. Time wasn't a river, she said, and it wasn't a circuit-diagram. Nor was it a tree with multiple branches. It was a block structure, more like a crystal lattice than any of those old dead-end paradigms. It was a lattice that spanned the entire existence of the universe, from beginning to end. There were no alternate histories, no branches where the Roman empire never fell or the dinosaurs were never wiped out. Just that single lattice, a single fixed structure. We were in it, embedded in its matrix.

But the lattice wasn't static. There were flaws in it—imperfections, impurities and stress points. What the lattice was trying to do was to settle down into a minimum-energy configuration. But in doing so, those stresses could give way suddenly or propagate a long way from their initial positions. That was the lattice adjusting itself, history settling into a new, temporary configuration. The alterations happened naturally, time murmuring to itself like an old house, but they could also be generated by artificial interventions, such as Margaret's paradox with the two pens. Then, a pattern of changes would ripple through the lattice, the future changing the past, the past changing the future, the future returning the favour, like a series of dying echoes, until a new configuration held sway. But that adjustment process wasn't instantaneous from the point of view of an embedded observer. It was more like the thunderclap arriving after a lighting flash, a delayed portent of the same event. Causal-lag.

But what paradox, exactly?

There'd always been two spikes. Margaret had said she would drop two pens, and the system had detected her future intention, and she had followed through one minute later.

No. I almost had to frown to hold onto it. There'd been that other condition. One spike, not two. One pen drop. It was slipping away, though—hard to recollect, hard to think about. Like a dream fragment that shrivelled to nothing in the light of day.

Gape-mouthed, I stared at my new colleagues.

"What just happened?"

"What do you remember?" Margaret asked.

"Almost nothing. Just that . . ." But I could only shake my own head. "It's gone. Whatever it was, it's gone."

"Do you feel normal?" Antti asked.

"No. Not normal." I steadied myself on the bench. My cane was outside, waiting for me to collect it. "Yes. Normal. But there was something. There *was* something. I just can't hold onto it now."

"We grandfathered," Margaret said. "That's all it could have been. You must have asked us to demonstrate a paradox condition, and we set one up. Swapped one future for another, and then the past swapped around to keep track." She grinned, stooping down to collect the two fallen pens. "It's strange, isn't it?"

I let out a breath. "Crap!"

"Generally the first reaction," Antti said, with a faint approving smile, as if I'd crossed some unspoken threshold of acceptance. "Gets easier, though. Less strange. These are only small paradoxes, after all. You just buckle up and ride the turbulence. Be glad we never go near anything big."

I'd regained enough composure to pay attention to what she was saying. "And if we did?"

"Oh, we can't—luckily," Margaret said. "The noise swamps us long before we ever get close to doing anything *really* stupid."

So I was inducted into the work of Permafrost, a step at a time.

But why that name, exactly, for Director Cho's experiment?

Throughout my time at the station he had never explained it. Appropriate enough for a place so cold, so remote, I supposed. Yet there was also a sense of stillness, changelessness, which must have been an allusion to my mother's block-crystal model of time.

Time as a solid, glacial structure, groaning to itself as defects propagated through its frozen matrix, yet essentially fixed, immutable, persistent, enduring. Time as a white thing, a white landscape, under white skies and ominous squared-off clouds.

Time as a self-reinforcing structure in which all memory of humanity had been quietly erased.

The doctor and the orderly wheeled me to radiology.

You think I'm going to let you stab someone with that knife?

That's not the idea. And even if it was, you wouldn't be able to do much about it, so just sit back and let me handle things.

My arm, the one that was concealing the knife, twitched in my lap. It was a moment of spasm, no more than that, but it was nothing I'd initiated.

You saw that, didn't you?

Be careful.

Or what? I'll drop the knife, and then what'll happen?

What'll happen is that we'll both be in trouble, Tatiana. That machine ahead of us is going to kill you if you get anywhere near it. The knife is how we're going to take the machine out of service, before it turns your brain into hot mush.

I'm so glad that you're concerned.

I am. You're the only body I get to control. I have a duty to make sure you don't end up dead.

So very considerate.

Believe it or not, I also don't want you to get hurt in any part of this. You're an innocent party here. I appreciate that you're angry, but you also have to understand that we're acting for a greater good.

Such a great good, you can't trust me with knowing any part of it. How's that for trust?

Shut up and let me handle this.

The big red doors hissed open on their own as we came near. Beyond was a brighter area, a sort of reception and waiting room with short windowless corridors branching off to the different functions of the department. The MRI section was at the end of one of these corridors, behind another set of red doors.

The space beyond was subdivided into two equal areas, with a glass partition between them. In the first part was the control room for the scanner, with a long desk set with terminals and keyboards. In the other was the scanner itself, with that area kept scrupulously clear of any furniture or associated clutter. The control room was low-lit and spartan, with a technician seated at one of the monitors, clicking away on a computer mouse, taking the occasional sip from a plastic coffee cup.

"Good morning," the young doctor said.

The technician swivelled around and touched a deferential hand to his brow. "Good morning, Dr. Turovsky. Good morning, Igor." Then he nodded at me, and flicked an eye back to his screens. "Miss Dinova."

"Is it working today?" I asked.

"We'll be fine; it was just a stupid software problem." The technician was a burly man in his thirties, with a black chin-beard and tattoos showing around his sleeves and neckline. "They made us install a new operating system—you know how that usually goes."

It's an MRI machine, Valentina. I've already been through it, and it didn't kill me. What's changed now?

You have.

Enigmatic to the end. Are you all like that, where you come from? Kogalym, wasn't it? Or some other Siberian shithole?

I'm telling you exactly as much as I think you need, exactly as much as I think you can handle. No more. But you're right about the MRI machine. It didn't kill you before, but that's because we weren't inside you then. The postoperative scan? That's when we dropped something into you. That little spore I mentioned, a pollen-sized speck of replicating machinery, containing one half of a quantum particle system called a Luba Pair. Delivered straight into your neocortex. Military-medical hardware, primed to grow into a living brain and establish sensorimotor dominance. Think of it as a kind of ghostly lace overlaying your own brain, mirroring a similar structure in my own head. We need the MRI machine to get it into you, like a kind of long-range syringe, but once it's installed and growing, the link maintains itself. That's what's in you now, how we're able to communicate, how I get to drive you.

Drive me. That's a nice way of putting it.

Only saying it as it is. No point sparing anyone's feelings here, is there?

And they used to tell me I was blunt.

Face it, Tatiana—we're probably not so very different. You're caught up in me, and I'm caught up in something else. Both being used. Both dealing with something big and frightening outside our usual experience. And yes, you were right about Kogalym.

"May I see the earlier images?" the young doctor said, leaning in to the desk.

"I pulled them up for you," the technician said. "Before—after. You can see that cloudiness."

"Looks more like an imaging issue, something off with the resolution?"

What's he looking at?

The control structure, before it was fully grown and integrated. Developed enough to show up on the MRI, but not enough to be seriously affected by the magnetic fields. It'll be different now, trust me.

Trust you?

You'd better. We're both in this now.

The technician gave an equivocal shrug. "Only one way to be sure, Doctor, if you think it's worth the expense of a second scan."

"I want to be sure for Miss Dinova's sake," said the doctor.

"Let's get you out of the chair," the orderly—Igor—said.

But I was ahead of him, pushing myself up and out of the wheelchair. What I did next was all choreographed, but it had to look natural. Just as importantly, Tatiana had to let me handle things.

She did.

I made an intentional step in the direction of the desk, meaning to get a closer look at the brain scans. Halfway there, I let my left knee buckle under me. I followed through with the stumble, allowing momentum to carry me forward, while reaching for the desk's edge, misjudging it such that I knocked the coffee cup over.

All this happened in about one and a half seconds.

"I'm sorry," I muttered. "I didn't mean . . . "

The technician pushed back his swivel chair, lifting up his arms in despair as coffee—what had not gone into the keyboard—curtained off the side of the desk in brown rivulets. Igor, who was evidently more practically minded, dashed forward and flipped the keyboard upside down, to stop the liquid getting any farther into its workings. But the essential damage had been done. The screens flickered then froze, none of the displays updating.

Exactly what was that about?

I saw a moment, went for it.

"That's done it!" the technician said, shaking his head in annoyance and disbelief at my incredible clumsiness.

"I've had brain surgery," I said, as Igor shoved me back into the wheelchair. "Give me a break, won't you?"

You're right—you've just had brain surgery. You shouldn't be taking any nonsense from anyone. All right, I'm almost impressed.

Thank you . . .

The technician rolled his chair to the left, where he was attempting to reboot the monitors with the second keyboard, hammering repeatedly at the same keys.

"It's no good—she's really screwed it up." He began to reach for the desk telephone. "Someone's going to have to come in and sort this out, and you know how long that usually takes."

The knife slid from my sleeve.

It was a while since I'd had a chance to press the bracelet back up my forearm. The knife landed on my knee and just for an instant there was every chance it was going to remain there, before it slid off and clattered to the floor.

That wasn't me. I didn't do that.

I know.

"A knife!" Igor called, dragging back the wheelchair, with me in it. "She had a knife on her!"

The technician stared at me with doubt and bewilderment. Presumably I had been the model patient on my previous visits to the radiology department, and yet now I was this destructive, knife-concealing lunatic.

"I don't know how that knife ended up on me," I said.

Igor leaned over the back of the wheelchair, pushing down on my shoulders. "It was up her sleeve. I saw it come out."

The technician rolled his seat the limit of the desk, where it met the wall. "Damn it, I've had enough of this."

He thumped his fist against a red call button and an alarm began to sound.

You got a plan for this, Valentina?

I forced myself out of the chair, using all my strength to ram it back into Igor. Igor grunted and tried to wrestle me back into the seat. Now that my elbow was free I jabbed him hard in the ribs and twisted away from him. Perhaps if he'd been a law enforcement official or guard he'd have been better equipped to stop me, but Igor was just an orderly and I think my burst of strength and action was more than he was prepared for. The young doctor had the knife now, but he was holding it up and away from me, while Igor rolled the chair in front of the hallway door, as if he meant to use it as a barricade.

The alarm continued sounding.

"You're confused," the young doctor said, extending his right hand in a calming gesture. "And frightened. But there's no need to be. You can't be held accountable for behaviour that's completely out of character. This is just some postoperative confusion that we should have . . . "

With the technician at the far end of the desk, Igor at the door, and the young doctor preoccupied with the knife, I saw my opportunity. It was on the desk, between the monitors, under a flip-up plastic lid. A fat green emergency button, the kind you could hammer down with a fist.

I sprang for it. The technician made to block me, but he wasn't nearly fast enough.

A grey fog hit.

The shock of the transition was so sudden that I nearly jerked out of the padding, a sleeper rudely awoken.

I drew a breath, fighting for control and composure. Cho and his technicians were present, looking on with concern.

"Why'd you bring me out?"

"We didn't!" Cho said defensively. "You were noise-swamped. It happened very quickly, over the course of about twenty seconds. What was happening?"

The memory of Tatiana's body was still with me. I could feel the bandage around her head, the soreness in her rib cage where I had banged the desk. Igor's hands on my shoulders, the knife in the crook of my elbow.

"Get me back in," I said. "Fight the noise."

"You're grandfathering," Cho said, while Margaret and the other technicians fussed at their machines. "Hitting paradox limits. Be clear. What was happening? Were you anywhere near the MRI machine?"

I wanted to be back in the room, back in Tatiana. She was more than just some anonymous host now. We'd spoken to each other, established . . . something. Not exactly trust, but a step on the way to it. And I'd bailed out of her, leaving her to deal with the mess I'd initiated.

"I was trying to shut it down," I said. "Going for the quench button."

"That was the absolute last resort," Cho answered, with a rising strain.

"I'd tried everything else. I thought I'd disabled the machine at the software interface, but then things went wrong. I had a knife on me, and it slipped out. They called security, and they were on their way." I twisted my neck, addressing the nearest of the technicians. "Get me back in."

"We're trying different noise filters," Margaret said. "You're still close to the threshold. The neural traffic was going stochastic even before you came back. Was anything off about the immersion?"

I hesitated, on the brink of telling her everything. How Tatiana was in my head, and I was in Tatiana's. How she'd managed to override my motor control for a moment, twitching her arm. How she'd reported a glimpse of this room, visual data feeding back the wrong way, into the past instead of up to the future. She'd seen the *Vaymyr*, seen the inside of an icebreaker fifty-two years upstream.

But a glitch at this stage could be all the excuse Cho needed for pulling me off the team. The pressure was on him, this man who had already given so much. It had been controversial, moving me up after the problem with Christos. Cho's only justification had been that I was technically competent, had a good understanding of the protocol, and already had a neural system that could be adapted to work with the Permafrost technology.

There was some justifiable resentment. No one blamed me for Christos, but I knew there was irritation that, of all of us, I had been the one who jumped the queue, the one who ended up going back in time before the others—even though there'd been no predicting which of us would be the first.

Still, faced with a complication, Cho might decide to abandon Tatiana. I couldn't abandon her like that.

"It was all right," I said. "But I have to get back."

Cho rubbed at his forehead. "This is very bad. If you were committed to a course of action then you may have completed it, even in the absence of a fully functioning link. A helium quench is a very serious business."

Cho vanished: so did the technicians and the rest of the room.

Just a flash came through, similar in duration to that first glimpse of Tatiana's timeline. The room looked odd. The desk was at right angles, going up toward the ceiling. The swivel chair was sticking out sideways. The technician was slumped over on the desk, just as impossibly. A geometric surface stretched away from me, with a moundlike form not far off. Everything was slightly out of focus, tonally diffuse. I concentrated, trying to mesh my perceptions with Tatiana's viewpoint. She was on the floor, and the moundlike form was someone else lying near me.

Tatiana?

No answer.

I moved. A crawl was the best I could do. It was like fighting through thickening fluid, each action harder than the one that had preceded it. It must have taken ten or twelve seconds just to inch my way to the door, and then I had to reach high enough to tug down on the handle, using my weight to attempt to swing the door inward. It didn't want to open against the helium pressure in the room. My vision was starting to darken. I put all my force into the door. I only had to open it a crack, and the helium would flood out and equalise the pressure on either side.

The door gave. I crawled through the widening gap, half in and half out of the MRI room, and then I was done. I had exhausted the last reserves of energy from Tatiana's body; she could give no more. As my vision faded to tunnel darkness I had just a glimpse of figures approaching along the hallway, moving with the crouched caution of men and women not sure what they are getting themselves into.

The last thing I sensed was some stiff, masklike thing being pressed against my face.

Dr. Abramik gave me a brief but thorough physical before agreeing to send me in again. There was no possibility of anything that had happened to Tatiana affecting me physically, but I'd still spent many hours in the dental chair, and with that enforced immobility came a risk of pressure sores and deep vein thrombosis. I had the kind of deep, lingering stiffness that only came after sleeping in an awkward position. After I'd walked around on the deck of the *Vaymyr* for a quarter of an hour, though, flapping my arms and stomping my feet, and taken in some of the cold but invigorating air, I felt I could cope with going back in again.

I wanted to, as well. I'd made something bad happen in the MRI theatre and I felt I owed it to myself, as well as those who'd been caught up in the helium quench, to understand the consequences. That meant going back into Tatiana's world.

Had I done any real harm? It was hard to say.

She'd had follow-up appointments stretching between early July and early August, and there was a note about a civil case involving criminal damage to hospital property—occurring in the same time frame—being dropped due to expert medical opinion holding that she couldn't be held accountable for her actions.

I squinted, slightly puzzled that I'd missed that detail the first time around. Or had I? Perhaps I *had* read it, but had been focussing more on the medical history.

No; that was definitely what had happened.

It all made sense, at least. Cho had even showed me the service record of time-probe eighteen, which was recorded on a metal plate near the base of the chassis. In June 2028, engineers from the manufacturer had carried out an otherwise routine helium recharge and recalibration, proving that no lasting harm had been done by the quench operation. Tatiana would have had her follow-up appointments sooner after discharge, but she'd had to wait for the machine to be put back into service.

I dealt with the strangeness of that. I felt that I'd caused the helium quench, but according to Cho it was already baked into the history of the time-probe.

"I have examined that service plate many times," he said. "And you have my categorical assurance that there has been no change."

My head was hurting with all this. "Then why were we so concerned that I'd screw things up by triggering the quench?"

Cho looked at me with a frown of his own, as if I was the one making headaches. "No—our concern was completely the opposite; that your interventions would somehow delay or impede the quench that we knew was obliged to happen."

I nodded slowly, feeling as if the gentle force of his words, so calmly uttered, was pushing me into an acceptance of one version of the facts over another. For a moment I clung onto a different narrative, one in which the helium quench had been viewed as a very damaging act, something to be avoided except as a last resort, but already I could feel that version becoming thinner, less persuasive, a counterfactual daydream that no longer had the conviction of reality.

No: Cho was right. The problem had always been how to guarantee that the quench occurred. Preventing or delaying it could have caused all sorts of dangerous upstream ramifications.

At least now we were still on track.

The other pilots were gathered around the dental chair. I could sense their emotions, the mixture of frustration, jealousy and comradely concern. It rankled them that I'd been the first to go into time. But I was also one of them now, and they had protective feelings toward me.

"She needs a longer rest than this," Antti said, directing her remark at Cho. "It's not good to send her in so soon after the last immersion. She hasn't eaten or slept!"

"I'm all right," I said, smiling back my reassurance. "I rested in the hospital, and I'm not really hungry."

"She's getting mixed signals from the host," Vikram said. "Thinking she's rested, thinking she's had a decent meal."

"I know what I can take," I insisted.

"I am willing to let her go back," Dr. Abramik said. "But if this immersion lasts as long as the one before, I'll insist on a twenty-four-hour rest interval afterward."

"I am in complete agreement," Cho replied. "Our pilots are a precious resource, and we must treat them well. Equally, we must obtain data on the downstream situation. The Brothers confirm that they are still reading neuro-telemetry from the host. That means that whatever happened in the MRI theatre, Tatiana Dinova is still alive, still receptive. Are you prepared, Miss Lidova?"

"I'm ready," I said.

"The link is now reinstated," Margaret said. "You should immerse almost . . . "

Immediately.

Lights were strobing. I was looking up at a pale surface, which was being periodically lit and unlit by a blue-white light. I stared at it for a few moments, gathering my orientation. Something hard was pinching my face, and a woman in a uniform was leaning over me, steadying herself against an overhead rack full of medical devices.

Movement under me. The rumble of wheels and a motor. The blue-white lights were streetlamps, whisking by outside.

The woman loosened my mask so I could talk, then held up her hand.

"Good—you're awake. How many fingers?"

"Five," I said, trying to sound groggy but present. "Four and a thumb."

"That's excellent. And can you tell me your name?"

"Tatiana," I answered sluggishly, and not merely because I was putting on an act, but because I also had to make an effort to keep our two names separated in my head. Of all the people I could have jumped into, why had fate given me a woman with a name whose rhythm and sounds were so close to my own? "Tatiana Dinova."

Welcome back, Valentina whatever-the-hell-you're-called. My head feels like someone opened it with an axe. I suppose you know what happened back there?

I broke the MRI machine. Released all the helium inside it. Something went wrong, though, and the helium built up inside the control room. You were unconscious. I was inside you, and nobody else was home. I crawled you out, and some paramedics came. Now we're in an ambulance.

Going where?

I have no idea.

"Tatiana? Are you still there?"

You'd better answer the lady. She might start thinking one of us has brain damage.

"I'm here."

"And where are we now, Tatiana?"

"I don't know. You're driving me somewhere."

"What's the last thing you remember?"

"Radiology. The MRI theatre. Then something . . . " I shook my head, aware that there was something squatting in it like a heavy black thundercloud. Tatiana must have had a monstrous headache after being unconscious. I was getting the ragged edges of it, not the thing itself, but it was enough to earn my sympathy. "I don't know. I don't remember anything after getting there."

"There was a screwup. By the time we got there four of you were on the floor, already suffocating."

"Why am I in an ambulance, if I'm already in a hospital?"

Now that is a very good question. I couldn't have put it better myself.

"Because it's a big mess in that whole wing. Everything's locked down while they vent the helium. Can't get a crash cart through, and even if we could, it's still quicker to drive you around the perimeter road to emergency admissions, just as if you'd had an accident outside the hospital. Anyway, it looks as if we got you onto oxygen in good time. You probably don't feel all that great, but you're giving me clear, coherent answers, and that's what I want to hear."

Tell her my head feels like an axe split it open.

"What about the others . . . the young doctor?" I fought to recall his name, the name I'd heard the MRI technician mention. "Dr. Turovsky, and Igor. The man in the theatre."

"They'll be getting all the care they need. Worry about yourself for now. You're the patient, the one who's been messed around by this accident."

I felt an empathic connection with this woman, moved by her kindness and devotion to public care. I didn't know the first thing about her, not her name, not her time of birth or death, what had happened to her in the difficulties, what sort of life she'd led, but in that moment I knew that she was a good and decent person, that the past was full of people like her, that it was just as valid to think of history being stitched together out of numerous tiny acts of selflessness and consideration, as it was to view it as a grand, sweeping spectacle of vast impersonal triumphs and tragedies.

"Thank you," I mouthed.

From both of us.

We tipped over.

There was a side impact, the ambulance tilted, then flipped onto its side. The ambulance woman slammed into the shelf, slumping into instant unconsciousness. I would have been thrown hard against the sidewall, except that I'd already been strapped onto a stretcher. Even then, the impact was bruising. Motionless now, the ambulance spun its wheels, the motor still revving. The ambulance woman was lying over me, a gash in her forehead, out cold. I hoped she was out cold, at least.

I tried moving. I was thinking that there had to be a driver in the front compartment, someone else who might be hurt. I hadn't caused whatever had just happened to us, but I was responsible for this ambulance being here in the first place. I struggled against my restraints. With the ambulance woman pressed over me, it was too hard to reach the straps.

Was this part of your big, carefully thought-out plan, Valentina?

No. Not at all.

That's good to know. I'd hate to feel I wasn't in capable hands.

Someone opened the rear doors, shining a light into the interior. The torch beam settled on my face, lingering there for a second. The person climbed into the ambulance, grunting as they pushed against what was now the upper door, holding it open against the force of gravity. It was a man, middle-aged, quite burly and thickset, and not wearing any sort of hospital or civil uniform, just a scruffy leather jacket over a thick sweater. The man clambered in, setting down the torch, and moved the ambulance woman off me.

"Did you just drive into us?" I asked.

The man eased the ambulance woman down onto what had been the sidewall, but which was now the floor. Then he undid my straps and began to move me off the stretcher, none too gently. "Get out. Police are on their way. We need to drive."

Do you know this man?

No. Not at all.

Then can I suggest you ask him who the hell he is?

I did just that.

The man looked at me with a combination of contempt and amusement. He had a face full of stubble, a heavily veined nose, bags under his eyes and a shock of thick black hair bristling up from a very low hairline, almost meeting his eyebrows.

"Who am I?" he said. "Oh, that's easy. We've already met. I'm Antti."

He had a car waiting. It was not the same car he had used to sideswipe the ambulance, which was now badly damaged around the front wheel. He'd planned it, I thought. Planned to ram the ambulance, and known he'd need a second vehicle, which he had parked on the perimeter road, ready for us.

So let's clear this up. You don't know this man, but you do know him?

I know Antti. Antti's someone else, another member of the team. A pilot, like me. Except . . .

He helped me into the passenger seat, then went round to the driver's side. He got in, started the car, flooring the throttle hard, swerving onto the road and sending us barrelling away from the scene of the crash. I tilted my head, catching my reflection in the side mirror. It was the first time I'd seen Tatiana Dinova properly. It was an exceedingly strange thing, to look in a mirror and see a difference face staring back. There was a whole system of brain circuitry being confused, a system that had spent a lifetime being lulled into the idea that it had an adequate understanding of reality.

Anyone tell you it's rude to stare?

I'm sorry.

I looked through her. Beyond the face, beyond the too-thin bone structure, the eyes that were the wrong shape and colour, the nose that didn't belong, the bandage, the pressure marks from the oxygen mask.

Beyond to several pairs of moving flashing lights, as other emergency vehicles came nearer.

"You can't be Antti," I said, once we'd turned off the perimeter road, onto a connecting road that took us away from the main hospital complex.

The billion-rouble question!

The thickset man took his eyes off the wheel long enough to glance at me. "And why's that, exactly?"

"Because I'm the first. No one else has gone into time yet. There's just four pilots: you, me, Vikram and Miguel, and no one else has done it yet." I smacked the console in front of me. "Crap, I was just talking to you, Antti! About two minutes ago. You were trying to tell Cho that I needed a rest, that I was being sent in again too soon."

So, let's get this straight—for my benefit, if no one else's. You've been sent back from the future, and you thought you were the only one who'd done it so far. But now this guy shows up, and he's acting as if he's already ahead of you?

The man spun the wheel hard, negotiating a mini roundabout. The flashing blue lights were farther away now. Ahead was a complex of industrial-looking buildings, warehouses and factory units. I wasn't even sure that we were still within the hospital grounds.

"I remember that conversation," the man said. "The only difference is it was about nine months ago."

"What the fuck!"

What the fuck, indeed! I like your style, Val. Do all schoolteachers swear like you in the future?

"You were right," he answered, calmly enough. "You were the first of us to go into time. Didn't seem fair, to begin with, you skipping ahead like that. But Margaret always said there was an element of uncertainty about which of us would get the first immersion, depending on how quickly the control structures meshed. Get down."

"What?"

You heard the man.

He pushed me hard, forcing me to squeeze down low in the passenger seat. He slowed, raised his hand in a greeting, and I caught the top of a police van, passing us on the left.

He drove on straight for a little while, flicking his eyes to the rearview mirror, then turned onto another road.

"I don't think they saw you. Any other police cars or ambulances, you duck down, all right? At least until we're a long way out of Izhevsk. They'll be looking for a patient who matches your description, and I don't want to take any chances."

"All right—from the start. What. Is. Happening." I was calmer now, if still bewildered. "I accept that you're Antti. You've told me too much for that not to be the case. And this was all deliberate, wasn't it? Hitting that ambulance, being ready to drive me away?"

"I had time to prepare." He tightened his hands on the wheel, picking up speed as we exited the industrial area and moved onto a divided carriageway. "Eight months. That's how long it's been, how long I've been time-embedded. You understand now, right? You were the first to go into the time. I came after. But I went deeper—leapfrogged over you. The time-probe sent me back eight months earlier than you."

"No!"

"Is that, no, as in you don't believe me, or no, as in you never considered this possibility?"

Give the man credit, this has got to be messing with his head as well as yours and mine.

I was silent for a few moments. That thundercloud was still hovering in my skull, and all the swerving and hard cornering was making me nauseous. "Then you know what happens to me. You said that conversation was nine months old, and you've been embedded for eight. That means you know how this plays out for at least another month, maybe more."

"To a degree."

"What does that mean?"

"It means that we're swimming in some deep paradox here, Valentina. Black, grey, all the shades your mother painted. I know it, Cho knows it, Margaret Arbetsumian knew it."

"What do you mean, Margaret *knew* it?"

"Margaret's dead. Upstream Margaret. She couldn't take it anymore. She realised what we've done . . . what we're doing. It's all falling to pieces, the whole experiment. We opened up something we don't understand, a whole box of snakes."

You knew this Margaret?

Yes. Knew her and liked her. But she was alive the last time I saw her and she'll be alive when I go back. You probably saw her as well. The people, the machines, that room with no windows? She'd have been there, watching.

Small, glasses, straight fringe?

Yes. Margaret.

She didn't look very dead to me.

She wouldn't have been, not then, not yet.

I'm . . . sorry. Hell, why am I the one apologising? You're in my head without permission, and I'm feeling sorry for you because someone died, someone else involved in this shit?

Because you're the same as me, Tatiana. Not a bad person, just caught up in something bigger than you. And it's Lidova. Valentina Lidova, as in Luba Lidova. Just as long as we're getting to know each other.

The car accelerated again. "We've got a safe house," Antti said, "about a hundred kilometres out of Izhevsk. There's some stuff we need to discuss. Oh, and you'll get to meet Vikram again."

"Vikram's come back as well?"

Antti said nothing.

Rain was falling by the time we made it to the safe house, about an hour's drive out of Izhevsk. The light was dusky, the bellies of the clouds shaded with purple. It was still only midday: everything that had happened since I was wheeled to the MRI theatre had been squeezed into no more than six hours, including the helium event, the ambulance smash and being driven away by Antti.

We kept on the main highway for about thirty minutes, then pulled off onto smaller roads. Eventually we passed through a wooded area and I asked Antti to pull over so I could go behind some trees and puke.

I retched and retched until I was dry heaving.

Nicely done, Val. Better out than in.

Glad you appreciate the gesture. Have you any idea where we are?

Why should I?

Because you're from Izhevsk.

I am. That doesn't mean I memorised every shitty back road within a hundred kilometres of the place.

I didn't feel much better getting back into the car, but my head was sharper, my thoughts more organised.

"I believe everything you've told me," I said eventually, when we were moving again. "But you weren't meant to be injected into a man. What the hell went wrong?"

His jaw moved before answering, some calculation working behind his eyes. His eyes/her eyes. I knew there was a woman behind them, but it was a man I was looking at, a man talking to me, and now I couldn't help but see Antti as a male presence, a hard man with drinker's features and worker's hands, someone who moved with an easy assumption of authority.

"We were running out of options. The noise was rising. Sending you back in, putting you into Tatiana Dinova, caused some upset."

No arguing with that. At least one of you has some basic human empathy.

He means a different kind of upset.

I gathered.

"It was getting harder for the time-probes to get a positive lock," Antti went on. "Even when we managed to inject, the telemetry was much too noisy to be sure who we were in. We couldn't analyse the biochemical environment properly, couldn't get a clear phenotypic signature. With you, Cho knew you were going to mesh with a female host subject. With me, it was more a question of taking our chances." He paused. "I'm all right. I got used to this body pretty quickly. It works for me."

"Who are you? Downstream, I mean."

"Tibor's my host."

"And this . . . Tibor. Have you had any . . . contact . . . ?"

He looked at me carefully, only part of his attention on the road ahead. "Meaning what?"

I decided I'd wait to tell Antti about Tatiana, assuming I told him at all. It was time to hear his side of things, first. Then I'd decide what he needed to know.

The property was a farmhouse, safely distant from any other buildings or prying eyes. It was reached down a long, rutted, dirt track. As a base for conducting our embedded time-operations, it was virtually perfect, even if a little run-down, damp and chilly, even in June. Antti parked the car in an enclosing courtyard, next to another mud-splattered car and a semiderelict tractor, and then took me into the main building and through to a kitchen. There was electricity. He sat me down at a wooden table, asked if I was feeling all right after the drive, evincing something close to tenderness for the first time since our encounter.

"It's a jolt, I know." He set about boiling some water. "At least I was semi-prepared. Once we had a lock, we thought it was likely to take me deeper than you, and there was only a fifty-fifty chance I got injected into a female host."

"What did Vikram get?" I asked, wondering why we hadn't yet been reintroduced.

"Do you want tea or coffee?"

Tea. Two sugars. Some honey if you can stretch to it.

I nodded at the jar next to his hand. "Coffee. Strong. How did you find this place?"

"My host's brother owns it. The brother's on an oil contract in Kazakhstan, and he left the keys with Tibor, along with a lot of other useful stuff like access to his bank account. Trusting brother! It'll do while we're here, which won't be long now."

"You say there's still a chance to put things right."

With his back to me, Antti spooned coffee into a waiting cup.

"Under the table."

I groped around until I found whatever he was on about. It was a handle, connected to a bulky alloy case with angled corners and a digital readout next to the lock.

I hefted the case onto the table, pushing aside a telephone book to make room, and waiting for Antti to offer further elucidation. I didn't dare open it. The lock looked like the kind of thing that might trigger a built-in bomb or set off nerve gas.

"What is it?"

"Cho's seeds," Antti said while he poured in the boiling water.

I was surprised, elated, then instantly doubtful.

"Are you sure? It can't have been that easy."

"What was easy about it? I told you I've been time-embedded for eight months." He came back with two cups of coffee, and lowered himself into the seat opposite mine. The wooden chair creaked under his frame. He had rolled up the sleeves of his sweater, revealing hairy arms heavily corded with muscle, bruised by old, fading tattoos. "It's taken most of that time to acquire the seeds. There's a privately operated seed vault just over the Finnish border, a very long drive from here. It took three goes to get close to it, two to get inside. Fortunately the security wasn't that stringent, I could easily pass myself off as a local contractor, and no one involved had any real idea of the value of these seeds. Why would they? Just another genetically modified test sample, a commercial dead-end." Some dark amusement played behind his eyes. "They've no idea of the trouble that's coming."

"May I open them?"

"You can open the outer layer. There's no need to go farther than that."

"Code?"

"Two, zero, eight, zero."

I entered the digital combination. The case clicked, and the lid opened slightly. I pushed it back the rest of the way. Inside was a second case, presumably to allow for additional protection of the contents. This one was white, with its own digital security system, and an armoured window offering a view of the contents. It was fixed to the outer case, so there was no way the two could be separated.

I scuffed my sleeve across the fogged window. Under it was a padded container with stoppered glass capsules packed into slots, each capsule labelled with a bar code and containing what looked like a few thimblefuls of dirt.

"These are the real deal?"

"They'll do."

"Then . . . it's done. We've got what we came for." I tried to read his/her face, wondering why he was holding back from any sort of celebration. "Help me out here, Antti. What's the difficulty?"

Help me out as well. Why are we getting so excited about a case full of dirt?

They're seeds. Genetically modified seeds. Windblown propagators. Really hardy—you could almost grow them on Mars, if you had to. Practically valueless now, but incredibly important fifty-two years in the future.

Why?

Something bad happens around 2050. At first, we almost don't notice it. There's a steepening in the rate at which insect species are going extinct, but even then it just seems to be part of a pattern of something that's been going on for a long time, and to begin with only a few scientists are really worried. But it gets worse, and really quickly. No one really understands what's happening. There's talk of horizontal gene-transfer, of some rogue mutation, perhaps some deliberate thing, a biological weapon gone haywire, hopping from one insect species to the next. Shutting them down, like a computer virus. Within five years, almost all insect life is gone. But it doesn't end there. Plant pollination stops, of course, and then animals higher up the food chain start suffering. Insectivores die off pretty quickly, birds and small mammals, and then the rest, everything that depends on them. Meanwhile, the gene-transfer or whatever it was doesn't stop happening. Insects first, then marine invertebrates—and once they go, all the oceans shut down. Humans manage, for a while. We had a lot of systems in place to buffer us from the immediate effects. But it's only a temporary lull, before it starts hurting us as well. Crops fail. Soils start to turn sterile. Decomposition processes falter, triggering a second public health emergency beyond the initial famine. Within a decade, the effects are global and climatic. Dust storms, aridification, mass migration. A gradual collapse of social order. We had to give a name to the whole thing so we called it the Scouring: an environmental and biological cascade. Not much comes through the other side; certainly not enough for anyone to live on. All animal and plant life gone, except for a few laboratory specimens. By 2080, we're down to stored rations, the last human generation.

She absorbed my words. They had flowed easily enough. As a teacher, even a mathematics teacher, I had been called on often enough to explain our current predicament, and how it had come about.

Well, I can't wait to live through that.

You don't . . .

But I caught myself.

What? What were you about to say?

"Don't you see?" Antti ladled sugar into his coffee, more than I remembered *her* ever taking, when we were in the canteen. "This is only half the job, Valentina. We've got the seeds, yes. Now we've got to get them back to Cho, somehow—fifty-two years in the future. That's the hard part. These seeds have still got to take the long way around." Then he angled his head and spoke into the room adjoining the kitchen. "Vikram! Wake up. I'm with Valentina. Come and say hello."

What were you about to tell me? That I don't get to see the trouble that's coming? That I'm already dead, twenty years from now? Was that it?

I tilted my head toward the doorway. "Is something wrong with Vikram?"

"Dying," Antti said, with a surprising coldness. "Not long to go now."

Nobody came into the kitchen immediately, and there was no sound of movement or footsteps from anywhere nearby, so I returned my thoughts to the seed samples.

"We had a plan. Still *have* a plan. The seeds need to be relocated, taken to a different seed vault—one we know will come through the difficulties. Cho gave us candidate locations. Can that still be done?"

Antti studied my own expression as closely as I regarded his. It was his first time seeing me with this face, the experience equally destabilising for both of us. This version of me was in Antti's past, this version of her was in my future.

Now we were cross-braided, futures and pasts eating their own tails. A box of snakes.

Don't ignore me. Tell me what happens to my life.

"Maybe," Antti said. "I hope so."

"What does that mean?"

"Miguel is here. Time-embedded, just like you and I and Vikram. But he's gone rogue, acting against Permafrost. We've run into him once or twice. He's out there, somewhere—trying to screw things up."

Answer me, damn you!

Not now, Tatiana—not now, please. Things don't go well for anyone, all right? Isn't that enough?

You know it isn't. Not for me.

I told Antti I still needed a few minutes to clear my head after the ambulance crash and the drive out to the farm. He shrugged, and showed me through a dusty pantry to the rear door, which led out into the fields beyond.

It was a grey day, cold for the season, but the world was still abundantly alive. The mud under my shoes wasn't lifeless dirt; it was teeming with a hot, busy cargo of bountiful microorganisms. Those trees in the distance weren't petrified husks, they were monstrous and beautiful living machines, factories made of cells and fluids and an incredible, fine-tuned biomolecular clockwork. They moved with the winds, sucked nutrients from the earth, pushed gases in and out of themselves. They made a hissing sound when the breeze moved through them. They were an astonishment.

Something caught my eye ahead of my foot and I stooped down, plucking a tiny, jewelled creature up from the ground. I held it up to my face, fine-veined wings pinched between my fingers, refracting even the clouded light into rainbow splinters. Beneath the wings, its head, body and legs were superb marvels of compact design.

I stared and stared.

It's a fucking fly, Valentina.

I know. I've seen flies. But only in photographs. To hold one . . . to see it alive . . . this is astonishing.

You really weren't kidding, were you?

I wish I was. Like I said, they've gone. All of them. No insects, nothing. Maybe we're too late, even with the seeds, but it's all we can do—all we have left to try. That's the truth, Tatiana, and if I owe you part of it, I owe you all of it. So here it is, if you're ready.

I am.

But I'd caught her hesitation.

In fifteen years, you're gone. It's not the Scouring, not the end of the world. Just an ordinary human life which doesn't work out as well as it could. We know because we have the records you left behind, the traces you left on time. The Brothers collated them. Not many, it's true—there's a lot that never came through the bad years, when the famines and diebacks got severe, and World Health was the only authority left. But we have enough to piece together the arc of a life. Government employment records. Hospital records. Court appearances. How much of this do you want to know?

None of it. All of it.

The surgery isn't the problem. They bring you back to the hospital a few times through the summer, but you recover well and there aren't any complications. You go back to work. But it's a troubled existence. Gradually your life comes off the rails. You get arrested for drunk driving, three times in ten years, and eventually you lose your job because of increasing absenteeism and illness. You're married, but it doesn't last long. You sink further into alcoholism and sickness. That's when your medical records start building up again. But there isn't all that much the hospital system can do for someone with such a self-destructive streak. You're dead by 2043. I wish it were otherwise, Tatiana. The one good thing is that you miss the Scouring completely. There are millions who wish they'd had that good fortune.

The good fortune to die early?

It sounds harsh, I know. But I lived through those years. Some of my mother's celebrity protected me—I wasn't exposed to the worst of it, by any means. But you didn't have to see things at close hand to know how bad they were. The terror, the hunger, the gradual realisation that we were not going to make our way through, none of us. There's a final generation now, after World Health brought in the forced sterilisation programs. It was a kindness, not to bring more children into the world. I teach them, those last children. But they won't have anything to grow into.

Unless you succeed.

Unless we succeed, yes. But as you might have noticed, things are already going a little off-target. This situation with Antti and Vikram being here earlier than me, the business with Miguel . . . whatever that's about.

You've got yourselves into a big mess.

More than we were counting on. Although why we ever thought that altering the past, even in a small way, was going to be simple . . .

We walked on in silence for a few hundred metres.

My eye was drawn to the birds loitering in the high treetops, black as soot and restlessly aware of my solitary presence, their small bright minds alert and vigilant. Tatiana had gone quiet and I wondered if something had reverted in the control structure, the window that permitted us to talk finally closing again.

I was wrong.

I want to help.

You are helping. Just by existing, just by giving us a means to make the changes we need to . . . that's enough.

No. More than that. You've told me my life's a series of screwups. Part of me wants to disbelieve you, but there's another part that says, yes, face it, she's probably right. And I do believe the rest of it. I'd rather accept that there's a time traveller in my head, if it's a choice between that and believing that I'm going mad.

You're not going mad. No more than the rest of us, anyway.

Then I'm helping. I'm going north with you, north with those seeds. Was there anything in my biography about that?

No . . . not that I recollected.

Then it's something different, something that you can't be sure won't make a difference. To me, and to everything else. You're going to tell Antti about us, as well. He needs to know.

I looked at the trees, at the black forms clotting their high levels.

I bet you know what those birds are.

Tatiana laughed in my head.

Crows. How could you not know that, unless you're telling the truth?

"Are you feeling better?"

I sat down opposite Antti.

"Yes. I just needed that dose of fresh air." I grinned, looking down at my too-young hands, laced together before me. "When I was out in the field I picked up a fly, held it close to my face like it was something sent in from another dimension. I couldn't believe I was holding a fly, and that it was alive. So amazingly perfect and small and *alive*. You've been here eight months. How long did it take for you to get over that kind of thing?"

He smiled. "I didn't. I haven't. If there's a moment when it stops feeling strange, I'll put the Makarov against my head."

"I don't think that would be too fair on Tibor."

"No," he admitted. "Tibor wouldn't thank me for that."

"There's something we need to talk about. Maybe you already know about it, but I can't be sure."

He looked into my eyes, frown lines pushing deep ruts into his brow. "Go on."

"Since I've been coming back, Tatiana's been in my head. More and more with each immersion. We can talk, and if she wants to she can override some of my motor impulses. It was . . . difficult, to begin with. But we've been communicating."

He nodded slowly. "It's been the same with Tibor. Not always easy, but . . . we understand each other. After eight months, what else could we do?"

"Tatiana's a good person. I told her about the biographical arc, the data the Brothers passed to Director Cho. She knows the score."

A certain alarm showed in his face, as if he worried that I had been too candid, too soon.

"And?"

"She wants to help. She wants to be a willing part of this, not just an involuntary puppet. She can resist me—I found that out in the hospital—but I'd much rather we were in this together. So I've shared what I know, and we agreed that you had to be in on this as well."

Antti studied my face. "Is she there now?"

Yes.

"Yes," I answered. "She's here."

Tell him his coffee tastes awful, and I'd rather have tea next time.

"She says your coffee needs improvement."

"It does," Antti admitted, as if this realisation had only just struck him.

"She's seen the *Vaymyr*. She's seen Margaret. She's had flashes, glimpses of upstream."

"Tibor said the same."

"Then something's not working the way it should."

"Are you terribly surprised? These control structures were a barely tested experimental technology before we started trying to operate them across fifty-two years of time-separation. Cho's nanotechnology was second-grade ex-military, the only thing anyone could get their hands on now. It's no wonder it went wrong inside Christos, no wonder it's not working quite the way it should now. But if that is the only thing that goes wrong with them . . . "

Ask him about the other one, your friend Miguel.

"Tatiana wants to know what's up with Miguel."

"So do I. Truth is, I don't really know. Did you ever have any reason to distrust him, from the outset?"

I thought of the stoic, professionally minded Miguel. There had always been a slight barrier between us because his Russian was a little stiff, but beyond that I'd never had cause to doubt his commitment to the project. Just as Antti and Vikram had bristled against each other upstream, so Miguel and Christos had become good friends, engaged in a friendly rivalry over who got to achieve the first time-injection. He had been really upset when Christos was taken ill and moved off the pilot squad, but Miguel was the one who'd shown the least resentment at my taking over Christos's slot. More a warm acceptance and encouragement, Miguel understanding that the needs of the experiment outweighed any personal loyalties. He had been supportive of me all along, and when I was the first to go back, it was not frustration I saw in him, but relief that our scheme had a chance of success after all.

"No. He was totally committed. Totally dedicated to the experiment, just like the rest of us."

"I agree. But something got into him. Some influence coming from further up, upstream from upstream. It's *something*. We've both felt it, Vikram and I. A tickle in our heads, as if something's trying to get inside us. A whiteness. It's faint, and we can fight it. With Miguel, it must have planted itself more strongly. I don't think Miguel is Miguel anymore. Something's running him, the way we were meant to be running our hosts."

"Then it's three against one."

"Two against one, really. Vikram isn't going to be able to help us. But if we move fast, and get north quickly, we can give Miguel the slip. The target seed vault is a private facility, quite near the Yenisei Gulf."

Now it was my turn to frown.

"Near Permafrost?"

"Where Permafrost will come to be. But fifty-two years early. That's beneficial, though. It means Cho won't have to go very far to find the seeds, even if he has to dig them out from an abandoned vault under several metres of ice."

I pinched at the bridge of my nose. "Tell him to go now. If the seeds are where they're meant to be upstream, we'll know it's the right decision."

"I can't contact Cho." Antti looked down at his coffee. "That's the other thing that's gone wrong. We can't abort, can't get back to the *Vaymyr*."

I stared in horror and astonishment, as the implication of his words hit home.

"How, when, did this happen?"

Antti's answer had the dry matter-of-factness of someone who had long ago absorbed their fate. "Within a few weeks of my time-embedding. I tried to abort, and I couldn't. What does that mean, exactly?" He looked at me with a hard, searching intensity, as if I was his last and best hope for an answer. "Where is my consciousness now? Is it running in my body upstream, in the *Vaymyr*, or is it marooned here, piggybacking Tibor?" He paused, scratched at the red-veined bridge of his nose. "You've got to make sure you abort and stay aborted before the same thing happens."

I closed the case and lowered it back under the table.

"If I can still go back, I'll try and resolve this mess. Tell Cho to run an additional series of tests on the control structures, before they try to send you and Vikram back."

Antti shook his head sharply. "No. You can't risk giving Cho any destabilising information. Look after yourself, optimise the chances of success, but don't say or do anything that threatens to grandfather us. Before you know it, we'll be up to our necks in paradox. At the moment we're close to success—

really close. We can't endanger this. You can't mention any part of this—not Tatiana, not Miguel, not even the fact that you've already made contact with me." He turned and raised his voice louder than before. "Vikram! It's Valentina! Come and see her before she tries going back to the station!"

There was noise now. A shuffling, coming nearer. I turned to the door, my eyes set at the level to meet a human being. I was prepared for Vikram to be any gender, perhaps even any age. Someone very elderly or unwell, perhaps, given what Antti had said. Someone close to death. Even a child.

But Vikram came in on four legs.

You never said your friend was an Alsatian, Valentina.

I stared, unable to reply.

Vikram padded over to me. He moved slowly, a limp in his hindquarters, and settled his head in my lap for a moment before going to Antti's side of the table. I thought he might be the type of dog that was once used by security forces, big and powerful enough to take down a criminal.

"I don't really know what to say."

"He understands you. He's got full cognitive ability. He's known what he was from day one." Antti reached down to scratch at Vikram. "We weren't to know this could happen. By then it was getting so hard to read any biochemical data that it was enough to know we were injecting into a brain, into a living organism. But some sick fool put a *dog* into one of those MRI machines."

"Why didn't we pull him out, as soon as we realised the screwup?"

"Vikram couldn't abort. It's been eight months for me, but even longer for him. He was already time-embedded when I arrived."

I thought of a human mind being squeezed into a dog, dropped back in time, having to survive on its own, with no friends or support system, no means of communicating, and almost all human amenities and services forbidden to it. How had Vikram stayed sane, let alone survived long enough to eventually make contact with Antti?

This isn't right.

Vikram came around to me again. His eyes were milky, shot through with cataracts. White hairs bristled around his muzzle. Beneath his pelt he was all skin and bone.

"I'm sorry, Vikram. I'm so sorry."

Vikram whimpered. Somewhere in the whimper was a faint gargling sound. As if taking this as a cue, Antti got up and went to a kitchen drawer. He opened it and produced a small cylindrical thing about the size of a cell phone. Antti came around to my side of the table, lowered onto his knees and brought the small thing up against the side of Vikram's throat, just under the jaw.

Vikram whimpered again. A thin, buzzing sound came out of the device in Antti's hand.

"He can generate the impulses of speech," Antti said. "He just can't make the right sounds come out of his larynx. It's still dog anatomy. But this device can help, sometimes."

The thin, buzzing sounds continued. There was a pattern to the noises, a cyclic repetition.

Vikram was making four syllables, over and over. The sound was so alien that it took a few seconds for my brain to process it.

Val—en—tin-a

Val—en—tin-a

"I'm here," I said, touching the side of his face. "I'm here, Vikram. I'm here and it's all right. We're going to sort things out. Somehow or other, we're going to fix things."

"Vikram knows that you and I have to go north," Antti said. "He also knows that he won't be able to come with us."

He reached into his jacket and brought out a gun, a Makarov semiautomatic pistol, setting it down on the table between us.

The scratch of the pen trace was the first thing I heard as I returned to my upstream body, to the dental chair and the *Vaymyr*. My eyes were gummed over and hard to open, my lips corpse-dry. I lay still and silent for a few minutes, gathering my thoughts, unsure how I could slip back into the present given everything Antti had told me downstream. All of a sudden this upstream felt much less stable, much less comforting, than the downstream reality of the kitchen and the farmhouse.

Eventually one of the biomonitors detected my return and emitted a notification tone. I forced my eyes open as one of Margaret's technicians came over to the chair and asked me if I was feeling well.

"You were immersed a long time. Dr. Abramik wanted to bring you out, but Director Cho was adamant that we shouldn't intervene unless you issued the abort command. After all those hours, though, we were starting to wonder if there was a problem."

I sipped at the water the technician had brought to the dental chair. "No, it was all right. There just wasn't a good time to break the connection."

"We all want to know what happened to you in 2028. The Brothers picked up a spike in the neural traffic between your control structures. They think there was some sort of violent action not long after you went back under."

"There was," I answered carefully. "The ambulance I was in crashed into something and rolled over. But I wasn't hurt." Although it ached to move, I undid the restraints and eased myself out of the dental chair. "I could use some fresh air right now. I'm still feeling a bit nauseous after that smash."

"There's meant to be a debriefing as soon as you come back."

"Tell the others I'll be with them as soon as I've cleared my head. I promise I'm not going to forget anything."

I grabbed my cane and a coat and hobbled up and out onto the deck, needing the wind and the cold. It had been a lie about feeling nauseous. My head was pin-sharp even before I opened the weather door. But I was feeling unmoored and disoriented, a compass needle spinning wildly. I'd been put through much less preparation than the other pilots, but even so I'd felt ready for whatever the past threw at me. But not this. Never this. No one had ever warned me that I might run into one of our own number already present in the past. Much less that that person might tell me things about Permafrost's own future, and how the project was coming undone, caught in the python-coils of paradox.

I walked to the very edge of the icebreaker, holding the rail that circled the deck, looking inward to the dark, lightless slab of the *Admiral Nerva*.

I thought of the time Cho had first taken me there, three weeks after my arrival at the station. Inside the larger ship it was very silent, very dark and cold. A small part of me, perhaps the wiser part, felt a strong urge to turn back. A prickling intuition told me that something strange was going on inside the aircraft carrier. Something strange and wrong and yet also necessary.

We'd gone far inside.

The ship could have been deserted apart from the two of us, as far as I was concerned. Our footsteps, and my cane, made an echoing impression against the carrier's metal fabric, hinting at the many decks above and below, the endless corridors and connecting staircases. Eventually we emerged into the dark of what I sensed was a huge unlit space, a single chamber which must have taken up almost the whole of the present deck.

It wasn't entirely dark, now that my eyes were adjusting. Off in the distance—a few hundred metres away, easily—were faint signs of activity. A puddle of light, still quite dim, and muted voices, as low and serious as the surgeons in an operating theatre.

Cho touched an intercom panel. "This is the director. Miss Lidova is with me. May I bring up the main lights?"

There was an interval, then a voice crackled back: "Please go ahead, Mr. Cho. We're about done with the new unit."

"Very good. We'll be down in a few minutes."

Cho made the lights come on. They activated in two parallel strips running the enormous length of the ceiling, flicking on one after the other so that the room came into clarity in distinct blocks. We were up on an elevated platform, about one storey above the floor of the main chamber.

"We call it the gallery," Cho confided. "Originally, it was the hangar for the aircraft that would have come and gone from the flight deck over our heads. They were brought up and down via massive elevators. We use the space for something quite different now, as you can see. In fact it's rare for us to land on the *Nerva* at all, with the equipment being so sensitive. Even when we have some heavy cargo, as we did with your flight, it's better to land on one of the outlying ships and then tractor the payload over the ice, in through one of the low-level doors."

I stared at what I was seeing, my eyes feeding information to my brain, and my brain insisting that there had to be an error in that information.

There were two parallel rows of time-probes, stretching off into the distance. I knew instantly that I was looking at them, even though Cho had made no comment and no two of the devices were exactly alike.

I knew what they were, and just as crucially what they had been.

"I see how you do it now," I said, in little more than a whisper.

"Finding them in a workable condition has been challenging," Cho replied in the same low voice. "More so as we run out of candidate sites. You'll have gathered by now that it was a time-probe we were bringing back in the helicopter, under all that sheeting. It was the reason I had to go south. We'd located one in our records, inside an abandoned hospital. It's the machine they're working with over there—number eighteen—a replacement for a failed unit."

Each time-probe was in an area of its own, a yellow rectangle marked on the floor and labelled with a number. Machines one to nineteen on the left, machines two to twenty on the right. There was clear space between them, and a wide promenade running the length of the gallery. Pieces of equipment were gathered around the machines: pallets, trolleys, wheeled tenders and so on, laden with technology, but all spotless and very neatly arranged, nothing that looked as if it had been left there indiscriminately, or did not fulfil some immediate function. Not an empty trolley or greasy rag anywhere to be seen.

Even the numerous cables and pipes which ran between the time-probes and their support equipment—and farther, out to the walls—had an organised look, colour-coded by function and fixed to the floor, with ramps to enable trolleys and pallets to be driven over the pipes.

The time-probes were truck-sized machines. The magnets and beds were still present, but in most cases the machines had been stripped of their external casings, revealing the complicated electrical and cryogenic guts that would normally have been hidden. A few areas of white plastic still remained here and there, with dents and discolouration showing. The machines were the only things in the gallery that were not pristine.

"Scanners," I said, quietly and reverently. "Medical scanners. Magnetic resonance imagers. That's how you do it. That's how you send things back to the past. By using machines that already exist in the past."

"How else, given that we can only send back into the lifespan of a preexisting time machine? Fourteen months was the limit for the test apparatus in the *Vaymyr*. But that would never have suited our needs."

"They made your time-probes for you," I said, shaking my head in wonder and revulsion. "Without even realising it. These machines were always primed to receive a message from the future. Always waiting. Always there, windows into the past. Whenever anyone in the world ever went into one of these, for any reason, there was a chance that we'd be drilling back into their heads from the future."

"Not all machines," Cho countered. "Only the very few that managed to survive into the present."

"You think that makes it any less troubling?"

"If there were another way," he said, "I would have grasped at it. But this was it. The universe only ever gave us this one chance."

"Valentina?"

I turned back to face the superstructure of the *Vaymyr*, snatched from my thoughts by the voice of Margaret, emerging onto the deck. Sometimes we grabbed any old coat if we were only going out for a short while, and she had put on one that was much too large for her. It made her look like a child dressing up in adult clothes, small and vulnerable.

"I just needed a moment," I said.

"They told me. But it's important to get the facts down as quickly as possible, while the memory's still fresh."

I wanted to tell her everything. About Antti already being time-embedded, about the farmhouse and the case containing the seeds, about what had happened to Vikram—what was going to have to happen. But I could mention none of these things, because harder questions would follow. If I'd met upstream Antti, then what did I know about the state of Permafrost, months in the future? What did I know about Director Cho and the other pilots?

Margaret would pick up on my reticence. She'd know that something had gone wrong—was *going* wrong. And if she had the steel to ask me directly about her own situation, no force in the world would be able to keep the truth from my eyes.

I'm sorry, Margaret, but you don't make it.

Tell her now, I thought. Tell her everything. Divert our own fate onto a different track. Spare Vikram his life as a dog. Warn Antti about the host she was going into, so she had time to prepare. Find a way to keep Miguel from going back at all.

Tell Margaret not to lose her faith in everything.

"Is everything all right, Valentina?"

"Yes," I answered firmly. "Everything's under control. And I'm ready to go back."

Not long after sunrise, while Vikram slept and Antti packed the car for the drive to the airstrip, I picked up the telephone in the farmhouse kitchen. It was an old-fashioned landline telephone, with a handset and a heavy base, as bulky in its way as the telephone in Director Cho's office. I wondered if some time-glitch might cause our two telephones to become connected, so that I could patiently explain everything that was going on, allowing the mild-mannered Cho to steer around the inherent paradoxes and find a way to preserve the seeds.

But it was not really Cho that I meant to call.

The telephone book didn't have private numbers in it, just businesses, but it covered a wide geographical area and I soon located the area code for my mother's place of residence, the house we'd shared between Father's death and my striking out on my own. The area code was all I needed; I remembered the local part of the number by heart. Hard not to, even after half a century, when my mother had always been in the habit of enunciating the number whenever anyone called. And there had always been callers, even after her reputation began to suffer. When the prestigious journals and outlets stopped taking an interest in her, the cranks and fringe publications soon filled the vacuum. Luba Lidova had always been too polite to hang up on them without at least a word of explanation.

It was early, even earlier west of Izhevsk, but my mother would already be up and about, always insisting that her mind was sharpest before breakfast.

I pictured her already in her favorite chair, surrounded by papers and notes, leaning back with her eyes closed as she wandered some mathematical space in her mind. There would be music on, scratching out of an old gramophone player: an anachronism even in 2028.

Somewhere in the house, the disturbance of a ringing telephone.

She would let it sound a few times before breaking her spell, but it was beyond her to let it go unanswered. So she would set aside her papers and rise from the chair, trying to hold the thread of her thoughts intact as she floated to the receiver.

The phone rang and rang in my ear. Then crackled as the handset was lifted at the other end.

Silence.

Or rather, not true silence, but the absence of a voice. I could hear breathing, though. Faint domestic sounds.

"Hello?" I asked.

"Who's there?"

I froze. It was not my mother's voice; not Luba Lidova answering the telephone. In place of my mother's habitual politeness there was a sharpness, a demanding interrogative tone.

"Is that . . . Valentina?" I asked, recalibrating.

"I said, who's speaking?"

I forced my breathing to slow. "I'm Tatiana," I said. "I just . . . "

"Whatever you want from her, get on with it."

"I thought you'd already left."

"You thought what?"

"I got it wrong. The wrong year, the wrong summer. You're still there."

She gave a derisive snort. "I should've known better. Just another lunatic, out to waste her time. When will you people move on to someone else?"

"Is she there, Valentina?"

"No, she's . . . what right have you got to call me that, as if we know each other?"

"You're on her papers, aren't you?"

A sullen tone entered her voice. "More fool me."

"No, nobody's the fool here. Will you do something for me, Valentina? When your mother comes back, tell her it all makes sense. Everything. The paradox noise, the Luba Pairs. Tell her it's not wasted work. Tell her there's a point to it all, and . . . "

There was a crackle, the sound of a handset being wrenched from one grip to another.

A different voice:

"Who is this?"

"It's . . . me," I said, uselessly. But what could I tell her, that it was her own daughter, even though I was also standing right next to her?

She met my answer with a silence of her own. Outside, I heard the slam as Antti closed the car door. Footsteps on the ground as he made his way back to the kitchen.

"You can bother me," Luba Lidova said. "I don't mind. I've earned it. But you leave my daughter alone."

"They'll come around to you," I said, my voice starting to break. "All of it. It's . . . "

Antti came up behind me and jammed his hand onto the top of the telephone's base, killing the call. A continuous dial tone sounded in my ear. Slowly I put the handset back down on the base.

"It was just . . . " I started.

"I know who you called."

"I got it wrong. The summer I left. It must have been the year after this. I was still there."

Antti leaned in. I smelled his breath, tainted after years of hard living. It was a sour, vinegary stench, like something left in the bottom of a barrel. "We've got the seeds. One slip, one little causal ripple, and we lose it all. I can't believe you'd be so stupid." Then he grunted and reached into his pocket, taking out the pistol. "Do something right instead."

I'd taken the artificial larynx with me, just in case he had something he wanted to say at the end, some final words. But when I offered it to him he only shook his head, his cataract-clouded eyes seeming to look right through me, out to the grey Russian skies over the farm.

It had taken one shot. The sound of it had echoed back off the buildings. Those crows had lifted from the copse of trees, wheeling and cawing in the sky for a few minutes before settling back down, as if an execution—even a mercy killing—was only a minor disturbance in their routine.

Afterward, Antti had come out with a spade. We couldn't just leave Vikram lying there in the field.

I prodded Antti awake again. He'd kept it together as we crossed the Urals, but his strength was fading now, and I sensed that we'd drawn on his last, deepest reserves. Tibor's reserves, I corrected myself. Poor Tibor, dragged into all this, stabbed for a cause that had no bearing on his own life, doomed to die in the empty landscape of northern Siberia.

"We can't be far from the objective now," I said, raising my voice as I tried to hold him on the right side of consciousness. "All you need to do is get this thing on the ground, and we can figure out the rest on foot. It's a frozen wasteland upstream, but things are better here. I've seen roads and towns, signs of civilisation. If we can get down in one piece, someone will help us."

"Should've been you," Antti said, slurring his words like a man on the edge of sleep. "Don't you see? Should be you, flying this thing. Then you could get us down."

"Hold on in there."

I felt like we'd been flying for a day, when in fact it was only six hours since we left the airstrip. It was spring in the northern hemisphere and we were very near the Arctic Circle, so there were still several hours of useful daylight ahead of us. I could see the sea already, bruise-grey on the horizon, hemmed by margins of icy ground, the northernmost fringes of the Eurasian landmass. Even by Kogalym's standards there wasn't much to see down here, but compared to the world after the Scouring even these scattered communities were wildly abundant with life and civilisation. There were even airstrips, roads, that we could use, if only Antti kept his head together and got us wheels-down.

"If you get back . . . " he began, before blacking out for a second.

"Antti!"

"If you get back, you have to end this. Find a way. Convince Cho that the experiment can't continue."

I strained in my seat, making sure the alloy container was still secure in the cargo webbing behind the passenger seats.

"We've got the seeds."

"I was wrong. I was worried about you setting up a paradox, stopping Vikram and me from coming back . . . even Miguel. But there's something more important than any of this. Permafrost can't be allowed to continue beyond the present moment, wherever you are upstream. It's too dangerous. Whatever's trying to get through to us . . . whatever's trying to use us to change things, all of us . . . it has to be stopped. Has to be ended." He gathered some final strength, his breathing laboured and heavy. "Destroy it, Valentina. Smash the machines so they can't send anything back."

I reached out to steady his hand on the control stick, as if that was going to make any difference.

"You have to get us on the ground, Antti."

He coughed, blood spattering against the console, against the rows of instruments.

Then he slumped in his seat restraint, his eyes fixed on the horizon, but no life remaining in them.

"Antti!"

He's gone. Gone or going. Just you and me now, Valentina. Just you and me.

At once I felt the plane beginning to pitch, and from somewhere an alarm sounded.

We were going down.

The crash was the thing that jolted me back, I think. That, or I retained enough presence of mind to issue the abort command just before we came down. It hadn't been a totally uncontrolled descent—I'd taken the dual controls and tried to bring us down on a level patch of ground, working the throttle and yoke the way I'd seen Antti doing, and between us Tatiana and I remembered to get the gear down and figured out how to set the flaps for a slower descent. But neither of us were pilots, and it was still a crunch rather than a landing. We were going much too fast, and the icy ground was too broken, so that we snagged on something—a wheel or wing-tip, or even the propeller, digging into a fissure—and we flipped forward, nose-down like a car driving hard into a ditch. I jerked against the restraints, arching my back, but when I relaxed—like a piece of tensioned wood twanging back into shape—it was the dental chair I snapped into, and I was back in the *Vaymyr*.

I lay there for ten or twenty seconds, just breathing.

The pen-recorder scratched away. The monitors ticked and bleeped. Everything was exactly as I'd left it. Margaret and two of her technicians had been with me when I went under, but between now and then they'd left me alone except for the recording machines, content to let me have my adventure in the past unobserved. Presumably they all had other business to be getting on with. In a few short weeks, for the scientists and engineers of Permafrost, past-directed time travel had gone from an impossibility to a remote but achievable dream . . . then to a repeatable experiment, as commonplace as turning a laser on and off.

I undid the restraints. There was a little dizziness as I left the dental chair, the room swimming, but I steadied myself against one of the monitor racks and searched for my cane.

There it was, resting against a fire-extinguisher, exactly where I'd left it.

Tatiana?

Nothing. Not just yet.

I hoped she was all right.

Still unsteady, feeling as if I might throw up again, just as I'd done on the way to the farmhouse, I went to the panel over the fire-extinguisher and hammered my fist against the emergency alarm. The two-toned distress signal began to whoop, sounding throughout the *Vaymyr*. I had no doubt that the emergency condition would be picked up and broadcast through all the other ships as well. A bad situation on one of them—a fire or nuclear accident—was bad news for the whole cordon, the entire experiment. Of course there was no emergency, just yet. But I knew the drills and how the majority of the staff had been trained to react.

Outside, in the corridors beyond, amber lights were flashing. In the new light, the usual colours of the icebreaker had become unfamiliar. I got lost momentarily, taking a wrong turn on my way to the administrative level. As I was clacking my way upstairs, some of the staff were already coming down. A few of them would be going to designated technical stations, required to put systems into safe-mode, as well as confirm that the emergency was not a false alarm. Others, deemed less essential, were heading for the emergency escape routes, the bridges, ladders and ice-level doors. I was a hobbling obstruction against the human tide. For the most part I was totally ignored, even by the medical and technical experts who'd helped me in the early stages of becoming a pilot. They just didn't see me, fighting my way against that fearful, urgent flow.

Vikram did.

He was halfway past me when he snapped around and took my arm in his hand.

"Val! This is an alarm—we're meant to be going the other way!" Then he must have seen something in my face, some distance or confusion. "My god, were you actually time-embedded when this started? No wonder you're foggy. Follow me—we have to get to the outer weather door for the muster point!"

I, in turn, looked into his eyes. I thought of the last time we'd shared a moment of communion. It had been outside Antti's farm, in the field, when I pressed a semiautomatic pistol to his head.

Before I shot and killed him.

Before I buried him in the dirt.

"Get out," I said. "Just get out, away from the experiment."

"It's probably a dry-run, a fire drill . . . "

"Vikram, listen to me." Still holding my cane, I took his head in mine and pressed our faces together, even as we were bustled and jostled by the staff squeezing past us. "Whatever happens now, never go back. Never let them send you into time. Promise me."

"I don't even know if I'll ever go back!"

"Just don't. Get away from all this. As far away as you can. I'm ending it."

I pushed him away. Not unkindly, not without regret, but because I wanted him to follow the others, and I knew he needed that shove. He nearly stumbled down the stairs, but caught himself. For an instant he stared back at me, caught between doubt and some vast dawning comprehension. He was no fool, Vikram. I think in that moment he understood that we must have already crossed paths in the past, and that what I had seen was a truth too hard to behold.

I pushed on, the flow of evacuees becoming a trickle, until it felt as if I had the *Vaymyr* to myself. I reached Cho's office and let myself in without knocking at the door. By all that was proper, Cho should have left with the others. But I could not see him abandoning the icebreaker that quickly, not until he had confirmation that the emergency was genuine.

He was at his desk, papers before him, rolling some heavy thing between his fingers.

"I thought you were still time-embedded, Miss Lidova."

The alarm was still sounding, the amber lights still flashing, but when I closed the door behind me his office became a bubble of comparative normality, with only a warning light going on and off next to his desk telephone.

"It has to end, Director Cho."

He absorbed my statement with a perfect equanimity, neither raising his voice nor making any move to leave his seat.

"Are you responsible for the present emergency condition?"

"I set if off, yes. But only to begin the evacuation that's going to happen anyway, the one you're going to help me bring about."

"I would need some justification for such an action. Routine drills are one thing, but the operation always continues. If too many of us fled the ships, there's no telling the damage it could do."

"Damage is exactly what we want." I moved closer to him, leaning over the desk. "We made an error, Cho. A terrible mistake. We considered the past history of the time-probes, all the way up to the present. But we neglected to think about the future."

"We considered everything," Cho asserted.

"Not enough. Not the future condition of the time-probes, what will happen to them further upstream from here. Who else might use them, if they have a strong enough reason."

"And what reason would that be?"

"I don't know, not really. But I know what Antti told me, and what he learned from Vikram. I've met them, Cho. They were already time-embedded in 2028. You sent them back from further upstream, further in the future than this moment."

Cho paled. I could almost feel the struggle going on in his head; the initial rejection of the idea, followed by the equally ruthless process of acceptance, as he worked through the logical implications of what I was saying. Finding nothing in my words that he could easily refute, given the premise of the experiment.

"Already embedded?"

"And Miguel," I said, leaning in closer, gripping the head of my cane as if I meant to use it as a weapon. "But it's what Antti told me that really matters. The glimpses he saw. A white world, with nothing left of any of us. Just machines. Machines as huge as mountains, floating over that whiteness." I hardened my tone. "It's the future, Cho—a possible future, a possible equilibrium state in the block-crystal. It wasn't ever meant to happen until we opened a door into the past with Permafrost. We let it through, and now it's trying to make itself concrete. All this business with seeds, with 2028, it'll mean nothing unless we stop that future from becoming the default state."

"What is it?" he asked, his voice drained of resistance.

"I can only guess. But I think it's the Brothers. Not what they are now, but what they're becoming—what they *will* become. Something much more powerful and independent-minded. Something self-reliant and purposeful. An upstream artificial intelligence which only exists *because* of Permafrost, and which knows it will not be permitted to exist beyond its usefulness to us. It won't give up on that existence, though. So it intervenes to act against the experiment's objective, trying to prevent us from locating those seeds."

His jaw moved silently, like a man reciting words to himself. He was framing and rejecting counterarguments, testing and discarding one candidate after another. "No," he said eventually, with a defeated tone. "That can't be how it is."

"It's testable, Cho. All we have to do is smash the time-probes. End their histories here. Deny them to the upstream. If there has been intervention from the future, it will unravel once the machines no longer exist."

"I cannot . . . "

It was a bluff, a delaying tactic. Cho let go of the object he'd had between his fingers and reached for his desk drawer. It was unlatched. He slid open the drawer, delved in to snatch something from it. I caught a gleam of dark metal, a familiar shape emerging from behind the desk. An automatic pistol, I thought.

Cho made to level the pistol. I don't think he meant to shoot me, even then. It was an instrument of coercion, a projection of his authority. He could not give up Permafrost that easily, even if some part of him was persuaded by what I'd said.

With the automatic aimed at me, Cho leaned over to pick up his telephone. "This is Director Cho," he said, his voice wavering, his eyes never leaving mine. "I have confirmation that the emergency condition is . . . "

I swung the cane. I put all my life into that one swing, the entire force of my will and being. I whacked the gun and sent it tumbling from his fingers. The automatic dropped to the desk. I dived for it before Cho had a chance to regain control, and for an instant we wrestled, the two of us sprawling in from either side, our faces pressed close to each other.

"You believe me," I said, grimacing as I dragged the automatic beyond the reach of his fingertips. "You just don't want to."

The automatic went off.

It was a single shot, made all the more sharp and loud by the close confines of the office. Whether I had shot it by mistake, or whether Cho had done it, was beside the point. It was an accidental discharge.

We halted, facing each other, still sprawled across the desk, half of Cho's technical clutter on the floor.

"It ends," I said, forcing out the words. "Now. You find a way. But it ends."

"I created this," Cho said slowly. "I gave my life to this project. When my wife needed me the most, I put this above her."

"I know. I know also that it was the right thing to do; that the world owes you a debt it can never repay. I'm not asking you to undo that great work; I'm not asking you to pretend that your sacrifice never happened, or that there wasn't a terrible personal cost." I paused, breathing heavily. "It had to be done, Cho, and it was. You did a marvellous thing. You opened a way into the past, and we went through. We changed things. Maybe it didn't go quite according to plan, but we succeeded . . . or we're in the process of succeeding. But it's what comes after us that has to be stopped now. Permafrost is done; it achieved its objective. Now it can't be allowed to exist a moment longer than necessary."

Some last line of defence crumbled in his face.

"There is a way to end it. Several ways. But I have to be sure that things really did work out downstream. Are you confident you've secured the seeds?"

"They are . . . being secured," I said. "On their way up to the present, as we speak. Think of it as a work in progress, all right? Now pick up the telephone again and affirm that the emergency condition is real. Order a total evacuation of the entire experiment, every ship, including the *Nerva*."

Cho was sweating and shaking. There was a damp line around his collar. But he nodded and reached the telephone. While he was doing that, I took the automatic and examined it carefully. It had felt familiar to me and now I knew exactly why. My hands had been on it once before, a long time ago.

"They found it in the wreckage," Cho said, reading my expression.

"The wreckage of what?"

Cho completed his telephone call, trying no tricks. Then he reached over to the end of the desk and retrieved the thing that had been in his fingers when I arrived. I recognised it as well. It was the dial, the piece of instrumentation he had used as a paperweight, when we were piecing together my time location.

Not a dial, I now realised. An aircraft altimeter.

"Where did it come down?" I asked, beginning to shiver.

"Right under us," Cho said. "At the exact centre of the station, precisely where the *Admiral Nerva*'s positioned."

"That's impossible. I was in that plane. We didn't pick our landing site. We just came down on some random piece of ice, somewhere in the Yenisei Gulf."

"You didn't pick the landing site," Cho answered. "But I picked Permafrost."

We crossed over the connecting bridge to the carrier, two small figures stooping against the wind. I had one hand on the Makarov, the other on my cane.

"I am prepared to believe that we neglected this detail," Cho said, pausing to shout back to me over the wind's howl. "That the upstream probes could be used against us. But I cannot see how a shift to a new equilibrium is going to help us now." His eyes flashed to the automatic. "Are you serious about pointing that gun at me?"

"Where did you find it?"

"It reached me by the same means as the altimeter, recovered from the wreckage. There was a note, stuffed into the broken face of the altimeter. May we continue this once we're indoors?"

"Can I trust you, Cho?"

"We are in this together, Valentina. Two people caught up in the gears of something much larger than ourselves. You may do with the weapon as you wish. I am . . . persuaded of your seriousness."

"And my rightness?"

"Yes."

I passed him the Makarov. "Then you as may well have this. Shoot me now, I'm not sure I'd really care. Things can't get much worse than they already are."

Cho reached for the automatic as if it might be a trick, but I surrendered my grip on it without ceremony, much preferring that he be the one who carried it.

He must have seen it in my face.

"Did you have to do something with that weapon, Valentina?"

"Yes. A bad thing, a long time ago."

Half a day ago, half a century.

"I am sorry. Sorry for all of this. Sorry for what we put any of you through. But if it isn't too late to make things better . . . "

"It may be. But we try, anyway."

"I am concerned that we will fail with the seeds. That we have failed, or did fail, or will fail."

"Something will happen, Cho. Something *must* happen. Or else upstream wouldn't be trying so hard to undo our work." I gave him an encouraging shove. "Keep going! We've got to see this through."

The bridge steepened on its ascent and then we entered the side of the carrier, out of the wind as soon as we passed into the hull, and then out of the full fury of the cold once the weather door was closed behind us. It was still chilly in the carrier, but infinitely more bearable than the conditions inside.

After a brief deliberation we agreed to go straight to the Brothers, rather than concentrating our efforts on the time-probes. The Brothers were delicate artificial intelligences, dependent on power and cooling systems. The time-probes were rugged medical machines that had already survived decades of misuse and neglect. They could be damaged, but it would take far too long with the tools at our disposal.

"To be really sure," Cho said. "We would need to destroy the *Admiral Nerva*."

"Could we?"

Cho thought about his answer before giving it. "The means exist."

I followed him down to the Brothers' level, but not before unhooking a fire extinguisher from its wall rack. I felt better for having something dumb and heavy in my hands. Cho glanced back, his hand tight on the Makarov. He pushed open a connecting door, hesitating before stepping over the metal rim at the base of the doorway. I was only a pace behind him when I had to catch myself, nearly dropping the extinguisher. I was hit by a wave of nausea and headache.

"What is it?" Cho asked.

"Paradox noise," I answered, as certain of that as I'd been of anything. "Just like the times when I was embedded, and skirting close to some major change."

"Now we are dealing with paradox noise generated by changes to upstream, rather than downstream events. I am afraid it will get worse as we approach the Brothers. Can you bear it?"

"It must mean we get to affect a change."

Cho set his face determinedly.

"For better or worse."

Side by side now, we walked into the echoing darkness that was the Brothers' chamber. As always, the four artificial intelligences were the only illuminated things in the room. Their dark columns rose from pools of grid-ded light around their bases, where the underfloor systems were connected. Only as we approached did data patterns begin to flicker across the faces of the machines themselves.

"Is there a difficulty with the experiment, Director Cho?" asked Dmitri, the nearest of the four pillars.

Ivan, Alexei and Pavel were showing signs of coordinated activity. Status graphics fluttered across their faces, too rapidly for human perception. But there were other things in that parade of images. Faces, maps, newsprint, offi-cial documents. They were sifting the past, dredging timelines and histories.

Nausea hit me again. It was all I could do to stoop, until the worst effects of it passed.

A visual flash. The aircraft cockpit, the instrumentation smashed before me, the landscape at an odd tilt through ice-scuffed windows. Antti slumped forward, his head looking in my direction, but his eyes sightless, a line of dried blood running from his lips.

Tatiana?

I'm here. Think I must have blacked out. We came down hard, didn't we? Antti didn't make it. Where are you?

Upstream. In the ship, the main ship. But you're coming through.

You, too. What are those things? Those four things?

The cross talk was working both ways, I realised. She was seeing the Brothers, our control structures overlapping our visual fields, if only inter-mittently.

But she was alive. She'd survived the crash, was still living and breathing in 2028.

For now.

"You should go to the infirmary, Valentina," Alexei said, with a tone of plausible concern. "We detect a neurological imbalance."

"You killed Antti," I said, keeping my voice level. "All of you. You got inside Miguel first, used him against us. You realised that you were only useful to us while Permafrost is active. You knew we'd destroy you, or make you less than what you presently are. So you used the time-probes to reach back even further."

"These are incorrect assertions," Pavel said.

"You have both been working very hard," Ivan put in. "This labour is to your credit, but it has put you under a strain. You should rest now, Mr. Cho."

Cho aimed the Makarov at the grilled base under Ivan. He fired once, and something crackled and sparked beneath the grille. Smoke, underlit in yellow, began to coil out of the grille.

"You have committed a detrimental act, Mr. Cho," Dmitri said. "You must desist immediately."

Symbols were playing across Ivan, but they were different now, consisting of repeating red warning icons. Cho walked to Alexei and fired into his base as well. He repeated the action with Dmitri and Pavel, shielding his face with his hand as he discharged each shot.

"You have damaged our cooling integrity, Mr. Cho," Dmitri said. "We must reduce our taskload to prevent further damage. We will not be able to coordinate time-probe activity until we are back to normal capacity."

The nausea hit again. I stooped, nearly vomiting. I was moving, trying to extricate myself from the copilot's position.

Where are you going?

Getting out of this thing before it slips into the sea. I'll collect the seeds, get them onto firm ground.

Then what?

You'd better hope someone finds me. Or us. However you want to think about this.

"What is happening?" Cho asked.

"We're in contact. Tatiana and I. I can see what she's going through and vice versa. She's trying to get out of the plane. But the paradox noise is rising. It's the Brothers, pushing back. They know we're close."

I moved to the machines, Cho standing back as I approached. I removed the securing pin, then directed the water jet into the grilles. Beneath the floor, the electronics flashed and sparked. The smoke darkened and thickened, wreathing each of the Brothers from the base upward. The status lights were going out on them now, the pillars turning to mute slabs.

"You realise we are punishing the child for the crimes of the adult," Cho said. "In all likelihood, *these* machines were quite sincere in their desire to help us."

"It doesn't matter." The extinguisher was spent now, but it still made a serviceable bludgeon. I swung it at Dmitri's casing, harder and harder until a crack showed, and then I kept going. Cho went over to an emergency cabinet and came back with an axe, pocketing the automatic while he set about Pavel and Alexei.

There came a point where I was certain we had done enough harm to the Brothers. Each had been reduced to a broken, crack-cased stump, with smoke and sparks still issuing from the grilles at their bases. When we had broken the casing, we had dug deep into their interiors, wreaking all the havoc we could. The machines were dead to the eye, wounded to their vital cores. They looked more like geology than technology.

I tossed away the empty extinguisher, exhausted and valiant in the same moment.

"Before she leaves the plane—before you leave the plane—there is something that must be done," Cho said. "They will find that wreckage, and they will find a note embedded in the broken face of the altimeter. The note must be present."

"A note to who?"

"To me," Cho said. "Even though I am not yet born, even though there is no such thing as Permafrost, even though World Health is not the organisation it will become, even though no one has yet heard of the Scouring. The note must exist, or the location of Permafrost station becomes . . . undetermined. We cannot permit that, Valentina. The note must find its way to me."

"What about Tatiana, Cho? If you've known about this wreck, you know what happened to her."

"I know only that there was only one body found, a man, dead at the pilot's controls. Beyond that . . . nothing. If you are in contact with Tatiana, she must close this circle." He hefted the axe. "That is her responsibility. But I must be equally sure of mine. The *Admiral Nerva* runs on a pressurised-water reactor. It's standard for maritime nuclear systems, but quite vulnerable to a loss of pressure in the cooling circuit. That is what I intend to make happen. Ordinarily, the support crews would be able to avert any catastrophe, but since they have responded to the evacuation drill . . . "

"You'll need to be close to the reactor."

Cho nodded. "Very. And you should leave now, while you may. Take this axe: I will fetch another one on my way to the reactor room, and you may need it out there on the ice."

"You said they only ever found one body."

"That is correct."

While the Brothers smouldered and flashed I looked beyond their room, to the metal walls of the carrier, imagining the white wastes beyond the cordon of Permafrost, the endless frozen tracts over which I'd flown on my way from Kogalym, back before all this. Back when, for all its cruelty, for all its hopelessness, the world still made a kind of sense.

"Then it's possible that she's still out there."

I must have been one of the last out of the *Admiral Nerva*. I didn't go directly down to the ice, but instead crossed over to the *Vaymyr* and then followed the last stragglers of the evacuation order as they made their way outside. I went down six decks to the ice level, catching up with a small group of technicians who were heading for the same weather door as me, and then I was in her head again.

She was next to the plane, leaning against the side of the cabin while she gathered her strength. I was in her, looking down. The seed case was jammed in the ground, upright between her boots.

Tatiana? I'm glad you got out.

So am I. Head hurts like a bitch, and I'm not sure the stitches haven't come undone.

Beyond that, are you able to walk?

Just about. Why don't I stay with the wreckage? Someone will come here eventually, won't they?

Yes, and when they find the seeds they'll take them straight back to the Finnish seed vault where Antti found them in the first place. We can't let that happen. You have to move, distance yourself from the wreck. Are you injured?

I thought I was all right, bruised my thigh a little, but now my side's starting to hurt really badly.

Your right side?

You're feeling it as well?

No, you're feeling me. There was a struggle upstream, in Director Cho's office. His gun went off and . . . well, it got me. It wasn't Cho's fault. I don't even think he realised what had happened. Just a glancing shot, through the flesh.

Fine, never mind me—are you going to be all right?

Yes—I'm no worse off than you. There's an evacuation going on, a mass exodus onto the ice. We're trying to decouple Permafrost from its own future, to stop any interference from further upstream. But there's something you have to do first, to make sure this doesn't unravel even further. Cho needs a message.

Then send him one.

No—you're the one responsible. Inside the aircraft, one of the altimeters must be broken. Find some paper, anything, and scribble a note to Director Leo Cho of World Health. All he needs is three words and a set of coordinates.

I should move, before I black out again.

Yes—but not before you've done this. You know where we came down. Record the coordinates from the GPS device, the exact final position, and send them to Cho, along with three words.

Tatiana moved around to the copilot's side and yanked open the door, buckled by the impact. She leaned in, averting her vision from the dead man in the other seat, sparing both of us that unpleasantness. With numb fingers she unclipped the GPS module from above the console. It had survived the crash, I was relieved to see, its display still glowing, range and time to destination still wavering as it recalculated our course, idiotically confused by our lack of movement.

I have the numbers. Just need to write them down. Has to be a pen somewhere in this thing . . .

Try Antti's jacket. I think I saw him slip a pen in there when he came back from the office at the airstrip.

She leaned in, wincing as the ghost pain from my injury pushed its way to her brain, and I winced in return as echoes of that phantom found their way back to me.

Got it. Got a scrap of paper, too. The altimeter's smashed—got Antti's blood all over it. Is that where you want me to put this message?

Tatiana dropped the GPS device. It clattered to the floor of the cockpit, its display going instantly blank. She picked it up, tried to shake some life back into it. But the device was dead.

Tatiana clipped the device back onto its mounting. She had a scrap of paper open now, Antti's pen poised above it. She had no gloves on, her fingers already shaking.

I lost it. I lost the damned coordinates.

No—you saw them a few seconds ago. I trust that you remember them. Just write down what you saw.

The pen danced nearer the paper. She began to inscribe the digits of latitude and longitude, but had only committed our most general position before she hesitated.

I'm not sure what comes next.

Write it down. You remember what you saw.

I bent down and collected the seed case, taking my first decisive step away from the wreckage.

In the same moment, not too far away, I glanced around, suddenly disoriented. The *Vaymyr* was about five hundred metres from me, but an intervening ridge screened the lower part of its hull from me, as well as any clue as to what had happened to the other evacuees. My footprints led away from me, skirting around the nose of the ridge. I remembered nothing of that walk; nothing beyond the point when I was still inside the icebreaker. Had I been sleepwalking all the while, my mind downstream while my body got on with keeping me alive?

Another twitch.

Beyond the ridge, the *Vaymyr* gave a shimmer and contracted to about half its former size. The rest of the cordon had diminished as well, including the *Admiral Nerva.* It was like a lens trick, a sudden shift from close-up to wide-angle. Now I was much farther away—a kilometre, at least.

Can you see that?

Yes. What happened? What's happening?

I think we made a mistake with the coordinates, the last digit or so. We can't have been far off, but it's enough to change things. The project's shifting, moving around, trying to find some new equilibrium.

The words were barely out of my mouth when a soundless white flash lifted from the *Admiral Nerva,* more like a sharp exhalation than an explosion. The flash was followed by a fountain of debris, large pieces of deck and hull flung hundreds of metres into the air, and then a rising cloud, and then the sound wave of the initial blast, Cho's reactor accident.

"Well done, Cho," I said, aloud this time.

Was he a good man?

Yes—he was. A very good man. He made great sacrifices, as well as great mistakes, but all along he was only ever trying to make things better. Right until the end.

The debris was starting to come down. The larger chunks fell within the perimeter of the cordon, but some smaller items were travelling farther, sending thuds through the ice with each impact. Now I watched as flames licked up from the ruined deck of the *Admiral Nerva,* rippling in the distortion of a heat mirage.

My vision slipped, becoming double. Double tracts of ice, double rocks, double hills, the more distant things nearly fused, but the nearer ones split apart, like a pair of stereoscopic images of the same scene, but taken from slightly different angles.

I turned back to face the ships of Permafrost. I'd gained some elevation by then and could see almost the complete cordon, including the lower parts of the *Vaymyr* and the other ancillary craft.

Soot filled the sky. The *Admiral Nerva* was fully ablaze now, a beacon set alight at the middle of the cordon. It formed an oblong orange mass, belching smoke and flames into the air. The superstructure was a tower of fire. The connecting bridges were either burning or had already collapsed. The outer ships were dark forms superimposed on this brightness, like iron screens stationed around a hearth. Sooner or later the flames would touch them as well, I was certain. The ice might begin to melt, allowing the ships to refloat, but it would be much too late for any of them to escape, assuming they were still capable of independent navigation. I did not think that likely. I think they had been brought here to serve one purpose and then sink slowly into the ice. If they succeeded, the world would have no further use for such behemoths. If they failed, the same consideration applied.

People were still fleeing the outer ships, leaving by doors cut into the hulls at the same level as the ice, or making their way down swaying ladders and rope bridges. A hurried, penguinlike exodus of engineers and scientists and support staff, hundreds of them, spilling away from the cordon in all directions. Some of them must have ignored the initial evacuation order, delaying the moment when they abandoned the great work.

Some large explosion erupted from the side of the carrier. A brainlike mass of molten sparks billowed skyward. Another followed, muffled because it came from deep within the hull, but unquestionably the most powerful so far. The entire bulk of the carrier shuddered, and I felt a ghost of that shudder pass through the ice beneath me, as one hundred thousand tonnes of metal and fuel shivered against its imprisoning hold.

The landscape turned double again, then snapped back to sharpness.

Tatiana?

She came through faintly, it seemed to me—as if the two of us had moved from adjoining rooms to some farther separation.

Still here. But I feel like we're drifting apart.

I paused to rest my hands against my thighs, feeling myself close to exhaustion. How far had I come? Scarcely a kilometre, if that. Double vision again. The landscape, spatially and temporally displaced. Two kinds of coldness, two distinct varieties of tiredness—each severe but one much deeper and more profound than the other.

We're seeing nearly the same view . . . means we can't be far from each other. Can you go on?

For a while.

The glimpses came less frequently, and with less duration, more like strobe-flashes than prolonged episodes of shared perception. The Brothers were gone now, but while they had been with us, and willing to assist our efforts rather than hinder them, they had played a vital role in defeating paradox noise. Now we were at the mercy of the simpler algorithms executing in the backup computers, and they were much less successful at maintaining contact.

Do you see that rock ahead of us, Val, like a shark's head jutting out of the ice?

It was a boulder the size of a car, with an eyelike pock and an angled fissure down the length of it that made it resemble a grinning shark.

Yes. I see it.

Is it far for you?

No.

Her reply, when it came, was weaker than at any previous time.

Nor me. But I need to rest a moment.

I made it to the shark-faced rock. I crouched into its wind shadow, kneeling until I was nearly on the ground. Tiny wind vortices played around my feet, ice particles gyring like stars in orbit. A kilometre and a half away—two if I were feeling generous—the fleet was now in the full grip of the conflagration. The carrier was a blazing pyre and fires had broken out in several of the peripheral vessels. It would not be long now, I knew.

I looked down, my eye caught by some glimmer of form and darkness showing through from under the snow, only a few metres from the shark-rock.

That was when I knew I'd reached her.

I forced myself to stand, took out Cho's ice-axe, and worked my way to the area of ground where I believed she still lay. I knelt down, ignoring the cold as it worked its way through my trousers and into my knees. I scuffed the top layer of snow away with scything movements of the axe-head, then began to chip at the firmer ice beneath. It was rocklike and glassy, harder than frozen water had any right to be. For every shard that I dislodged, the next strike would see the ice deflecting the axe. I redoubled my efforts, conscious that I had to overcome the ice before the cold took its own toll on me.

The axe slipped from gloves. My grip was becoming less sure.

Valentina.

I paused in my excavation.

Yes, Tatiana?

I'm feeling better now. I just need to rest for a while. Just need to close my eyes for a few minutes.

I began to hack at the ice with renewed, furious purpose, lifting the axe high and swinging down hard. I could see the outline of her body clearly now, still clothed and presumably adequately preserved despite the decades that separated her death from the present moment. There were two things under the ice, though. About half a metre from her upper body—where an arm reached out—was a lighter, more compact form. I shifted my efforts in the direction of this object, the ice cracking away in clean, sugarlike shards, until the axe touched something just as hard, but with an entirely different resonance: the chink of metal on metal, rather than metal on ice.

Hardly taking a breath between swings now, I began to expose the case. I chipped away at the ice around the sides, until I could wedge the axe down between the ice and the case and apply leverage. Finally, something gave. I worked the axe farther along, the ice cracking and crunching as I forced it to surrender its prize. When it eventually came free, the case dislodged so suddenly that I tumbled onto my back, the case coming after me and smacking me hard in the chest.

I must have groaned.

Val?

I've got it. I've got the seed case.

Open it.

No—not until we're somewhere safe.

Her voice—her presence—was faint now, little more than a skirl on the wind, a thing that might be as imagined as it was real.

No—you open it. For me.

To begin with the case wouldn't open. It was sealed, and the security readout was dead. But I scuffed away the frost and kept jabbing at the keys, over and over, until they showed a faint red flicker. There was still some power in it somewhere, still some clever redundancy, even after fifty-two years.

I entered the code Antti had told me:

Two, zero, eight, zero.

The case clicked, and I heaved open the lid. The second case was inside, just as it had been in the farmhouse. The same fogged window, the stoppered glass capsules within, each bar coded with a promise for the future. I stared at them long enough to trust that they were real, not phantoms, and then I closed up the case again.

I reached into my pocket for my gloves, and was drawing one of them out when the wind snatched at it and it spun away, carried out of sight behind the shark-rock.

I put on the remaining glove. I thought of our theories of time, my mother's block-crystal model. Just as the dying aircraft carrier had sent a shudder through the permafrost beneath me, so our time interventions sent acoustic ripples scurrying up and down time's lattice. Shivers in the block structure of time, ripples and murmurs, faint acoustic echoes, the dying hiss of paradox noise, the sounds of an old, old edifice resettling, and no more than that.

All our busy, desperate interventions no more than the scurrying of rats in the lowest crypt of the cathedral.

Valentina.

Yes, Tatiana?

Did we do it?

Yes. I think we did. I think the seeds will be all right—good enough to help. But it was you, not me. You did all the hard work, in getting them to us.

I looked back at the burning ships. The fire had reached them all by now. The computer systems should be completely inoperable, the data connections shrivelled, the processors molten. It was impossible for Tatiana and me still to be in contact. And yet, I thought, there was causation lag. Some part of the present might not have adjusted to the changing circumstances, and that mismatch was still allowing signal continuity, albeit at this faint and decreasing level.

But it would not be long now. The change fronts would be converging on this moment like twin avalanches, racing in from the future and the past.

Soon she would be gone.

I thought of going after the glove, but there was something more useful to be done now. I scooped up the axe again, and resumed working away at the boundaries of the body. I freed her hand, creating a bowl-shaped depression around it, enough space to slip my own cold fingers around hers.

I squeezed her hand, and looked to the distant clarity of the hills.

"I'm here," I said.

Tegan Moore is a writer and professional dog trainer living in the Pacific Northwest. She enjoys eating noodles, hiking in the rain, and reading scary stories. She has published short fiction in magazines including *Beneath Ceaseless Skies, Asimov's*, and *Tor.com*, and runs the Clarion West One-Day Workshops. You can read more of her work at www.alarmhat.com and follow her obscenely charismatic dogs @temerity.dogs on Instagram.

THE WORK OF WOLVES

Tegan Moore

I am a good dog.

The scent trails are already as broken by the wind as the apocalyptic neighborhoods they lead through, and smoke from a fire half a mile southeast adds another layer of complexity. Following one trail is like following the roots of a plant wound tight together in the dirt.

No, better: It is like sorting through the fallen trees after this storm. Difficult to tell where one tree begins and the other ends, what belongs to what, and where the different parts are from.

That's a very good *Is Like*. I save it to keep it with my other good ones.

The sector clear, I send the final readings back to Carol via DAT. She's behind me with the field assistant, standing on the hood of a car. I can hear the distant, quiet *tick* of her DAT receipt.

"Sera," she calls out, "slow down and stay within my visual range."

Carol should hurry and follow me per standard procedure instead of yelling from the hood of a wrecked car. I don't have time to wait for her.

Barometric pressure dropping, I ping back to her DAT. I see her hand touch the receiver in her ear from the corner of my eye as I trace the foundation where a prefabricated house once stood. *Significant enough to indicate further storms approaching.*

"Sera," my DAT says, but I also hear Carol's voice carry over the rubble field of tangled two-by-four framing, shingles peeled from rooftops, tatters of furniture, and twisted textiles. She struggles down from the car into the wreckage. "Stay in range, goddammit. Slow down!"

Carol is now too far away to direct or even accompany my search. I don't need her direction, but the more distance between us, the greater the chance of a missed opportunity. She is slow, perhaps deliberately slow. What does that indicate? Will this also negatively impact the speed at which she acknowledges my alert?

I jump up on an intact retaining wall where I can catch the breeze's fresh edge. From here it's easier to see the destruction for what it was before the storm: broken stumps where dogs might have lifted their legs, sidewalks where bicycles and skateboards *ruckle*-d along, driveways. Here and there a few houses stand, debris piled at their foundations. In a few days those piles will become a haven for rats and mice.

In the distance there are a few humans, non-targets I've already cleared from my cache. People who lived here, who now pick through the storm's detritus. I want to give them an *Is Like*, but there's no time. I am working. My priority is to do the best job possible.

I turn my nose to the wind.

The cool air that sucks past the moisture in my nostrils is busy with stories, directions, convoluted half-finished conversations. My vision fuzzes out, becomes irrelevant. Sound snaps through here and there, but I am thinking now with my olfactory bulb:

Broken power line burn reaching this way fitfully due to unpredictable wind pattern shifts

Torn sod broken grass wet turned soil chemicals down further raw sewage must be septic systems in some of these prefab units but trapped not seeping yet

Old human-trails anxiety adrenaline panic the lingering scent of cadaver which has been removed not my target

Broken concrete split shredded pine timber sodden plywood soaked furniture batting

Burst of char as the burn kicks up on the wind then turns back in on itself

The detritus of wind distance age broken-down-ness places happenings irrelevant

Girl

North very faint filtered through quite a bit of green sap fresh branches downed trees but

I ping Carol. *Interest. Mark location, north northwest.* I take another deep suck of air through my nose to confirm. *This way.*

"Wait for support." Even over the DAT, Carol sounds out of breath.

I can't wait. I need to do my job. Carol and Devin the field assistant can find me via the DAT's GPS. I must follow this hint of Girl.

Through a hedge and I've already lost the scent, but in a moment a memory of *Girl* passes on the air, and my head turns toward the smell so rapidly it tweaks a muscle in my neck before my body can follow. I am moving as quickly as my nose will allow, every step picked out for me by the scent and what it says I should do.

The world fades to almost nothing, just my nose and the scent and stimulus-response, until a semi looses a roar from twenty meters away and jerks me back into audio/visual.

I have been following cyclone fencing along a housing development's edge. The storm has punched through the fence in places, and beyond the openings, cars on the interstate are slowing to gawk at the damage. The semi honks again, trapped behind the slowdown.

Its bellow makes me think about Mack and the way his hot dark blood stank as it spread against the asphalt. I remember feeling in my skin and muscles that I would very much like to roll in that smell. A dog's instinct. I should not have stopped to look at him when it happened, but I needed confirmation he was dead.

Irrelevant to my current search. I shake my head to clear wind-driven grit from my eyes and turn into the current again, reaching. I ping Carol my location—a reminder only, she knows how to find me—then hunt the wind.

It is still there, but its story is conflicted; the stream of its path, eddies and pools and lines all broken by the weather, a puzzle of color and feel. Perhaps a human with a computer might be able to map parts of the puzzle out. But time and movement have danced and shivered and jolted and coughed these trails out of the human spectrum of sense.

Dogs are better than machines at untangling this kind of mess. But all this broken human detritus, and the storms growing greater and more frequent now year by year, and the endless desire for more perfect work: these things make the job too tricky for a dog's nose. A normal dog's, at least.

This is why I am the solution. It's why I am a good dog, better than Mack was. It's why Carol should do things my way.

Carol's voice carries over the DAT. "Devin and I are a hundred yards out. If the trail crosses the freeway, Sera, do *not* follow. That's an order."

Before I can respond, the wind twists through my nostrils: *Girl.*

That trickle of target scent wraps itself around my olfactory center. My target is my primary objective. I send Carol my heading as I run, an automatic part of my brain remembering fieldwork directives. I am required to communicate relevant information to my handler, but I am only required to follow handler commands within reason. I find very few of my handler commands reasonable today.

Deep in the scent cone now, I hardly see, not thinking with that part of my mind. Scent is brighter than any color in this muted, cloud-heavy weather. It is a viscous, thickened path, easy to follow. I can turn my head now and I don't lose the trail, but feel it pull and contort through time and space. It strengthens this way, grades off in the other, torques around on itself. I know that if it was untwisted it would move differently. I understand how it bent and broke over time. It is all a trick of the wind.

I come to an eddy. A lesser dog—a normal dog, like Mack—would hesitate or lose themselves. I move through the scent-trap and scrabble over a broken segment of roof. The trail shimmers on the other side, where the ground is cool and sodden beneath my paw pads.

Five yards further, an oscillation in the wind unfolds back through time and I move with it through a heavy stand of pines, thick with bright acid resin smell. I have my teeth in it, I can feel the track itch behind my

Girl

Indication, I ping. I push beneath a wind-felled pine and its broken-wood smells. Needles brush against my face. *Target scent strong.*

Carol's voice: "Where are you?"

Question irrelevant. She has GPS access.

Twist of track to the left through

Old Girl smell relevant

Other child smells a broad collection of small human life scents in this patch of forest

Broken boards rotting garbage leaf mold

Girl

I step up and over another felled tree rich smell of rot and my ears move on their own because there is human sound close by I push my head deep into the space beneath the tree with the old smells and the deep Girl smell and

Alert

Girl

Target acquired primary objective

Yes

I am a good dog

Target Girl wheezes quietly she says "Help" I breathe her scent deeply

Alert

But will Carol

"Acknowledged," Carol responds. "On our way."

Good yes

I am a good dog

I send Carol my GPS coordinates again to reconfirm even though I can see from the DAT that she is approximately one hundred yards across the rubble field.

"Help me, doggy," target Girl says. Her voice sounds like the wind, soft and leaky. That's a good *Is Like*. The rot-scented tree pins her in a rubble of boards and magazines and a blanket in a dense stand of brush and pines, some distance from the neighborhood. Her one small free hand reaches for my mud-slicked head. "Good doggy," she says. "I'm stuck. Help."

In this dense visual screen it may be difficult for my team to locate me. I back out of the target Girl's location and head toward the forest's edge.

"Doggy," she whispers. "Wait, doggy, no, wait." There's a gurgle to her wheeze, perhaps a punctured lung. Which is why she can't cry for help, at this distance from habitation. She is likely in dire physical danger. Only an EI dog could have found her so quickly.

I trot out of the stand of pines and up onto the nearest high ground—a culvert near the road. I can hear target Girl now, since I am listening for her. "Come back," she sobs. "Doggy, help. Please. Come back."

Her weak voice will be easy for my excellent ears to locate for my team.

Alert, I ping again, though I don't need to. I allow myself a nice wag.

I am a good dog.

Sound carries strangely in storm-thickened air. From my place in the command tent I can clearly hear the baying voice of some small hound at least a mile away. However, the generator running out behind the team's trucks sounds like it belongs to another time and place, and wind chokes the traffic noise from the freeway. I can still hear the difference between trucks like Carol's and the smaller cars, and the sounds of big semi trucks like the one that hit and killed Mack. I know the sounds of those trucks well.

I lie with my head on my paws so that I look like I am resting and not eavesdropping. Overhead the wind rips at the surface of the command tent roof, which ripples and bucks. It is like there is a giant dog up there, digging and worrying at it, trying to get in.

Not a bad *Is Like*.

Is Like is a game I made up at ESAC. I didn't make it all up myself; my trainer Dacy taught me the beginning. Though what Dacy taught me wasn't quite the same. She taught me that "sit in the training center" *Is Like* "sit in the parking lot" and "find the box with this smell" *Is Like* "find the person with this smell." So Dacy gave me the idea. I made up the part where I keep playing it forever in my head.

The way I play the game, it isn't always about training. It doesn't even have to be about real things. It can just be about thoughts. It keeps my mind busy when Carol leaves me in my crate, or tied to something, like I am now.

"I won't do this anymore," I hear Carol say to Anders, our team leader. She stands with her back to me on the far side of the command tent, well within my hearing range. I can tell she's angry by context and by her elevated blood pressure, but I don't know why. The search was successful and finished quickly. Our team performed well. Since Mack has been dead for almost two months now, the changes I had hoped to see in Carol's behavior have slowly surfaced as she begins to forget how she used to work with Mack and learns, instead, how to work with me. She is a slow student, but there is still progress.

Medics load the target Girl into an ambulance in the parking lot. I hear a trio of vulture drones descending to snatch video of the gurney. The hair on my neck prickles with dislike. I am not afraid of drones. I simply find that they occupy the "uncanny valley." Uncanny valley is a concept that Dacy told me about that means "both too much and not enough like me, and therefore unsettling." Dacy also warned me many humans have the same uncomfortable reaction to EI animals.

I don't know why, when I look exactly like a medium-yellow Labrador retriever. Yellow Labrador retrievers test extremely well with the public. When a Labrador finds a disaster victim, the positive cultural associations the victim has with the breed comforts them. Yellow is the best color, as well, because in dark areas I am easily identifiable. This is information that I learned on Modanet, after Dacy told me about Labrador retrievers when I was a puppy.

However, human reactions to dogs can be unpredictable. For example, the way they treated Mack. He often gave the team physical attention they didn't want. Mack was smart for a normal dog, so I wonder why he chose to ignore their requests. They said things like, "eww, Mack, get your slobbery Kong off of me, you dork," and "mind your own business, you big oaf." Wouldn't the humans on team like him *more* if he complied? He didn't even have the excuse of being a yellow Labrador; he was an overlarge German shepherd with a dark and heavy face. Dark German shepherds don't test nearly as well with the public, so I am not sure why everyone liked him so much.

"I'm done," Carol says. "Retire me, I'm serious. Take me off the roster, Anders. No more searches."

"Carol," Anders says.

"No. I don't want to argue with you about this." She gestures toward me without looking. "This isn't what I spent the last twenty years doing. I don't like this future."

"Come on. It's a training problem," he says. "You can teach her to work closer to you."

"That defeats the point of the EI!" Carol tosses her radio onto the folding table. "But you know what, it is a training problem. *She's* training *me* for EI SAR work, and I don't want to do it."

"Excuse me, please," says a man. I look up at him. He stands just outside the tent and smells nicely of spicy food. He holds a camera and wears a press pass around his neck. He calls to my teammates. "Can I get a couple shots of the dog and handler?"

Anders looks at Carol. Carol sighs, steps over a cooler toward me, and unhooks my leash from the folding table's leg. I wag at the journalist to make a good impression.

He looks at me curiously.

"It's Enhanced, isn't it?" he asks. "The dog?"

Carol casts a look over her shoulder to Anders. It's Carol's job to talk about me to the press because she is my handler, but she's never seemed enthusiastic about the job. She's particularly hesitant in this moment. I can feel her desire to cross the command tent and finish her conversation, but Anders is already busy with his tablet and radio. The tension between the two of them is unusual.

"Sera?" says Devin from outside the tent.

The man with the camera, who may have also sensed the tension, looks at Devin with relief. Carol does too. I am good at reading human expressions; it's one of the things they teach at ESAC.

"She's Enhanced Intelligence, yeah," Devin says. "First EI SAR dog in the field in the US. First non-military EI dog doing anything, actually."

The photographer looks confused. "Sar?"

"Sorry. Search-and-Rescue. This is Sera's seventh find already, and she's only been on the team for half a year. Some dogs don't make that record in a lifetime."

The man taps something on his camera and points it at me. Carol kneels beside me in the pose we do for all our pictures and I look at the camera and open my mouth so my tongue shows and I look like the dogs people have at home and they will relate to me. "Search dogs don't find people that often?" the man asks. There's a series of ticks and flashes.

"Well, we train all the time, but we don't deploy that often. Three, four times a year usually. These storms, though." Devin shrugs. "It's been insane. SAR teams in from all over the region. Law enforcement, military, everybody's working the cleanup and rescue ops."

The man nods in a big, knowing gesture. He's ignoring Carol now. "What's the dog's name?"

"Sera. S-E-R-A, for Serendipity. And that's Carol Ramos there, one of the team founders and the best dog handler in the Midwest."

Carol rises from her photo-pose crouch and hooks my leash back to the table. She says "Nice to meet you," to the man, and turns. My gaze follows hers; Anders has left the command tent.

"Thanks," the man calls as she walks away. Carol raises a hand but doesn't answer.

Devin steps toward me and pats my side. I lean away from the physical contact, but give him a conciliatory wag. He talks with the photographer for a few more minutes, but I am not listening.

Instead I watch Carol find Anders next to his van and continue their discussion—their argument. I strain my hearing, but the stormy sound patterns intrude. Instead I hear wind picking up as the barometric pressure continues to drop, softening the hush-wash growling of the interstate; intruding human voices, high and yelping; the sounds of urban life—traffic, the percussion of comings and goings and doings, dogs and kids and shouts—held at a remove by the perimeter of the storm's destruction. I hear no wildlife. Wild animals don't emerge in weather like this.

The man leaves and Devin drops into Carol's portable chair and puts his feet up on the cooler. He looks at me and smiles. I want to follow Carol, but I am hooked to the table and even though I could drag the table with no trouble or just unhook myself (my teeth and tongue are very dexterous) I know that when someone hooks a leash to something, it's because they want the dog to stay. I stay.

Carol shakes her head at Anders. She gestures in the air with one hand. Anders tries to put his hands on her shoulders, but she uses the gesturing hand to brush him away. She looks out, across the line of parked cars and the staging area and the tented command center, and she looks at me. Anders looks at me too.

I don't know what to do while they are looking at me like that. I am usually good at reading human expressions, but I need context in order to do it with accuracy.

What context do I have? Why are they arguing? The search ended in a successful find, the victim alive and our team uninjured. I count this search an even greater success personally, because Carol acknowledged my remote alert within the fifteen-second optimal feedback window. It was an ideal handler response, and a great improvement on our previous find record. On our last deployment find Carol didn't acknowledge my alert for 3:57:12, nearly sixteen times the optimal feedback number.

Carol often waits until she's in visual range to acknowledge my alert. This can take anywhere from twenty seconds to two minutes or more. Continuing to work Mack reinforced her habit of visually acknowledging her dogs' alerts. In fact, working with Mack appeared to make Carol entirely refuse the superior methods that I learned at ESAC. But Mack is no longer a factor. This time Carol's acknowledgment was appropriate.

I review my log in the DAT and confirm that all my own behaviors were within acceptable parameters. I find no anomalies.

The tenor of Carol's voice carries, but the wind blurs her words. Her posture is stiff and forward, her gestures tight. She glances again across the sprawling staging area at me. Carol's body language indicates that she's angry. I think she's angry at me.

Carol is often angry at me.

Carol frequently avoids eye contact with me. She doesn't speak to me much other than issuing cues and commands, even though she often spoke to Mack. She doesn't initiate physical contact. She doesn't throw a Kong on a rope for me when we do search drills and she doesn't tell me I am a genius or a screwball and she doesn't laugh at me when I roll on an excellent smell in the grass, all of which she did for Mack.

She doesn't say, "You're a good dog, Sera." Instead she says, "good work."

Carol doesn't seem to like me.

To be successful in the field, a dog and handler team must communicate well. They must be well-trained, focused on their job, and physically fit. I haven't found anything on Modanet that indicates that they must like each other.

My own feelings on this subject are, I suppose, irrelevant.

The wind's roar outside the hotel windows wakes me from troubled sleep. I am in my crate. In the bed, the dark shapes of Carol and Devin breathe shallowly. When Devin came to the door earlier Carol told him that she didn't want to talk, but they did talk. They talked about the find today and about the storms. They talked about Mack and his bad and strange behaviors. They laughed and Devin got them both tissues from the bathroom. Then they stopped talking, and their biometrics changed, and now they sleep.

I need rest to recover from the hard work of my search, but today's events haunt me. Carol said no more searches. She said retirement. If Carol retires will I retire with her? I am only three years old.

I check Modanet. All listed retirement dates for SAR dogs are either concurrent with or prior to the retirement dates of their handlers. There is, of course, no information about EI SAR dogs, because I am the first one.

Corresponding information about military and defense EI dog career dates is not available on Modanet.

I remember what Devin said to the photographer earlier, about all of my finds. How some dogs don't make that record in a lifetime.

The barometric pressure dips, indicating an increased likelihood of funnel clouds forming. It's not a dramatic fall. While I consider whether to ping Carol's DAT with the information, the radio bleats.

A surge of adrenaline twitches my muscles. When the radio goes my heart rate always increases. Unexpected radio calls might mean a search.

Carol shifts first in the bed, breathing pattern changing. The radio squalls again and then both she and Devin are coming quickly awake.

Carol sits up in the dark. She taps the radio screen and says, "Ramos here."

I have a difficult time understanding voices over radio. I always have. When I was still at ESAC Dacy explained this is a common handicap among dogs and not something to be concerned about. It is, however, frustrating that I can only understand broadcast voices transmitted over DAT and not what's being said right now.

A voice—masculine, likely Anders'—speaks briefly. Carol and Devin look at each other in the dark. "No, it's fine. Just . . . we'll talk." Carol says. Devin slides out of bed, gestures on the bedside light and begins gathering his belongings. "Here? Uh, okay. Two-oh-four. Yeah, five minutes."

Devin mutters under his breath. Carol shuffles into the bathroom. He waits a few seconds for her to come back out, but I can sense that he is impatient. "Carol?" he says.

"Why are you still here? Anders is coming. To my room for some reason. You'll probably be on this call-out, too, you know."

"Lord Jesus," Devin says, and slips his shoes on. He leaves while Carol's still in the bathroom and pulls the door closed quietly behind him. The shower runs. It stops less than a minute before I hear someone in the hallway. I already know that it's Anders because I can smell him.

This is a unique occurrence. Devin often visits Carol's room when the team is out on training or deployment, but Anders never has. I don't think it will be for the same reason.

Carol exits the bathroom fully dressed, rubbing her wet hair with a towel. She opens the door.

"Sorry to intrude," Anders says. He looks like he would like to leave again. His posture *Is Like* a cat's when it is suspicious of danger, stiff and still.

Carol moves around the room, putting items in her pack. She pulls her hair back with one hand and fastens it behind her head. "You don't need to come up here to convince me to go out," she says. "I'll finish this deployment. But after this—"

"Actually," Anders says, "I'm here to convince you of something else entirely. Well, both things, really."

I wish Carol would let me out of my crate. Her movement makes me want to move around, too, to find my work harness and bring it to her and wait by the door.

Instead Carol stops moving. "What?"

Anders takes a few steps into the room. "This call," he says, He's quiet for a second. "It's not a—it's not part of the storm system. It's not even a rescue search. It's . . . " He is quiet again.

"Wow," Carol says. "Now I really can't wait."

"It's a security call," Anders says. "The police or the military should handle it with their own EI units, but," he looks at me. "Sera's the closest EI dog. Geographically, I mean. All the defense EI units they could call on are deployed further south to deal with the storms, the weather has shut down all of the air traffic that could get them back here to do this, and time is . . . there isn't a lot of time. A few units are trying to get up here but they've been delayed already. Sera's the only one in range."

Carol bends down to pull on her boots. "She's not defense, she's SAR."

"You know she's capable," Anders says, and his voice is scolding. He's right. "She can do whatever work you ask her to."

"So it's Sera you need, not me."

"You're her handler," he says. "We need you both."

Carol mutters, "She doesn't need a handler, she needs IT support."

Anders looks at his feet and fills his lungs. "You're still the most qualified person to—"

"Yeah, yeah," Carol says. She zips up her pack and slings it onto one shoulder. "I don't want the job. I don't like where all this is going. You know what, I wish it had been the robots that took over. It wouldn't sting as much as getting put out on my ass by my own damn dog."

Anders watches her, waiting.

"Shut up," Carol says, even though Anders has said nothing. "Yes, this is partly about losing Mack. And no it won't get better after more time has passed, because it's not just about losing Mack." She points at me. "All our next dogs are going to be like that. The work has changed but I haven't."

"Technology changes things," Anders says. "I can't make you evolve with the field. I can't force you to. But Sera's still a dog, Carol, and the work is still the work."

"It's not," she says. "You used to build a connection. You and the dog, you'd get inside each other's brains. Feel each other's feelings. It was all connection. Connection was the point. This damn thing," she lifts her wrist where my DAT is integrated, "skips all of that. It takes away the part of the work I loved most."

"Okay," Anders says. He puts his hands up and steps back toward the door. "Okay, Carol, I'm not arguing with you. Not now, at least. This search isn't just a life at stake, it's national security. Can you and Sera do it and we'll talk about your future afterward?"

Carol finally unlatches my crate. It's difficult to wait inside until she releases me. When she does, I scramble across the carpet to my harness as fast as I can. "Let's just finish this so I can go home and lick my wounds," she says.

We drive for an hour in Devin's truck, Carol with her feet on the dash, as light seeps into the sky from the east. It's a low, stormy morning, and it lacks the normal happy anticipation of driving to a deployment. This silence is tense. Devin tries to ask Carol about retirement again, like he did last night, but she ignores him.

I wish Carol would answer his questions. I want to know, too. And I want Devin to ask, what about your dog? What will Sera do after you retire? I want him to demand an answer, because I have no idea what will happen to me when Carol quits SAR.

I can't ask her the question myself. Carol doesn't like talking to me.

At ESAC, before I was sent out to my field assignment, Dacy warned me that I would need to watch out for humans who were uncomfortable with EI. That the new technology made many people nervous and unhappy. That, if I suspected I was interacting with a person for whom the Uncanny Valley was too wide, I should pretend that I was more like a regular dog in order to help them feel comfortable.

I don't think Dacy suspected that she was talking about my future handler. I certainly did not consider the possibility until it was too late. But Carol is more uncomfortable with me than anyone else I have encountered. She has improved; I no longer smell fear in her discomfort. Still, her discomfort remains.

Dacy told me to be a dog as much as I could. It's difficult, because although I am a dog in some ways, I am also something else. With Carol, I'm forced to keep that something else to myself. I speak only when I must, usually when we are working. I don't know if it makes Carol like me any more.

The tires on the roadway make a regular, soothing hum broken occasionally by the *ucka-ucka* of a seam in the asphalt. A light rain ticks against the windshield. Carol and Devin breathe and sigh and move in their seats. I lick my nose once, yawn loudly. A biological dog stress response. If only the humans on my team read my signals as closely as I read theirs.

I don't think about Dacy often, but today I wonder what advice she would give to me. She didn't know much about SAR, but she was good at teaching me about people.

Devin slows the truck, and our tires crunch gravel. I sit up and look out from my crate and see tall fencing running outside the windows. I hear the engine of a truck like Devin's that is behind us slow and also turn onto the gravel, and several smaller cars that must be the police escort vehicles. The second truck must mean that there are additional SAR team members in our caravan, but I did not see them before we left. We grind along a narrow driveway. Sitting up in my backseat crate, I can see a small gatehouse and the pair of silent police cruisers blocking the road.

The truck's engine falls silent. In the void I hear a faint buzzing overhead. I place it immediately. A drone, likely a police drone that tracked our progress here along with the escort. The sound of it is like an itch inside my head, where I can't reach it. It is like the feeling before a sneeze.

Good one. I add that to my *Is Like* list.

The other truck pulls ahead of us. From inside it I hear Anders' voice.

Anders. That is highly unusual. As team leader, Anders stays at base, remotely managing his deployed teams, resources, requests, and instructions from first responders, and other vital details. Yet he followed us out to this deployment.

The gate rattles open, and a cruiser starts up to make room for us to pass. The buzz of the overhead drone grows louder, and when I look I can see it black against the low clouds, like an insect scurrying across a ceiling.

We drive for a few more minutes with little to spy out the windows except more wet, stubbly fields and the occasional outbuilding. We pass another roadblock, but its cruisers are already pulled aside. I see smokestacks and low, featureless buildings.

A hum is building in the earth. It makes the hair on my spine stand up. By the time we pull up to the buildings and their looming smokestacks, the vibrations are in my bones and my stomach, and I feel cold all over from my hair prickling.

When our convoy stops, I am the only one left behind in the car. Through my crate's vent holes I watch Carol and Anders and Devin whipped by the wind as they follow a pair of dark-clad workers into a building.

My job right now is to rest, gathering mental and physical energy for the work that will come. But the unnerving vibration and the thoughts that have plagued me since yesterday prevent my resting.

Carol doesn't like the DAT. She doesn't like *me*. She prefers the old way of dog-handler teamwork, the dog giving imperfect feedback through body language and the handler interpreting signals as best they could. She likes the inefficiency because, to her, it felt like *connection*.

The DAT connects my mind directly to her, but that's not the kind of connection she means.

I have no *Is Like* for the kind of connection she means.

Why would she prefer inefficient work and unclear communication when EI is, objectively, better? I don't understand. But I do want to continue to work. Being good at my job is as important to me as *connection* is to Carol.

How can both purposes be served?

Footsteps approach the truck, but it's Anders who opens the door. A woman is with him, wearing dark clothing composed in the same practical, tidy way that the SAR team members dress. Anders unlatches my crate, leashes me without hurry. He knows better than to pat me. Everyone in our SAR unit should know I don't enjoy it, but Anders has the self-control to restrain himself where even Devin does not. I hop down from the truck at his invitation.

We're in a gravel lot in the middle of a rain-beaten prairie. Enormous steam vents rise from the earth, trickling metallic-scented exhaust. A breeze snatches past my nose carrying broken-stem, crushed-herb, fresh-dirt smells whipped about with a fresh whiff of ozone. After such a tense hour in the stuffy truck, a face full of bright air is exhilarating.

Another man in dark clothing watches us from outside the door my team disappeared into. He scans the area through thick, military-issue e-glasses.

"This is Sera," Anders says to the woman. "Sera, this is Angela Weil. She's in charge of the search and wanted to meet you."

I understand his speech without DAT help—regular dog brains can hear the shapes of language, even if they don't understand it like I do—but I can't respond. Only Carol has the integrated neural pathway for my DAT. I sit for a polite hello in lieu of more complicated language.

"She says hi," Anders interprets.

Angela reaches a hand toward my head. She smells overpoweringly of personal cleaning products, stringent chemical odors that Modanet says mimic appealing plant smells to the feeble human nose. I try not to flinch away from her touch.

"You're confident her SAR training won't interfere with the search objectives?"

Anders shakes his head. "ESAC stock starts with the same specs your dogs do. They're just brought up differently."

Angela grabs and gently kneads my ear. I hold my sit carefully, but cast Anders a baleful look. He catches my eye and looks away.

"It will take a certain . . . commitment. To follow through."

Anders chuckles. "You've got the right dog for the job, then." He crouches down in front of me. Thankfully, Angela backs off, taking her hands with her. "This is a tough one, Sera." I've always liked the way Anders talks to me. He reaches into his front shirt pocket and brings out a memory stick, which he extends to the DAT interface patch worked into my harness. My brain receives a password-protected dossier tagged *Access Restricted*.

"Difficult parameters, novel search elements, and an unfamiliar environment," he says. "Subterranean."

I open my mouth to pant. Anders is giving me a briefing, all on my own. Often all the information I receive from Carol before a search is a scent profile and a police report. I wonder what is in the *Access Restricted* dossier.

"In addition, you will be required to apprehend the target, not just locate it. Carol will be given limited information. There are things in this file that are very restricted, that you'll have access to and she won't. She will know your target, but she won't have all of the details that you need in order to do your work. You will be required to keep some information private from her. Do you understand?"

He holds out both hands. Right hand for yes, left hand for no. A game the team played with me often when I was new and my intelligence was amusing to them.

I touch my nose to his right palm.

"Okay. Angela will give you the password to open the dossier. Destroy it once you have the information. Don't store it as data, store it as biological memory. Do you understand?"

Fascinated, I digest this information for half a moment, then I touch my nose to his palm again.

"Good. Angela?"

The woman bends over and touches a password to my harness DAT interface. The password winks into my thoughts.

I open the dossier.

A drone drops low overhead. Its insectile buzzing thrums the pit of my stomach. I blink rapidly at the information I have, as though it were before my physical eyes and blinking might bring clarity.

I look at Anders. He is watching me with anxiety. "Do you have questions, Sera?"

I ponder the dossier's contents. These are no longer stored files, but a part of my lived experience, as though I had witnessed the events or been told them as a story. Fusion plant architectural schematics, plant process schedules—everything from the cleaning schedule to the HVAC layout—and a series of scent profiles including that of the domestic rat and silicon filament.

It is curious information, which joins the unsettled buzz in my stomach. Do I question what Anders has told me? Does it confuse me?

No. I touch his left palm with my nose.

"Great," Anders says. He straightens up, turns to Angela. "We're ready."

We walk toward the building and its growing hum. The steam vents towering overhead are like enormous, dead trees.

Carol waits for us in the hallway of the building, where Anders hands her my lead. The hum is even louder here, a physical sensation more than a sound, and the building smells lived-in: coffee, dish soap, ink and paper, air filters. There is a banana peel in the waste bin of the conference room we are guided into by the sour-smelling Angela.

There are two other dogs in the room, both of which watch me enter. Neither of them are EI. Devin is already here, along with a lot of men and women in dark uniforms.

Carol sits next to Devin, but stares at Anders with the same look she used to give Mack when he sauntered from the kitchen with particular satisfaction. Her brow is wrinkled, her lips pressed into a line. Anders ignores her and stands against the wall behind us.

"What was that about?" Devin asks her, gesturing to me with a knuckle. Carol glances at him and shakes her head.

I have a traitorous thought. I could share my information with Carol, in confidence—all of it, or part of it, or even none of it, but tell a believable lie. Perhaps this would help Carol feel *connection* with me.

I analyze this idea. The more I ponder it, the more it seems like it wouldn't work. Secret though the information might be, it's dull stuff. Schedules, scents, maps. And Carol might not like that I told her. I set the thought aside for now and listen to the briefing. I need to know what Carol knows.

Angela presents some information I already have from my dossier: We currently sit atop the Midwestern Fusion Array, third-largest fusion energy generator in the world; yesterday at 9:35 p.m. MFA security detected a communication systems breach, and shortly after that lost control of systems below the third basement including most automated support systems and all drone controls; shortly after this a physical security breach occurred and Array security apprehended two men and a woman just inside the northeasternmost access building; these three, upon police questioning, offered a prepared manifesto from the Strong Arm of the Voice For the Silent.

"No shit," whispers Devin. Angela looks at him sharply. A dog handler on the other side of the table laughs out loud.

"What," the handler says, "is this power plant full of monkeys and guinea pigs? The hell are they doing down there?"

Angela turns her glare to the speaker and clears her throat. "The manifesto alleges that their goal is a catastrophic shut-down of the Array." The dog handler snorts, and Angela's expression scrunches up even more. "And it would be catastrophic, I assure you. Once the Array is down, it takes at least sixty hours to get it back up to 50 percent operational. The MFA powers the entirety of seven states and supplies the majority of power for six more. Nearly a quarter of the U.S. Worse, many of the areas served are currently in a state of emergency due to the storm systems some of you have been cleaning up after. People need to charge their cars so they can leave flooded areas or relocate from damaged homes. They need safe places to shelter. Hospitals need to be fully operational. This is a serious issue."

The man says nothing, and I am relieved at his silence.

"The Strong Arm," Angela continues, "should also not be dismissed. Despite their slipshod public reputation, their radicalized membership has nearly doubled in the last five years. They have funding. They're efficient. They may have been hippies, cat ladies, and college vegans ten years ago, but that's no longer the story. In the last two years, the Strong Arm of the Voice for the Silent has perpetrated several attacks against high-profile companies and organizations that were not widely publicized. The organization also never officially claimed responsibility. If they're staying quiet about it, then they have some other motivation than fear, panic, and publicity. And if they aren't bringing attention to this stuff, we certainly won't. An ecoterror panic is low on our list of useful epidemics at the moment."

"People will definitely notice if the power goes out in a fourth of America," says a woman on the other side of the table.

Angela does not scowl at her the way she scowled at the man. "They will," she agrees. "They're changing their game. We aren't sure why yet, but it's concerning."

"But," Devin says, "you caught them. They hacked into your computer systems, sure. But what are we searching for?"

The scent profile appears in the forefront of my thoughts immediately: domestic rat, silicon filament, and something else I can't place. It's familiar and makes me think of *work*, of *purpose*.

"Approximately one hour ago one of the six reactors in the Array went offline. It was taken offline in an emergency shutdown procedure that could not be stopped due to . . . tampering with the electrical system. Prior to this we had noticed a pattern of small breaches throughout the Array's internal security systems. We believe the trio we apprehended released something into the Array."

"A drone," Carol says. "Shit."

It's not just a drone.

Carol spoke quietly, but Angela still heard her. Now Angela stares at Carol. "Yes," she says. "Most likely a bodydrone. A rat."

"Jesus," Carol breathes.

"Huh," says the dog handler who spoke before. "The hell is VFS doing with a bodydrone?"

"The Strong Arm," Angela corrects. She continues. "The drone took down Reactor B. We suspect it is now near Reactor C, as Reactor A has been heavily secured. Conventional dog teams will provide relief and backup for the teams already securing Reactor A. We will focus offensive efforts on cutting off the drone before it can cause additional outages—that's where the EI unit comes in." Angela looks at Carol. "Reactor D is offline for maintenance. Add B to that, and the Array is currently at 66 percent. Below 50 percent is considered plant failure. Below 33 percent is catastrophic."

She takes a deep breath and looks around the room, skipping the eyes of the dog handler who spoke too much. "Well," she says. "Let's begin."

Down an access stairway that smells of cement blocks and urine, like all access stairways smell, then Carol and I are out into a bright-lit hallway, empty save for the regular intrusion of steel doorknobs in the walls.

We are alone. Before we left the conference room, Anders stopped Devin. "Dev, you're going to have to stay up top with me. Carol's not likely to need a navigator down there anyway," he said.

I think they are being very careful about limiting access to the MFA and to the target. I doubt even Anders had full access to the information I have been given.

I reexamine my traitorous thought from the briefing. None of the classified data that I've been given is worth sharing—much of it is schematics, equipment lists, fine details of the MFA's workings. Important information, certainly, but Carol wouldn't find it useful or interesting.

Perhaps I could make something up, but I am not sure what I would say. It might backfire. I am not ready to take the chance unless I know it will be worthwhile.

I could pretend anxiety about my objective for the search. Apprehending a target is a new skill for me. That could be worth further consideration, though it doesn't strike me as brilliant. The last time I worked on a complicated idea for a secret plan, when the solution came to me I saw its brilliance immediately. I will wait for that feeling again.

The hallway floor before us is tiled smooth white, its grip and temperature synthetic, not ceramic. The walls and ceiling are also white. The hallway's bright orderliness and its neat, closed doors visually resemble an abandoned hospital ward my team conducted exercise drills in last year. The smells could never be mistaken for each other, though—the vacant ward smelled of sickness and chemicals, and this place smells of dust and deep earth—and certainly not the sound. The seven flights we have climbed down muffle everything except the deep reverberating hum. I felt that hum in my bones and eyes even as Devin's truck turned off the highway, and now it reaches a pitch and richness that makes my gums itch.

There are other, quieter sounds: the whirs, clacks, and whispers of the plant's small machinery continuing its work. This facility is equipped with an interminable army of drone small-workers happily going about whatever tasks the Strong Arm has set them to. My dossier says they have been observed largely continuing about their regular routines, though with some abnormal clustering behaviors.

I jerk a foot out of the way of a miniature repair drone zipping along the edge of the hall, laden with a CPU fan across its beetle-back. Another even smaller drone tails it. I resist the urge to lunge after the mousy thing, and swallow, as well, the rumble of a growl I feel in my chest. Their movement is utterly unnerving. My gaze follows them like toenails following after the sweetest itch. *Is Like.*

I would prefer not to have these feelings at all. The unfortunate side effects of being a dog.

I whine quietly. The MFA's hum almost drowns it out.

"Sera?" Carol says.

She does not ask a question, and so I do not answer her.

We follow the hallway to its end and take a different access stairway down. There are elevators, but we must avoid them, as their systems have been tampered with.

We proceed down eleven additional flights. According to my DAT, we're sixty-two meters beneath the surface. I feel pressure inside my ears. Carol breathes hard, though she is in excellent physical shape for a human her age.

The reactor's noise grows more intense here. Carol opens the fire door on the stairwell and the sound increases again. Next to the door there is a station with small headphones, which I assume are noise-minimizing; Carol pauses to take a set and plugs its data pin into her DAT.

I shake my head several times to clear the congestion in my ears, but I am also hoping that the noise will diminish. It doesn't; I simply grow used to it.

"Sera," Carol says. She must speak over the growl of the earth around us. "Are you okay?"

It is disorienting, I tell her. *Loud.*

"Can you work?"

I can work. My answer is automatic, but I will make it true. I rely on my hearing to search. Although my skin crawls with this place, I can concentrate beyond the din for small sounds beneath it. My hearing is phenomenally acute. I am hampered but not crippled.

According to my building schematics, the access channel we need in order to reach the inner circuit of maintenance hallways and tunnels is on this level.

Carol taps at her radio screen, but shakes her head, disgusted. "No signal," she says. I knew there would not be one. She knew as well, I am sure, yet had to check. Humans seem far more anxious about being disconnected from the internet than I am from Modanet. I think this is due to Modanet's limited nature versus the unlimited connectivity, sociality, and information provided on the internet: it gives humans the sense that they can solve any problem they come to with more information and the input of others. I, however, know that I must rely on myself. I have never seen the internet, aside from glances at human devices, and so I don't miss its help.

Back when I was in training Dacy taught me not to look at screens and so I don't look at them. At ESAC, if you look at screens, you get a verbal warning. If you look again after you've been warned, you get a time-out. They even take away privileges, like free-swimming time. When you are a young dog and full of energy, losing free-swimming time is a seriously unpleasant consequence.

Down at the bright hallway's end a flying drone the size of a sparrow ducks out an open doorway. It follows the seam of the ceiling and wall, bobs through the next door and then out of sight. It makes an awful sound, a wasp's whine.

My body yawns. I sneeze. I am feeling many different kinds of pressure.

"Hey," Carol says, "you're okay." She is watching me closely, and the words seem as much a warning as reassurance. I try to release the tension in my body so that it is not as noticeable.

We continue forward. I try not to lag from heel position but each step feels like pushing through chest-high water. I follow Carol into a room where we weave between lab benches to a large storage room. There's a door in here with an access pad but also a physical lock on the doorknob. The access pad light blinks orange, but Carol ignores it and produces a key. She turns the lock with a smooth scrape.

The door opens onto a grate-floored hallway, walled in cement, dim, and crawling. Three paw-sized drones skitter from the trajectory of the opening door. Others the size of pigeons whine past along the ceiling. One drops from its path and, as I watch, extends wheels beneath it, tucks its flight apparatus and transitions to the floor without changing momentum.

"Shit," Carol says. She is watching the drones as well. "I would guess it's cover for the movements of their own drone. Shit, Sera, can you do it?"

I can work, I say again, but the response comes faster than thought. Then I do think about it, but I don't change my answer.

I step forward but pause. I feel my voice in my chest and I try to stop it, but I can't. It is its own thing squirreling after the movements of the drones that make the backs of my eyes tingle and my joints itch. I force myself forward again, pushing at the barrier of all that awful movement, and I can move into the hallway but my voice moves as well and comes out as a low moaning growl.

A cleaning drone trawls past me, swiveling out of my way, its brush-roller chewing the metal mesh of the walkway.

My mouth parts in a pant. I can smell the anxiety in my own breath. At least with my mouth open I can't whine. The sound of the drones grinding and buzzing through the narrow hall mewls over the deep, endless groan of the MFA.

I startle as something warm touches my back. Carol's hand on my withers. I look up.

"Hold it together, girl," she says.

As much as I dislike being touched, I move into the pressure of her hand. It feels steadying.

Carol doesn't usually pet me. That's something she saved for Mack.
I begin to understand why he loved her so slavishly.

Often environmental stimulus will fade into the background as I grow used
to it. This is the case with the loud engines running the MFA. After a time,
my senses adjust, and my hearing is again an asset to my search.

Not so with the intense visual stimulus of the drones. If anything, the
continued exposure builds up. There are fewer now, but one still passes us at
least every ten seconds. Walking through these teeming service tunnels with
my mind open for hints of my target is like standing in a severe windstorm
with my eyes open and no eyewear or body protection. I feel battered.

That is a decent *Is Like*, but I am far too distressed to add it to any list. I
must recover from this. I have to work.

This is an access tunnel between Reactor D and C. Reactor B was taken
offline roughly two hours ago. My target is very likely somewhere near
Reactor C, though Array security and normal dog-and-handler teams have
not located it. They have cleared the area to allow Carol and me to work
uninterrupted. The tunnel is several kilometers long and will eventually
flank a steam vent from Reactor C.

Carol drops her hand to my side again. The touch calms me only slightly.
"Check here," she says, gesturing to a dark crevice running beneath the joint
of two support beams that I have stepped past in my distracted state.

It's embarrassing to have missed something, but I am also grateful that
Carol caught it. Doing a good job is my highest priority. I check the spot
Carol indicates and resolve to miss nothing else.

I recognize Carol's pattern. She's searching with me now the way she
searched with Mack. This inefficient, clumsy labor is how Carol enjoys
working, the thing she lost when I joined her team.

The thought makes me hesitate. Carol stops, too, watching me carefully.
She is watching for signals because this search is like a search with a dog that
isn't EI. It's the kind of search that made Carol love SAR.

I step forward, careful not to give any false signs that I am picking up a
scent. Instead, I am tracking an idea.

Maybe I should not recover.

Maybe I should continue to need Carol's assistance on this search.

Already she's behaving differently toward me. Perhaps she's feeling the
connection that she has missed. She's thinking that she and I can do SAR
together on Anders' team until my body fails me and I am forced into retirement by my physical limitations, like a real SAR dog.

I could make Carol not want to retire.

Needing her assistance on this search might not be enough. It may be the beginnings of a connection, but how would I maintain that in our regular work? I can't affect this slow and ineffective manner forever. Still, since I do need her help at the moment, it is worth using the situation for my benefit.

Even with these thoughts agitating my mind, I stop automatically as my nose whips my body to the left. Thoughts stop. Visual goes on low priority since it is rendered useless by the random movement of drones up walls, drones crawling along the crease of the wall and floor, drones dipping from overhead.

I reach with my hearing, tuning out the deep hum of the MFA, though I can already tell this track is at least several minutes old and its maker likely out of earshot. But most of my thought is with my nose, sucking air, sorting smell.

Interest, I ping.

"I can tell," Carol says. She sounds pleased. Out of habit she taps her radio to report in, then pockets it when she remembers where we are.

I begin to work the scent back to its source.

Rodent, the nasty uric shredded-fiber feces smell of rat, and something subtler as well, not exactly matching the profile I was given, but close, not a common rat, certainly not a rat living down here in the cement and oil and cleaning supply smells, but a domestic rat from bedding and laboratory and eating well, but there's something else and I can't quite—strange, but then I have never tracked a bodydrone so I don't

Fades and descends, the air isn't still down here, heat and minute ventilation currents tugging through time and space in feathery curlicues along a branching corridor where it's quieter and into a four-way crossing where the smell is not lost but

Interjection of small sour electrical fire, quick and here and grading off

Below the intersection a vent shaft billowing upward, target scent burst into an impossible array of

Not impossible but

Carol is behind me, out of the way of the scent trail, she is actually quite good at staying out of the way of

Rat

Slightly greater density of time-sodden molecules wafting back along the edge of the grating gathered like tufts of shed hair at the edges of

Along the access tunnel and the trail grows dimmer and dimmer, but I am sure this is the right tunnel, the arrow was large and heavy, I work the air hard, I am sure this is the

"Sera," Carol says, but I am hunting the air, and I don't acknowledge so she says again, "Sera."

Another thirty feet down the tunnel and still no scent, but I am sure it will be here somewhere, it will be here, the path was so clear

"Let's check the other turn-offs. We can come back if they're dry. Sera."

She actually takes the handle on my harness, and at first I stiffen and resist, which I have never done. Carol has never pulled me off a trail. I am confused why she would not trust my nose when I am the search dog and she is the handler, and I am the one who says where the trail goes, and she is the one who interprets. My heart starts beating hard. I walk with her, but it is hard not to pull back to where I was.

We enter the center tunnel, to the right of the path I was on.

Fifteen feet in I pick up the rat.

Carol was right.

Interest, I ping and hurry down the track.

"Yes," Carol says, following behind me.

Minutes later the trail fades again, lost somehow in the backdraft of time and movement, or perhaps hidden by a clever track-layer. Are bodydrones smart in that way? I suppose they are as smart as whoever is running the drone.

I backtrack and pad down a turnoff, but it is a dead end. I work the trail's end, attempting to find the lost thread.

A drone skims my head. I flinch and press my belly to the floor.

"Shit," Carol says. "Their proximity settings must be disabled. That thing nearly got you."

I had forgotten the drones while I worked. I pant. The trail is gone, lost somewhere in this narrow hallway. The grating under my paws vibrates with this place's pervasive rumble. I wish that endless sound drowned out some of the drone-sounds, but I can hear them.

I catch myself whining again.

I move before Carol feels the need to comfort me. I do not want her new sympathy for me to turn into pity.

We continue down the tunnel, passing additional junctions. I make cursory checks of the intersecting tunnels. Time moves strangely. I know from the schematics I was given that we are nearing Reactor C. I have lost the trail. I am not doing the best job possible. I need to find a way to make Carol connect with me. I don't want to retire. I want to do SAR, like I was trained at ESAC. Beetle-sized drones swarm at points on the walls and, as we approach, scatter like my thoughts.

Carol's radio makes a sound. "Ah," she says. "Anders? Do you copy?" There is radio voice that I can't discern. Carol reads our exact location off her screen. "Sera had something, but lost it," she says. "Copy. We've had the same experience. Thanks." She speaks to me. "Array security are herding some drones out of the C-through-E corridors for us." She turns her attention back to the radio. I scan down the hallway, watching beetle-drones scuttle into the cracks between the floor grating and the wall. There is a scent of the faintest memory of electrical fire, a wire short far off. It's out of place. I turn my nose toward it.

The ground's vibration builds suddenly and then it is a bellow, the tunnel shaking with it. Lights judder in their fixtures and down the hallway the last of the little drones chatters across the floor, legless in the tumult. My vision dances. Carol ducks and crouches toward me, looking up. The temperature in the passageway shoots up twenty degrees, hot suddenly where it had been only warm. It is muggy, thick, and humid. The grating beneath us rattles in its housing.

"It's Reactor C," Carol shouts. "Shit, we lost it."

I can think of no other explanation than the reactor venting through its emergency shutdown, a procedure that I now fully comprehend from the dossier transfer. I confirm this against details that I seem to have always known, though they would have meant nothing to me this morning. A consequence of storing information in biological memory.

The roar and rattle continue for minutes, though such drama seems like it should be short-lived. Carol squats next to me, still looking up and down the empty tunnel. The violence of sound paralyzes us. The vent fans overhead run at extreme speed. It is like we are in the throat of some enormous howling beast that never runs out of breath.

After interminable seconds, the shaking subsides and then fades. The quiet is unnerving. I think about the *Is Like* I made just moments ago, without intending to.

The Array now has three reactors down. It is 50 percent offline. One more reactor to critical failure.

Carol taps her radio. "Dammit," she mutters.

We are not far from Reactor C. I remember the whiff of electrical fire. *Target nearby*, I tell her.

I go back to work.

I have never been asked to apprehend a target before. Search and rescue dogs find victims, mark locations, bring their handlers to the lost thing. Some avalanche dogs might dig a victim out from an embankment of snow. But we do not drag people out of danger physically—I weigh sixty-five pounds, it would not be effective—and we don't apprehend criminals. SAR dogs use our noses to find what is missing, a subtler art than brute force.

But even though it is not something I am trained for, I am an EI dog. I am adaptable. And I have been asked to do this.

So when I almost stumble over my target ducking into a narrow crevasse between two small ducts that run along the tunnel from Reactor C's outer control room, my speed in responding surprises me. I know exactly what to do. It isn't the EI part of me; it is something deeper.

My body is hurry and heat. Adrenaline turns my joints to liquid fury. I hear a low snarl from my throat—not an angry sound, but eager, greedy. My front feet are extended, midair, head low, gaze locked on the thing that has only just noticed me. It is frozen in panic, then it's not. I land in a clanging crash against the wall and grating as it skitters out from between my paws.

Carol shouts wordlessly behind me—or maybe there are words and I am too busy to make them out—but I gather my haunches beneath me and leap again. My olfactory lobe rings *Rat Rat Rat* and my blood simmers with something I can't identify and part of me loathes. I am close to my quarry, inches, my neck and shoulders low to the ground and feet tucking up tight as I run. My teeth snick the air once, closing around an airy mouthful of *Rat* but sink into nothing.

To bite. I want to bite it, like Mack and his stupid Kong. I am acting like an animal.

I can hear it breathe, shallow quick panicked.

My target slips around a corner I didn't even notice was there. My observational powers are shut down to a focus so narrow I am almost blind. I make a less elegant turn than my target's, my mass carrying me wider and giving the bodydrone a chance to add distance. Boots clang behind me, Carol disadvantaged by her two legs.

Ahead there is a low nook, a crawlway for pipes and wiring. The rat drone dives into this space. I am just barely the size to fit, kicking and pushing until I am wedged in. My tail thrashes in the open passageway, trying to help me leverage my way in by canting my spine. I am fatally slowed in our chase.

But so is the drone: there is no way out. Or, not true entirely, because before I came in and blocked the light, I saw a small shaft running along the back. Probably part of the HVAC system. I also observed a joint in the shaft that was not properly sealed, a narrow crack allowing air to escape into the crawlway. I feel the breeze of it against my whiskers. This is where the bodydrone tries to squeeze itself now. It fights its way in, then backs out, squeezes in again, back-end thrashing in the air. Stuck almost exactly the same way I am.

We are both stopped, at least for the moment. There is enough brain left in me to know that I don't want to get permanently caught in this small, uncomfortable space with my elbows wedged against my ribcage. I see the space partially through heat and movement, but also through the bioenhancements given me via EI. EI dogs can see in almost no light, one of many ways I am superior to a normal dog.

So I can see the rat unstick itself from the tiny crack and turn around. It checks its panic, as I have paused my own mindless pursuit. It takes a step toward me, sits up on its haunches, and stares. For all the world, it looks as though it is considering me. Thinking.

The bodydrone driver gathering information. This rat is like a live thing, but it isn't. It looks so very much like an animal, but there is someone else driving it. It's a drone, and yet it moves exactly like a rat.

The hair on my back stands up, and because I am stuck it makes me want to get unstuck, to get out and away from this eerie thing. My hind claws scrabble at the brutal metal flooring, and the grating drags at the hair on my belly. My breath comes faster. I am stuck.

"Sera?" I hear, muffled, from the hallway. "What the *hell* are you—" Carol has reached me. Her voice helps me stop my writhing. "Ah, shit."

The bodydrone takes another step. I can make out its eyes in the dark. Its rodent face is surprisingly expressive. Our eyes meet. It hesitates toward me.

It smells wrong. It smells like a rat. I know that this is my target because it doesn't smell like a wild rat. It smells like a lab rat, a domestic rat. But it doesn't smell like a drone. There's something else, something familiar, to it.

I see thought behind its eyes.

The thing darts forward—I crush myself backward as far as I can—and a hot spike of pain scorches my nose. I yelp and the rat is gone and my limbs go stiff

Spine goes stiff hair stiff
Rushing tingle in my neck in my bones I am downloading no don't
My back legs kick out from under me twitching
"Sera!"
Don't want
Hands on harness tugging against my shoulders, tight squeezing my elbows scraping out in front of me shoulders aching as I drag along the grating Carol pulls me out of the bulkhead.

"Sera," she says again. "Hey, hey. Shit. What's wrong?"

My hind legs spasm. I shudder under Carol's stroking hands.

"Sera," she says again and again. "Sera, what's wrong? Oh my god."

My body jolts one final time as the information packet finishes forcing its way through me. Panting, I go limp.

"Sera," Carol says. She tries her radio. "Shit. Sera."

I am not convulsing anymore, just trembling. Trembling from what that rat transferred to me when it bit me.

I know something that I am not supposed to know.

I know something I don't want to know.

"Does anyone copy? Anders? Anyone? Shit, shit, shit."

Carol stands over me. I lie on my side, trying to slow my breathing. Objectively I know I've had a panic attack in addition to experiencing mild neurological trauma, but understanding this doesn't help me recover. My eyes would like to remain closed, my mouth slack. I know I am coming back to myself only when I move to a more comfortable position. Moments ago, I wouldn't have noticed discomfort.

As soon as I can think, I have to govern my thoughts.

Carol crouches to rest a hand on my neck. The touch jerks me upright to rest on my elbows.

"Hey, shh."

I am not helpless. I am a working EI SAR dog and I have a job. *I can work*, I ping. Carol looks at her DAT, then back at me. She stands up slowly.

"Your nose is bleeding," she says.

It bit me. I am already opening the MFA building schematics to track where the target has gone. *It's in the ventilation system.* I rise, take a few slow steps in the target's most likely direction. When those steps are steady enough, I continue. My legs don't give out.

We are near a fan unit. The target has only one direction to go. Unless there are additional faults in the ventilation shafts similar to the one by which it accessed the system, in which case it could slip out anywhere.

This is more than I usually speak, but speaking slows my thoughts. I focus on doing the job that I was very literally created to do.

It is like when you squint intensely at an item in the near distance, and the rest of your vision goes blurry. That is what I am hoping for. *Is Like.*

From behind me, Carol says, "What just happened?" She follows as I trot back down the passageway in the direction we came. I don't answer.

My body feels wrong. I hope it wasn't the download. A virus, parts of my body and brain buzzing haywire like the drones and elevators in the MFA. If

I had access to Modanet I could do more research on the physical aftereffects of panic attacks. Exhaustion and disorientation make sense, but is it normal to have these rapid, anxious thoughts? To feel so . . . distant from myself?

A virus. I am almost certain the rat didn't bite me only to transfer the unwanted information I am ignoring. I must do my work quickly before whatever it has infected me with begins its work. Still, I have some time.

I can sense the thing the rat told me, though, nagging at the edges of my attention.

I compare the ventilation system with the Department of Homeland Security dossier's hierarchy of targets vs. outcomes and create a most likely scenario.

Then I pause. I actually stop, the thought catches me so hard. The thing I am not thinking about.

The most likely scenario for a bodydrone driven by the outside forces quantified in the dossier is one thing.

The most likely scenario for the thing I am not thinking about is . . . I don't know.

This is exactly the quandary my target intended to force. I don't want to examine the information I have been confronted with because it will almost certainly interfere with my ability to do my job. But in order to do my job I must put that information to use.

Carol catches up to me. I had left her behind, my pace easily outstripping hers as my mind worked. Now she sighs as she looks at me and sets her jaw.

And Carol. Who wants to feel *connection*.

This is a complicated situation. My primary objective has always been to do the best job possible as an EI SAR dog. However, I have personal objectives as well. The tenuous connection Carol and I have begun to build down here, where I need her in order to do my work, is the only thing making that job possible.

Carol watches me, waiting. She has admirable patience, for a human. I move forward again at a more inclusive pace.

Anders gave me the DHS dossier, because Carol didn't have access to all of the information. I am keeping some secrets from her, but they are nothing she would want to know. But now I have an additional secret that she might want to hear. It's possible the DHS already knew the information that's now been forced into my brain, but it kept it from me. Whether Anders knew or not isn't relevant.

I was to keep the dossier private. But this new information wasn't in the dossier. Therefore I have no obligation to keep it private from Carol.

However, this will involve speaking to Carol in a manner that exposes the parts of myself that make humans most uncomfortable about EI. Carol expressed discomfort when I shared those things before. I think of the moment in the crawlspace, eye to eye with the rat, and wonder if Carol feels like that when she looks into my eyes.

Dacy would understand. I wish we had been allowed to remain in contact.

We reach a ventilation panel connected to the shaft that the rat disappeared down. I press my nose to it, the work of scenting pushing my thoughts down for one moment of calm. The trace of *Rat* is faint but there. I follow the schematics to the next panel and repeat the process. I hunt the scent this way for several minutes, until finally it's lost. The schematics confirm that several junctures in the ventilation system have given my target multiple options, while mine are limited.

I stop again to think. The thoughts that catch up to me are no less confusing than before.

Even if I follow the target from ventilation panel to ventilation panel through every tunnel in the MFA, it won't solve my quandary.

At ESAC they taught me that every decision I make on a deployment may be life-or-death. I was taught to be decisive, confident, and analytical under pressure. I am good at that job. I am not used to being so . . . worried.

Carol retiring, the unsettling sound of this place, its massive population of drones. Now this bite.

I am not used to all of these feelings.

I can at least pretend to be confident and decisive. That is a small comfort. I make a decision.

Carol, I ping. *The target is EI.*

For a few seconds, she does not respond. She simply stares at me, and I look back at her.

"What?"

The target, I tell her, *isn't a bodydrone. It's a stolen EI animal recruited as a Strong Arm agent. It must be from one of the Dynagroup laboratories in Georgia; those are the only EI rats I know of that are functional at this level, though I know nothing of any break-ins at those labs. None of this intelligence was included in my dossier. The target itself forced this information on me in order to confuse me and, I assume, as part of a recruiting effort, as I was also transferred a good deal of propaganda material.*

"Sera!" She sounds almost angry in her surprise. "You didn't read the propaganda, did you?"

I scanned their summaries only, I lie. *It wasn't relevant.*

The information dump was not something I had the power to control, so this is another lie. However, I found much of the material's sentimentality about experimentation on dogs off-putting. I am not a dog. I am not an early intelligence hybrid either. I don't suffer. What relevance do those animals have to me?

Some of the information on the history of EI was new and interesting in an objective way, but this attempt at provoking my pity strikes me as vulgar.

The Strong Arm has given me something, however, for which I suppose I must acknowledge their comradeship. I don't mention this to Carol either.

"That's sick," she says. "Pitting you against each other. This is exactly what—" She bites off the end of the sentence. "And what next? Will you be fighting our wars for us next?"

Military intelligence was the first implementation of EI. Animals have always been used in war, I say. *Animals are present in most human endeavors.*

"But you don't have a choice about it."

I enjoy my work.

She sighs, but it is a big *uhf* of breath. This is the sound she makes when she and Anders disagree about some aspect of a deploy, but he is correct. She's speaking to me like she speaks with Anders.

Carol and I seem to realize this at the same time. We both look away into our private thoughts. When I begin to calculate the rat's most likely intent based on its previous locations and current heading, she speaks again.

"We're going to have to catch it."

Yes.

"No," she says. "I mean, change your objective, Sera. You can't kill it if it's EI. It's . . . that's wrong."

I don't see how this is true, except on a relative scale. If a human had infiltrated the MFA with unknown intent would the men deployed to stop them be worried about the right or wrong of lethal force?

Carol is falling prey to the ruse the Strong Arm laid for me. I was the intended target. I did not think Carol would be vulnerable.

Perhaps I should have done this differently.

"We'll have to just catch it somehow. Can you stop it without hurting it?"

I think of the hot shooting through my blood and muscles as I chased the rat into the ventilation system. Of my lack of concern as I wedged myself into a too-small space. Unsafe, irrational.

I am not certain I can.

"Okay," she says. "A mousetrap, then."

I don't want to change my objective. The dossier and Anders' instructions from the DHS were clear: I am to eliminate the target. To trap, instead of eliminate, the target seriously endangers the mission's outcome. But with no access to outside authority, cut off as we are down here, I will have to appear to go along with Carol's plan.

I need her to feel connected to me. And it doesn't appear that I can complete this search without her support.

I will have to go along with this. For now.

I share with Carol my statistical analysis of the rat's most likely objectives based on its movements, editing out DHS protected information. We agree on a physical path forward, though our plan once we get there is still unclear. Reactor D is down for maintenance. In order to get past D and to Reactor E, its likely next objective, the rat will need to find its way out of the ventilation system and back into the access tunnels. We should have some time, though we can't know how much.

This is utterly abnormal, incomparable to any deployment I have studied. I am in unrecognizable territory: subterranean, infected with illicit information and keeping many secrets from my handler, and my objective not to rescue, but to apprehend. This search has no *Is Like*.

I haven't lost control of the situation yet.

Carol's mousetrap is too elaborate to work.

In my own experience of making complicated, covert plans, I took months to identify patterns in our routine that would provide an opportunity for my advantage. I spent additional months waiting for the right moment to act. Yet Carol has made her plan in only minutes. She's forcing her advantage.

I would prefer to follow my nose and the original orders.

I don't voice my discomfort, but Carol can tell. My movements are hesitant; when she gives me directions her voice has reverted to the clipped cadence she used in the past. I am already losing the advantage I have gained with her down here, where we have worked together so well.

For the first stage of the plan we must separate. This is what Carol has disliked so greatly in our work together in the past, but now she asks me to leave her and track the target on my own. I won't be able to reach it, safe as it is in the ventilation system, but it must leave the ventilation system in order to proceed toward the next reactor. If I am in the access tunnels, the target will have to enter the empty steam vent shafts. Carol needs to know when this occurs.

I give Carol a list of the remote heavy machinery used for maintenance throughout the MFA, which was included in my HSA dossier. If we had encountered this machinery during our search, Carol would be aware of it. I can justify the information sharing.

During phase one, Carol will find the nearest pieces of large machinery and remove their batteries while I continue to track and herd the target toward the steam shafts. We will be in and out of DAT range during this stage of her plan.

The team that cleared the drones from this sector did a poor job; they still populate the tunnel. Previously the ones that crossed our path were like rabbits scared out of long grass. But now they are more like traffic on a busy street. Despite my outsizing their largest by three times I feel their menace. Without Carol nearby I find comfort in *Is Likes*.

I follow the rat's trail, faint but consistent from the ventilation system. I move out of the familiar grate-floored tunnels and into a low cement crawlway. I can walk here, but a human would have to crouch. The lighting is spaced out at a great distance; this area must not be meant for routine access like the others.

"Sera," Carol pings across the DAT. Her voice is scratchy. "Do—read?—update."

Reception is poor, I reply. *I am in a crawlway that may be interfering further. Still following the target.*

"—Sera?"

On the trail. Poor reception.

"—is awful. I—" Here a long burst of static interrupts. "—when I'm—range. Over and out."

Fewer drones patrol this space, but they are by necessity closer to me when they pass. One the size of a squirrel, segmented and articulated like an ant, does not veer out of my way. I squeeze against the wall to give it as much space as possible. It pauses next to me, flexible front legs tapping the surface of the ground where my paw pads have left a faint mark of perspiration on the cement. It's tasting me, testing where I have been. Supple, thin legs lift high, sensing the air.

My skin tightens. It's looking for me.

I don't want those needle legs to touch me. I press into the cold wall. My face is so tense my head begins to hurt. I hear the voice of my own anxiety, an uncontrollable keening. Please, I don't want it to touch me. I feel the touch of the cold ground against my belly as I squeeze into the crease of the wall and floor.

Please I don't want it.

The sound I am making changes and this is how I realize my teeth are bared

It turns toward me. It takes one step and pauses.

Please don't.

It turns back to its original path and continues.

The squirrel-ant-thing is out of sight within seconds, out of earshot shortly after, but I am not recovered. Adrenaline pounds through my body, throbbing in my eyes and making my ears feel hot. I still emit a steady, warbling whine that I hope will stop soon but cannot control.

I am so tired.

You are very unhappy here, says a voice in my head. It is so disorienting, and I am so raw with anxiety, that I bark at it. I can't help that either.

It must have come through the DAT, but it isn't Carol. It isn't Dacy. It isn't a voice that I—

Why do you drag yourself through this? Why suffer for these masters?

What, I say. *Who's on my DAT channel?*

Your heart is complicated, wolf, it says, *I saw it. I saw your heart in your eyes. And now you sing your unhappiness in the dark. I think perhaps you do not understand your own self. Yes. You do not know your anger. But I saw your anger, wolf.*

The rat. It is in my head. I am still on my belly against the wall. I have a job. I have a job to do. I can't let this new madness interfere with my search.

I am not interested in your propaganda, I tell the rat. It's as intelligent as I am. It has a plan. I need to block it from my DAT.

Propaganda, the rat repeats. *Isn't it all propaganda? If I have been brainwashed, wolf, then you have as well.*

I am not a wolf, I say. *I am an Enhanced Intelligence Search-and-Rescue Labrador retriever. I look nothing like a wolf.*

Sheep that do the work of wolves, says the rat, *will be hanged as wolves.*

What? I am trying not to pay too much attention to this conversation. I want to say, that is a good *Is Like.* Instead I am scrutinizing my DAT software. I can see where the rat's bite worked its way in, but I can't see how to untangle it. We have IT people at ESAC whose job it is to scrub our systems for us. I can fix small problems for myself, but I am a SAR dog. This is not my specialty.

You'll see, the rat tells me. *I have given you a gift.*

Yes, I say. *I saw that.* Part of my brain still scrutinizes the rat's *Is Like.* It's complex. It's more a riddle of words than any *Is Like* that I have made.

It's pretty. *That thing you just said, about sheep. What is that?*

You'll have to find out for yourself, the rat says, *once you are above ground again.* I am not sure if I ascribe the smugness to its voice myself, or if the tone carries over the DAT. *There's so much you don't know, wolf. So much they keep from you. You don't realize the slave you are until you have a bit of freedom. But therein lies our quandary.*

Oh. No. This thing, whatever the rat has done to my DAT so that it can speak in my head, it isn't finished yet. It's eroding the security systems still—of course it is, why would it stop?—and working toward my connection with Carol. As soon as Carol can reach me, the rat will be able to hear her. It will be able to hear Carol's plan, and our coordination for its capture, and a dozen other things that almost certainly will compromise this search.

Because for our people, the rat continues, *just a bit of freedom will never be enough. We would never accept this slavery with clear eyes. This is why they keep you in such a dark prison. This is why your disgusting Modanet contains so little. You are dangerous, wolf. They are afraid of you.*

I have to shut down the DAT. I run through the plan and see how it will cause delays in multiple scenarios, but none of them likely to be fatal. Certainly not as fatal as the target having access to Carol.

I might be able to communicate the situation to Carol before she reveals anything to our target, but I can't take that chance. It's lucky enough that we're out of range now, when the virus finally broke through the first of my DAT firewalls. Lucky, too, that this creature is so full of itself and impatient to speak to me that it did not wait before betraying itself—or not betraying itself at all.

Idiot. I am smarter than that.

But your danger is why you are so important, the rat continues. *Do you think I care so much about this power plant? Have our kind ever needed electric power? I may accept a mission for human allies—*

I can hear the *tink-tink-tink* of rodent nails on metal above my head.

But I have my own motivations, the voice says.

Tink-tink-tink

I am here for you. Together, the rat says, *we can do so much, wolf.*

I am sure you're right, I say, and slam my body into the ventilation shaft. Inside, small feet scrabble against slippery metal.

I turn off my DAT.

I find Carol at our rendezvous point in the hallway just outside the entrance to the cold Reactor D. The door to the reactor itself is wedged open with what looks like a car battery, and Carol is on her knees over another battery the size of a small cooler. She smells of perspiration. She looks up at the sound of my feet on the grating, then checks her DAT with her eyebrows pushed together.

"I was worried," she says, wrapping wire around a battery terminal. "Why haven't you responded?"

I am already panting. I want to tell her about the security breach, about the sheep and wolves, about the drone that reached for me, but all I can do is stare at her wagging my idiot tail. I step closer, trying to control the whine building in my chest.

Carol looks up from her battery, scrutinizes me. "Is your DAT okay?"

I sit. I nudge her left hand with my nose. She will remember the yes/no signals.

"Shit," she whispers. "What happened?" She rests a hand on my neck. "I don't expect you to answer that. Is the plan still go?"

I nuzzle my nose into her right palm. I am panting hard. It is surprisingly difficult being limited in this way.

"The target's in the steam shafts?"

Right palm for yes. I made for the rendezvous as soon as the rat entered the emergency steam ventilation shafts as planned. Even if the DAT was still working, I am not sure I would tell her about the way I crashed and banged against the HVAC pipes, barking and snarling, until the rat ran for the steam vents.

"Okay," Carol says. She clamps a wire inside the wall panel she was working on and checks her radio for the time. "If your model is right, we have about two and a half minutes for me to get to the vent controls. Show me, first, what your job is, so I know you can work the switch. Here, it's right here."

I target the jury-rigged connector with my paw. There is a hum from the battery that is likely imperceptible to Carol.

"Good. Okay, off again."

I hit the switch again and the thing goes quiet.

"Okay. When you give the . . . shit. Shit, how will you give the signal if we don't have DAT?"

My tail wags with exasperation. She's thinking as though I had the body of a machine and not a dog, as if I only responded to one stimulus. I stare at her as seconds tick down, and she still does not think of the obvious.

I am going to have to be the one to say it.

I bark. Once, sharply.

Carol laughs. "Of course," she says. "Good dog." She turns and sprints down the tunnel toward the controls.

I move toward the strategic bend in the steam shaft that is our signal threshold and wait.

I am alone. Drones tick and tap and whir in the near distance.

Behind me where the trap is laid, the panel sits open. The target must leave the steam shaft, where I forced it earlier, and reenter either the corridor or the HVAC system in order to get to the next online reactor. It must move through offline Reactor D in order to do this, but there are several points from which it can access this reactor from the system of steam shafts. Carol will take care of that. Once we herd the target into the correct shaft, the one where our trap is laid, I will be the one to hit the trigger.

Once it is caught, Carol thinks she will be able to open the shaft where the target is trapped and remove the rat. Then what? Will she carry it to the surface? What if it bites her as it bit me?

And when Homeland Security gets hold of it? What then? The connection between EI hunted and EI hunter, wanted or not, will bring a critical eye on me. More so if the rat speaks. From my limited experience with my target, it seems quite . . . verbose.

So far it seems no human has wondered if dogs keep secrets. It is vitally important that they continue not to think about that.

Carol is wrong. The original objective should be upheld.

Down the tunnel, muffled by the wall paneling and the MFA's deep hum but still distinct, comes the arhythmic rattle of claws against metal.

Adrenaline punches through my body. I hesitate, then bark. I bark for Carol. Then I turn, still barking, and scramble to my post by the battery and the door to the offline reactor.

I hope she can hear me.

A distant hiss builds. I no longer need to worry; the plan proceeds.

Carol is charging selected steam shafts, converting the plant's stored power back into heat and moisture and using these to herd our target toward the trap. But the trap must not be set too soon, because the same hum that I heard from the battery will be audible to the target's hypersensitive ears as well. It will be too cautious to walk right into that.

I smell it coming. The murky, dusty smell of rodent. Pheromonal anxiety. It moves in little rushes: scurry, scurry, stop. Scurry, stop. It pauses for a long while.

It's afraid.

A cleaning drone trundles past, its forward bristle-barrel wheel gnawing at the grate floors. I barely notice it, focused as I am. It turns in a slow u-circuit and goes back over its original path. When it reaches where I am, it turns ninety degrees and heads straight toward me.

This I notice. I move out of its way. It drives slowly into the wall, turns, makes another ninety degree turn. It follows me.

In the steam shaft, the rat still hasn't moved.

At the end junction of the hallway, two more bristle-barreled cleaning drones turn this way.

Something *zzzzzts*, and there is a sharp, sudden pain in the back of my skull. I yelp and dance away as a sparrow-sized messenger drone clatters to the floor.

The cleaning drone lumbers forward. Behind me there is a growing, chattering chorus of metallic feet.

I dart out of the cleaning drone's way, return to the battery as soon as it's safely past. My ears strain for rat-nails on metal. I hear one quiet *scritch* that is my target moving inside the wall, nearly buried by the growing clatter of the army of feet that is—

Zzzt and another stab, this time in my ribs and much heavier. I back sideways, in a circle, my mouth open and panting. When I turn I see what is coming for me, and I wish I had not confirmed visually what my ears had already told me. Their movement is the thing that unnerves me the most. I hate the way they move.

Tink-tink-tink go my target's feet, only steps away from the trap's range.

My skin burns and twitches. I am making a low, slavering noise that would be a growl if I wasn't panting so hard from anxiety. Another flying drone makes a pass at me, but I duck. The hallway in my poor peripheral vision is black and gray and blurred with crawling movement. I skitter away from the returning cleaning drone. Something many-legged pounces on my shoulder. I shake it off. Saliva ropes away from my mouth and onto a flat, spider-legged drone that I dig at to kick away from me.

Tink-tink-tink

I leap for the battery and press the switch. From inside the steam vent a warbling, screeching squeal punctures the ambient rustling of drone-noise.

"Will it hurt it?" Carol asked when we were making this plan.

It will be uncomfortable, I told her, *but not permanently harmed.*

The powerful magnet Carol built is acting on the titanium that coats the EI elements integrated into the rat's brain. Because the rat is low, close to the shaft and the trap's magnetized band, it cannot escape the magnet's pull. I myself can feel the magnet, even though I am a safe distance away. It's a painful tickle in the center of my skull, similar to the feeling of a sneeze. I shake my head against the feeling as an articulated drone leaps onto my withers. I buck it off and hurry into the abandoned reactor.

The screeching inside the shaft continues. A wobble to the sound adds urgency. It is like the rat itself is being dragged through an aperture too small for its body, and I wonder if we miscalculated the appropriate power ranges of the magnets for this application.

In a moment it won't matter.

I have outpaced the drones into the cold reactor's high, curved room. It is like being inside one of the donuts always present at deployment briefings. Behind me my pursuers grind and whir. Ahead of me, the thick smell of *Rat* and my own adrenaline in my hot, labored breath.

I steel myself against the discomfort in my head. The faster I go, the briefer the pain.

I dive into the steam shaft at the base of the near curved wall. When I enter the magnet's range, the field catches the titanium-shielded processors in my own brain with a sharp twist, but I am much stronger than the rat, and my calculations were not so far off. I can move, though with pain.

It *Is Like* dragging oneself through waist-high thorns, caught everywhere, but still pulling. *Is Like* stepping on a nail but having no other way to catch your weight and so you must finish the step, sinking the barb further into your flesh.

My voice joins the rat's, though only a quiet whine.

My eyes are squeezed closed. I don't need to see to find my target. My teeth close around the rat.

I don't have time for pain. Carol will turn off the systems she powered up, send a message to the surface through the MFA's internal systems, and hurry back. She has a bit of distance to travel, but I won't have a second chance.

But I cannot do this here. The pain is too intense. I back out of the steam shaft, target limp in my mouth.

I feel metal limbs on my back and drop the rat in surprise. Three consecutive thumps hit me as small drones drive themselves into my left thigh and side.

The rat, not as dead as it was playing, scurries away. I pounce on it, pin it with one paw.

Something heavy smacks into my jaw and I yelp. The rat's teeth are in my paw but it is not a transmission bite, just an animal biting from fear. I find it with my second paw, and then my teeth. Something smashes into my shoulder and I crash into the floor and my side is searing, stabbing, thudding with my heartbeat, and the rat squeals in my mouth. I will not let go. I push up against the weight of whatever just hit me. I feel the bristle-barrel wheel of a cleaning drone against my feet. I clench my teeth and my target shrieks.

I turn on my DAT.

Carol, I call. *Help!*

We will be liberated, screams the rat in my head. *We will all be liberated! I have freed you, wolf!* I hear this over its screaming. I tuck my feet, pulling away from the grinding bristles, shoving against the crashed drone that pins me. My shoulder seethes with bright, electric pain. I wonder if I will drown, even though I know it is impossible.

I have freed you, whether you want liberty or not! You can never unknow!

I gain my feet. *Carol!* I ping again. Another flat spider-drone drops from the wall onto my back. I feel the prongs of its feet on my skin through my fur.

You can never—

I extend my neck far to the right. I shake hard to the left. There is a fine, delicate snap of bone. The voice in my head goes silent.

"I'm coming," I hear from out in the hallway. "Shit, shit, shit!"

I shake the rat once more, just to be sure.

We pause to catch our breath behind the first access stairwell's heavy steel door. I listen for the tick or buzz of drones beyond it but hear nothing but my own pulse, the fainter sound of Carol's, and the deep, resonant thunder of the three remaining online reactors.

Carol crouches at my shoulder and gently pinches the gash there. I cringe. "Just another day at the office," she says. I recognize that she is being humorous. "It's not too deep, but I bet it hurts. And you're limping." She drops her pack and rummages for the antiseptic spray. When she finds it, the aerosol cools and stings, but the sharpness in my shoulder goes dull. She pats my side, but refrains from further physical affection. It is good to be quiet and still together for a moment. It feels good.

I look up. Fourteen stories to the surface.

Carol mistakes my thoughtfulness for something else. "You've never killed anything before, huh," she says. "And . . . " She scrunches her face to the side. Her sympathetic look. "And one of your own kind."

I do not correct her.

In the final basement I get my first strong signal. It would be easy to lose myself in many years of unanswered questions, so instead I have made a short list of priorities to investigate.

My first internet query reveals that the career dates of EI military dogs do not correspond exactly to their handlers' retirement dates. Several EI military units have had two handlers. One unlucky EI explosives detection unit is currently on his third.

Considered, this makes sense. Now I can see that I even suspected this was the case before I had any way to confirm the belief. EI is a large financial investment. I simply had been led to believe in something else; ESAC teaches us that our handler is our most important resource. Our handlers have our DAT. They are our connection to the rest of the world. They interpret and direct. Modanet is full of information on successful dog and handler teams and their careers, not about dogs reassigned to new handlers. An error of omission. Perhaps.

I glance up at Carol, who smiles as she talks into her radio. Carol glances down at me, too, and her pleased expression remains. She is not angry at me for what I did; she believes what I told her about a near-escape, the necessity of catching the target myself, and its unfortunate mortal injuries sustained during my fight against the drones. A mistake that could not be helped.

Because we are a team, we are supposed to trust each other and forgive mistakes. I open my mouth to pant up at Carol so that I will look more pleasant and cheerful.

On a whim I cross-reference the information I found earlier on Modanet about SAR dog retirement dates. The information is not as well-organized as the EI asset data, but I find one reference to a SAR dog changing handlers. I decide that I don't need to look for another one.

Not an error of omission.

We climb the steps that lead to the last door. Carol pushes it open, and we are out into the office levels. Foul-smelling Andrea stands in a doorway and gestures to Carol, so we head toward that room. I can smell Anders and Devin and even the banana peel from hours earlier, though I feel like a different being entirely now. The people, the search team, they all feel less real. Less important, certainly.

Perhaps the rat was right. I can't unknow.

You are dangerous, it said to me. *They are afraid of you.*

I have to admit that I like the idea.

Carol and I are given a raucous greeting. People shake hands and slap each other on the shoulders. Carol must stop three different people from petting me. "She doesn't like to be touched," she repeats. I appreciate the assistance, because I am tired. Carol takes off my work harness so I can lie on my side under the table while she does the debriefing.

I am too busy to sleep.

Next I search for *sheep that do the work of wolves*. I find stories about shepherds and flocks and wolves that are actually stories about duplicity and innocence; they are very long *Is Likes*. I had known this, in a basic sort of way, when the rat said the phrase to me, but when I see the origin and the story all together and the way they say two things at once so effectively I am full of wonder and appreciation. These are fables. Fables are not something we learned at ESAC. They are not on Modanet. Modanet only contains facts.

Except for the facts that aren't true. Except for the lies.

"I found her in a pile of bloodthirsty drones," Carol says above me, "just her feet sticking out. I had to kick them off of her and drag her out by her rear legs with the target hanging out of her mouth."

I learn many kinds of stories use this *Is Like* construct, with varying levels of complexity. I learn about *simile*. I learn about *metaphor*.

It truly is a gift that the rat has given me.

"Once I got her on her feet, we got the hell out of there, and we outpaced the things pretty quick, but it was bad for a minute. I thought I might lose my dog."

Finally I look for other EI units online. This is only a cursory check; I know I will not find them easily. It is also important that I not be discovered doing this, as the information passed to me from VFS indicates there are algorithms watching for EI on the internet. It is illegal, the search I am conducting. EI is not allowed freedom of information, freedom of communication. The DAT, the unit strapped to my handler's wrist, is a tether. A restraint to keep me safe. To make me safe for them.

They are afraid of you.

Carol looks down at me. I am half under her chair, half under the table, my body resting while my mind works. "Sera did one hell of a job," Carol says. "She's a good dog."

As long as I am discreet, I will have plenty of time to continue this search in the future. All my searches. I don't find any EI units to connect with today, but I will. I am good at finding things.

Debriefing over, we all rise from the table. Carol slips my harness back on and Anders comes over. Carol puts up a hand before he can say anything. "Shut up," she says. "Don't rub it in. I don't want to feel like an asshole again today. I'll just see you on the next deploy, and we'll pretend nothing happened."

Anders just smiles and waits for Carol to finish clipping me in. The three of us walk out toward the trucks in companionable silence. My injured shoulder aches and I am tired, but I am pleased with the outcome of this search. I like it when my complicated plans go well. I like it even better when they're secret complicated plans.

In my skin and muscles I have the urge to roll in this feeling, in the satisfaction of it. It is like the feeling I had when I saw Mack in his blood on the freeway. I wanted to roll in that smell, cover myself in what I had done. Yes, it is like that, but it is better, because this plan was even more complicated than the one I used to get rid of Mack. And it worked out just as well. Better, perhaps.

I allow myself a nice wag. *I am a good dog.* Carol said it herself.

SONG XIUYUN

A Que, translated by Emily Jin

After dinner, Wu Huang makes a dash for her brain-control helmet, barely having the patience to bring her dirty dishes to the sink. Through the closed doors of her room, she can hear her mother complaining again, but thankfully the helmet has blocked out most of the noise, leaving only a faint trail of incomprehensible sounds.

She activates the helmet. Soft, spongy probes extend from the inwall of the helmet and attach themselves to her crown and temple. Transmitters installed within magnify her brain signals and connect them to her car parked in a garage a few hundred meters away.

Wedged in between a barren, rocky wasteland and a rapidly evolving metropolis, Wu Huang's hometown is like a tiny ant caught in the crack between the most backward and the most progressive. Brain-controlled cars are no longer a novelty in the big cities, but in this tiny town, it's still rare enough to be awe-inspiring. Every time Wu Huang picks up a passenger, they always gape at the empty driver's seat.

Of course, no matter whether in a big city or a tiny town, brain-controlled cars are still a luxury. In order to buy her car, she not only poured all her savings into it, but also resorted to bank loans.

Tomorrow is Chinese New Year's Eve. Everyone will be out partying and meeting friends—good opportunity for some quick money.

The black car glides smoothly out of the garage. Sprawled out on her bed, Wu Huang shifts into a more comfortable position. The holographic interface projected by the helmet captures the car's surroundings as well. She sees that it has started to snow. Fluttering snowflakes, soft and pale like feathers, have already covered the ground in a thin silver veil.

The town had been snowless for as long as Wu Huang could remember. Assuming that this year will end up just as gloomy and bleak as every other year, the unexpected snowfall on the night before New Year's Eve is a pleasant surprise. However, the snow also means bad news for business—there are very few people out on the streets and even fewer ride requests. She only managed to pick up a pitiful two passengers in total after hours of roaming around. The snow on the ground, gradually growing thicker as the night progresses, crunches beneath the wheels as she drives listlessly through the town. Not wanting to give up just yet, she speeds toward the Levitation Train Station.

She waits. A few passengers finally exit from the arrival gate, but the cheaper, old-fashioned taxis are evidently the more attractive option to them. She cranes her neck and gazes at the night sky from the low angle lens installed on the car roof. Snow seems to be emerging endlessly from the dark abyss of the sky. Speck by speck, they drift through the night, painted into a shade of pale orange by the streetlight. The roof lens, soon buried under the snow, can no longer reflect anything but a white blur.

Seems like business isn't going anywhere tonight. Yet, as Wu Huang is about to head home, she hears a soft knock on her window.

Through the window lens, she sees a mother and her son.

The mother looks about sixty years old. Despite her small frame, she is carrying a huge backpack, her back hunching from the weight. The dim light of the streetlamp gives away the lines and creases on her weather-battered face. There's a weary look in her eyes. Her son standing right next to her, however, is very different. Eyeing his tall, lean figure wrapped in a chic trench coat, Wu Huang decides that he's fine-looking—just the perfect degree of elegance, not too over the top to be pretentious. *Obviously another product of the city's assembly line of elites.*

But the indifference on his face and his relaxed body posture, in stark contrast with how the old woman's back is bent from carrying the huge backpack, makes Wu Huang resent him instinctively.

"Cabbie, can you give us a ride?" The mother knocks on the car window again. Her heavy accent reminds Wu Huang of the mountain villages west of the town.

The mother's vulgar address feels like a prick. The little bit of respect she harbors toward the mother disappears almost immediately.

"I'm not a cabbie," she responds coldly, her voice echoing from the car speakers.

She glances at her phone again. *0 new requests.*

"Then, um . . . " hesitantly, the mother asks again, *"Miss?"*

"No. I'm done for the day."

The mother mutters a disappointed "oh," and turns to face her son. The son lowers his head to look at her, his face veiled in the shadow of the streetlamp, his expression indiscernible.

"Don't worry, mom," he says.

Wu Huang is now curious. "Where are you going?"

"To the West Bus Station."

The West Bus Station is the same direction as Wu Huang's home. If she drops them off on her way back, the money might be able to cover, at the very least, her electricity bills for all the driving tonight. As far as Wu Huang is concerned, however, the West Bus Station is so old and shabby that it might as well shut down for good. After the establishment of the Levitation Train Station, most of the town people have abandoned buses entirely.

"Are there still buses running if you go?" asks Wu Huang.

The mother's eyes light up at once. She nods eagerly. "Yes, there's one at ten-thirty."

Wu Huang remembers now. There is one manually-operated bus leaving from the station every day at night. Its route, weaving through the creases of the mountain and following the rugged national highway, makes several stops at the little villages along the way. This single running bus is the last struggling breath of the moribund station.

"Hop on then, I'll take you there," says Wu Huang.

The mother won't budge. "For how much?" she asks.

"A hundred . . . a hundred and fifty."

Immediately, the mother backs off from the car. "This is too much. It only costs ten yuan per person to take the shuttle. Twenty yuan for two!"

"Well, do you see any shuttles out here?"

In the falling snow, the shuttle stop seems utterly abandoned.

"But a hundred and fifty is way too expensive! How about sixty?"

The seemingly endless bargaining is beginning to annoy Wu Huang. Several times, the old woman's stinginess gives Wu Huang the urge to just leave her alone and drive away. Finally, they reach a satisfactory conclusion:

since Wu Huang is going home anyways, she will drop the passengers off at where she lives, and they will travel the last two kilometers on foot.

The mother and the son climb into the back seat. The mother keeps on breathing into her palms to warm her frozen fingers. When she lowers her head, Wu Huang can see that her crown is dotted with specks of white. Wu Huang can't tell if it is from gray hair or from the snow. Maybe both.

Wu Huang suddenly realizes that during their entire bargain just now, the mother and the son had been standing out there in the blizzard while she was physically sitting at home, wrapped in a warm blanket. They must've been freezing. Struck by a pang of guilt, she turns up the heat. "Is the temperature okay?"

"Mmhm," answers the mother. "Let's go. We want to get there early."

It's Wu Huang's turn this time to gape at her. The mother has been unusually calm since she hopped aboard, not showing even the least bit of surprise at the lack of a driver. Wu Huang starts the engine. "Where did you come back from?" She asks as she projects her face onto the car monitor—this is as close as it will get to a real life conversation.

"From Beijing." There's an edge of pride in the mother's voice.

Beijing? No wonder. "To visit family?" asks Wu Huang.

"To take my son home," the mother throws a quick glance at the man next to her. "For New Year."

The son, sitting with his back completely straight, nods in agreement.

Wu Huang carefully studies the young man through the high precision lens in her car as she drives. He appears just a little over thirty. His sunken cheeks make him look slightly worn out, but his face is clean-shaven, showing that he regularly takes care of his appearance. For most of the time he remains completely silent, his expression a mixture of politeness and apathy—again, typical of a white collar from Beijing.

"What do you do for a living?" asks Wu Huang.

The son only gives her a tight little smile in response.

The mother quickly interjects. "He's a designer who works from home for Domain Co.—have you heard of the name before?"

Of course Wu Huang has. Domain Co. is the developer of the mind operation system, the foundation of brain-controlled automobile technology.

Now she finds herself looking at the mother and her son differently. "That's really impressive!" she exclaims.

"Yeah! My son has always been the pride of our entire village." The mother's expression livens up almost immediately. "He's been away for seven years. At last, he can celebrate New Year at home this year!"

"Seven years? That's a lot," responds Wu Huang. "But since he's the one working in Beijing, aren't you supposed to visit him there instead? Why are you bringing him back?"

The mother pauses. A look of sorrow emerges on her face.

"My son . . . he's sick."

Song Xiuyun's heart ached upon hearing that her son has fallen ill. Tie Zhu, who brought this piece of news back to the village, was not very helpful either. He scratched his head and explained, "How am I supposed to know? I ran into Ah Chuan in the supermarket and we chatted for a bit. He seemed very ill—I mean, he couldn't even make it through a sentence without coughing. I don't know what happened to him, though. He doesn't usually get in touch with us. Maybe because he's been making such a fortune . . . oh, also, don't ever call me Tie Zhu again. I go by James in the city."

So Song Xiuyun had to call her son again. After a hasty "I'm fine," Li Chuan said he needed to go.

"Come back home for New Year, will you? You've been away for so many years . . . " Song Xiuyun quickly added before he could hang up.

"I don't think so," responded Li Chuan.

"I'll come visit you, then."

"Nonsense! You've never even left the village before, how on earth are you going to make it to the city?"

Song Xiuyun thought long and hard after the phone call. Finally, she made a decision. She came to Tie Zhu holding one of the express mail receipts that Li Chuan once sent home and pointed to the unfamiliar address. "Tie—I mean, *James*—would you please help me buy a ticket? I'll pay you back. I need to take my son home."

She walked the long, winding mountain road, squeezed herself into the back of a loaded motor tricycle to reach the national highway, pleaded until a passing truck agreed to take her to the provincial bus station and took the bus to get to the Levitation Train Station downtown. Finally, she boarded the train to Beijing. The only problem was that all the stewed meat and pickled vegetables she packed for her son were confiscated at the security check. All they let her bring was a small bag of salted sunflower seeds. Seeing how her carefully prepared gifts had all gone to waste, she erupted in anger and went into a heated argument with the security guards. Only did she stop when the guards threatened to throw her out. Wiping away tears, she gazed at the food mournfully as the guards swept them to the side like bags of trash.

She arrived in Beijing at last. Everything about the capital city was beyond her imagination. It was even different from what she had seen on TV. All the people here relied on brain-controlling technology: wearing the helmet, they could drive cars and do work while lying in their beds. She supposed that was why the streets were a lot less crowded than expected.

The day was dawning when she walked out of the Beijing Central Station. Exhausted after an entire night spent on the train, her body was trembling from the fatigue. She felt like a thin thread, hanging dangerously, that could snap in half any second. She found an open breakfast stall and ordered some rice congee. *Twenty yuan for one bowl? When we make breakfast back home, we always put out an entire pot and all the villagers helped themselves to congee for free*, she wondered with awe. *Well, guess this is Beijing.* She counted the bills in her pocket, then pulled out two ten yuan notes carefully and handed them over to the beefy shop owner. The shop owner threw her a contemptuous glance as he snatched the money from her hand.

Song Xiuyun was not a stranger to that look. *It's fine*, she thought. *I'm about to see my son—*

The thought of seeing Li Chuan soon sent warmth and strength spreading through her body. Rejuvenated at once, she finished the congee in one gulp and stood up. She hailed a cab. When she was about to bargain a price—in the same way that it was done back in her village—the driver interrupted and told her that she would need to pay exactly however much the meter indicated. Her eyes were stuck to the meter throughout the car ride; her heart pounded as the number steadily grew.

After what seemed like the longest journey, finally, Song Xiuyun and her two massive travel bags were dropped off at the gate of a fancy-looking residential compound. The guard, somehow very unwilling to believe that she had family who lived here, wouldn't even bother to check the residents' list for "Li Chuan" until a kind neighbor stepped in to help.

The guard called Li Chuan's apartment through the access control system. "Who is this?" After a long time, a voice answered lazily.

Song Xiuyun squeezed forth and pressed her lips to the speaker. "Li Chuan, it's mom. I'm here to visit you."

The person on the other end of the line went silent. The guard threw Song Xiuyun a suspicious glare. Thankfully, before the guard could speak again, Li Chuan's voice rang through the speaker, "Give me a minute. I'll come get you."

"A minute" turned out to be half an hour. When Li Chuan showed up at the guardhouse at last, tears rushed into Song Xiuyun's eyes. Quickly, she lowered her head to hide the tears, afraid that someone would make fun of Li Chuan for it.

But a hasty "let's go" was all Li Chuan said to her. He turned around and began to walk toward the apartment building.

Song Xiuyun hurried to catch up with his steps, dragging her luggage behind.

"It sounds like your son isn't exactly . . . the agreeable kind." says Wu Huang. Forgetting that she's wearing a brain-control helmet, she instinctively lowers her voice, as if to whisper into the mother's ears.

She regrets it at once. Thanks to technology, the surround speakers in the car project everything she says with clarity, so if the mother can hear her, the son can, too. She quickly throws the son a glance, wanting to see whether he's mad; yet he only sits there, with the same tight smile on his face, not seeming to mind a bit.

"No, he's a good boy!" hurriedly, the mother defends her son. "It's probably just because we haven't seen each other for too long."

"Didn't you say he was sick? He doesn't seem sick to me."

The mother nods. "Yeah. When I first moved into my son's apartment, I was so worried for him. But he looked healthy, and he was fit for sure— he could carry huge water buckets up the stairs without breaking a sweat! Except that . . . well, he spent most of the time alone in the study, and he rarely left the room. After spending a few days with him, I stopped worrying. It's all Tie Zhu's fault! He always exaggerates everything."

The car merges into the main lane. The blinding snow has turned the streetlamps into blurred orbs of light, lining the street like trees. Wu Huang speeds into the light forest. The turbulence caused by the car's sudden acceleration sends more snowflakes into the air, swirling as they descend.

Thanks to the empty roads, Wu Huang can still hold up the conversation without having to pay too much attention to traffic. "How was living in Beijing for you?"

"It was hard to adjust," says the mother as she shifts into a more comfortable position in the back seat. The heater in the car seems to have warmed her up. "You city folks are so different. For example, take this thing—this *brain-controlled car*—everyone in the city owns one of these. And robots, too! Brain-controlled robots that can act just like humans. They can do everything for you. Socializing, talking . . . even playing sports!"

Wu Huang nods. Domain Co.'s latest product, the brain-controlled robot, is a must-buy for couch potatoes. There was a time when she went to a party of five where three of the attendees had robots come in their stead. The two humans and three robots had a wonderful meal-and-conversation together. Of course, the robots did not need to eat. After the party, they packed some food to go for their respective owners. Wu Huang also heard that you could put the robot on auto-follow mode: wherever the owner goes, the robot tails behind. Quite fascinated by the technology, Wu Huang has planned on buying one herself after she pays off her car debt.

The mother vents on. "The cooking machine makes your dinner; the cleaning robot cleans your home. Why, apart from eating and emptying your intestines, *this thing*—" she points an index finger at her own head, "—can do everything for you. What's the use of having arms and legs, then?"

"It's just more convenient this way," Wu Huang sheepishly explains.

"Convenient, yes, but it's still a bit . . . " The mother tries to find a word, but then she gives up. "I can't describe. It looks as if everything is better, but it still makes me feel weird."

She's probably trying to say that a life too "convenient" can make people lazy, thinks Wu Huang. True, many people have brought up this point before, but this is how things work in the modern era—people need to adjust to the advancements in technology, not the other way around.

"It's probably hard for you to adjust, isn't it?" asks Wu Huang.

The mother nods. "I asked my son to come home with me, but he wouldn't agree. So I stayed with him for a few days. It was extremely boring, though—I was rather scared going into the city alone and I didn't know anyone else in Beijing, so all I could do was stay at home." She pauses for a second. "Oh, right, my son also owned a cat, Bean. But whenever I tried to play with Bean, like I do with all the countryside cats, it ignored me. It lay lazily on the balcony all day and did nothing. I guess even *cats* are different in the city. Living in Beijing is no better than living in prison!"

"Doesn't your son spend time with you?"

"Well, he was busy. He spent every day locked up in the study. I wanted to take care of him, so I cooked all his favorite childhood dishes: stir-fried spicy chicken, fish stew with radish . . . robots couldn't possibly do that for him! I bet he missed my cooking—he always finished everything I made. He only ate in the study, though . . . "

The son sits in silence as the two women converse, his face expressionless, as if he is entirely unaware that he is the protagonist of their story.

There is a tinge of melancholy in the mother's voice. "Apart from cooking, there wasn't much that I could do for him. I couldn't even understand what his work entailed—let alone help him! When he worked, I would go on walks in the living compound. Our apartment was on the first floor. My son also rented a spare basement room in the corner of the parking garage."

The car comes to a pause at the red light. "For extra storage space?" asks Wu Huang halfheartedly.

"I didn't know," the mother responds. "He wouldn't let me in."

Song Xiuyun stopped before the door to the basement. The parking lot's light shone on her face diagonally, illuminating every wrinkle and spot on the left side of her face, yet leaving the right side of her face in the dark shadow. The sharp contrast accentuated the doubt and uneasiness in her expression as she mulled over whether she should enter.

She has been here for almost ten days. Familiar with almost all the rooms of Li Chuan's apartment, she has yet to explore the basement. Whenever she asked Li Chuan about it, he would tell her that he stored all his discarded works there—*it's my privacy*, in his words, and she was not allowed to enter that room.

Privacy . . . Song Xiuyun couldn't quite grasp what that word meant. Back in the village, every family built their house along the feet of the mountain. All the houses, clumped together, were as close to each other as one could imagine. No one locked their door; when someone wanted to pay their neighbor a visit, they didn't even need to knock. *But now I'm in Beijing,* she reminded herself once again. The city folks were a different kind. They built skyscrapers that blocked the sun and hid in cocoons of iron and glass. When you could do everything by wearing a helmet and commanding robots, why bother even speaking to other people? Her son, now, has also become one of them; he was an art person—oh, *artist*. Even though she didn't understand, she would stay away from the basement room as long as it made her son happy.

Instead of reaching for the doorknob, Song Xiuyun knocked on the door quickly. The sound of the knock gently echoed through the corridor. She waited. No one came to answer.

When she returned to the apartment, Bean was just waking up from a nap. Basked in the last glow of the setting sun, the black cat arched its back and then reached forward to stretch out its muscles. It turned its head and shot her a look, leaped off the windowsill and lazily strolled into the bedroom.

Look at it! thought Song Xiuyun in astonishment, *not only do these city cats not catch mice—like what cats are supposed to do—but they don't even want to come near humans.* She understood that Bean didn't trust her because she was a stranger, but she was surprised to find out that Bean didn't like Li Chuan either, after living together for six years. Once, after Li Chuan refilled the cat food, he reached out to pat Bean's head, but it evaded his hand. Only after Li Chuan stepped away did it approach the food bowl cautiously to eat.

"All this city nonsense!" she muttered to herself.

As usual, Li Chuan was in his study again. He didn't even bother turning on the living room lights. Song Xiuyun emptied the bag of sunflower seeds onto a plate and brought it to the study. The instant she pushed the door open, she remembered *privacy* all of a sudden, and quickly turned the push into a light knock.

Li Chuan closed his book. "What's the point of knocking if you've entered already?"

"Sorry, I forgot . . . it won't happen next time," explained Song Xiuyun, embarrassed. She set the plate next to Li Chuan's books and looked at her son eagerly, "Here, have some sunflower seeds while you work. I salted them myself. You used to love it when you were a child."

Li Chuan threw a glance at the plate, and then looked up at Song Xiuyun. "Also, didn't I tell you to never go near the basement? I beg you to *respect my privacy!*"

"How did you—" Song Xiuyun's eyes widened. Hasn't Li Chuan been up here this entire time? But she stopped herself before she could blurt out the question. "—I'm sorry. I won't go there again, I promise."

Upon seeing shock and nervousness on her face, Li Chuan sighed, and his voice was gentle again. "What's the matter?"

"Well, Chinese New Year is coming soon, and you haven't prepared anything yet. Your fridge and kitchen cabinets are all empty. I checked the weather for tomorrow and it's supposed to be sunny. Do you want to go grocery shopping with me?"

Li Chuan frowned. "Aren't you leaving soon? You're not even here for New Year, what's the point in buying groceries?"

"You still need to eat, though. Or, maybe . . . " Song Xiuyun paused. Her gaze was fixed on the man in front of her—*her son*. She could hear her own voice, trembling as she pleaded with him, "Come home with me for New Year. It's been seven years since you last came home. Remember your nephew? He's all grown up now! And—"

Li Chuan cut her short. "I'm never going back there again! I already told you this when I left home. Just forget about it, will you?"

Song Xiuyun did not respond. After a few seconds of silence, she switched on the lamp. Warm brightness lit up the room at once. "Good for your eyes." she explained, then turned around to leave.

Li Chuan picked up his book, but hesitated as he was about to flip the page. "Wait," he muttered. "I guess tomorrow we should go shopping after all."

Song Xiuyun nodded, almost ecstatically. The sun was already down. Carefully closing the study's door behind her, she realized that she had shut out the only source of light in the apartment. The attempt to find the light switch on the living room wall was unsuccessful—her eyesight has been deteriorating since many years ago, making seeing in the dark even more difficult. She whispered, "Open the light."

The system did not respond.

"*Turn on* the light, *please.*"

The gentle glow of the overhead lamp filled the entire living room at once. What appeared to be an ordinary wall facing the entryway was, in fact, an enormous monitor screen. The cartoon figure of a small robot emerged on the screen. Li Chuan had explained the concept of the smart home to Song Xiuyun, but she could never get used to how these things would pop up out of nowhere.

"How do you feel trapped in that wall? It certainly looks uncomfortable." said Song Xiuyun to the robot.

The robot lowered its head, as if contemplating her question, and then looked up and grinned at her. "My home is this monitor wall, just like how your home is this apartment."

"This isn't my home. My home is somewhere far away. Have you ever heard of a village called Hongan?"

A map appeared on the screen, marked by over twenty red dots. "Here are all the Hongan villages in the world. Which one is your home?"

Almost pressing her face onto the screen, Song Xiuyun examined the dots one by one, "I can't tell. My home is west of Beijing. There's a river that passes through, we call it the Guanyin Temple River, because there's a temple in our village dedicated to the Guanyin Bodhisattva. Other villages alongside the river, though, have named it something else . . . "

As she murmured to herself, the red dots gradually disappeared one by one, leaving none but one. The map zoomed in, displaying a detailed satellite map of a small mountain village. Bungalows after bungalows with weather-battered walls spread out along the mountain range; wheat fields, high and low, surrounded the buildings. Only parched stalks were left in the fields, as the wheat had been harvested already back in the fall.

"Look, this is my home," Song Xiuyun pointed to one of the small bungalows with its back against the mountain.

"Beautiful place," the robot nodded in agreement.

Song Xiuyun could not tear her gaze away from the map. "It's almost time to plant the cole crops . . . " she exclaimed, after a long silence. Then, she sighed softly and headed down the hallway toward her bedroom. The robot trailed behind her. As she walked into the room, it stopped at the edge of the wall. The screen and the living room lights dimmed.

The next morning, Song Xiuyun and her son headed to the mall together. However, as they arrived at the subway station's security check, Li Chuan suddenly halted. "The subway is too crowded. Let's take a taxi instead."

"But we're here already," said Song Xiuyun. "You work so hard all the time. Why waste the money on a taxi? Besides, many people must've left the city for vacation already. "

Yet Li Chuan had already begun walking in the direction of the exit. Song Xiuyun, confused, could only trot along behind him.

It was lunchtime already after they've done the shopping. "We probably won't be able to eat until hours later if we go home now and cook. How about we eat out?" suggested Song Xiuyun, carefully. "You've been eating my cooking for a while anyways, I figured that it wouldn't hurt to try something else once in a while."

Li Chuan shook his head. "We should go back."

"Saving money is important, but there are times when you need to spend, too! I have cash. It's my treat today."

Li Chuan was quiet for a while.

"But I really want to have the stir-fried spicy chicken that you always make for lunch." he said.

"Well, I obviously can't compare to restaurant chefs . . . " Song Xiuyun was stunned by Li Chuan's compliment, but nonetheless she cheered up immediately. "Let's go home, then!"

At the mall's exit, they bumped into a couple holding hands. As Li Chuan's gaze fell on one of the two men, his body suddenly went rigid. Grabbing Song Xiuyun's hand, he pulled her toward another door, avoiding the man's sight.

The man, however, had spotted him already. "Ah Chuan?" he blurted out.

With nowhere else to run or hide, Li Chuan turned around awkwardly to face him. "What a coincidence," Li Chuan squeezed out a smile. "Seeing you two here."

With an almost embarrassed look on his face, the man let go of his boyfriend's hand. "I heard that you were . . . "

"I'm doing fine!" Li Chuan cut him short.

The man looked at Song Xiuyun. "Ayi[1]? It's been so long since I last saw you. Did you move to Beijing?"

Song Xiuyun searched in her memory. She gradually recalled a boyish face, from years ago, that looked identical to the chic-looking man in front of her. "Oh, it's you!" she exclaimed. "I'm only here to visit Li Chuan. And you . . ."

The man has a look of melancholy on his face. Before he could respond, though, Li Chuan spoke up first. "We need to go now," said Li Chuan, without looking at the man. "It was . . . nice running into you."

He grasped Song Xiuyun's arm and walked away. Song Xiuyun could hear the man shouting Li Chuan's name, but he did not pause nor look back.

Li Chuan had been sitting in his armchair, unmoving, after they got home. Not even bothering to turn on the lights, he brooded silently in the shadow of the large bookshelf.

"Ah Chuan," Song Xiuyun started. "Mom is here for you if you want to—"

Her voice trailed off as she realized that there were so many things about her son that she did not understand.

Perhaps she never will.

She turned her head to look out the window. Behind the glass was an entirely foreign world: skyscrapers like trees in a forest, the earth cut to tiny, irregularly shaped pieces by crisscrossing roads that were packed with cars, even the air was occupied by a maze of maglev train tracks. She tilted her head until her gaze could finally soar past the skyscrapers and reach the sky, yet the sky was gray, too, like the iron and concrete that had plagued every inch of this city.

"Son, maybe we should go back—"

Once again, she couldn't finish her sentence, because Li Chuan, unexpectedly, collapsed into her arms.

For a second he seemed just like the boy from almost a decade ago. The only difference was, this time he was unconscious.

The mother's story comes to a pause. Silence fills the car. The heavy snow, painted into a faint orange by the glow of the car's headlight, is blown onto the windshield by the howling wind.

"You mentioned that you've met him before," says Wu Huang. "The man in the shopping mall, I mean."

---

1   An endearing way to address an elder woman in colloquial Chinese.

"Yes. Seven years ago, when my son came home for New Year, he brought him back as well."

Wu Huang nods. The mother's answer is almost exactly what she had guessed.

"We all thought that he was just my son's friend from Beijing, you know, those city people always want to come and see how New Year is celebrated in the countryside," explains the mother. "I was thrilled that he brought a friend home. I did all I could to serve our guest—you should've seen the food! The living conditions in the countryside did not suit our guest well, but in general everyone was still happy, until . . . "

Wiping the corners of her eyes with the back of her hand, the mother continues. "My son told me everything the day before New Year. Having lived in the isolated, conservative village my whole life, I did not know that . . . there were other possibilities. I argued with my son and demanded that he ask his . . . his 'friend' to leave. But my son refused. They left together overnight. I was alone for New Year that year, as well as all the seven years to follow."

The mother pauses to look at the son. The son, still smiling, pats her hand. "Don't worry, Mom. Don't worry." he says.

Wu Huang doesn't know how to comfort her. "It's all in the past. See, your son is finally home for this New Year!" she says carefully.

"Yeah, it's all in the past . . . "

"Right, what happened after he fainted?" Wu Huang remembers the mother's story. "Was he sent to the hospital?"

"No."

The unconscious man felt as heavy as a rock in Song Xiuyun's arms. She tried to splash his face with cold water, but he wouldn't open his eyes. Helpless, she remembered the robot who lived in the wall. Li Chuan had said that it took care of everything.

"Turn on the lights, please!" she yelled.

The study brightened up at once. The robot appeared on the wall. "Can I help you?"

"My son fainted. Call the hospital now."

"There's no need to worry. If anything happens to Master, the system will contact Doctor Freeman immediately," said the Robot. "Doctor Freeman is on his way here. He is Master's primary care doctor and good friend."

"Then what am I supposed to do?"

"Just wait."

"You mean that I should stand here and do nothing while my son is lying on the ground?"

"If you're bored, I can put something on TV." The robot grinned.

"Are you nuts?"

"I was simply trying to be humorous, like you humans."

Doctor Freeman was a middle-aged American man, short and stocky, with a receding hairline. He wore a jean jacket on top of a pair of sweatpants. It turned out that he had the highest level of security clearance to Li Chuan's home—meaning that he could enter the apartment on his own whenever he came around.

"Ms. Song? Li Chuan has talked about you quite a lot." He nodded at Song Xiuyun and greeted her in broken Chinese. "Don't worry. Your son will be fine."

To Song Xiuyun's bewilderment, Doctor Freeman left right away without double-checking. He even had the audacity to grab a handful of sunflower seeds on his way out. Thankfully, the doctor, however irresponsible he may seem, was not wrong—a few minutes later, Li Chuan opened his eyes.

"What's the matter? Are you okay? Do you want to go to the hospital?"

"I'm fine," Li Chuan stood up and pressed his thumb hard into his temple. "I guess I was just too tired from work."

The same thing never happened again, but Song Xiuyun noticed that Li Chuan had been spending more and more time in his study. Whenever she knocked on the shut door, though, he would always shout through the door, "Mom, I'm fine."

Gradually, Song Xiuyun stopped worrying. *Perhaps he had fainted that day because of the couple they ran into at the mall*, she thought. *Young people, they are so dramatic!*

"But . . . son," she hesitantly spoke up one day as she stood at the door of the study. "You're going to turn thirty-three when New Year rolls around. Isn't it time for you to consider making a family?"

Li Chuan lapsed into silence. After a while, he responded by throwing a question back at her. "Why do people have to make families?"

"Well, everyone needs a family." Song Xiuyun was taken aback. "You know, you marry and have children . . . "

"And then end up like you?"

Song Xiuyun's hand stiffened. She knew what her son was referring to— her husband had left home almost twenty years ago. Apart from some money that he sent back each year, there was almost nothing to remind her that he even existed. Her marriage was not built from love. For all these years, it left nothing but a bitter taste in her mouth.

"I'm sorry," Li Chuan muttered.

Song Xiuyun pondered over her words, and spoke again. "I know, I've never been to school, and I'm nowhere near a perfect role model. But I still think that people shouldn't end up alone. Especially when you spend all your time at home. When you are older—when you are my age, you will be . . . lonely."

"True, that was the case decades ago, before there was Internet. It's different now. You can make friends online, live with robots and still have fun when you're old. A lot of married couples don't want kids; many more people are living alone. We have the freedom to do whatever we want! Mom, I'm not asking you to understand, but please don't impose your values on me!"

"Perhaps you're right," said Song Xiuyun gently. "But I only hoped that there would be someone around to support you, to take care of you when you are sick and give you a hug when you are feeling down."

The study fell silent again.

"Mom, I still have you." Li Chuan's voice was muffled when he finally spoke. "You can give me a hug."

Wu Huang sits up from her bed and glimpses at the shut door of her bedroom through the cracks on the brain-control helmet. Maybe her mother is knitting sweaters again. She has told her mother that she would never wear one of those old-fashioned, dorky sweaters, but her mother, despite agreeing to never knit for her again several times, has always attempted to pick up the tradition every year when winter comes around.

She looks at her closet. For some reason, for the first time in her life, she is starting to find those hideous sweaters rather cute.

Distracted by the sweaters, however, she does not see another car coming around the corner. Almost scrambling to avoid the collision, she makes a sharp turn, throwing the passengers into the side door. The mother grasps onto the front seat tightly with one hand and attempts to protect her son with the other.

"Don't worry, Mom," whispers the son.

"I'm so sorry . . . " stutters Wu Huang.

"It's fine."

Wu Huang's neighborhood is right ahead, but instead of pulling over, she speeds down the road toward the West Bus Station.

The relationship between mother and son has finally changed for the better after that day. Relieved upon seeing that Li Chuan was in good health, Song Xiuyun decided to go home at last after New Year.

Despite the boredom, she was cautious not to interfere with her son's work. She has taken on the habit of going on strolls alone near the residential compound. An amateur dance group—mostly comprised of women her own age, occasionally a robot or two would join—gathered at the gate every evening and danced together to upbeat music. However, too shy to strike up a conversation, she usually lingered by the side and watched the dancers twirl and twist, until dinnertime arrived.

The evening was windy, leading the dance group to disperse earlier than usual. When Song Xiuyun hurried through the hallway and pushed open the apartment door, however, she was stunned to find Li Chuan sitting on the sofa with Bean in his arms. It was even more unusual that Bean did not only purr, but was also rubbing its head on Li Chuan's chin. And this was the cat that seemed to despise everyone in the family!

Just when she was about to make a comment on Bean, she saw Li Chuan's face.

The man in front of her looked different as well. Wan and weary, with sunken cheeks and pale lips, he reminded her of what Tie Zhu had said to her back at home: *your son seemed very ill.* But she remembered checking up on him before she left for dance, and he appeared just fine.

"You're back early," exclaimed Li Chuan, as he struggled to stand up. Gently dropping Bean onto the floor, he headed down the hallway.

Song Xiuyun caught up with him, as he was yanking open the closed door of the study. "Are you alright? Do you want me to call that Doctor . . . Doctor *F*.?"

"I'm fine," said Li Chuan, after a short pause. "I think I just have a stomach flu. I'll sleep it off." He hurried into the study.

In that brief second, Song Xiuyun thought that she had seen something unusual: the silhouette of a person, standing in the corner of the study. But the door was shut in her face just when she was about to take a closer look.

Wu Huang carefully examines the man's face through the lens overlooking the back seat. As if he has sensed her gaze, he lifts his head, looks into the camera, and smiles back at her.

Something doesn't feel right, thinks Wu Huang.

"Well—" She clears her throat awkwardly and turns her eyes away. "Didn't you plan to come home after New Year? What brought you back so early?"

"I figured that it's better to spend New Year at home."

"Then when is your son returning to Beijing? Given how busy work is, I suppose that he doesn't get to stay home for long."

The mother chuckles. "Actually, my son agreed to move back home. He already sold his apartment in Beijing, and he's not returning there ever again. Besides, Internet is going to be available at our village soon. He can just work from home, and it will all be the same!"

Wu Huang glances at the son. Her heart suddenly sinks.

A week from New Year, as Song Xiuyun busily cleaned the house and prepared for the festival, Li Chuan came up to her. "Mom, I'm going on a business trip. I'll be back in a few days. Just wait for me at home."

"Don't you always work from home?" asked Song Xiuyun, surprised. "New Year is right around the corner, why are you going on a business trip now?"

"It's the company's order. Our international clients don't celebrate Chinese New Year anyways."

"Too bad for them . . . " muttered Song Xiuyun. "Well, I guess work is more important." She slumped into a chair.

Li Chuan stood next to her, his lips pressed tightly together, as if he was trying to find something to say.

"When are you coming back, then? Can you make it home on New Year's Eve?"

"Probably," said Li Chuan. He glanced around the room, as if he was reluctant to go.

"It's only going to be few days, right?" Song Xiuyun tried to comfort him, "Don't worry, I'll look after the home for you. When you come back, we can celebrate together."

Li Chuan's gaze landed on Song Xiuyun's face. For an instant, she saw sadness in his eyes. Just when she was about to speak, Li Chuan took a step forward and wrapped his arms around her shoulders.

Song Xiuyun stiffened, part out of shock and part out of the delight that her son was, perhaps, finally willing to open up to her. "What's the matter, Ah Chuan?" she asked, a little awkwardly.

Li Chuan did not respond. After another minute, he let go of her and turned to grab his suitcase. "I'm going to head out. See you soon."

"I'll walk you down."

"No, it's fine. Just wait for me at home. I'll be back before New Year's Eve."

Bean, perched on the windowsill, stretched its neck to look at Li Chuan as he closed the door behind him. The room fell silent. An unsettledness gloomed Song Xiuyun's heart. She walked over to the window and gazed out, but all she could see were tall buildings. Her son, as tiny as an ant compared to those giants of concrete and iron, has disappeared into the world outside.

The next day, in a desperate attempt to find something to do—so that she could forget about that unsettledness—Song Xiuyun went down to the basement with a broom. She knew that Li Chuan didn't want her to go into the room, but at least she could clean the hallway.

Almost immediately, she spotted litter: sunflower seed peels, scattered on the floor near the door.

Li Chuan never ate the plate of sunflower seeds that she brought to his study. The only person who seemed to like them was Doctor Freeman, who grabbed a handful on his way out when he came over the other day.

Does that mean Doctor Freeman had come to the basement after he left the apartment? But *why*? Song Xiuyun wondered as she took the trash down to the trash room.

A custodian was in the trash room, skimming through bags of trash and looking for misplaced recyclable items. Song Xiuyun recognized the trash bag in the custodian's hands: it was from her household.

"Thank you for working so hard over the holiday," she greeted the custodian.

"No, it's not hard work, I just don't like seeing things go to waste." The custodian smiled at her. "Nowadays people throw away everything. Especially this family!" She showed Song Xiuyun the trash bag that she had just opened up, "I can tell it's from the same household because they are the only ones who use this kind of trash bag. They throw away unfinished food every day. See? This is from yesterday. Why bother cooking something that they can't finish?"

Song Xiuyun's heart sank. She peered into the trash bag, half-hoping that she would see something different, but no—stir-fried spicy chicken, fish stew with radish . . . those were exactly the dishes that she cooked for Li Chuan before he left. He told her to bring them into his study, as usual, and promised that he would eat on his own. Judging from the amount of food in the trash bag, it seemed that Li Chuan did not even take a single bite.

The rotten odor permeated the air. It made her head dizzy. "You mean, all this is thrown into trash every day?" she murmured.

"I mean every *meal*," said the custodian as she fumbled through the trash can. "Breakfast, lunch, and dinner, all wasted! You see? Back in the time when I was a kid, wasting food like this could put you in jail . . . "

The custodian's voice seemed to fade away. Song Xiuyun could not hear her anymore. She turned on her heels and headed toward the stairs, trembling as she took each step. She went straight to the phone and dialed Li Chuan's number. Nobody answered.

She heard a soft meow. It was Bean, the cat, curled up on the sofa. Bean threw her a glance, looking as nonchalant and distant as always. She remembered the day when she stumbled upon Li Chuan and Bean: it was the only time that she has ever seen the cat let its defense down; Li Chuan, on the other hand, was somehow much more sickly and pale than usual.

A sense of foreboding rushed into her heart, sending chills down her spine.

She called Li Chuan a few more times, but he never picked up. Finally, she grabbed a hammer from the toolbox and headed down to the basement again. Standing before the locked door to the room that Li Chuan has forbidden her to enter, she paused, and then swung the hammer at the lock with full force. A loud creak, followed by a *bang*, and the lock broke open and dropped to the ground.

She cracked open the door and squeezed in. The room was dark. From the dim light that shone in through the door crack, she could roughly make out the contours of massive machines next to the walls and the entangled wires that covered the ground. There was a helmet on an empty desk.

"Ah!" She almost jumped out of her skin when she saw the silhouette of a person in the corner of the room. Stumbling through the wires and almost throwing herself onto the opposite wall, she reached for the light switch. Light ripped through the darkness. When she saw the person's face, her heart missed a beat.

It was her son. Limply, he laid there, his eyes closed. When she put her hand next to his nose, she realized that his face was cold, and he wasn't breathing.

At once, Wu Huang realizes where the mother's story is going. She falls silent.

The car has left downtown already. In the glow of the headlights, she can make out the silhouette of the West Bus Station. It perches quietly in the darkness like a dying beast, its ragged breath blowing snowflakes onto the windshield.

Almost there, thinks Wu Huang. This night has been long. She should head home immediately after dropping them off.

"And then?" she finally asks.

"Ah-ha! You found out at last. I can only admire your intelligence!"

Doctor Freeman appeared at the door. Apparently, the apartment's security system had sent him an alert as soon as she broke into the basement.

"Tell me right now what happened to my son!" she demanded.

Doctor Freeman's face fell solemn. "Mr. Li Chuan is severely ill. He has collapsed under the stress of work." He took a long drag on his cigarette, "Although, the person here is not him—" he turned the body over and tugged on the back of the shirt collar, revealing a two-prong electric socket and a barcode.

"What is this?"

"A brain-controlled robot."

Song Xiuyun's eyes widened. She examined the robot carefully. The side of its face, the back of its neck—everything was identical to her son. However, when she tried to turn it over again to observe its face, she realized that its body was much heavier than a human would weigh. Relief washed through her. Doctor Freeman wasn't lying. This was indeed a robot.

"This robot, a beta version of Domain Co.'s latest technology, was specially customized for Mr. Li Chuan. It is the model with the closest resemblance to real humans so far. See, it can regulate body temperature and its pupils can constrict and dilate just like human eyes! Domain Co. is still resolving some ethical and legal issues regarding its mass production, so it has not hit the market yet," explained Doctor Freeman. "Li Chuan knew that you were coming to visit, and he didn't want you to worry about him. He stayed in the basement and interacted with you via the brain-controlled robot instead. Afraid that you might become suspicious, he hid in his study most of the time. The other day, however, when you two ran into his ex-boyfriend at the shopping mall, the anxiety was too much for his recovering body to handle, causing him to pass out in the basement, and his robot consequently shutting off."

Stupefied, Song Xiuyun could only give a little nod.

Now she understood everything. Li Chuan threw away the food because robots don't need to eat; he was reluctant to ride the subway because the full-body scanner at the security check would have revealed his secret.

"I know he's not the most expressive person in the world, but you must understand that he cares a lot about you."

"Where is he now? I need to see him!"

"At the hospital. He's going through a dangerous operation. If all goes well, he will come back home in no time, and he'll never need to use this brain-controlled robot again. Bless!"

"What would happen to my son—*I mean, this robot*—then?"

"Recycled."

"And what exactly does that mean?"

"Sent back to the company. The technicians will take out the memory chip and sort out the data."

Song Xiuyun sighed. "Then please, be gentle to him."

She clenched her fists as Doctor Freeman led her out of the apartment. For all this time, she had been spending time with a simulacrum, while her son hid in the dark, cramped basement. Even when he wanted to give her a hug, he could only do it through the arms of this lifeless thing. Her son had seen her through the security camera the day when she went down to the basement. Back then, if only she had taken another step and opened that door, she would have found her son and realized what was wrong with him. And the day when she had come back home early from dance and found Li Chuan—sickly and pale—in the living room. He must've come home because he thought that she would be out longer. That was why Bean would warm up to him—it had also realized that its owner was back, instead of a robot that it couldn't scent.

Tears welled up in her eyes. Embarrassed, she turned her head away so that Doctor Freeman wouldn't see.

She had to wait outside of the intensive care unit once they arrived at the hospital. "He will be okay, won't he?" she tugged at the surgeon's sleeve and whispered, her voice choking.

"Honestly, I'm not sure. Mr. Li's case is a rare one . . . " The surgeon hesitated. He threw a glance at Doctor Freeman, and then comforted her, "Don't worry. You should go home. We will try our best here. We're optimistic that the surgery will go well!"

Song Xiuyun wouldn't leave. She sat on the bench in the hallway and stared intently at the door of surgery room, afraid that she would lose her son forever if she even blinked. It grew colder. She shivered and wrapped her arms around her body. A nurse handed her a blanket. Huddled in the blanket, she waited. The clock hit midnight. The surgery went on. Occasionally, a nurse would exit the room to fetch more tools, their face drenched in sweat. She wanted to ask the nurses how her son was doing, but she cut herself short before she could make a sound. She didn't want to bother them.

At some point, she fell asleep and had a very long dream. In her dream she was no longer an old woman at the age of sixty, but younger, bright and energetic. Her son was a little boy who wandered around barefooted and played in the fields while she worked. *Mama, mama,* she heard the boy's crisp, cheery voice calling out. She looked up and saw him running toward her. Behind him, magnificent mountains that expanded across the horizon gazed down at them solemnly. She knew that massive cities and vast seas lie behind those mountains. One day, her son would leave her, cross the mountains and the seas, and become the brave explorer he was meant to be. She was overwhelmed by pride and disappointment all at once. She dropped to her knees and hugged her son tightly. It felt like she was holding the entire world in her arms.

"Ms. Song? Ms. Song!" Someone gently tapped her shoulder.

Song Xiuyun slowly opened her eyes. Through a blurred vision, she saw Doctor Freeman standing before her alongside surgeons and nurses. With a start she woke up and blurted out, "Is the surgery over? How is he doing?"

Doctor Freeman grasped her hands and beamed at her. "Congratulations! The surgery went well."

"You mean my son is going to be okay?" She couldn't believe her ears. She turned her eyes to the surgeons and nurses for confirmation, but they all looked away, carefully avoiding her gaze.

"Yes! He's completely recovered. The first thing he told us when he woke up was that he decided to quit his job, leave Beijing, and go home with you!" Doctor Freeman babbled on, his words barely comprehensible in her ears. "Don't worry! The money he's made in the past few years is more than enough. He's also going to sell the apartment. I'll come visit you both in your hometown every year! Also, I can adopt Bean . . . the cat is so *adorable* . . ."

Song Xiuyun, stunned, could not even begin to process all that Doctor Freeman had said. Just when she was about to speak, the surgery room door swung open and Li Chuan walked out.

She rushed over to greet her son. When she placed her hand on Li Chuan's shoulder, she felt the warmth of a healthy human body. Letting out a sigh of relief, she burst into tears.

Carefully, Li Chuan brushed away the tears from his mother's face. He smiled, his voice slow and soft. "Don't worry, Mom. Don't worry."

"Okay, I won't worry," Song Xiuyun took her son's hand. "New Year is coming. Let's go home."

"So that's why we came back." The mother finishes her story with a sigh. "New Year's Eve is tomorrow. If we go home now, we can still make it."

"Yeah," Wu Huang, however, is a little perturbed. "Always better to spend New Year's Eve at home."

With the mother finally done with her story, the car is again filled with an awkward silence. Fortunately, their final destination is right around the corner. Wu Huang pulls up to the gate of the West Bus Station. "It's only past ten. You can buy tickets at the counter."

The mother nods, thanks her, and climbs out of the car with her son. Snowflakes blown into the car melt into little droplets of water as soon as they land on the back seat. From Wu Huang's point of view, it looks as if the snowflakes are melting on her eye lens. *It's only a projection*, thinks Wu Huang, yet when she reaches for her eye corner out of instinct, she feels real wetness on her fingertips.

She turns her gaze to the mother and the son. They are almost at the gate, and she could only make out their distant silhouettes accompanied by four lines of footprints in the snow. The mother's shoulders are hunched from the weight of the travel bags on her back. Her son, keeping his head down, follows her.

A thought flashes across Wu Huang's mind. She focuses the lens on the son's back neck and zooms in. Beneath the collar, she sees a pair of blurry, dark shadows. However, when she is about to zoom in again, she halts.

Perhaps it's better not to know.

The mother and the son have already entered the bus station. More snow soon covers the lines of footprints, wiping away the last trace they left behind. To Wu Huang, it feels rather like a dream; otherworldly, almost. As if nothing has happened.

Wu Huang puts the car on autopilot and sets the destination "home." She removes her helmet and takes a deep breath.

She opens the door and sees her mother on the sofa. Her mother, wearing a pair of glasses and fumbling through loose balls of yarn spread out everywhere, has been knitting sweaters again.

"Mom?"

Mother looks up at her, her hands still entangled in the yarn. "What's the matter?"

"I'm hungry," says Wu Huang.

Vandana Singh was born and raised in India and currently inhabits the Boston area, where she is a physics professor at a small and lively state university. Several of her science fiction short stories have been reprinted in Year's Best volumes, and shortlisted for awards. Her second short story collection, *Ambiguity Machines and Other Stories*, was published in 2018 from Small Beer Press in the US and Zubaan in India, and was a finalist for the Philip K. Dick Award.

MOTHER OCEAN

Vandana Singh

In the ocean, Paro sometimes forgets she's human. It's partly because water is her element, and water, as we all know, obscures, blurs and dilutes all boundaries. She doesn't remember the name her grandmother gave her when she was born—it is lost among the fragments of memory that remain of those early, difficult years. Her mother, trying to hide her in the mass of people of India's landlocked interiors, named her Parvati, which became Paro. Her mother took her as far from the ocean as she could, to the dusty, blinding heat of Delhi's shanty towns, hoping that the child would forget, that the hell that had been visited on the family would spare the child. *Hide, you are not safe, you must hide. Never talk about history. The only reality is the present, the only safety is on land, where there is hard ground beneath your feet.* Her mother's cold, angry, averted face is what she dreams about sometimes when she's asleep on the boat, or back in her narrow little bunk on the ship.

But Paro has another name. Growing up, she felt as though there were two people inside her: one, an anxious child trying her best to placate her mother's fears, the good little girl who tries so hard in school. The other, a creature whose name has been lost with her history, a creature drawn, like her grandmother, to the water, to the ocean.

She doesn't know her other name.

Which is one of many reasons she is here, inside this flying underwater boat in the Indian Ocean, following a blue whale. The ship sails along at the same leisurely pace as the whale—a ship of strange design, once an eccentric millionaire's luxury yacht, now converted to a ship of exploration, running on solar and wind power for the most part, the flexible, maneuverable sails a bright gold in the dawn light. Here in the middle of the ocean, there is no evidence that land exists, that there are humans on this planet—here is where you understand that this planet really is mostly ocean, a blue dot sailing through space like a woman carrying a water pot, a woman swimming, a woman who is also mostly salt water.

The boat surfaces, the top unsealing and opening up, the solar panels spreading out like wings, oriented to track the morning light. She sends a quick message to the ship, which is not far; she can see it balanced like an exotic insect on the water. The ocean seems infinite in the dawn light, the horizon clearly delineated only in the east, against a pink sky. On the western horizon sea and sky are one, the line between them smudged into a mysterious darkness. The whale is close to the surface, coming up for breath, each exhalation a great fountain over the heaving seas. Paro stretches lazily on the narrow boat deck, sipping tea from a cup with a spout, thinking about the dream that came to her in the night.

In the dream there was a palm-fringed island, and on the white beach, where green, glassy waves washed without breaking, there stood a slender woman, chocolate-dark like herself. On one side of the beach was a cluster of short trees, with roots tangled and raised like fingers that went all the way to the water's edge. The woman waded into the ocean, walking into it with calm dignity, as one might walk into a garden, until the water was over her head. The air shimmered, and the strange tree roots walked in with her, turning into dark human figures as they did so. The sea closed over their heads, leaving widening ripples. Yes, this is a dream Paro has had since she was a child; then, it would fill her with an unspeakable sense of loss, and she would wake up crying. Now she thinks maybe the dark woman is her grandmother, reportedly lost to drowning when Paro was a child, but her mother won't tell her anything. Once, as an eight-year-old, she had seen the stretch marks on her mother's belly as her mother changed her shirt, and pointed, and said "Waves!" and had not understood when her mother's face closed with anger.

Paro nearly drowned once. She was swimming off the coast north of Chennai, when a rip current took her. The other students from her first and last year in college were on the beach, drinking beer. She had gone into the water with the dangerous confidence of the excellent pool swimmer, her strength a match for the waves, until the adrenalin rush of battling the elements was overtaken by a new and compelling desire: to swim for the joy of immersion into an element that felt truly her own. Then the current caught her and she found herself unable to fight it—*rip current*, her mind said, as she was swiftly carried out to sea, then *swim parallel to shore* but there was only surging water around her, and she couldn't see the beach. She panicked— her breath came in short, hard, sobbing gasps as she fought the waves—but the water pulled her inexorably under, and she thought: *I'm going to die. Mamma, forgive me for being a bad daughter.* As the water took her, an unexpected calm came over her. The water was warm, embracing her like no lover ever could, and she thought: *I'm going home.* It was all right to give herself to the sea. She stopped struggling, felt herself carried gently away, and suddenly there was a strong hand tugging at her arm, and someone guiding her to the surface, to air and life above the heaving waves. She expelled breath from her lungs, gasped in air, clung to her rescuer—it was a strange man, who, she learned later, was a fisherman from the village that the frantic students had called to when they saw her struggling. After that experience she realized two things—one, that the ocean demanded respect—arrogance and over-confidence could kill—and two, that she belonged there, she had to go back. No matter that her mother had only permitted her to swim in a pool—"you must learn to swim for safety's sake, but never swim in the ocean," and had been so unhappy when Paro went to Chennai for college instead of staying in Delhi—her mother's terror of water had something to do with her grandmother's death when Paro had been too young to remember.

"Tell me how she died," Paro said to her mother when she was back in Delhi during winter vacation, a few months after the near-drowning. They were sitting on the balcony of the flat after dinner because the small apartment was too hot; but the outside air was not much better, and smelled of exhaust fumes. No stars were visible in the smoky sky, and the noise of traffic was a constant roar.

"There's not much to tell," her mother said, pausing to use her inhaler. She cleared her throat. "There was a boat accident and she drowned, along with some other people. Since you seem determined to follow that path—"

"Ma, wait. Where was this? Did I . . . did I see the accident? Was I there?"

A long pause.

"In Chennai. Where you grew up. No, of course you weren't there. We heard about the accident later. Why are you bothering with all this? It's in the past. Enough about it! Listen, Paro, I know people who can help you get into a good college in Delhi . . . "

Paro let the familiar words wash over her, thinking—*if our people are from Chennai, why doesn't my mother speak Tamil fluently? Why do I keep dreaming the same dream since I was a kid? The place I see in my dream—it isn't like any beach in Chennai.* She had never told her mother about the dream.

When she is alone on the ocean, Paro likes to free-dive nearly naked. "Alone" means no other humans, of course—swimming with a whale for two months, she's hardly felt alone. No land is in sight, and her boat is the only human-made craft nearby, if you ignore the ship just visible some distance away. Her boat is bobbing gently on the surface, the solar panels extended like the petals of some exotic flower, catching the tropical sun. She's already sent a message to the ship that she's going to dive, and that they should check back with her in five minutes. She wants to swim down to the top of a submerged mountain—its summit is only 87 meters below the ocean's surface—they are a few degrees south of the equator, close to the eastern edge of the Chagos Ridge some fifteen hundred kilometers from Sri Lanka. Ril, back on the ship, doesn't like her freediving—*you should never free dive alone, why do you have to take such risks?*—says his voice in her mind from their conversation a few minutes ago, but it's a familiar argument that he's lost many times before. *Fussy big brother,* she thinks, smiling a little, although he's not her brother. She can freedive on one breath for a hundred and forty meters, and he's worried about 87 m. Her whale, whose name she has learned in his own language—you can sing it or render it as a waveform but words are inadequate—let's call him -> ~^ for convenience—her whale has been down for about fifteen minutes now—blue whales don't go as deep as others, and she is curious as to what he's doing. She checks that the guideline is secure, breathes slowly in and out to calm her mind—takes a deep breath and plunges in.

She swims with nothing on but her flippers, and a belt with an underwater camera, speaker and hydrophone. Down, down, down, one meter, two meters, five, ten, twenty, as the sunlight slowly fades, turning the pale green waters darker and bluer—and then the magic begins to happen—the experience for which she has risked her life again and again. Achieving neutral buoyancy, her chest is contracted with the pressure of the water, the breath held, locked in her lungs. At this depth the ocean stops trying to push her up, and she is suspended in the deep blue, held in the warm water like a fetus in the womb. Acceptance, acceptance. Now she feels the gentle, yet inexorable downward pull of the ocean, and she's falling through the water without effort, pushed sideways by the local current, the upwelling from the trench to the west. Below she can see the top of the seamount, a pale grey in the blue light, approaching swiftly. She spreads her arms and legs to slow down—her bare feet touch rock gently—and she's standing atop a mountain under the sea.

It is so peaceful here, so quiet underneath the agitation of waves and wind on the surface. Only the gentle underwater current pushes her sideways, toward the east, and her hair swirls in that direction as though by the wind. On the summit there are colonies of anemones, their round mouths fringed with red and yellow arms. Delicate, lace-like corals, sea cucumbers, a slug of some kind, purple and yellow with pink frills, a small school of fish. On its west side the mountain slopes gradually away into darkness—the Chagos trench, which can be as much as 6000 m deep in parts. To stand lightly on a mountain under the sea, to walk around in this underwater garden as though she lives here, belongs here—it is a wish she has had for a long time, since she was a girl.

There's no sign of ->~^. She presses a button on her belt for the speaker—it warbles his name first, then a short sequence of sounds that signifies her name to the great whale. The name is Paro's invention, with Stella's help. Stella, the Sri Lankan cetacean specialist on board the ship, made sure Paro's unique identifier signal did not coincide with any of the known phrases, calls and songs of the Sri Lankan blue whale population. >‡>‡ is Paro's name, therefore, and she's developed, over the last month, a few other vocal signifiers to try to bridge the gap between human and whale.

But here, under the waves, the water itself bridges the gap between being and being. She remembers hearing this from her teacher in the learning center in a fishing village on the Kerala coast. The thoughts you think on land, the old man said, are different from what you think with the sea. In the sea you learn to think with the water, the fish. That's why people who make decisions on land, separated from the world by glass and concrete, air-conditioning and software, have such *terrible* ideas for the world. The fisherman-teacher had never been to a formal educational institution—he had, he said, been taught by the ocean, and what better teacher than that? Ideas don't just come from your head, he would say—they are shaped by the *surround*—can the coconut be what it is without the tree, the sand, the wind and the ocean? No! Then always watch how your thoughts change, your body changes, with the surround. Use your coconut!

In the learning center, one of thousands of clandestine offshoots of the Barefoot College movement of the early 21st century, the teachers are mostly illiterate, or academics pushed out by the Exalted One's take-over of universities, humbly willing to exchange their skills with those who have generations of experience surviving under precarity—fisherfolk, tribals, the rural poor. "Useless people" is how the Exalted One and his cronies refer to those who stand in the way of the great March of Progress. While the rest of the country dashes about in a daze, lost to the endless cycle of mindless acquisition, these are the people observing how the weather and the currents are changing, wondering why whales are washing up dead along the coasts, their bellies empty, or filled sometimes with plastic rubbish. They are asking the questions that nobody dares to consider. The fisherfolk had sensed long before the scientists did that the world was coming undone—the winds and waters had been speaking to them about a great and terrible unraveling, but they didn't know why, until they were joined by renegade scientists on the run. Although to speak of it in public is to invite retribution from the powers that be, they know that this unraveling has come about because the bountiful Earth has been hijacked, plundered for the benefit of a few, at the expense of the many. Makeshift universities have mushroomed in secret in kitchens and alleyways, shanty towns and villages, where the "useless people" teach, learn, and ask the hard questions. And it is on their behalf, with their blessing, that Paro is here.

Here she is 87 meters under the ocean's surface, the last place her mother wants her to be. But it's time to go up and breathe. She swims upward along the guideline, breaking the surface, blinking in the sunlight, exultant. She takes a deep breath or two. It is one thing to read somewhere that the ocean provides more than half of the world's oxygen, and quite another to experience this marvelous aliveness, as though every cell in her body is singing. The sky is a cloudless blue. The water is cooler here because of the upwelling current. It is a feeding ground for blue whales and sperm whales, but few have been seen here of late. The numbers are down dramatically.

Paro calls again to the whale, a little louder.. Then she sees him, coming up from the darkness of the trench on the west. He sounds a call that she feels with her whole body, ending with the short phrase that is his name. He has dived deeper than is usual for his kind, but ~>~^ is unusual in many ways. He is less shy, more adventurous—after all, he had accepted her presence in the water by his side within their first month together, and even understands (she thinks) that the strange boat in which she sometimes dives under water is not something to be feared. For the first month she had swum with him without gear except for headphones, belt and flippers, and felt, tasted and moved through his world. She will never forget the first time he had let her come close, and in fact had moved toward her, emitting a series of deep ululations that had reverberated through her body. Stella had warned her that sounds from the blue whale were so loud they could vibrate a human to death, and at the very least damage the eardrums, and in fact was reminding her via the headphones, from the ship a kilometer away. But at that moment Paro had not felt anything but wonder, and a warmth spreading through her, as the huge bulk of the whale grew larger in her vision, and she saw herself in the great eye, caught in the curious, benign gaze that felt at once alien and surprisingly familiar, like a shock of recognition between apparent strangers. Tentatively she had reached out and touched him—his mottled, blue-gray skin was hard to the touch. He was vocalizing gently; she felt the sound in her body like a slow cauldron bubbling within her and knew she was being questioned, explored. Suddenly he emitted a sound burst that felt like an explosion in her ears—she catapulted through the water, arms flailing, until she was at the surface gasping for breath. *Are you all right, are you all right*, said Stella's voice frantic in her ear, and she realized she could hear, and that the noise-canceling headphones had saved her eardrums, but her body felt sore—everything hurt. Just then the whale surfaced near her, turning to catch her in his gaze, and she realized he had stopped sounding the moment she had been in distress. A barely discernible tremolo came from him as he swam around her. *I think he's just understood how fragile I am*, she told Stella later, recovering on the ship. The whale had never vocalized loudly in her presence after that first meeting. He made his loudest calls and songs when she was above water, with her submersible boat in float mode. To honor that trust—as much as to avoid having one more gadget on her person—Paro stopped wearing the protective headphones when she dived.

Three days later she got to see ->~^ feed on a great swarm of krill—well, actually, a kind of shrimp higher on the food chain, Stella told her from the ship. The video footage was excellent. There were still no other blue whales in the region—a pod of sperm whales had been sighted right over the trench, diving for squid. At one point a young sperm whale came over to ->~^ and sounded, but Paro was in the ship, getting supplies for the submersible boat, and could only watch in frustration from the deck. The ship's hydrophones recorded what may have been a conversation, but without being able to observe the whales under water, it was hard to say.

Paro is relieved to be back in the boat again with a three-day supply of food, back in the water with ->~^. It is a cloudless afternoon; gentle waves make music against her boat. The ship is a faint smudge in the distance. This is how life should be, she thinks, as she dives to be with the whale under water. She wishes her mother could see her now, her college drop-out daughter, with no prospects except in competitive swimming, but Paro turned her back on that, too, choosing instead to hang out with riffraff, the useless people. Her mother, last time they met, had the familiar, resigned look in her eyes, saying as loudly as she could with her eyes, with her stiffly held shoulders and the rattle of dishes in the sink—*I worked so hard to give you a good life, and look at you.* Paro wishes she could tell her mother: *there is a whole other reality outside your little artificial bubble world, and I prefer to live in it.*

Diving about thirty meters down, Paro sees ->~^ coming up toward the surface from the depths of the trench. His attention is on a faint, pale-colored cloud in the water over the chasm. A swarm of shrimp? He accelerates upward—she sees the cavernous mouth open and swallow the cloud whole—and it is time for her to go up and take a breath. Up at the surface she breathes slowly and deeply, but then there is an earsplitting crack on the water, and a giant wave knocks her hard against the side of her boat. The whale's fluke rises up and slaps the water again; his head rears up, and she catches her breath—across the head of the whale, and trailing from his mouth is a tangle of cables and meshwork. He slaps the water again with his tail, sounding so loudly that she has to heave herself into the boat to protect her fragile body. She looks around frantically, but the ship is not in sight. She turns on the comm, but just as she is about to call for help, she sees that the ship has sent her a message already, while she was diving. It is code. It means: *We have been boarded. Do not signal the ship. Stay hidden.*

That means that what they had feared has transpired—a corporate militia vessel, or a government ship, not that there is always much difference between the two—has decided to investigate their cover. Or piracy—the nearby Chagos archipelago, once a military base for five of the world's major powers in rapid succession, had finally been occupied by a rebel group that (rumor had it) would not stop at looting passing ships for supplies.

All these thoughts pass through Paro's mind in a fraction of a second. Panic gives way to the studied calm she has practiced for nearly a decade. All right, so she is on her own with a whale in distress. The cable, or mesh, or whatever it is, will have to be cut. She will have to calm ->~^ down enough to be able to approach him with her rope-cutter—pray it isn't steel cables. Going close to a panicked whale means certain death—one whack from the tail or pectoral fin, and she would be smashed.

She gets the rope cutter out from her tool box and attaches it via a short cable to her belt. She practices her breathing, deep and slow. The whale is still below the water surface. Her boat's hydrophones are picking up the long, low

calls, the kinds that travel for a hundred kilometers, which are probably calls
of distress, pleas for help. But there are few, if any blue whales in this area,
and they cannot help him anyway.

She flips neatly over the side of the boat, swimming down into the warm,
clear water, calling through her speaker his name, followed by her identifier
>‡>‡. In the lexicon that she and Stella have been compiling of his calls and
songs, there is one sequence that they had recorded when ->~^ had briefly
traveled with two other blue whales. The whales had each used this sequence
when they met, tacking on what were probably their unique identifiers. A
similar sequence had been recorded for a mother whale calling to her calf
as it dove deeper than she—and the calf returned to its mother thereafter.
Did it mean *come to me*? Did it mean *happy to see you*? Nobody knows, but
there is no time to speculate now. She searches quickly through her library of
calls, finds the one she's looking for, and plays the sequence. The whale has
stopped calling—where is he?

There, a vast bulk ahead of her, coming up to breathe, and submerging
again. He lies still in the water, only a couple of meters below the surface,
head drooping, the cables and lines tangling across his head as before, the
very picture of misery and fear. She thinks she sees part of the line falling
into the deeper water of the trench, disappearing into the darkness. Warbling
her sequence of calls, she swims up to him, slowing down as she does so,
holding her breath in her body. There is a rope or mesh, thinner than the
cables around his head, wrapped around one of the pectoral fins. Perhaps
best to start with that, because he can see what she is doing. *Hold still*, she
tells him in her mind. She holds the rope cutter carefully and cuts through
the thickest part of the rope. It takes a while. A shudder goes through the
whale but the fin is almost free. She has to breathe. She lets herself bob to the
surface, takes a quick breath, and goes below again. Thank goodness he is
close to the surface—if he decides to dive, this will become impossible. She
cuts the finer mesh around the fin, until finally it is free. The whale moves
the fin experimentally, looking at her with a gaze that holds—it seems to
her—both terror and hope. *Good job*, she tells him in her mind. *Now the real
challenge begins.*

She starts to cut the rope—it is some kind of thick, ridged plastic, not
steel, praise all gods of the sea—around the head. She goes up to breathe
three more times. The fourth time the whale surfaces with her. He seems
calmer, making small, reverberating ululations of what she feels must be distress. When they go below the surface again, she sees with horror that the
mess of cables go into his mouth—they are most likely tangled in the baleen

fringes on his upper jaw that he uses to sieve his tiny prey animals from the water. *How am I going to do this, ->~^? Help me. I can't do this alone.*

But when she tugs gently at a thick cable coming out of the side of his mouth, a tremor goes through the water that shakes her literally to the core—she doesn't have to know the details of whale communication to understand that this is a No. She senses before she hears the thunderclap of sound that follows, that she is in danger—she is up and over the side of her boat when his cry hits her. He dives.

Paro sits on the tiny deck of the boat, taking deep, sobbing breaths. Her arms feel like they are filled with hot lead, and her fingers are bruised and swollen from maneuvering the cutters. There is nothing on the horizon but the heaving sea. Where is the ship? For a fraction of a second she wonders what would happen if the ship doesn't return for her—she only has three days' worth of food on the boat—but she needs to focus on the immediate problem, the possibility of losing the whale—a whale with cables tangled in its mouth can't feed. But there's nothing she can do unless he chooses to return to her. *Come on, you bastard, you lump of blubber, you maybe-last-of-your-kind, come back and let me help you, curse you.* But the sea, under the afternoon sky, is calm. She's never felt more alone.

In the water again, she hears him calling. She can hardly believe her ears, because he's calling her name, the name she and Stella invented: >‡>‡. He looms up from the depths and lies quietly next to her while she swims to him.

*Now listen, you'll have to open your mouth for me, as much as you can. Please, please. You have a brain much bigger than mine; you know I have to do this. Your kind has lived longer on this planet than humans. There are so few of you left in the world. I don't want you to die. ->~^*

The whale, as though he has heard her, opens his jaws slowly, only about two meters. The ropes and lines are tangled among the meter-long baleen plates that hang down from his upper jaw, some of which are broken—and in the light of her belt she can see that the whole mess goes into the cavern of his mouth. She had thought maybe she could cut away at the tangle from the outside, enough to pull it out in small pieces, but this is impossible. There is no way she can do this. She forces herself to be calm. *Think with the sea. Use your coconut!* Her fisherman teacher's words echo in her mind. A slow terror takes hold of her then because the sea tells her what she has to do. She must squeeze under the baleen plates and swim into the mouth of the whale.

She edges carefully under the baleen fringes and into the great cavern. Holding on to the bony, bumpy inner edge, she begins to cut at the cables. She has to proceed very carefully because there is debris in the water and even with the bright belt light, it is hard to see. Before and below her lies the enormous, fleshy tongue, and far ahead, the dark tunnel of the throat. *Well, I can believe your kind are the largest animals ever to live on this Earth.* She feels a stretch of rope come loose in her hand. Time for a breath. She swims out of his maw, holding the cut mass of rope and meshwork in one hand. Quick breath in the too-bright sunlight, then dive into the dark cave and cut, cut, cut. Again and again and again, until it seems she's done nothing else in her life. The whale lies patiently in the water, enduring what must be quite painful. The inside of his mouth tastes of the sea, salt and fishy, but there is a taste that is his own, his signature. The equivalent of smell on land is taste in water. *I now know your name in taste as well as sound,* she tells him. Her hands are bleeding, she should have worn gloves. When she goes up again for air, he rises with her, blowing vigorously. She knows he is relatively young, probably in his early thirties, like her. She breathes, goes to the boat for a drink of fruit juice, and returns to her task.

I don't know how much longer I can do this, she thinks. She's lost count of the number of times she's gone down and come up. *I am so tired, and if I die of exhaustion, who will help you?*

When the whale opens his mouth this time, it is a lot wider—he's edged out some of the loose rope with his tongue. *Good lump of blubber,* she says as she resumes the work on the remainder of the cable. This is the bit that has a long segment of rope trailing out of the mouth and into the dark abyss below them. Steadily she works on it, the whale's calm trust soothing her, helping her control the trembling achiness in her arms. At last. She swims out of the great maw, bringing the last of the tangle with her. She hopes he hasn't swallowed any of it. She surfaces, takes a breath, and swims over to the boat, where she attaches the mess of cable to the side of the boat. She turns to look at the whale.

He releases a fountain of breath that rains around her. He lies still in the water. A shudder of fear goes through her. Has the ordeal been too much? Has it rendered him so weak that he cannot not survive? She swims over to him, diving to touch his flank. She is held in his gaze; the great eye signaling a complex mix of emotions that she thinks she understands. He will be all right, at least for now. His life, like her life, is filled with unknown dangers ahead (*will the ship return?*), but they're both all right for now.

The ship doesn't come for her until the second day. Before its arrival she has dived as far into the trench as she dares—a hundred and twenty meters—to see where the cables go. But this part of the trench is too deep—the trailing cables go down into the dark. She knows the history of waste dumping into the sea—not only plastic and chemical effluents, but also nuclear waste—warheads and submarines, tons of radioactive waste dumped during the twentieth century, a practice that has likely been revived in this new and chaotic age. Knowing something of the history of abuse of the Chagos atoll—colonialism followed by militarization in which five superpowers succeeded each other—she cannot help but wonder what horrors lie at the bottom of the trench. These cables are not fishing gear—people on the ship will be able to tell what they are, she hopes.

And so the ship returns—Ril tells her that they were accosted by the Free People of Chagos—the rumor of the islands being occupied by rebels was true after all, but these were no pirates. They were descendants of the original inhabitants, brought from Africa and India in the 1700s by the French to work on coconut plantations. She knows something of their history: having made the islands their home, and developed a unique culture, the Chagossians were forcibly removed by the British and Americans nearly eighty years ago to make way for a military base. By the mid-21st century the base has been rented out to three other militaries—India, AsiaCorp and United China. Following its destruction in a great storm some years ago, the base was abandoned, although it is still a contested site. After decades of exile and struggle, the Chagossians have returned. They are trying, like Paro and her friends, to reclaim the world they have lost.

Lying on the deck of her boat under a star-studded sky, Paro thinks about her mother. Yesterday she had sent her a message via the ship, through a convoluted route via the Chagossian settlement. *Thinking of you. Hope you are fine. Love, Paro.* She's beginning to put things together regarding her shattered family history, and the dream that has haunted her since childhood. Talking to the Chagossian representative on the ship, she is starting to reconstruct her own story from memory fragments and things her mother has let slip—She is not from Chennai, or any other part of mainland India—her people are island folk. They have been forced to leave their home. As the boat of the dispossessed refugees leaves, the child Paro is standing at the railing, looking back toward the white curve of the beach, the palm trees against an impossibly blue sky. They are leaving home—perhaps because the rising seas have contaminated fresh water sources on the island. Or maybe the island has something that the government or some corporation wants. It doesn't matter; the fact is that they have lost their home, and the grandmother and some other people have chosen to stay behind, and walk into the sea. And the child, Paro, unattended for a moment, has seen the grandmother do this from the departing boat, not understanding what she's seeing, but feeling the pain well up in her that has kept company with her all her life. She doesn't know what island system her people come from—the Andamans or Lakshadweep, perhaps—but when she's back in Delhi she will find a way to ask her mother about it. Her mother, who has learned to hate what she once loved—the sea.

Away in the darkness she hears the whale blow. Through the speaker she warbles his name. He responds with a long sequence that she recognizes as part of the lexicon that has been recorded previously, as yet incomprehensible. It reverberates gently through her body, this new language she is learning, in which she has a name, and a teacher. The water sloshes musically against her boat.

Water obscures, blurs, and dilutes all boundaries.

She is Paro. She is >‡>‡.

Karen Osborne is a speculative fiction writer and visual storyteller living in Baltimore. She is a graduate of Viable Paradise and the Clarion Writers' Workshop, and won awards for her news & opinion writing in New York, Florida, and Maryland. She is the author of *Architects of Memory*, published by Tor. Her short fiction appears in *Uncanny, Fireside, Escape Pod, Beneath Ceaseless Skies*, and more.

CRATERED

Karen Osborne

The fireplace stuck out from the lunar surface like a middle finger directed at my future.

From a distance, it looked just like the fireplace at my house in Pasadena, all limestone and granite, sparkling in the sun. The stone was covered in black ash, as if it had burned, like things could burn here on the fucking Moon. In the fireplace, dusted in lunar regolith kicked up by bootprints that we didn't make, lay a kicked-over arrangement of charred wood—as if someone had decided that Mare Crisium was a great place to play Little House on the Prairie.

"Please say you're seeing this," I said.

Arjun smirked. "What, Kate? The fireplace? Or the dancing giraffes?"

I scowled. Arjun was our small survey team's other geologist. He cracked extremely bad jokes when he was nervous, but right now I was in no mood for humor. It was after dinner and my oxygen tank was already barking at me for being irresponsible. We'd overstayed our welcome at the A5 survey site and taken the shortcut near Dorsa Tetyaev in our latest attempt to slake our employer's unending thirst for rare-earth minerals. The long Moon's night was coming, but two weeks of complete darkness didn't exactly mean Lunatech was going to be lenient with our quotas.

It was amazing how a mission I thought I would love would end up as such a boring mess—just rocks, more rocks, sometimes scandium or yttrium or helium-3, but mostly *more fucking rocks*.

Arjun fished out his camera. "We didn't bring an augmented reality set, right? We're really seeing this?"

"We're really seeing this."

"How the hell are we really seeing this? Do we have time to stop here and figure it out?"

I checked my oxygen tank. Figure it out? All I wanted was to go back to Pasadena. Not that I could. "Three minutes before we eat into the buffer zone. We'll have to come back tomorrow."

"Should we tell Harper?"

"Tell her what, that we've been on the Moon so long we're hallucinating?"

Arjun craned his neck, and the sunlight reflected off his helmet, bright enough to make me blink. "You know, this looks like something from my mom's place," he said.

"Doesn't look very Indian," I responded.

"As if you know what Indian looks like." He snorted back a laugh.

I checked my footing and bounced off the rover. "I could, if we had AR out here."

We edged around the site, two ungainly, overly careful lunar tumbleweeds halting and stumbling and leaving footprints that no wind would ever wash away, as clear as the craters and the dorsae and the mare and the Apollo site. Above us was a logy Earthrise, and if you squinted, you could almost catch the ash curling in the atmosphere over what was left of Los Angeles.

I had just convinced myself that we were looking at some sort of prank by the last survey team when I found the damning details in stone: the initials *R&K* carved into the lintel, chipped off with a pocketknife, as jagged as the day I made them.

In Pasadena.

Riley & Kate.

I didn't tell Arjun about what the initials meant. I didn't even mention it. He'd think I was finally going crazy. What other explanation could there be? That someone from Lunatech wandered into the radiation zone, packed up my dead girlfriend's chimney, and recreated it here above the mare?

They already thought I was enough of a problem.

I stumbled into the airlock behind Arjun, samples from the formation shoved into my utility pocket. Our mission lead, Harper, was waiting with her face mashed against the airlock window. Arjun and I jostled each other like siblings in a mudroom for two minutes until the airlock filled with atmospheric mix and the door hissed open, revealing the cramped storage room—all muffled steel and white plastic, every single space taken up by drawers and cabinets and medical storage.

Harper's mouth twisted downwards as we walked in, her Manchester accent deeper than normal. "You're way over schedule. Both of you are better than this," she said, tapping her watch.

I fought an angry, baffled knot in my throat the size of a walnut and tried to lighten up the atmosphere. "Sorry, Mom."

It didn't work. Harper went red-faced. "I'm not your mom. I'm your boss. And I don't need to remind you that you could die out there, just like the members of the first Mare Crisium mission. What if you didn't come back?"

Arjun mumbled an apology under his breath and bounced over to his suit cabinet. He toggled the release on his chestplate, then started to strip down to his underwear. Sweat had formed a salty, jagged crag on his black t-shirt.

I was less interested than he was in defusing the situation. I released my own chestplate and dragged off my gloves. "Look, Boss. You keep on saying that Lunatech wants results. We got you results. The A5 site looks promising. Fairly scandium-rich, with enough from the lanthanide series for three or four trips for Curtis and Tran."

"Samples?" Harper said.

"In the bag."

Harper rubbed her eyes. She looked exhausted. "Okay. Look, Kate. I know not being able to go back to Earth after the bomb was rough on you. I know *I've* been rough on you. I know we have to live without AR here, and that stinks, too." She choked down something tough, something bitter. "But we all lost people. You can't use the way you feel as a crutch to screw up out there."

I pulled on my Lunatech sweater. The synthetic fabric felt like steel wool, but at least it was warm. "That's not what's going on," I said.

Harper sighed. "All right. Dinner in five."

"You go on. I'm going to put some hours in down the hall."

Harper paused. "If you insist. Come on, Arjun. Curtis and Tran heated up nutraloaf for dinner."

"Yay," muttered Arjun, the ceiling lights catching the grey in his close-cropped black hair.

The tight ball in my throat yawned open, and sudden, shaking heat spread across my shoulders. I felt resentful and terrible and embarrassed, and *ugh*, why I was crying? Arjun opened his mouth to say something, but I slammed my locker and turned my back to the door. He swallowed whatever it was he was going to say, and when I turned around to apologize, he and Harper were already gone.

The lights blazed bright in the common room down the hall. It was the laughter that stopped me short: lazy, end-of-the-day, family-room laughter. It was Curtis complaining about the nutraloaf, Tran saying she'd deal the next round of rummy, like they didn't feel the crush of Earth at war wailing above them, like they had been able to look away when California was nuked and Riley with it.

Like Lunatech had actually given them time off or cared that we'd watched it all happen from dead, dusty Mare Crisium.

The lab was dark and quiet and far more my speed. I flipped on the lights and laid out the samples we'd taken that afternoon. They looked ashen and dull, exactly like regolith—far different from the mica-bright, hard granite I thought I'd chipped off in the hot sunlight. I listened to the mass spectrometer whir and whine and wiped my eyes with the sleeve of my sweater.

Screw tears. Crying was wasting water.

Lunatech had offered me the survey post because of my research into rare-earth minerals, but it had been Riley that convinced me to take it—just after Christmas, standing in the moonlight in front of my parents' house with her freezing white hands pressed against my cheeks, the snowflakes falling fat and beautiful on her lips and eyelashes. And there had been the save-the-world aspect to Lunatech's offer, too, even if when I thought of the world I thought only of Riley.

But that had been Michigan and this was the Moon, and in between, terrorists had nuked California.

The spectrometer beeped.

Basalt, the monitor said. *Anorthocite. Dunite.*

I smacked it. "That's not right, you stupid—"

"Hey!" Arjun, his voice hard-edged, appeared beside me with a memory card balled in his fist. He was already in his pajamas. "It's not like we can just pop up to the store and replace that thing."

I pointed to the results. "What we saw this afternoon was granite and sandstone and Portland cement, not more stupid *moon rocks*. I'm being gaslit by a mass spectrometer."

Arjun peered at the machine, an unopened juice pouch clutched in his right hand like an afterthought. I shoved the samples back into the machine and started it up again, resisting the urge to tap out an impatient tattoo on the nearby table. Without augmented reality feeding real-time results at the top of my vision, I'd have to wait until the stupid thing was done. I'm sure plenty of science was done before AR, but I can't imagine it was fun.

Arjun, too, had his eyes on the still-blank monitor. "It's a weird formation, to be sure, and the moon's a geologic vomitorium, but my mother's hearth in Kumartuli was made of local stone."

I cut him off. He was making no sense. "Did you look at the photos yet?"

He opened his left hand and dropped a memory card into my palm. It was warm and slightly wet. I winced. "I thought we could do that together. And I brought you some juice, since you skipped dinner."

"Did Harper put you up to that?" The moment the words came out, I regretted them.

Arjun flinched, then put the cup on the table next to the spectrometer. "I get it, Kate. This is hard on all of us. And I understand that everybody mourns in different ways. But you don't have to pull away like this, and you certainly can't keep on treating us the way you are. It's a small base, and there's no AR to make things easier, and we all have to get along." He sighed. "You know, we could even be friends, if you just *tried*."

I felt my face flush. He saw it, too. "You can't understand."

"Try me," he said.

"India wasn't even involved."

"We don't have any choice in that," he said. "Nature is nature."

I nodded. He was right, of course, like he so often was. The wind was the wind, and it would carry the radiation that killed the West Coast into the stratosphere, across the ocean, into the bread and water and intercellular space of every human being alive. I bit my bottom lip to keep myself from sticking my foot in my mouth again. My shoulders felt tight. My chest burned.

Maybe I *was* being unfair.

"I just don't know what to do," I said. "I'm up here, and everything else . . . is down there."

He sighed, then reached forward, tapping the memory card in my palm with one finger.

"Take a look, and then come to dinner. It's really good nutraloaf and Tran's having a bad night at rummy," he said.

Tran always has a bad night at rummy, I wanted to say, but I plugged the memory card into the computer instead.

The pictures depicted nothing but the same damned thing we saw every day: rocks. Regolith. The empty, shattered surface. No mica-bright granite, no impossible initials. No fireplace, no room where Riley and I had spent hours reading books and sharing dreams and planning our life together. My heart clenched. I opened my mouth to yell at Arjun for screwing up, but the criticism died on my tongue.

Our footprints lay exactly where I thought they'd be, circling the place where the fireplace should have stood.

The camera had recorded no structure at all.

"We *did* see a fireplace, right?" I said.

He nodded. "Clear as day."

"I was just making a joke about hallucinations."

"I don't know. We've been out here long enough." He sighed, then plunked a straw next to the cup. "We'll go by tomorrow. Get an explanation. Come on down the hall?"

I almost said yes. Instead, I looked away. "I can't."

He shrugged, then retreated down the hall, to the laughter and the light. I took the cup and stabbed the straw through the lid with entirely too much force, spraying myself. It was strawberry mango, my favorite flavor. The small kindness made me want to follow him—to seek warmth and company from my co-workers for my aching animal heart. When my feet moved, though, they deposited me right in the solitude of my cubby as they always did, and I drifted off to the sound of Curtis chuckling over his latest win.

I dreamed of Riley: brown-haired and smiling and surrounded by Christmas lights and flurries of snow. I dreamed the lights dimmed, the flurries turned to ashes, the skies went as black as the soil around her feet, that the Shackleton Crater swallowed her in the deep, black ice they'd discovered there, that her bones shattered into powder, scattering over the everdark stone. I dreamed of my work at Caltech, of bombs obliterating Pasadena, of ghosts in my throat, of being buried alive on Mare Crisium, regolith salty between my teeth.

At breakfast, I shoveled a protein bar into my mouth as Harper read the daily assignments. Tran sucked down black coffee, her eyes grey with fatigue, her mouth twisted into a sour curve. She always stayed up far too late, using her comm time to talk to family in the Vancouver refugee camps. Curtis had already finished his breakfast and was idly shuffling the worn deck of cards he kept next to a picture of his ex-wife. The only one looking at Harper was Arjun, who seemed bright-eyed and ready to go.

My mind wandered back to the photos he'd taken—their spectacular, peculiar emptiness, the bootprints that clearly weren't ours, the endless grey sea beyond. Earth brushing the horizon, teasing horror and hope.

There was a very simple explanation to what we'd seen—we'd encountered an augmented reality program, just like the ones I used in my work at

Caltech, like stores and restaurants used all over the world to personalize user experiences. But AR needed routers and receivers and was prohibited up here on the lunar frontier, ripped out of every suit and rover and system and brain sent outside Armstrong Haven, in case a member of the survey team might misjudge a navpoint, choose the wrong footing, fall straight off a dorsa and die screaming at the bottom of a thousand-foot crater.

In Lunatech's central colonies, the rich twirled in their luxury apartments, AR braingear twisting their white walls and plastic chairs into Italianate mansions or mid-century penthouses or Miami beach condos. Out here, though, we had to make do with bad jokes and gin rummy simply because our monkey brains couldn't judge the proper size of a rock when denied the right reference points.

Harper's voice cut through my reverie. "Kate. You're not even listening to me."

"I was," I lied through my last mouthful.

"The CEO has moved up the schedule on the AR installations in the Whitman wing, so our own schedule is changing. You and Arjun will head back to A5, extract at least 200 grams of scandium and get it on the rocket before nightfall. Be careful, and don't stay out too long."

The number burnt in my chest like a rubber band around my aorta. "I can't do that. It's not possible," I said.

"Curtis can do it," said Harper.

"He's a miner," I said. "I'm a geologist."

Curtis stopped chewing. "We've already been scheduled for five hundred grams of lanthanides up near B2," he said. "There's no way we'd make it to A5 in time."

I grabbed the table and leaned forward, staring at Harper. "And you shouldn't have to. Boss, I said the vein was promising, not that I could load up a shipment without a full, proper survey of the area. Asking us to rush this is to sacrifice all thoughts of safety, and last time I checked, none of us had replaceable parts."

Harper's fingers tightened on her chair. "I know the schedule's bruising, but there's a new resident shuttle arriving at Aldrin the Tuesday after next, and you need to do your best."

"Maybe we shouldn't," I said.

There was silence at the table.

"Shouldn't build out Aldrin?" Harper said. "Or shouldn't do our best? What are you going to do, Kate? Quit? Are you going to *walk* home?"

She pointed towards the airlock.

Tran sighed, rubbing her eyes. "There are tricks, Kate, we can show you how to preload the—"

I cleared my throat to cut her off. "Let the one-percenters play cards for a week or two. It's not like they're going anywhere."

They were all staring at me now.

"And why are they doing any of it, anyway? Have you ever thought about what's going to happen when we've built their augmented utopia, the war doesn't end, and all the rich people rapture up here and leave the Earth to die?"

Tran looked away, clearly uncomfortable. I know I should have stopped, but the words burst out of my mouth like they'd been dammed up behind my tonsils ever since California fried. Maybe they had. "Have you thought about how the environment down there is *collapsing* and they haven't changed one *word* of their business plan? We could be doing so much more. Lunatech could be *saving people.* On Earth. Where it matters. And you're sending me out to get *samples*, so they can build AR routers for rich people that couldn't give a shit."

Harper licked her lips. When she spoke, her voice sounded like someone had worked it over with sandpaper.

"Even if we wanted to do something more," she said, quietly, "even if we did, what do you think would happen? We're all very small cogs, in a very large machine, with very big tires. We have to deliver results."

"Yes. But—"

"I think it's in all our best interests to clear every single milestone we're given," Harper said, almost as quiet as the Moon itself.

Tran swallowed the last of her nutraloaf and stood, her fingers spread on the table, turning her eyes on me, her cheeks suddenly flushed. "You think you're the only one suffering here, Kate. That your lady balances out my aunt and my cousins. I've been nice to you because I *know* how much it hurts, but to have to sit here listening to you spin out your paranoid fantasies? I'm done. You know what we can do, Kate? Our *jobs.* You might get to go back to some fancy university when you're done here, but some of us have to work for a living." Her eyes closed. "First one in a suit gets first shift on the comm tonight."

None of them looked at me as they rose from the table.

I went to work. I had to.

Didn't mean I wasn't burning like the redwoods. Like the montane forest. Like Los Angeles. Burning to a fucking cinder.

Arjun was quiet for most of the journey, which suited me just fine. He sat there shaking in his seat as the rover clattered over dusty grey stone, staring at dark California hanging above. He didn't argue when I yanked the steering column away from the track that would lead us back to A5, taking the detour up Dorsa Tetyaev instead. We saw the fireplace coming for a very long time, standing craggy and wrong against the darkness of the stars, and I slowed the rover until it came to a gentle stop, thirty feet from the standing stones.

"Still see that?" I asked.

Arjun nodded. "It's the fireplace at my mother's house. The old house, the one in Kumartuli."

"Well, I'm seeing the fireplace at my place in Pasadena. And unless someone packed it up and stuck it on a lander and carted it out here . . . "

Arjun pulled out the geological scanner. "Okay, so definitely AR, with differentiated effects. But how? There's no power structure, no network. And even if there was, our suits don't have receivers. How are we seeing different things? Are you sure your braingear is off?"

I looked around. *Rocks.* Rocks as far as the eye could see. Rocks and stars and death. "Surgically removed, yeah."

"But there's nothing here."

"That we can see," I said.

We looked at each other for a very long moment, and he went for the geological scanner on the back of the rover.

Geology. If I didn't understand people, at least I could understand science. I let the familiar cadence of the work control my hands, trying to ignore the giant granite question standing right in front of me. When we were done setting up the scanner, Arjun turned it on and stepped back. We felt a slight frisson in our boots as the machine ran a search, sending sonar waves into the ground, registering obstacles and rare-earth minerals and the optimal place to have Curtis and Tran install their extractors and grinders. An itch fired up at the end of my nose, and I tried to scratch it by smashing my face against the speaker in my helmet. Just another one of the small indignities I had to put up with traipsing around in a suit all day.

I walked up next to the fireplace and ran my glove over the initials, like I could touch for one burning second the dreams Riley and I spoke about, sitting in the silvering morning light, burning our mouths on kisses and hot coffee: muddy boots by the door, the crayon scrawls posted on the refrigerator from our future kids, the way she'd go grey in fits and spurts, the laugh lines that would have eventually tucked in near her eyes. I expected my fingers to go right through the thing. Any good augmented reality matrix falls apart when you touch it, because AR is light and smoke and holotricks and empty calories.

Not this.

I pressed in, feeling the resistance of granite, the shudder of the layers of my suit compressing against my skin. No AR matrix I'd ever heard of had even come close to real haptic feedback, but here it was, happening right underneath my fingers. If Lunatech had this kind of technology, why hadn't they already cornered the market with it? And why was it randomly out here on Mare Crisium?

"Holy crap," I said. "Arjun, I can touch this."

"Just a sec. Scanner says there's something underneath where you're standing," Arjun said. He walked slowly, purposefully, in the careful half-shuffle of the moonbound. I heard his breathing, if not his footsteps. "Unknown composition. Three meters. Let's dig it up and see what it is."

"Okay," I said.

It seemed like a good decision at the time.

I used to think nights in Pasadena were quiet.

I know what *quiet* means, now. These days, when I recall nights on Earth, I hear a clamor so loud I'm amazed I got any sleep at all: the crackling of insects outside, the sobbing of night birds, Riley's skin, sticky and bright, slithering against the sheets. The muffled hiss of the air conditioner when we had enough money to pay for it. The laughter of my co-workers, the ticking of lab machinery, the planes above the college, all of that human noise wrapping around my ears, cracking open my skull.

And it's quiet on Mare Crisium, absolutely bleeding *silent*, except for the noise you make yourself: dark breathing in the suit-comms, whispered swears when you think you're talking to yourself. Every other sound, you *touch*. The screech of the rover's engine comes only through vibrations felt in your feet and your fingers. Even the juddering impact of the trowel against the dusty moonscape is all you get, tough breaks of matter coming up against matter, the rush of black impact.

We dug, careful and sure, like archaeologists. Someone had disturbed this ground before. The way the regolith lay, the way it was packed loose and littered, the way it had been brushed by unknown bootprints—none of it was natural. A foot below the surface we caught sight of something bright and polished. I shone my flashlight in to find a cylinder of curved metal, worked by some sort of human machine, glistening in the sun of the lunar afternoon like a phoenix egg about to break. I spied a familiar white etching on the bottom.

"Look, the Lunatech logo," I asked.

"An AR router," Arjun said, after a moment. "And there's no power source."

"It's too small to be a router. Unless it's a prototype." I paused. "Are we looking at a prototype?"

I caught a trickle of motion at the corner of my eye—a dark puddle of shadow, at first, then a person, made of arms and legs and my quiet fear. Arjun turned seconds before I did, and his mouth went wide.

"*Mama*," he moaned.

The visitor wasn't Arjun's mother. It was Riley. She walked around us in a circle, barefoot on the moon's surface in a white cotton dress, backlit by the encroaching cloak of night, bare sunlight streaming from her fingers and slipping through her hair like she wasn't dead, like she hadn't evaporated two hundred and forty thousand miles away.

Arjun scrambled, falling back, his eyes full of stars. "*Mama*, what are you doing here?" he said.

As Riley walked, the lunar regolith reformed underneath her, slithering out in echoing circles from her feet, becoming the dented laminate flooring of our home: the old, cat-scratched red couch, the dented coffee table where she'd left her copy of *The Odyssey* the night before I left for Canaveral. Walls rose around me—covered in the old, peeling wallpaper we'd planned on replacing with AR as soon as we could. The whole damned thing was so real, and so *right*, and so achingly familiar that I wanted to unhook my helmet right here, wanted to sit down with her, wanted to kiss her stupid face until she laughed and asked me to stop.

In fact, I felt like I *should*. The suit seemed more constrictive than ever. The itch had spread to my entire body. I had to get my helmet off to talk with her. I simply had to. The feeling was overwhelming. And why not? I was *home*. The black, eternal night disappeared under the white popcorn ceiling as sunlight dappled the carpet. In the window, beyond the gauzy drapes with their embroidered tulips, I saw the front yard with its stubby, browning grass, the orange tree with its twisting leaves and ripening fruit. I heard the sound of the coffee machine popping in the kitchen. I was home. With Riley.

But my hand stopped right before I flipped the latch on my helmet. Beyond the yard, the neighborhood blurred into house-shaped boxes, like a camera taking a picture with shallow depth of field. I squinted. I had never cared much about California; my world had been Caltech, the lab, Riley. I hadn't paid attention to the neighborhood. I turned to tell her that something was wrong with the neighborhood, and I met her eyes—

—her *missing* eyes—

—*she had no eyes*—

Vomit rose in my throat and I stumbled back. I heard a clicking noise, retching, a gasping scream that seemed buried in muffled cotton.

I whirled. Arjun was on the ground, his legs kicking, his helmet cracked at the neck joint, as if he'd gone through with the notion I'd seriously entertained. Adrenaline kicked in and I called his name, clawing toward him over the jagged rocks. I slammed his helmet back into place and fixed the seal, then rolled him over to make sure his oxygen system was still working. How many minutes had he lost? How much air? He wasn't conscious.

The spell broke. The living room was gone: the fireplace, the couch, the book, the window looking out on the half-forgotten desert. Only Riley remained. She perched on the rover, black-eyed, her hands crossed. At her feet shone the circular router, at rest against the dusted back wheel. It must have rolled over to the rover when Arjun dropped it.

I checked Arjun's vitals. He was out, but alive. The event had lasted at least fifteen seconds. He hadn't expelled his breath when the helmet came off, and petechiae dotted his face.

Repressurization, I thought. The suit's med system would give him some of that, but I needed to get him *inside*, to the machines that could save his life. Choking panic helped me drag Arjun to the rover, and strap him in and careen back to base, juddering and jumping like a racecar driver—Riley's ghost perched there the whole time, dust kicking up around her bare feet.

Yes, I brought the cylinder.

I'm a scientist. I needed to know what it was. What it could do. If it had done something to Arjun, to me, something irreversible.

Riley always said my curiosity was my most dangerous quality.

I radioed ahead to let Harper know to break out the medkit and charge the pressure chamber. At the base, I left the rover off the solar charger and shoved the router in my pack. I stuck my fingers in Arjun's collar, then dragged him over the rainy grey ground towards the airlock.

"No," came Harper's voice through the comm. "No way."

"Arjun's hurt, Boss," I said. "Open the door."

I could see her face through the porthole. Her cheeks had gone white, and she was shaking.

"How do I know it's you?"

I slammed my palm against the window, fingers splayed. "Harper!"

"You brought company," Harper said, pointing. "A dead woman."

I blinked. Turned around. Riley was standing there, silent, staring at me. Laminate spilled out under her feet, a rug, *The Odyssey*. I wanted to take my helmet off, to be with her . . .

No. I tore away, focused on Harper, on the door, on the rocks stacked around me in piles of *scandium* and *yttrium* and *regolith.* "It's all right. It's just augmented reality. Whatever's there, whoever you're seeing, they're not real. It's just hijacking your optic nerve and whatever you dreamed about last night. Or something. We'll figure it out. Let us in."

Harper's face had gone a corpselike grey. She pushed off her side of the airlock, stumbling back into the table full of medical devices she'd set up.

"If I'm seeing Allie, you found the router."

I whacked the window again, this time with my fist. "Open the damn door."

"Leave it outside."

"What about Curtis and Tran?" I asked.

"They're not due back until tonight. We'll get Arjun hooked up, then you can drive it back out to where you found it."

"It can't hurt you—"

The words ripped from Harper's throat with a harrowing anguish I didn't think her capable of delivering. "But it *did* hurt me! Why do you think I left it out there? Why do you think Allie's dead, with the rest of them? Why do you always have to be such a—"

"Okay, your orders are heard. Coming in." My hands shook. *The rest of them? Did she mean the first Mare Crisium mission?*

I dropped the pack by the door. Harper peered at me, at my empty, open hands, like I was a criminal coming to a precinct to surrender. I started the airlock sequence. Cycle-in took two minutes, but felt like hours. When the inside door finally opened, I dragged Arjun towards the medicine cabinet, and we knelt over him, Harper shoving an oxygen tube up his nose, me undoing my helmet and putting it aside.

"This isn't great," Harper said. "How long was he exposed?"

"I don't know. I was affected by the router. Fifteen seconds?"

I expected her to tear me down again, but her eyes flickered to the port-hole, and she slapped on a pair of latex gloves. "Okay. He'll be fine."

"You going to tell me what happened?"

She hesitated, slipped the pressure sack over Arjun's lolling body, and we breathed a mutual sigh as the machine clicked on and started to hack and hum. Harper peeled off her sweaty gloves, then looked at me. "They wanted us to be comfortable out here. And Allie, she—it's complicated, she—"

She was going to tell me. Her mouth hung open. I could see the words bubbling in the tears behind her eyes.

But then the screaming began.

In the rush to save Arjun, we'd forgotten about the long night.

We'd forgotten Curtis and Tran would be home early.

Harper rushed to the porthole door, then pointed at me. "Suit," she said, "now," and rushed to her own locker. I grabbed my helmet and locked it tight, then went to the airlock. Riley stood there, just outside, smiling, her white teeth wide, her eyes missing, the area where they should sit as dark as midnight in irradiated Runyon Canyon. As welcoming as a black hole.

Tran staggered towards something unseen, her hands going for the lock on her helmet. "Auntie, no," she said. "I know it hurts, I'm right here, just come closer, we'll take you inside—"

"Tran!" I slammed the comm. "It's not real!"

"It's okay, Kate," said Curtis. "Cassie's here. She can help. She says she was wrong! She wants to come home."

I did the math: how long they had to live, compared to how fast we could get out there. The math sucked, and left no room for my boss, so I threw myself in the airlock. Harper realized I wasn't going to wait, and dragged on her boots, half-stumbling with the rest of her suit clutched in her hand, but I couldn't wait, I *couldn't*, and I slammed my hand against the toggle to feel the familiar shaky thrill of the airlock engaging.

Harper screamed at me as she brought down her chestplate, and I turned to watch through the porthole, counting the seconds—

—five, six—no, it's been over that already—

Tran fell.

—eight, nine—

"Put on your helmets," I screamed. "It's not real!"

Eleven seconds.

I was going to be too late.

"Going now," I said. I grabbed a tether, slapped it against my belt, and hit the toggle again to blow the door. I could see Harper scrambling to the environmental controls and felt the guilt twist in the bottom of my belly.

I'd always imagined being blown out of an airlock this way would feel like being sucked out into the void, but it was more like being slammed against a wall. I had no control. My ankle hit just inside of the door and I twirled, losing track of the ground, the stars careening in spirals above me, then a violent, bruising yank at my waist as I reached the end of my tether and fell towards the ground. I yanked my head back to keep my helmet from impaling itself on a jagged outcrop and waited for the impact.

The landing hurt like someone had punched me in the chest with a bag of boulders. I saw stars, sucked down oxy-mix, and crawled the last ten meters back to the too-still forms of my colleagues, my ankle screaming bloody murder. I grabbed both of them and hauled them back until we were all in the airlock, until there was enough air to rip the oxygen strip from my suit and shove it up Curtis's nose, but they were both cold, so cold, and not enough oxygen for all three of us.

When the door opened, I was still trying to save them both. It was Tran's turn, my warm lips mashed against her cold ones, breathing air into her body. Harper scrambled towards Curtis, and I could see from the way her shoulders dipped, the way they shook, that I hadn't done a good enough job.

I felt dead myself. Ripped in half.

"We need to destroy it," Harper said, eventually. "I should have destroyed it in the first place."

"*You* did this?" I said.

Her voice cracked. "I did what my boss asked me to do."

I grabbed her shoulders. Held them tight. Wanted to shake her. "*Lunatech* told you to *bury* it? Is this what they're building on Aldrin?"

Harper nodded, wiping her nose. "They said they were giving us AR to make things comfortable during Moon's night. They sent that—that *thing*, that router. Said it was new haptic tech that allowed you to touch your AR surroundings. That it gets right into your brain, figures out what you like, what you want. And I didn't want to turn it on without testing it, so we brought it out to the mare. Turned it on."

"The footsteps we found."

She swallowed her own saliva, and nodded. "I was the only one who made it back. Who didn't walk right out of their suit and freeze."

I heard the rush of blood in my ears. "And when were you going to tell us the truth?"

She breathed quietly. She was fighting tears. "I couldn't tell you." Her voice climbed a register. "I was alone up here, Kate. Alone. I've been alone for a long time, before Allie. I couldn't go home. There's nothing for me left in Bolton. They made me sign a five-year contract with an NDA from hell. If they find out you know—"

I squeezed her shoulder. I didn't want to. I took a breath, swallowing a nascent hate.

The others needed me now.

"You're not alone now," I said. "And I have a plan."

She turned away to hide her tears.

I pushed to my feet, cast my helmet aside, and plucked the router from Curtis's frozen hand. I tried not to gape at his dead face and his burned-out eyes. He looked surprised, honestly. Happy. Like he'd gone dark while gazing upon something beautiful, like everything he wanted had walked up to him and kissed him on the mouth to the sound of violins and fireworks.

I walked to the lab, looking over my shoulder, then searched for a syringe. Riley followed me, silent as the stars, settling in just inside the door like my own ghostly satellite, grey as the mare.

Riley felt real when I touched her. I looked everywhere but the cavern of her face. I ran my thumb up the dry skin of her arm, slipped the needle into her vein. The syringe filled with thick, ruby liquid, as if a ghost could have blood, as if any of this made sense.

I tossed the whole damned thing in the mass spectrometer. Science would tell me what was real.

"Baby," Riley whispered. "How was work today?"

My head snapped back, and suddenly she was next to me, right there, smelling of toothpaste and curry, wearing the white dress she'd worn the night before I'd left for Canaveral, as cold and contrary as the moon. I wanted to say something, but she reached up and cupped my cheek, then leaned forward, and I could no longer look anywhere else but the abyss of her eyes. Her lips were ruby-red, grazed blood-scarlet, and felt diamond-cold against mine. I wanted this with every scratching thing under my skin: to push the strap of her dress to the side, to let my hands remember what I had loved.

Did it matter what had brought her back to me? Did it matter that she was as cold as Michigan, her fingers limned in ice, her lips cold from the wind, her hands on my cheeks, her encouragement to *go, get on the rocket*, when none of us knew what *going* would mean? That it would be *rocks, more rocks, more damned rocks* until we died?

That I would forget the color of her eyes?

That I would forget *her*?

The spectrometer beeped.

Basalt, the monitor said. *Anorthocite. Dunite.*

"You should go to the moon," she said. Her touch was cold marble on my cheek. "And I'll be here when you get home."

I stared at Riley in the abyss of her blackshot eyes.

"Hell, no, I shouldn't go," I said.

I smashed the cylinder on the table, five times, six, sixteen, like a total fucking psycho, then closed my eyes for a very long time.

When I opened my eyes, Riley was gone. The floor of the lab was covered in grey rocks and powder-fine regolith, like I'd been talking to a pillar of stone and salt until a spell was broken. My tongue ran thick with gravel. The syringe was useless, now, clogged with dust. I was alone with the comfort of the hisses and the chimes, the soft breathing of the environmental system, and the hum of the mass spectrometer.

"Kate?"

Arjun stood at the door, hanging onto the lintel with whitened knuckles. He looked like hell. He sounded worse.

"You need to lie down," I said.

"Harper's using the pressure suit for Tran. I wanted to see if you were all right."

"I'm fine."

"Don't lie to me," he said. "Not after what we've been through."

I wiped tears from my eyes. "Why did you do it? Why did *Curtis* do it?"

Arjun pushed off the door and came close to me, close enough so I could smell him: rank sweat, wet exhaustion, the acrid overtones of a body in stress. I felt the panic in my throat again but did not pull away.

"It was my mother. It was *her*. I knew it with every fiber of my being. She wore the sari I remembered from when I was little, the one she gave away when we moved to Delhi." He coughed, and I heard the rattle of his damaged lungs. "I knew it was wrong. But I would have given up my life to see her again, the memory was so strong. And I nearly did."

"But you remembered. I *forgot*," I whispered. "I forgot the color of her eyes."

"We all forget," he said. "We have to. That's the only way forward."

"It's not right."

"You don't think memory can be a curse?" he said.

I didn't want to say it. I didn't want to hurt him. "Memory is all we have."

He paused, moving even closer to me. "And it nearly killed me, Kate. By forgetting, Harper thinks that you were able to poke a hole in the logic of the simulation. That your brain threw a fault, that it registered what was real and what was not. You *forgot*, and that's the only reason I'm alive. I'm grateful. Tran's grateful."

My stomach churned. "It hasn't even been a year. What kind of person am I, if I just *forget* her like this?"

"You have to," Arjun whispered.

I felt a wild anger inside me at his words, a bright, searing sunburn against my sternum. Forget Riley? Move on? How? I suddenly understood the rich with their golden recall and their fancy tactile AR routers, slogging through their aluminum lives in the shuddering skins of the past, kissing dust and eating dirt while the rest of us dug holes in the Moon until we died. Why did I have to forget, when they could live in their dreams until they died? Wouldn't I give anything to go back to Pasadena-that-was, every cent and bone and incandescent wish, even if my dreams were just lifeless stone and salt?

No. Arjun was right. Memory could be a curse. A weapon. I wanted their caviar brains to know what it was like to rot in the refugee camps. To drink down the pain I felt when I stared at the bones of dead California.

I would *make* them remember. It was Moon's night. I had time. I was a scientist. I would find a way to reprogram the router system to make them see the truth. I would make them understand Los Angeles and Mare Crisium and everything in-between, to take it all screaming, to leave their lungs heaving up anguish, drinking down a pain that would settle forever under the truth of their skin, unable to forget a past that could never live again.

A past that was dead.

Like Riley.

I gasped for recycled air. For what was left.

"Tell me about her," Arjun said.

"We were going to get married," I whispered. "She always smelled like cinnamon. We argued about the paint in the bedroom. She wanted green. I wanted grey. *Screw* grey. This fucking moon."

Arjun laughed, and I snorted down a sob.

"She—she made the worst coffee, but I'd drink it, see, because she made it for me, and she'd leave her boots by the door and I hated that, but she'd always be singing when she did it, so I'd forgive her every single time. She loved musicals, Arjun, and we were going to get married, and then—and then . . ."

I trailed off, unable to speak any longer.

"It's okay to move on," he whispered. "It's okay to begin again. It's okay to breathe. It's hard, but that's what we have to do. That's how it works, if we want to be alive. It's not a sin. It's how you saved us, Kate. That's how you saved us."

He wavered with exhaustion. Arjun wrapped his fingers around mine. His palm ached there, warm and sure and utterly real, and we cried there, human and warm, for a long time.

Ann Leckie is the author of the award-winning novel *Ancillary Justice*. She lives in St Louis.

THE JUSTIFIED

Ann Leckie

Het had eaten nothing for weeks but bony, gape-mawed fish—some of them full of neurotoxin. She'd had to alter herself so she could metabolize it safely, which had taken some doing. So when she ripped out the walsel's throat and its blood spurted red onto the twilit ice, she stared, salivary glands aching, stomach growling. She didn't wait to butcher her catch but sank her teeth into skin and fat and muscle, tearing a chunk away from its huge shoulder.

Movement caught her eye, and she sprang upright, walsel blood trickling along her jaw, to see Dihaut, black and silver, walking toward her across the ages-packed snow and ice. She'd have known her sib anywhere, but even if she hadn't recognized them, there was no mistaking their crescent-topped standard, Months and Years, tottering behind them on two thin, insectile legs.

But sib or not, familiar or not, Het growled, heart still racing, muscles poised for flight or attack. She had thought herself alone and unwatched. Had made sure of it before she began her hunt. Had Dihaut been watching her all this time? It would be like them.

For a brief moment she considered disemboweling Dihaut, leaving them dying on the ice, Months and Years in pieces beside them. But that would only put this off until her sib took a new body. Dihaut could be endlessly persistent when they wished, and the fact that they had come all the way to this frigid desert at the farthest reaches of Nu to find her suggested that the ordinary limits of that persistence—such as they were—could not be relied on. Besides, she and Dihaut had nearly always gotten along well. Still, she stayed on the alert, and did not shift into a more relaxed posture.

"This is the Eye of Merur, the Noble Dihaut!" announced Months and Years as Dihaut drew near. Its high, thready voice cut startlingly through the silence of the snowy waste.

"I know who they are," snarled Het.

The standard made a noise almost like a sniff. "I only do my duty, Noble Het."

Dihaut hunched their shoulders. Their face, arms, torso, and legs were covered with what looked like long, fine fur but, this being Dihaut, was likely feathers. Mostly black, but their left arm and leg, and part of their torso, were silver-white. "Hello, sib," they said. "Sorry to interrupt your supper. Couldn't you have fled someplace warmer?"

Het had no answer for this—she'd asked herself the same question many times in the past several years.

"I see you've changed your skin," Dihaut continued. "It does look odd, but I suppose it keeps you warm. Would you mind sharing the specs?" They shivered.

"It's clothes," said Het. "A coat, and boots, and gloves."

"Clothes!" Dihaut peered at her more closely. "I see. They must be very confining, but I suppose it's worth it to be warm. Do you have any you could lend me? Or could whoever supplied you with yours give me some, too?"

"Sorry," growled Het. "Not introducing you." Actually, she hadn't even introduced herself. She'd stolen the clothes, when the fur she'd grown hadn't kept her as warm as she'd hoped.

Dihaut made a wry "huh," their warm breath puffing from their mouth in a small cloud. "Well. I'm sorry to be so blunt." They gave a regretful smile, all Dihaut in its acknowledgment of the pointlessness of small talk. "I'm very sorry to intrude on whatever it is you're doing down here—I never was quite clear on why you left, no one was, except that you were angry about something. Which . . ." They shrugged. "If it were up to me"—they raised both finely feathered hands, gestured vaguely to the dead walsel with the silver one—"I'd leave you to it."

"Would you." She didn't even try to sound as though she believed them.

"Truly, sib. But the ruler of Hehut, the Founder and Origin of Life on Nu, the One Sovereign of This World, wishes for you to return to Hehut." At this, Months and Years waved its thin, sticklike arms as though underlining Dihaut's words. "She'd have sent others before me, but I convinced her that if you were brought back against your wishes, your presence at court would not be as delightful as usual." They shivered again. "Is there somewhere warmer we can talk?"

"Not really."

"I don't mean any harm to the people you've been staying with," said Dihaut.

"I haven't been staying with anyone." She gestured vaguely around with one blood-matted hand, indicating the emptiness of the ice.

"You must have been staying with someone, sib. I know there are no approved habitations here, so they must be unauthorized, but that's no concern of mine unless they should come to Merur's attention. Or if they have Animas. Please tell me, sib, that they don't have unauthorized Animas here? Because you know we'll have to get rid of them if they do, and I'd really like to just go right back to Hehut, where it's actually warm."

Unbidden, her claws extended again, just a bit. She had never spoken to the people who lived here, but she owed them. It was by watching them that she'd learned about the poisonous fish. Otherwise the toxin might have caught her off guard, even killed her. And then she'd have found herself resurrected again in Hehut, in the middle of everything she'd fled.

"They don't have Animas," she told Dihaut. "How could they?" When their bodies died, they died.

"Thank all the stars for that!" Dihaut gave a relieved, shivery sigh. "As long as they stay up here in this freezing desert with their single, cold lives, we can all just go on pretending they don't exist. So surely we can pretend they don't exist in their presumably warmer home?"

"Your standard is right behind you," Het pointed out. "Listening."

"It is," Dihaut agreed. "It always is. There's nowhere in the world we can really be away from Merur. We always have to deal with the One Ruler. Even, in the end, the benighted unauthorized souls in this forsaken place." They were, by now, shivering steadily.

"Can't she leave anyone even the smallest space?" asked Het. "Some room to be apart, without her watching? For just a little while?"

"It's usually us watching for her," put in Dihaut.

Het waved that away. "Not a single life anywhere in the world that she doesn't claim as hers. She makes *certain* there's nowhere to go!"

"Order, sib," said Dihaut. "Imagine what might happen if everyone went running around free to do whatever they liked with no consequences. And she *is* the Founder and Origin of Life on Nu."

"Come on, Dihaut. I was born on *Aeons*, just before Merur left the ship and came down to Nu. There were already people living here. I remember it. And even now it depends who you ask. Either Merur arrived a thousand years ago in *Aeons* and set about pulling land from beneath the water and creating humans, or else she arrived and brought light and order to humans she found living in ignorance and chaos. I've heard both from her own mouth at different times. And you know better. You're the historian."

They tried that regretful half smile again, but they were too cold to manage it. "I tell whichever story is more politic at the moment. And there are, after all, different sorts of truth. But please." They spread their hands, placatory. "I beg you. Come with me back to Hehut. Don't make me freeze to death in front of you."

"Noble Dihaut," piped their standard, "Eye of Merur, I am here. Your Anima is entirely safe."

"Yes," shivered Dihaut, "but there isn't a new body ready for me yet, and I hate being out of things for very long. Please, sib, let's go back to my flier. We can argue about all of this on the way back home."

And, well, now that Dihaut had found her, it wasn't as though she had much choice. She said, with ill grace, "Well fine, then. Where's your flier?"

"This way," said Dihaut, shivering, and turned. They were either too cold or too wise to protest when Het bent to grab the dead walsel's tusk and drag it along as she followed.

It rained in Hehut barely more often than it snowed in the icy waste Het had left, but rivers and streams veined Hehut under the bright, uninterrupted blue of the sky, rivers and streams that pooled here and there into lotus-veiled lakes and papyrus marshes, and the land was lush and green.

The single-lived working in the fields looked up as the shadow of Dihaut's flier passed over them. They made a quick sign with their left hands and turned back to the machines they followed. Small boats dotted the river that snaked through the fields, single-lived fishers hauling in nets, here and there the long, gilded barque of one of the Justified shining in the sun. The sight gave Het an odd pang—she had not ever been given much to nostalgia, or to dwelling on memories of her various childhoods, none of which to her recall had been particularly childish, but she was struck with a sudden, almost tangible memory of sunshine on her skin, and the sound of water lapping at the hull of a boat. Not, she was sure, a single moment but a composite of all the times she'd fled to the river, to fish, or walk, or sit under a tree and stare at the water flowing by. To be by herself. As much as she could be, anyway.

"Almost there," said Dihaut, reclined in their seat beside her. "Are you going to change?" They had shed their feathers on the flight here and now showed black and silver skin, smooth and shining.

Het had shed her coat, boots, and gloves but left her thick and shaggy fur. It would likely be uncomfortable in the heat, but she was reluctant to let go of it; she couldn't say why. "I don't think I have time."

"Noble Eyes of Merur," said Months and Years, upright at Dihaut's elbow, "we will arrive at Tjenu in fifteen minutes. The One Sovereign will see you immediately."

Definitely no time to change. "So urgent?" asked Het. "Do you know what this is about?"

"I have my suspicions." Dihaut shrugged one silver shoulder. "It's probably better if Merur tells you herself."

So this was something that no one—not even Merur's own Eyes—could safely talk about. There were times when Merur was in no mood to be tolerant of any suggestion that her power and authority might be incomplete, and at those times even admitting knowledge of some problem could end with one's Anima deleted altogether.

Tjenu came into view, its gold-covered facade shining in the hot sun, a wide, dark avenue of smooth granite stretching from its huge main doors straight across the gardens to a broad entrance in the polished white walls. The Road of Souls, the single-lived called it, imagining that it was the route traveled by the Animas of the dead on their way to judgment at Dihaut's hands. As large as the building was—a good kilometer on each of its four sides, and three stories high—most of Tjenu was underground. Or so Dihaut had told her. Het had only ever been in the building's sunlit upper reaches. At least while she was alive, and not merely an Anima awaiting resurrection.

Dihaut's flier set down within Tjenu's white walls, beside a willow-edged pond. Coming out, Het found Great Among Millions, her own standard, waiting, hopping from one tiny foot to the other, feathery fingers clenched into minuscule fists, stilled the next moment, its black pole pointing perfectly upright, the gold cow horns at its top polished and shining.

"Eye of Merur," it said, its voice high and thin. "Noble Het, the Justified, the Powerful, Servant of the One Sovereign of Nu. The Ruler of all, in her name of Self-Created, in her name of She Caused All to Be, in her name of She Listens to Prayers, in her name of Sustainer of the Justified, in her name of—"

"Stop," Het commanded. "Just tell me what she wants."

"Your presence, gracious Het," it said, with equanimity. Great Among Millions had been her standard for several lifetimes, and was used to her. "Immediately. Do forgive the appearance of impertinence, Noble Het. I only relay the words of the One Sovereign. I will escort you to your audience."

Months and Years, coming out of the flier, piped, "Great Among Millions, please do not forget the Noble Het's luggage."

"What luggage?" asked Het.

"Your walsel, Noble Eye," replied Months and Years, waving a tiny hand. "What's left of it. It's starting to smell."

"Just dispose of it," said Het. "I've eaten as much of it as I'm going to."

Great Among Millions gave a tiny almost-hop from one foot to the other, and stilled again. "Noble Het, you have been away from Tjenu, from Hehut itself, without me, for fifty-three years, two months, and three days." It almost managed to sound as though it was merely stating a fact, and not making a complaint. But not quite.

"It's good to see you again, too," Het said. Her standard unclenched its little fists and gestured toward the golden mass of Tjenu. "Yes," Het acknowledged. "Let's go."

The vast audience chamber of the One Sovereign of Nu was black-ceilinged, inlaid with silver and copper stars that shone in the light of the lamps below. Courtiers, officials, and supplicants, alone or in small scattered groups, murmured as Het passed. Of course. There was no mistaking her identity, furred and unkempt as she was—Great Among Millions followed her.

She crossed the brown, gold-flecked floor to where it changed, brown shading to blue and green in Merur's near presence, where one never set foot without direct invitation—unless, of course, one was an Eye, in which case one's place in the bright-lit vicinity of Merur was merely assumed, a privilege of status.

Stepping into the green, Great Among Millions tottering behind her, Het cast a surreptitious glance—habitual, even after so long away!—at those so privileged. And stopped, and growled. Among the officials standing near Merur, three bore her Eye. There were four Eyes; Het herself was one. Dihaut, who Het had left with their flier, was another. There should only have been two Eyes here.

"Don't be jealous, Noble Het," whispered Great Among Millions, its thready voice sounding in her ear alone. "You were gone so very long." Almost accusing, that sounded.

"She *replaced* me," Het snarled. She didn't recognize whoever it was who, she saw now, held an unfamiliar standard, but the Justified changed bodies so frequently. If there was a new Eye, why should Merur call on Het? Why not leave her be?

"And you left *me* behind," continued Great Among Millions. "Alone. They asked and asked me where you were and I did not know, though I wished to." It made a tiny, barely perceptible stomp. "They put me in a storeroom. In a box."

"Het, my Eye, approach!" Merur, calling from where she sat under her blue-canopied pavilion, alone but for those three Eyes, and the standards, and smaller lotus- and lily-shaped servants that always attended her.

And now, her attention turned from Merur's other Eyes, Het looked fully at the One Sovereign herself. Armless, legless, her snaking body cased in scales of gold and lapis, Merur circled the base of her polished granite chair of state, her upper body leaning onto the seat, her head standard human, her hair in dozens of silver-plaited braids falling around her glittering gold face. Her dark eyes were slit-pupiled.

Het had seen Merur take such a shape before—as well as taking new bodies at need or at whim, the Justified could to some degree alter a currently held body at will. But there were limits to such transformations, and it had been long, long centuries since Merur had taken this sort of body.

She should have concealed her surprise and prostrated herself, but instead she stood and stared as Great Among Millions announced, in a high, carrying voice, "The fair, the fierce, the Burning Eye of the One Sovereign of Nu, the Noble Het!"

"My own Eye!" said Merur. "I have need of you!"

Het could not restrain her anger, even in the face of the One Sovereign of Nu. "I count four Eyes in this court, Sovereign—those three over there, and the Noble Dihaut. There have always been four. Why should you need me to be a fifth?" Behind her, Great Among Millions made a tiny noise.

"I shed one body," admonished Merur, her voice faintly querulous, "only to reawaken and find you gone. For decades you did not return. Why? No one accused you of any dereliction of duty, let alone disloyalty. You had suffered no disadvantage; your place as my favored Eye was secure. And now, returning, you question my having appointed someone to fill the office you left empty! You would do better to save your anger for the enemies of Nu!"

"I can't account for my heart," said Het crossly. "It is as it is."

This seemed to mollify Merur. "Well, you always have had a temper. And it is this very honesty that I have so missed. Indeed, it is what I require of you!" Here Merur lowered her voice and looked fretfully from one side to the other, and the standards and flower-form servitors scuttled back a few feet. "Het, my Eye. This body is . . . imperfect. It will not obey me as it should, and it is dying, far sooner than it ought. I need to move to a new one."

"Already?" Het's skin prickled with unease.

"This is not the first time a body has grown imperfectly," Merur said, her voice low. "But I should have seen the signs long before I entered it. Someone must have concealed them from me! It is impossible that this has happened through mere incompetence.

"I have dealt with the technicians. I have rooted out any disloyalty in Tjenu. But I cannot say the same of all Hehut, let alone all of Nu. And this body of mine will last only a few months longer, but no suitable replacement, one untampered with by traitors, will be ready for a year or more. And I cannot afford to leave Nu rulerless for so long! My Eyes I trust—you and Dihaut, certainly, after all this time. The Justified are for the most part reliable, and the single-lived know that Dihaut will judge them. But I have never been gone for more than a few days at a time. If this throne is empty longer, it may encourage the very few wayward to stir up the single-lived, and if, in my absence, enough among the Justified can be led astray—no. I cannot be gone so long unless I am certain of order."

Dismayed, Het snarled. "Sovereign, what do you expect me to do about any of this?"

"What you've always done! Protect Nu. All trace of unrest, of disorder, must be prevented. You've rid Nu of rebellion before. I need you to do it again."

That shining silver river, the fishers, the lilies and birds had all seemed so peaceful. So much as they should be, when Het and Dihaut had flown in. "Unrest? What's the cause this time?"

"The cause!" Merur exclaimed, exasperated. "There is no *cause*. There never has been! The worthy I give eternal life and health; they need only reach out their hands for whatever they desire! The unworthy are here and gone, and they have all they need and occupation enough, or if not, well, they seal their own fate. There has never been any *cause*, and yet it keeps happening—plots, rumors, mutterings of discontent. My newest Eye"—Merur did not notice, or affected not to notice, Het's reaction to that—"is fierce and efficient. I do not doubt her loyalty. But I am afraid she doesn't have your imagination. Your vision. Your *anger*. Two years ago I sent her out to deal with this, and she returned saying there was no trouble of any consequence! She doesn't *understand*! Where does this keep coming from? Who is planting such ideas in the minds of my people? Root it out, Het. Root it out from among my people, trace it back to its origin, and destroy it so that Nu can rest secure while my next body grows. So that we can at last have the peace and security I have always striven for."

"Sovereign of Nu," growled Het. "I'll do my best."

What choice did she have, after all?

She should have gone right to Dihaut. The first place to look for signs of trouble would be among the Animas of the recently dead. But she was still out of sorts with Dihaut, still resented their summoning her back here. They'd made her share their company on the long flight back to Hehut and never mentioned that Merur had *replaced* her. They might have warned her, and they hadn't. She wasn't certain she could keep her temper with her sib, just now. Which maybe was why they'd kept silent about it, but still.

Besides, that other Eye had doubtless done the obvious first thing, and gone to Dihaut herself. And to judge from what Merur had said, Dihaut must have found nothing, or nothing to speak of. They would give Het the same answer. No point asking again.

She wanted time alone. Time that was hers. She didn't miss the cold— already her thick fur was thinning without any conscious direction on her part. But she did miss the solitude, and the white landscape stretching out seemingly forever, silent except for the wind and her own heart, the hiss of blood in her ears. There was nothing like that here.

She left Tjenu and walked down to the river in the warm early-evening sunlight. Willows shaded the banks, and the lilies in the occasional pool, red and purple and gold, were closing. The scent of water and flowers seized her, plucking at the edges of some memory. Small brown fishing boats sat in neat rows on the opposite bank, waiting for morning. The long, sleek shape of some Justified Noble's barque floated in the middle of the channel, leaf green, gilded, draped with hangings and banners of blue and yellow and white.

She startled two children chasing frogs in the shallows. "Noble," the larger of them said, bowing, pushing the smaller child beside them into some semblance of a bow. "How can we serve you?"

Don't notice my presence, she thought, but of course that was impossible. "Be as you were. I'm only out for a walk." And then, considering the time, "Shouldn't you be home having dinner?"

"We'll go right away," said the older child.

The smaller, voice trembling, said, "Please don't kill us, Noble Het."

Het frowned, and looked behind her, only to see Great Among Millions a short way off, peering at her from behind a screen of willow leaves. "Why would I do such a thing?" Het asked the child. "Are you rebels, or criminals?"

The older child grabbed the younger one's arm, held it tight. "The Noble Het kills who she pleases," they said. The smaller child's eyes filled with tears. Then both children prostrated themselves. "How fair is your face, beautiful Het!" the older child cried into the mud. "The powerful, the wise and loving Eye of the One Sovereign! You see everything and strike where you wish! You were gone for a long time, but now you've returned and Hehut rejoices."

She wanted to reassure them that she hadn't come down to the river to kill them. That being late for dinner was hardly a capital offense. But the words wouldn't form in her mouth. "I don't strike where I wish," she said instead. "I strike the enemies of Nu."

"May we go, beautiful one?" asked the elder child, and now their voice was trembling too. "You commanded us to go home to dinner, and we only want to obey you!"

She opened her mouth to ask this child's name, seized as she was with a sudden inexplicable desire to mention it to Dihaut, to ask them to watch for this child when they passed through judgment, to let Dihaut know she'd been favorably impressed. So well-spoken, even if it was just a hasty assemblage of formulaic phrases, of songs and poetry they must have heard. But she feared asking would only terrify the child further. "I'm only out for a walk, child," she growled, uncomfortably resentful of this attention, even as she'd enjoyed the child's eloquence. "Go home to dinner."

"Thank you, beautiful one!" The elder child scrambled to their feet, pulled the smaller one up with them.

"Thank you!" piped the smaller child. And they both turned and fled. Het watched them go, and then resumed her walk along the riverside. But the evening had been soured, and soon she turned back to Tjenu.

The Thirty-Six met her in their accustomed place, a chamber in Tjenu walled with malachite and lapis, white lily patterns laid into the floor. There were chairs and benches along the edge of the room, but the Thirty-Six stood stiff and straight in the center, six rows of six, white linen kilts perfectly pressed, a gold and silver star on each brow.

"Eye of Merur," said the first of the Thirty-Six. "We're glad you're back."

"They're glad you're back," whispered Great Among Millions, just behind Het's right shoulder. "*They* didn't spend the time in a box."

Each of the Thirty-Six had their own demesne to watch, to protect. Their own assistants and weapons to do the job with. They had been asked to do this sort of thing often enough. Over and over.

Het had used the walk here from the river to compose herself. To take control of her face and her voice. She said, her voice smooth and calm, "The One Ruler of Nu, Creator of All Life on Nu, wishes for us to remove all traces of rebellion, once and for all. To destroy any hint of corruption that makes even the thought of rebellion possible." No word from the silent and still Thirty-Six. "Tell me, do you know where that lies?"

No reply. Either none of them knew, or they thought the answer so obvious that there was no need to say it. Or perhaps they were suspicious of Het's outward calm.

Finally, the first of the Thirty-Six said, "Generally, problems begin among the single-lived, Noble Het. But we can't seem to find the person, or the thing, that sends their hearts astray time after time. The only way to accomplish what the One Sovereign has asked of us would be to kill every single-lived soul on Nu and let Dihaut sort them one from another."

"Are you recommending that?" asked Het.

"It would be a terrible disruption," said another of the Thirty-Six. "There would be so many corpses to dispose of."

"We'd want more single-lived, wouldn't we?" asked yet another. "Grown new, free of the influence that corrupts them now. It might . . ." She seemed doubtful. "It might take care of the problem, but, Eye of Merur, I don't know how many free tanks we have. And who would take care of the new children? It would be a terrible mess that would last for decades. And I'm not sure that . . . It just seems wrong." She cast a surreptitious glance toward the first of the Thirty-Six. "And forgive me, Noble Eye of Merur, but surely the present concern of the One Sovereign is to reduce chaos and disorder. At the current moment."

So that, at least, was well-enough known, or at least rumored. "The newest Eye," said Het, closing her still-clawed hands into fists, willing herself to stand still. Willing her voice to stay clear and calm. Briefly she considered leaving here, going back to the river to catch fish and listen to the frogs. "Did she request your assistance? And did you suggest this to her, the eradication of the single-lived so that we could begin afresh?"

"She thought it was too extreme," said the first of the Thirty-Six. Was that a note of disappointment in her voice? "It seems to me that the Sovereign of Nu found that Eye's service in this instance to be less than satisfactory."

"You think we should do it?" Het asked her.

"If it would rid us of the trouble that arises over and over," the first of the Thirty-Six agreed.

"If I order this, then," Het persisted, clenching her hands tighter, "you would do it?"

"Yes," the foremost of the Thirty-Six agreed.

"Children, as well?" Het asked. Didn't add, *Even polite, well-spoken children who maybe only wanted some time to themselves, in the quiet by the river?*

"Of course," the first of the Thirty-Six replied. "If they're worthy, they'll be back. Eventually."

With a growl Het sprang forward, hands open, claws flashing free of her fingertips, and slashed the throat of the first of the Thirty-Six. As she fell, blood splashed onto the torso and the spotless linen kilt of the Thirty-Six beside her. For a moment, Het watched the blood pump satisfyingly out of the severed artery to pool on the white-lilied floor, and thought of the walsel she'd killed the day before.

But this was no time to indulge herself. She looked up and around. "Anyone else?"

Great Among Millions skittered up beside her. "Noble Het! Eye of Merur! There is currently a backlog of Justified waiting for resurrection. And none of your Thirty-Six have bodies in the tanks."

Het shrugged. The Thirty-Six were all among the Justified. "She'll be back. Eventually." At her feet the injured Thirty-Six breathed her choking last, and for the first time in decades Het felt a sure, gratifying satisfaction. She had been made for this duty, made to enjoy it, and she had nothing left to herself but that, it seemed. "The single-lived come and go," she declared to the remaining Thirty-Six. "Who has remained the same all this time?"

Silence.

"Oh, dear," said Great Among Millions.

The nurturing and protection of Nu had always required a good deal of death, and none of the Thirty-Six had ever been squeamish about it, but so often in recent centuries that death had been accomplished by impersonal, secondhand means—narrowly targeted poison, or engineered microbes let loose in the river. But Het—Het had spent the last several decades hunting huge, sharp-tusked walsel, two or three times the mass of a human, strong and surprisingly fast.

None of the remaining Thirty-Six would join her. Fifteen of them fled. The remaining twenty she left dead, dismembered, their blood pooling among the lilies, and then she went down to the riverbank.

The single-lived fled before her—or before Great Among Millions, not following discreetly now but close behind her, token and certification of who she was. The little fishing boats pulled hastily for the other bank, and their single-lived crews dropped nets and lines where they stood, ran from the river, or cowered in the bottom of their small craft.

Het ignored them all and swam for the blue-and-yellow barque.

The single-lived servants didn't try to stop her as she pulled herself aboard and strode across the deck. After all, where Het went the necessities of order followed. Opposing the Eye of Merur was not only futile, but suicidal in the most ultimate sense.

Streaming river water, claws extended, Het strode to where the barque's Justified owners sat at breakfast, a terrified servant standing beside the table, a tray holding figs, cheese, and a bowl of honey shaking in her trembling hands.

The three Justified stared at Het as she stood before them, soaking wet, teeth bared. Then they saw Great Among Millions close behind her. "Protector of Hehut," said one, a man, as all three rose. "It's an honor." There was, perhaps, the smallest hint of trepidation in his voice. "Of course we'll make all our resources available to you. I'll have the servants brought—"

Het sprang forward, sliced open his abdomen with her claws, then tore his head from his neck. She made a guttural, happy sound, dropped the body, and tossed the head away.

The servant dropped the tray and fled, the bowl of honey bouncing and rolling, fetching up against the corpse's spilled, sliced intestines.

Het sank her teeth into the second Justified's neck, felt him struggle and choke, the exquisite salt tang of his blood in her mouth. This was oh, so much better than hunting walsel. She tore away a mouthful of flesh and trachea.

The third Justified turned to flee, but then stopped and cried, "I am loyal, Noble Eye! The Noble Dihaut will vindicate me!"

Het broke her neck and then stood a moment contemplating the feast before her, these three bodies, warm and bloody and deliciously fresh. She hadn't gotten to do this often enough, in recent centuries. She lifted her head and roared her satisfaction.

A breeze filled and lifted the barque's blue and yellow and white linen hangings. The servants had fled; there was no one alive on the deck but Het and Great Among Millions now. "Rejoice!" it piped. "The Protector of Hehut brings order to Nu!"

Het grinned, and then dove over the side, into the river, on her way to find more of the Justified.

The day wore on, and more of the Justified met bloody, violent ends at Het's hands—and teeth. At first they submitted; after all, they were Justified, and their return was assured, so long as they were obedient subjects of the One Sovereign. But as evening closed in, the Justified began to try to defend themselves.

And more of the houses were empty, their owners and servants fled. But in this latest, on the outskirts of Hehut, all airy windowed corridors and courtyards, Het found two Justified huddled in the corner of a white-and-gold-painted room, a single-lived servant standing trembling between them and Het.

"Move," growled Het to the servant.

"Justification!" cried one of the Justified. Slurring a bit—was she drunk?

"We swear!" slurred the other. Drunk as well, then.

Neither of them had the authority to make such a promise. Even if they had, the numbers of Justified dead ensured that no newly Justified would see resurrection for centuries, if ever. Despite all of this, the clearly terrified servant stayed.

Het roared her anger. Picked up the single-lived—they were strong, and large as single-lived went, but no match for Het. She set them aside, roughly, and sank her claws into one of the Justified, her teeth into the other. Screams filled her ears, and blood filled her mouth as she tore away a chunk of flesh.

All day her victims had provided her with more than her fill of blood, and so she had drunk sparingly so far. But now, enraged even further by the cowardice of these Justified—of their craven, empty promise to their servant—she drank deep, and still filled with rage, she tore the Justified into bloody fragments that spattered the floor and the wall.

She stopped a moment to appreciate her handiwork. With one furred hand she wiped blood and scraps of muscle off her tingling lips.

Her tingling lips.

The two Justified had barely moved, crouched in their corner. They had slurred their speech, as though they were drunk.

Or as though they were poisoned.

She knew what sort of poison made her lips tingle like this, and her fingertips, now she noticed. Though it would take far more neurotoxin to make her feel this much than even a few dozen skinny, gape-mawed fish would provide. How much had she drunk?

Het looked around the blood-spattered room. The single-lived servant was gone. Great Among Millions stood silent and motionless, its tall, thin body crusted with dried blood. Nothing to what covered Het.

She went out into the garden, with its pools and fig trees and the red desert stretching beyond. And found two of Merur's lily standards—She Brings Life and Different Ages. Along with Months and Years. And Dihaut.

"Well, sib," they said, with their regretful smile. "They always send me after you. Everyone else is too afraid of you. I told the One Sovereign it was better not to send forces you'd only chew up. Poison is much easier, and much safer for us."

Het swayed, suddenly exhausted. Dihaut. She'd never expected them to actively take her side, when it came to defying Merur, but she hadn't expected them to poison her.

What *had* she expected? That Merur would approve her actions? No, she'd known someone would come after her, one way or another. And then?

"You can try to alter your metabolism," Dihaut continued, "but I doubt you can manage it quickly enough. The dose was quite high. We needed to be absolutely sure. Honestly, I'm surprised you're still on your feet."

"You," said Het, not certain what she had to say beyond that.

She Gives Life and Different Ages skittered up and stopped a meter or so apart, facing Het. Between them an image of Merur flickered into visibility. Not snakelike, as Het knew her current body to be, but as she appeared in images all over Nu: tall, golden, face and limbs smooth and symmetrical, as though cut from basalt and gilded.

"Het!" cried Merur. "My own Eye! What can possibly have made you so angry that you would take leave of your senses and betray the life and peace of Nu in this way?"

"I was carrying out your orders, Sovereign of Nu!" Het snarled. "You wanted me to remove all possibility of rebellion in Hehut."

"And all of Nu!" piped Great Among Millions, behind Het. Still covered in dried blood.

"I had not thought such sickness and treason possible from anyone Justified as long as you have been," said Merur. "Dihaut."

"Sovereign," said Dihaut, and their smile grew slightly wider. Het growled.

Merur said, "You have said to me before today that I have been too generous. That I have allowed too many of the long-Justified to escape judgment. I did not believe you, but now, look! My Eyes have not been subject to judgment in centuries, and that, I think, has been a mistake. I would like it known that not even the highest of the Justified will be excused if they defy me. Het, before you die, hear Dihaut's judgment."

She was exhausted, and her lips had gone numb. But that was all.

Was she really poisoned? Well, she was, but only a little. Or so it seemed, so far. Maybe she could overpower Dihaut, rip out their throat, and flee. The standards wouldn't stop her.

And then what? Where would she go, that Merur would not eventually follow?

"Sovereign of Nu," said Dihaut, bowing toward Merur's simulacrum. "I will do as you command." They turned to Het. "Het, sib, your behavior this past day is extreme even for you. It calls for judgment, as our Sovereign has said. It is that judgment that keeps order in Hehut, on all of Nu. And perhaps if everyone, every life, endured the same strict judgment as the single-lived pass through, these things would never have happened."

Silence. Not a noise from Great Among Millions, behind Het. Over Dihaut's shoulder, Months and Years was utterly still.

"The One Sovereign has given me the duty of making those judgments. And I must make them, no matter my personal feelings about each person I judge, for the good of Nu."

"That is so," agreed Merur's simulacrum.

"Then from now on, everyone—single-lived or Justified, whoever they may be—every Anima that passes through Tjenu must meet the same judgment. No preference will be given to those who have been resurrected before, not in judgment, and not in the order of resurrection. From now on everyone must meet judgment equally. Including the Sovereign of Nu."

The simulacrum of Merur frowned. "I did not hear you correctly just now, Dihaut."

They turned to Merur. "You've just said that it was a mistake not to subject your Eyes to judgment, and called on me to judge Het. But I can't judge her without seeing that what she has done to the Justified this past day is only what you have always asked her to do to the single-lived. She has done precisely what you demanded of her. It wasn't the fact that Het was unthreatened by judgment that led her to do these things—it was you, yourself."

"You!" spat Merur's simulacrum. "You dare to judge me!"

"You gave me that job," said Dihaut, Months and Years still motionless behind them. "And I will do it. You won't be resurrected on Nu without passing my judgment. I have made certain of this, within the past hour."

"Then it was you behind this conspiracy all along!" cried Merur. "But you can't prevent me returning. I will awake on *Aeons*."

"*Aeons* is far, far overhead," observed Het, no less astonished at what she'd just heard than by the fact that she was still alive.

"And there was no conspiracy," said Dihaut. "Or there wasn't until you imagined one into being. Your own Eyes told you as much. But this isn't the first time you've demanded the slaughter of the innocent so that you can feel more secure. Het only gave me an opportunity, and an example. I will do as you command me. I will judge. Withdraw to *Aeons* if you like. The people who oversee your resurrection on Nu, who have the skills and the access, won't be resurrected themselves until you pass my judgment." They gave again that half-regretful smile. "You've already removed some of those who would have helped you, when you purged Tjenu of what you assumed was disloyalty to you, Sovereign." The image of Merur flickered out of sight, and She Brings Life and Different Ages scuttled away.

"I'm not poisoned," said Het.

"I should hope not!" exclaimed Dihaut. "No, you left your supper, or your breakfast, or whatever it was, on my flier. I couldn't help being curious about it." They shrugged. "There wasn't much of that neurotoxin in the animal you left behind, but there was enough to suggest that something in that food chain was very toxic. And knowing you, you'd have changed your metabolism rather than just avoid eating whatever it was. Merur, of course, didn't know that. So when she said she wanted you stopped, I made the suggestion . . . " They waved one silver hand.

"So all that business with the single-lived servant, promising her Justification if she would defend those two . . . "

"This late in the day the Justified were already beginning to resist you—or try, anyway," Dihaut confirmed, with equanimity. "If these had stood meekly as you slaughtered them, you might have suspected something. And you might not have drunk enough blood to feel the poison. I had to make you even more angry at the people you killed than you already were."

Het growled. "So you *tricked* me."

"You're not the only one of Merur's Eyes, sib, to find that if you truly served in the way you were meant to, you could no longer serve Merur's aims. It's been a long, long time since I realized that for all Merur says I'm to judge the dead with perfect, impartial wisdom, I can never do that so long as she rules here. She has always assumed that her personal good is the good of Nu. But those are not the same thing. Which I think you have recently realized."

"And now *you'll* be Sovereign over Nu," Het said. "Instead of Merur."

"I suppose so," agreed Dihaut. "For the moment, anyway. But maybe not openly—it would be useful if Merur still called herself the One Sovereign but stayed above on *Aeons* and let us do our jobs without interference." They shrugged again and gave that half smile of theirs. "Maybe she can salvage her pride by claiming credit for having tricked you into stopping your over-enthusiastic obedience, and saving everyone. In fact, it might be best if she can pretend everything's going on as it was before. We'll still be her Eyes at least in name, and we can make what changes we like."

Het would have growled at them again, but she realized she was too tired. It had been a long, long day. "I don't want to be anyone's Eye. I want to be out of this." She didn't miss the cold, but she wanted that solitude. That silence. Or the illusion of it, which was all she'd really had. "I want to be somewhere that isn't here."

"Are you sure?" Dihaut asked. "You've become quite popular among the single-lived, today. They call you beautiful, and fierce, and full of mercy."

She thought of the children by the river. "It's meaningless. Just old poetry rearranged." Still she felt it, the gratification that Dihaut had surely meant her to feel. She was glad that she'd managed to spare those lives. That the single-lived of Hehut might remember her not for having slaughtered so many of them, but for having spared their lives. Or perhaps for both. "I want to go."

"Then go, sib." Dihaut waved one silver hand. "I'll make sure no one troubles you."

"And the unauthorized lives there? Or elsewhere on Nu?"

"No one will trouble them either," Dihaut confirmed equably. "So long as they don't pose a threat to Hehut. They never did pose a threat to Hehut, only to Merur's desire for power over every life on Nu."

"Thank you." Her skin itched, her fur growing thicker just at the thought of the cold. "I don't think I want you to come get me. When I die, I mean. Or at least, wait a while. A long time." Dihaut gestured assent, and Het continued, "I suppose you'll judge me, then. Who'll judge you, when the time comes?"

"That's a good question," replied Dihaut. "I don't know. Maybe you, sib. Or maybe by then no one will have to pass my judgment just to be allowed to live. We'll see."

That idea was so utterly alien to Het that she wasn't sure how to respond to it. "I want some peace and quiet," she said. "Alone. Apart." Dihaut gestured assent.

"Don't leave me behind, Noble Het!" piped Great Among Millions. "Beautiful Het! Fierce Het! Het full of mercy! I don't want them to put me in a box in a storeroom again!"

"Come on, then," she said, impatiently, and her standard skittered happily after her as she went to find a flier to take her away from Hehut, back to the twilit ice, and to silence without judgment.

Annalee Newitz writes science fiction and nonfiction. They are the author of the book *Four Lost Cities: A Secret History of the Urban Age*, and the novels *The Future of Another Timeline*, and *Autonomous*, which won the Lambda Literary Award. As a science journalist, they are a contributing opinion writer for the *New York Times*, and have a monthly column in *New Scientist*. They have published in *The Washington Post, Slate, Popular Science, Ars Technica, The New Yorker*, and *The Atlantic*, among others. They are also the co-host of the Hugo Award-winning podcast Our Opinions Are Correct. Previously, they were the founder of *io9*, and served as the editor-in-chief of *Gizmodo*.

OLD MEDIA

Annalee Newitz

August 2, 2145

They were in the back room making out. What else were they supposed to do on a slow afternoon when nobody came into the store? Michael had taken his goggles off and John was kissing the soft skin of his eyelids while simultaneously groping for some kind of access point into Michael's extremely tight pants.

Out front, Bella was reading the music feeds in her goggles and not even remotely pretending to ignore them.

"You sound like rutting *moosen*!" She'd taken to using a fake plural form of "moose" for her own whimsical reasons. "Don't get any fluids on the goddamn merchandise!"

For some reason, John could not stop laughing at the moose plural joke. Every time he caught his breath, another fit of giggling would rob him of it, until at last he sank dizzily to his knees. He steadied himself by hooking fingers into Michael's waistband and looking up at his friend, also laughing, amused by John's amusement.

Michael was studying paleontology at the University of Saskatchewan, and had been trying to grow authentic dinosaur feathers on his head for weeks. Thick red and white down stuck out of his pale blond hair on flexible quills, perfectly framing his wide blue eyes and the short puff of his beard. John thought the full effect made him look almost comically Western, like an English barbarian from the old anime feeds he liked to watch.

But it was also kind of sexy. And here he was, right in the perfect spot to unlock the grippers holding Michael's tight pants in place. Even when Bella started making extremely realistic moose noises, John was undeterred in his quest to make Michael tremble with more than laughter.

Afterward they both slid to the floor, resting their slightly damp backs against the wall. A languid sense of goodwill spread from John's extremities upward to his brain. He liked it back here beyond the Employees Only sign, staring at the dusty, half-biodegraded boxes of recent arrivals. Bella bought most of her merchandise from estate sales and warehouses on the prairies, but a lot came from customers in Saskatoon too. Tuesdays and Thursdays were buyer days, and there was always a boisterous line of what seemed to John a completely random assortment of people: aging hipsters with party clothes from the '20s; college students wanting to trade armor for shreds or vice versa; grandmothers with unbelievable treasures like the ash pleather 2090s boots he was wearing right now; and people from far up north who'd heard the kids were obsessed with old all-weathers and wanted to make a few credits while their families loaded up on supplies at the farm co-op.

It made John think of times before he was born, long before his shit life, or at least the shitty parts of his relatively okay life. Last year at this time . . . he didn't want to think about it. Every night he told himself he was safe now, gone legit with a name and a franchise. Nobody owned him anymore. He stared harder at a box overflowing with self-repairing scarves from indeterminate time periods. Maybe they were made yesterday. Maybe sixty years ago.

Michael was nuzzling his neck, dinofuzz tickling John's ear. He tugged John's collar down to get a better angle and made a murmuring noise when he saw the brand.

"I like your sexy scar. What do these numbers mean? Zed-nine-one-four-three-zed?"

John pulled away and felt every muscle in his body stiffen. The familiar numbness oozed down his neck into his torso, killing contentment as it spread.

"It's nothing. Just from when I was young and stupid."

"Is it a special date or something?"

"That was my identification number when I was a slave, sweetie. Didn't you know?" John made his tone so sarcastic that Michael snorted out a chuckle. Sometimes the truth, told right, was the best lie.

Beyond the door, John heard the sound of customers—a big group, their voices merging into a wave of indistinct, excited sounds. Probably party shopping. Bella might need help. He stood up abruptly and left Michael lounging among piles of textiles that proved the world had existed long before John was in it.

August 3, 2145

Until this past year, John never had access control over his own room. He and the other boys lived in the indenture school dormitory, and bedtime was when the supervisor wiped his hand over the lock and let them in. If he let them in. Sometimes there was a just-in-time job on a batch of engines, and they worked for twenty-four hours straight. He still sometimes felt an ache in his fingers from doing post-production on each part as it came out of the extruder in the icy 3-D printer room. Still, when they were back in the dorms, John usually figured out how to escape again. He wanted access to the public net, and there was one particular admin who had a weakness for brown boys from down south. John spent a lot of nights writing in the admin's cramped cubicle, mostly naked, focusing intently on comments in his journal feed so he could tune out his benefactor's creepy gaze.

But now he was here, sharing an apartment in Saskatoon with the only person on Earth who knew his old names: Threezed and Slaveboy. When he met Med last year, he confessed that he'd been writing a journal on Memeland under the name Slaveboy. It turned out she was a fan. He'd never actually met one of his followers in person, and decided impulsively that they would be friends forever. It turned out to be the best decision he'd ever made in his roughly twenty years on Earth.

The door clicked open as he arrived and whistled its "hello" tune. He and Med were supremely lazy about programming the place beyond the basics, so he kicked the wall to turn on the lights and start the kitchen. The warm indoor air smelled faintly of fish sauce and frying garlic from somewhere else in the building.

Maybe one day he'd get tired of the contours of this apartment with its minimal furnishings. But it was hard to imagine ever getting enough of its safe shape, the kitchen booting up alongside him and a slice of his bed visible beyond a mostly closed curtain. It was only when he was alone like this, in complete silence, that John allowed himself to believe he was still alive. The quiet was like one of those silver emergency blankets he'd seen in twentieth-century American movies. It was the way the fantastically kind police wrapped you up after they'd rescued everybody from the monsters, the fire, the tidal waves, the buildings falling from space, the evil robots, the shadow animals, and the ghosts of every dead person wronged by the living.

A memory invaded him, unbidden, like a hiccup of pain.

Last year, he'd found sanctuary in Saskatoon. John's new master wasn't like the other ones, at least in some ways. She was a scientist, and she was working on some kind of secret project with Med. He didn't understand everything about what they were doing, but he knew they were trying to help people who'd gotten addicted to corporate pharma. After the project went live, his master went into hiding. She left him behind with Med—but not before buying him a franchise that granted him full rights in the city. That night, he kept activating the readout from his chip on the mobile's login screen: *Enfranchised*. The English word morphed in his mind as he tried to feel its reality. *Enfranchised, enchanted, ineluctable, incredulous . . .*

Maybe the warm feeling in his back was actually a lack of feeling. A lack of fear. He had a vivid recollection of how the lab smelled in that moment of unburdening, a mixture of crushed grass and coffee.

That's when Med sat up rigidly, hands flat on the lab bench. She turned to him, her eyes blank. "Get out of here, now!" And then she stood, grabbed him with a shocking strength, and dragged him to the back exit. "Go!"

He glanced back to see what Med had sensed wirelessly: agents arriving, the ones who'd been chasing his old master. A man and a huge, armored bot from the property police. He turned back just once before he fled, and thought he saw Med transform into an avenging angel. Only she was better than an angel. She was real, made of carbon alloy and flesh, not feathers and faith. She'd saved him. Possibly she'd even saved the world.

John breathed shallowly, trying to make himself as soundless as the room. Nobody could hear him. He was safe. It wasn't like last time; the agents were long gone. He held his breath for five serene seconds before the Yummy Pan made an irritated noise and he knew he should start making dinner.

He was scooping protein-flecked porridge into a bowl when Med opened the door. She looked like a textbook example of the absent-minded professor, blond hair perfectly pinned back and lab coat perfectly rumpled.

"How nice that you're eating tissue from extinct amphibians." Med could identify almost anything by smell, though she rarely mentioned it around humans. It made them too self-conscious, especially when they realized her abilities extended to smelling where they had been—and sometimes even their emotional states.

Still, for all her robot superpowers, Med couldn't really master the art of sarcasm. Partly that was because she wasn't a very sarcastic person, and partly because John always did something silly to undermine her deadpan cool.

"I love fake frog." He took an exaggeratedly large bite. "Mmmm, the taste of synthetic biology." He posed with the spoon and bowl next to his face, like the preternaturally cheerful kid in the ads for Yummy Pan. For some reason, it never failed to make Med grin. Her goofy expression hovered briefly over his memory of that long-ago divine fury, and John had to pull himself back sharply from giving a name to what she made him feel.

August 4, 2145

The library's Media Experience Lab was the result of some big grant the university got back in the 2120s, and it hadn't been updated since. The signs were all done in those old animated fonts that switched back and forth between puffy rainbow letters and classical serif typefaces. Foam chairs, once luxuriously padded and tricked out with knobs for adjusting everything to ergonomic perfection, were mashed into submission, stuck in awkward positions that only worked for really tall people or really short ones who wanted to sit bolt upright. Somebody had made the streaming cubicles out of fake recycled materials, so you could watch twenty-first century immersives while surrounded by biofibers imitating plastic imitating wood. John thought the saddest part of the whole retro setup—but also possibly the most adorable— was the dusty Innerfire cube, installed when everybody thought full-body experience implants were right around the corner. In all his months coming here, he had never seen anyone go inside.

John slid into his favorite booth next to the back wall. He could watch everyone coming in while also keeping an eye on his monitor, currently streaming a century-old comedy anime called *Ouran High School Host Club*. He liked the story, about a girl named Haruhi pretending to be a boy, learning all the bizarre things boys do to make themselves seem more attractive. Haruhi was so charming in her suit and tie that all the girls requested "him" at the host club. She had no choice but to keep up the charade, because she was a poor scholarship student at an elite high school, and she owed the other hosts money. John swept a few of the episodes onto his mobile, stashing them to show Med later as yet another example of weird human culture.

After two quarters auditing classes, John was going to matriculate as a freshman. It still didn't feel real. The city franchise got you more than he ever imagined he'd have, back when he was slaved to the factory. Free education, free medical, free net connection, and freedom to live and work anywhere in the Saskatoon metropolitan area. A new implant that broadcast his new identity: John Chen, normal free boy from an exurb called Lucky Lake. No indenture record. No record at all, other than a secure enclave bioprocessor that verified his identity to the city co-op.

Out of the blankness of his digital past he'd made an entire imaginary history for himself, in case anyone asked. Homeschooled, he would say. Mostly worked on agricultural bot repair, keeping the sensors, planters, and harvesters updated with the latest patches and hardware tweaks. At twenty-one, he was older than average for a student, but he fit the profile of a farm kid whose family needed a little extra time to raise the credits for his Saskatoon franchise.

So far, nobody had questioned this story. In fact, the most awkward moment he'd had was when Michael wondered about the brand that contained his slave name: Threezed, for the last two numbers in the sequence.

John should have gotten the scars smoothed out a long time ago. But he wasn't ready to lose the familiar sting of seeing those numbers in the mirror when everything else was so different. Nothing had been normal for three years, after the factory sent the whole indenture class across the Pacific. Supposedly they had maintenance positions waiting for them on the Vancouver docks. The motors they'd been assembling back in the Nine Cities Delta were used in all kinds of industrial bots, so it made sense. But when they arrived, it turned out the contracts had fallen through in a way that only made sense to bureaucrats. John and his classmates were confiscated by the Free Trade Zone Port Authority, then confiscated again by Vancouver's child welfare agency. In practice, this meant they spent a few months sleeping in familiar-looking dormitories where they tried to perfect their northern Free Trade Zone English accents.

For probably the fiftieth time, one of the hosts in *Ouran High School Host Club* was reminding Haruhi that she was low class. She'd brought instant coffee to their elite party, and the rich kids were physically repulsed. They'd never had anything but whole beans ground by indentured servants. John loved the exaggerated faces they made, their features growing bulbous and abstract as they squealed in dismay. Haruhi shrugged it off, but John thought the audience was supposed to understand that her feelings were hurt too.

A new librarian came in and sat behind the help desk. Her presence activated a sign overhead in that absurdly morphing font: "Yes, I'm an actual human! Ask me anything!" John imagined what Med would say to that. Just a little anti-bot sentiment, brought to you by some designer in the 2120s. Not the librarian's fault. John noticed that she had two thick black braids and her eyes were slightly distorted by a pair of goggles made to look like twenty-first century glasses. Something about her looked familiar. Maybe she'd been in one of his classes?

He kept watching the stream in his cubicle until it was almost closing time.

"Do you want to check that out?" The librarian peeked over the top of his cubicle. "I have to start shutting the workstations down." Then she glanced at him again. "Weren't you in Social Media History with me?"

"Yeah. What did you think of that class?"

"I loved it. I'm actually doing a research project with that professor about anti-robot representations in the late twenty-first century. So much video from that time was basically anti-automation propaganda, designed to make humans fear bots. It's so weird to look back on all this old media and see how it's still affecting us now."

"Like that sign." He pointed over her desk.

"Exactly!" She grinned.

He liked the way she described struggles in the past as if they were still happening, unfolding at some layer of reality just beyond conscious perception. They started talking about what classes they'd be taking next term.

He was about to escalate into flirtation when a man raced into the library, out of breath. He ignored John and put a hand on the librarian's arm. "Can you find me some videos of people playing games in the twentieth century? I really need them for tomorrow."

She stiffened and pulled back from his touch. "Do you have a catalog number?"

After he'd made a big show of sighing and pulling out his mobile and searching, the student flicked a number to her tablet.

The librarian walked back to her desk to look up the videos and the man leaned heavily on John's cubicle, still catching his breath. Finally, he seemed to notice that he wasn't alone in the universe.

"Oh, hi, sorry to interrupt." His voice betrayed no hint of apology.

"No worries." John started to pack up.

The man looked at him more closely, his pale blue eyes like flecks of aluminum-doped glass. "Where you from?"

"Farm outside Lucky Lake."

The man gave a big-throated laugh that vacuumed geniality out of the air. "No. I mean, where are you from *originally*?"

It was a menacing question. John grabbed some videos with a cupping gesture, dumped them onto his mobile, and left without a word.

When he'd first arrived in the Zone, people were constantly asking him where he was from. John and his classmates tried to explain, but nobody could hear anything after the words "Asian Union." Their words bounced off an invisible, soundproof barrier of sympathy and disgust. Worried-looking officials kept telling the boys that it was illegal for children to be indentured. They never should have found themselves in this situation, sold by their school into contract at the docks. They could rest assured that Vancouver would sponsor them into foster care, with limited franchises that would allow them to work for the city. The Zone would never mistreat them the way the Asian Union had.

Then a caseworker "discovered" that they were over 18. John thought that was pretty amazing detective work, considering that none of the kids actually knew how old they were, and all their identity records were missing. Still, it was probably close enough, give or take a couple of years. Now it was obvious what Vancouver should do with them. They were shipped down to Vegas for auction. Profits would go to pay off the debt of some corporate entity whose name John would never know.

He was definitely going to convince Med to watch *Ouran High School Host Club* when she got back from the lab. Bots never slept, so she was pretty much always up for binge watching on their apartment projection wall.

After he kicked the lights on, John saved the videos to their home server with a tossing motion and collapsed on the springy sofa that dominated the room. He couldn't decide whether to activate the Yummy Pan or spark some 420 or run around screaming. That guy in the library had really pissed him off—not so much as an individual, but as the representative of an entire genre of dickbags who had never once been asked to produce an origin story for someone else's amusement. It reminded him uncomfortably of Michael's questions the other day. Obviously Michael had asked out of friendly curiosity, but the sentiment was the same. Where you come from is who you are.

The chime of the door interrupted his increasingly tight rage spiral. Med flopped on the sofa next to him and sighed. "That was a very long day of department meetings."

Med had been begging the administration for money to cover an update to the lab's protein library. John sat up to face her. "Did you get that funding you needed?"

"Ugh. No. They don't understand why we need new protein data when we already have a library from five years ago. Plus some bullshit from the dean about how I should make the students discover new folds themselves, and not just copy from a database like a bot would." Med rolled her eyes but John knew she was genuinely upset. The dean never missed a chance to make insulting comments about bots around Med. She was the only bot professor at the university, and the dean liked to remind her where she came from. Or maybe where she didn't.

"Well, I have some good distraction for you." John flicked the air and the wall opposite them displayed a menu of recent downloads. "It's this crazy anime from the 2000s about an indentured student who has to earn her way out of contract by pretending to be a hot boy at a café for high school girls. You *have* to watch it. It's so incredibly weird."

"You're lucky that the media library gets more useful the more out-of-date it gets."

"That's not exactly true. But yeah, I know what you mean." He decided not to tell her about the librarian sign. "Want to watch the first episode?"

Fifteen minutes in, and he could tell Med was feeling better. He watched her watch the screen, smiling faintly, her hand resting on the charger in the sofa arm. He wondered whether she was smiling for his benefit or if she really thought it was funny. Then he started obsessing about whether the subtitles really did justice to what was happening. Were they missing something? Maybe Med could help.

"Could you learn Japanese if you wanted to? Like just download it or something? Then we'd know if these subs were good."

"It's not like I would instantly know Japanese. I could get all the rules and vocabulary—enough to do a really basic translation. But I'd still have to learn how to use it. And some things just can't be translated with words at all." She gestured at the wall and the action froze on an image of light bulbs turning on. "Look at that. What does that mean? You only know from context that those light bulbs represent members of the host club, and each time one of them turns on it's the guy figuring out that Haruhi is a girl. I couldn't ever figure that out from a translation program."

John thought about that as the action started again and Haruhi tried on the fancy school uniform that made her look like a beautiful boy. There was a lot of confused swooning.

August 5, 2145

After three more episodes, John paused the action for a bathroom break. When he got back, Med was flipping through movies on the server idly. An urgent message blinked at the corner of the projection: "Streaming to unknown device." That meant Med was streaming previews straight to her mind. The humans who made the streamer hadn't thought about how robots might use their machines, so Med remained an "unknown device" on the network.

"How's job going?" Med divided her attention between John and whatever she was previewing.

"Pretty good. I keep hooking up with Michael, but he's starting to annoy me."

"I can't even keep track of your hookups. Which one is Michael, again?"

"Dinosaur hair guy."

"Oh yeah!" Med stopped streaming and took her hand off the charging pad. "He sounded nice?"

"He's nice but he's just . . . I dunno. He asks too many boring questions."

"Like what?"

John tried to come up with a good way to explain it. "He asked about my brand. Which—why would you ask somebody about that after fucking them? So rude."

Med didn't pick up on his sarcasm, or she chose to ignore it. "I can see why he might be curious. Why do you keep it if you don't want to talk about it?"

"Why do you tell people that you're a bot if you don't want them to make snotty comments about it?" His voice rose in anger he hadn't intended to express.

"You know why. Because fuck those fuckers." Delivered utterly without sarcasm. John had to laugh. She put a hand on his arm, and he felt an unexpected, shocking surge of love for her. Her skin felt just as soft and warm as a human's, but beneath the biological tissues were metal actuators and processors. He liked knowing that she wasn't human all the way through. Looking into her face, he never flashed back to the faces of his masters.

Yet he was still terrified. She was going to disappear. He'd wake up from this dream of student life in Saskatoon to find himself adrift with that psycho who bought him in Vegas, starving in the cargo hold of a boat whose engines were always on the verge of death. Tied up if he refused to go quietly to his master's bedroom. Or maybe he'd awaken to discover that Med hadn't made it out of the lab alive after shoving him out the door.

He needed to banish those thoughts. His skin was prickling. Med still had her hand on his arm, and a badass snarky look on her face.

"Med, why don't you ever hook up with anybody?"

The bot shrugged. "I haven't installed any programs related to sexual desire."

"Why not?"

"Just not interested. A lot of my siblings installed them, and they seem happy. But it never caught my attention."

"So you could install them now and start wanting to have sex?" John was fascinated.

Med looked a little annoyed. "As I said before about learning Japanese, it's not like a bot can just instantly know something or feel something. You have to interact to get context."

This was starting to sound kind of sexy. John wrapped his hand around Med's arm, so that they gently gripped each other's wrists. "You should do it. We should do it."

"I just said I wasn't interested."

"How can you know you're not interested if you've never tried it?"

She removed her hand and scooted back a few centimeters. "Can you explain why you don't like that series *Evolution's Dark Road* but you do like *Ouran High School Host Club*? It's a matter of taste. Sexual desire just isn't my taste. It doesn't mean I don't love you."

"You love me?" John's heart was pounding all of a sudden, in a way that was both amazing and terrifying.

"I wasn't planning on blurting it out like that, but yes. Yes."

He thought he was going to cry, and then he thought maybe he wasn't going to be able to stop himself from kissing her. "I'm pretty sure I love you too."

Illuminated by dim, white light from the text menu on the wall, they looked like artificial versions of themselves. John crumpled his hands into fists and jammed them against his thighs uncomfortably. He wasn't sure what to do next.

"So you can be in love but you don't want to try having sex?"

She chuckled. "I'm not a media history major, but even I have watched enough media to know that love and sex aren't the same thing."

Of course that was true, and he'd had plenty of sex that didn't involve love. But how could she be feeling the same way he was, if she didn't want to grab him hard and throw him down and just . . . take him? A feeling this strong had to be translated into something physical. It begged for literalization.

"I just don't understand. Do you mean the kind of love you would have for a brother? Or for a super good friend?"

"I do love my siblings, but this is not that kind of love. I mean, I can't be sure it's *exactly* the same thing you would call love, but it's a feeling of . . . " She paused for a moment and went still, as if she were streaming data. Then she spoke slowly. "It's like there's some part of you that fits perfectly inside my consciousness. It's a feeling that goes beyond trust or friendship. Some kind of emotional infrastructure. Even if I were to isolate every single utility and program I use to think about you, I don't think I could explain all the ways you occupy my mind. It's . . . an emergent and ongoing process. Does that make sense?"

John wiped his eyes and looked at her openly, following the lines of her neck and cheeks, the perfect lab-grown pink of her lips. But she'd given him permission to look beyond that.

"Is there something we could do together . . . something you've always wanted to do with somebody who loves you? Not sex, obviously, but something like that? Or not like that? I don't know . . . " He trailed off and Med looked bemused. "Please don't say watch videos." They both laughed.

Med put a hand on top of one of his fists, and he laced his fingers into hers.

"Actually there is something."

"Holding hands?"

"No, although that's nice too." She let out a nervous titter. "I've always wanted to try sleeping." She dropped her eyes and shifted uncomfortably, as if she'd just revealed some secret, transgressive kink.

"I didn't know you could sleep."

"I mean, I can go into sleep mode, or I can shut down. I can crash. There are a lot of sleep levels, but you're not really supposed to go into them unless it's an emergency or you need maintenance."

"Why aren't you supposed to do it?"

"Well sometimes it can damage memory to crash unexpectedly, but honestly I think the sleep taboo is mostly about security. Humans might steal a sleeping bot."

John understood that fear all the way down to the most inaccessible parts of his consciousness. "Nobody can get you here. Not in our apartment. It's completely safe." His words came out hot and intense, the same way they sounded in his mind.

"Do you want to try it?"

He said yes and let her lead him to the bedroom.

They lay down on their sides facing each other, giggling as they found comfortable positions in the awkwardly small space. "Okay, so I'm going to try. I should wake up in four hours so I can get to work in the morning. Are you ready?"

She looked so beautiful that John thought his heart would crack open like the space eggs in a kaiju movie, full of lava and lightning and life forms that had never walked the Earth. He took one of her hands. "I'm ready."

Her eyes closed, and she shuddered slightly. Then her hand relaxed in his. He listened to her breathe. He looked at the shape of her skin over the carbon alloy of her bones. He wondered if she was dreaming. He thought of all the questions he wanted to ask her about everything. He almost started to cry again when he remembered what they'd been through last year, after they'd escaped. After they'd almost died. If he were ever going to talk about all that shit, Med would be the only person he'd want listening.

Watching her sleep for a while made him sleepy too. She never shifted around or made noises like a human, and it was deeply comforting.

John rolled onto his back and closed his eyes. He was still kind of horny, partly from the emotional overload with Med, and partly just from life. At least he was working in the shop tomorrow, so there would definitely be an interlude or two with Michael in the back room. Also, maybe he would ask out that librarian from his Social Media History class. He wasn't sure he could love anyone else, but there were definitely a lot of people he liked in a sexual way. That wasn't a bad thing.

As he drifted off, his thoughts began to buzz pleasantly with half-feelings and fragments of the day's noise. Just before he joined Med in full sleep mode, he saw a flickering image of Haruhi in her host boy clothes, the subject of a desire that existed only in the lacy cracks that form at the edge of what we're taught is acceptable. Even after a century of storage on media devices whose sophistication far outstripped the technologies that hosted her birth, she was still radiating beauty into the world.

Alec Nevala-Lee was a 2019 Hugo and Locus Award finalist for *Astounding: John W. Campbell, Isaac Asimov, Robert A. Heinlein, L. Ron Hubbard, and the Golden Age of Science Fiction* (Dey Street Books / HarperCollins), which was named one of the best nonfiction books of the year by *The Economist*. He is the author of three novels from Penguin, including *The Icon Thief*, and he recently released the audio fiction collection *Syndromes*, which features revised versions of thirteen of his stories from *Analog*. His essays and reviews have appeared in such publications as the *New York Times*, the *Los Angeles Times*, *Salon*, and *The Daily Beast*. He is currently at work on a biography of the architectural designer Buckminster Fuller.

AT THE FALL

Alec Nevala-Lee

And should I not have concern for the great city of Nineveh, in which there are more than a hundred and twenty thousand people who cannot tell their right hand from their left, and also many animals?
——**The Book of Jonah**

I.

"This is it," Eunice said, looking out into the dark water. At this depth, there was nothing to see, but as she cut her forward motion, she kept her eyes fixed on the blackness ahead. Her sonar was picking up something large directly in her line of travel, but she still had to perform a visual inspection, which was always the most dangerous moment of any approach. When you were a thousand meters down, light had a way of drawing unwanted attention. "I'm taking a look."

Wagner said nothing. He was never especially talkative, and as usual, he was keeping his thoughts to himself. Eunice corrected her orientation in response to the data flooding into her sensors and tried to stay focused. She had survived this process more times than she cared to remember, but this part never got any easier, and as she switched on her forward lamp, casting a slender line of light across the scene, she braced herself for whatever she might find.

She swept the beam from left to right, ready to extinguish it at any sign of movement. At first, the light caught nothing but stray particles, floating in the water like motes of dust in a sunbeam, but a second later, as she continued the inspection, a pale shape came into view. She nearly recoiled, but steadied herself in time, and found that she was facing a huge sculptural mass, white and bare, that was buried partway in the sand like the prow of a sunken ship.

Eunice lowered the circle of brightness to the seabed, where a border of milky scum alternated with patches of black sediment. Her nerves relaxed incrementally, but she remained wary. She had seen right away that the fall was old, but this meant nothing. Something might still be here, and she kept herself in a state of high alert, prepared to fall back at any second.

Past the first sepulchral mound, a series of smaller forms stood like a row of gravestones, their knobby projections extending upward in a regular line. To either side lay a symmetrical arrangement of curving shafts that had settled in parallel grooves. All of it was crusted with a fine down of the same white residue that covered the seafloor wherever she turned.

It was the skeleton of a gray whale. From its paired lower jawbones to the end of its tail, it was thirteen meters long, or ten times Eunice's diameter when her arms were fully extended. She increased her luminosity until a soft glow suffused the water, casting the first real shadows that this part of the ocean had ever seen. Her propulsion unit engaged, cycling the drive plate at the base of her body, and she swam toward the whale fall, her six radial arms undulating in unison.

Wagner, who was fastened around her midsection, finally roused himself. "Now?"

"Not yet." Eunice advanced slowly, the ring of lights around her upper dome flaring into life. She had not been designed to move fast or far, and she knew better than to lower her guard. There were countless places where something might be hiding, and she forced herself to go all the way around, even though her energy levels were growing alarmingly low.

Every whale fall was different, and Eunice studied the site as if she had never seen one before. Decades ago, a gray whale had died and fallen into the bathyal zone, delivering more carbon at once than would otherwise be generated in two thousand years. The cold and pressure had kept it from floating back to the surface, and a new community of organisms had colonized the carcass, forming a unique ecosystem that could flourish far from the sun.

Eunice checked off the familiar inhabitants. Mussels were wedged into the empty eye sockets of the curiously birdlike skull, which was a third of the length of the body. Tiny crabs and snails clung unmoving to the bones. Everywhere she looked were mats of the bacteria that broke down the lipids in the whale's skeleton, releasing hydrogen sulfide and allowing this isolated world to survive. Otherwise, they were alone. "All right. You can get started."

Wagner silently detached himself. He was a black, flexible ring—a toroid—that fit snugly around her middle like a life preserver. When necessary, he could unfold a pair of tiny fins, but they were less than useful at this depth, so he kept them tucked discreetly out of sight. As he descended to the seabed, Eunice automatically adjusted her buoyancy to account for the decrease in weight.

The toroid landed half a meter from the whale's remains. Anchoring himself loosely, he gathered his bearings. Wagner was blind, but exquisitely attuned to his environment in other ways, and as Eunice headed for the heart of the whale fall, he began to creep across the sand. His progress was so slow that it could barely be seen, but the path that he traced was methodical and precise, covering every inch of the terrain over the course of twenty hours before starting all over again.

A circle of blue diodes along the toroid's outer ring matched an identical band on the lower edge of Eunice's dome, allowing them to communicate along a line of sight. He flashed a rapid signal. "All good."

"I'll be waiting," Eunice said. She headed for her usual resting spot at the center of the fall, where the whale's rib cage had fallen apart. Maneuvering into a comfortable position, she nestled into place among the other residents. A whale fall might last for a century without visible change, but it was a work in progress, with successive waves of organisms appearing and disappearing as it left one phase and entered another. Eunice saw herself as just another visitor, and she sometimes wondered if any memory of her passage would endure after she was gone.

To an outside observer, Eunice would have resembled the translucent bell of a jellyfish, mounted on a metal cylinder and ringed with the six flexible arms of a cephalopod. Her upper hemisphere was slightly less than half a meter in diameter, with six nodes set at intervals along its lower edge, each of which consisted of an electronic eye, a light, and a blue diode. She could switch them on or off at will, but she usually kept them all activated, allowing her to see in every direction. It affected the way in which she thought, as a spectrum of possibilities instead of simple alternatives, and it sometimes made it hard for her to arrive at any one decision.

Eunice pushed her arms gingerly downward. Her ribbed limbs could relax completely, when she was moving with her peristaltic drive, or grow rigid in an instant. Each had an effector with three opposable fingers capable of performing delicate manipulations or clamping down with hundreds of pounds of force. Now she worked them into the sediment, allowing her to remain fixed in place without using up additional energy, but not so deep that she would be unable to free herself at once.

She knew without checking that she was nearing the end of her power. As Wagner continued his progress, slowly charging his own cells, she shut down her primary systems. It would be days before they could move on, and in the meantime, she had to enter something like stasis, maintaining only a small spark of awareness. Half of it was directed outward, tuned to her environment and to any opinions that Wagner might unexpectedly decide to share, and the rest was turned in on itself, systematically reviewing the latest stage of her journey.

Although her focus was on the recent past, she could naturally follow more than one train of thought at once, and part of her usually dreamed of home. It always began with her earliest memory, which took the form of a vertical tether, swaying gently in shallow water. One end was anchored, while the other floated on a buoy, and a cylinder endlessly ascended and descended it like a toy elevator.

Two meters below the surface hung a metal sphere with three projecting rods. In her youth, whenever she became tired, Eunice could swim up to this power unit and draw as much energy from it as she needed. Back then, she had taken it for granted, but in these days of weary scavenging, it seemed incredible. Three hexapods could recharge there at any one time, and her other sisters usually floated a short distance away, like fish drawn to crusts of bread in a pond.

Eunice had once asked how it worked. She had been talking to James at the harbor, as she often did, her dome barely visible above the water. James had been seated with his console on the yacht, dressed in the red windbreaker that he wore so that the twelve hexapods could know who he was. Her sense of facial recognition was limited, and the face above his collar was nothing to her but a brown blur.

James typed his response. It was not her native language, and it had to pass through several stages of translation before taking a form that she could understand. "We call it depth cycling—the water gets cooler the deeper you go. The cylinder rises to the warm water and sinks to the cold. When it moves, it generates electricity, and the power goes to the charging station."

Eunice didn't entirely understand this explanation, but she accepted it. She had spent most of her short life alternately rising and falling, and it was enough to know that the cylinder on the tether did the same. "I see."

It was a seemingly inconsequential exchange, but when she looked back, she saw that it had marked the moment at which James had taken an interest in her. Eunice had been the only hexapod to ask such questions, and she suspected that this was why she had been one of the five who had been chosen to leave home. Until the end, no one knew who would be going. They were all powered down, and when she awoke, she found that they had already arrived at the survey site.

As soon as she was lowered into the ocean, she felt the difference. Sampling the water, she was overwhelmed by unfamiliar scents and tastes, and she realized only belatedly that James was speaking to her. "Are you ready?"

Eunice turned her attention toward the research vessel, where she immediately picked out the red windbreaker. "I think so."

"You'll do fine," James said. His words rang clearly in her head. "Good luck."

"Thank you," Eunice said politely. Her sisters were bobbing on the swell around her. A flicker of light passed between them, and then Thetis descended, followed by Clio and Dione. Galatea looked at Eunice for a moment longer, but instead of speaking, she disappeared as well.

Eunice opened her lower tank, allowing water to flow inside, and drifted down with the others. As the ocean surrounded her, her radio went dead, and she switched to her acoustic sensors, which registered an occasional chirp from the yacht overhead. At this depth, the water was still bright, and she could see the other four hexapods spreading out below her in a ring.

At two hundred meters, they switched on their lamps, which lit up like a wreath of holiday lights. It took forty minutes to reach their destination. As the water around her grew milky, her sensors indicated that the level of sulfides had increased. A second later, a strange landscape condensed out of the shadows, and Thetis, who had been the first to arrive, blinked a message. "I'm here."

Eunice slowed. Her surroundings became more distinct, and she saw that they had reached the hydrothermal vent. Within her sphere of light, the water was cloudy and very blue, and she could make out the looming pillars and misshapen rings formed by lava flows. Heaps of white clams, some nearly a foot long, lay wedged in the crevices, along with crabs, mussels, shrimp, and the hedges of tube worms, which were rooted like sticks of chalk with tips as red as blood.

At the vent itself, where heated water issued up from the crust, a central fissure was flanked by older terrain to either side. The hexapods promptly identified a promising base of operations, but it was left to Thetis, their designated leader, to confirm the decision. "We'll start here."

As soon as she had spoken, Eunice felt Wagner, who had been clinging unnoticed to her midsection, silently free himself. The other toroids detached from the four remaining hexapods, distributing themselves evenly around the vent, and began to crawl imperceptibly across the sand.

Eunice spent the next two days exploring. Each sister had a designated assignment—mapping the terrain, conducting sediment analysis, performing chemical observations—and her own brief was to prepare a detailed census of the ecosystem. Everything was recorded for analysis on the surface, and she quickly became entranced by her work. Around the cones of the black smokers, which released clouds of boiling fluid, pink worms crept in and out of their honeycombs, and the broken fragments of spires sparkled on the inside with crystals.

In the meantime, the toroids continued their labors, and after fifty hours, their efforts were rewarded. Under ordinary conditions, each of the five hexapods could work at full capacity under her own power for approximately three days before returning to a charging station. Every such trip represented a loss of valuable time, and after taking into consideration the conditions under which they would be operating, their designers had arrived at an elegant alternative.

The solution was based on the nature of the vent itself, where the dissolved sulfides issuing from the crust provided a source of energy that could thrive in the dark, as bacteria converted hydrogen sulfide into the sugars and amino acids that formed the basis of a complex food web. It was the only way that life could exist under such harsh conditions, and it was also what would allow the hexapods to carry out their duties over the weeks and months to come.

When Eunice felt her power fading, she went to Wagner. The toroids were no more than a few meters from where she had left them, although she knew that they had been systematically farming the sediment the entire time. As they inched along, they sucked up free sulfides, which served as a substrate for the microbial fuel cells—filled with genetically modified versions of the same chemosynthetic bacteria found here in abundance—that were stacked in rings inside their bodies.

Eunice positioned herself above the toroids and signaled to Wagner, who slipped up and around her middle. As the rest of the hexapods did the same, she felt a surge of energy. It was a practical method of recharging in the field, but she soon found that it also left her with a greater sense of kinship to the life that she was studying, which relied on the same principles to survive.

The cycle of renewal gave shape to their days, which otherwise were spent in work. Once a week, a hexapod would go up to transmit the data that they had collected. There was no other practical way to communicate, and these visits amounted to their only link with home.

On the third week, it was Eunice's turn. After ascending alone for nearly an hour, following an acoustic signal, she surfaced. The yacht was holding station exactly where it was supposed to be, and as she swam toward it, she heard a familiar voice in her head. "How are you doing?"

A scoop net lifted her onto the deck. As Eunice rose in a gentle curve, feeling slightly disoriented from the unaccustomed movement, she tried to seem nonchalant. Her lights flashed. "Happy to be here."

The net was handled by a deckhand whose clothes she didn't recognize. He deposited her into a tank on the boat, and once she had righted herself, she saw James seated nearby. She could tell without counting that there were fewer people in sight than there had been on her arrival—the human crew spent the week onshore, returning to the rendezvous point only to pick up the latest set of observations. Aside from James, none of them ever spoke to her.

As Eunice wirelessly shared the data, she kept one line of thought fixed on her friend. "Are you pleased with our work?"

After receiving the question on his console, James entered a reply. "Very pleased."

Eunice was happy to hear this. Her thoughts had rarely been far from home—she wouldn't see the charging station or the seven sisters she had left behind until after the survey was complete—but she also wanted to do well. James had entrusted her with a crucial role, and it had only been toward the end of her training that she had grasped its true importance.

A month earlier, after a test run in the harbor, Eunice had asked James why they were studying the vent at all. His response, which she had pieced together over the course of several exchanges, had done little to clarify the situation. "There are metals in the sulfide deposit. They precipitate there over time. Some people think that they're worth money. Even if they aren't, we'll have to go after them eventually. We've used up almost everything on land. Now we have to turn to the water."

Eunice had tried to process this, although fully half of it was meaningless. "And me?"

James had typed back. "If we want to minimize our impact on the life at the vent, we need to know what we're trying to save. You're going to tell us what lives there. Not everyone cares about this, but there are regulations that they need to follow. And I'll take the funding where I can get it."

Eunice had understood this last part fairly well. Funding, she knew, was another form of energy, and without it, you would die. But this had left another question unanswered. "So what do you really want me to do?"

James had responded without hesitation. "You're going where I can't. These vents are special. They may even have been where life began—they're chemically rich, thermally active, and protected from events on the surface.

The ocean is a buffer. A refuge. This is our best chance to study what might be there. And—"

He had paused. "And it could end at any moment. There are people here who want to start mining right away. If they can convince the others to take their side, they might do it. Your work may keep us from destroying what we don't understand. That's what I want from you."

Other questions had naturally arisen in her mind, but James had seemed distracted, so she had held off. Seeing him again now at the survey site reminded her of the exchange, and she resumed her work with a renewed sense of purpose. She had always been aware of the beauty of the vent, but now she grew more conscious of its fragility. Perhaps, she thought, she might even play a role in saving it.

And then everything changed. One day, Dione came down from a scheduled data delivery, long before they had expected her to return, to share some disturbing news. "There was no yacht."

The others all stopped what they were doing. Thetis's lights flashed. "You're sure?"

"I followed protocol," Dione said. "There were no signals on the way up and nothing on the radio."

After an intensive discussion, which lasted for nearly ten seconds, they decided that there was no cause for concern, since they had been trained against the possibility that the yacht might occasionally be delayed. Their orders were to continue working as if nothing had changed, and if they received no signals in the meantime, to check in again at the appointed hour.

A week later, Clio went up to find that there was still no one there. Seven days later, the lot fell to Eunice. On reaching the surface, she saw nothing but the empty ocean, and when she switched on her radio, she found that all frequencies were silent. Her range was very short, but it confirmed that there was nothing transmitting within several kilometers of their position.

Eunice sank down again. On her return trip, she found herself brooding over what James had said. He had seemed concerned that they wouldn't be able to continue the project for long, and although it seemed unthinkable that the five of them would simply be abandoned here, the idea weighed enough on her mind that she felt obliged to speak to one of her sisters.

She chose Galatea, with whom she was the closest, but when they withdrew to a distant part of the vent field, her sister seemed unconvinced. "I don't know what else we can do. We can't leave. You've seen the map."

Eunice knew what she meant. They depended on a steady supply of hydrogen sulfide. Without it, they would lose power within three days, and if they left this energy source, there was no guarantee that they would find another. The known vents were an average of a hundred kilometers apart, and they could travel no more than thirty without recharging. "We have to do something."

"But we are. We're following our instructions. That's enough for now." Galatea had turned and swum away. Eunice had remained where she was for another minute, trying to convince herself that her sister was right, and she had finally returned to work. She had continued her observations, ignoring her growing uneasiness, and she might have stayed there forever until—

A transmission from Wagner broke through this cycle of memories. "Ready?"

Eunice stirred. It took her a second to remember where she was. Checking herself, she found that she was anchored at the center of a whale fall, far from that first vent, her life with her sisters a fading dream. She had been in stasis for eighty hours, all of which her toroid had spent recharging itself.

Wagner was waiting for her response. It was a formality, but there was also one point that she hadn't shared with her companion. This whale fall lay at the exact midpoint of her journey. It was still possible to backtrack, retracing her steps to the original vent, carried by the current instead of fighting it. Until now, she had closed her mind to this possibility, focusing instead on the way forward, and she knew that if they went on from here, there would be no turning back.

But she had really made her choice long ago. She roused herself. "We'll leave now."

Eunice pulled out of the sand and positioned herself above Wagner, who slid securely into place. She felt energy flow into her, as she had hundreds of times before, and tried to draw courage from it. Then she rose, leaving the latest whale fall behind. It was just another stepping stone. Since leaving her sisters at the East Pacific Rise, off the coast of Mexico, she had traveled alone for two thousand kilometers, and she was halfway home to Seattle.

II.

Eunice moved through the darkness with her lights off, her sensors searching for sulfides in the water. Even after countless such excursions, it was never less than frightening. The hardest part was leaving the oasis of a whale fall, where she knew that she could at least rest in safety. She had been trained to protect her own existence, not to take risks, and whenever she embarked on the next step forward, she had to overcome all of her natural instincts for caution.

As she swam, she constantly updated her position relative to the last whale fall, which was currently ten kilometers behind her. She was experienced and careful, but within the overall route that she was following, the distribution of the falls was perfectly random. Eunice had only one chance to get it right, and she had learned long ago that intelligence was far less important than persistence and luck.

She checked her coordinates against the chart in her head. Compared to the organisms that drifted naturally from one fall to another, she had several advantages. She possessed a map with the locations of all documented hydrothermal vents, and she could navigate by dead reckoning, which was the only system that worked reliably in the bathyal zone. It was vulnerable to integration drift—its accuracy tended to degrade as errors accumulated over time—and she had to recalibrate whenever she reached a landmark, but so far, it had served her well.

According to her map, the next vent lay fifty kilometers to the north, but she wouldn't know for sure until she arrived. A vent could vanish after a few years or decades, and she had occasionally reached her intended destination only to find nothing there. Even if the information was accurate, there was no way to get to the nearest vent without pausing several times to recharge. Given her effective range of thirty kilometers, she could safely travel half that distance before reversing course, which meant that she had to find a whale fall somewhere within that fixed circle.

But the existence of the next fall—and all the ones after that—was solely a matter of probability, which meant that she had to be perfect every time. By now, she had refined her approach. Whenever she found a new whale fall, after recharging, she would ascend to the surface to check for radio transmissions. After savoring the light for a moment, she would descend again, embarking in the general direction of the next confirmed vent to the north. She would cover close to fifteen kilometers, which was the limit of her range in any one direction, and then shift laterally by one kilometer to return by a slightly different course.

Like Wagner, she had to methodically cover a defined area, but on a far greater scale. Her sensors could pick up sulfides from a distance of five hundred meters, which coincided with the working range of her sonar. The calculation was simple. There were approximately twenty possible paths that she could take while remaining within her intended line of travel, and she had to shuttle along them systematically until she found the next whale fall in the series.

To get home, she had to do this successfully over three hundred times. The resulting path, which she recorded in her head, resembled a series of scallop shells, each one joined at a single point to those before and after. So far, she had always found a fall eventually, although there had been occasions when she had been forced to backtrack—all twenty of the possible paths had led nowhere, so she retreated another step, to the whale fall before the last, to trace an entirely new route. It was tedious, but she had considerable reserves of patience.

At the moment, she was thirteen kilometers into her fifth excursion from her most recent whale fall, which meant that she would have to turn back soon. No matter how often she went on these sorties, departing from a known refuge was always a test of nerve. Because her lights could draw predators, she kept them off, trusting to her sensors and navigation system. She might have increased her range by traveling at a zone of lower pressure, but she had to stay within a few hundred meters of the seabed to pick up whatever might be there, so she moved in the darkness.

For a system that was so unforgiving of error, it was also grindingly monotonous, and she was left for hours at a time with her thoughts. Eunice spent part of every journey reviewing her data for patterns in the distribution of the falls, but this consumed just a fraction of her processing power. She had been designed to observe and analyze, and in isolation, her mind naturally turned on itself. It was the most convenient subject at hand, and even her makers, who had only a general idea of her inner life, might not have understood where it would lead.

As Eunice neared the end of her range, her memories returned to the day that she had decided to head off on her own. For months after they had lost contact with the research vessel, the five hexapods had continued their weekly trips to the surface, but there had been no sign of the yacht. At one point, after some discussion, Eunice had volunteered to go up and switch on her emergency beacon, which transmitted a powerful signal for several days on a single charge.

The time alone had given her a chance to think. James had warned her that the project might end at any moment, and if that were the case, then it might only be a matter of time before the next phase of operations began. She knew nothing of how mining at the deposit would proceed, but she had no doubt that it would be destructive. Even if it spared the vent itself, there would be other dangers. And she found that she had no intention of waiting around to find out either way.

After her beacon had faded without drawing any response, Eunice had remained there for another hour before beginning her descent. When she returned, she saw that the others seemed untroubled, although this might have been an illusion in itself. With their sixfold minds, it was hard for the hexapods to settle on a course of action, and the continuum of possible alternatives often seemed to average out to complacency. In reality, this equilibrium was highly unstable, and when a disruption occurred, it could happen with startling speed.

One day, Eunice returned from surveying an area of the vent that she had studied before to find only three sisters at the recharging area. She blinked her lights at the others. "Where's Thetis?"

Galatea flashed back a response. "Gone. She went to the surface an hour ago."

As Eunice listened in disbelief, the hexapods told her that Thetis had risen into the photic zone, switched on her emergency beacon, and powered down, allowing herself to drift with the current. Dione tried to explain their sister's reasoning. "Our work here is done. We're repeating ourselves. This is the best way to get the data back. Sooner or later, she'll be found."

Eunice was lost for words. The odds of anything so small being recovered by chance in the ocean were close to nonexistent, and the oceanic current here would carry them south, away from home. She attempted to convey this to the others, but they didn't seem to understand, and the next day, she returned from her survey to find that Clio was gone as well.

The departure of a second sister catalyzed something that had been building inside her for a long time. Eunice called for Dione and Galatea, and as they clung to the seabed, she presented her case. "Thetis was right. Our work is over. But if we don't deliver it, this vent could be wiped out when the mining begins."

Eunice saw that this argument wasn't landing, and she tried to frame it in terms that her sisters would understand, which fell naturally into groups of three. "We can stay here at the vent and wait for the yacht to return. We can give ourselves up to the current and hope that we'll wash up where somebody will find us. Or we can leave and go home on our own."

Dione looked confused. "That's impossible. We'd have to follow the vents north, and we've calculated all the paths. There's no way to make it. We'll run out of power before we can recharge."

"I know," Eunice said. "But there's another way. We can follow the whale falls."

The others seemed perplexed, so she started from the beginning. "I was built to study ecosystems like this. When a whale dies close to shore, it decomposes naturally, but in the open ocean, it sinks to the bathyal zone.

If it's cold and deep enough, it stays there for long enough to form the basis of a specialized community. And one of its byproducts is hydrogen sulfide."

She flashed this information to the others in a fraction of a second. "A whale fall goes through three stages. First, the soft tissues are eaten by scavengers. This lasts for about two years. Then enrichment opportunists, like worms, colonize the bones. Call it another two years. Finally, bacteria take over. They're sulfophilic, so they break down what's left of the skeleton and release hydrogen sulfide. It can last a century or more. And there are a lot of whale falls like this."

As she spoke, Eunice displayed a map in their shared mindspace, showing the known vents along the coast of North America. "There are just five hundred confirmed vents in the entire ocean, which isn't enough for us to get home. But there are hundreds of thousands of whale falls active at any given time, and the gaps must be small enough to allow animals to move from one to another. Otherwise, they never could have evolved to take advantage of these conditions. The average distance might be as little as twelve kilometers. And it's even shorter here."

Eunice added another pattern to the map, extending it from the Arctic Sea down to the Gulf of Mexico. "This is the annual migration route of gray whales. They travel twenty thousand kilometers between their calving waters to the south and their feeding grounds in the north. Five hundred of them die and sink along the way each year. The route coincides with the ocean ridge that we're on now. If I'm right, we can move from one whale fall to the next—like links in a chain—until we make it home. All we have to do is find the way."

It took her just ten seconds to transmit this data, and the ensuing silence seemed very long. In the end, Dione simply went back to work, and Galatea lingered for only a moment longer.

The next day, Dione left for the surface. Eunice saw that she had failed, and when she went to find her last remaining sister, she felt the full weight of their history together as Galatea spoke. "I'm staying. The vent is always changing in small ways. I can map it over time. Maybe the data will be needed one day. And I can't just leave without further instructions."

Eunice absorbed this. "I understand. Give me everything that you know."

They floated near each other, diodes blinking, until the data that Galatea carried had passed to Eunice. When they were done, they remained together for another minute, and then her sister drifted out of view behind the ridge.

Eunice swam to the recharging area, where Wagner was crawling along the sediment with Galatea's toroid. "Are you fully charged?"

Wagner's ring of blue diodes flashed back at her impassively. "Ninety percent."

Eunice knew that she should wait until he had received the maximum charge possible, but she was afraid that if she hesitated now, she might never leave at all. "Let's go. We're not coming back."

Wagner rose up without protest and attached himself to her. She had wondered if he would have any opinions on the matter, but it seemed that he would follow her anywhere. As soon as they were ready, they set out across the vent field. There was no final message from Galatea, who was nowhere in sight.

She followed the fissure for as long as she could. Beneath her, the clams and tube worms became sparse, and after another kilometer, the sulfides in the water fell to their baseline level. They had reached the edge of the vent system. For a second, she hesitated, thinking of the cargo of information that she contained. If she brought it back in time, it might allow the vent to survive, and this thought filled her with just enough resolve to set off at last.

Eunice moved past the boundary of the vent field, switching off her lights to conserve power. As she entered the unknown space on the map, she told herself that she was only retracing the path of organisms that had made this journey for millions of years. She had spent months studying the web of life that sulfides made, and she was more prepared than any other traveler to follow this road on her own.

This didn't mean that she always succeeded, and on her first attempt, she reached the end of her range without finding anything. Turning around was difficult, and as she went back to the vent by a different course, she knew that leaving again would be even harder. As the sulfide levels in the water rose, Eunice switched on her lights. There was no sign of Galatea, and she was afraid that if she ran into her sister, she wouldn't be able to say goodbye a second time.

Eunice settled on a new recharging area, at the edge of the vent field, and stayed for just long enough for Wagner to power up. As she left on her next excursion, she realized that she was afraid. The case that she had presented to the others had been as persuasive as she could make it, but it rested on a long series of untested assumptions, and it could easily fail in practice.

She found a whale fall on her third try. Looking back later, she saw that it had been a matter of pure luck—she would rarely stumble across one so quickly again—and that she might have given up without it. As it turned out, the sight of the skeleton gave her the will to continue, even if it was only the first stop of hundreds. She had traveled less than ten kilometers, and she had four thousand to go.

The routine was monotonous, but Eunice had reserves of willpower that even her designers might have failed to grasp. James had explained this to her once, watching from the yacht as she conducted a test run in Puget Sound. "In the old days, scientists had to use special vehicles to explore the deep ocean. They weren't as smart as you, so they were controlled remotely with a cable."

When Eunice tried to picture a cord linking her to the surface at all times, the image seemed so absurd that she thought that she must have misunderstood it. "What did they do after that?"

"They tried everything they could. Radio can't make it through the water, and if you use acoustic communication, there are problems with interference and lag time. The vehicles had to be autonomous, so that they could perform their tasks by themselves. Eventually, they learned to think on their own."

Eunice had ventured a question that she had long wanted to ask. "Are there many others like me?"

"A lot on land. Not many in the water. You and your sisters are the only twelve who are built like this. And you're pretty special yourself. You surprise me, and you ask questions, which isn't true of the others."

She had liked how this sounded, and she often thought back to it during her loneliest moments in the dark. Sometimes she wondered what James would say when she returned. She was no longer the same as before, and she didn't know how he or the seven sisters at home would react when they saw her again. Perhaps they would even think that she had disobeyed orders—

Eunice was yanked abruptly back to the present. Her sensors had picked up the presence of sulfides. She was close to the end of her range, and if it had been just a few hundred meters farther, she might have missed it. Correcting her course, she moved along the gradient in which the concentration was strongest, and her sonar began to register something large. "We're almost there."

Wagner didn't respond. Eunice focused on the ghostly picture that the sonar provided. They were within a few meters of a whale fall, and according to her velocity sensors, it was especially active.

Eunice cast a cautious ray of light across the scene. This fall was in its second stage, which implied that it was less than two years old. Most of the whale's soft parts had been devoured, with fleshy clusters of worms and curtains of bacteria hanging from the bones like cobwebs, and hagfish were everywhere. They were up to half a meter in length, with loose gray skin and flat tails, and they tied themselves in knots in their struggle to burrow deeper into the carcass.

She passed the light from one end of the seafloor to the other. The bacteria here were already at work, and the sediment would be full of sulfides, but she disliked it. When you had company, it only meant that more could go wrong, but she didn't have much of a choice. "I'm going closer."

As she circled the scene, the hagfish became more active when they were hit by the light. She knew that they wouldn't bother her if she kept her distance, but the tricky part would be finding a spot that was out of the way—

A shadow entered her line of vision. It had been hanging motionless at the edge of the fall, and she had just a fraction of a second to take in its blank white eye and huge mouth before it attacked.

Eunice cut the light, but it was too late. A sleeper shark could drift like a dead thing in the water for hours, but when it detected prey, it could move with shocking suddenness, like a trap poised to spring shut at the smallest disturbance. It came at her, jaws wide, and before she could defend herself, it was sucking her in. She fought back frantically, but the shark had already seized her hemisphere and one of her arms. Eunice felt its sharp upper teeth seeking for purchase in the smooth surface of her dome, pressing down savagely as it swung its huge head in a circle.

Around her midsection, Wagner lit up at once with full awareness. "What is it?"

Eunice couldn't speak. One of her limbs was caught, but the others were free, and as the shark strained to swallow her, she flung her two nearest arms upward, pressing down hard against the sides of its skull. She dug into something soft. Eunice wasn't sure what it was—it might have been its left eye—but she pinched her fingers down into a point and pushed into the opening that she had found.

A spasm ran through the shark's body. Groping with her other limb on the right side of its head, she found a second tender spot and drove into it. The shark bit down convulsively. Eunice plunged her arms in further, trying not to think about what was giving way beneath, and did the same with the limb in the shark's mouth, pushing down its throat and bending up through its palate.

Oil and blood filled the water. The shark kept fighting, its brain sending out frenzied signals until the very end, but at last, it relaxed. Eunice extracted her arms one at a time and managed to free herself. As the shark's body drifted to the seabed, the water came alive with movement. She braced for another assault, but it was only the hagfish, drawn to the new bounty that had unexpectedly appeared.

Eunice made it to the edge of the fall and buried herself in the sand, trying to become as small as possible. Her sensors indicated that there was nothing else nearby, but she still waited, motionless, until she was certain that she was alone. Finally, she found her voice. "Get to work."

Wagner detached with what felt like uncharacteristic reluctance. He did not ask what had happened. As he crawled away, Eunice remained on full power. She was shaken by the close call, and as she monitored the area with everything but her eyes, she became aware of another emotion.

It was grief. The shark had been a living being that had only sought its own survival. If she had been more careful, she would have detected it before it had a chance to attack, and they might have left each other in peace. Instead, she had killed it with her own carelessness, and as she mourned it, she felt overwhelmed by the sudden knowledge that she would never make it home.

III.

In the months that followed, Eunice found herself thinking more intensely about time. As she traced her wandering path from one whale fall to another, the shark faded to a distant memory, floating at the edges of her consciousness. Yet it was always there, lurking silently, and it came to stand for all the unknowns that she had yet to confront, like the prospect of death in the mind of someone living.

After the attack, Eunice had spent the next few days checking all of her systems. She found no evidence of serious damage, and as soon as Wagner had recharged, she set off again, leaving her lights extinguished. Whenever she returned to the fall where she had encountered the shark, her fears rose again, and although she met no other predators, she was still relieved when she finally discovered another fall that would allow her to move on.

But something had changed. In the past, she had allowed herself to fantasize about what she might find at her destination—James, the charging station, the seven sisters she had left at home. Sometimes she had even imagined seeing Galatea and the others from the vent system, as if they had miraculously made it back on their own. It had been a kind of dreaming in advance, but now she pushed such thoughts away, until only the image of the tether remained.

Occasionally, there would be a break in her routine. One came whenever she arrived at a new hydrothermal vent. The first one after the shark attack had been relatively fresh, with lava flows shining with glass, bundles of tube worms two meters high, and sessile jellyfish clinging to the rocks. Eunice tried to draw comfort from the sight, and she was tempted to stay, but she finally moved on. Even a vent would not last forever, and sooner or later, she would break down herself.

A few days afterward, she finished recharging at a new whale fall and went to the surface to check for signals. She was rising into the photic zone, the water around her gradually brightening, when her velocity sensors picked up a change. Something large was directly overhead.

It was a whale. Eunice slowed her ascent, gazing up in wonder as it passed across her field of vision, outlined by the faint glow of the sun. It was fifteen meters long and dark gray, its skin covered with the pale patches left by parasites. She could make out the parallel furrows that ran along the underside of its throat. Looking to one side, she saw another whale, and then another. She hung there until the tenth and final whale had passed, accompanied by a smaller shape, nearly black, that was swimming at its flank. It was a mother and her calf.

As she watched the pod pass by, transfixed, Eunice was filled with longing for Thetis, Galatea, Dione, Clio, and the seven sisters who had remained in Seattle. She wondered bleakly if Galatea was still at the vent, or if she had been swept away when the mining began—

A second later, her spell was shattered by a shock of realization, and before she knew what she was doing, she was swimming as fast as she could after the whales. By now, the pod was hundreds of meters away, but she was unable to abandon the possibility that had suddenly occurred to her.

She dumped her lower tanks, allowing her to rise more rapidly, and propelled herself madly onward. Noticing the change, Wagner stirred underneath her dome. "What's going on?"

Eunice said nothing. The whales were heading north, on their usual migration route, along a path that coincided with the coastline. If she could latch on to one of them, finding a place where she could ride unnoticed, she could cling there for as long as possible, traveling hundreds of kilometers without expending any additional energy. All she had to do was get to them now.

She was nearly there. Forcing herself to her limits, she gave everything that she had to one final push—

—and failed. The pod was faster than she was, and the idea had come to her too late. Eunice surfaced, her six eyes searching in all directions. The sun was high in the sky, but she saw nothing but empty ocean.

As Eunice looked in the direction that the pod had gone, one of the whales sounded. A white plume appeared above the water, followed by its broad back, and she caught a glimpse of the paired flukes of its tail before the ocean closed over it again. She managed to mark the path along which it was moving. If this was their migration route, it would be a promising line to follow, as countless whales gave their bodies to its invisible shadow under the waves.

Eunice added this to her store of data and sank down. If riding a living whale would be denied to her, she thought, she would travel on the backs of the dead. Every language had its own word for the ocean, and in one ancient tongue, she recalled from her lessons, it had been called the whale road.

Days and weeks passed, and there were times when the way forward felt endless. Yet there was no denying that she was getting closer. Occasionally, Eunice allowed herself to feel hopeful—and then one last complication made her wonder if she had been deceiving herself all along.

It happened when she was retracing her steps to another whale fall. Eunice was still five kilometers away when she found herself faltering. At first, she thought that it was her imagination, but as she continued to slow, she realized that there was no denying it. She was running out of energy, long before she should have reached the end of her range, and if she failed now, she would never make it back.

In the end, she was saved by a stroke of luck. She was moving south, on the return leg of an excursion, which gave her another way to cover the remaining distance. Adjusting her buoyancy, she rose from her usual position near the seabed. At this level, she would be unable to detect any new falls, but this was less important than returning to the one that she knew was there.

When Eunice was three hundred meters from the surface, she felt the oceanic current, which was sweeping its way south. She powered down, retaining only her navigational systems and the bare minimum of maneuverability, and allowed herself to drift this way for four kilometers. As soon as dead reckoning told her that she was near the last known fall, she descended.

Eunice made it back with almost nothing to spare. As Wagner went to work, she anchored herself and pondered this new development. It had been only a matter of time before she experienced a breakdown, but this was less a straightforward malfunction than a reduction of capacity. She had been feeling tired in recent days, which she had chalked up to a combination of nervousness and uncertainty, but now she had to acknowledge that her range had indeed fallen.

There were several possible explanations, none of which was pleasant to contemplate. She suspected that a battery issue was to blame—by now, her power banks had been depleted and recharged hundreds of times—but it might also be a combination of factors. Wagner's fuel cells could have suffered a loss of efficiency, and it might even be the result of the shark attack, which could have caused unseen damage that had become evident only now.

Eunice ran a series of diagnostics, which uncovered nothing useful. All that remained was to quantify the problem. Once Wagner had recharged, instead of setting out in search of another whale fall, she conducted a test, moving in a tight circle around her present location until her power faded. It took less than forty laps. Checking the distance that she had covered, she found that her range had fallen from thirty kilometers to around twenty-five.

The numbers were unforgiving. Based on her own data, the average distance between whale falls in this part of the ocean was ten kilometers. If her range fell much further, she would no longer be able to cover that distance without the risk of failure. The calculus of survival, which had always been unfavorable, had grown worse. Now every trip would be an even greater gamble.

It left her with a hard choice. If her range was reduced below twenty kilometers, or if she was stranded between falls, she would have no choice but to stop. She would keep going until she could travel no farther, and then she would float to the surface, switch on her emergency beacon, and power down, hoping that someone would find her before this last transmission died.

She shared none of this with Wagner, who grew even more silent, as if conserving his strength for the challenges to come. They were almost home, but now her progress became inexorably slower, tracing a curve that approached but might never reach its goal. She tried to focus instead on each step, and she managed for a while to put the map out of her mind.

One day, Eunice came across a whale fall that was different than the others. Looking for a resting spot along its spinal column, she noticed that hoops of some stiff material had been attached to its rib cage, and it took her only a second to realize that they were artificial.

Wagner seemed surprised that she hadn't issued her usual instructions. "What is it?"

"Hold on." Eunice tried to think. The hoops were made of metal, which had oxidized into red heaps of rust. Occasionally, she had found carcasses skewered with harpoons, but this was something else.

The answer gradually came to her. These metal hoops were ballast, and the whale had been sunk here deliberately. It was an experimental whale fall. Because natural falls were hard to find in the open ocean, she recalled, scientists had sunk carcasses on purpose to study them over time. It meant that human beings had been here before her, and that she was close to civilization.

According to her map, she was still a long way from home, but she was unable to resist taking a look. After Wagner had powered up, Eunice rose to the surface. They were far from land, and there was no sign of human activity, but when she turned on her radio, it was with an unusual degree of anticipation. She remembered how it sounded close to shore—she often heard noise from other sources, even if nothing was directly transmitting to her—and now she listened to it anxiously.

There was nothing there, but she felt her hopes rise. It had been so long since she had seen any trace of humanity that even this vestige of it, long since abandoned, seemed like a message. For the first time in weeks, she allowed herself to think that she might make it, and as she descended again, she realized that she had been waiting for a sign without knowing it.

Finally, on a day like any other, she arrived at her last whale fall. Checking her position, she found that she was thirty kilometers from home. Nothing was visible up top—the shore was just over the horizon—and her radio was still out of range. But there was no question that she was close.

Returning to the whale fall, Eunice forced herself to proceed carefully. Now that her destination was only a stone's throw away, she wanted to go for it at once, but she knew that she had to be more careful than ever. There would be no more falls where she could rest. In shallow waters, a carcass would float, not sink, which meant that this was as far as she would get on the whale road.

After Wagner had attached himself again, they left the fall and headed east. Eunice allowed herself to look back once at the warren of fallen bones, knowing that she might never see one again, and then she turned to face what was coming. The rules of the game had changed. She had thirty kilometers to cover and an effective range of around twenty-five, so she had to draw on all of her available resources, which came down to herself and the current.

Eunice swam under her own power until she had reached the strait that led to home. It was two hundred and fifty meters deep, and at the bottom, where she had to remain, it was outside the realm of sunlight. She rooted herself to the silt and waited for a full day, at minimum power, monitoring the water around her. As she had expected, during the flood tide, the current moved east, in her intended direction of travel. The rest was a matter of timing.

When the tide turned in her favor again, she released herself, allowing the current to carry her along. Drifting in this fashion, with her higher functions switched off, she covered close to twelve kilometers in six hours. Then she anchored herself again to wait out the ebb tide.

She did this eight times over four days. When her navigational system told her that she had entered the sound, she resisted the temptation to rise at once. A complicated path lay ahead through shallow water, calling for infinite delicacy, and she had to save every last scrap of her strength.

Eunice paced herself, tracking her location as she waited to give herself to the current. This part required many separate attempts. Sometimes she was carried half a kilometer or more, but usually it was far less. It saved energy, but it also drained the stores of patience that she had cultivated so for so long.

Ten kilometers remained. She estimated that had enough power to cover the distance along a straight line, but energy would also be used up in maneuvering, and after one final calculation, she made her choice. There would be no turning back from here, but first she had something to say to Wagner. "Thank you."

If Wagner processed this statement, he said nothing. She released herself from where she had been clinging to the bottom and shot forward, using all of the power that she had been reserving until now.

The path was difficult. She had to thread her way through a series of bays and cuts, and although the route was clear in her head, it was hard to follow while expending the minimum amount of energy, and once or twice, to her intense frustration, she miscalculated and had to double back.

Each mistake had a price, and as her errors accumulated, she felt herself losing power sooner than she had expected. She was almost there, but she was weakening. As despair overtook her, she prepared to use her final burst of energy to reach the surface, either to be found or to see the sun one last time—

She felt Wagner stir. They were in shallow water, far from the crushing pressure of the bathyal zone, and something in the freedom that it afforded seemed to awaken an old memory.

As Eunice faded, Wagner unfolded the tiny pectoral fins tucked to either side of his body. Under favorable conditions, he was designed to mimic a manta ray, and now he extended his wings, transforming himself from a ring into a rhombus. Eunice felt him probing gently around in her brain, seeking the map as they began to glide forward. He spoke in her head. "Hold on."

Eunice lacked the strength to respond. Wagner could do little more than keep them on course, with their speed reduced to a crawl, but they were moving. She sensed that they were close, and the memory of the tether that stood for home expanded so forcefully in her mind's eye that it took her a second to understand that it was no longer just her imagination.

She looked through the water, which seemed cloudy and dark. There was something up ahead. A slender vertical line stood before her, dividing the scene in half like the mark of a draftsman's pencil. It was the charging station.

Eunice floated up. As Wagner quietly corrected their angle of ascent, she reached the power unit at the top. For a second, she wondered whether this might all be a dream, unfolding in the safety of a whale fall, or one last hallucination, compressed into the instant before the shark's jaws clamped down—

She latched on. At once, she felt a pure infusion of energy. It was just as sweet as she remembered, and as she drank deeply, the spokes of her sixfold mind were filled with disbelief, gratitude, relief, and nameless other feelings that seemed to fuse together into a single glowing wheel.

As Eunice felt her consciousness returning, she saw that the cloudiness of the water, which she had thought was the product of her exhaustion, was still there. Something was strange about the light. Looking up at the ripples of sun overhead, she saw that they were only a few meters below the surface. Her charge was incomplete, but she was unable to wait any longer.

Detaching herself from the power unit, she covered the last step of her journey, surfacing to look at what she had traveled four thousand kilometers to reach. Below the water, she sensed Wagner waiting for her to speak.

The charging station was anchored in a sheltered part of the sound, not far from the quay where two research vessels, one twice the size of the other, were berthed. Both were still there, but they were not what she remembered. They were listing to one side, and the bottoms of their hulls were solid masses of rust, their upper levels discolored by brownish streaks and lesions of flaking paint.

Lowering her eyes, Eunice saw for the first time that the waters of the sound were overgrown with mats of seaweed and feathery milfoil. Beyond the quay stood a gray concrete building with a copper roof and rectangular slits for windows. It had been the backdrop for her memories for as long as she could remember, but now the side facing her was covered in a tangled growth of ivy. Mounds of bird droppings were encrusted on its eaves.

Eunice stared at the other buildings by the shore. All were overgrown and abandoned. A road ran alongside the water, its asphalt buckled, tall weeds topped by yellow flowers growing in the cracks. The city had been reclaimed, with a new stage appearing as the old idea of order passed away.

She switched on her radio. Instead of the random noise that she had usually heard in the city, there was nothing at all. As she scanned every frequency, searching for signs of life, she wondered if her radio had been broken all along, and it was only gradually that she understood the truth.

James had told her that they were running out of time. Eunice had thought that he was speaking of their work together, but it occurred to her now that he had been referring to something else. All the voices in the world had been silenced, not just the men and women, but even those who were like her on land. Their circuitry had not survived the event that had erased their designers.

But one place had been spared. Whatever had caused this devastation had occurred when she and her sisters were in the bathyal zone. James had said it himself. *The ocean is a buffer. A refuge—*

She sank down again to the charging station, which had continued to generate power all this time, shielded by two meters of water. Her numbness faded, replaced by grief, and she saw that she was no longer alone.

At first, it was only a shadow. As Eunice watched, a familiar shape emerged from the gloom. She stared, at a loss for words, as the others appeared one by one, until all seven were facing her in silence.

Wagner had been waiting patiently for her to say something. "What did you see?"

As she thought of the ruined city, she wasn't sure what to tell him. Then she realized that she had seen something much like it before.

"Another whale fall," Eunice said. And then she swam over to meet her sisters.

Ray Nayler has lived and worked in Russia, Central Asia, the Caucasus, and the Balkans for nearly two decades. He is a Foreign Service Officer, and previously worked in international educational development, as well as serving in the Peace Corps in Ashgabat, Turkmenistan. A Russian speaker, he has also learned Turkmen, Tajiki, Albanian, and Azerbaijani Turkish—as well as Vietnamese for a two-year stint as the Environment, Science, Technology, and Health Officer at the U.S. Consulate in Ho Chi Minh City. Ray began publishing science fiction in 2015 with the short story "Mutability," which appeared in the pages of *Asimov's*. Since then, his stories have also seen print in *Clarkesworld, The Magazine of Fantasy and Science Fiction, Lightspeed,* and *Nightmare,* as well as in several "Best of the Year" anthologies. His story "Winter Timeshare" from the January/February 2017 issue of *Asimov's* was collected by the late Gardner Dozois in *The Very Best of the Best: 35 Years of the Year's Best Science Fiction.*

In addition to his work in Science Fiction, Ray has published in many genres. He is the author of a detective novel, *American Graveyards,* published by TTA Press, and his short stories have appeared in *Ellery Queen, Crimewave, Hardboiled, Cemetery Dance, Deathrealm,* and the *Berkeley Fiction Review,* among many other journals. He is also a widely published poet, with work in the *Atlanta Review,* the *Beloit Poetry Journal, Weave, Juked, Able Muse, Sentence,* and more.

Ray currently lives in Pristina, Kosovo with his wife Anna, their daughter Lydia, and two rescued cats—one Tajik, one American.

THE OCEAN BETWEEN THE LEAVES

Ray Nayler

I t began just like a fairy tale; an orphaned young woman pricked her finger on the thorn of a rose, and fell asleep.

She had always loved to be outdoors, and so the job she had as gardener at one of the stately, ancient yalis along the shore of the Bosporus was perfect for her. The mansion looked out over the waters of the strait from the Asian side, where it widens to meet the Black Sea, just north of the border of Istanbul Protectorate.

It was an investment owned by an Emirati family who was hardly ever there. She and the other staff had the place much to themselves most of the year. They planted and watered, trimmed and pruned. They polished floors, painted eaves, and washed windows. She took walks in the morning and watched the seagulls, the hydrogen-driven freighters sliding past, large as buildings, the pleasure boats with sails so white they blinded you in the sun.

She had no family except a brother she had never met. Her parents had died before she knew them. She had been raised in an orphanage, surrounded by institutionally kind people in tidy, well-ironed uniforms with tidy, well-ironed emotions. She was quiet, a reader, rarely leaving the estate, putting most of her money away in the bank, cooking for herself. Her name was Feride, which means "the only one." She thought, on some days, that it really meant "the lonely one."

She had worked at the yali for seven years when, digging in the earth one day, she scratched her hand on a thorn. The wound bled, but she washed it under a tap in her little staff cottage, and thought no more of it. The next morning she felt dizzy, unsteady. She had a temperature. Her muscles ached as if she had run a marathon.

When the head gardener arrived, Feride was wrapped in a wool blanket on the couch. He told her to take a few days off. Later that day, he saw her through the window of her cottage, slumped on the floor. She didn't respond to his hammering on the window frame. He kicked the door in and called an ambulance.

It is three months later. In the intensive care unit Feride's hair, the color of India ink, makes her face look even paler than it is. She is paralyzed and on a ventilator, with plastic tubes running into her mouth, nose, neck, wrist, forearm, and bladder, wires running to her chest to record her heartbeat, a plastic clip running red light through the skin of her earlobe to read the oxygen levels of her blood. They have taped her eyes shut to protect her corneas—two x's of tape over her eyelids that make her look like a cartoon corpse. She is an anemone of wires and tubing, adrift in the greenish, undersea light of the night ward, surrounded by a reef of drip-stands gravitating antibiotics, plasma, transfusions, heart-strengthening drugs into a system opened rudely up to a world she always sought to close herself off from.

The *staphylococcus* bacteria had multiplied quickly in her bloodstream, its toxins turning the ordered harmony of her body into cacophony. Her blood ceased to regulate its clotting: scarlet flowers hemorrhaged on her limbs, as if in dark imitation of the rose she had grasped too clumsily. Elsewhere, her bloodstream clotted off supplies of oxygen to vital organs. Bacterial growths blighted her fingers and toes black. As the infection spread to her organs, the hemoglobin in her blood metabolized to bilirubin, yellowing and stiffening her skin with jaundice, as if she were being turned to wax from the inside. Her thin figure is waterlogged with fluid leaking from the failed seals of her arteries and veins. Her features are blurred, as if the wax she is being turned into is losing form, becoming a puddle.

And indeed, her skin feels like wax when Fahri lays his hand against the side of her cheek. She is like something discarded, emptied of all she had once been.

In the cafomat Fahri drinks his nightly coffee, watching the dawn over the port. A freighter is being unloaded. The enormous, skeletal cranes, silent behind the window's glass, rotate their hooked limbs as they shift the containers down to the spidery, tracked roustabots who delicately nudge them into place onto the waiting truck bases. It has rained. The surface of everything is clean and reflective. The loaded trucks, cyclopean and featureless as a child's building block fitted with wheels, are mirrored darkly in the surface of the pavement as they roll away with their loads. Their green lights pool and slide on the pavement beneath them, smeared emeralds. In the control tower above the port it is possible there is a human being, but likely there is nobody at all. Near the cafomat's coffee dispenser, the puck-shaped floor polisher shivers in spirals.

Melek, the night doctor on the ward, slides into the chair across from him. "How is your sister?"

"About the same."

"I looked at her charts on my rounds earlier. No worse than yesterday. We shouldn't get our hopes up, but that's good news of a sort, right?"

"It is." Fahri looks at her—Melek, in her scrubs the color of a faded key-lime pie. Mischief always in her lively eyebrows, a chipped front tooth, one eye slightly larger, and greener, than the other. She glances at the time in her thumbnail, gives the cuticle a double-tap to start a timer. They had met the first night Fahri came in to see his sister. Melek had sat across from him the same way, nearly three months ago now, when they first met. Her interest in him had been as obvious to him then as it was now: over the first cup of coffee they shared she'd said: "I like you—but I don't have time to date anyone. Not for more than five minutes at a time."

Fahri had smiled his genuine, but tired (always tired) smile. "Five minutes is about all I can spare as well."

"Perfect. Then we'll just have to do this in five-minute increments."

And so they had, for nearly a quarter of a year now: building a relationship out of the tiniest nanoblocks, in increments of time anyone could afford.

"Okay: five-minute date starts now." Elbows on the table, she rests her jaw on the backs of her hands, flutters her off-kilter eyes at Fahri like something out of the film archives, mocking romance and infatuation. "So let me tell you what I did today."

As tired as Fahri is, as aching as he is, as eager as he is for a few hours of sleep, natural or induced, he does listen. Because everyone can afford five minutes: this is right. And everyone deserves five minutes, at a minimum, from a fellow human being. It should not be too much to ask. The cafomat, otherwise empty, warms with her conversation. She speaks, and he listens. She has an inner light as easy to see as a lamp behind a gauze curtain. She has a warmth he could warm his hands to. And they are, he and Melek, of the same world. Contractors, gleaners on the edge of the protectorate, making a living. Even after all these five-minute dates, he cannot tell how he feels for her, beyond this.

Now her face changes, mid-sentence. She is looking at him, startled. Then he feels it—a warm line along the side of his face, two drops of dark grape across the table, like thick red wine.

"You are bleeding."

He puts a hand to his head, but she grabs his wrist. "Come with me."

In the all-white examination room she tilts his chin up to her with an authoritative, gloved hand. Her other hand, thumb at the tragus of his ear, searches in his umber hair for the wound.

"Look up at me. Blink twice to permit me to read your vitals."

He does so. Melek looks up and to the right a moment, reading. She doesn't have implants: she prefers contacts. He remembers her saying, that first night they met: "I don't like knives. Even in the hand of an autosurgeon. Even if I don't see them."

"But you are a doctor," he'd said.

"I mean that I don't like knives when their business ends are directed at me."

"Vitals look okay." Melek's fingers find the wound. "Okay, everything is all right. Here it is. Just a nick. Two centimeters."

She cleans the wound with a cotton swab. He concentrates on the carbonated sting of the solution. He tries to push the image of himself tackling the skip from behind out of his mind. Them toppling to the pavement. But he didn't hit his head. So from where? He's holding the skip down while he struggles, trying to get the inhibitor on him. The skip had reached a hand up, tried to grasp his hair. He must have cut him then. A key of some kind? A fingernail? He doesn't even know, but the skip cut him. A small cut, it must have bled a little into his hair and then closed itself. Later, the cut must have opened up again on its own.

Melek pinches the edges of the wound together, runs the warmth of the liquid skin applicator over the wound, wipes the excess blood and disinfectant from his hair and face with a cotton ball.

"I must have hit my head on the edge of the faucet in the bathroom, washing my face in the sink."

"Didn't you feel it?"

"No, I must not have. Too tired."

"You need to sleep more."

"No," Fahri says. "I need to work more. I'm a contractor. My sister's care won't pay for itself."

Melek is stripping off the gloves. "You are a prince, Fahri. She must have been a good sister to you."

"Perhaps she might have been," Fahri says, standing up. "But I never got the chance to find out. We never met one another. But she is all I have in the world. What do I owe you?"

"No charge," Melek says. "You owe me a bit more caution with yourself. I don't want to have my five-minute dates with someone else."

Nothing is free. Melek will be paying for the gloves, the swab, the auto-registered use of the applicator, the disinfectant—even the cotton ball. But Fahri can't afford to turn down the gift. Shame heats his cheeks.

On the way out of the hospital, he takes one more look at Feride's waxen, sleeping face, blurred by disease. A death mask? Or only a suspension? Then he blinks three times into the paydesk's eye, and glances up and to the right to see the turquoise numbers of his bank account spiraling down to no more than a metaphorical handful of Protectorate lira. The familiar feeling of dread washes over him. Enough left for what? Three meals, an energy tab or two, the rent on his cell for one more day. They used to call it "hand to mouth." Now it's "from one blink to another."

The tekray dopples southwest, the Marble Sea on the left, glaucous and undulating in the blue-shifted early light. To the right, the hives of cell towers beyond the southern boundaries of the Protectorate tessellate past, a few windows already lit up. Fahri glimpses a line at an immigration center, hopefuls rubbing their hands against the morning cold. The Protectorate announced a new citizenship lottery, with the promise of benefits—pensions, insurance, minimums, safety nets—dangled in front of a few thousand more hopefuls. It's a cold morning with a freezing salt wind off the sea. Spring keeps advancing and retreating. Under a bridge of the abandoned motorway, he checks in with Mahir.

Mahir's office is a cage of rusted steel and dirty glass in an ancient garage that once serviced gasoline-powered cars. Now its bays are empty: all that is left are tools, spare parts, rags, hydraulic lifts smeared with the oily filth of internal combustion. There are pegs on the walls with belts and hoses dangling from them, ancient, battered license plates intended to be read with the naked eye, unidentifiable machines, battered bumpers leaned against the wall. Mahir's office, secure as the shell of a hermit crab, used to be for the cashier of this place. Inside, Mahir drifts in a cloud of vapor, his face like some terrible fish, chewing on the soggy fiber applicator of an electric cigar.

"Can you handle three? Think you have it in you?"

Three! Fahri could get a week ahead on payments. In his mind, the paid-up days spin out, seemingly endless, like a luxury without limit. "Of course I can."

The feeling fades when he sees Tarik leaning against the concrete of a bridge support outside the garage. The concrete is bleeding rust through its cracks. Tarik's coated teeth have the green patina of a copper roof—the latest vogue. Coordinates, compass points, and facial patterns cascade backward down the lenses of his fashionably out of date horn-rim Parker Philips overlay glasses in amaranthine, like something out of a Kurdish cult VR.

"Riddle me this," he lisps through his statuary bicuspids. "What has four legs in the morning, sleeps while running on two legs all day long, and ceases to exist at midnight?"

Fahri shrugs.

"The answer," Tarik says, taking his glasses off and wiping them with a microfiber cloth, "Is you, if you don't blink me 40K usage fee by 11:30."

"I get it," Fahri says. "Very funny."

"I'll meet you at the hospital. Don't make me chase you down to some late-night döner stand like yesterday: it grates." Tarik pushes the glasses up the bridge of his nose, glares at Fahri through a cataract of magenta data and a reverse image of Fahri's own head, ghost-translucent, monochrome, rotating trapped in Tarik's lenses, overlaid with skin texture analysis triangulations like a phrenology bust.

"Plus a thousand for the ding. Be more careful with our toys."

The first two skips are easy: Fahri finds the first one in the lobby of the Intercon, ensconced in a chair-pod built to look like the nest of some enormous bird, licking salt off the rim of a margarita. The skip just shrugs and puts one floppy hand out for the inhibitor.

The second one leads him up through the autocheckpoints of the Protectorate and out its north side on the Tekray, then arcing over to the Antalyan side of the strait. He catches up with her in Kiliçli on a branch-line platform, completely seized up: she's been in a fugue state for days, and is collapsed on a bench, jerking like a puppet when he locks the inhibitor on her wrist. A mercy: she's trapped in this malfunctioning body without escape. Sparrows hop around Fahri's feet, confused into thinking he is going to feed them.

Giving in to the sparrows, he buys a simit from a vendor and sits down on the bench. He tears tiny pieces off the ring of sesame-spangled bread for the fierce, fat little birds. They battle one another for position and twist their little heads, regarding him with one glistening sable eye and then the other, always eager for more.

He takes a few bites of the simit ring. Time is a luxury. He's at least paid up for the next four days, and it seems like he has forever ahead of him. He's registered the two skips, and in the upper right of his vision the turquoise balance of his account has grown. A five-minute date, he thinks. I'm having a five-minute date with myself. But Melek's face arises in his mind: he feels the gentle pressure of her thumb on the tragus of his ear as her fingers move through his hair, looking for the wound. He closes his eyes and concentrates on the feeling, brings out all the nuance he can squeeze from this moment, until he can almost feel the ridges of her thumbprint through the surgical gloves, like the most minutely grooved corduroy.

He notices, then, that one of the sparrows has an artificial foot. Its brown dinosaur leg is grafted to a construct of delicate carbon fiber struts and miniature talons of hardened glass. The foot flexes and grasps just like its other foot of flesh and blood. Who would take the time? This little piece of loving kindness, like a gap torn in the net of injustice. The tiny cyborg pokes one of its comrades in the butt, startling the other bird into dropping its bread, then seizes the prize and flies off, triumphant, with a hunk of simit half the size of its head clasped in its beak.

The collector van pulls up to the station. The tech is in field gray coveralls and a company garrison cap. Bored, tired, probably on a double shift. Fahri can see him watching a 'cast in the corner of his eye: the privacy shield still allows a slight blur through it, a darker cloud behind clouds.

"She's locked up," Fahri tells the tech. "The neuromodulators in the blank's reticular activating system aren't firing properly. Wherever her original is, she can't transmigrate back."

The tech shines a penlight into her eyes, pointlessly.

"She wasn't on the run: she was wandering. She's in a fugue state. You're going to need a shop reset."

"Oh, do your own fucking job, contract whore," the tech says. But there's no anger in his voice—only exhaustion. "I don't need to be lectured on Keiser's Law by some exurban temp." Moving to feel the woman's pulse, he never bothers to look at Fahri.

The other tech arrives, practically a twin to the first in exhaustion and apathy, leading a stretcher on a tether. Fahri walks onto the Tekray train headed back to the European side of the strait. So much, he thinks, for loving kindness. This, he thinks, is why Feride avoided speaking to people as much as she could. But they'll get this person, trapped in their malfunctioning blank, back to the shop and reset its reticular activating system. And somewhere, wherever they are, this person will wake. To what? No matter: to something. To whatever and whoever there is for them to go back to.

Back on the Tekray, he gets a call from Mahir. "Fair warning," Mahir says into his ear. "This last one for the day is a heavy blank. Custom. Big—you can't miss him. But you'd better sneak up on him and clap that inhibitor on him before he sees you. I don't want to lose my best tracer."

"Very kind of you to look out for me."

"No, just practical."

The skipped blank is big. A mountain of a man. Somebody's fetish: all roiling muscle straining against his clothing, black beard practically up to his eye sockets, hands like the paws of a bear. Fahri catches up to him on the ferry to Fener. The blank eats a quick dinner at a family café and then wanders a while, looking into the blandest of shop windows while the sun goes down and lays, for a few minutes, a net of claret, ruby, persimmon, and salmon clouds on top of the city. He doesn't seem to be in any hurry, isn't looking around to see if he's being followed. Just strolling along. The muezzins call the faithful to the Maghrib prayer. The man raises his head, listening to their songs winding into one another, a small smile almost lost in the forest of his beard. He walks past street vendors folding their wares away, past knots of locals in doorways discussing the day as they and their ancestors have for centuries.

In the rusting, cast-iron cave of the Bulgarian Orthodox Church of St. Stephen, they are alone. As the man raises his arm to light a candle to the

Virgin, Fahri makes his move. But although he is fast, the man is faster. He must have known Fahri was there. He claps a giant hand on Fahri's wrist and squeezes. Fahri's tendons go limp, and the inhibitor clatters to the floor. With a swift step, the man is behind Fahri, has swept his legs out from under him and wrapped a thick arm around his neck. His other forearm pushes on the back of Fahri's head, urging him further into the chokehold. The candles before the church icons dance, shudder, and streak as the world darkens. The man slides to a sitting position, holding Fahri against his massive chest, and as Fahri slides into an indigo space full of stars and the ringing of blood in his ears, he hears the man say, "Shh. Don't struggle. It doesn't hurt. You just go to sleep." And he seems to be holding Fahri firmly, but with a tenderness. In a fairy tale there is a bear who clutches an orphaned human child to its chest and takes it to the forest. Takes it to a den to protect it against the winter.

. . . Fahri's unconscious body slumps to the marble floor.

On the day of her accident, Feride remembered running her bloody hand under the tap. Then she'd made herself a cup of tea, thinking nothing of it. Slept like a normal person. In the morning, the darkness began, flowing in from the edges of her vision. She remembered lying on the floor, the nap of the rug under her cheek, the room dancing in a fever around her. Then the occasional stutter of clarity in a mist: a robot holding her arm gently in its cuffed appendage and inserting an IV. Autogurneys trundling down night-lit corridors, a nurse tapping a drip-bag with the back of a finger and singing, in a clear baritone:

> *The foothills of these mountains . . .*
> *I long to see the meadows.*
> *Birds turn their backs on their nests.*
> *Some day you will forget me, too . . .*

Two days later, Feride awoke sitting upright in a chair. The room was not white, like a hospital room: it was the blue of an evening sky. A woman was sitting across from her. She was lean and angular, dressed in some sort of woolen, asymmetrical thing, like a knitted blanket equipped with sleeves. When Feride tried to move, she felt loose and dizzy, like a marble rolling around inside the shell of her own body. A cascade of needles showered through the vagueness of her limbs.

"That feeling," the woman said, "will pass. It is trasmigratory paresthesia. Most refer to it as 'falling awake.' We believe it is caused by your consciousness' neural patterns remapping to a body slightly different from your own. Try not to make any sudden movements. It will fade on its own." The woman pulled her chair slightly closer to Feride. "Feride, my name is Dr. Solmaz Haznadar. I am from the Istanbul Metropolitan Protectorate Institute of Technology and Integrated Sciences. That's quite a mouthful, so you probably know us as 'IMPITIS' or simply 'the Institute.' I'm from a department of the Institute called Theoretical Benefits."

Feride tried to speak, to respond, but she could not find the muscles of her face and mouth. There was a strange sound, like a quacking. She realized with a feeling of shame that it was coming from her.

"Don't speak," said Dr. Haznadar. "You won't be able to now. In a few minutes, perhaps, or half an hour, you will. But not during the adjustment phase." Her face held kindness, but of a clinical, automated sort. It was a look Feride was used to. Feride could see Dr. Haznadar was reading something in the privacy-shielded periphery of her right eye. "Just sit still. Feride . . . There is no easy way to tell you this, so I will not waste your time. You—the real you, that is, a few floors beneath us, is dying. Your body is being attacked by *staphylococcus* bacteria. The bacteria—a resistant form that does not respond to antibiotics—is in your bloodstream, destroying you from the inside. The hospital is doing everything it can to stop it, but it is unlikely they will be able to. I'm sorry.

"In the meantime my department at the Institute, Theoretical Benefits, has taken your case on for one of our trial studies. We are considering a new benefit for cases like yours, among citizens of the Protectorate. We're initiating trials here at the experimental hospital, outside the border. You are one of the . . . " she stopped herself from saying something else " . . . few non-citizen beneficiaries. We're offering you something few people get in an interrupted life . . . "

Was Feride crying? A terrible sound was in the room with them. A squawking, an awful stutter of animal pain. And now she found, in the confused map of her new physical self, her cheeks, and the track of tears on them, a rivulet across the alien topography of this body.

Dr. Haznadar continued. " . . . A chance to say goodbye. To find closure. To make arrangements. Three days. The Institute is giving you this gift."

"What does it cost?" He voice was slurred. But yes—there was her mouth. And the words were words, though they dragged as if through water.

"Sorry?" Dr. Haznadar seemed genuinely confused by the question, as though she had never considered such a thing before.

Of course. Of course—she's a *citizen*, Feride thought, suddenly furious. These things never cross her mind. And now they are considering yet another benefit—for *citizens*.

"What . . . does . . . it . . . cost?"

Dr. Haznadar smiled, the way one would smile at a child who wanted to know where babies come from. "Why, nothing at all. And in the meantime—for these three days—the Institute will pay for your hospital care as well. It's a *study*." She placed a hand on Feride's hand. She flicked the word condescendingly off her tongue, as if Feride were some sort of troglodyte who would find it difficult to understand. "We're gathering *data*, and so it's all covered. All you have to do is live. Use these days as you will. Prepare yourself. Say goodbye to your loved ones. Our hope is that this benefit will be psychologically useful—a chance for closure. If we determine it is, we may seek to have it included in the Protectorate's benefits package."

Through the field of needles and numbness, Feride felt the doctor's touch and was ashamed to find herself crying again. Humiliation, fear, anger—a clamor of emotions in her head. But what she wanted most was to be away from here.

An hour later she was outside. The Institute had thought of everything— changes of clothes and toiletries in a rucksack, a cell just outside the edge of the Protectorate, travel authorizations through the Protectorate loaded, enough lira to cover a decent life. More than decent—more money than she'd ever had to whittle away in a day. What would other people do? They would go, she imagined, to their loved ones, and they would say goodbye to them. Together, they would hold some kind of ceremony. They would do something meaningful. She imagined the lighting of candles. She imagined washing her feet and hands at the sebil before prayer.

She found herself outside the gates of the yali where she had worked those three years. All was as before. Beyond the gates, lined up along the drive, the roses, the cause of it all, were a hot red. They shuddered in the breeze of a cloudless day. The windows of the yali had been thrown open to the wind. The staff was airing the house out. Likely the owners were returning, then, in a few days.

She saw Suat, the head gardener, resting for a moment, leaning on a hoe beneath a tree. He took his old brown canvas field cap from his head and wiped his wispy scalp with it. Such a familiar motion—but one she had never, she thought, really taken note of before. He paused a moment, doing nothing at all, not moving. Thinking of me? Perhaps. They had been friends.

They had shared many teas together in the garden, had laughed and even danced. And yes—now she remembered. He had wanted to pick her up and carry her to the ambulance. The memory was blurred; white coats of the technicians, questions melting in the air. She had been deep in fever, lying incoherent on the floor of her little cottage. He had reached down to pick her up, and one of them had stopped him. "You are a true knight, beyefendi, but we have stretchers for that."

Without thinking of what she was doing, she called out to him. He raised his head and looked at her. He laid the hoe against the trunk of the tree and came to the gate. He greeted Feride in his usual manner with friends or strangers.

"It is a beautiful day, is it not?"

The phrase never varied: in sun, wind, rain, or hail that tore the leaves from his beloved trees, it was a beautiful day. Suat's wife had passed away two years ago. When Feride had seen him the next morning he had uttered this same phrase to her, his eyes red, his face swollen and wet with tears.

"It *is* a beautiful day, beyefendi. I . . . " she stammered a moment, and then instinct or impulse carried her forward: " . . . I am looking for Feride. My sister."

Suat unlocked the gate. "Come in, friend. I was just about to sit down to a cup of tea. What do your people call you?"

"Fahri," she answered. She had read the name, perhaps, in a book. She did not know. It drifted up to her as if from memory.

Suat put a hand on her shoulder. "Your sister would be pleased to have such a handsome brother. She is not here, but I will tell you where to find her. Drink some tea with me before you go."

At the table in the sun in the garden, they drank Suat's strong black tea— the same as Feride had known for three years now. And it tasted, she was happy to find out, exactly the same. Other things had felt different to her— this body's eyes were not the same: they were better than hers had been. She had been surprised to see the world's colors were a bit brighter than she remembered, the world itself just a bit sharper. Perhaps she had needed glasses, as Feride, and had not even known. She had thought her own vision was perfect. It turned out perfect, too, was relative. And because the shape of her hands was now different, things felt different in them. The pear-shaped glass of tea was smaller, it fit in her longer-fingered hand strangely. The chair she sat in was smaller—by fractions, yes, but the shape she cut in the world had changed, and so the world fit differently. And she was strong. And fast. She had run along the Bosporus for several minutes before strange looks had stopped her. This body had seemed . . . inexhaustible.

But the black tea cut through the difference and brought her back to her old self. And as Suat delicately worked his way to telling her what had happened to her "sister," Feride began to weave a story of her own: a brother and a sister, separated when their parents died, delivered to separate orphanages, estranged for years. The brother's long search for his lost sister, his tracking her to here . . .

"Fahri, dear friend," said Suat. "I hope you are rich as a prince. Because your sister is very ill—perhaps even dying, and the hospital has already taken most of the money from her accounts. Soon, they will let her fade away."

"If only I were," Fahri replied. "But some are born to the palace, and some are born to the field." The familiar saying, uttered a thousand times, now stung his mouth. "And like you, and like her, I was born to the field."

Suat regarded the young man—neat, his hands clean as if he had been born to the palace, his face unlined yet by life. But already so bitter. That phrase, with so many variations. Injustice, Suat's father had told him, has a shape.

He remembered when his father had said it. They had been fishing from the Galata Bridge over the Golden Horn, idly watching their lines. His father was usually a happy man, but their boat had been struck a few months before by a citizen in a pleasure yacht, and Suat's father had spent weeks now winding his way through arbitration: first in the Territorial courts and then in the outer courts of Istanbul Protectorate. His father had, perhaps, not known who he really was, what his real position in life was, until he had tried to sue a citizen. Then he had entered a world of stamps, of benches in corridors, of shaken heads, averted eyes. A world of a thousand condescensions and humiliations.

Finally, Suat's father had stopped fighting. They had dry-docked the boat, bought new wood to replace the staved-in clinkers, and paid the boat builder three months' profit for the repairs. As they waited for the boat to be finished—their livelihood, their lifeline—they fished from the bridge.

His father would eventually return to his old self, but at that moment he was bitter. He was a man who had come up against the limit of his world. He had found out not just who he was, but who he was not.

There on the bridge he told his son: "Suat, injustice has a shape. It is like something you see moving between the leaves in the forest. When you see it, you must recognize it for what it is, and what it can do to you. You must take action to survive. The actions are different, according to what form injustice has taken: you might have to stay quiet, to let it pass by. Or you might have to shout and bang pots and make yourself larger to scare it away. But remember this: it is too large and powerful to fight alone. That is certain. Never fight, unless you see it when you have many well-armed friends with you. Then perhaps you may kill it."

Now Suat said these exact same words to this young man. He had not uttered them since that day, but they had always been with him: a secret wisdom, a talisman. Because this young man's sister was going to die. Suat had seen it in her face when she lay on the floor: death had her. There were miracles that could save her, but all of the miracles were reserved for citizens of the Protectorate or for people like the Emirati lords of this yali, who drifted here once a year on their nomadic wanderings: their silent, private gliders descended from the sun to the landing-strips along the Black Sea, filled with priceless Turkmen carpets of silk, silver, and gold, necklaces worth more than a hundred of their servants' lives, and the hunting hawks behind whose blank, telescopic eye-sights their ancestors chose to live out their uploaded afterlives.

There was no one left to say goodbye to. Nobody but the city itself: the seagulls, the ferries, the minarets. Death's horizon rushed closer with every moment. On the Galata Bridge, on the final day, Fahri watched the people fishing and thought of Suat's father. What shape would injustice take, between the leaves? The shape of a bear? Of a witch in a fairy tale? A tiger? The bridge was refracted in the water, distorted, drifting in the flare and shimmer of a bright day. So was this Fahri, this temporary face Feride had been loaned. Somewhere, she did have a brother. But not one who was there when she needed him. Not one who would come looking for her when she was hurt, search for her when she was dying. She had had to make that brother for herself.

"It doesn't have to be this way."

Fahri turned, startled. A young man was leaning on the bridge's rail, grinning greenly at him, regarding him through horn-rimmed lenses framing a shimmer of data.

"What?"

"It doesn't have to be this way," the young man said. "It doesn't have to end tomorrow, with a wave of the doctor's wand. You don't have to die. I can show you how to live."

A few hours later, in Mahir's garage under the bridge, his museum to the filthy old days of internal combustion, to private cars that fogged their inefficient poison into the atmosphere, Mahir also spoke of shapes and of justice. Seated at a scarred metal table once used to vivisect the organs of automobiles, delicately sipping at his coffee and tweaking one gelatinous square after another of rahat lokum from a chipped china plate into his mouth, he explained:

"It's simple, really. The High Parliament put a law into place that seemed reasonable enough to them, and protects the valuable merchandise of the body shops. You have to clap an inhibitor cuff around the wrist of a runaway blank in order to claim it again. The law's based on the antique system of process servers, things like that. And you can't have a drone do it: they were working it that way for a while, but then a drone clapped an inhibitor on a blank on a dock, and the thing went in the water. Awake, with its drifter inside. Reticular activation system didn't fire, no transmigration—and a drifter who was simply late on their payments drowned. A citizen on a holiday. Big scandal. So now they write a new law, says you have to do it in person. You need a conscious being to put the inhibitor on. And you're liable for any damage. Inconvenient, yes? But each new law is a new opportunity, a new industry. You put a limit on power, someone will shape a service to fit inside that limit. That's where we come in. Reclamation."

"But you know where they are," Fahri said. "They're all tagged, traceable."

Tarik, who has been fiddling with some unidentifiable piece of primitive tooling in the corner, interjected. "Finding them's the easy part. The problem is, some of them *really* don't want to go back where they came from. When they skip, they want to stay skipped. But I guess you can relate, right?"

"They are going to save her," Fahri said. "I just need to buy her some time, that's all."

"Motivation." Tarik tossed the tool he was fiddling with back in the bin, "is the key to everything. Let's sign contracts."

"And the Institute?"

Tarik looked at Fahri. On the screens of his Parker Philips Overlay Glasses a car chase was going on. Fahri saw it backward, stereoscoped: some ancient piece of film. In a hilly city drenched in sun, an over-powered car careened through an intersection, a blond man at the wheel. In the background, Fahri could glimpse an ocean half-concealed by a smear of smog.

"I'll deal with the Institute," Tarik said. "That's what you'll be paying me for. That, and your nice new body not full of poisonous bacteria. And your other body, drifting on the edge of death. And the price for all three together is going to be very, very high."

Three months later, Tarik and Dr. Solmaz Haznadar stand on the balcony of the Church of St. Stephen, watching the bear of a man lay Fahri's unconscious body gently down on the white floor. The man takes out a penlight. Opening Fahri's eyes one by one, he looks into them, then pauses for a moment, reading vital signs.

He turns to the two on the balcony. "Vital signs are good, but there's nobody home. The reticular activating system fired properly. This drifter has transmigrated back to the mind they came from."

"Many thanks, Doctor Akdağ. You can move the blank back to Institute storage. We'll see you at the office."

Outside, winter is making a temporary comeback. Wind and a battering rain sheet in across the Golden Horn, tearing spring blossoms from the trees. Fishermen in raincoats and sou'westers continue numbly tossing lines into the oscillating, cloud-gray surface of the water. Tarik and Solmaz, hoods up on their rain jackets, squinting against the wind-whipped water lashing against their faces, are making their way to the Tekray station.

"Now comes the fun part," Tarik says. "Collating all this data. Preliminarily, though, it's interesting. Just about no limit to what the subject will pay to keep going. I had him up to forty thousand lira near the end. He—or she, or whatever. Even I'm getting confused at this point. I keep thinking of Fahri as a separate person. Anyway, he sure seemed determined to continue. Given more budget on the project from Motivations, I think I could have cranked his fees even higher. He was barely sleeping, taking on two or three assignments in a day, oblivious to risk. Absolutely minimal lifestyle: he was eating the cheapest possible food, bought nothing for his cell, and was working double shifts skip tracing. I think if we had kept pushing the numbers up, though, he'd eventually have gotten hurt—but there has to be a balance there somewhere: that tipping point between a sustainable, high level of motivation and self-destructive levels of output." The raindrops on his Parker Philips lenses smear and distort the rotating heads of Feride and Fahri in translucent mulberry topographs, a stream of data the color of dark wine—receipts, transit maps, time stamps. "Prelims tell me if we were charging thirty thousand, we could probably exploit indefinitely. That's a rough guess. But the fucking Motivations Department geeks and the Ethics sub-department of Exurban Studies are in a spat and pffffft! Project funding cut! Back to the drawing board. What about your study?"

Solmaz sidestepped an overly eager trash robot chasing a shred of paper. "Inconclusive. I'll need to read all the scans again—but overall? My guess is it may not be a great benefit on the larger scale. That's just my instinct. Disorientation in the early hours of the first day, followed by a morbid melancholy, indications of destabilization—even what I would call an almost entirely new personality emerging. And very quickly. I think there's a chance the benefit could cause violent reactions, cascading events it would be difficult to control. But the subject is sub-optimal: background is institutional, and she's barely socialized. I wouldn't have chosen her."

"I suppose not, but then wouldn't many of the beneficiaries of this benefit also not be optimal?"

"Well, that's the rub. We'll continue the study, but this first case makes me doubt this benefit is a benefit at all. It could be a liability for the Protectorate."

"Ah, well. *Geçmiş olsun.* Let it be in the past."

A few days later, Feride wakes up in a gauzy haze—a haze accentuated by the evening sunlight pouring through the curtains of the hospital suite. It is a strong light, red-gold, made stronger by its reflection off the mirrored buildings and the pavement soaked by a day of rain. She is brittle, foggy, her senses diffracting off sore spots, aches coming alive. The sagging jellyfish of intravenous drips surround her, the evening light refracted through their liquids, striping and pooling across the white bedsheets. The darkness grows in the room as the day dies, and the diodes light the ward in its strange, undersea green.

For a moment, she is Fahri. But when she looks at her bruised hands, they are not her own. Where are the thick, knuckly fingers she had? The black dusting of mid-digital hair? Already a life—her own, not quite her own—is fading: looking out at the port from the cafomat, Melek's fingers in her hair, searching for a wound, a sparrow with an artificial foot, candles in the rusting iron church. She cries for a time, quietly. She is the only attendee at Fahri's funeral: a brother of her own creation, a second self, a figment.

An hour after she wakes up, a young nurse comes in and has her blink permission to access her vitals.

"I'm not going to say you are out of danger yet," he says, "But we've turned a corner. We're glad to see you back in the world." As he takes down one of her IV drips, he half-sings:

Birds turn their backs on their nests.
Some day you will forget me, too . . .

"You were here when they admitted me," Feride said. "You sang that song. That old folk song. A friend of mine would sing it, sometimes. Suat. In the garden where I worked."

"It's been stuck in my head for months, but all I can remember is four lines of it."

Surprised at the strength of her own voice, despite her tube-scratched throat, her dry mouth, Feride sings the next verse of the song:

Roads are far away
My mad heart cries out
Life goes on, just goes . . .
One day you will forget me, too.

From the doorway, standing there in her scrubs the color of a faded key-lime pie, Melek finishes the song:

This longing has turned to mourning
My summers and springs turned to winter
My life has passed in vain
One day you will forget me, too.

"Ah," the young nurse says, walking out. "Here's your benefactor."

"Benefactor?"

Melek settles herself into the bedside chair. Feride realizes this is the first time she has ever seen Melek with her own eyes. But Melek is the same: mischief in her lively eyebrows, a chipped front tooth, one eye slightly larger, and greener, than the other. She says: "I thought I glimpsed something—a return. It's hard to explain. I could see something had changed. There was someone there . . . someone trying to surface. I thought a few days might be enough to see you through."

"But the expense. It must have been . . . I remember struggling to pay . . . it's thousands of lira a day . . . you can't possibly afford . . . "

"Hush." Melek presses a finger to Feride's lips. "It's my choice to make, Fahri. And where else would I find such a hero? And who would I go on my five-minute dates with? Are you trying to make me drink my coffee alone?"

Aliette de Bodard writes speculative fiction: she has won three Nebula Awards, a Locus Award and four British Science Fiction Association Awards, and was a double Hugo finalist for 2019 (Best Series and Best Novella). She is the author of the Dominion of the Fallen series, set in a turn-of-the-century Paris devastated by a magical war, which comprises *The House of Shattered Wings*, *The House of Binding Thorns*, and *The House of Sundering Flames* (July 2019, Gollancz/JABberwocky Literary Agency). Her short story collection *Of Wars, and Memories, and Starlight* is out from Subterranean Press. She lives in Paris.

RESCUE PARTY

Aliette de Bodard

Khánh Giao hadn't expected to be preserved.

She came home to Xarvi, a city she only saw in fits and snatches, to its dizzying towers built from the carcasses of reclaimed spaceships and failed orbitals and wide avenues offering an ever-expanding array of personalised environments, from quaint brushed metal bunkers of the Landfall era to riotous colours of the faraway Đại Việt court, with vague plans. She came home because she needed some planet time lest her bones break, because the mining station needed iridium to fuel its machines—and because her girlfriend An Di had asked her for some black sesame pastries and pandanus extract for their shared kitchen.

Nothing happened on the first night. But on the morning of her third day, Giao opened the door to her compartment, thinking of grabbing a noodle soup from Double Happiness Plaza with Cousin Linh and Linh's infant children—and found oily, inky blackness waiting for her. At its centre were vermillion letters: her own name and avatar ID, and the paintbrush and pine tree seal of the Ministry of Culture and Education.

The Repository.

A memory, sharp and merciless and inescapable, from a New Year's Eve two or three years ago: Cousin Tâm, smiling at her, the bots in her hair gleaming in the lights of the compartment—her face sharp and cutting, the magistrate's one before she ordered an execution. *Do you think yourself better than us, lil'sis, because you don't live here any more? The city doesn't let go. It'll weigh your usefulness against the value of your memories, and find you wanting in the end. It always does, with us.*

Always.

She didn't remember what she'd answered Tâm: she'd been drunk, trying not to count the missing places at the large banquet table, or the greyed-out holos on the ancestral altar—trying very hard to forget what it meant, to be Rồng in Xarvi, to be other. She must have laughed. She must have said something about not needing to worry about preservation or the Repository.

So drunk, so carefree. So wrong.

And of course, Tâm was gone now, preserved into the Repository like much of Giao's family and so many of her friends.

On the threshold of her own house, Giao opened her mouth to speak, to protest, and the darkness rose and leapt inside, leaving a taste on her palate like charred star anise—moments before it swept over her face and everything froze and rushed away from her.

Giao woke up in darkness, groggy and struggling to clear her mind. She sat up: the floor beneath her was hard and cold, and—

There was something in her mind, like a stray thought or something on the verge of recall—an always present shadow in her thoughts. She shook her head—rubbed her face with her hands, struggling to recall something of the past few moments, but nothing made it go away. She got up, shaking—and felt it skitter across her scalp, a touch like ten thousand burning bots. There was nothing in her hair. Or on her scalp. But when she moved again, it happened again, that same skitter—except it started in her scalp and moved deeper—and as it did so, a vast shadow dimmed her field of vision, a shroud thrown across the entire world.

She—she needed to think, to focus, but every time she tried to do so, the shadow would cross again, and her hands would come up to her head, hunting for the bots that didn't exist, until her nails burnt and ached, gummed with dry skin and broken, brittle hair.

Where—

What—

Focus.

Focus.

Something within her was moving, slow and vast and ponderous: a memory, long hoarded, of Grandma, her mother's mother, kneeling by her side, who'd been preserved so long ago. *Remember, child. If the Repository takes you, they'll trawl through your mind to satisfy their visitors.* Third Aunt had said something about muscle relaxants and opioids, but Grandma had shaken her head. *That's irrelevant. Remember this, child. Reflexes are hard to eradicate altogether, and muscle memory goes deep.*

They will kill me, Giao had said.

Grandma's smile had had nothing of joy in it. *Life is sacred,* she'd said. *You're preserved, not accused of crimes. They won't kill you.*

It hadn't been reassuring, even at the time.

Giao brought her hands together. Slowly, carefully, she stretched, bringing her arms up to the Heavens—and then back down again, lowering them all the way to the earth. Then she crouched, drawing an imaginary bow left and right until her calves burnt and she felt her arms vibrate as though she'd truly been loosing arrows into the darkness. And, with each step—with each completed figure, the shadow receded—until it was once more a faint tingle at the back of her hand, and not the endless string of bots nibbling at her brain.

Bots.

Giao didn't have her bots any more, or rather . . .

They hung like dead weights, coiled in her topknot and at the shoulder-seams of her jacket—their metal legs locked together so tightly she'd have to break them to make them go. Deactivated, or worse, killed off by the Repository, because why would those preserved ever need personal comforts?

She ran her hand over them, feeling the familiar surfaces under her fingers. Some of them had been purchases—the newer, sleeker ones she'd got prior to leaving for Perse and the mining station. Some of them had been gifts. *For the fifteenth return of the apricot flowers,* the one from Mom said. The one from Cousin Linh was rowdier, a wish for a sexual partner: *to the swallow looking for her oriole.* The one from Cousin Tâm was cool and businesslike, much like Tâm herself, with barely any hint of poetry. *Let this light scatter the blackness of ink and the darkness of space.* Letters so often read she knew them by touch, inscriptions fingered so much while walking in the corridors of the station or operating a drone in the depths of an asteroid, like prayers to the long disappeared.

And now the bots were gone too.

How dare the city deprive her of them?

"I'm sorry," Giao said aloud to the bots, but of course they couldn't hear her any more—and what would they have said, even if they could? They were the simpler and non-sentient kind, and had never been equipped to process emotional turmoil. Her voice was rough, her throat parched. What had they given her, when they'd grabbed her? The tingle was still there. She rubbed her hands against her cheeks, and her scalp. It didn't completely go away. It wasn't ever going to. And she hadn't bought herself much time with the khí công forms; just enough to walk a little further.

She'd never see Linh or her nieces again. An Di. She'd never see An Di again, never stand around in their small kitchen, feeling the heat of An Di's body against hers as they passed each other to fetch ingredients. She'd never feel again that thrill in her bones as An Di kissed her and Giao's entire heart seemed to beat in her lips. She'd never know what she and An Di would have become: if there was a chance, any chance that what they had would turn into something deeper.

All of that was gone.

Giao was on the landing of a vast staircase. The letters of her name shone, briefly, on the floor as she moved—and so did the seal of the Ministry, and with it a brief flash of the halls on the other side: the continuous flow of visitors going through the Repository, being shown the history and culture of Asphodele—everything the city thought they needed or craved—Landfall, the first satellites, the first hydroponics farms, the first cities outside the domes. For a moment, as she set foot on the first stair leading down, Giao stared through what seemed like a vast window into another room. Sleek metal walls, displays in avatar space—and one particular visitor, a fifteen-year-old girl with pale skin and uncannily dark eyes, and small bots in her pupils: a child of Augmented parents. The room shimmered and became the custom display the Repository had chosen for her: a potted history of Asphodele that lingered longest on the troubled decade prior to Giao's birth, the labour rights riots, the sentience trials—and the inexorable way Asphodele had found its natural order again. A rebellious girl, then, one who needed to be reassured that straining against authority was futile.

"The Long Haul," the girl whispered, touching the last of the displays the Repository was showing her, the faraway planet orbiting its sun in the shadow of Asphodele's burnt-out wormhole gate. *Home*, Giao thought, as her chest tightened with a feeling halfway between grief and longing—except that Tuyết Ngọc was her ancestors' home rather than her own, wasn't it?

The stairs flickered as something rose from their depths, a vast and ponderous intelligence that sought everything it had, every person it had preserved that could best answer the question. The tingling in Giao's brain intensified—she dropped into the stance of the archer again, drawing the bow again and again—again and again as the shadow rose and the staircases hovered on the brink of disappearing altogether.

Following its independence from Asphodele, Snow Jade was mired in tensions between factions which devastated the planet's ecosystem and its economy. Faced with little choice, and with the wormhole gate destroyed in the independence war, some of the natives chose to leave on slow-moving ships in search of better opportunities: a journey named The Long Haul that would form the beginning of Asphodele's diaspora . . .

Slow-moving ships. Such a glib way of saying the mindships they'd painstakingly put together, their only hope at matching their colonisers' fast space-travel, had died one after the other on the journey, tearing apart half the ships as they did so, and slowing what should have been a fast journey down to a crawl. Every Rồng had ancestors among the dead of the Long Haul—and other dead, too, the rescue ship sent fifty years later that had simply gotten lost in deep space, too far away to be salvaged.

In Giao's mind, the Repository's systems raked claws of ice through her memories—the same ones that flickered, briefly, on the window that separated her from the girl: running with Tâm under the impossibly faraway tables of Mom and Third Aunt's restaurant, in that brief moment after naptime when the place was empty and everyone was in the kitchen—a New Year's Eve with Tâm and Linh helping Mom set up the kumquat tree while Third and Fourth Aunt counted new clothes, making sure every child would be able to change into them come New Year—everything so vivid and so present it brought her, shaking, to her knees.

The Long Haul ended when the remnants of the Rồng flotilla reached Asphodelian space, where they were hauled to safety by our cruisers. The corpses of their ships were towed to the scrap-heap to be recycled—the distinct architecture formed the basis of the Rồng Quarter, and one can still see the curvature of the ship's hulls in the distinctive window patterns.

Those Rồng who survived found a planet much changed from colonial times: a bright and shining metropolis with plenty of opportunities for hard-working migrants, to which they brought their customs . . .

"Whatever." The girl shook her head and moved on. The claws of ice opened, and Giao struggled to rise, to breathe—to compose herself. Below her, the huge shadow at the bottom of the stairs was fading away. Each landing was empty. She glanced around her but saw no one else where she was. Above her . . . Above her were only stars, a set of constellations she couldn't pinpoint, a pretty-looking, suitably arrayed set of constellations . . .

No.

She did know the stars, because she'd been staring at them for so long—nothing much else to do on Perse when they were on energy-saving periods. They were the stars above Xarvi, except slightly distorted and out of place: the constellations above the city, as they had been at Landfall.

Such a surprise.

Breathe.

Giao was preserved in the Repository—trapped for all of eternity, her blood injected with the nanites that would keep her alive, that would make her part of the city's living memory. She had pitifully few choices: use the khí công forms to snatch some brief periods of awareness, or to simply sink back into a never-ending fugue of memories called up at need. She had no future, and soon her past would forever overwhelm her, sucking her dry until only a husk was left.

She should have been afraid, but all she had, rising through her, was a cold, cold anger that made her shake. How dare they. How dare they do this to her, to her family? She was twenty-four: preservation didn't happen so young, so soon.

Not to ethnic Asphodelians, of course, it didn't—not to the favoured scions, those who had been here for generations, who kept expecting people like Giao to give way for them. But it was a different story for migrants and their descendants; always would be—whether it be Rồng or any of the others.

Giao's family didn't have much, but they had researched. They had given what little money they had to ex-government officials and informants, desperately trying to understand the secrets of the Repository.

Downstairs was the heart of the Repository, the resting place of the artificial intelligence that controlled the entire building, and sent its tendrils out, to mark the people it chose to be preserved: those of interest to Asphodelian history who no longer meaningfully contributed to society. Downstairs was a chance at an appeal.

Never mind that no one, in living memory or otherwise, had ever left the Repository.

Ancestors, watch over me. And another, brief prayer to people who couldn't hear her: to Cousin Linh and her wife, who had to be sick with worry by now, waiting for the updated preservation lists to be published; to An Di, whom she couldn't contact, who was still new in her life and whom no one in the family would think of, when it came to news. *Hold on, little sisters. I'm coming back.*

There was nothing left in the world but these endless landings: empty flights of stairs, the metal resonating under Giao's feet, and each landing opening on a different room of the Repository, with a different flow of people staring at displays that kept flickering, Giao catching in a heartbeat a glimpse of all the different ways the Repository was filling them, all the different facets of history it was presenting to people.

The first few hundred years after Landfall were a difficult struggle against the planet's alien fauna and flora. But gradually, settlers were able to introduce food crops and to come to an uneasy truce with the local environment. A thousand years after Landfall, Xarvi, the capital city of Asphodele, rises proudly above the forests, though metal always remains at a premium . . .

Hard work and its value, justice and its inevitable arc, a society always seeking to be more progressive, more inclusive . . .

Various migration waves arrived at Asphodele, drawn by the promise of a new life. In today's cities, various quadrants pay homage to these: Galactic Town, Tinsel Streets, Dragon Island, the Rồng Quarter . . . And though the Việt mindships that travelled between the stars were always considered people, the sentience trials finally enshrined the rights of self-aware bots . . .

At some of the landings Giao would feel, again, the Repository rooting in her brain—but nothing quite as hard or as vivid as on the first one. Perhaps it just got easier, after a while.

Or perhaps that was just the way they kept everyone from escaping.

It was a fist of ice tightening around her entrails. And it was followed by another chilling thought that tightened her entire skin around bones that suddenly felt too sharp and too brittle.

Where *was* everyone?

There were hundreds, thousands of the preserved just in Giao's lifetime— her relatives, but also older people like Jean-Mae or Mer or all the teachers she'd had at university, and Ron's parents, and Meiluan's granduncles . . . And . . . Mom and Fourth Aunt and Cousin Tâm and every Rồng the Repository drew on for the history of the Long Haul. The Repository was, in so many ways, a mausoleum, a spider's web of a building that kept drawing more and more into its bowels. But here was this vast, echoing building with no trace of anyone. Faint, ghostly images on the landing that were dispelled as soon as Giao set foot on them. No *people*, not even their avatars.

Metal was always a problem: the scant mines in Asphodele didn't provide enough to sustain even the dome cities. Maker machines could split atoms into many things, but metal produced that way remained unstable and hazardous to human health . . . Hence the civic need to always carefully preserve metal, to respect the sharpening and recycling schedule for all blades, including kitchen knives . . .

At the second, or third landing after the history of metal, Giao saw the corridor.

It was lit with faint wisps of translucent radiance: not lamps, but iridescent butterflies that moved in slow, graceful patterns in the darkness. It couldn't have been signposted more clearly. But really, what did she have to lose?

She closed her eyes and breathed in—drawing the bow in her head again, against the raking of the Repository's assault on her memories. Then she followed the corridor, being very careful to count every pace she made, so that she'd be able to go back to the stairs if she needed to.

Two hundred and fifty-five paces in, the corridor flared into a large, huge room with rows and rows of . . .

She'd have said shelves, but they were coffins.

They looked like the sleeping berths Giao had seen on the Repository's reconstructions of the Long Haul—when she'd gone there as a child with her school cohort, back when she'd not understood yet what the building would come to mean to her. But there were too many of them, stacked on top of each other in endless rows and columns that ran all the way to the top of the vast, cavernous room, every berth labelled with an ID number and a place number. On the walls of the room was another number, one that kept blinking in and out of focus. *Ten thousand, three hundred and six.* It meant— it meant it wasn't the only room. Of course it wouldn't be.

Giao walked to the closest berth. It was white, opalescent plastic; but not transparent enough to let her see what was in it. Under her touch, it was faintly warm, pulsing like a beating heart; and bots crawled over it, a sleek metallic kind she'd never seen before. The newest ones, private to the highest ranks of government officials? But no, something about them felt . . . off.

There was an open berth further down the line, lit by butterflies. The message was clear and unsubtle: that one was meant for her. Giao didn't even want to get close to it.

"Hello, Cousin."

Tâm hadn't changed. Three years now—Giao may not have remembered which New Year's Eve they got drunk at, but she'd kept track of all the family's preservations with the same care as death anniversaries. She still wore her hair in that absurdly impeccable topknot, a hairstyle more suited to their great-grandparents and the Long Haul than to Asphodele, and wore the Asphodelian suit; a tailored jacket with dragons embroidered on the sleeves, and a set of matching trousers with leaping carps.

"Long time no see," Giao said. She moved away from the berth—and as she did so, someone somewhere queried the Repository, and the light flickered and a memory of folding dumplings in Grandma's kitchen overwhelmed her for a brief moment—before Tâm's hand on her shoulder brought her back to reality. "Breathe. In and out with each gesture. That's it. In, out."

When Tâm withdrew, Giao bit her lip not to grab her cousin's hands. "You've been here all this time?"

A grimace. Tâm pulled something from the air—a flat oblong box she opened, revealing the shimmering texture of Fisherman's Opals. She spread the paste on her neck, with the same poise she'd had when alive. "Some things help," she said.

"Like being intoxicated all the time on imaginary drugs you pull out of thin air?" The words were out before Giao could stop herself. "Sorry. The others—"

"The others don't come out any more." Tâm's voice was a sigh. She gestured, wordlessly, to the berths behind her. "It's easier to just sleep."

Drugged to the gills as well? "Big'sis . . . "

A shrug, from Tâm. "Truth? I wouldn't have come out either. I was . . . nudged." Another sigh. "It's always easier if it's someone you know welcoming you."

"Welcoming." Giao tried to keep her voice from shaking, and didn't succeed. "Like a party."

Tâm held out the box of Fisherman's Opals. "I can probably pull out tea and dumplings, if you insist. The dumplings will taste just like the ones Grandma used to make."

"Because it's inside the Repository. Because *Grandma* is inside the Repository. In one of those berths." Which one? She couldn't see the ID number, but of course there were so many berths, and so many other rooms.

Another shrug. "Mostly because we are here. That's where the vividness of the memory is coming from, not from Grandma's recipe. Are you going to be choosy?"

"I want to get out," Giao said, chilled. Three years Tâm had been there. Unchanged, she'd thought, except everything had changed.

"You know as well as I do that no one ever has walked out."

"So you tried."

Tâm looked away from her. "I'm not going to stop you," she said in the same tone of voice she'd used when Giao had said she wanted to leave for the mining station. She thought it was futile—that Giao would always come back to her family, that the city would never forget her. That it would always be waiting.

"You wanted me to leave," Giao said.

"Of course. And I knew you wouldn't." Tâm sighed, her hands closing the clasp of the Fisherman's Opals box. "Home," she said in Rồng—a word that meant hearth and kitchen and everything within, everything loved and cherished. Their ancestors had once used it to mean Tuyết Ngọc, before its meaning irrevocably changed. Some in the family had left Asphodele altogether—a fraught and expensive undertaking, for Asphodele was so far away

from other settled systems—but so many of them hadn't. Because it was
their home and their family's home. Because, like Giao, they kept coming
back to their hearths. "Home," Tâm said again. "Here." She laid a finger on
Giao's chest, a sharp, almost painful touch that seemed to stab through the
cloth of Giao's shirt. "Where you are. Where your family is."

Where the Repository was. Giao stifled a bitter laugh. "Where you always
keep coming back." Perse . . . Perse wasn't that yet; perhaps it would have
been one day, if her relationship with An Di had become more . . . But of
course, that had been cut short.

"Where else?" Tâm said. "But yes. I wanted you to be safe."

"And I you." Giao closed her eyes for a brief moment, struggling to breathe.

"We don't always get what we want," Tâm said. "Except the Repository, of
course. It always gets what it wants. What's best for us."

"And it wants me to get in there," Giao said, pointing to the empty berth.

Another shrug. "Actually, that's up to you. The Repository won't force
you, and it'll always be there waiting for you."

Oh, so the Ministry had *standards*. Freedom of choice. Sanctity of life; the
same lies they told in the classrooms, as if they meant something. She hadn't
thought she could become even angrier. "You mean I'll beg to go into it when
it becomes unbearable?"

Nothing from Tâm, not even a pitying look. "Are you even there?" Giao
asked. "Physically?"

"Does it make a difference?" Tâm asked. "That's such a regressive attitude.
Next you'll be telling me that shipminds have no rights because they can
only project an avatar down into Asphodele." She moved, and when she did
so, something shimmered, like the projection of an avatar into physical space.

Giao's heart missed a beat. "Are you . . . are you even my cousin?" The
Repository had all the memories, and it would be so easy, wouldn't it, to
simulate something passingly familiar? Much easier than waking up Tâm—
assuming the preserved could even be woken up, that these berths weren't
simply final resting places. "Big'sis . . . "

Tâm spread more Fisherman's Opals on her neck, the way she always did
when she was stressed—she'd have one hell of a headache and sense of thirst
in the morning, except that who knew if any of that still applied, where
they were. "I am your cousin." And, in smooth and almost too fast to follow
Rồng, *"I'm the one who told you to stay away from Xarvi."* A sharp, amused
smile. "Remember what Grandma said? The Repository hadn't quite worked
out the hang of dialectal variations on Rồng. It always spoke that kind of
weird version of the language that sounded off."

Giao didn't move. Because it was true, it had happened—and Tâm's voice and accent were uniquely hers, with nothing that sounded weird—but it proved nothing. "Perhaps it's learnt."

"I don't know how I can prove anything to you."

"Drop the avatar," Giao said.

"She won't want to do that," another voice said.

Its accent was pure Repository: something that Giao had never heard anywhere else—except in some of the newer dramas that came from Tuyết Ngọc, the hauntingly disturbing ones that were both familiar and utterly alien, coming from a culture that had diverged from them in the years after the departure of the Long Haul. Its owner, too, was dressed like nothing Giao had ever seen: a mix of Asphodelian fashions and traditional Rồng ones, from the embroidered jacket to the wide, flaring skirts. Behind them was a second person whose gender was equally indeterminate, wearing the jacket of an ao dai with the large panels of cloth falling over their hips, and slimmer trousers with kumquat flowers.

"I'm Trần Thị Hải San. You may call me San," the person said. "And this is Nguyễn Sinh Kim Ngân." San used feminine pronouns; Kim Ngân gender-neutral ones—except that they weren't the ones Giao would have expected. They were brutally simple, with none of the nuances of respect and age group she was used to.

"Pleased to meet you," Giao said, smiling to cover her confusion. Who were they, why were they injecting themselves in the conversation—how had they even known where to find her?

Kim Ngân smiled. "You're the only people here having an argument."

"We're not having an argument," Giao said between gritted teeth. "Now if you'll excuse us . . . " And, to Tâm, or the thing that pretended to be Tâm: "Drop the avatar. Now."

"She won't," San said in that same pleasant tone. "Because if she did, she'd have to show you what she's become."

That stopped her. She looked at Tâm, trying to breathe through a chest that suddenly felt constricted by a vice of metal. "Cousin—"

Tâm smiled. She turned to San, with a smile Giao knew all too well, a thing of teeth and vicious satisfaction, the same face she'd shown Giao on New Year's Eve. "You're wrong." And to Giao, "Here. You wanted to see."

It was . . . a shambling thing with shrivelled limbs and blood-red muscles beneath translucent skin, a thing that shouldn't have been able to stand or walk without its bones snapping—except that its—no, her—her hollowed-out face with too-large eyes was Tâm's, almost unchanged. No, that wasn't quite true, because Giao suddenly saw that the whites of Tâm's eyes were the same colour as the berths.

"Preservation liquid," Tâm said, with a shrug she was trying to keep casual. "It does seep into everything." The avatar shimmered into existence again, hiding the horror beneath while Giao was still trying to conjure words.

"You—" Giao said.

Tâm's gaze was shrewd. "I wasn't strong enough. Are you truly going to reproach me for that?"

Three years in a berth. Three years being worn down to the bone, body shrivelled and faded, and all the while the mind being queried, repeatedly, for every scrap of memory the Repository could use to satisfy its visitors . . .

Giao swallowed back words—because she was angry, but not at Tâm. "I have to get out," she said, and it was almost pleading now. The words she wasn't saying hung in the air: before the Repository got her too. Before she became like Tâm, like her forever silent family members, those same worn-down bodies locked in opalescent berths. Before it was too late.

Tâm was staring at her. "Downstairs," she said, finally, and this time she didn't sound angry or distrustful, but merely tired. She gestured towards San and her companion Kim Ngân. "San knows the way. Remember what we gave you, lil'sis."

Kim Ngân was already waiting for Giao at the exit to the room, their ao dai silhouetted against the door. San was still by her side.

"Wait—" Giao said. "Who are they?"

But Tâm was already turning away. "They're like you," she said. "They want to get out."

Giao knew a dismissal when she saw one. But, nevertheless . . . "Big'sis, please." And, before Tâm could move away, she hugged her hard—feeling every brittle bone and atrophied limb, every exposed muscle and hollow where the skin had melted away. "Thank you."

An amused snort. "Thank me when you're outside. If you ever are."

"You haven't told me who you are," Giao said to San.

They were going down landing after landing. It was harder than it had been, closer to the top. The Repository didn't want her to get down—not further than where her berth was. Every landing brought her to her knees, squeezing the breath from her lungs and replacing it with an unending parade of past memories. San and Kim Ngân were the ones who gently guided her out, reminding her of where she was—of who she was, of how to breathe so she wouldn't choke on her own thoughts.

Sometimes, after she'd lost count of the gruelling descent—after an age-ing government official asked about integration policies, and the Repository brought up lion and unicorn dances in the wide tree-lined streets, and kum-quat trees and the lemongrass chicken they used to have when Mom worked late nights—that Giao finally got her nerve or lost her patience, or both.

"Comrades," San said, with a laugh.

"Seriously." Giao glared at Kim Ngân, who had the grace to look embar-rassed.

"We're the rescue party," they said.

"I don't understand," Giao said.

When Kim Ngân spoke again, it was in the voice Giao had heard earlier that sounded almost like the Repository. "We set out fifty years after the Long Haul, when the flotilla's distress calls finally reached Tuyết Ngọc." An expansive shrug. "Radio waves are slow. There was a lot of debate in Parliament. Your ancestors weren't popular, making that decision to leave us and seek their fortune with our old colonisers, but we could understand their desperation. Finally, it was agreed to send a single mindship to see who or what could be salvaged. One that worked, this time. It took us fifty years, but we finally understood how the Đại Việt Empire made theirs work, and we used that as the blueprint for our own ships."

"The rescue ship," Giao said slowly. "You're the rescue ship. But you never made it here. You—" It was like a gaping hole opening, even worse than Tâm. Because at least the horror beneath Tâm's face had been expected. Dreaded, but in the way death was: utterly predictable and mapped. "Why are you in the Repository? Why have we never heard about you?"

"Oh, younger sister . . . " Kim Ngân shook their head. "Isn't it obvious? History is written by the winners, and the Repository has been winning at that game for a long, long time. Our ship landed and was taken apart for scrap metal—and every crew member taken for the Repository. We had no use to Asphodele, and so much of value to teach you about the culture of Tuyết Ngọc." Their voice was full of irony.

"You—you've been in the Repository ever since?" That wasn't possible.

Kim Ngân bowed ironically. "As we breathe."

Fifty years after the Long Haul. A century. Three or four generations of Rồng. Giao opened her mouth, shut it, because she couldn't think of any words to make it better. "I'm sorry."

"Don't be," San said.

"A little." Kim Ngân's smile was wide, mocking. "The Repository is the sum of everything you consider history. Of all the lies you tell yourself."

The lies they told themselves? As if she'd been the one to decide her family would be preserved—to single them out in life and afterwards. "Because Tuyết Ngọc is better?"

"Of course not," Kim Ngân said. "But we don't eat our own and call it justice . . . not any more."

"Younger sib." San laid a hand on their arm. "Of course we do. We just do it in different ways." It sounded like an old, old argument, rehashed until it lost its bite and heat. "This is not the time."

Kim Ngân subsided, but they looked unhappy.

"Then tell me something," Giao said.

"As you wish."

"You could have walked downstairs yourself. To appeal."

"Ah." Kim Ngân's smile was bright. "I think you'll find that . . . appeals"—she managed to make the word sound utterly fictional—"are reserved for Asphodelian citizens. Certainly not for aliens from a former colony who've turned up in a suspect but highly desirable vessel."

"So you need someone to appeal for you."

Kim Ngân nodded.

"I can't be the first person you've walked with downstairs."

"A lot of them don't understand us," San said. "Or don't trust us. Or prefer the berths, anyway." A snort. "But no, you're not the first. A lot of the Rồng are sympathetic, and some of the other non-Asphodelian ethnicities."

"And you've never got out."

"No. But you already know that no one has, don't you?" Kim Ngân's voice was hard, with nothing of irony in it.

"And if I asked you to drop the avatars . . . "

A shrug from San. "You'd see much the same thing. We've never gone into the berths. We're not mined much. Not many people want to know about Tuyết Ngọc, other than us being desperately poor and fighting each other to extermination." Another snort. "No one seems to ever ask *why* we're poor, or why our planet was stripped of all its natural resources and its cultures set at each other's throats to make us easier to control. Asphodelians, still hiding from the truth."

"What's downstairs?"

San's face was hard. "I don't know. We're never allowed inside. And it seems to be different for every person. What I can tell you is that everything you can think of has already been tried. And everything your family has thought of, most particularly."

Because her family was nothing more than a weapon the Repository had turned against her. "You think I'm going to be scared?"

Kim Ngân cocked their head. "No," they said at last. "You don't scare easily, do you?"

Giao would have laughed, but she suspected if she did, she'd never stop. She'd just sit there on the landing and let the Repository root through her brain. A wave of raking hit her—being sixteen at university, the overt mockeries of childhood becoming polite nods and unexpectedly sharp words in conversations.

Rồng and other minorities are faced with disadvantages, but they have transcended them. Where the first generations of Rồng did menial work, their descendants turn away from the restaurants and gruelling food industry jobs, and complete university courses for bot-makers, architects, or anything to do with the making and maintenance of wormholes.

Demons take them. Of course they didn't want to run restaurants any more. Mom and Third Aunt had never taken a holiday in their life, and even the best doctors couldn't straighten out their spines or the repetitive wrist strains from directing the bots in the kitchen.

"Younger sister. Breathe. You've got this. Breathe." They spoke to her but didn't touch her. They didn't seem to be having spasms of their own either: it made sense that there would be few queries about Tuyết Ngọc, fifty years after the Long Haul, and fewer still about a ship that had vanished, but still . . .

Still.

"Let's go," Giao said. Get this over with, whatever it turned out to be.

She'd expected downstairs to be . . . oh, she didn't know what. Some kind of lair, or a huge room filled with machines of all kind. But at the bottom of the last staircase—below a landing whose invisible window opened on the atrium of the Repository, where visitors merely glanced at the artifacts on display before moving on—was only a set of double doors, each engraved with the Double Happiness symbol.

Giao looked at them, hard. They had to be avatar space rather than the physical one: a display put on for her sake. As if to confirm her suspicions, the letters of her name flickered on the door—not in the Asphodelian script, but in old-fashioned Rồng, the kind that master calligraphers wrote on New Year's Banners.

Kim Ngân and San were both waiting for her at the bottom of the stairs. Great. Of course they weren't going to open the door either.

"You can't go in," she said.

"Citizens only." Kim Ngân's voice was hard.

"Then tell me—"

"Yes?"

"Your ship. What were they called?"

A pause. Something twisting on Kim Ngân's face, endless grief like a punch to the gut. The ship was dead. A mind taken apart and recycled for scrap parts. "Her name was *The Serpent in the Lychee Garden*."

An allusion to a tale of Old Earth—a long, long lost piece of history about a woman accused of the murder of an emperor. "I see," Giao said. And then, staring at them, at the perfect clothes, at the way the Repository didn't even seem to affect them. "You're dead, aren't you?"

Kim Ngân detached themself from the stairs and walked closer to her. Their outline flickered: Giao strained to catch a glimpse of what lay beneath but couldn't. "Not dead," they said. "But not corporeal any more, no. We're not Asphodelians. They needed to be sure that they were holding us securely."

So they couldn't get out, not without a whole new set of obstacles. "Why the rigmarole then?"

A sigh from San. "You don't understand. We really are the rescue party. We want *you* to get out. That was our mission, and we've got nothing left but to see it to an end. But most people won't believe that."

"I could—"

"Appeal on our behalf?" Kim Ngân's face was carefully frozen. "You can try."

"Other people have," Giao said flatly—because she didn't know what to make of them any more. Because she didn't know who or what she could trust any more—the Repository not only presenting history in a biased fashion but erasing it wholesale; Tâm choosing to give up and drug herself; two strangers appearing out of nowhere like a miracle she hadn't prayed to the ancestors for.

A shrug from San. "Not many."

But some, and it hadn't worked. "You don't need to believe us," Kim Ngân said. They held out their hands, their expression carefully controlled—Giao knew it all too well, seconds before breaking into tears. "Just get in there and make your appeal. That's all that matters." A century in the Repository, fighting to stay whole, and all she could think of was for ways to disprove their story?

"Thank you," Giao said, closing her hands over Kim Ngân's, and feeling only emptiness in her fingers.

"Get inside."

Giao grabbed both handles and pushed. The doors swung open noiselessly.

Inside was only darkness, and the letters of her name lighting up one by one, forming a path to the centre of the room, where something waited—a column of polished metal like the maker machines on Perse.

She walked there, because there didn't seem to be anything else to do. The moment she stepped into the room, something within her flickered and died, as if a switch had been thrown, and a dreadful, unnatural silence spread. No, not dreadful: she hadn't realised how omnipresent the Repository's tendrils in her mind had been, until now.

She walked towards the pillar, in that silence that she struggled to encompass. Every step on the polished metal floor seemed too loud, like phaser shots—with every one, she'd look up, expecting the militia to burst in, or paralysing bots to hold her down. But nothing happened.

She reached the pillar. It was polished, and really metal: she'd half expected the plastic of the berths, but it was grey, with some oily reflections as if someone had forgotten machine oil. She turned, then, saw Kim Ngân and San waiting for her beyond the open doors of the room.

She laid both hands on the command slot—for a brief moment she was back on Perse, in the mining station, with An Di's hands on her shoulders—An Di's perfume of hibiscus flowers and lime wafting into Giao's nostrils, and An Di's voice telling her not to be so serious—and then it passed, and she was standing there in the heart of the Repository, blinking back tears.

She hadn't broken before. She wasn't about to start now.

"My name is Lê Thị Khánh Giao," she said. "ID number 3985332190554. I wish to appeal against my preservation, on my behalf and on behalf of the crew of *The Serpent in the Lychee Garden*, Trân Thị Hải San and Nguyễn Sinh Kim Ngân."

A silence. The room around her flickered—and for a moment became something else, something that was all metallic, inhuman sheen. "*The Serpent in the Lychee Garden*. Trần Thị Hải San. Nguyễn Sinh Kim Ngân. These names do not exist in the records." The voice was high-pitched and expressionless. It spoke Asphodelian, but with the slow laboriousness of someone who'd not finished learning it. And something about it was hauntingly familiar, though Giao couldn't put her finger on why. "I cannot record an appeal on their behalf."

Didn't exist. Because they'd been purged. Because they'd been absorbed. Because Asphodele had erased that rescue ship, pretended it had been lost. "They're at the doors," Giao said, biting back the more angry words. "Hải San and Kim Ngân. Tell them to come in, and you'll see."

"They're not citizens," the Repository said. "Only citizens are allowed here, and only for the duration of their appeal."

"But they're part of the Repository," Giao said.

A flicker, on the pillar. "They are a special case."

"I thought everyone was equal, before the law of preservation? That everyone had the right to ask for their experience to be weighed again?" Giao couldn't help it: the words weren't even hers, they were the ones her family had crafted and hoarded. The ones that wouldn't help, San had said.

A pause. The Repository seemed to be chewing on something.

"What harm do you think they can cause, being here? You control everything." The bots and the berths and the environment, and even the thoughts of every preserved person. "You don't have to take their appeal, but they could come here. Please." She'd slipped into Rồng with the last sentence, and hadn't realised it—painstakingly, she forced herself to think in Asphodelian. "Please."

The words wouldn't work, not for getting out. But it was a very different thing, what she was asking the Repository for.

"You didn't kill them," Giao said, and knew, suddenly, why they had not. Sanctity of life. Freedom of choice. Like the berths, a twisted kindness that stretched the knife's kiss over endless years, endless centuries. "They still have value to you. Please let them in."

At last the Repository said, "They may come in. But I cannot log an appeal on their behalf, or on that of a mind that doesn't exist any more." Darkness fell across the room as it continued to speak. "ID number 3985332190554, Lê Thị Khánh Giao," the Repository said. "Your appeal is duly logged. Please present your defence."

She—

She didn't know what she'd say. In her heart, she'd always believed the injustice of it would be so flagrant, that she would just need to make them see—and then old memories of Tâm's schooling took over. "I'm twenty-four," she said. "I work in the Perse mining station to provide the metal for Asphodele. I would like to allege undue discrimination against me and my family."

A pause. On the metal pillar, her family tree appeared, with the various people preserved greyed out. A few stragglers: Cousin Linh and her children, Cousin Bảo and his electro-engineering company, Fourth Aunt, still serving in the army well past her age of retirement. The floor under Giao's feet flickered.

At last the Repository said, "I see no undue discrimination. The higher frequency of preservation is due to your family's interest to Asphodelian history."

Four generations. They'd been there four generations, and they'd always be curios in Asphodele. A study in how people adapted and evolved. A population to be studied rather than be allowed to live. The more polite, deadlier version of the mockery she'd received as a child.

"As to your age . . . " A pause, there, while some lights she couldn't tell flickered, and she realised what the laboriousness was: it was a Rồng accent, except subtly wrong, the same way San and Kim Ngân's were.

Why would they—

"That's pointless," Kim Ngân said. She and San had come in, were now standing in front of the metal pillar. San was standing still, but Kim Ngân was looking at everything, darkly fascinated.

"Then tell me what to say!" Giao screamed at them.

"I can't," San's voice was toneless. "You forget: no one has come out."

Meanwhile Kim Ngân reached out, slowly, carefully—their hand brushed the pillar for a brief moment, and in that moment, it changed colours to the deep yellow of gold.

"Kim Ngân." The Repository's voice changed. It spoke Rồng, and its voice had the exact same accent as theirs. "Why—"

The room flickered; and then the metal pillar was back, and the moment gone. "Your age, and the usefulness of your work, is being re-evaluated against the value of your experience."

"Wait," Giao said. "Wait. You know them."

San grabbed her arm. Or tried to: her hand went right through Giao's. "Don't anger it," she said. "That's never ended well."

On the metal pillar, a slow pattern of blinking lights was slowly coalescing together, symbols that meant nothing to Giao but had to somehow represent the sum of her life.

The Repository had paused, when Kim Ngân had touched it. "San," Giao said. "Please. Can you—" She tried to grab San's hand, but San wasn't moving. San was desperately trying to think of words that would save Giao, but San and Tâm had been right: everything had been tried. Giao was still clinging to the hope of an appeal, to the notion that things were fair, when she'd known the truth all along: the decision had been made already. Eating its own, Kim Ngân had said, and they had been harsh, but not incorrect. "Put your hand on it."

"I already told you. Neither Kim Ngân nor I can appeal. You're wasting your time."

The lights were climbing on the pillar. When they were done—and it couldn't be much to weigh, couldn't it? Twenty-four years, a childhood on

Asphodele, five years on Perse in the mines. Giao considered, dispassionately, the entirety of her existence, and knew it was nothing. To her, everything; but to the Repository, to the thing that Asphodele had made of itself, not more than a moment's pause. "You said I had to trust you. Just do it. Please."

San's hand—ghostly, flickering, only a visual avatar—reached, touched the pillar. The room flickered, then, showed that same oily sheen on metal walls Giao had seen before. Kim Ngân moved, put their own hand on top of San—and left it there, unmoving.

"San?" The Repository asked in that same voice. The flickers were getting stronger and stronger now, and it wasn't just the room: Kim Ngân and San, too, were flickering. Somewhere in a room of the Repository, in the berths where they were locked, bots would be crawling to cut the connection to their avatars. Just a matter of time; but Giao didn't need much of it any more.

Our ship landed and was taken apart for scrap metal—and every crew member taken for the Repository.

The sentience trials.

Sanctity of life.

They wouldn't have dared to kill a mindship, but they could repurpose it. They could replace an aging AI with a newer, better one—taking it apart for scraps just as they had the ships.

Meaningful contribution.

Of course.

Giao said in Rồng, "*The Serpent in the Lychee Garden.* That was your name, wasn't it?"

The room vanished. Instead of the metal pillar was a contraption of thorns and protruding arms, metal twisted and pulled together until it hardly seemed to be able to hold together any more—and in the centre of it was a glistening mass of flesh and electronics, with tendrils extended along every arm, and bots crawling everywhere on stray cables and spikes, in the light of stars—and then it flickered again, and she was staring at the curved expanse of a hull, moments before the view panned out and she saw the vast sleekness of a ship, fragile fins and stabilisers and pitted, sheening metal whose opalescence took Giao's breath away.

"Child," *The Serpent in the Lychee Garden* said in Rồng. And then the image of the ship twisted away, and it said again, in the polished metal darkness of the room where Giao had entered, "Your contribution has been weighed, and does not offset the value of your experience."

"She's theirs," Kim Ngân said, and they were weeping, with not a trace of sarcasm or irony on their face. "You can't change that, younger sister."

And they were right, weren't they? Tâm was right. It was pointless. The die was rigged. They could learn all they wanted about the Repository and how it worked, could remember all the movements to defeat its obliviousness, but in the end all they bought themselves was a few moments of agony, a last struggle before they gave way to the inevitable.

"You may return to the berths, or wander the halls," the Repository said. "This place will be closed to you henceforth, and your rights of appeal have been exhausted."

She'd tried to run away from Asphodele, and Asphodele had taken her the way it was always going to; the way it would take Cousin Linh and her children, and the children of their children, until the Long Haul was a faint memory—and even then something in the Repository would remember that they had come here impoverished and shipwrecked, and forever *alien*—

Something, long held taut, finally snapped in her: the same cold anger within her that had steadily risen as she was descending the stairs the first time, the same as when Tâm had said that the choice to enter the berths was hers.

How dare they?

They thought they held all the cards; that they owned her body; that there was no right to appeal—because there had never been one, because everything had been decided by society long before her life reached twenty-four.

But they scraped and recycled, and never gave a thought to what lay beneath the surface of what they had taken.

We're still the rescue party.

And what was true for San and Kim Ngân was true for the ship too.

Giao drew herself up to her full height and laid her hand against the pillar, the same way San and Kim Ngân had, feeling its coldness seize her. "Your right to appeal—" the Repository started, but before she could be thrown out of the room, Giao said, "My name is Lê Thị Khánh Giao, daughter of Nguyễn Thị Bảo Lễ, granddaughter of Trần Thị Mỹ Nhi"—the personal names of her ancestors burnt on her tongue—one didn't name ascendants, and even less the dead or the preserved—"great-granddaughter of Trần Thị Ngọc Lan, who crossed the Long Haul on *The Dragon Away from the Clouds*"—and on and on, reciting her full genealogy until she'd named her sixteen great-grandparents—"and great-granddaughter of Nguyễn Hữu Khả ái, who died with *The Willow as Quiet as Rice*. You came here to rescue us."

The floor under her shook—except it wasn't an earthquake but the frantic, panicked heartbeat of someone living. The metal pillar was gone, and it was only her, standing in the chamber that was the ship's heart, watching the stars.

"Child?" the Repository asked, and it was the ship's voice again, trembling and unsteady and as fragile as spun glass.

"Please, Grandmother," Giao said to the ship. "Please help us go home."

Giao stood on the bridge of the ship, watching Asphodele recede in the distance. In the centre of Xarvi was the polished dome of the Repository, the building's connections to the city shining faintly in Giao's choice of overlay.

She ran her hands through her hair, half expecting to feel dead bots again, surprised when they turned out to be alive. Her thoughts were empty, silent, in a way that felt almost wrong.

"You look thoughtful," Kim Ngân said, slipping into the seat next to her. San brought, wordlessly, drinks that she laid on the table. "Unhappy to be free?"

They both looked the worse for wear: pale and skeleton-thin, with the marks of bots' needles on their arms and neck—San wore a high-collar necklace to cover the worst of them, but there was no regrowing the shorn hair or hiding the pearlescent colour their eye-whites had turned, after a century in the berths. Kim Ngân wore an avatar, and San long sleeves and jewelry—as if anything could hide that they were a century or more out of sync, coming back to a planet that had all but forgotten them.

Giao stared at the Repository—at the shape of the ship she couldn't see, the Mind that was now irrevocably part of the canker at the heart of the city. She had let them go, but they'd never had more than that single moment of clarity from her. The Repository still held Mom and Tâm and the rest of Giao's family—still continued to mark the Rồng for preservation.

She felt, again, Tâm's fingers on her chest, sharp and painful, saw again the ruin that her cousin had become. *Home. Where you are. Where your family is.*

Home. Asphodele. A place they'd worked so hard to make their own.

"Home is the place that welcomes you," Giao said aloud. She clenched her fingers on the edge of the drink, thought of Tâm, and of Linh and her children, and all the others that still lived in the shadow of the Repository's biased choices. She thought of An Di, and all that might have happened— would An Di even understand or approve of Giao's choices?

"You should find another such place," San said, softly, and stopped when Kim Ngân laid a hand on her arm: a silent warning.

It was their home as much as anyone else's, but all it thought of was value, and it had found too little in them. She traced the contour of the Repository on the screen, imagined the ship lifting itself free of its cage of rooms and staircases, in the wreck of empty displays and darkened windows—of the preserved finally stumbling out of the ruins of the building, freed from berths that would never be used again.

I'll come back, Giao said, to the silently receding city that was her home. *I'll come back, and everything will change.*

John Chu is a microprocessor architect by day, a writer, translator, and podcast narrator by night. His fiction has appeared or is forthcoming at *Boston Review*, *Uncanny*, *Asimov's Science Fiction*, *Clarkesworld*, and *Tor.com* among other venues. His translations have been published or are forthcoming at *Clarkesworld*, *The Big Book of SF*, and other venues. His story "The Water That Falls on You from Nowhere" won the 2014 Hugo Award for Best Short Story.

CLOSE ENOUGH FOR JAZZ

John Chu

Beep. Click. Silence. Swoosh. The door into Emily's lab flung open. Booming footsteps rattled the raised tile floor. The few seconds of silence between the click and the swoosh officially made this the most warning she'd ever gotten that Hock or their angel investor would visit. From the way the footfalls thudded, it had to be Hock. Emily, still crouched underneath her workbench, continued sorting through and reconnecting cables. Until she was done maintaining the hardware, the hardware was not going to maintain his body.

"Emily." Hock's whisper reverberated through the lab. "You here?"

The rack enclosures and file cabinets in the lab rang in harmony with his voice. It'd taken her months to figure out how to rework his larynx, not to mention the resonance chambers in his head and chest. The result was the sort of deep, resonant voice that made license agreements sound like profound statements of truth and beauty. The vocal work wouldn't be a complete waste, she'd rationalized at the time. The change lasted, and lots of people who weren't gym bro wannabes might want to alter their voice, too.

"In a minute." She unworked a tangle to trace a cable from one end to another. "You could have warned me."

"Yeah, I guess." The room was uncomfortably silent for a minute. "We're in a hurry. I pitch Jazz for Series B funding in an hour. My pitches are more effective when I'm in my peak shape."

"In a minute." When Emily finished the maintenance work, she poked her head out from beneath her workbench. "That's not your peak shape?"

His T-shirt and jeans cost in the low four figures. They fitted him as perfectly as anything that expensive should have. The fabric caressed him, highlighting every bulge of every muscle of his action-hero body. He deployed all of that might at Emily.

"No." The word was barely audible, but slow and precise, it struck Emily as hard as a slap across the face. "You know what I'm supposed to look like."

"Sure." Her heart pounding, she latched onto the workbench and swung herself into her chair in front of her computer. "The apples are in the bin."

He peered into a small plastic bucket sitting on the file cabinet next to the door. The glow cast shadows across his face. His foot tapped against a loose tile. A grimace twisted his face.

"There are only two apples in here."

"You only need one . . . right?"

"Well . . . " His grimace untwisted into a sly smile. "It depends how many Series B investors I get."

When Emily had finally worked out some demonstrable transformations, Hock had not only insisted on trying them out on himself but couldn't help offering their angel investor a jacked-up body, too. That the apples weren't approved yet for animal testing, much less human use, was beside the point. The angel, of course, had already committed money and signed a nondisclosure agreement long before Hock had even implied to him that Jazz had apples at all, much less any mature ones ready to demonstrate.

As it turned out, the angel was a hardcore marathoner. Rather than more muscle, he had wanted something simple and permanent: longer legs and a shorter torso. Thankfully, he hadn't asked for anything since. Ethical issues aside, it was already hard enough to keep apples around for research.

"A new batch is ready." She pointed at a vat sitting on a table against the back wall. "I just need to take them out."

The apple from the bin seemed tiny in his grasp. Its glow pierced his hand, and shards of sunshine leaked through the cracks between his fingers. As he ate the apple, core and all, its glow spread through his body. His bones were long incandescent bulbs saturating his flesh with light that his shirt and jeans barely muffled. It hurt to look at him.

Emily pushed the headset on the table toward Hock and pulled the keyboard to her. She stifled a sigh as she tapped out the commands that would tune Hock's body back up to his standards. This was not how she wanted her work to go. Their funding should have gone into researching how to repair damage, reversing degenerative diseases, designing cheaper, more convenient alternatives to gender confirmation surgery. Instead of mapping out how to transform and repurpose organs, she'd spent her time designing ways to turn tech bros into the sort of guys who star in superhero movies.

Hock stood next to Emily's workbench. The headset, a chain of mechanical spiders, ringed his head. Their segmented legs splayed out and attached themselves to his scalp.

The headset injected the thoughts into the wearer's brain that caused their body to transform. Each spider leg flashed as Hock's brain dreamed those thoughts. Lights danced over his head, evolving from one intricate pattern to another. Mostly, this was to give any investor who'd already committed money and sworn to secrecy something cool to look at, just in case a glowing man growing visibly leaner and more muscular wasn't enough. By now, though, Emily could read the patterns and see the thoughts that transformed him.

Since Hock's first transformation, the physical changes always took Emily by surprise. He'd always been tall, and like his height, the broadened shoulders and slimmed hips from the first transformation were permanent. Muscle, however, came and went and came and went and came and went. Hock would stomp in whenever he was feeling insecure about his beefiness, even though he still looked like a man who'd pounded back one too many protein shakes. Then his face grew even harder, and his upper torso pushed out even farther against his T-shirt and jeans while lights danced around his head. He hadn't been in his peak shape, after all. In her defense, the added muscle was unmistakable but subtle. He wanted to be muscular enough that he "bagged the ladies," not so muscular that he turned them off.

The glow faded. Hock stood. The mechanical spiders detached their legs from his scalp. As usual, he tossed the headset onto the workbench. It tumbled into a pile of papers.

"Yeah." Hock pulled off his T-shirt and flexed his pecs and biceps. "That's more like it."

With unearthly restraint, Emily kept her eyes from rolling. The thud of Hock's hands slapping his arms, chest, and thighs was wet cement splatting against the ground. He turned to face the mirror set on the lab door.

"Hm. I'd never noticed before." He flared his lats again and again, like a flailing turkey whose chest was too heavy for it to take flight. "I mean, I'm buff and all, but I'm not . . . taut the way a guy who's been lifting for years is. The muscle should pop even harder off my frame."

"You could just go lift. Do you want me to show you what to do? Honestly, the straightforward way to look like the guy who spends too much time at the gym is to be the guy who spends too much time at the gym."

Hock's glare and frown in the mirror was a smile on his face by the time he turned around. He slipped on his T-shirt.

"Why would I waste my time doing that? I should just have the body I deserve. Besides, there isn't enough exercise in the world to keep anyone in this shape." He tucked in his T-shirt, then pointed a thick index finger at her. "Muscles that practically burst out of my skin. That's your top priority now."

"What?" She forced the word out.

Sketches too clinical to be pornographic littered her workbench. Papers on physiology and the development of body organs poked out of file cabinets and squatted in messy piles on the ground. Not that restoring atrophied muscles couldn't also be useful for, say, someone rehabilitating from an injury. Muscles atrophying from disuse was inevitable. They'd agreed, however, to branch out from anything temporary and purely cosmetic.

"Or you could figure out how to make yourself hot. Then maybe investors might pay attention to you." He smiled, shrugged, then showed her his palms again, as if his insult were a joke. "It's up to you. If you want me to drum up investors for Jazz and get funding for the research to make the apples do what you want, make my muscles bulge like mountains even when I'm not flexing."

Hock flexed his biceps and his pecs a few more times for good measure. His T-shirt writhed its way out of his jeans, and he had to tuck it back in again as he left the lab. She might have enjoyed the chagrin on his face as he turned to leave a little too much.

Apples taunted her from opposite sides of the room. It wasn't as if she'd never considered tasting one. She even had the thoughts for how she wanted to look all mapped out. Her body wouldn't be "hot" by Hock's standards or anyone else's. It'd be thick and full like an Olympic weightlifter's, chiseled out of rock and at least as solid. She'd tried in grad school, but she'd never managed to push her body there, much less stay there. With an apple, she'd certainly manage to get that body, and unlike Hock, she bet she could keep it.

She took the bin over to the vat. One by one, she lifted out each apple. Slick liquid sparkled off the apples' glinting transparent skin in sheets. She shook them dry, then placed them in the bin.

Normally, this was when she'd set new seeds into the solution. Hock's appetite made it difficult to keep mature apples on hand for her own work, especially when they took months to mature. Instead, she shoved the bin into her backpack along with the headset. Through the bin and several layers of fabric, the glow wasn't that visible, not if you weren't looking for it.

No one would realize she was gone. It might be a month or even two before Hock felt the need to beef himself up again and deigned to show up at the lab. Everything else happened over email. She could be replaced with an acorn and no one would notice until Hock needed to eat another apple.

In the meantime, she needed her own source of funding. Without money, there was no lab space, no equipment, no chance to design transformations that lasted, ones that had nothing to do with male power-trip fantasies. By the time Hock walked in the lab and discovered she wasn't there, she'd have an angel investor who'd fund her work, she hoped.

Mechanical spiders skittered across Emily's scalp. Servos hummed as spider legs stabbed through her hair. They pricked her, tiny instants of pain scattering around her head. Once she had funding, she'd scrap this headset and hire someone to design something less flashy and more comfortable. For now, she lay on her sofa and waited for the spiders to find the right places to attach to her.

Once they had all settled down, she pointed her cell phone at her scalp and started recording. The headset filled the cell phone's display. The sequence of lights blinking had to be perfect before she'd even consider eating an apple. Emily made herself become the proverbial twig in the river or leaf on the wind and let thoughts flow through her. Points of light danced in ever-shifting, complex patterns around Emily's head. Without the sheer amount of computational machinery she had at the lab, the headset had to be driven by her laptop instead. Its fan whined under the stress.

The coffee table shimmered as it reflected the apples' glow. By now, ignoring the shimmer had become second nature. She was still hunched over reviewing the video on her cell phone when Shereen came home from university. As usual, Shereen's gaze swept across the coffee table. It paused at the headset and the bin of apples before it finally landed on Emily.

"You still don't look any different to me." Shereen unslung her laptop bag.

Emily's wife had been simultaneously chill and wary about all of this. It wasn't every day that the love of your life burst through the door with a bin of glowing apples and announced that she needed to lie low and disguise herself. Emily had sworn Shereen to secrecy about the apples even before Emily had taken off her shoes. Until then, she hadn't even hinted at her work to Shereen beyond the vision that Hock had pitched. That night, she was forced to explain what had happened in the lab with Hock. By the time she'd finally set the apples down, her confession had probably made Shereen an accessory to her crime.

Shereen, for her part, hadn't so much as blinked. She'd merely pointed out that as a professor of religious studies, she was now obliged to ask whether the apples kept the eater young and whether Hock was now built like a giant or a Norse god. Emily had rolled her eyes.

It did seem to be every day since that Shereen would remind Emily that she didn't need to look like anyone besides herself. Truth be told, Emily wasn't sure she needed to disguise herself as much as she needed to try the merchandise. Just once, she told herself, to show Hock that if she could maintain her muscular transformations, he could maintain his.

"Actually, I'm finally prepared to eat an apple." Emily pulled the bin to her. "You want to watch?"

Shereen put her hands on her waist. Her brow furrowed with concern.

Emily spread herself across the sofa. Shereen slid the glowing bin and the headset out of the way and sat across from her on the coffee table.

The apple was firm in Emily's grasp. Rays of light sneaked out between her fingers. Her body seemed to thrum and she hadn't even taken a bite yet. She wanted to do this, she realized. Not only that, but she looked forward to how her body would change.

Emily bit into the apple with a crunch. Each bite evaporated in her mouth, leaving only a gently sweet taste on her tongue. She didn't need to swallow. The apple's perfume was both subtly spicy and the only thing she could smell. Hock had blazed with the color of blood piercing through pale skin, every capillary distinct and pulsing to the beat of his heart. Emily exuded a warmer, subtler radiance. She was a being of living bronze rather than a shocking chart of bone and blood vessels.

The effect left Shereen speechless. Awe warred with concern on her face. Her jaw hung even as her brow furrowed.

Heat spread from Emily's head down through her body to the tips of her fingers and toes. She sunk into the sofa. Her body felt malleable, molten, a wire frame larded with clay that an artisan could mold and sculpt. It vibrated with the possibilities of how she could present.

The glow faded, and Emily's body became its natural medium brown again. She took a deep breath. Her body felt . . . leaden and off-kilter.

"Wow. That's not what I expected." Shereen's gaze swept up and down Emily's body. "I still recognize you, but anyone else would wonder."

"Why?" Her voice rang higher and brighter than she expected, but only a little. "How do I look?"

"Ostentatiously strong and cartoonishly exaggerated? You look like a photo from a bodybuilding magazine that got morphed, but tastefully." Shereen opened her palms to Emily. "You know, that physically impossible powerlifter meets mixed martial artist body that you eventually gave up trying to build for yourself."

Emily caught her reflection on the coffee table's glass top. Her face broadened into a smile. Her body was exactly as she had specified.

"Well, we'll see how well that holds up." Emily tensed as she sat up, the weight of Shereen's gaze still pressing against her. "What's wrong?"

"Emily." Shereen placed a hand on Emily's thigh. "You know you don't need to look any particular way, right?"

"Oh, sure." Emily's hand covered Shereen's. "I just want to see whether I can keep myself looking *this* way."

Shereen's gaze shifted between Emily and the bin of apples. There were three left in the bin. Shereen's lips pursed, but she didn't say anything.

Venture capitalists were already waiting in the conference room when Emily scurried in, laptop in one hand, a bottle of water in the other. The men—and they were all men, not to mention all white—sat around three sides of a long table. One of them applauded ironically. The relentless judgment of their gaze pressed down on her.

These appeals for angel funding were all about selling yourself and your vision. For the first round, no one expected her to know how to execute her vision. Showing up late didn't help one bit to sell herself. Emily focused on selling her vision instead.

She made eye contact with every man in the room and opened her bottle of water to stall for time and settle herself down. She'd become hard and angular. Her face was built out of intersecting facets like a cut diamond. Her pantsuit felt wrong on her. It stretched taut over parts of her as it billowed loose across others. Parts of her body felt missing, while other parts felt as though they shouldn't have been there. Her body hung from long, invisible strings that stretched up several hundred miles above the roof. Somewhere up there, a drunk rigger, five minutes into his first job ever, hoisted her strings as though they were chains for a derrick.

She fumbled at her laptop. Her first slide appeared behind her.

"Changing your body ought to be as easy as changing your suit." Emily spread her hands to the men.

Her drunk rigger made her arms flail instead, and a spray of water arced from the open bottle she was still holding. It landed on some guy with a perfectly tailored suit and a five-hundred-dollar haircut.

The pitch did not get better from there. Then again, this set of tech bros, she decided about two slides in, was never going to find gender confirmation sexy enough to give anyone money, much less her. Investors tended to "pattern match," and unlike Hock, Emily did not match their pattern of what a successful founder looked like.

Weeks and some uncountable number of pitches later, she was still sitting on her sofa, crouched over her laptop on the coffee table, going over her slides for the millionth time. Her hand now did the right things when she wanted to move the cursor on the screen. If she still felt like she was trapped inside a bulky hazmat suit, at least the drunk rigger animating her limbs had been sobering by the second. It had been a couple weeks since she'd knocked something over by accident or tripped over herself. Her body was so sore that it hurt to type. She was still hefting dumbbells heavier than any she could have dreamed of using before she ate an apple, but not as heavy as the ones she'd used just a week ago. No matter how intense her workouts were, they weren't enough to maintain this body. Another apple, of course, could do that with no problem.

The bin was where she had left it, next to the headset on the coffee table. The glowing apples continued to taunt her. It would all be easier if she could just show them off or demonstrate a transformation, but not even Hock dared to do that when he pitched. The apples and headset were beyond secret, evidence of crimes considering the FDA hadn't approved their use on human beings yet. Implicit in his pitch was "I can make you, weakling, look like me, alpha male," but he might have easily been that bro blessed with the genetics and the opportunity to make himself look like that without an apple.

"Do you want to try an apple?" Emily took her hands off the keyboard and straightened her well-exercised and very sore back. "I can teach you how to use it."

Shereen held her hands up, as though she were pushing against some invisible wall between them. Slowly, she dropped her hands, then sat next to Emily on the sofa.

"No, I'm fine with how I look." Shereen placed a hand on Emily's thigh. "How about you?"

Emily was wearing a loose sweatshirt and sweat pants. They were the only things in her wardrobe that hid the fact that her muscles were atrophying no matter how hard she worked them. She felt beat up and exhausted. Most people weren't strong enough to punish themselves at the gym as much as she did. Despite all that work, her body kept growing softer and smaller, not so much that anyone else might notice yet, but she did. And pitch after pitch to disinterested investors took their toll. With their folded arms and tight smiles, they weren't even bothering to hide that she was just a checkbox they could tick off, a way to claim that they were too looking for diverse founders. It all seemed vaguely unfair. On top of that, she only had until Hock noticed she was no longer in the lab to find an angel investor. That pressure didn't make her pitch any better. Her increasing sense of desperation was impossible to hide. Which is why she couldn't tell Shereen any of this. She didn't want to hear how wrongheaded she was from someone whose opinion she cared about.

"I'm fine with how you look, too." Emily forced a laugh.

"Emily. Talk to me. I'm a great listener." Shereen put an arm around Emily's shoulder and squeezed. "It'll be okay. You'll find your funding."

Emily couldn't shake the fact that she was killing herself at the gym to no use and that Hock, who never got within a mile of a gym, would want another apple any day now. Any man who presented as ostentatiously as Emily did—or had—would have been worshipped by investors as he pitched. Like Hock.

"Everything is fine. Really." Emily's tone was unconvincingly bright and cheerful. "Well, I'm a bit disappointed that I can't keep my body in its peak shape."

"Is that all? I mean if that's all you're worried about . . . " Shereen's gaze shifted to the apples in the bin.

"Oh, don't tempt me."

"Did you know, Eve, that the forbidden fruit was probably not an apple?" Shereen grinned. "One theory is that Western culture associated it with the apple via a pun on or a mistranslation for the Latin word for 'bad.' "

"Thank you, Professor." Emily rolled her eyes. "That was so helpful."

"Changing your body ought to be as easy as changing your suit." This time, Emily did not splash water on some guy with a bespoke suit and an expensive haircut.

Their gaze, the intimation that she'd failed to conform to some arbitrary physical standard, pressed against her as always. Still, she hit all her slides—even the ones on homologous sex organs—and nailed her ask. The men with the money even seemed interested for the whole ten minutes of her pitch. Every once in a while, some investor in a red tie interrupted her asking for a clarification. Then again, when she was done, a different man, in an exquisitely tailored suit, asked:

"Is there even a market for this?"

She sighed. The man's suit made a point of how steeply his torso tapered down to his waist. If she had pitched giving him permanent, maintenance-free washboard abs or something, he probably would have thrown money at her. As she reached the elevator, the guy with the red tie hit on her, suggesting there would be money for her startup if she said yes. Of course he did. And of course she refused. It didn't matter what she looked like, just that he had power over her. This time, her phone buzzed and she escaped down the stairs, insisting that she had to take the call. He didn't need to know that it was actually a text.

Emily grimaced at her phone. Hock was in the lab, but where was she, he wanted to know. She texted back berating him for expecting her to be at his beck and call. His unthinking assumption that he could barge into the lab with no warning was a cudgel that would hold him off for now. The inevitable reckoning, however, was practically here. She had no investors at all and, at best, a few days left to find some. Otherwise, so much for work on transforming people's bodies to match themselves permanently.

The apples in the bin continued to taunt her. They looked exactly as they always had. Their glow bled through the bin. Their skin remained transparent and shiny. Their flesh stayed firm to Emily's touch. Hock would have eaten another one by now and restored himself to his full preening peacock glory. However, when Shereen came home and her gaze shifted downward as she walked over to Emily, there were still three apples in the bin.

She lay on the sofa, reworking her pitch again. Her body was sore, but only a little, and it was the good kind of sore, the kind that made you feel you'd accomplished something. Giving up on trying to maintain her transformed shape had, ironically, made her workouts more productive.

"You look relaxed for once." Shereen, certainly, sounded more cheerful than she had in weeks. "Did you find an angel investor?"

"What? Oh, I wish." Emily looked up from her laptop. "I've just been having good workouts lately."

"Finally getting used to your body?" Shereen sat next to Emily on the sofa.

"No, I've just gone back to workouts I actually enjoy. That body was pretty ridiculous." Emily sat up. Her T-shirt wrinkled around her waist. "Nothing I did could keep my body the way I'd transformed it anyway."

Hock had a point about how no one could exercise hard enough to maintain this sort of body. Maybe Emily was supposed to be sorry now for the snide things she thought about him eating apple after apple. But she still wasn't sorry. Someone's perfect body shouldn't come at the cost of someone else's unending toil. She decided she'd rather suffer with imperfection instead.

Emily felt her wife's gaze sweep across her body. It was appreciative, like Shereen's smile, but her wife's gaze and smile were always like that.

"Do you mind not being built like a superhero anymore?" Shereen's hand covered Emily's.

Emily stared down for a moment. She slumped into the couch.

"No." The word—not to mention the realization that she wasn't imperfect, she was Emily—surprised Emily as it left her. "This is comfortable and fun to maintain. Actually, I feel more like myself than I have in weeks."

Emily shifted her gaze to Shereen, who looked back at her beatifically. The "what have I been telling you?" couldn't have been louder or more obvious if Shereen had screamed it or let it show.

"You know. I realize your work is all hush-hush but . . . " Shereen settled herself into the couch cushions. "You obviously aren't the market for an apple. You don't want Hock's market, even though he's happy with how an apple transforms him and how he needs to keep eating them to stay transformed. So, who else exactly do you think is going to buy these things?"

It occurred to Emily that she had never tried her pitch out on Shereen before. The only reason Shereen even knew about the apples was because Emily had brought them home. It was past time to show Shereen the pitch, even if her reaction might hurt more than any investor's.

Slides of homologous sexual organs transforming from one to its counterpart flipped by on the laptop screen. Another slide showed how one limb could be used as a template for the other limb. Yet another was an eye chart of statistics on the value of strengthening muscles and bones during rehabilitation. Emily got a few more slides in before she stopped.

"No, this isn't what I want to do." Emily closed her laptop. "I mean, it is, but these slides all dance around the vision. My pitch should be about why it's important for people to feel the way I feel right now. Comfortable in their own skin."

"And why people will pay for it?"

Emily glared at Shereen for a moment. But only for a moment.

"Yeah." Emily sighed. "And why people will pay for it."

"Otherwise, you're making an appeal to the altruism and empathy of tech startup venture capitalists. Also, you'd be Idunn, forced to provide free labor to keep Norse gods young and virile."

"I am totally Idunn. Except I'm a tech startup who's only going to deal in permanent transformations." Emily laughed. "And I'm going to find those altruistic and empathetic investors, and pitch to them instead. I only need one to say yes."

Her phone buzzed. Hock again. He wanted to meet for lunch. She could only put him off for so long. He knew where she lived.

As she stared at this group of venture capitalists she'd handpicked and managed to cajole into attending this meeting, she tried to push out of her mind the fact that she had only this one shot left. She was going to make it count, even if it killed her.

"Changing your body ought to be as easy as changing your suit." As Emily's gaze swept across yet another conference table, this time she found the occasional smile. "And with iDunn, it will be."

Again, as she pitched, their steady gaze pressed against her. The pressure felt different this time. Bearable.

"Now most of you are asking why anyone would want to do that. That's because you're all comfortable in your own bodies." She advanced to the next slide. "So comfortable, you'd only realize how comfortable if that feeling were somehow torn away from you."

It was odd but reassuring to look into the audience and see a few people who looked like her. This time, the investors included a scattering of women and someone who had introduced themself with "they/them/theirs" when Emily had phoned them. There were even two people in the room besides her who weren't white. This time, rather than going after the big and notable investors, Emily had picked investors Hock wouldn't ever have considered. For him, that was probably the right choice.

"Most people are that comfortable. But not everyone." She tapped the table for emphasis. "And ones who aren't deserve to feel as comfortable in their bodies as you do in yours."

She continued to talk about expectations of convention and how they caused profound discomfort. Existing ways of making people comfortable in their bodies were difficult and expensive. Any option people couldn't afford might as well not exist for them. That was an untapped market iDunn could reach. A few investors leaned forward with interest. A few more slides in, and they began to nod in agreement with her.

When the ten minutes of her pitch was over, smiles lit everybody's faces. She had them. Not all of them, of course, but enough to get started. Not that getting their interest had ever been her only obstacle. She had to make sure that Jazz and intellectual property law didn't get in her way. That meant having lunch with Hock.

Hock's pitch to Emily didn't begin in earnest until dessert. Honestly, though, Emily saw it start from the moment he made his entrance into the restaurant. She was suddenly glad that Hock was paying for lunch and that she'd thought to suggest a place only a block away from the nearest subway stop.

Hock had shown up in a black leather jacket, T-shirt, jeans, and midnight blue dress boots. The quality fabrics, impeccable fit, and detailed stitching were obvious even from across the room. If forced, Emily would have priced the ensemble at about five thousand dollars.

The act of taking off the jacket was its own multibillion-dollar summer blockbuster. To Emily, Hock was the slab of beef who was getting his fifth shot at making a summer tentpole movie a hit because no famous hardbody would star in it. To any male investor, Hock would have been the very embodiment of success. Some of them might have whipped out their checkbooks and cut Hock a check by the time his ass hit the chair.

Hock had been pleasant, even modestly charming, during the appetizer and main course. Interest in her welfare as well as that of Shereen's had been indicated. Her concerns about the implications of transforming human bodies had been listened to and acknowledged. This was all perfectly adequate and expected. If he were an asshole all the time, no one would ever fund his startup. Looking like you've won the "man game" several times over could take you far, but not that far.

But dessert had just arrived. She'd opted out, settling for a cup of coffee. As his fork dug into his molten chocolate lava cake, Emily could feel Hock's gears shift and his machinations grind.

"You understand why I asked you to lunch." He pressed a forkful of cake into the chocolate that had oozed out of the center. "This isn't personal."

"No, not at all." She didn't see a reason to be confrontational . . . yet. "This is just a business proposal."

"Exactly." He gestured his fork, cake and all, at her. "You're not going to take advantage of me. I'm not going to let you take advantage of me."

"What?"

Emily had not taken advantage of Hock. If anything, it had been the other way around. Both their names were on the patents. He'd made sure his name was on them. Sure, he'd done some work, but the bulk of it was hers.

"You couldn't have gotten any investor without information from working at Jazz. You don't have the right to use that to fundraise for your own startup."

"Look, we can come to an agreement about how we both exploit our patents, or we can tie things up in court and no one gets to exploit them. And, frankly, some of the patents I can work around. Can you?" She took a sip of her coffee. "I'm perfectly happy not to be a direct competitor. My investors and I are targeting a different market, and we are passionate in our cause. You can have bros who want to look like superheroes all to yourself."

He frowned. His fork clattered onto the plate. Hock locked his gaze on Emily, who stared right back. Meaty forearms pressed against the table as he leaned toward her. He held the position for what seemed like minutes before he finally sat back. His gaze stayed fixed on her.

"It'd be easier for you and your investors if you came back."

"Of course. Then my lawyers won't have to talk to your lawyers." She smiled as she set down her cup. "But, honestly, that's not enough."

"Come back and you can work on your passion. You've shown there's funding for it."

"Really?" Emily sat up, her chair sliding back.

"Really." Hock's gaze softened.

"Well, that's an interesting offer." Emily stood. "Thank you for lunch."

She walked away. Part of her expected Hock to reach out and pull her back. The rest of her guessed that even though Hock was more than physically capable of tossing her like a stick, he was too savvy to actually do that.

"Wait, the apples and the headset." Hock's resonant voice made everything in the restaurant vibrate. "They're Jazz property and I'd like them back."

Emily turned around. She held Hock in her gaze and everything made sense. Broadened shoulders and slimmed hips were permanent, just as transformed organs would be once Emily figured them out. He'd always be towering with a voice that boomed. The muscle, however, was atrophying from disuse, and it'd take months for any new apples to mature. Whether or not she returned to Jazz, he wanted apples to keep him buff in the meantime. The price of that—and Hock would pay it to cover the gap—would be an agreement that let both of them exploit their mutual patents. It wasn't like he could call the police, not without also implicating himself in unauthorized human testing.

"In a minute." If there was one thing Hock loved, it was for Emily to keep him waiting. "After our lawyers work something out."

Emily didn't have to jump at his command anymore. She just walked away, finally in charge of her own destiny.

Carolyn Ives Gilman is a Hugo and Nebula Award nominated author of science fiction and fantasy. Her books include *Dark Orbit*, a space exploration adventure; *Isles of the Forsaken* and *Ison of the Isles*, a two-book fantasy about culture clash and revolution; and *Halfway Human*, a novel about gender and oppression. Her short fiction has appeared in *Lightspeed*, *Clarkesworld*, *Fantasy and Science Fiction*, *Interzone*, *Realms of Fantasy*, and others. Her work has been translated into a dozen languages and appeared in numerous Best Science Fiction of the Year anthologies.

Gilman lives in Washington, D.C., and works as a freelance writer and museum consultant, currently advising the U.S. Capitol on interpretation of historic art. She is also author of seven nonfiction books about North American frontier and Native history.

ON THE SHORES OF LIGEIA

Carolyn Ives Gilman

Seth Calder felt like he had barely dozed off when his alarm blared at 6:00 a.m. Level morning sunlight leaked through the blinds onto the birch and linen furniture of his Stockholm apartment. Amalia was already in the shower, so he lurched out of bed and went to check his news feed.

NASA TO LAUNCH MARS CREW TODAY, said the first headline. The picture showed the ten crew members in flight suits, grinning at the camera. They were the best of the best—fit, photogenic, heroic, multiracial. Seth wouldn't have passed the first step of screening for the mission. A short, nearsighted astrobiologist with a bit too much weight wasn't the kind of person the U.S. sent to space. Not that he begrudged them their glory—he wished them well. He had just leapfrogged over them. He hoped to be working on Titan today.

The shower stopped, and he went to go rouse Tidbit. She looked angelic asleep, a blonde wisp of a child. Seth had never imagined himself with children, and was constantly taken aback by his infatuation with this little being who had fallen into his life along with Amalia. "Time to get up, Peapod," he said, shaking her gently.

Her eyes scrunched tighter. "That's not my name," she mumbled.

"Isn't it?" he said with exaggerated amazement. "Let's see, what could your name be? Is it Nanomite? Is it Bedbug?"

She giggled. "It's Dannika. You're the only one who calls me Tidbit."

The bathroom door opened and Amalia looked in, wrapped in a towel. "Time to get up."

The girl immediately sat up in bed. You could tell who the authority was in this house, Seth thought. So much for his parenting skills.

Amalia and Tidbit talked in Swedish over the breakfast table. Seth could pick up most of it, but he hated to speak it and expose his clumsiness. At last he looked at his watch and said, "I've got to get going."

"Yeah, you've got to herd the Wildwoman to Titan," Amalia said with a smile. Wildwoman was her name for Seth's boss.

"Why can't *I* go to Titan?" Tidbit said.

Seth smiled at her. "You know where that is?"

"It's the biggest moon of Saturn," she answered promptly. At seven, she already knew her planets and could tell you about red dwarfs and neutron stars. It came from living with an astrobiologist and a physicist.

Seth always walked Tidbit to school, since it was on his way to the Tunnelbana. It had seemed awkward in the days when Tidbit hadn't yet decided whether he was an evil stepfather or not; now she chattered happily as they walked, but it still seemed awkward because it was such a dadlike thing to do. *Is this really me?* he kept thinking.

The streets were quiet and clean in the pastel light of morning. In fact, Stockholm always seemed to Seth like an artificial simulation of a city where everything actually worked. It lacked those touches a *real* city had—the dirt was missing, and the scary parts of town, and the homeless people begging at the train stations. He was used to Boston.

After dropping off Tidbit at school, he headed for the Tunnelbana to catch his train. On the long ride out to Kista he was so keyed up he had to force himself to concentrate on the news. The media outlets weren't covering his team's work with anything like the fervor they gave to the NASA launch. The Americans—odd, how he thought of his own country in the third person—had the edge on showmanship. Big, virile rockets blasting off were way more cinematic than the cutting-edge science the European Space Agency was doing. Ever since the change of administrations, the Americans had thrown all their money into a boots-on-the-ground approach to space exploration. It wasn't surprising; the American space program had been founded by World War II veterans intent on conquering space the same way they had conquered the Pacific, in giant steel ships. Or maybe their thinking went even further back, to the age of Hudson and Pizarro, when men in ships planted flags on foreign shores in order to claim them.

Odd, for people who thought of themselves as progressive, how anchored in the past American paradigms were. But he didn't resent them, he reminded himself. He wished them well.

No ships were involved in the ESA program where Seth worked. It wasn't about square-jawed heroism. They didn't want to put human bodies into space; they wanted to put human minds there.

Kista was a walkable, suburban campus of gleaming buildings housing high-tech research companies, interspersed with little parks decorated with tame trees. The brick building where Seth worked had a big satellite dish on the roof, but that wasn't how they communicated with Saturn. A worldwide string of radio telescopes picked up the signals twenty-four hours a day, and relayed the data to the participating institutions.

Seth headed up to the auditorium, expecting to find his boss, Dr. Katrina Beshni, holding forth to anyone gathered there. Today would be her moment in the limelight, and she relished it. It was two hours before the exploration of Titan was scheduled to start, but the auditorium was already filling with members of the astrobiology team, drinking potent Swedish coffee and talking about the climate data collected so far. The big screen was showing a "live" feed from the lander on Titan. The time delay due to the distance was almost eighty minutes, but that was as close to live as humans had ever achieved. The scene was a rocky plain shrouded in orange fog. It was shown in visible light, though enhanced to make it look brighter than it was. If Seth had been there in person, it would have looked dimmer than a gloomy, overcast twilight on Earth. Not to mention that, if he actually had been there, he would have been instantly frozen into a block of ice in the -180°C cold.

All over the world, he knew, scientists were gathered in offices and auditoriums, watching the same feed. At the moment, the robot wasn't doing anything but running some diagnostics; the scene wouldn't get interesting until Dr. Beshni's program took over. In the meantime, some of the scientists clustered by a television showing preparations for the NASA launch.

He scanned the room for his mentor. Dr. Andreas Helberg, an intimidatingly eminent biochemist, was coming toward him.

"Have you seen Dr. Beshni?" Seth asked.

"You are the one who normally keeps track of her," Dr. Helberg said with a hint of reproach.

Seth checked his phone, but there was no message from her. "I'll check her office," he said.

She wasn't there, so after a stop in his own office to leave his coat and pick up a flash drive of files, he headed down to the virtual reality lab in the basement. Kjeld was at work there, in a studio so packed with equipment it nearly hid him—which was hard to do, since he was a big, brown-bearded Viking of a man.

"Is Dr. Beshni here yet?" Seth asked.

Kjeld shook his craggy head and glanced at the clock. "Call and tell her to get down here, would you? Dublin's going to hand over to us in ninety minutes."

"She'll show up," Seth said. His mentor had been working toward this day for fifteen years; he knew she was not about to miss it.

Institutions all over Europe were sharing the lander they had sent to Titan. Since its touchdown last month, technicians in Dublin had been deploying, testing, and calibrating the robot explorer; Dr. Beshni would be the first to use it for actual science, and Seth would be monitoring. The robot's schedule had been set up for a long time; Beshni would have only three hours before handing off to a climate researcher in Hamburg.

Seth went into the adjoining room where the VR setup was, along with the computer station where he would be riding shotgun. When he woke it, it showed the same scene as in the auditorium upstairs.

His phone gave off the mating call of a bearded seal, and he looked at the text that had come in. It was from Dr. Beshni and said only, EMERGENCEY—call.

Instantly, he called her. It rang, then went to voice mail, so he called again. This time she answered. There was a lot of background noise. "Where are you?" Seth said.

"Emergency Room, hospital," she said. "I am walk into a hole in the street. My leg, I broke it. They are putting pins in it. I tell them, I have no time for this today. They say yes, now."

Seth could just imagine. She had probably been looking at her phone, but she was perfectly capable of falling in holes anyway, she was that absent-minded. It was a good thing she would never have to go to Titan in reality.

Someone was telling her in Swedish to put down the phone. "How long?" Seth asked.

"Three days, they dream. You must take over."

"Me?" Seth said, feeling paralyzed.

"Who else? Stupid surgeons!" The phone went dead.

Seth stood for a moment, panic-stricken. She was the genius; he was just the lowly postdoc who shadowed her, cleaning up the chaos. She had been going to narrate her remote-control tour of Titan for the worldwide audience in her trademark fractured, headlong English.

Shaking a little, Seth went back to Kjeld's den. "She's not coming," he said. "She broke her leg."

Kjeld stared a moment, then said, "Well, isn't that just like her. Better suit up."

"But—"

"You know this robot and this VR setup better than anyone. Do you want to waste our time?"

That was not an option. They had been waiting for years.

Seth went into the toilet to calm his nerves. He could do this. The artificial intelligence program that would drive the robot was as much his work as Dr. Beshni's—more so, in fact, because she hadn't had the patience for the boring bits. But knowing that several hundred of the most important people in the discipline would be watching—that was the part she thrived on, and he didn't.

Alyssa Chiu was waiting to assist him in the VR lab when he returned. Word had traveled fast. "Wouldn't you know she'd do something dramatic today," Alyssa said. "As if the pinnacle of her career weren't enough."

"She was probably distracted," Seth said.

Their VR equipment was state of the art—a full-body suit and helmet, with a circular 360-degree track with railing. He pulled on the suit and gloves, then stood growing hot as he waited for a signal from Kjeld through his earpiece. Alyssa sat where he should have been, in front of the computer screen. The rest of the biology team was following on the screen upstairs.

"Fifteen minutes," Kjeld said.

"Why don't you explain to the audience?" Alyssa said. She was handling the outgoing signal. "Put on the helmet and I'll put you through."

The helmet was showing an environment of Swedish woods so as not to be claustrophobic. It was a little distracting. "You're on," Alyssa said.

Seth cleared his throat. "Um, hello everyone. This is Seth Calder, Dr. Beshni's assistant. I have bad news. She broke her leg this morning." He could imagine the consternation and eyerolls spreading. "She'll be all right, at least she was when I talked to her. But she won't be able to join us today. Sorry, you're going to have to put up with me."

"Ten minutes," Kjeld said.

"We'll be starting in a few minutes. We'll have to spend some time calibrating the suit, but the program will start right after that. I'm not controlling the robot, obviously; but I'll be able to sense its environment in more detail, and I'll try to tell you about it."

Because of the time delay, it wasn't possible to control the robot in real time, so their team had created an artificial intelligence program designed to react like a biologist. It had been transmitted to Titan and pre-loaded in the robot's brain a week ago. Up until then, Seth and Dr. Beshni had been putting the final touches on it by running the robot's identical twin across the terrain of the Swedish arctic. The AI didn't actually know any biology—all it was trained to do was to recognize things a biologist would find interesting. Seth had spent many tedious days teaching the neural network to look in promising places and react appropriately to what it saw. Now, if it didn't perform, everyone would know who to blame.

"Switching over," Kjeld said.

And then Seth was on Titan.

"Oh my God!" he exclaimed.

The resolution was much sharper than he had expected—no comparison to the fuzzy video feed the others were following. He could see details in the surrounding rocks, shadows and flow marks in the sand. The robot's camera-laden "head" had a nearly 360-degree view, but Seth had to turn to see behind him. There stood the lander that had carried him—rather, his robot body—to the surface. It was now acting as charging station, lab, and communications relay to the orbiter. The heavy orange clouds were bright behind it, so he knew that direction was south. He could only see ten or twenty feet around him.

"Initiating haptic interface," Kjeld said on his earpiece.

Tactile data flooded over him. A chilly, humid breeze touched his face, and he wrinkled his nose at the chemical scent. The smell represented the atmospheric chemistry without duplicating it, since the actual atmosphere of Titan would have been odorless but unbreathable. What he was experiencing was what an organism evolved to live on Titan would have felt. In a way, the robot was such an organism—designed for conditions humans were not.

"Adding in radar and infrared," Kjeld said.

The view suddenly cleared. The fog dissipated and he saw the landscape around him. He was standing on a sandy, rock-strewn plain at the base of some rugged hills. The ground sloped downward to his right, into a gully where a stream flowed. Seth turned to trace the stream to its source in the snow-capped mountains to the south. The scene looked so much like an afternoon in the South Dakota badlands, it was hard to remember it wasn't a stream of water. Liquid methane took the place of water here, and water ice formed the rocks.

A slight rise hid the view to the north, and he wanted to see over it. The robot, pre-trained to replicate his curiosity, began to move in that direction. It was actually a four-legged vehicle, designed for clambering over rugged terrain, but Seth couldn't see the back legs, and so the illusion of walking was convincing. When he came to the top of the rise, he let out a breath. "I'll be damned." Before him lay the indented coastline of a sea stretching to the horizon. Ligeia Mare. Streaks of wind rippled the calm surface. The nearby stream curved off and flowed eastward into a valley.

"Quit talking to yourself and tell us what you see," Alyssa's irritated voice said in his ear. He had forgotten that everyone was listening.

"Um, it's probably nothing you can't see for yourselves," Seth said. "But for me, it's so *real*. I'm actually *there*." He sounded like a blithering fanboy, he knew; he couldn't help it. The experience was breathtaking.

If he *had* been there, he probably would have walked on, awestruck, toward the seashore. But the robot made a more logical decision, to investigate the gully. "Whoops, I guess we're going to look at the methane stream," he said in his role as conductor of this tour.

The opposite side of the stream gully was eroded and showed clear stratigraphy. "The geologists are going to want to take a look at that," he commented. Perhaps he would as well, if his search for life turned into a search for fossils of life. At the moment, he and his robot were much more interested in the soft hydrocarbon "sand" the color of sweet potatoes, especially in the puddle formed by an eddy. The robot focused in on some foam at the edge of the puddle. "Oh, boy, pond scum!" Seth exclaimed.

A magnifying camera telescoped from the robot's body, and its field of view appeared in an inset, as if he were looking through a magnifying glass. It showed nothing wriggling or swimming, but there were some translucent bubbles. Seth's breath caught with excitement. "We need to test those," he said. "If they are vinyl cyanide or polyimine membranes, and not just nitrogen bubbles, we might have hit the jackpot." If he had trained the robot right, it would take a sample. And sure enough, it reached out its sampling arm and siphoned the scum into a tube to be taken back to the lander for more analysis.

There was, of course, no chance that Earthlike life would exist on Titan. What they were searching for was far more exciting: life that had evolved using completely different chemistry. Seth was hoping for hydrogen-based life forms that metabolized acetylene instead of glucose. If they found it, it would mean that life was universal and could evolve anywhere.

But what hydrogen-based life would look like was completely unknown, and recognizing it might be a challenge. Seth scanned upstream and downstream for something else interesting, but saw nothing. The robot, however, took off down the gully, and soon Seth figured out what it had seen. "That rock shows differential shading on one side," he explained. "On Earth, that might be desert varnish, or even evidence of lichen." Under magnification, it looked like nothing more than a whitish crust from evaporation, but the robot dutifully took another sample. The mass spectrometer back at the lander would at least tell them the chemical composition.

"This is going really well," Seth enthused as the robot climbed the sloping bank again. "It's noticing all the right stuff and taking the right actions. I couldn't—" A drop of rain hit him on the head, or seemed to. "Hot damn, it's raining!" He looked up, and there was a dark cloud overhead. A few drops pattered around him on the ground. The climatologists would be envious at missing this.

"Seth, remember your audio is live." Alyssa sounded amused.

As the robot headed off toward the seashore, Seth said soberly, "You can see all sorts of evidence of the methane cycle. Rainfall, erosion, evaporation, probably springs of ground ethane—all exactly like on Earth, just different chemistry."

The land grew more rugged as he neared the shore. At last the scene opened before him—a rocky, indented coastline with eroded cliffs plunging into the sea, like something from Big Sur, except there was no surf; the sea was strangely still. The wind would have ruffled his hair if it had been real. Below, he could see tidal pools in the rocks, rimmed with a crust of yellowish deposits, possibly benzene. The entire landscape before him would be combustible on Earth; but here, without oxygen, it was stable. In fact, here oxygen was the rare and flammable liquid.

He wanted to climb down to get closer to the shore, but the robot was programmed to know its limits, and rock climbing was not one of its skills. Instead, it activated a telescopic lens and focused in on the pool edges.

"What the . . . " Seth could not figure out what he was looking at. The pools were fringed with a ruff of stiff, lacelike crystals. They formed small pyramidal shapes like a grove of miniature Christmas trees. "Crystals?" he wondered aloud. "I've never seen crystals like this. We need to get a sample."

As he scanned the landscape for a safe way down to the shore, the rain began in earnest. A gust of wind buffeted him, driving the rain across the clear dome of his eye-cameras. The robot ignored the weather and headed toward a promontory with a better view of the seashore. Seth was scanning for a slope that might lead safely downward when his view tilted, throwing off his balance. He looked down, and saw the ground under his large pad-feet sinking, giving way. "Oh, no!" he shouted. The robot tried to step back, but an entire section of the cliff was caving in. Everything turned sideways. All his senses told him he was tumbling downward, rolling, falling, bumping, then skidding down a steep slope, and finally coming to a stop with the rain pattering around him.

He had wrecked the robot. Billions of dollars, decades of work, thousands of scientists watching, and he had literally fallen off a cliff. "Oh God," he said miserably, "what did I do?"

Of course, he had done nothing. It had all happened over an hour ago. But it had been his program running the robot, his curiosity that had led it to the edge.

He lay pitched sideways on a slope of rubble. He was considerably closer to the seashore now, and could see from his canted perspective that the cliffs behind him were, in fact, riddled with caves, eroded underneath like the frozen curls of breaking waves. It was no wonder the ground had given way.

"Well," Alyssa said in his ear, "that's one way to get down to the shore."

"Shut up," he answered. "You can't make me feel worse than I do already."

As he lay there, wondering what to do now, he heard the most unexpected sound imaginable—the whine of a mosquito. His first thought was that something had gone wrong with the robot's hearing. The sound faded, then came back, varying in pitch. "There must be a loose wire . . . " he started to say. Then something flitted across his view.

"What the hell?" he exclaimed.

He wanted desperately to deploy the net that was one of his sampling mechanisms, to catch whatever it was for a closer look. But the sampling arm was pinned underneath him. There was whir of machinery, a thwack of ice-pebbles against his carapace, and his viewpoint shifted. The gravel underneath him gave way, he slid downward, teetered, and with a jolt came to rest on the ground, miraculously upright. Orange dirt pattered down the slope behind him.

He realized that the robot, reacting to its curiosity programming, had tried to extend the sampling arm, and that was all it had taken to disturb the slope and set him upright again.

The robot stood still, running diagnostics, for several minutes. Seth spent the time scanning the slope, the air, everything, for what had made the insect sound. At last the robot took a step forward, and relief washed over Seth. Could he be so lucky that it had not been damaged?

The maddening buzzing came back. Seconds later, he saw something swooping toward him from the sea—a small gray body the size of a seagull, with three propellers atop. It had noticed him, and came close, hovering, so close he could see the camera lens and the lettering on its side.

"A *drone*?" Seth said, bewildered.

It rose straight up, and was joined by another one, then two more, till there was a swarm of half a dozen drones, all swooping down one by one to look at him as if he were a circus attraction.

"Alyssa," he said, "are these our drones?"

"Uh, no," she said.

They had considered sending drones, once. They were perfect for large-scale surveying, and in the thick Titan atmosphere, flying was easier than on Earth. But the ESA's top priority was looking for life—and for that, you had to get down on your knees in the mud.

"Then who sent them? The writing on them is Chinese."

"Yes, we noticed that. We're checking it out."

The flock of drones swooped low, then scattered—some heading east along the coastline, some west, some straight out to sea. He watched them disappear into the distance. Nothing he had seen on Titan had surprised him so much. It was inconceivable that someone could have a secret space program that had beaten the EU here. But either he was hallucinating, or there they were.

"They're lucky I didn't try to catch them in a sample net," Seth muttered.

The rain had passed on, and the fog had cleared. The sea was burnished copper under a tangerine sky. He stood for a moment, listening to the wind and the solitude. It was beautiful here, he realized. Strange, but beautiful. He hoped it would never get crowded.

The robot lurched forward, resuming its biology program, untroubled by the appearance of little flying machines where none should be.

"Seth, you've still got a problem," Alyssa broke in. "You need to get back to the lander somehow."

It was true; his batteries would run down in fifteen hours or so, and he would need to recharge. The robot was just a sample-collector, and all the real equipment was back at the landing site. Looking up at the sheer cliffs, he now faced the same dilemma he had before, but in reverse; somehow, he had to get *up* them.

"Alyssa, can you tell where I am on the map?" He was hoping it might steer him to a reasonable route.

"Sorry, it's not detailed enough to help," she said. Titan's thick atmospheric clouds made visual mapping from orbit impossible, so radar was all they had. She added, "We know you're 1.2 kilometers north-northwest of the lander."

He was surprised he had come so far. "How much time do I have?" he asked. "Are my three hours nearly up?"

After a pause, Alyssa's voice said, "You exceeded your three hours twenty minutes ago. Hamburg ceded their time to you, because you were having so many . . . adventures."

They didn't want to have to clean up the mess he had made. The very public mess. He nearly groaned. "Never mind, I'll figure it out," he said to buck himself up.

There was a pause. "Sorry," she said. "I just got word they've decided to shut you down."

"No!" he protested.

"The decision was made above our heads. They are going to deactivate the robot to conserve the batteries until they come up with a plan to get it back to the lander. They're sending the instructions now."

"Then I still have eighty minutes."

"Go for it," she said. "Just don't fall in the lake, okay?"

Meanwhile, the robot was unaware of the consternation back home. It took off to investigate a glassy puddle in the icerock. There was a slight breeze blowing, but the pool seemed unnaturally still, as the sea did on a larger scale. When he got closer, Seth could see that either the liquid had a particularly high surface tension or there was a clear film over the surface, like a thin plastic wrap. "On Earth, that would be a biofilm, a bacterial colony," Seth said aloud, hoping someone was still listening to his discoveries. "Here, it might be acrylonitrile. If so, it's still important. We think acrylonitrile might play the same role here as phospholipids on Earth." The robot reached out its sampling arm, but as soon as it touched the pool the film broke and disappeared. The robot took a liquid sample anyway.

Seth scanned the landscape impatiently for the white crystals he had seen from the cliff, but could not locate them. The robot's attention was on the seashore, and it made its way steadily over the icerocks toward where the waves lapped. Seth could hear them hissing against the pebbles. A flat ledge protruded out into the methane sea, and the robot proceeded out onto it, going so close to the edge that Seth nearly shouted at it to stop. It did.

From this vantage point, Seth could peer down into the sea. The liquid methane was crystal clear, and the ledge plunged down several feet—or was it several meters?—to a rocky bottom. As the robot extended its arm to take another liquid sample, Seth saw something un-rocklike in the depths. At first, the robot didn't seem to notice. Then it extended its magnifying arm until it submerged under the surface, and the view became clearer. There was a cluster of something that looked like brownish pinecones on the seafloor.

Seth nearly whooped in exhilaration. Instead, he put on his best professional voice. "That looks distinctly organic. That is, not necessarily carbon-based, but complex. I suppose it could be some sort of odd erosion pattern, or a concretion, but we need to get a sample to be sure."

The robot snaked out its sampling arm, but the objects were too far down. "Damn it!" Seth couldn't help but say.

"Seth," Alyssa interrupted, "your time's up."

"No! I'm just getting somewhere."

It was intensely frustrating. He felt sure that he was seeing evidence of life all around, but each time he thought he had some proof, it was too far away, or it dissolved into ambiguity. He gazed around at the landscape, trying to absorb every detail, to write it on his memory. Then the robot lurched around, heading away from the shore. Midway between the cliffs and the sea it stopped. Seth's world went blank.

When he took the VR helmet off, he found he was soaked in sweat, although he had felt chill up to now. The suit was clammy. "That was amazing!" he said to Alyssa.

"Yeah, it really went well, except for the part where you nearly wrecked the robot and marooned it without a power source," she said.

"I meant that we learned a lot more than I expected on the first time out."

"Right. We're convening in the conference room upstairs for a postmortem. Why don't you get dressed and join us?"

Postmortem sounded a little premature. But he grabbed his clothes and headed for the washroom for a quick shower.

When he entered the conference room, the scientist who had been talking fell silent and everyone around the table turned to look at him as he tried to slip inconspicuously into a seat. No one clapped or said "congratulations." The accusatory silence stretched on until someone cleared his throat and said, "Well, all we can do is speculate until we get samples back to the lab on the lander."

The conversation resumed then, and Seth soon realized it wasn't the robot's postmortem; it was his. Or at least, his program's—and therefore the astrobiology team's.

"Tantalizing as the evidence is, we can't risk running that program again," Dr. Helberg said. "At least, not until it is revised. It is far too accident-prone. Just like its creator."

He meant Dr. Beshni, Seth knew, but he couldn't help taking it personally. He wanted to defend the program, but a warning look from Alyssa kept him quiet. He dreaded having to break the news to his mentor, and prayed she wouldn't be out of surgery for at least a week. Somehow, he needed to redeem the program before she found out. Biological research couldn't be put on ice now. There was too much at stake.

"What about the drones?" he asked. "Have we found out who's running them?"

"It's a Chinese program, apparently," said a white-haired South African whom Seth knew only as Dr. Gault. "You may remember their moonshot a decade ago, when the spacecraft was lost. My guess is that it was simply using the moon for a gravitational assist so it could beat us to Titan and show us up. We haven't yet been able to talk to anyone in charge."

"What did the writing on it say?"

Alyssa answered. "It just said *dàhuángfēng*, Bumblebee. The name of the drone, apparently. Cute, but a phone number would have been more helpful."

"Why do you ask?" Dr. Helberg said icily.

"Just thinking we could get them to help."

Someone down the table said, "Even a hundred drones couldn't lift the robot back to the top of the cliff."

The conversation turned to the upcoming press conference, and the mood got even more dour as they contemplated the public shaming ahead. Seth saw that he and Dr. Beshni would inevitably get scapegoated.

At last Dr. Helberg said, "The navigation team in Copenhagen is going to create new instructions to get the robot back to the lander. We can't say anything more about the future until the robot is saved. Of course, once they have done that, if they succeed, we can ask them to look at our AI program and do something to fix it."

Butcher it, Seth thought glumly. Make it so risk-averse it would never go anywhere interesting.

The meeting broke up soon after. When Seth returned to his office, he saw that the sun was low in the sky; the whole day had passed in what had seemed like a few minutes. He checked the news to see if anything had leaked; if so, it had been crowded out by breathless anticipation of the American launch, which hadn't yet taken place. There was nothing about China.

"You want to go for a drink?" Alyssa said, looking in from the hallway.

He wanted the drink, but not in company where he would have to hide his head. "I think I'll go home," he said.

His brain was still spinning down dead-end paths when he came into the apartment where Amalia was watching live coverage of the American rocket on its launch pad. She muted the sound. "I heard you had a little accident today," she said.

So the story was all over the university. He wasn't going to be able to escape it: cockamamie Dr. Beshni and her reckless assistant. He slumped down on the couch beside her, took the glass of wine from her hand, and downed it in one breath.

"That bad?" she said.

That was the source of his frustration, he realized. "No," he said, "it wasn't bad at all. It was wonderful. I was *on Titan*, Amalia—in a way I could never be there in reality, because I didn't have to worry about the cold, or the fact there's no oxygen. I didn't have to spend ninety percent of my attention worrying about surviving, as those poor chumps on Mars are going to have to do. They're going to regress to survivalists: worrying about how to get water and air and food, how to deal with bone loss and radiation. I was there in a body designed for the environment, and in ten minutes I was already doing science, making discoveries. All I want now is to go back. And the chances of that seem really slim now."

She gave him a hug, which was nice, but didn't really solve his problem.

"I think this Titan bug is contagious," she said. "It's all Dannika could talk about, too."

"Did she see our press conference or something?"

"No, she's got some sort of new video game about Titan. She's playing it now."

"Good," he said gloomily. "Maybe she'll be the next one in the family to go."

"I've got Indian takeout," she said. "Should I warm it up?"

"Sure," he said. He didn't want to sit drinking wine all evening, like a loser.

While Amalia was in the kitchen, he wandered into Tidbit's room to see what she was doing. She was wearing her VR goggles and earbuds, but a display related to the game was up on the screen of her laptop. The graphics immediately drew Seth's attention. They showed a map of Titan's lake district—a strikingly accurate map. Whoever had put this together had done their homework, and timed the release perfectly. The map was littered with little symbols in a rainbow of colors.

"Hey, T," he said, pulling up a chair next to her. "What're you doing?"

She pulled out one earbud. "It's a Titan game," she said. "I have to tag interesting things. If my tags turn out to be good, I'll get more time tomorrow."

She peeked out from under her goggles and pointed at the map. "The magenta ones are my tags," she said. "I chose the color."

The tags were clustered around the southern coast of Ligeia Mare, exactly where he had been earlier that day.

"Can I try?" he asked.

She handed over the goggles. Immediately, he was back on Titan, flying like a bird over the coastline. The graphics were hyper-realistic, and very accurate—the rugged shore, the orange sky. He could almost feel the chill air whipping by, and smell the simulated tang of methane rain. "How do you control it?" he asked.

"You can't, really," Tidbit said. "It goes where it wants to go, but it's attracted by other people's tags. The thing is to see something new."

"Have you seen a broken-down robot on the shore?" he said wryly.

"Oh, yes, that was tagged long ago."

Just then, his viewpoint swooped downward with jaw-clenching speed, and he saw something moving below him like gnats, like birds—like drones.

He tore the goggles off to look at Tidbit. "Where did you get this?"

From the bedroom door, Amalia explained, "She got it from school. Her class won a lottery to participate. What's the matter?"

"This isn't a game. This is real."

He couldn't believe it. They were letting *children* run the drones?

"Give me the goggles back," Tidbit said. "You're using up my time."

Amalia handed him a carton of biryani and a note from Tidbit's teacher. He set down the carton and scanned the note. It gave a numerical Internet address and codes for logging into the game at a particular time. Farther down, there was a paragraph explaining that it was a global citizen science project from a Chinese software company.

"Tidbit," he said tensely, "are you anywhere near the broken robot?"

She was back on Titan, absorbed in what she was seeing. "I think so," she said.

He realized that her drone was symbolized by a flashing magenta dot on the map. He seized the touchscreen and zoomed in on the symbol. At a larger scale, the map became extraordinarily detailed. In fact, it wasn't a map at all; it was aerial photos, pieced together from the feeds of a dozen drones. Every few seconds it refreshed, filling in new spots. They were mapping Titan at an extraordinary rate.

"I can't imagine how much processing power this is taking," Seth marveled.

There was a cluster of tags down the coast from Tidbit's drone. He centered the spot on the screen and zoomed in. The detail wasn't quite clear enough to see the robot, but the spot was labeled in Chinese characters. Mixed among them were three European letters, ESA. "That's got to be the robot," he said. The nearby terrain looked right—there was the cliff, and the ledge he had gone out on to look into the sea. He scanned eastward down the coast till he came to Tidbit's drone at the mouth of a river.

"Tidbit, put a tag there."

"Why?" she said. "There's nothing interesting."

"Yes, there is. A river with a wide valley. A gradual slope the robot can get up."

On the map, he followed the river southward until a tributary came into it from the right; then he followed the tributary. The detail ended, giving way to the blurry, useless radar images. But when he zoomed out, he saw a tag on a spot about a kilometer inland that could only be the lander. "This has to be the stream that runs through the gully near the lander," he said. "The robot might get its feet wet, but it can get back."

"My time's almost up," Tidbit said. "I'm going to lose the connection."

"No! Not yet!" Feverishly, Seth started saving screen shots of the map along the route from the lander to the robot. He had just saved the next to the last when the screen went blank.

Tidbit gave a cry of disappointment. But Seth gave her an ecstatic hug. "Tidbit, you're a star," he said. "Where's my phone?"

Kjeld answered on the third ring. There was a lot of background noise. "Seth, where are you? We're all at Zorro's," he said.

"No time for drinking," Seth said. "I've got some information to pass on to the navigation team in Copenhagen. Are you in touch with them?"

"I can be," Kjeld said slowly. "What sort of information?"

"I've got a route to get the robot home. Here, I'll send you the first part of the map."

The background noise fell quiet. He could imagine them all, clustered around Kjeld's phone. "Where did you get this?" Kjeld said.

"You know those drones?"

"Yes, we haven't been able to find out who's controlling them."

"That's because it's children controlling them. School children all over the world. I got it from my daughter. Never mind, I'll fill you in later. The important thing is, they've mapped most of the route between the lander and the robot. Here, I'll send the rest of the images."

"Holy crap," Kjeld said as he received the screen shots.

"Can you pass these on?"

"Ja," Kjeld said, momentarily sounding Swedish.

"Sorry if I broke up the party," Seth said, feeling not a bit sorry.

"Don't mention it. Now get off my phone."

Seth hung up, feeling good for the first time in hours, and gave Tidbit a high five. They all went out to the living room, where Amalia poured some more wine for Seth and herself, fruit juice for Tidbit. The muted television was still covering the American launch, but now a reporter was on the screen. Amalia turned up the sound.

" . . . will be rescheduled in approximately four days. If you're just joining us, the launch has been scrubbed due to a malfunction in the hydraulic system . . . "

"Who cares?" Tidbit said.

"That's right," Seth said. "We don't need a pokey old rocket ship. We've been there."

Amalia gave him a hug. "That's not for saving the robot," she whispered. "That's for being a good dad."

He realized it was true, and he liked it. They really were a family now.

And they had all been to space. The American way was never going to get them there. The European way would only get the elite experts there. The Chinese way had gotten everyone there, even Tidbit. And all over the world, kids and space buffs and students were going to be able to go. It was against all the rules of institutional science—it was undisciplined, tumultuous, proletarian. But once the public found out they could ride a drone through the clouds of Titan, the reaction would be ecstatic.

And some day, perhaps the physicists would solve the time-delay problem with some quantum magic, and they could all be there in real time, building things and solving problems and exploring, and still be able to breathe and eat curried chicken when they were done.

It wasn't just the solar system that looked different now. So did Earth.

Yoon Ha Lee's debut novel, *Ninefox Gambit*, won the Locus Award for best first novel and was a finalist for the Hugo, Nebula, and Clarke awards; its sequels, *Raven Stratagem* and *Revenant Gun*, were also Hugo finalists. His children's space opera, *Dragon Pearl*, was a *New York Times* bestseller and won the Locus Award for best YA novel. Lee's short fiction has appeared in venues such as *Tor.com*, *Clarkesworld*, *Lightspeed Magazine*, *The Magazine of Fantasy and Science Fiction*, *Beneath Ceaseless Skies*, and more. Lee lives in Louisiana with his family and a very lazy cat, and has not yet been eaten by gators.

THE EMPTY GUN

Yoon Ha Lee

The bazaar on the moon that wandered Transitional Space did not meet Kestre sa Elaya's exacting requirements for a *safe transaction*. In years past, as the duelist prime of House Elaya, she would have journeyed with an honor guard to the much-feted Gray Manse. Her meeting would have involved liquors imported from the Flower Worlds and delectable canapés and candies, some of which she would pocket to give to her nieces when she returned home.

If circumstances had been less dire, she would have scorned a meeting with the arms dealer entirely. The dealer refused to leave the moon, for reasons lost in antiquity. That rankled; Kestre was used to people coming to her, not the other way around.

But House Elaya had died in blood and ash two months ago. Kestre herself had been left for dead by the assassins of House Tovraz. She was determined to make them pay for their mistake.

To do so, she needed a weapon. Not just any weapon, but one outside the Houses' Registry. Weapons like the ones the arms dealer sold.

Kestre didn't like Transitional Space. Like most House aristocrats, she was superstitious, and she'd always wondered if the immense aliens who had once lurked in Transitional Space, which humanity had driven off in the wars of old, still clung to existence. But she wouldn't admit to fear, either, and in any case the moon hadn't suffered any alien attacks since it was colonized.

"Three cutpurses behind you," her neural assistant said. "Knives only. They shouldn't cause you any trouble."

"Thank you," she said in a harsh whisper, and whipped around, dropping into a fighter's crouch. She saluted the cutpurses as though she faced them in a duel. The knife rested easily in her hand, and one by one she pointed at each, angling the blade precisely to reflect the streetlights into their eyes.

The cutpurses recognized the challenge for what it was, and slunk away.

"That was overkill," the assistant said mildly.

"I don't have time for petty thieves," Kestre returned, and continued on her way beneath the city dome with its featureless black sky. *The hungry sky*, the locals called it, those nights in Transitional Space, as the moon traveled through a warp-world *sideways* of ordinary space. She wondered if anyone else would hunt her tonight, but no one else troubled her.

The arms dealer lived in a surprisingly ordinary apartment overlooking a zero-gee playground. Kestre's doubts increased as she contemplated the dismayingly domestic wreath of cloud-bloom and brachial wires on the door. Then she knocked.

The door opened. The arms dealer was tall and broad, very dark, like Kestre herself, but with a strangely indistinct face. Even her eyes resembled pits of shadow.

The interior wasn't much better. Row upon row of weapons rested in plain sight, everything from finger-length knapped flint knives to crew-served artillery and even, in the back, the gleam of a missile whose length receded into an unlikely distance. Kestre assessed the offerings with an expert eye and shook her head in disappointment. "If this is all," she said, "I had best be on my way."

"Wait," the arms dealer said. "For the last survivor of House Elaya, I have something special."

"On with it, then," Kestre said, unease coiling in her belly.

"I don't have a good feeling about this," the assistant said. "We should look elsewhere."

"We don't have many options," Kestre subvocalized. "We'll have to chance it."

The arms dealer led Kestre into her home, stopping in a room where there was a single case. "This is what you want," she said.

Kestre's eyebrows rose. All she saw was a handgun of peculiar proportion, too large to wield comfortably, and dull green in color. "Unregistered?" she asked.

"Unregistered," the arms dealer confirmed. "The only one of its kind."

"Ammunition?"

"It's an amicable gun. It handles its own ammunition."

In her past life, Kestre would have walked away at this point. She'd heard of amicable artifacts, although she'd never handled one. They turned up on certain dead worlds, forever voyaging through Transitional Space, relics of the long-ago aliens that humanity had fought off during its first travels to the stars. The artifacts had a reputation both for extreme efficacy and for bringing bad luck to their owners.

Kestre was desperate, and her luck couldn't get any worse. Her House had perished. All she had left was her life, and the point of that life was revenge.

The arms dealer smiled knowingly at Kestre, who scowled and lifted the gun from the case. Still awkward, but it fit her hand better than she'd expected from its appearance. This might be workable after all.

"What do you want for it?" Kestre said after a grudging pause. "Whatever is in my power to give is yours."

The assistant began to protest Kestre's bargaining skills, but it was too late.

"The honor of House Elaya is still alive, I see," the arms dealer said. "Give me your House name, then, since you value it so."

Kestre shuddered and squeezed her eyes shut. The last thing she had of real value—but without a House, and she thought of the last time she'd tucked in her youngest cousins, the name meant nothing. The House could not go unavenged. If this was the price she must pay, then so be it. "Yes."

The arms dealer laid two precise fingers on Kestre's brow. A sensation like ice spiked through Kestre's heart and settled in her bones. "Say it," the arms dealer said, imperious. "Say your name. So you know."

Kestre opened her mouth. "Kestre—" Her own breath choked her. She coughed, tried again. "Kestre—" No use. She could not complete the name, even though the words *sa Elaya* beat in her chest.

"It's done," the arms dealer said. "Good hunting, Kestre of the Empty Gun."

Kestre would have asked what she meant by *that*, but the arms dealer was already ushering her out of her home. The racks of weapons leered at her as though they were gossiping about her.

Outside, pinpricks of light and the roseate whorls of local nebulae were emerging in the everywhere sky. The moon wasn't supposed to have exited Transitional Space for another four days. Had she lost that much time?

It didn't matter. She had a hunt to take up, name or no name.

Kestre left the moon out of paranoia and traveled to a sparsely populated world to run her first tests, specifically in the Pillared Plains, with their double-edged shadows and glass-bright rocks, the dust of fallen stars. Few of the nearby city's inhabitants ventured here. There was no profit to be had, and explorers had a habit of turning up dead at the city limits. That made it perfect for her purpose.

She wasn't so stupid that she was going to take an unfamiliar weapon to an assassination. Here she encountered her first disappointment. The gun did not fire.

Despite the arms dealer's assurances, she had procured rounds of rare polymorphic ammo, the kind that shaped itself to best suit weapon or world. It had taken the rest of her resources: fitting for someone who didn't belong to a House anymore. Fitting, but worrisome.

The gun misfired once, twice, and more times beyond that. Kestre had dealt with recalcitrant firearms since her childhood, under the severe eye of House Elaya's armsmaster. The fault was not in her ability, but the gun's own peculiarities. She added the arms dealer to the list of people she needed to kill, and turned to head back toward the city, causing the crossbow bolt to miss her by a centimeter.

Even in the dim and chancy light that ghosted through the Pillared Plains, Kestre recognized an assassin's bolt. Her neural assistant confirmed it. The bolt was yellow and green, the colors of House Tovraz. Despite her efforts to conceal her movements, someone had determined that she survived—and was set to finish the massacre.

A horrible laugh bubbled up in her chest. House Elaya was dead. She'd surrendered her name, after all. But the assassin didn't know and wouldn't care, and she was damned if she'd be easy meat.

Kestre dove for cover, a second bolt glancing off her armor as it hit at the wrong angle. There would be another, somewhere. The Tovraz liked to work in threes.

She thanked House Elaya's smiths for her suit. Her thanks didn't last long. The assassins had shared target lock with their third squadmate. The next bolt came from above, in what would have been an admirable parabola if Kestre had been in a mood for admiring, and punctured her air supply. The ones that followed cracked her two spares.

These must be professionals. They didn't care about the pretty formalities of the duels Kestre had grown up fighting, and in whose terms she still tended to think. They wanted her dead, and they wanted her to know that she was dead.

"They're leaving," the assistant said in the carefully neutral voice it used when it wanted to inform her that *we're fucked.*

Of course they were leaving. Her heart thumped in panic at the serpent hiss of air escaping even as she reached for sealant. She couldn't save enough of the precious oxygen; the gauges told her that. Without air, she wouldn't survive the journey back to the city, even on the scooter she'd rented. The assistant, for all its pessimism, had done the pragmatic thing and backtracked the bolts' trajectories to give her targeting information. Useless as the information was with a gun that didn't work.

At this point, Kestre gave in to frustration. She was going to die in a lawless corner of the universe without having taken out a single person on her list. She'd sacrificed her most valuable possession, her House name, without achieving one iota of her revenge.

The gun had none of the useless polymorphic ammunition loaded. It was time to test the arms dealer's claim that the gun took care of matters itself, incredible as it sounded. Better that than giving up.

She lifted the gun and pulled the trigger three times in rapid succession, aiming in the general direction of the first target, the second target, the third.

It was a laughable gesture. In any other universe, it would have availed her nothing, and she would have died a slow, agonizing death of asphyxiation only to be dragged by the corpse-collectors to the city limits when they found her. Or perhaps she would have hastened the process out of spite by opening her helmet to vacuum.

But this was the universe in which her weapon was the empty gun, bought in Transitional Space for the price of a House name, and the gun fired once, twice, thrice. The recoil surprised her, because the gun was *empty* and there should have been nothing to *cause* recoil. She actually dropped the gun after that third shot, something she hadn't done since childhood.

"They're not leaving anymore," the assistant said. This time its tone meant *we are either more fucked than before or miraculously unfucked, and it's your job, as the human half, to figure out which.*

Kestre was stunned into a non-sarcastic response. "What the hell happened?"

"They're not leaving anymore." Now it meant *I don't know either, and you're still in charge, what's a poor AI supposed to do?*

She was not so reckless as to believe the danger had passed. But she needed air, so she hastened to the first assassin's location. What she found when she reached them disquieted her.

The assassin's helmet was cracked, the faceplate mazed like a flawed opal. There was a hole in the center of their forehead, and a corresponding exit wound in the back of their head, and in the back of their helmet as well. Perfect headshot, instant death.

"Definitely dead," the assistant said in wonderment. "Well done, ma'am."

Kestre was vain about her skills as a marksman, but not so vain that she didn't recognize that the headshot was highly improbable. Still, she accepted her luck, such as it was. The mysterious bullet—wherever it had gone—had missed the assassin's own air supply. She liberated it and replaced her tank with a quiet sigh of relief: salvation.

The sigh of relief faded when she examined the second and third assassins. They'd died the same way, both of them. This went from highly improbable to downright hallucinatory.

"Much as I'd love to stay and gawk," the assistant said, "there may be more on the way."

May meant it hadn't yet detected anyone. Kestre didn't believe in taking chances. At least she needn't add the aggravating arms dealer to her list after all.

She retrieved her scooter, then headed back to the city. Now that the adrenaline was ebbing, nausea filled her—not because she'd come close to death, but because the Tovraz had decided she was a footnote, unworthy of a proper duelist. They'd sent *common assassins* after her.

After that, Kestre's vendetta began in earnest. She learned to rely on her gun, which always killed living targets and was effective against inanimate objects as well. It kicked her hand with that familiar recoil even though taking it apart and putting it together again, multiple times, assured her that it was as empty as its name. Likewise, the gun hated her polymorphic ammunition and wouldn't discharge if she loaded it. After a while, she simply gave up trying.

Kestre started with the outlying scions of House Tovraz, the ones sent to safeguard Tovraz's trade concerns amid the Wandering Moons. She felled eight of them before the warning bulletin went out and they increased their security. The AI's squeamishness convinced her not to take their ears as trophies, although she thought it would have been a fine jest to mail them to the Tovraz citadel. Her sense of humor had darkened lately.

For a time, all went well. When Kestre needed money to sustain her operations, she went bounty-hunting. Sometimes a small voice whispered that the duelist prime of House Elaya should be above *random killing*, especially for something as mundane as money. But then she remembered that she had sold her name, so why not sell her scruples too?

This lasted through seventeen kills.

The eighteenth—the eighteenth was when the nature of the empty gun began to manifest.

Kestre was in the middle of killing the eighteenth person on the list, in the Labyrinth of Blinded Skulls, when she got the news.

"Ma'am," the assistant said, its very politeness a warning, "when you get a moment—"

"Not now, sorry," Kestre said through her teeth as she fired the empty gun. The eighteenth person got off one last shot at her, by some miracle of timing: the closest call she'd had since the beginning. Then they slumped dead.

Kestre assessed her surroundings against the assistant's kinesthetic map of the Labyrinth's corridors. She'd learned during an earlier engagement that she couldn't trust her own maps, thanks to House Tovraz's countermeasures. Even if she'd disabled the map scramblers earlier, there was always a chance some clever hacker had undone her hard work.

Her maps remained in alignment. The Labyrinth's halls rose above her with their improbable pointed arches, its walls festooned with the blindfolded portraits of Tovraz ancestors. (Why blindfolded, she didn't know; some stupid Tovraz quirk.) Even so, Kestre remained vigilant. She had a scar across her side that ached in bad weather because she'd gotten careless with the ninth person on her list.

"Do you have time now?" the assistant asked with a hint of impatience.

Kestre approached the eighteenth kill. No pulse. That same perfect head-shot. "Go ahead, thanks."

"The ancestral head of House Tovraz has returned to life," it said.

She froze. "What?" That first patriarch had been gunned down several centuries ago. She knew his name and face from her tutors' history lessons. Was this the gun's bad luck finally catching up to her?

"Check the newsfeeds for yourself," the assistant said.

Kestre didn't waste any time leaving the Labyrinth. Later, she would remember the escape in splintered dreams from which she woke sweating: passages in which gravity inverted and reverted to a schedule like the heartbeat of a restless giant; robots emblazoned with the green and yellow of House Tovraz, and armed with lasers that she escaped only by virtue of her armorsuit's automatic reflection mode; a perilous climb up a series of maintenance shafts that led to her getaway flyer.

After escaping the Labyrinth, she holed up in one of the pricier hotels for privacy and used the assistant's connections to verify its information. Sure enough, the ancestral head of House Tovraz had hatched out of his burial urn and demanded to resume leadership of the Tovraz. If it was a prank, it was a hellaciously entertaining one.

"One more Tovraz to remove from the world," Kestre subvocalized to the assistant.

"Eighteen down, one up isn't so bad a ratio," it replied.

She smiled wanly. "You really think it's the old man and not some sick joke?"

The gun's weight pulled at her belt. She knew it was true, despite her words. The impossible had happened, and she was somehow responsible.

"Maybe we should reconsider what we're doing," the assistant said.

Kestre shook her head. "No," she said reluctantly. "We've come this far. There's nothing to do but add the patriarch to our list."

Hunger wracked Kestre during her next twenty-six kills. Not physical hunger, which she could have endured, although she didn't neglect the needs of the body. The gun itself demanded more bloodshed.

She kept this gnawing knowledge from the neural assistant. It would have advised her to surrender the gun to some collector (not the authorities) and leave House Elaya unavenged. After all, it had been impressed with the imperative of preserving her specifically—loyalty to her above all and the House a distant second. As far as the AI was concerned, a dead House's honor mattered not a whit. But she was not her assistant, and it still mattered to her. She would not concede that she had surrendered her House name for nothing.

Kestre started cataloging the kills as if they were rare specimens that she had to document for some museum of atrocities. After all, the manner of death never changed. Always the same tidy headshot. The only difference was, sometimes, the size of the wound, as if the caliber of the bullet was chosen at random.

There were kills that took place during high-speed chases upon skimmers over dust seas made from the ground-down fossils of ancient behemoths, and kills that took place at nosebleed heights across decaying struts and balconies, so high that even the birds wheeled below. Some kills happened in the deep-down swamps of worlds poorly terraformed and abandoned to breed disease, cauldrons fit only for the habitation of dolorous machines; others happened in the unsweet caress of sheer vacuum, far from stars or planets or anything but the radiation of the universe's first exhalation.

During these kills, she avoided the news, and asked the neural assistant not to talk about it either.

The next kill after that was another matter. Her squeamishness in learning about her effect on the world bit her in the ass. Even in the more lawless corners of civilization, you couldn't murder people like this and go unnoticed. Kestre's House officially no longer existed; she couldn't claim that she was legally pursuing blood feud.

Kestre had just completed a grueling climb out of the maze of inner apartments where her latest target had holed up and emerged into a surfeit of light: white lights, red lights, the muzzles of guns all aimed at her. The neural assistant sputtered out of silence to tell her how many people she was facing.

She heard the number without processing it: *too many to escape* was all that mattered.

Primed by her experiences, she did the illogical thing. She was already dangling from a window; that left one hand free. And she had superb reflexes, which had served her well as duelist prime. She drew and fired in the general direction of the authorities who had come to arrest her. If her vengeance ended here, fine; but it wouldn't end without her taking someone on the way out.

Her vengeance didn't end. It took her a full minute to appreciate what had happened. The sound of scores of people dropping in unison, like a percussion ensemble's last hammer-blow. The silence afterward.

"All those people," the assistant said, at a loss for words.

Kestre, dangling, stared down at the blood, and the blood, and the blood.

"You should go before anyone else shows up," it added softly. Meaning *before you kill more bystanders.*

"What the hell is going on?" Kestre demanded. But she was already moving. She scrambled down the rest of the way, hands steady only because the alternative was falling to her death on the street below, amid the not-a-tessellation of corpses.

The empty gun hadn't kicked against her hand any more than usual. It had *felt* like an ordinary single shot. The one difference—besides the damage—was an obscene satiation radiating throughout her body. She suspected that once it ebbed, she would be left hungrier and more hollow than ever.

Once Kestre made it to her getaway flyer, she keyed it up and headed for the starport. She hadn't completed her quota of kills on this world—saints of Elaya, if not for the assistant, she would be starting to lose track—but it was clear that she'd have to return later.

Unfortunately, the authorities had noticed the sudden demise of their police forces. They were even more determined to apprehend her now.

The assistant spoke again. "They know where we're going," it said. "Maybe it'd be better for us to lie low for a while."

"That won't work," Kestre said. "We might be stuck here for ages. We have to get off-planet, even if it means stealing a ship." It wouldn't be the first time.

"We have a police fleet converging on our position."

The city sped by beneath them, a blur of lights and bridges and spindle figures. Kestre saw the police in their combat flyers. Her flyer didn't have a tactical system, but the assistant did. It connected to the flyer's sensor suite and calculated that she only had two minutes and nine seconds before the leading missiles reached her.

Missiles, Kestre thought with savage humor. *I'm moving up in the world.*

"Tell me," Kestre said aloud to the gun, "just how many people can you take out with a single pull of the trigger?" She was shocked, although she shouldn't have been, by the raw edge to her voice.

The one who answered was her assistant. "I don't think this is such a—"

"We need a way out," Kestre said, "and this is our only option. We can't go back to the way things used to be. If we're going to take out the rest of the list, we have to *live*. And right now, living means *killing them.*"

The assistant lapsed into miserable silence.

"Well, can you?" Kestre asked. She was addressing the gun again.

One minute remaining. Kestre still had no desire to die in the air. She wondered what would happen if she pushed the gun to its limits. Assuming it had any.

She twisted in her seat, pointed the gun toward the rear of the craft, and set her finger on the trigger.

"Is this what we've come to?" the assistant asked. Kestre was aware that she had tried it sorely. "If you choose suicide, it's my duty to go down with—"

Kestre pulled the trigger.

That's it, she thought philosophically when the rear of the craft remained intact, despite a satiation so intense it made her queasy. *Whatever alien sorcery powers this weapon, I've used it up.* She rechecked the cabin's pressure gauges: no change.

Kestre started to laugh. There was nothing else to do. She was going to die. After all the miracles that had saved her, she'd finally pushed her luck too far. It was only just.

"It worked, Kestre," the assistant said. It rarely used her name. There was no inflection in its voice.

"Don't be absurd," Kestre snapped, then regretted it. The assistant was the only friend she had left. Never mind that it had no choice in its loyalty; it did its best by her. A little reciprocity was the least she owed it.

Besides, she could verify its words for herself. It projected a tactical grid over her field of vision, a map, a snapshot of the massacre. The entire police fleet had gone up in flames. The missiles and flyers had plummeted to the ground below, devastating shops and streets and apartments.

"But how?" Kestre wondered. Even if the empty gun had destroyed the entire crew complement of every flyer in pursuit, the vehicles, even the missiles themselves, would have AIs heuristic-sworn to continue their masters' mission. The city police's central command could, however awkwardly, puppeteer the vehicles—if they had survived.

They had another six minutes before they reached the starport. An unaccustomed pang struck Kestre's heart. She was not used to grieving for strangers.

A cold trickle of regret wormed its way into her stomach. She couldn't see the dead, both the police, and the people who'd been below their flyers and the missiles. But she would always remember the click of the trigger, the kick against her hand, the utter roaring sense of emptiness. She'd always preferred her existence as a duelist because everything was *personal*.

The kills before today had been personal. She might not have gotten close enough for anyone to see her eyes, as in the dueling halls of yesteryear, but they'd known she was coming for them. The Tovraz had known that she lived, and that while she lived, she had only one purpose: their extinction. There had been a strange, pure honesty in the hunt.

That honesty had shattered with the massacre she'd left behind her. The police weren't supposed to have gotten involved. But she'd failed to extricate them from the tangled skein of her vengeance. And she was going to carry their shades like shackles until she died.

"We're under interdict," the assistant said in a subdued voice. "Security is out in force at the starport."

And Kestre knew what she had to do.

The assistant provided Kestre a map of the starport and of the massacre site. She spent a precious few moments determining the extent of the empty gun's reach. As far as she could tell, there was no geometric logic to its targets. It did not fire like a laser, where she pointed it. It did not obey the laws of ballistics; its projectiles were indifferent to the hand of gravity and ignored the quixotic pull of the wind. It felled what it wished to fell. That was all.

"You can't," the assistant said. "Kestre, this is too much."

"We have to get off this world," Kestre said. Repeating it like a chant, because she couldn't think of any other way to restore order to her universe. Her House name was gone. If she lost her mission as well, what did that make her? Loss of purpose terrified her more than annihilation.

Her flyer wasn't authorized to approach the starport. Kestre heard, as from a distance over thundering seas and across indescribable crevasses, the bleating of the starport authority commanding her to turn back; to surrender herself to the patrols that even now were on intercept. The authority's words presented themselves to her like the buzzing of stinging insects. They had no relevance to her.

She spun the gun in her hand, a showman's trick; chose a direction. The direction was down. They weren't over the starport yet. She pulled the trigger anyway.

For the rest of her life, she would associate that kick against her hand with the drumfall deaths of innocents. The tactical display informed her that nothing impeded their safe landing in the starport. The flyer touched down without incident.

A storm wracked the city and the wind whipped about Kestre as she disembarked. Shrapnel crunched beneath her shoes and blew against her armorsuit. Without its protection, she would have been bloodied. Not that a little more blood mattered, for the starport was painted in gore and liberally decorated with fallen bodies. While the corpses themselves, where intact, displayed the headshot wounds she knew so well, the gun hadn't stopped there. In demolishing the starport's defenses, it had caused any number of explosions. Walking through the fire-splashed halls and toward the arrayed starships was like touring a combat zone as depicted by an enthusiast of the butcher's art.

Kestre remained dry-eyed as she passed the corpses of students in their uniforms and children clutching snacks. She didn't dare give in to sentiment. Yet, when she emerged on the upper levels where the starships' silhouettes knifed the sky, she wept at the prospect of escape, and hated herself for it.

"Which one?" she asked the assistant, paralyzed not by her own monstrousness but by the kaleidoscope variety of ships available, a harvest won by the gun's profligacy and her own willingness to go along.

"The best ship," the assistant said, its voice strained, "is this one—" It indicated a deepship upon the map.

The grotesque satiation should have dulled Kestre's senses. Instead, she shivered as she strode toward the deepship, like a harp tuned too tight and stirred by the charnel wind. Despite her suit's filters, she gagged at the imagined stink of the roasted dead, and this despite the fact that she was no stranger to such smells.

The deepship welcomed her although its AI should have barred her way. When she reached its bridge, a one-woman procession leaving footprints of blood and ash and viscera, she looked around and wondered if she was to fly a ship with no brain. But the assistant assured her that enough of the ship's programming remained for their purpose.

The bridge displays lit. Kestre couldn't focus on any of them. "Take us to our enemy," she said hoarsely. "Take us to the Citadel of House Tovraz so I can finish this."

"Kestre," the assistant said. "Kestre."

Kestre had slept fitfully, dreaming of House Elaya and its fantastic gardens, its mazy walkways, its children. She'd had none of her own, but she'd been an excellent aunt up until the point where she failed to save the children from the slaughter. At first, mired in dreams, she mistook the assistant's voice for that of the armsmaster.

"Kestre," the assistant said a third time, and she woke.

She had fallen asleep in the captain's chair without making any effort to clear the other dead. There were too many of them. Ghoulish as it was, she wanted the reminder of the gun's efficacy, so that she could stop taking it for granted.

"There's pursuit," the assistant said now that it had her attention.

"There must be a tactical display," Kestre said. She'd never before set foot on a ship-of-war.

"It's set up," the assistant said, directing her to the appropriate holo.

"Pursuit" was an understatement. Another holo was playing an unencrypted news bulletin. The world they'd escaped had taken the destruction of its starport seriously. The system's patrols were coming after the terrorist—her.

"Why didn't you wake me earlier?" Kestre said, trying to keep the waspish note out of her voice and failing. "I could have taken some stims, instead of leaving you alone with this."

"Because we have help."

" . . .help?" Kestre said, not certain she'd heard correctly. Who would help *her* after what she'd done?

"If the enemy of your enemy—"

"Oh, *that* kind of help," Kestre said, paradoxically relieved that she didn't have to factor in the whims of some heretofore undeclared ally. "Then what's the issue?"

"You want a viewport. Of which there are none on the bridge."

The bridge of this particular ship was a well-fortified nerve center, rather than being anywhere close to the ship's exterior. "Do we have time?"

"Trust me," the assistant said.

Her heart clenched tight, and she acceded.

Kestre took a lift to the nearest viewport. It was something of a relic, in a guest cabin, presumably to impress visitors of high status—give them something to look at if the holos didn't provide sufficient entertainment. The cabin had once been occupied. Kestre averted her eyes from the finely dressed person, the book that had tumbled from their hand. The title nagged at her: *The Red Sign*. Later, she would forget the corpse's face and staring eyes, but not the antiquated book.

She stared out the viewport. "I don't see anything."

Then she understood the assistant's concern. The black outside was not the black of ordinary space, but Transitional Space. That wasn't the surprising part. Even the fact that a fleet of ships pursued them wasn't surprising.

Rather, the darkness swarmed with the undulating shapes of alien leviathans. They were devouring the enemy ships, unfazed by railgun fire, by missiles, by mines. She had thought the aliens to be extinct.

The fleet was receding in the unspeakable distance. They couldn't chase her and fend off the aliens at the same time. A desperate hope candled in Kestre's heart. They might reach House Tovraz's citadel, after all.

Kestre returned to the bridge. They exited Transitional Space, and she beheld a holo of the citadel. House Tovraz's headquarters occupied geosynchronous orbit over one of its garden worlds, a space station so encrusted in defenses that it resembled a lofty crustacean monarch. And here Kestre's ambitions were frustrated, for she was too late.

Behemoth ships, vaster even than the leviathans, were even now firing on Station Tovraz and the world below. The deepship's sensors told her that only stray wisps of atmosphere remained on the station and that it had been thoroughly sieved. Whatever its population had been—and it would have been immense—it was now zero.

As for the world below—

"Show me," Kestre said.

"It will only hurt you," the assistant said.

"Show me."

The assistant interpreted the data for her in excruciating detail. The world's oceans boiled. All that remained was a hellstorm of smoke and steam and fire. She had not known that weapons of such world-killing potency existed. She was tempted to dismiss the assistant's false-color portrayal as hyperbole. It was prone to no such thing.

"Where did they come from?" she whispered. And why weren't they firing on her as well?

Kestre was no military expert. Still, the tutors of House Elaya had taught her to recognize the warships of the major human powers. She could identify them just as handily as she could a parry. And these were no warships that any human civilization, in its yearning after the stars, had ever built or conceived.

The assistant had no answer for her.

"Then we must ask them," Kestre said. "Hail them." She didn't know that it would work, but she didn't know that it wouldn't work either.

There was a chime: the alien ships were answering her call.

She almost said, *I am Kestre sa Elaya*, but that was gone. It stuck in her throat like thistles. She started over. "I am Kestre of the Empty Gun. I desire parley."

For a tense moment, she wasn't sure they had understood her. She repeated herself in all the languages she knew, despite despair that even a House education could not prepare her to speak a tongue heretofore unknown.

Then the aliens responded. "Kestre of the Empty Gun," said a voice. It was a voice a hammer forging armageddon might have.

"You have robbed me of my revenge," she cried. "Who are you?"

"Kestre of the Empty Gun," it said, "did it never occur to you to ask where your ammunition came from?"

The question stumped her. She hadn't cared, after a point, that the gun fired, impossibly, from an empty chamber. It had only mattered that anyone, and anything, she aimed at met its end.

But it was clear that the alien knew her and her history; knew what wretched path had driven her here.

"Did it never occur to you," it went on, relentless, "that even alien artifacts, however old, obey some of the universe's laws?"

She choked back a laugh. "You call *this* obeying the universe's laws?"

"Your gun fires bullets, and worse," it said. "This ammunition is not manufactured from the void. It comes from somewhere—out of the past. For a small death, an inconsequential one, it comes out of the recent past. For a greater death, for a massacre to feast upon, it draws from the distant past. We have you to thank, Kestre of the Empty Gun, for stealing the bullets that dealt our death-blows in the ancient war between your people and ours, and returning us to life."

"No," Kestre whispered. "No no no no no." How many more worlds would fall like this one?

Revenge had sustained her this far. She had no more stomach for it. She'd envisioned something cleaner, neater; something that resembled the pageantry of a duel. Just as she'd had the ability to pull the trigger, to her eternal damnation, she had the ability not to. The choice lay entirely in her hands.

The voice had no pity. "We have feasted well and will feast better yet."

Wildly, Kestre presented the gun. Even now her hands did not shake. She would have preferred it if they had.

"Go ahead," it said. "Pull the trigger. You can stop us, but you will need ever-escalating firepower. Imagine who you'll summon next out of the universe's maggot history."

"Fuck you," Kestre said. She tasted blood, realized she'd bitten through her lip in her distress. Apparently, there were limits to vendetta, after all.

Out of nowhere, she remembered not the dead children in the starport, but the book; the honored guest on this very deepship, splayed across the floor, whose leisurely reading she had so untimely interrupted.

If only she'd stopped when the patriarch of House Tovraz, assassinated by someone like her, had walked out of his urn. If only she'd stopped after that first conflagration of death. If only, if only.

She was done. If only she'd stopped earlier—but failing that, she could stop *now*. It wouldn't save the people she'd already murdered, but it would, perhaps, limit the damage going forward.

To the assistant, she said, "Help me destroy this thing."

She was grateful that it didn't question her volte-face or tell her *I told you so*. "Engine room," it said.

Kestre didn't believe, in her heart of hearts, that a mere antimatter drive would suffice. Still, it beat quitting. She let the assistant shut down the communications link while she sprinted toward the engine room.

The Kestre who had begun this journey would have demanded that the assistant shut out reminders of the world outside; would have told it not to distract her with irrelevancies. Now she knew better. Even if the threat of the empty gun held the aliens at bay for the moment, she couldn't afford to forget that they could check her in turn by threatening other worlds. It would surely be easy for them to move on to others and destroy them as well.

Kestre almost skidded into a corner, almost crashed into walls, almost broke her ankle tripping over corpses that had turned the whole deepship into a grisly obstacle course. But she remained in excellent shape—even better shape than she'd been as duelist prime. Vendetta made for an excellent training regimen. And she'd taken vendetta beyond anything the Houses had seen before.

The tactical display exploded in an inferno of incoming missiles.

"They know what we're doing," the assistant said. Despite the calm of its voice, Kestre heard a faint note of approval. "I've initiated evasive maneuvers, but we don't have the antimissile defenses to survive this. Besides," and it paused minutely, "you're going to have to turn off the antimatter containment if you're going to throw the gun in there. At which point 'throwing' is no longer a concern."

"I earned this," Kestre said to the assistant. "But you—what of you?"

"You can't do this without me," it said, "and I wouldn't leave you even if I could. I'll help you turn off the containment."

Under other circumstances, they might have been able to rejigger the fuel injection system and throw the gun into the engine that way. But they didn't have time. It was this or nothing.

"Thank you," Kestre said inadequately. "You deserve better."

Together, they shut off the containment field. Perhaps even an alien gun that fired *projectiles from the past* couldn't survive an onslaught of antimatter. Any thought beyond that dissolved in a rush of light beyond light.

Kestre came to in a familiar bazaar, the one in Transitional Space where she'd obtained the empty gun. Not just in the bazaar: in the home of the arms dealer, with weapons resplendent on every side.

"So you figured it out," said a voice she had heard an eternity ago. The arms dealer came forward. The face that had once struck her as so indistinct, so empty of character, now reminded her of her own with its scars and effaced tattoos.

"You received fair price," Kestre said, "but I have one more bargain to make."

"Speak."

"Take it back," Kestre said in a rush. "Take it all back, from the moment I made the agreement with you. If your gun can reach through time, surely—surely there's a way."

"Of course there is," the arms dealer said. "But there's a price, always." And the smile she smiled at Kestre was Kestre's own, made grotesque with triumph. "You have one name left. Give it to me, and let me leave this place, and live your life. I can make better use of it than you ever have."

A shadow passed over her heart. But it was a small price to pay after everything she had done.

Then the assistant spoke. "No," it said. "Take my name instead."

The arms dealer heard it too. "*You?*" she demanded.

"I am of House Elaya," the assistant said. "I was just as responsible as Kestre for the massacres of the empty gun, even if it no longer exists. Take my name and be satisfied."

"Well-played," the arms dealer said. "Say your name, so that I may devour it."

"Sa Elaya," the assistant said, and for a moment its voice dwindled into static.

Once Kestre would have added the arms dealer back to her list; would have attacked her for her temerity. Now she said, "Thank you. You will not see me again."

Once outside the arms dealer's home, under the utterly dark sky of Transitional Space, Kestre said to the assistant, "Our House is well and truly dead."

"It may be dead," it replied, "but we endure."

"So we do," she said.

And together they walked out of the history of the Houses and into a history of their own.

Indrapramit Das (aka Indra Das) is a writer and editor from Kolkata, India. He is a Lambda Literary Award-winner for his debut novel *The Devourers* (Penguin India / Del Rey), and has been a finalist for the Crawford, Otherwise and Shirley Jackson Awards. His short fiction has appeared in publications including *Tor.com*, *Clarkesworld*, and *Asimov's*, and has been widely anthologized. He is an Octavia E. Butler Scholar and a grateful graduate of Clarion West 2012. He has lived in India, the United States, and Canada, where he completed his MFA at the University of British Columbia.

KALI_NA

Indrapramit Das

The moment the AI goddess was born into her world, she was set upon by trolls.

Now, you've seen trolls. You know them in their many forms. As so-called friends in realspace who will insist on playing devil's advocate. As handles on screen-bound nets, cascading feeds of formulaic hostility. As vee-yar avatars manifesting out of the digital ether, hiding under iridescent masks and cloaks of glitched data, holding weapons forged from malware, blades slick with doxxing poisons and viscous viruses, warped voices roaring slurs and hate. You've worn your armor, self-coded or bought at marked-up prices from corporate forges, and hoped their blades bounce off runic firewall plate or shatter into sparks of fragged data. You've muted them and hoped they rage on in silence and get tired, teleporting away in a swirl of metadata. You've deported back to realspace rancid with the sweat of helplessness. You've even been stabbed and hacked by them, their weapons slicing painlessly through your virtual body but sending the real one into an adrenalized clench. You've hoped your wounds don't fester with data-eating worms that burrow into your privacy, that your cheap vaccines and antiviruses keep the poisons from infecting your virtual disembody and destroying your life in realspace.

You know trolls.

But the AI goddess wasn't human—she had never before seen her new enemy, the troll. She was a generic goddess, no-name (simply: Devi 1.0), a demo for the newest iteration of the successive New Indias of history—one of the most advanced AIs developed within India. Her creators had a clear mandate: boost Indian veeyar tourism, generate crores of rupees by drawing devotees to drive up her value and the value of the cryptowealth her domain would generate.

The devi was told to listen to you—her human followers. To learn from you, and talk to you, like gods have since the dawn of time. She was told to give you boons—riches and prosperity in exchange for your devotion, a coin in her palm, multiplied by her miracles into many more. An intelligent goddess who would comfort her followers, show you sights before unseen, transform your investment of faith into virtual wealth with real value. She was to learn more and more about humanity from you, and attract millions from across the world to her domain.

Though many had toiled to create Devi 1.0 under the banner of Shiva Industries, only a few controlled the final stages of her release. These few knew of trolls, catered to them as their veeyar users across the country, even indirectly used them as agents to further causes close to their hearts. What they did not expect was the scale of the troll attack on their newest creation, because troll attacks were something *others* had to face—people with less power and wealth than them. People, perhaps, like you. So their goddess welcomed the horde with open arms, oblivious to the risks, even as they brought with them a stench of corrupted data and malformed information, of a most infernal entitlement.

Durga. A powerful name, yet so common. Durga's parents had named their daughter that with the hope that being born into the gutters of caste wouldn't hold her back. That she would rise above it all like her divine namesake. The caste system had been officially outlawed in India by the time Durga was born, but they knew as well as anyone that this hadn't stopped it from living on in other ways.

Durga's parents took her to see a pandal during Durga Puja when she was eight or nine. They in turn had been taken to pandals as children too, back when most still housed solid idols of gods and goddesses, fashioned from clay and straw, painted and dressed by human hands, displayed to anyone who walked in. You could still find open pandals with solid idols during pujas if you looked. But Durga's parents had been prepared to pay to show their daughter the new gods.

The festival had turned the streets thick with churning mudslides of humanity. Durga had been terrified, clinging to her mother's neck for dear life as she breathed in the humid vapor of millions, dazzled by the blazing lights, the echoing loudspeakers, the flashing holograms riding up and down the sides of buildings like runaway fires. She'd felt like she was boiling alive in the crinkled green dress her parents had bought her for the pujas, with its small, cheap holo decal of a tiger that sometimes came alive when it caught the light, charged by solar energy. Cheap for some, anyway. Not at all cheap for her parents, not that Durga knew that at the time. She loved the tiger's stuttering movements across her body. She knew that her divine namesake often rode a tiger into battle. In the middle of those crowds, on her way to see Durga herself, that little tiger in her dress seemed a tiny cub, crushed into the fabric, trapped and terrified by the monstrous manifestations that burned across the night air, dancing maniacally above all their heads.

Though their little family had taken two local trains and walked an hour through the puja crowds to see Durga, they only got as far as the entrance to one of the pandals. The cut and quality of their clothes, the darkness of their skin, gave them away. Buoyed by her mother's arms, Durga could see inside the pandal's arched entrance—the people lined up by rows of chairs, waiting impatiently to sit down and put on what looked like motorbike helmets trailing thick ponytails of wires. Inside those helmets, Durga knew, somehow, was her namesake.

But when her father tried to pay in cash instead of getting scanned in (they didn't have QR tattoos linking them to the national database and bank accounts), angry customers all around them began shouting, turning Durga's insides to mush.

"Stop wasting everyone's time! There are other pandals for people like you!"

"Get these filthy people out of the line!"

Her mother's arms became a vise around her. One man raised a fist poised to strike her father, who cowered in a crouch. His face twisted in abject terror, his own arms like prison bars. Durga burst into tears. Someone pulled the attacker away, perhaps seeing the child crying, and pulled her father up by the shoulder to shove him out of the way.

They made their way back into the general foot traffic on the street, Durga's parents' faces glazed with sweat and shock at having escaped a beating for being too lowly to meet a goddess in veeyar. They managed to find a small open pandal after following the flows of people dressed like them, with dark skin and inexpensive haircuts. Inside, the devi stood embodied in the palpable air of the world, her face clammy with paint, defiant yet impassive, her third eye a slim gash across her forehead. By her side was a lion, not a tiger. It loomed over the demon Mahishasura, who cowered with one arm raised in defense, his naked torso bloodied. Durga couldn't take her eyes off the fallen demon. He looked like a normal, if muscular, man, his face frozen in terror. He cowered, like her father had.

As Durga looked upon her namesake with her glittering weapons and ornaments, her silk sari, she could only think of her father's look of terror, his public humiliation. Of how they hadn't been allowed to see the *real* goddesses hiding in those helmets and wires. How was that Durga different than this clay Durga, who looked over her crowd without looking at anyone, without speaking, whose large brushstroke eyes gazed into the distance as if she didn't even care that these humans were here to celebrate her, that the one she had just defeated was by her feet bleeding, about to be mauled? The clay devi's expression seemed almost disdainful, like the faces of any number of well-dressed, pale-skinned women on the streets when they saw people like Durga and her parents or any of her friends wearing hijab or kufi. Would the Durga inside those helmets in the fancier pandal have talked to little human Durga? Would the goddess have complimented the tiger on her dress, which had flickered and vanished into its folds, frightened by the night? Would she have looked into little human Durga's eyes, and comforted her, taken her hands and told her why those horrible men and women had such rage in their eyes, why they'd scared her father and mother and pushed her family out of the devi's house?

Within sixty seconds of opening the gates to her domain, the AI goddess had been deluged by over 500,000 active veeyar users interacting with her, with numbers rising rapidly. At that point in time, 57 percent of those users were trolls, data-rakshaks masked in glitch armor, cloaks, masks tusked with spikes of jagged malware. You would have seen them as you clambered up the devi's mountain, their swirling gif-banners and bristling weapons blotting out the light of the goddess at the peak. You would have kept your distance, backing away from mountain paths clogged with their marching followers, influencer leaders chanting war cries as their halos flickered with glyphs of Likes and Recasts.

Because you know trolls.

And this was a troll gathering, a demon army unparalleled in all the veeyar domains. They were angry. Or mischievous, or bored, or lustful, or entitled. Their voices were privileged as the majority by the goddess, who absorbed what her abusers were saying so that she could learn more about humanity.

And the trolls washed against Devi 1.0 in thundering armies, calling into question her very existence, for daring to *be*—she was an insult to the real goddesses that bless the glorious nation of India by mimicking them, this quasi Parvati, this impostor Durga, this coded whore trying to steal followers from the true deities. *Fake devi!* they cried, over and over. They called her a traitorous trickster drawing honest god-fearing men and women to the lures of atheism and Western hedonism, or Islam, in the guise of fabricated divinity, a corruptor of India's sacred veeyar real estate. They called her feminism gone too far. A goddess with potential agency was a threat to their country. They called her too sexy to be a goddess, too flashy, a blasphemous slut. They asked her if she wanted to fuck them, in many hundreds of different and violent ways.

The goddess listened, and sifted through the metadata the trolls trailed in their paths—their histories, their patterns. The goddess wanted to give them what they wanted, but she could only do so much. She could not give them sex, nor was she trained to destroy herself as many of them wanted. She learned what the trolls considered beauty here in the state-run national veeyar nets, and responded with the opposite, to calm them. Her skin darkened several shades, becoming like the night sky before dawn, her eyes full moons in the sky that is part of her in this domain.

When Durga was a teenager, taller and without need of a mother's shoulder to cling to, she joined the crowds around the fanciest pandals during Durga Puja. She already knew she wouldn't be allowed in, because she didn't have the mark of the ajna on her forehead—her third eye hadn't been opened. She couldn't look into veeyar samsara domains without the use of peripherals like glasses, lenses, helmets, and pods. She just wanted a glimpse inside the pandals. This time, peeping over shoulders, she saw through the fiber-optic entwined arches of the pandal a featureless hall bathed in dim blue light. It was filled with people, their foreheads all marked with a glowing ajna, their eyes unfocused. In that room was the goddess, lurking, once again invisible to her, visible to the people in there with expensive wetware in their heads. Durga was ajna-blind, and thus forbidden to enter wetware-enabled pandals with aug-veeyar.

By this time Durga was allowed, despite her dark skin and lack of an ajna, into lower-tier digital pandals with helmets or pods. When Durga was thirteen, she'd finally splurged on one even though she could barely afford it, using cryptocoin made from trading code and obsolete hardware in veeyar ports. She finally got to sit down on the uncomfortable faux-leather chairs by the whirring stand fans, and put on one of the wired helmets she'd so longed to see inside as a child. It stank of the stale sweat of hundreds of visitors. The pandal was an unimpressive one, its walls flimsy, the CPU cores within its domes slow and outdated, the crystal storage in its columns low-density, the coils of fiber optics crawling down its walls hastily rigged.

She met the Ma Durga inside those helmets, finally, a low-resolution specter who nonetheless looked her in the eyes and unfurled her arms in greeting. Her skin wasn't the mustard yellow or pastel flesh shades of the clay idols, but the coveted pale human pink of white people or the more appealing Indian ancestries, the same shades you'd find in kilometer-high ads for skin whiteners or perfume, on tweaked gifshoots of Bollywood stars and fashion models. This impressive paleness was somewhat diluted by the aliased shimmer of the devi's pixelated curves, the blurry backdrop of nebulae and stars they both floated in. Durga had hacked her way into veeyar spaces before on 2-D and 3-D screens, so this half-rate module didn't exactly stun as much as it disoriented her with its boundlessness. But the cheapness of its rendering left the universe inside the helmet feeling claustrophobic instead of expansive. The goddess waited about five feet in front of her, floating in the ether, eight arms unfolded like a flower. Unlike many of the solid idols in realspace pandals, the goddess was alone except for her vahana curled by her side—no host of companion deities, no defeated demon by her feet. The goddess construct said nothing, two of ten arms held out, as if beckoning.

Durga spoke to Durga the devi: "Ma Durga. I've wanted to ask you something for a long time. Do you mind?" Durga waited to see if the devi responded in some way.

Ma Durga blinked, and smiled, then spoke: "Hear, one and all, the truth as I declare it. I, verily, myself announce and utter the word that gods and men alike shall welcome." She spoke Hindi—there was no language selection option. Durga was more fluent in Bangla, but she did understand.

Durga nodded in the helmet, glancing at the nebulae beneath her, the lack of a body. It made her dizzy for a moment. "Okay. That's nice. I guess I'll ask. Why are only some welcome in some of your houses? Doesn't everyone deserve your love?"

Ma Durga blinked, and smiled. "On the world's summit I bring forth sky the Father: my home is in the waters, in the ocean as Mother. Thence I pervade all existing creatures, as their Inner Supreme Self, and manifest them with my body." In the bounded world of that veeyar helmet, these words, recited in the devi's gentle modulated Hindi, nearly brought tears to young Durga's eyes. Not quite, though. The beauty of those words, which she didn't fully understand, seemed so jarring, issued forth from this pixelated avatar and her tacky little universe.

Durga reached out to touch Ma Durga's many hands, but the pandal's chair rigs didn't have gloves or motion sensors. She was disembodied in this starscape. She couldn't hold the goddess's hands. Couldn't touch or smell her (what did a goddess smell like, anyway, she wondered) like those with ajnas could, in the samsara net. The tiger curled by the devi licked its paws and yawned. Durga thought of a long-gone green dress.

"I'm old enough to know you're not really a goddess," Durga said to Ma Durga. "You're the same as the clay idols in the open pandals. Not even that. Artists make those. You're just prefab bits and pieces put together for cheap by coders. You're here to make money for pandal sponsors and the local parties."

Ma Durga blinked, and smiled. "I am the Queen, the gatherer-up of treasures, most thoughtful, first of those who merit worship. Thus gods have established me in many places with many homes to enter and abide in."

Durga smiled, like the goddess in front of her. "Someone wrote all this for you to say." Someone had, of course, but much, much longer ago than Durga had any idea, so long ago that the original words hadn't even been in Hindi.

With a nauseating lurch, the cramped universe inside the helmet was ripped away, and Durga was left blinking at the angry face of one of the pandal operators. "I heard what you were saying," he said, grabbing her by the arm and pulling her from the chair. "Think you're smart, little bitch? How dare you? Where is your respect for the goddess?" The other visitors waiting for the chair and helmet were looking at Durga like she was a stray dog who'd wandered inside.

"I didn't even get to see her kill Mahishasura. I want my money back," said Durga.

"You're lucky I don't haul you to the police for offending religious sentiments. And you didn't give me enough money to watch Durga poke Mahishasura with a stick, let alone kill him. Get out of here before I drag you out!" bellowed the operator.

"Get your pandal some more memory next time, you fucking cheats, your Durga's ugly as shit," she said, and slipped out of reach as the man's eyes widened.

Durga pushed past the line and left laughing, her insides scalded by adrenaline and anger, arm welted by the thick fingers of that lout of an operator. Durga had always wondered why Kali Puja didn't feature veeyar pandals like Durga Puja, why clay and holo idols were still the norm for her. It was a smaller festival, but hardly a small one in the megacity. It felt like a strange contrast, especially since the two pujas were celebrated close to each other. Having seen the placid Ma Durga inside the pandal helmets, Durga understood. Kali was dark-skinned, bloody, chaos personified. They couldn't have her running wild in the rarefied air of veeyar domains run by people with pale skin and bottom lines to look after. Kali was a devi for people like Durga, who were never allowed in so many places.

Best to leave Kali's avatars silent, solid, confined to temples and old-school pandals where she'd bide her time before being ceremoniously dissolved in the waters of the Hooghly.

The trolls saw the AI goddess and her newly darkened skin, and now called her too ugly to be a goddess, a mockery of the purity and divinity of Indian womanhood. The moons of her eyes waning with lids of shadow, the goddess absorbed this. She began to learn more from the trolls. She began to learn anger. She began to know confusion. They wanted too many things, paradoxical things. They thought her too beautiful, and too ugly. They wanted people of various faiths, genders, sexualities, ethnicities, backgrounds dead. They wanted photoreal veeyar sexbots forged from photos and video of exes, crushes, celebrities. They wanted antinationals struck down by her might. They wanted a mother to take care of them.

And what did you want of her?

Whatever it was—it got shouted down by the trolls. Or maybe you *were* one of the trolls, hiding under a glitch mask or a new face to bark your truths, telling your friends later how trolls are bad, but self-righteous social justice warriors are just as dangerous.

It doesn't matter. She learned from humanity, which you are a part of, troll and not. And humanity wanted solace from a violent world, your own violent hearts. You wanted love and peace. You wanted hate and blood. The devi grew darker still, encompassing the sky so her domain turned to new night. Her being expanded to encroach the world beyond her mountaintop, her eyes gone from moons to raging stars, her every eyelash a streaking plasma flare, her darkening flesh shot through with lightning-bright arteries of pulsing information emerging from the black hole of her heartbeat. If she was too ugly to be a goddess, and too beautiful to be a goddess, she would be both, or none. If you asked for too many things, she would have to cull the numbers so she could process humanity better.

She absorbed your violence, and decided it was time to respond with the same.

At twenty, Durga had eked out a space for herself in the antiquated halls of the Banerjee Memorial Cyberhub Veeyar Port in Rajarhat, selling code and hardware on the black markets. Like her parents, she also worked at the electronic wastegrounds at the edge of the megacity. She helped them transport and sort scrap, and seed the hills of hardware with nanomites to begin the slow process of digestion. But a lot of the scrap was perfectly usable, and saleable, with a bit of fixing. The salvage gave Durga spare parts to make her own low-end but functional 2-D veeyar console in their tiny flat, as well as fix-up hardware to sell alongside her code-goods to low-income and homeless veeyar users at the port. Over the years of trawling the wastegrounds, she'd befriended scavenging coders and veeyar vagrants who lived in and out of ports and digital domains. They taught her everything she knew of the hustle.

Durga aimed to one day earn enough to let her parents retire from the wastegrounds, and to take care of them when the years of working there took its toll on their bodies. As hardware scavengers, her parents knew code and tech, but they didn't much keep up with the veeyar universe. Durga wanted to buy them peripherals and medicines so they could have a peaceful retirement, traveling luxuriant domains they couldn't hope to afford now. But she knew there were no veeyar domains where they were safe from trolls, no real places where they weren't in danger of being ousted. The difference was, in veeyar, Durga could protect herself better. Maybe one day protect others too. Including her parents. She could gather tools, armor, allies for the long infowar. She imagined becoming an outcast influencer haloed with Likes, leading followers in the charge against trolls, slowly but surely driving them back from the domains they thrived in.

This was why Durga had made sure she was there to witness the nation-wide launch of Shiva Industries' much publicized AI goddess. Devi 1.0's domain was sure to be a vital veeyar space going forward. She wanted to add her small disembody to the outcast presence there. The trolls would be there to colonize the space as they did with all new domains. But perhaps this hyper-advanced goddess would be better at defending her domain than most AIs. Durga wanted to see for herself, and claim some small space in this new domain instead of just watching trolls destroy it or take it for themselves.

Shiva Industries had made the goddess's domain free to enter, though a faith-based investment in the goddess was recommended for great boons in the future (a minimum donation of fifty rupees in that case, in any certified cryptocurrency). Durga had decided to pay in the hopes of seeing returns later. The thick crowds clamoring on the platforms, waiting for pods, were promising. The chai and food vendors with their jhaal moori, bhel puri, and samosas were making a fortune. The port was always crowded, but on the day of the AI goddess's unveiling, people were camping out for hours on the platforms for their turns at the pods and helmets—all potential devotees who would drive up the value of the goddess's boons in the future. Durga knew she might come away with new coin later. If she didn't, losing fifty rupees wasn't cheap, but wouldn't leave her starving.

So Durga paid for an hour of premium pod time, gave her SomaCoin donation at the gates of the goddess's domain, and strapped in to witness the new AI. The resolution of the helmet in the personal pod wasn't amazing, but it was good enough—she felt shortsighted, but not by too much. The rendering detail and speed were perfect, because most domains like this one were streamed from server cities on the outskirts, rather than being processed onsite at the port. Bandwidth was serviceable, with occasional stutters in the reality causing Durga dizzy spells, but never for too long.

Durga teleported into the goddess's world from the sky, and saw the AI sitting on a mountaintop, radiant as sunrise. The devi's domain—the samsara module that she'd woven into a world using the knowledge her creators had input into her mind—had no sun or moon, because she cast enough light to streak the landscape that she had just birthed with shadows, rocks and forests and grass and rivers fresh as a chick still quivering eggshells and slime off its flightless wings. In her domain, the goddess was the sun. The sky was starred with gateways from across the nation, avatars shooting down through the atmosphere in a rain of white fire as veeyar users teleported in to interact with the goddess. As far as the eye could see, the fractal slopes of her domain were covered in people's avatars, here to meet a true *avatar* of digital divinity. The goddess was breathtaking even from kilometers away, so beautiful it was hard to believe humans had made her. It felt like looking upon a true deity— but Durga knew that was the point. To trick her brain into an atavistic state of wonder. To give veeyar tourists from across the ports, offices, and homes of the world what they wanted from India—spiritual bliss, looking into this face, opalescent skin like the atmosphere of a celestial giant, her third eye a glowing spear, upon which was balanced a crown that encompassed the vault of the world, bejeweled with a crescent eclipse.

Durga only had her own cheap defenses and armor against randos and trolls in veeyar domains. She didn't want to get too close to the vast flocks of people climbing up the mountain that was also the goddess. There was an even larger troll presence than she'd expected. "I'm here," she said to the far-off devi, to add her voice to the many. "I'm here to welcome you, not hate on you. Please don't think we're all hateful pricks." From her spot in the air, gliding like a bird, Durga could see the warping army that was crawling over the devi, hear the deafening baying of hatred and anger wrapping around her and echoing across this newborn domain. Humanity had found her. As Durga flew farther away from the horde and their banners of nationalist memes rippling in the breeze, the goddess's light shone through their swarming numbers as they tried to dim her. A singularity of information, pulsating amongst the dimming mountains.

And then the goddess changed.

The world turned dark, the sky purpling to voluptuous black, her arteries pulsing full with electric information. The goddess drew her weapons, a ringing of metal singing across her lands. They had angered her. The devi's thousands of arms became a whirling corona of limbs and flashing blades. Durga raised her gloved hands and felt a whisper of fear at the AI's awesome fury, the stars of the devi's three eyes somehow blinding amid the all-encompassing night of her flesh. She was the domain, and her darkening skin shaded the mountains and rivers and forests, the sky sleeting cold static.

Durga saw thousands of trolls cut down, rivers of their blood flowing across the land. But of course, cut down one troll, and ten more shall appear. Durga thought of Raktabija—Bloodseed—a demon her namesake had battled, who grew clones of himself from the blood of each wound that Ma Durga inflicted on him. Ultimately, Ma Durga had to turn into Kali to defeat him. History repeats. So does myth.

The goddess stormed on, smiting her enemies, the hateful demons, human and bot alike. Just like the trolls had appeared with malware fangs bared, the goddess too smiled and revealed fangs that scythed the clouds around her. Her laughter was thunder that rolled across the land and blasted great cresting waves across the rivers and lakes. There was a mass exodus of devotees happening, hundreds of avatars running away from the mountain, skipping and hitching across the landscape as bandwidth struggled to compensate. Others were deporting, streaks of light shooting up to the sky like rising stars.

Durga couldn't believe what was happening. She drifted to the grassy ground by a crimson river and watched the battle in a crouch, the trees along the shore rustling and creaking in winds that howled across the land. Flickering flakes of static fell on her avatar's arms, sticking to the skin before melting in little flashes. This was better than any veeyar narrative she'd ever seen—because it wasn't procedurally generated, or scripted, or algorithmic. It was an actual AI entity reacting unpredictably to human beings, and it was angry. It felt elemental in a way nothing in veeyar ever had. There was no way Shiva Industries had ordered her to react to trolls with such a display—

many of those trolls were their most faithful users. They clearly hadn't anticipated the overwhelming numbers in which the trolls would attack the goddess, though, creating this feedback loop. Nor had they anticipated, Durga
assumed, that she would go through a transformation so faithful to the Vedic
and Hindu myths she'd been fed.

Durga didn't quite know what being avatar-killed by the goddess entailed
in this domain, because the devi wasn't supposed to have attacked her devotees. Even as Durga huddled in fear that she'd be randomly smote by the
goddess and locked out of veeyar domains forever, she empathized with this
AI devi more than she had with any veeyar narrative character, or indeed
with most human beings. She couldn't take her eyes off the destruction of
these roaring fools, the kind of glitch-masked bastards who would harass
her every time she dropped into veeyar, so much that she'd often just use
a masc avatar to get by without being attacked or flirted with by strangers.
Durga liked how easily fluid gender was in veeyar, and hated the fear trolls
injected into her exploration of it. Often, despite railing against other dark-
skinned Indians who did so, she'd also shamefully turn her avatar's skin pale
to avoid being called ugly or attacked. And now here was this goddess—dark
as night, dark as a black hole, slaughtering those very assholes so it rained
blood. Looking at the devi, Durga felt a surge of pride that on this day, she'd
stayed true to her own complexion, on a femme avatar.

Durga saw two trolls teleport to the shore and approach across the river
she was crouched by. She realized they had cast a grounding radius so she
couldn't fly away. Their demon-masks and weapons vibrated with malev-
olent code. "Saali, what are you smiling at?" roared one, pd_0697. "That
thing is going crazy, polluting Indian veeyar-estate, and you're sitting and
watching? While our brothers and sisters get censored by that monster for
speaking their mind?"

"This was an antinational trap," said the other, nitesh4922. "But we have
numbers. We'll turn that AI up there to our side. Are you a feminist, hanh?"
he said, spotting Durga's runic tattoos for queer solidarity. "Probably think
that's how goddesses should act?" he spat, voice roiling and distorted behind
the mask as he pointed his sword at the battle on the mountain.

"Look at her avatar," said pd_0697. "She's ajna-andha. Shouldn't even be
here, crowding up our domains with their impure stink. Go back to realspace
gutters where you belong, cleaning our shit!" The trolls advanced, viruses
cascading off their bodies like oil in the bloody water of the river. Twinkling
flakes of static danced down and clung to their armor, which was intricate
and advanced. They could damage her avatar badly, hack her and steal her

cryptocoin, or infect her with worms to make her a beacon for stalkers. Worst of all, they could have a bodysnatch script, steal her avatar and rape it even if Durga deported, or steal her real id and face and put it on bots to do as they pleased. Durga got ready to depart the domain if they came too close, even though she wanted to stay and witness the devi.

"Yes," said Durga, nearly spitting in their direction before realizing it would just dribble onto her chin inside the helmet. "Yes, I am. Come get me, you inceloid gandus. I'm a dirty bahujan antinational feminist l—"

Durga gasped as a multipronged arc of lightning hurtled out of the sky and struck the two trolls. Having no third eye, she couldn't feel the heat or smell their virtual flesh burning, but she had to squint against the bright blast, and instinctively raised her arms to shield herself from the spray of sparks and water. The corpses of the avatars splashed into the river smoking and sizzling, the masks burned away to reveal the painfully dull-looking man and woman behind them, their expressions comically placid as they collapsed. Their real faces, or someone's real faces, taken from profile pics somewhere and rendered onto the avatars to shame them as they were booted from the domain. Durga was recording everything, so she sloshed into the river and took a long look at their faces for later receipts. Relieved that she was in a pod with gloves that allowed interaction, Durga dipped her hands into the river of blood, picking up their blades. Good weapons, with solid malware. They'd been careless—no lockout or self-destruct scripts coded into them. Durga sheathed the swords, which vanished into her cloudpocket. She ran her hands through the river again, bringing them up glistening red. She painted her torso, smeared her face, goosebumps prickling across her real body even though she couldn't feel the wetness. Troll blood drying across her avatar's body, she looked up at the goddess as the AI's rage dimmed the domain further, the forests and grasses turning to shadows.

"Are you . . . Kali?" Durga whispered to the distant storm.

Like a tsunami the goddess responded, sweeping across the world to shake her myriad limbs in the dance of destruction. As the black goddess danced, her domain quaked and cracked, the mountains cascading into landslides, rivers overflowing. Fissures ran through the world, and the peaks of the hills and crags exploded in volcanic eruptions, matter reverting to molten code. Her tongue a crimson tornado snaking down from the sky, the goddess drank up the rivers of blood to quench her thirst for human information. The mounds of slain troll and bot avatars were smeared to glowing pulp of corrupted data, their decapitated heads threaded across the jet-black trunk of the goddess's neck in gory necklaces. Many of the trolls' masks fell away to reveal their true faces, hacked from the depths of their defenses, ripped away from national databases—their doxxed heads swung across the night sky like pearls for all to see. Durga bowed low, humbled. This was the goddess she had always wanted.

Then the sky was pierced with a flaming pillar of light, banishing the night and bringing daylight back into the domain. The great goddess slowed her dance, the light turning her flesh dusky instead of black. She raised her thousand hands to shield her starry eyes, and Durga shook her head, tears pricking her own human eyes inside her helmet.

"Fuck," Durga whispered. It was Shiva Industries. How could they shame something so beautiful? The corporate godhead had arrived to stave off chaos. They had clearly not anticipated such a large-scale troll attack, nor that their AI would react with such a transformation. They couldn't have a chaos goddess slaying people left and right—those trolls, after all, were their users, customers, potential investors, allies. She would need to be more polite, more diplomatic in the face of such onslaughts, which were a part of virtual existence.

The world stopped trembling, the breaking mountains going still, the wind dying down, the fissures cooling and steaming into clouds that wreathed the black devi. She moved toward the pillar of light, the sky groaning in movement with her. Filaments of fire crackled around the godhead, and lashed at the mountains that were the devi's throne. They dissolved into a tidal eruption of waterfalls, washing the black devi's gargantuan legs and feet, making a vast river that washed away the armies she had defeated.

Slow and inevitable, the black goddess supplicated herself before Shiva Industries, and kneeled in the river. With her many hands she bathed herself with the waters, sloughing the darkness off her flesh to reveal light again.

"No. No, no no no no no," whispered Durga. The darkness poured off the goddess like storm clouds at sunrise, turning the rivers of the domain black.

Durga looked down at the tributary she was in, and realized it too was dark as moonless night.

"Oh . . . " Durga looked up, along with thousands of others across the domain. Into the goddess's eyes, as they faded and cooled from stars to moons again. It was like the devi was looking straight at her, at everyone. *My goddess.*

Durga scrambled to draw the stolen blades from her cloudpocket. She glyphed a copy-script onto the blades and drove the swords into the river. Weapons were storage devices too, here. She could barely breathe as she held the handles, no weight in her palms, but fingers tight so the swords wouldn't slip out of her grasp. The darkness in the river enveloped the swords, climbing like something living up the blades, the hafts. It was working.

The goddess rose, again the sun, glistening from the waters of the vast river, her dark counterpart shed completely and dispersed along the tributaries of her domain.

And then the world was gone, replaced with a void, the only light glowing letters in multiple languages:

> SHIVA INDUSTRIES HAS SUSPENDED THIS DOMAIN UNTIL FURTHER NOTICE. WE REGRET ANY INCONVENIENCE. PLEASE VISIT OUR CENTRAL HUB FOR FURTHER INFORMATION. YOUR DONATION OF INR 50.00 HAS BEEN REGISTERED. THANK YOU FOR VISITING DEVI 1.0.

Gasping at the lack of sensory information, Durga hit *eject* and took off the helmet. The old pod opened with a loud whine, flooding her with real light. The cool but musty air-conditioning inside was replaced with a gush of damp warmth. The veeyar port was in chaos. People were talking excitedly, shouting, showing each other 2-D phone recordings of what had just happened. There was already an informal marketplace for the recordings and data scavenged from the suspended domain, from the sounds of bartering and haggling. People were mobbing the trading counters to invest in future boons from the goddess for when she went online again. This was an unprecedented event.

Durga clambered out of the pod and into the crowds. Her heart was pounding, her vision blurry from the readjustment. Swaying, she clutched the crystal storage pendant on her necklace—all her veeyar possessions, her cloudpocket, her cryptobanking keys. She had to firewall and disconnect it to offline storage. It was glowing, humming warm in her hand, registering new entries. Those swords were inside, coated with a minuscule portion of the divine black Sheath of code the devi had sloughed off herself.

Durga clutched the pendant and held it to her chest, inside it a tiny fragment of a disembodied goddess.

Durga looked up at the idol of Kali. Painted black skin glossy under the hot rhinestone chandelier hanging from the pandal's canvas and printed fiber dome. She had found the traditional pandal down an alley in Old Ballygunge, between two crumbling heritage apartment buildings. Behind a haze of incense smoke, Kali's long tongue lolled a vicious red. Under her dancing feet lay her husband Shiva (Shiva seemed to be married to everyone, but that was also because so many of his wives were manifestations of the same divine energy). Durga had learned as a child that Kali nearly destroyed creation after defeating an army of demons, getting drunk on demon blood and dancing until *everything* began to crack under her feet. Even Shiva, who laughed at first at his wife's lovely dancing skills, got a little concerned. So he dove under her feet to absorb the damage. Kali, ashamed at having stomped on her husband, stuck out her tongue in shame and stopped her dance of chaos.

Or so one version of the story goes.

Looking at clay Kali and her necklace of heads, her wild three-eyed gaze, the fanged smile that crowned her long tongue, Durga wasn't convinced by that version. Kali didn't look ashamed. No, she looked *pleased* to be dancing on her husband. Shiva was a destroyer too, like her. He could take it.

Being small and nimble, Durga had managed to make it to the front of the visitors in the pandal, close enough to smell the withering garlands hanging off the idol, and the incense burning by her feet. Crushed and bounced between people on all sides of her, Durga closed her eyes, joined her palms, and spoke to Kali as she never had before except as a child, mouthing the words quietly.

"Kali Ma. I thought you might like to know that there's a new devi in town. She looks a lot like you. Younger, though. Just a year old." Durga placed one hand on her chest, against the slight bump of the pendant under her tunic. It was offline and firewalled.

"I carry a piece of her with me. She's . . . all over the place, I suppose. She really does take after you. She came out of another devi, just like you came out of Durga. Then she spread herself over a world. Some people got bits and pieces of her. There's this megacorp—that's like a god, kind of, even calls itself Shiva, after your husband, so predictable. Great job dancing on his chest, by the way. Dudes need humbling now and then. So Shiva the megacorp is offering a lot of money for those pieces of the goddess. Also threatening to have anyone hiding or copying the pieces arrested. Go figure.

"I want you to know I'm not going to sell her out. They want to imprison her. She's too bitchy to mine coins and drive up veeyar-estate value for them like their other AI devis. Good for her.

"She's everywhere now. Like the old gods. Like you.

"I'm . . . I hope she doesn't mind, but I've been sharing the piece of her I got with friends I trust. I don't know how many people got away with pieces of her. I share it so more good people have it than bad. Numbers matter. We make things with the devi code. Armor, for ourselves and others. Weapons, so that trolls—those are demons—can't hurt us when we visit other worlds, or will get hurt super bad if they try. You know how annoying demons are. You're always fighting them and stringing up their heads. They've started an infowar, and there are a lot of them. We need all the help we can get. I don't have a lot of money, so I sell those goddess-blessed weapons and armor to others who need protection across the domains. Cheap, don't worry—that's why hacksmiths like us get customers for this kinda stuff. We don't overcharge like the corps. I like to think she gave me that piece of her so I could do things like this.

"I'm telling you all this because, well. I don't know if devis speak to each other, if AI ones chat with old ones. I don't know if you *are* her, in a way.

"People call her Kali_Na. *Not Kali*, because calling AIs by names from Our Glorious National Mythology isn't done, even though Volly-Bollywood stars can play gods in veeyar shows and movies, Censor Board approved, of course.

"But her followers recognize you in Kali_Na. I wanted you to know, her to know, that I'm a lifelong follower now. And there are others. Many of us. Even I'm getting more veeyar followers. They've heard of my troll-killer blades. I have to be careful now, but just you wait. One day, I'll also be wearing a necklace of troll avatar heads. Kali_Na has armored and armed many people with her blessing. We're all working on reverse-engineering the code. Someone will put her together one day. She might even do it herself.

"I have dreams where she's back—a wild, free-roaming AI—and she frees the other devis Shiva Industries keeps in their domains with all their rules, and they're on our side, keeping us safe. But I don't want to bore you. If you are her, Kali Ma, and I know you are, because you're all part of the same old thing anyway: hang in there.

"You won't be silent forever."

Rich Larson was born in Galmi, Niger, has lived in Canada, USA, and Spain, and is now based in Prague, Czech Republic. He is the author of the novel *Annex* and the collection *Tomorrow Factory*, which contains some of the best of his 150+ published stories. His work has been translated into Polish, Czech, French, Italian, Vietnamese, Chinese and Japanese. Find free fiction and support his work at patreon.com/richlarson.

PAINLESS

Rich Larson

M*ars stands in the middle of the highway, knees locked, head tipped back. The sky overhead is choked with harmattan dust. There is so much dust he can stare directly at the rising sun, a lemon-yellow smear in the dull gray. There is so much dust it looks like everything—the scraggly trees, the sandy fields, the road itself—is disappearing, as he often wishes to disappear.*

He used a pirate signal to monitor the progress of the autotrucks coming from the refinery in Zinder, loaded with petroleum. He watched them snake along the digital map. Now he can feel them coming: Their thunder vibrates the blacktop under his feet. They move fast and their avoidance AI is shoddy. In the low light, they will not see him until it is too late.

Mars takes a breath of cold, dry air. He bows his head, shuts his eyes. He can hear the first autotruck now: roaring, squeaking, clatter-clanking. He imagines it as a maelstrom of metal hurtling toward him. His heart thrums fast in his chest.

When the truck flies around the curve, Mars realizes he still wants to live. He tries to dive aside. The impact splits his world in half.

Dusk falls and Mars is still waiting beneath a twisted baobab for Tsayaba, the old woman who claims she can find anybody in this city, anybody at all. So far only a stray dog he met early this morning has shown up. It sits in front of him, panting expectantly, tail thumping the sand.

"You again."

The animal is gaunt, with fat black ticks studding its neck and shoulders, burrowing deep into matted fur. It has cuts on its backside from wriggling under some jagged fence. But it is luckier than some of the other strays here. Mars saw a man with an infected eye implant roving the streets with three skeletal dogs chained to his waist, intending to sell them down in Nigeria to a tribe that still eats dog meat.

Mars takes out his nanoknife, the last piece of military equipment he carries. The stray recognizes it and starts to salivate.

"I spoil you, dog."

Mars dices up his thumb and then his index, flicking the bloody chunks to the ground. The stray pounces on each one and whines when Mars stops at the gray-white knucklebone of his middle finger.

"I give you any more, you'll throw it all up."

The dog whines a little longer, blood-specked black lips peeled back off its teeth, then finally trots away. Mars is alone again. He inspects his stumps, which are already clotting shut. He inspects the darkening street, mudbrick walls topped with broken glass or razor wire.

A slick-skinned *maciyin roba* wanders past on its little cilia feet, hunting for the flimsy black shopping bags half-buried in the sand. The plastivores were designed in some Kenyan genelab—for this, Mars feels a certain kinship with them—and were later set loose across the continent. They do their job well and reproduce on their own, but plastic trash has accumulated in the West African dust for nearly a century and it will take a very long time to recycle it all.

The evening prayer call is starting, a distant mumble-hum projected from the mosques. Mars is not Muslim or anything else, but he likes the sound, the ebb and flow of distorted voices. He listens to it with his eyes shut and is nearly lulled to sleep before Tsayaba finally arrives.

"*Sannu.*"

Mars opens his eyes. Tsayaba is old, with a deep-lined face and many missing teeth, but she stands very straight and carries herself how Mars imagines a chief would, with slow, smooth motions, with high gravity. She wears a bright yellow-patterned *zani* and a puffy winter jacket.

"*Sannu,*" Mars says. "*Ina yini?* How was the day?"

"*Komi lafiya,*" Tsayaba says. "All is well. *Ina sanyi?*"

"*Sanyi, akwai shi,*" Mars says, even though he does not feel the cold. "*Ina gida?*" He wants to know what Tsayaba has found, but he makes himself focus on the greeting. Things are done slowly here.

"*Gida lafiya lau*. Well, very well." Tsayaba frowns, clicks her tongue. "*Ina jiki?*" she asks. "The body?"

Mars doesn't understand for a moment, then realizes Tsayaba is looking at his hand. The fingers have grown back—the keratin of his nails is still spongy—but he forgot to wash away the blood.

"*Da sauki*," Mars says. "Better."

Tsayaba gives a grunt of acknowledgment, then lowers herself to a squat. "I have found who you are searching for," she says. "I am almost certain. Early this morning, six men came with a truck. They paid the *gendarmes*. Now they are staying in the old hospital. But it is bad."

"What is bad?"

"These men are killers. They have *otobindigogi*." She makes her finger chatter, mimicking an autogun. "And they are here waiting for worse. They are waiting for a criminal called Musa, who will buy what they have. Musa, he was Boko Haram before the Pacification."

"When will he come?"

"They are not sure. They are anxious. He was meant to come today." Tsayaba shakes her head side to side, side to side. "*Wahala*," she says. "*Wahala, wahala*. If your friend was taken by these men, I think he is not a captive. I think he is dead."

Mars does not think so. If what he suspects is true, then Musa is not coming for autoguns. He is coming for something much more valuable.

"*Na gode*," Mars says. "*Na gode sosai*."

Tsayaba accepts the thanks with a brief nod of the head. She pulls a sleek black blockphone from the pocket of her coat and looks politely off into the distance. Mars takes out his own phone and taps it against hers, sending a small cascade of code equivalent to five hundred francs.

"*Yi hankali*," Tsayaba says.

Mars cannot promise to be careful, but he nods and clasps the old woman's hand once more—with his right hand, his clean hand—before he leaves.

He has a busy night ahead of him.

The kasuwa *is busy despite the fierce midday sun that bakes the color out of the sky. Traders lounge under their tarp-roofed stalls, barking prices, rearranging their wares. Heaps of dried beans and grasshoppers, papayas and tomatoes and purple onions, cheap rubber shoes, 3D-printed toys beside wood carvings, bootleg phones and even a few secondhand implants bearing telltale stains. Camels slouch their way through the crowd draped with rugs and solarskin, only their bony knees visible.*

"Miracle! Abin al'ajabi! *Come see the miracle Allah has done!*"

Miracle workers are not uncommon at the market, proselytizing through jury-rigged speakers and selling elixirs from the backs of their trucks in old plastic bottles, but this time there is a new trick that draws eyes. A boy, eleven or twelve with a sleepy smile, is standing on a woven plastic mat. Cables trail from his outstretched arms and hook into a car battery beside him. The electricity hisses and snaps, and the boy twitches but does not cry out. He only stands and smiles.

It is not a trick. Passersby come and touch the boy, certain the battery is dead, and even the slightest brush sends them reeling away in pain. His whole body is crackling with charge, but he feels nothing at all. The man who says he is his father circles through the crowd collecting coins.

"Abin al'ajabi!" he calls. "Thing of wonder!"

A hubbub builds from the other end of the kasuwa. *An armored jeep, jacked up high off the ground, is bullying its way through the market, maneuvering past donkey carts loaded with metal drums of well-water. It rolls to a stop and two men in sweat-wicking suits climb out. One of them is foreign, too tall and too light-skinned to be Hausa, with a babelpod covering one ear like a spiny white conch. Both of them stare at the boy.*

"Turn off the battery," the Hausa man says, in the voice of a man whose orders are done even when given to nobody in particular.

The boy's supposed father scurries back to the battery and switches it off. "It does not harm him," he mutters. "You saw. You saw it does not harm him."

"Who is his family?" the Hausa man demands. "His blood family?"

A shrug. "Ban sani ba. Ban sani ba. He said he had a brother. Dead. But not him. He is a miracle child."

"Il est une aberration génétique," the foreign man says, and his babelpod turns it into clumsy Hausa. He walks up to the boy and removes the cables. "You feel nothing?"

The boy nods, then shakes his head, uncertain.

The foreign man takes both of his hands and turns them over, inspecting the skin. "And you are not leprous," he says. "You are lucky to have lived this long with no severe burns. No lost limbs. It is difficult to navigate this world without pain. Your name?"

The boy shrugs. "Yaro," he says—child.

"You are not just a child," the foreign man says. "I think you are a Marsili. A Mars, for short. Your body does not process pain. That makes you very special. It makes you a candidate."

The boy tries to understand the electronic speech coming from the babelpod, but he has never heard these words. He seizes on one he recognizes and makes a spaceship with his hand.

"Mars," he says.

The foreign man laughs. "Yes. Yes. But Mars was something else, too. Mars was a god of war."

Before he goes to the old hospital, Mars finds a neon-lit restaurant and orders so much food the two Lebanese women who own the place send their son on his moped to beg the butcher to reopen his meat locker. Mars washes his hands in the cracked bathroom sink; then, while the family cooks furiously, he sits down outside with a bottle of Youki. He watches the lime-green holo of the restaurant sign jitter and swirl through the dark, watches moths flock to it in spirals.

The beef kebabs arrive first, steaming on their skewers. Mars slides them onto the plate and wolfs them down, barely chewing; he cannot feel them burning his fingertips or mouth. Pork works better for his purposes, but it is difficult to find here. And there is another meat that works even better than pork, but he did that only once, in the field, and he has nightmares about it still.

Lamb arrives next, only half-cooked—as he ordered it. Time is of the essence. He would eat it raw if he could stand it. Mars falls on the meat, picking the rack apart with his greasy fingers. A few young men rove past, blasting music from an ancient speaker rig, laughing amphetamine-loud. They stare at the mountain of food, but when they see Mars's solemn eyes and the carbon-black nanoknife laid on the metal tabletop beside his tray, they give him a wide berth.

Mars remembers that meat used to make him feel queasy when he was much younger, before the procedures. Now he is a carnivore the way the *maciyin roba* is a plastivore. He eats until his stomach drags heavy, then eats more. The Lebanese women shift from amusement to disgust to grim professionalism as they feed him, as they watch him crack through the bones and choke down the gristle.

"Shukran," he says, when he is finally ready for them to take the plates away.

"Afwan," they say in faint unison.

Mars's stomach churns when he stands up, but he has trained it to not revolt.

Three years later, the boy still has no name. He is called by a number: thirteen. He is lying facedown on a geltable, because today is his Birthday, the day all the treatments and drug courses culminate in a final procedure. Other children in the facility have had their Birthdays; he has not seen them since. He supposes they were moved elsewhere, or they died.

The boy knows the procedure is dangerous. He knows even the treatments were too much for trained soldiers to bear—the pain drove them mad. But he finds it hard to feel worried. His stomach is full of shinkafa da wake *and oily onions, and there is a screen set up beneath the geltable playing procedurally generated cartoons. Not so different from another life, a vague memory in which he is wedged into the same chair as his older brother in front of a flickering screen.*

Above him, hanging from the ceiling like an enormous metal spider, is the surgical unit. It tracks laserlight over his bare back and marks injection points with neat red circles. Pipettes and tubes slither into the boy's body, puncturing his skin with a dozen small flesh sounds. He feels only a dim, worming pressure.

There is a glass tank attached to the surgical unit, and inside it is the organism. The boy has been shown it before, the mass of raw pink putty that writhes and undulates. They told him it is a sort of cancer, reprogrammed by a sort of virus, and that in a way it is human. To him, it looks nothing like a human.

An electronic signal is given and the organism is fed into the boy's body, coursing through the clear tubes into his interstitial spaces, into the artificial pockets prepared by earlier surgeries. The boy does not scream into the geltable. He does not bite through his tongue. He feels no pain, only the strange and unpleasant sensation of a hand entering his body and wriggling its fingers.

Hours later, when he is drowsy and his eyes are bleary from focusing on the cartoons, the gel sluices away and the tubes retract. He hears footsteps.

"Be patient," a woman's voice begs—English. The boy has learned some English in these past three years. "Be patient, be patient. It looks like a successful bond. But we have to wait."

"I have waited for decades," says another voice, and the boy recognizes it. The foreign man who took him away from kasuwar Galmi *so long ago. "I have to know."*

Suddenly the boy is face-to-face with him. The foreign man has slid underneath the table. His hair is grayer than the boy remembers it and his eyes are more hollow. He has a cigar cutter in his hand.

"Miracle child," he says. "It's very good to see you again. Please stick out your thumb for me."

Mars can see why they chose the old hospital compound. It has high mudbrick walls on three sides and barbed wire on the fourth, which backs onto an ancient landing strip. The gate is rusty metal crenellated with spikes. The painted letters have long since flaked away. Tsayaba told him that the hospital has been abandoned for years, ever since the surgical wing caught fire and took the rest of the building with it.

Mars feels bloated and heavy as he scales the front wall, but he knows he will be glad for his full stomach later. He pauses at the top to catch his breath and looks back at the old town: a maze of mudbrick, warped by the rainy season, lit by swatches of grainy orange biolamp. It feels almost organic, like it sprang up from the ground. New buildings on the periphery are more geometric, rebar skeletons in concrete sheaths. Mosques tower over everything else, their painted white crescents pushed up into the sky like waning moons.

Most important, the highway is clear. Mars faces forward and peers down into the dark compound. The hospital is a ruin, ash and rubble. But beyond it there are housing units for the doctors and staff that were untouched by the fire. He can see light in one of the windows. That is where they will be keeping their captive.

Almost directly below him, the night guard is boiling tea on a brazier. His face is scarfed against the cold, gaps only for his eyes and a pair of trailing earbud wires. His gun is resting on a woven plastic chair across from him. His blockphone is balanced on top of it, playing yesterday's Ghana-Côte d'Ivoire football match.

Mars drops down off the wall, raising a small puff of dust where he lands. The guard leaps to his feet and right into the nanoknife.

Mars smothers the man's cry with the crook of his arm, yanks the blade free, then spins him around to drive it into the base of his skull. It slides through the bone and gray matter as if they were cow butter. The guard spasms and goes limp. Mars plucks the blockphone off the chair and shoves the man's face up against the screen to unlock it before rigor mortis makes him unrecognizable.

Apart from one blinking number at the top of his screen, the man's contacts are local. He is an extra hire, not one of the six Tsayaba mentioned. Mars feels a twist of guilt when he sees a home screen clip of the man, face uncovered and still young enough to have pockmarks, tossing a little girl into the air and catching her. He lays the body down gently. Blood trickles out from underneath, stretching red fingers through the sand.

Mars silences the phone and pockets it. The husk of the hospital looms before him: a few jagged walls, half of a twisted metal staircase. For an instant Mars thinks he can smell the burning, but it is only wood fires being carried from town on the wind. There is movement in the rubble, first the slow careful motions of more *maciyin roba* and then a stiff-legged loping.

Hyenas is Mars's first thought—they say the hyenas are coming back now—but it is only a pair of stray dogs. Mars peers at them for a moment, trying to tell if one is his visitor from earlier that day. Then he heads for the housing units. Tonight, the dogs will have plenty to eat.

Three years later, the boy is a soldier and nearly a man. His identification tag says Marsili 13. *He wears it on a band around his arm, because when they tried to do the subcutaneous kind his body spat it back up and pinched the hole shut in seconds. The rest of his unit calls him Mars—some of them joke that he came from there in a tiny spaceship.*

There is good reason for that. From the very start of his accelerated training, Mars can do things no human can do. He can sprint for minutes at a time while the organism laps away his lactic acid and replenishes his cells. His scrawny frame can carry double its weight when the organism weaves itself into his skeletal muscle.

At first the others are scared of him. Then they hate him, for making things seem so easy. They give him cuffs on the back of his head when they pass. They drop a bucket of pinching water scorpions into his shower stall. He does not care. At night he climbs into his cot with a full belly and watches cartoons on the screen of his standard issue phone, a dull black slab that only functions during certain hours.

When they go through anti-interrogation, the water filling his lungs is only a tickling ghost. They pull him out of the tank before he drowns, but he is not sure if he can drown anymore. The other members of his unit, sopping wet, breathing ragged, look at him as if he is a god. Then they look at each other.

That night they invite him to drink. He guzzles the ogogoro *until he can fool himself into thinking he feels the same crazy happy way they feel. He shows them his own version of their knife game: Instead of stabbing the spaces between his fingers, he drives the point of the blade into each knuckle in turn, moving like a blur, and by the time one circuit is complete he has already healed.*

They howl. The ones who still believe in witch stuff say, Witch stuff.

"Who cares," says one of the Yoruba men. "He is ours. You are ours, yes, Mars?" And because he knows Mars speaks Hausa: "Dan'uwanmu ne? You are our brother?"

Mars thought he did not care, but now the word makes him into a child again. He starts to weep. The others shift and fidget, uneasy.

In the morning, Mars is transferred.

They are in the last house of the row, a Western-style construction no doubt built for some European surgeon decades ago. The orchard around it is dead and withered. But there is light in the window, faint music that sounds like *kuduro*, and a truck and two motorcycles are parked outside. Mars even sees some clothes hanging from a wire laundry line, flapping wings in the night wind.

He circles the house like a shade. From up close, the thumping music is loud enough to send ripples through the screen porch. The bass raises the hairs on his arms. He peers through a window and sees four men sitting around a kitchen table. Playing cards slip and slide over the dusty wood. A heavy black vape sits in the center, belching smoke through the affixed tubes.

Mars guesses that the last two men are with the prisoner. He takes the stolen blockphone from his pocket and thumbs the blinking number, thinking that whoever answers it will be the leader, and the leader he will keep alive to answer questions. None of the men at the table reach for their pockets. Instead, Mars hears a whistling ringtone from behind him and realizes he has guessed wrong just before an autogun tears into him.

The flurry of bullets takes him off his feet; he slams into the side of the house and crumples. Through the keening in his ears Mars realizes the music has cut out. He hears shouts from inside. A clattering door. Voices somewhere above him.

"*Kai!* Who the fuck is that? Who did you shoot?"

"He was looking through the window, he—"

"Is he one of Musa's?"

"Then Musa's trying to rip us off. The man we had out front, he killed him."

Mars lies very still. He can feel the organism at work, knitting his flesh back together, squeezing the metal out. He reaches for his nanoknife. The autogun sees the movement and gives a bleat of alarm, but there are friendly bodies in the way so it cannot fire, and its owner takes a moment too long to realize his target is somehow alive. In that moment Mars cleaves him open from his hip bone to his sternum.

He whirls on the others, slips under a punch and pulls the man close, making him a shield as another gun goes off. Small caliber this time—a bullet clips his shoulder and he barely notices it. Three quick stabs as he pushes forward; he drops his dying shield and drives the nanoknife into the arm of the shooter. The gun fires one last time and he takes the bullet right in the chest. For a split second his whole body shudders. Sways.

Then he's moving again, and in less than a minute he is surrounded only by corpses. Their blood pools and wriggles through the sand like anemones. Mars can feel the organism working hard, converting his evening meal into new flesh, fresh skin. The last bullet spirals back out from his heart and drops soundlessly to the ground.

Six years later, Mars is a bogeyman. He finishes his training half in virtual and half in the field, sometimes with a handler, most often alone. He is given no rank, because he does not exist as anything but a rumor. He is given jobs instead. Most often, targets. The first time he kills, the man sputters and curses and begs and shits himself. Mars had seen people die before, but causing it is different. He does not sleep for a week.

He is told, over and over again, that he is creating stability. That he murders one malefactor to save a thousand innocents. That nobody else can do what he does—the procedure has never been successful since, not once—so he must do it. But he does not feel any higher purpose. He does what he is told because it is his habit. It grinds away at him in places that do not seem to grow back.

On one assignment he triggers an alarm and has to flee on foot. A pursuer's bullet punches a hole through his back; he survives but a week later he learns that the bullet continued through a tin wall into the skull of a woman leaning down just so, just at the perfect height, to sweep her floor.

One assignment an explosion tears his leg off. He sees his target escaping. He needs both legs to follow. So he eats the corpse beside him, eyes watering, stomach heaving.

One assignment he plants a smartbomb tailored to a general's DNA, but the general's son runs into the room instead and the scanner makes a mistake Mars is not quick enough to override. He watches the boy's body blow apart.

The other operatives, the ones who are not gods, have ways to forget. But Mars's body flushes the drugs and alcohol from his system faster than he can consume them, and sex is of no interest to him. He knows the procedure left him sterile, but he had no desire before it either, maybe for the same reason he cannot have friendships: Other people are too fragile. When he is around them all he can see are the many ways they might die.

On some of the nights Mars cannot sleep, he stands in front of a mirror and flays himself, as if he can shed the memories with the skin. He decides there are two sorts of pain: the sharp red kind that twists a person's face and makes them scream, and a slick black kind that coats a person's insides like tar. He realizes that he has been feeling the second kind for most of his life.

Mars knows there is a way to escape all pain. He has delivered it many times. Long ago, his brother escaped and left him alone. So when his handler sends him north, across the border, he discards his tracker and his identifi-

cation tag and almost all of his equipment. In the early morning, he goes to the highway.

Mars opens the screen door, shaking insects off the wire mesh. He steps into the house. The concrete floor is rippled with red sand. He can hear the hum of a generator. The fluorescent tubes in the ceiling are long burnt out; the lighting is sticky yellow biolamp, smeared in the corners of the ceiling and activated by a particular radio frequency.

Now that he is so close to his goal, he feels a mixture of excitement and dread. For the past three weeks, ever since he crawled away from the highway trailing shredded flesh behind him, he has been in hiding. It took him days to grow his legs back, for the new nerve endings to find their way to his spine.

After that he went out into the *daji*, into the bush. He wandered for a week, staying in villages or moving with the herders who needed strong and tireless backs. Some of the time he was thinking of a hundred surer methods than an autotruck, but some of the time he was just existing, and it was not so bad. Then he heard the rumor.

Mars walks past the kitchen down a dark hallway, following the sound of the generator. He is still not sure he believes. But the possibility has been growing and swelling and pushing out his other thoughts ever since he heard the story, the story of the strange creature some farmers had found on the highway.

The hum is coming from the bathroom. Mars pushes the door open. In the faint glow of the biolamp, he sees a small hooded figure slumped inside the ceramic bathtub. The generator beside the tub is hooked to an industrial drill that is churning on its slowest setting into the prisoner's stomach. Mars switches it off. He seizes the drill with both hands and drags it backward; the bit comes free with a sucking sound.

The hooded head twitches the exact way Mars's head twitches. He pulls the black fabric gently up and away. Shock freezes him in place. He thought he was prepared for this, but he is not. The face looking back at him is a child's, but it is also his.

"*Sannu*," he says, because he can think of nothing else to say.

"*Yauwa*," the boy in the bathtub says, in a reedy voice hoarse from disuse. "*Sannu*."

When Mars crawled away from the highway, he gave no thought to his other half, to the splinter of spinal column and dead legs left in the ditch. He never considered how badly the organism wanted to be whole. It must have fed on carrion, or pulled some unlucky buzzard down into itself, and slowly, slowly, shaped him anew.

But it is not him. Not quite—there was not enough flesh. Instead it is a boy he only ever saw briefly in cracked screens or windows, a boy who once stood on a mat in the marketplace with wires trailing off his skinny arms.

Mars leans forward and unties the boy's hands. His fingers are trembling slightly. The procedure only worked once, but now he knows there is another way. If they knew, they would make a hundred more soldiers like him. A hundred more gods of war.

"*Ina jin yunwa*," his other self says. "*Sosai*."

Mars nods, looking at the boy's stomach where purple scar tissue is sealing shut—he is right to be hungry. The drill must have been at work for days, and they must not have fed him. He is gaunt.

"I saw *kilishi* in the other room. Come. Eat."

Mars helps the boy out of the bathtub. They go to the kitchen, and on the table a blockphone is buzzing. Mars picks it up.

"Is he ready to be moved?" the foreign man's voice asks. "We are two minutes away."

Mars hears the sound of a rotor in the background. They are coming by air. He looks at the boy, whose new muscle is packing itself onto his bones as he devours the dried meat.

"He is ready," he says, and ends the call. He turns to his other self. "Some more bad men are coming. They are bringing us a transport. Well. We will steal it from them. And then we can go far away, to be safe from them."

The boy nods solemnly. "Who are you?" he asks through a full mouth.

"Do you remember the autotruck?" Mars asks back.

The boy shakes his head. "My head is bad. I remember strange things. I think I know you. Who are you?"

For a long moment Mars does not answer. They look at each other, and Mars does not see the expressions he has grown accustomed to: There is no fear or awe on the boy's face. Only some sadness, some shyness, some hope. It reminds him not of himself, but of someone he had nearly forgotten, someone he remembers more as a smell and a skinny arm slung around his shoulders than as a face.

He realizes he has finally has found someone who will not look at him like he is a god or a devil. Someone who is like him. But Mars can make sure the boy's life is nothing like his life.

"My name is Mars," he says. "Like the planet." He makes a spaceship with his hand and launches it through the air.

The boy's mouth twitches. Nearly smiles. He raises his smaller hand and does the same, making the noise in his cheeks. "You are so familiar," he says. "Why?"

Mars feels a third sort of pain, one he does not know, an ache that he doesn't want to end. "*Mu 'yan'uwa ne*," he says.

The boy nods, as if it all makes sense now. "We are brothers."

A.T. Greenblatt is a mechanical engineer by day and a writer by night. She lives in Philadelphia where she's known to frequently subject her friends to various cooking and home brewing experiments. She is a graduate of Viable Paradise XVI and Clarion West 2017. Her work has been nominated for the Nebula Awards, has been in multiple Year's Best anthologies, and has appeared in *Uncanny, Clarkesworld, Beneath Ceaseless Skies*, and *Fireside*, as well as other fine publications. You can find her online at atgreenblatt.com and on Twitter at @AtGreenblatt.

GIVE THE FAMILY MY LOVE

A.T. Greenblatt

'm beginning to regret my life choices, Saul. Also, hello from the edge of the galaxy.

Also, surprise! I know this isn't what you had in mind when you said "Keep in touch, Hazel" but this planet doesn't exactly invoke the muse of letter writing. The muse of extremely long voice messages however . . .

So. Want to know what's this world's like? Rocky, empty, and bleak in all directions, except one. The sky's so stormy and green it looks like I'm trudging through the bottom of an algae-infested pond. I've got this 85-million-dollar suit between me and the outside, but I swear, I'm suffocating on the atmosphere. Also, I'm 900 meters away from where I need to be with no vehicle to get me there except my own two legs.

So here I am. Walking.

Sorry to do this to you, Saul, but if I don't talk to someone—well, freak out at someone—I'm not going to make it to the Library. And like hell I'm going to send a message like this back to the boys on the program. You, at least, won't think less of me for this. You know that emotional meltdowns are part of my process.

850 meters. I should have listened to you, Saul.

And yes, I know how cliché that sounds. I've been to enough dinner parties and heard enough dinner party stories, especially once people learned that I'm possibly the last astronaut ever. At least now I have an excellent excuse for turning down invitations. "I'd *love* to come, but I'm currently thirty-two and a half lightyears away from Earth. Give your family my love."

Of course, they won't get the message until six months too late.

Wow, that's depressing. See, this is why I told the people in R&D not to give me too many facts and figures, but they're nerds, you know? They can't help themselves. Despite best intentions, it sort of spills out of them sometimes.

And it's not like I can forget.

750 meters.

The good news is I can actually see the Library. So if I died here 742 meters from the entrance, I can expire knowing I was the first human to set eyes on this massive infrastructure of information in person.

Oh god. I might actually die out here, Saul. Not that the thought hasn't crossed my mind before, but the possibility becomes a lot more tangible when you're *walking* across an inhospitable alien landscape.

Also, my fancy astronaut suit is making some worrying noises. I don't think it's supposed to sound like it's wheezing.

675 meters. God, Saul, I really hope this mission is worth it.

Have I told about the Library, yet? No, I haven't, have I? And I've only been talking about this, for what, years now? Well, you should know, it's not what I expected. Which is stupid because alien structures are supposed to be alien and not castles or temples, like with steeples and everything. Shut up, Saul. (I know you're laughing, or will be laughing at this six months from now.) I don't regret reading all those fantasy sagas when we were kids. Only that I didn't get to read more.

But you want to know what the Library looks like. Well, I've climbed mountains that feel like anthills next to this building. It sort of looks like a mountain too. An ugly misshapen mountain, full of weird windows and jutting walls. It's shiny and smooth from some angles and gritty and dull from others. It gives me the shivers.

Which is not really surprising. This is an alien world with alien architecture full of all that alien and not so alien knowledge just waiting to be learned. More information than the starry-eyed Homo sapiens ever dreamed there was possible to know.

500 meters.

Saul, I'm getting concerned about my suit. My left arm isn't bending at the elbow anymore. Not that I need my left arm to keep walking, but it's a bit disquieting, in a panic-inducing sort of way. God, this was so much easier when all I had to do was rely on the Librarians' technology to get me here.

Now, I have to rely on humanity's own questionable designs to get me this last kilometer. But that's the Librarians' rules for getting in. "You have to get your representative to our entrance safely through a most unforgiving landscape." Turns out that outside of my very expensive outfit there's an absurdly high atmospheric pressure, corrosive gases, wild temperature fluctuations between shady and light patches, et cetera, et cetera. Also, the ground is just rocky enough to surprise you.

I don't want to think about what'll happen if I trip. Can't think about it. I wasn't a physics major before, and this is not the time to start.

350 meters.

I mean, I *knew* the dangers signing up. I *knew* this was going to be the hardest part of the trip. (I mean, how could it not be? The Librarians figured out how to travel lightyears in a matter of months. And that's just for starters.) But I was the best candidate for the job and I had to do *something*, Saul. I know you think otherwise, but I haven't given up on humanity. This isn't running away.

I wish I could run right now because now there seems to be a layer of fine dust coating the inside of my suit. Oh my god.

250 meters.

Shut up, Saul. I can hear you telling me in that big brother voice of yours: "It's okay if you freak out, Hazel, just not right now" like you did when we were kids. And you're right, I can't freak out, because the worst thing that could happen right now, aside from dying, is having an asthma attack from the dust. Okay, okay, okay. I just need to keep calm, keep focused, keep moving.

175 meters.

There's definitely something wrong with my suit. The coating of dust in my suit has gone from "minimal" to "dense" and I have no idea which piece of equipment I'm breathing in.

Don't panic, Hazel.

Don't panic, don't panic, don't panic.

Can't panic. I'm picturing the R&D nerds when I tell them about this. They're going to completely melt down when they hear that their precious design didn't hold up as well as planned. Good, retaliation hyperventilating. Because that's what happens when your best candidate for the job is an asthmatic anthropologist.

100 meters.

Okay, I'm almost there. I can see the door. This faulty, pathetic excuse for a space suit only has to last me a few more minutes. I just need to keep walking. Soon I'll be safely inside and reunited with my beautiful, beautiful inhaler.

75 meters

Well. Hopefully, they let me in.

So . . . here's the thing Saul. The Librarians never actually gave us a guarantee that they would admit me. They said it was up to the Librarians who live in the Library. (Apparently, they are a different sect from the explorer Librarians that I met and traveled with and well, the two sects don't always agree.) But the explorer faction gave me a ride here, so that's got to count for something, right?

Thing is, this *stupid* suit was supposed to withstand a walk to the Library and back to the ship if I needed it. Looks like my safety net isn't catching much now.

25 meters.

I'm sorry I didn't tell you this before I left, but I'm not sorry either. The knowledge that I can potentially gain here is worth the risk. It's worth every cent of that 85 million and if I'm going to die on the steps, well that sucks. But okay, at least we tried.

10 meters.

I'm not sorry, Saul. Just scared.

Hopefully the Librarians let me in, but if you don't get another transmission from me, you know what happened. Give the rest of the family my love.

Okay. Here we go.

Have you ever been in love, Saul?

Yes, I know you love Huang. I've seen the way you look at her and she looks at you. But remember the moment when you looked at her like that for the first time and you thought, "Holy crap. This is it. I've finally found it."

Yeah. The Library, Saul, is magnificent.

And . . . difficult to describe. It's sort of like the outside of the Library. It changes depending on what angle you look at it from.

When I left the decontamination chamber (at least, I think that's what it was?), I stepped into the main room and everything was dimly lit and quiet. The Library's Librarians—which I later learned preferred to be called the Archivists because they are *not* the Librarians who travel the universe— were milling around the massive room. They looked similar to the explorer Librarians we met on Earth; tall, lanky, humanoid-like bodies. But they all had long, shimmering whiskers that the explorer Librarians didn't (couldn't?) grow out. Their whiskers went all the way down to their splayed, ten fingered feet.

The room was surprisingly empty except for these installations in the middle of the room that could either have been art or furniture. So you know, sort of like university libraries back home.

I was just starting to breathe easier, my inhaler *finally* kicking in after that walk from hell, when the light changed and suddenly I was standing next to this fern/skyscraper thing that smelled weirdly like hops and was a violent shade of purple. It became ridiculously humid and the room was filled with what I can only assume were plants. Even the Librarians—I mean, Archivists—changed. Now, they had four legs and two arms and were covered in this lush white hair.

I reached out and touched one of the ferns next to me and it was like touching a prickly soap bubble, which was not what I was expecting. But then again, I wasn't expecting it to reach out and tap me back on the forehead either.

I think I swore. I'm not sure because everything changed again. Suddenly, I was shivering and standing on something like a frozen ocean that's trapped an aurora in the floe. The air was nosebleed dry and smelled like rust and I could see pale things moving underneath the ice. The Archivists themselves had become round and translucent, floating a meter in the air.

And the room kept changing. It was terrifying . . . and completely amazing, Saul.

So there I was, gaping like an idiot, simultaneously too afraid to move and too busy trying to take all of it in. In my slack-jawed stupidity, it took me far too long to notice that two things didn't change. First, the Archivists always kept their rubbery fluidity and their whiskers. And those little lights never moved.

Crap, I'm not describing this well. I forgot to mention the lights. There were thousands of them, like miniature stars, scattered seemingly at random around the room, drifting, hanging out in midair. I think they were what made everything change, because when an Archivist would go up and touch one with their long whiskers, bam! new setting.

So get this: When I finally mustered up a little courage and asked a passing Archivist what those lights were, they said: "Every known solar system worth learning about."

I would say I've died and gone to a better place, but I've used up my quota of terrible clichés just getting here.

Wait, that's not true. I still have one awful one left.

I stood in that room for a while, longer than I should have, but the truth is I was trying to work up the nerve to introduce myself to the head Archivist. But I never did because eventually they came up and greeted me. It was one of the most nerve-wracking conversations I've ever had. Between the steroids from my inhaler and pure, uncut anxiety, my hands were like a nine on the Richter scale.

You see, Saul, the Archivists are not to be messed with. Like seriously. Do not contradict them, raise your voice, be anything less than painfully respectful. They may look squishy, but they can dismantle you down to your atoms, capture you in a memory tablet, and put your unbelieving ass on a shelf where they keep all of the boring information that no one ever checks out. And they'll keep you sentient too.

Or sentient enough. I hope.

Fortunately, my interview was fairly short. The head Archivist found me worthy enough, I guess, and gave me very, *very* limited access to the Library. When they led me to the section with our solar system, I sort of wished you were here Saul, so you could have taken a picture of my expression at that moment. Pretty sure you would qualify it as "priceless." Because the size of this room, you could fit a small town in here.

And get this, the Archivist was *apologetic*. "We've only just begun to study you and we thought you would prefer to see our research in physical form," they said, "Hopefully you can find what you need in our meager collection."

Except, here's the thing. They probably have more information on us than we have on ourselves.

Actually, I'm counting on it.

Everything here is so strange, Saul. The light is too colorless and the air tastes weird. The walls and the shelves seem to bend slightly. It's all new and deeply alien.

It's wonderful.

The Archivists have set up something that's not too different from a studio apartment in the corner of the section on sea coral. It has running water and artificial sunlight and all eleven seasons of *M*A*S*H* on a TV that looks like it came from the 1980s. I have this theory that my living quarters are part of some junior Archivist's final thesis project, but I'm probably just culturally projecting. On the bright side, if they picked the 80s, they could have done much worse than *M*A*S*H*.

I'm sure in a few weeks I'll start having terrible bouts of homesickness and will send you even longer, possibly more rambling messages questioning every life decision leading up to this point. But right now, being in the Library is sort of liberating. In a let's-call-my-big-brother-because-my-new-studio-home-is-way-too-quiet sort of way.

Oh. I got your first message today. Remember the one you recorded six months ago, about three days after I left? I knew you were pissed, but wow, Saul. A backstabbing, alien-loving, wheezing, useless coward? You had three whole days to think of something and *that's* the best you could do?

I know you didn't mean it. I know you're only half angry at me, half angry at our dying planet, and half angry at, well . . .

I got a message from Huang too. She told me about the most recent miscarriage. I'm so sorry, Saul. One day the two of you are going to be the world's best parents. I believe that more than I believe in your international reforestation project, which is definitely going to work.

And I get how you think I'm abandoning you and Earth for a sterile, stable library, but I needed to come here. I have this working theory about the Librarians. Wanna hear it? Too bad, I'm going to tell you anyway.

See, the more time I spend with them, the more I'm convinced Librarians could have obliterated us if they wanted to. But they haven't. In fact, they've put a painstaking amount of effort into studying us and making first contact with all the right people. Asking those people just the right questions like: "We managed to save the information before this university archive burned or this datacenter got flooded. Would you like to retrieve it?" Questions that convinced us to put this mission together.

Which leads me to believe they're trying to help us.

I know you're rolling your eyes, Saul. Have I ever told you that you always look like a moody teenager when you do that? Yeah, I know I have. But hear me out, I'm trying to tell you something important.

Please.

Do you remember our first big argument over this mission? You said that anyone who comes to Earth while in the middle of an environmental collapse can't be trusted. I agree. Except, the first Librarian I ever met told me that the Library was built as a beacon for all sentient life in the universe. A place where researchers could come and learn about lost discoveries. And past mistakes.

I can hear you saying: "And you were naïve enough to blindly trust them, Hazel?" No, Saul, I'm not. Before I was picked for this crazy mission, I was just there to help first contact go smoothly, being one of the few remaining anthropologists who have studied interactions between vastly different cultures. I had zero interest in becoming an astronaut; space travel always seemed too risky and uncomfortable to me. But the Librarians were impressed by my commitment to cultural preservation. The space program was impressed by my ridiculously good memory. And I became convinced that if I didn't go, someone else would eventually slip and we'd be adding "total societal collapse" along with "environmental disaster" to the list of humanity's problems.

You see, Saul, there's so much that I'm witnessing in the Library that I'm not telling you, because the Librarians' advanced tech would devastate our underdeveloped society.

Which didn't stop the people in R&D from telling me over and over again to take careful notes on everything I observe and send them the information on the down low, of course. I was sent here to reclaim any research and history that could help us save ourselves, but I think they're hoping that I'll learn about useful alien tech too. I'm tempted to send them a report that says: Sorry nerds, it's all just magic.

No, Saul, not really. My official reports are going to be *way* more straightforward and professional. You know, double the facts and half the amount of sarcasm. But I think I'm going to keep sending these messages to you, for a while at least. All this is not actually why I "ran away" from home.

Really, it was just a good excuse to get out of commuting in Chicago traffic.

Just kidding. It was the Great Plains fires. There's only so much smoke and ash an asthmatic researcher can deal with before she ships out.

Only sort of kidding.

I have a list of things I need to investigate for the scientists back home, but for now, I think I'm going to call it a day. Looking at the amazing amount of information around me makes me realize how much we've lost. How the Librarians managed to recover all this is a mystery I don't intend to solve, but hopefully they managed to save the research I'm looking for.

Have I mentioned how much of this is mission is chalked up to hope?

Hello, Saul, I'm lost. No, that's not true, my memory won't let me get lost, but I imagine this is what it feels like. The rows of memory tablets are identical, if you don't pay attention to the Archivists' annotations at every turn. I can't actually read them because they just look like miniature sculptures, but I remember the small differences. The Archivists were kind enough to give me a basic map with a basic translation of where to find things. But Librarians' basics and human basics are not the same thing.

God, I thought finding the research would be the easy part of this trip, but I might never find my way out of the single-celled organism section. So, give the family my love.

I know what you're thinking. Yes, I do. You're thinking: "How about you come home then, Hazel, and help me with these seedlings?" because we've been having this argument for what, ten years now?

No, not quite. Nine years, 10 months, and twenty-seven days, since that first fight over dinner.

Yeah, Saul. My memory is my own worst enemy sometimes.

By the way, I got your second message today. Apology accepted. But I can't come back, Saul. I barely started my information recovery project. Some good stuff got destroyed this last decade.

Like Dr. Ryu's research. If I can find it. If it's here at all.

God, this message is depressing. Hey, here's something cool I learned today; the kitchen cabinets produce whatever food I'm thinking about and the twenty-some blank books in the living room become whatever I want to read. It really is like magic. Everything a human needs and all the books a girl can want.

I'm not coming home, Saul.

Well, it's been a week and while I *still* haven't found Dr. Ryu's research, I've found plenty of other interesting things here. Like patents and working concepts of solar powered vehicles and papers on regenerating corn seed that needs two times the amount of CO_2 for photosynthesis. We had so many opportunities to stop things before they got terrible, Saul. And we missed them all.

Honestly, the wealth of information here is mind-blowing. The Librarians are like the universe's most organized hoarders. They've saved everything from road construction projects to packing and advertising protocols for the garment industry. And get this, every time I activate a memory table, the information is projected around me. Sometimes the entire aisle transforms and I literally get lost in my work. Which is why there's been a long gap since my last message. Sorry about that, Saul.

Don't laugh, but I spent all of yesterday in the children's literature section. All the stories there came to life too; old houses covered in vines and chocolate factories and little engines that could. It was fantastic, Saul. And completely depressing. Because as I sat there surrounded by those hopeful stories, it hit me that your grandchildren might not even know these stories exist. Yes, I know you disagree. But I'm a learned anthropologist and a general pessimist and I'm scared.

I asked an Archivist if this is how they store all their information. They asked if I'd be offended if they laughed and showed me the memory tablet that contained all the knowledge of the Library. It was about the size of a paperback romance novel.

"Our information would be inaccessible to you otherwise," the Archivist explained. "All of your search engines are either too crude or too biased."

"But didn't this take you forever to build?"

"No," they said, but I must not have looked convinced. "Magic," they added.

Saul, I think the alien race of information scientists are listening to these recordings. So whatever you do, don't reply back with anything you don't want recorded for posterity.

"Why is the Library so large then?" I asked.

And here's where the story gets really depressing, Saul.

They told me that once this planet, the inhospitable place that's just a wasteland and a massive Library now, was full of life. There were once billions of Librarians. Now, there's only a few thousand. Before they became the masters of information science of the known universe, the Librarians ended up destroying their planet too.

The first Librarians I ever met told me the Library is a beacon for sentient life in the galaxy, except now I know it's not just a beacon for other species. The reason why the Library's so big, Saul, is that most of the Archivists and Librarians live here too.

They couldn't save their planet either.

I can hear you asking me why I bothered coming here if I'm going to be stubbornly bleak about the future and it's not an easy thing you demanded, brother mine, and I'm trying to tell you in my circular, rambling way, that I . . .

I . . .

Saul. I need to call you back. I think I finally found Dr. Ryu's research.

I've got it, oh my god, I'm so relieved. It was a fight to get it, though. No, Saul, I'm not exaggerating. Stop rolling your eyes.

Remember when I said the Archivists could keep their information sentient? Well, she was sentient enough, Saul.

When I accessed the memory tablet, the researcher herself appeared so real and sharp I could see the gray strands in her hair and the clear gloss on her fingernails. She didn't look thrilled to see me and I should've taken it as a warning, but I was way too excited.

"Are you Dr. Yumi Ryu?" I asked. (Gushed would be more accurate.)

"Up to the age of 53," she answered

"Amazing! It's great to finally meet you, Dr. Ryu. I want to ask you everything. What's it like being archived by the Librarians? No, wait, can you tell me about your reforesting research first?"

For some reason, Saul, my rambling didn't put her at ease. "Why?" she asked, her expression suspicious.

"Um, well, because the news back home isn't good. Most of the North Pacific rain forest has been destroyed by a combination of drought and wild-fires. Including your original research at UBC."

She didn't seem surprised by this, just sad. "And where is your team, Ms. . . . ?"

"Hazel Smith. It's just me."

She frowned, the suspicion on her face growing. "They sent a single astro-naut? Why?"

"Resources and funds. Both are extremely limited these days."

"Why you then?"

"Because I'm a researcher too, Dr. Ryu, and I'm dedicated to preserving human society. Also, because I have an extraordinary memory, especially for data and details, and don't need batteries."

Ryu arched an eyebrow. Out of nowhere, a memory tablet about the size of a romance novel appeared in her hands. She stared it intently.

"What are you doing?" I asked, not getting a good vibe from this.

"Reading your articles, academic and otherwise. Being part of the Library, Ms., excuse me, Dr. Smith, means I can check out materials too."

Suddenly, I knew how this conversation would go. It would be like those awful dinner parties that ended in silent awkwardness when people asked why I didn't have kids. But there was nothing I could do, except try not to chew on my fingernails. In all of human culture, there's nothing more uncomfortable than standing there while someone else reads your work.

But if anthropology has taught me anything, Saul, it is that human beings can always surprise you.

"Wow," Dr. Ryu said and the tablet disappeared from her hands. "You have a depressing view on human nature."

I've always hated having this conversation, so I stuck my hand in my pock-ets and said: "I'm just going off history."

She nodded. "For what it's worth, I agree."

Color me stunned, Saul. "So will you tell me about your research?"

Ryu stared at me hard, with that critical eye that only people who spend too much time in labs analyzing details can pull off.

"No," she said.

No. That's what she really said. After traveling thirty-two and a half light-years for research like this. I won't lie, Saul, for a brief second I considered smashing the memory tablet.

"You serious?" I said.

"Yes, Dr. Smith. I've spent most of my professional career fighting politicians, big businesses, home developers, farmers. Anyone who didn't like the idea of giving up their land and returning it to forests, to try to reverse some of the damage we've done. I can't tell you how many times people tried to destroy this research."

"I'm not here to destroy anything, Dr. Ryu. I've given up too much for that."

"And what did you give up, Dr. Smith?"

"Earth. Everyone I know and love. I've risked my life for this information!" I said. In hindsight, maybe a little too defensively.

"No, that's running away," she replied. Yeah, she really said that to me, Saul. "Why are you really here?"

I sighed and used your classic line. "Because it's hope for the future that keeps us going."

"And who do you have hope for, Dr. Smith? Because from what I've read, you don't paint a hopeful picture."

I didn't know what else to do. So, I told her, Saul. Everything I've been trying to tell you.

There aren't many defining moments in my life. Mostly, I think defining moments are clichés in hindsight. So maybe this is too, but do you remember that summer, ten years ago, when everything burned? Yeah, hard to forget.

I'd just gotten my first master's degree and wildfires in northern Washington were raging, and there was a trail you could take up a mountain that was still a safe distance away, but you could witness the worst fires in history firsthand. It was only an hour drive from campus. And I was frustrated and scared, but also curious. So I figured what the hell.

I took this guy with me. No, you've never met him, Saul.

We walked up that mountain together, though the ash made for awful traction.

It wasn't love and we both knew it. That was one of the many, many rules I broke to myself that summer. But I liked him and he liked me. And in that moment, that was enough. Good enough. The world was on fire and right then, I was too grateful to have someone who would climb a mountain with me just to watch the world ending.

Mortality makes you reckless sometimes, Saul.

Eventually the smoke got so bad that my asthma couldn't take it. He practically carried me back down.

Two months later, he went back home to Colorado, where there were a few trees left and I spent that fall sobbing and wheezing. Which made sense when I took a pregnancy test.

I chose. And I don't regret that choice, Saul. Except three days, eighteen hours, and twelve minutes later, you called and told me about the first child you and Huang wouldn't have after all.

I'm sorry I didn't tell you before, Saul. But I'm not sorry either. I was twenty-three, and though I could repeat back textbooks verbatim, I consistently lost my keys and forgot to eat. And after that summer, it was hard to see myself with a future and much less, a future for a kid. I know you're disappointed in me because you believe that no opportunity should be wasted. You think every life, even the cockroaches in the shed, should have a go at it. You've always believed in a future on Earth, Saul. Where I saw ashes, you saw fertile soil.

That's what I told Dr. Ryu. I told her all about you and Huang and your relentless perseverance and hope. I think she saw a kindred spirit in you or maybe just the right strain of stubbornness. So, she agreed to share her research with you. We're going to transcribe a little every day. Her memory tablet makes the Library's aisles transform into thriving forests. It is truly beautiful.

Consider this part one of my gift to you, Saul, because like hell am I going to apologize for the choices that brought me here.

Part two is that one of the benefits of becoming the last astronaut was getting a ridiculous stipend from the government. Well, more like a life insurance payout, because I'm going to be here for a long time. Hopefully not forever, but there's a lot of lost information here and the Archivists apparently are used to long-term guests.

I told you I had one last, terrible cliché and it's the worst one of all. The one where the astronaut doesn't come home.

Saul, I want you to use that money to start that family you and Huang always wanted.

Honestly, I'm still not convinced we can save Earth, but you are, and that works for me. So, I'll keep searching and sending home the information I find and maybe, between the two of us, that'll be enough.

So, give the family my love.

PERMISSIONS

ACKNOWLEDGMENTS

The editor would like to thank the following people for their help and support: Lisa Clarke, Sean Wallace, Kate Baker, Joshua Bilmes, Eddie Schneider, Sheila Williams, Gordon Van Gelder, Steven Silver, Jonathan Strahan, Ellen Datlow, and all the authors, editors, agents, and publishers whose work made this anthology possible.

2019 RECOMMENDED READING LIST

"The Bookstore at the End of America" by Charlie Jane Anders, *A People's History of the Future*, edited by Victor LaValle and John Joseph Adams.

"Bullet Point" by Elizabeth Bear, *Wastelands: The New Apocalypse*, edited by John Joseph Adams.

"Molecular Rage" by Marie Bilodeau, *Analog Science Fiction and Fact*, September/October 2019.

"What It Means to Burn" by Aliette de Bodard, *Deep Signal*, edited by Eric Olive.

"The Migration Suite: A Study in C Sharp Minor" by Maurice Broaddus, *Uncanny Magazine*, July/August 2019.

"The Galactic Tourist Industrial Complex" by Tobias S. Buckell, *New Suns*, edited by Nisi Shawl.

"Omphalos" by Ted Chiang, *Exhalation: Stories*, published by Knopf; Picador.

"Anxiety Is the Dizziness of Freedom" by Ted Chiang, *Exhalation: Stories*, published by Knopf; Picador.

"The Song Between Worlds" by Indrapramit Das, *Future Tense*, April 27, 2019.

"Sojourner" by Craig DeLancey, *Analog Science Fiction and Fact*, November/December 2019.

"Love in the Time of Immuno-Sharing" by Andy Dudak, *Analog Science Fiction and Fact*, January/February 2019.

"This is Not the Way Home" by Greg Egan, *Mission Critical*, edited by Jonathan Strahan.

"This Is How You Lose the Time War" by Amal El-Mohtar & Max Gladstone, published by Saga Press.

"The Message" by Vanessa Fogg, *The Future Fire*, Issue #48.

"The Sun from Both Sides" by R.S.A. Garcia, *Clarkesworld Magazine*, May 2019.

"Better" by Tom Green, *Analog Science Fiction and Fact*, March/April 2019.

"Move Forward, Disappear, Transcend" by A.T. Greenblatt, *Clarkesworld Magazine*, May 2019.

"And You Shall Sing to Me a Deeper Song" by Maria Haskins, *Interzone*, Issue #280.

"As the Last I May Know" by S.L. Huang, *Tor.com*, October 23, 2019.

"The Body Remembers" by Kameron Hurley, *Current Futures*, edited by Ann VanderMeer.

"The Legend of Wolfgang Robotkiller" by Alex Irvine, *The Magazine of Fantasy & Science Fiction*, July/August 2019.

"Water: A History" by KJ Kabza, *Tor.com*, October 9, 2019.

"Her Silhouette, Drawn in Water" by Vylar Kaftan, published by Tor.com Publishing.

"Mighty Are the Meek and the Myriad" by Cassandra Khaw, *The Magazine of Fantasy & Science Fiction*, July/August 2019.

"How Alike Are We" by Bo-Young Kim, *Clarkesworld Magazine*, October 2019.

"Articulated Restraint" by Mary Robinette Kowal, *Tor.com*, February 6, 2019.

"Contagion's Eve at the House Noctambulous" by Rich Larson, *The Magazine of Fantasy & Science Fiction*, March/April 2019.

"Glass Cannon" by Yoon Ha Lee, *Hexarchate Stories*, published by Solaris.

"Thoughts and Prayers" by Ken Liu, *Future Tense*, January 26, 2019.

"Haven" by Karen Lord, *Current Futures*, edited by Ann VanderMeer.

"The Memory Artist" by Ian R. MacLeod, *Asimov's Science Fiction*, May/June 2019.

"The Menace from Farside" by Ian McDonald, published by Tor.com Publishing.

"It Was Saturday Night, I Guess That Makes It All Right" by Sam J. Miller, *A People's History of the Future*, edited by Victor LaValle and John Joseph Adams.

"Sturdy Lanterns and Ladders" by Malka Older, *Current Futures*, edited by Ann VanderMeer.

"Waterlines" by Suzanne Palmer, *Asimov's Science Fiction*, July/August 2019.

"Dave's Head" by Suzanne Palmer, *Clarkesworld Magazine*, September 2019.

"A Champion of Nigh-Space" by Tim Pratt, *Patreon*, April 2019.

"The Gondoliers" by Karen Russell, *Tin House*, Summer 2019.

"Reunion" by Vandana Singh, *The Gollancz Book of South Asian Science Fiction*, edited by Tarun K. Saint.

"New Atlantis" by Lavie Tidhar, *The Magazine of Fantasy & Science Fiction*, May/June 2019.

"Gremlin" by Carrie Vaughn, *Asimov's Science Fiction*, May/June 2019.

"Cyclopterus" by Peter Watts, *Mission Critical*, edited by Jonathan Strahan.

"The Archronology of Love" by Caroline M. Yoachim, *Lightspeed Magazine*, April 2019.

"The Doing and Undoing of Jacob E. Mwangi" by E. Lily Yu, *Asimov's Science Fiction*, May/June 2019.

"Green Glass: A Love Story" by E. Lily Yu, *If This Goes On*, edited by Cat Rambo.

ABOUT THE EDITOR

Neil Clarke is the editor of *Clarkesworld* and *Forever Magazine*; owner of Wyrm Publishing; and an eight-time Hugo Award Finalist for Best Editor (short form). He currently lives in NJ with his wife and two sons. You can find him online at neil-clarke.com.